HADES AND PERSEPHONE

LEE SAVINO

STASIA BLACK

Text copyright © 2024 Lee Savino and Stasia Black
All Rights Reserved

ISBN: 978-1-64847-100-1

No part of this book may be reproduced in any form or by any electronic or mechanical means including information storage and retrieval systems, without permission in writing from the author. The only exception is by a reviewer, who may quote short excerpts in a review.

This book is a work of fiction. Names, characters, places, and incidents either are products of the author's imagination or are used fictitiously. Any resemblance to actual persons, living or dead, events, or locales is entirely coincidental.

FREE BOOK

Lee's dark lumberjack romance, Beauty & the Lumberjacks, is free right now for newsletter subscribers

Grab it here: https://BookHip.com/WZLTMQX

Beauty & the Lumberjacks

After this logging season, I'm never having sex again. Because: *reasons*.

But first, I have a gig earning room and board and ten thousand dollars by 'entertaining' eight lumberjacks. **Eight strong and strapping Paul Bunyan types, big enough to break me in two.**

There's Lincoln, the leader, the stern, silent type...

Jagger, the Kurt Cobain look-alike, with a soul full of music and rockstar moves...

Elon & Oren, ginger twins who share everything...

Saint, the quiet genius with a monster in his pants...

Roy and Tommy, who just want to watch...

And Mason, who hates me and won't say why, but on his night tries to break me with pleasure...

They own me: body, mind and orgasms.

But when they discover my secret—the reason I'm hiding from the world—everything changes.

CONTENT WARNINGS

Abduction and captivity of heroine, non-con/reluctance, stalking, mafia violence and assault, sexual assault and murder (historical), murder, torture, gun violence, BDSM, primal play.

PART I
INNOCENCE

Find the Persephone and Hades playlist here: https://geni.us/Innocenceplaylist

PROLOGUE

Persephone knew she was dreaming.

She stood on the rooftop of a high-rise, goosebumps rising on her skin at the glorious view. Beside her stood the man who gave her everything, his face shadowed.

"It's beautiful." The city lights glittered like jewels in a black velvet night. The whole world laid at her feet.

"It's mine," Hades told her. "Everything you see belongs to me."

She wore a red dress and heels with slender straps winding up her legs. Her wrists bore silver cuffs. Her ring flashed red as she tucked a strand of hair behind her ear.

"Everything?" She leaned against the ledge, striking a pose. The old Persephone, country girl Persephone would never be so brazen. The old Persephone was a sheltered virgin, sweet and naive.

The old Persephone was dead.

Hades's footsteps echoed as he stalked to her. "Everything." The lines beside his grey eyes crinkled.

He grasped her hips and lifted her onto the ledge. Giggles escaped as her chest tightened. Before her stood the man she loved. Behind her, a dark expanse. An endless chasm.

"Hades." She clutched his broad shoulders. The wind ripped at her garments and tugged her golden hair.

He caught her wrists and forced her hands back.

"Do you trust me?"

"Yes," she whispered. Her fingers fluttered. The garnet in her engagement ring caught the light.

Hades moved closer as if to kiss her. She angled her face toward his—

—and he shoved her off the ledge. Her hands reached for him, her dress streaming around her floating body as Hades grew further and further away.

The night rose up, surrounded, swallowed her. The city lights swirled, a dizzying kaleidoscope. One by one, the lights went out and Persephone tumbled into darkness.

Persephone jerked awake. Hades's dark head was on the pillow beside hers, the shadows under his eyes lighter with sleep. The sight of him anchored her, grounding her spinning senses, the weightless sensation. If she closed her eyes, she was still falling.

Smoothing her pillow, Persephone settled in. In the dark confines of Hades's bedroom, she was safe.

Safe from everyone but him.

1

6 *months earlier...*

PERSEPHONE SAT COLORING with little Timmy when his parents started up in the other room. Again.

"You know I hate this shit, Diana. I don't see why I have to go."

"Maybe because I expect my *husband* to support me when my firm wins a big case!"

Persephone grabbed her phone and turned on the playlist Timmy loved best. He was three years old and apart from the occasional tantrum, he was a sweetheart. It wasn't his fault his parents didn't know how to use their inside voices.

The opening strains of *I'm Walking on Sunshine* started pounding out of her phone's surprisingly good speakers, drowning out the parental dramatics in the other room.

"Roly monster time!" Persephone said, grabbing Timmy out of his chair and lifting him in the air. Whew, she was getting some serious ab and arm muscles out of this job.

Timmy giggled and she breathed out in relief. Distraction managed.

She put Timmy on the floor and he immediately assumed the position, lying down on his back in the center of the playroom. Persephone cleared out the toys around him so he had a clear space to move and wouldn't hurt himself by rolling over stray Legos and Magna-Tiles.

"Persephone roly monster too," he demanded, except he couldn't say his 'r's so it came out sounding like 'Se-fy wowy monsta too.'

Persephone pursed her lips like she was thinking about it, but she grinned and dropped to the ground, lying down next to him.

"You ready?" she asked.

"Yes!"

"All right. Staaaaaaaaaaaaart rolling!"

They both started rolling across the floor. The giggles began immediately. The playroom was huge, especially considering the Donahues lived in the prime real estate of the Upper East End. They could afford a live-in nanny like Persephone, so they obviously weren't hurting when it came to their bank account. Too bad the money didn't seem to be able to buy them happiness.

Timmy finally reached the wall and Persephone kept on rolling until her body smashed into his. "Uh oh! Collision! You know what this means."

Timmy squealed when she started tickling him.

"You gotta escape and start rolling again. That's the only way out."

She shifted him so he could wriggle over the top of her and off the other side. He started to roll away.

"Chase me. Chase me, Se-fy!"

"Oh, I'm coming." She gave him a fair head start before rolling, her long blonde hair catching crazy static electricity the more she did it.

As she finished a roll and started to twist into another, she caught sight of a figure standing in the door and yelped.

"Daddy!" Timmy cried. "Daddy, come play wowy monsta with us!"

Persephone yanked down the hem of her shirt that had ridden up and got to her feet.

Mr. Donahue was looking at her, not his son. He was in his mid-forties, an architect who was always well-dressed and put together, if a little overly fond of hair gel. He was holding a glass of scotch. "Looks like you can have the night off after all. I decided not to go out."

"Oh." Persephone blinked. "Thanks." She had asked for the night off a couple of days ago. Some of her friends, fellow nannies she'd met at the park where she took Timmy every day, had invited her out. But Mrs. Donahue told her no because her firm was having some celebratory dinner tonight. Which apparently Mr. Donahue had just begged off from. Eeek. As desperately as she needed this job, the family dynamics could get seriously weird sometimes.

But who was *she* to judge family dynamics? She and her mom qualified for the screwed-up family Olympics.

"Daddy. Daddy!" Timmy ran up and started tugging on Mr. Donahue's pants leg. "Come play."

Persephone looked between Timmy and Mr. Donahue. He was always asking her to call him Paul, but she preferred Mr. Donahue.

"Are you sure it'd be okay?" she asked, eyes flicking toward the door. Mr. Donahue noticed and glowered, taking a swig of his scotch.

"Go. Have a good time. You're young. You deserve a gods damned night off now and then." She flinched at his tone and he paused and ran a hand down his face. "Jesus, I'm sorry. Seriously. I'll put Timmy to bed." He offered a tired smile. "You're officially off duty."

Persephone bobbed her head. "Thanks. I really appreciate it."

She hadn't done much else other than work, aka spend time with Timmy, since she got to the city six weeks ago.

As much as she loved the little guy, she'd come to the city because she wanted to live bigger. To see the world. To have friends.

To live free.

She bent down and gave Timmy a kiss on the head. "See you tomorrow, monster."

He made a roaring noise and she made one back.

She snagged her phone and hurried out of the room and up the stairs to shower and get ready.

She texted Helena when she got to her room: I CAN COME TONIGHT AFTER ALL!

It was several minutes before Helena texted back. WE'RE MEETING AT THE STYX AT 10.

Ten? She was usually in bed by ten. Timmy was usually jumping on her face at five-thirty in the morning. Some days earlier.

Her thumbs moved clumsily over her phone screen. Unlike her peers, she hadn't grown up with a cell phone glued to her side. She was still getting used to all the marvels of technology. Back at the farm, they hadn't even had TV. Much less internet or cell phones. No, mom wouldn't dare have any of the outside world corrupt *her* daughter.

Persephone shook her head angrily and hit send on the message. SOUNDS GREAT. SEE YOU THERE.

She pushed play on the music again, leaving it on the Timmy playlist. Smashmouth's *All Star* came on.

Let go of the past. She wasn't on the farm anymore. She was in the big city. Living on her own. She had a job, a cell phone, friends, and now a night out on the town. This was what life was supposed to be.

Her head started bopping along to the music. Then her hips. Then she was dancing around the room and laughing, arms spread wide.

She was *free*.

And tonight she'd go dancing and maybe meet a cute boy. The whole world was in front of her and she was ready to meet it, arms wide open.

2

3 *Hours Later*

OH GODS, how had it all gone so wrong, so fast? Persephone lifted a hand to her head as the lights of the club swirled and danced in a crazy pattern. She shook her head and staggered, sluggish and bleary in the rowdy pit.

Helena. She needed to find Helena. Or Europa.

She was supposed to ask them if she could sleep on their couch tonight.

Because she couldn't go home.

Ha. Home. What a crock.

It had never been her home. And now she couldn't go back there.

Not after *Paul* had waited up for her and accosted her at the bottom of the stairs when she tried to leave to meet her friends.

The house had been dark, Timmy asleep and Diana still out at her dinner.

Paul had been drunk, that much was clear. He'd leaned against the wall of the foyer, blocking the front door so she couldn't leave.

"You're so beautiful, Persephone. I think it's time to stop with all the pretending."

Persephone had tried to edge around him and get to the door.

"I need to go, Mr. Donahue. My friends are expecting me."

"Paul," he said, slamming his hand to the wall behind her head, boxing her in. "How many times do I have to tell you? Call me Paul."

His breath had been sour from the scotch. He'd reached up a hand to touch her face and she'd shoved it away.

"Stop it!" she'd hissed incredulously. "What are you doing? You have a wife! And a beautiful little boy."

But he crowded her in with his body. "I can't stop. I love you, Persephone. You drive me crazy. Seeing this tight little body." He put a hand on her waist and squeezed. "Hearing the shower earlier and knowing you were up there, naked."

She tried to twist away from him but he grabbed her with both hands and shoved her against the wall.

He kissed her.

Or, well, she should say, he smashed his mouth against hers and tried to shove his fat tongue between her lips.

She'd kneed him in the balls and shoved him backwards. "I quit!" She'd fled with only her phone, the small bit of cash she had shoved in her bra, and the clothes on her back.

And she'd come here.

Only to find her so-called *friends* could barely give her the time of day. They were too busy flirting with guys at the bar. She tried to tell them what had happened. Helena made a few sympathetic noises, then said Persephone should get drunk and forget all about it.

Persephone had stared at Helena. What did she expect? She barely knew these girls. So they'd talked a few times at the park while their charges played on the playground. She'd built it up to be more in her head because well, she'd never had friends. It had felt monumental to have girls she talked to and hung out with regularly. But to these girls, she was no one. Barely a blip in their busy lives full of friends and lovers.

So, doubting herself, she'd wimped out of asking to crash at one of their places. She told herself she'd do it at the end of the night. Besides, maybe Helena was right. Maybe loosening up and having a good time tonight was the answer. Maybe everything wasn't as dire as it all felt.

So she'd let a guy buy her a drink just like they did in the books and on TV—she'd been doing a lot of catching up in the last six weeks—and tried dancing.

But he must have gotten her order wrong. She'd asked for cranberry juice but there must have been alcohol in it because she felt weird. Really weird.

She stumbled forward and only barely caught herself from head-butting a chick who was dancing seductively up and down on a guy like she was a stripper and he was the pole.

Persephone fumbled in the side of her bra for her phone. Why couldn't she feel her fingers? Her hand was a clumsy stump.

Okay, this was starting to really freak her out. She was never drinking alcohol again.

She frowned as she finally got hold of her phone and pulled it out. Everything kept going in and out of focus. And the lights. Too bright. She winced and stumbled her way through the crowd.

She'd text Helena. Maybe they weren't best friends, but she was one of the only people Persephone knew in the city.

And Persephone needed to lie down. This day had officially been *too long*. It needed to be over. Now.

It took her three tries to swipe the right sequence of dots to unlock the phone. She squinted blearily at the little screen. It kept moving and dancing. It was hard to figure out which screen was the real one. She stabbed at it with her weird stubby hand but couldn't seem to do anything right.

She felt frantic and sleepy at the same time. She needed help.

She finally got to the text app, somehow. Thank the gods, thank the gods.

Tears of relief flooded her eyes.

But when she started to type a message, she fumbled the phone and dropped it.

"Shit!"

The club floor was a dark abyss. Would she even be able to find it—

"Hey, I remember you. Did you drop your phone? I saw you from over there." A man dipped down in front of her and came up with her phone. She could have hugged him.

She tried to say, "Thank you," but her tongue was thick and it came out more like *tank ya*.

She squinted up at him as the strobe lights flashed their way and she winced. Still, she could see it was the nice guy from earlier and she relaxed. He hadn't laughed or looked at her funny when he asked to buy her a drink and she said she was only drinking cranberry juice.

"I think I—" she started, but the world dimmed.

The next thing she knew, the nice guy's arm snaked around her, supporting her weight as he led her around the edge of the crowd.

"Let's get you to the restroom so you can splash your face," he was saying. "I texted your friend to meet you there."

Persephone nodded. Talking was too much work. *Walking* was too much work but she fought to stay up on her feet and to keep stumbling along beside the nice man. He was strong and solid beside her and she clung to him with the little bit of strength she had.

She lifted her head and was blinded by the lights again. It was too much. All too much. The music pounded in her head with the force of an icepick. She needed quiet. Dark. She'd even take Mama's cellar over this.

The thought made her feel hysterical.

Look how far I've come, Mama. The big city is as scary as you said after all.

No. Today was a bad day. She focused on lifting her feet. One and then the other. Holding on to the man to stay upright.

Gods, it felt like they'd been walking *forever*. Weren't they to the bathrooms yet?

She finally hazarded looking up again. And frowned when she saw they were in a hallway. She twisted and looked over her shoulder.

Wait, they'd passed the bathrooms. She tried to dig her feet in. She needed to let the man know he'd made a mistake.

"Bathr—" she tried to say but he cut her off.

"Shh, quiet, kid. Everything's gonna be fine. Just fine."

But his voice didn't sound right. More like he was talking to a child he was annoyed at.

"No." She shook her head. Not right. This wasn't right.

She tried to pull away from him but his fingers closed around her arms like talons, and instead of gently leading her, he was yanking her forward.

Stop! Help! she screamed in her head. But only little whimpers came out.

He was shoving her out the back door of the club. The cool night air hit her like a thousand tiny needles and she finally managed a shriek.

But it was too late. The door closed behind them as quickly as it had opened.

"Shut up, bitch," the man said, pulling keys from his pocket. There was a black car parked in the alley not far away and the lights lit up as he pressed a button on the fob.

No! No, no, no.

Persephone tried to fight. In her head she was fighting tooth and nail. Screaming and flailing and clawing.

But outwardly, she must not have been putting up much of a fight because the brute lifted her slender body with no problem at all. He shoved her in the back of his car, face first into a leather seat. The car door slammed.

He didn't even bother to restrain her. He didn't have to.

She was helpless as he hit the gas, tires screeching. She was tossed against the back of the seat and, when he stopped, she was dumped into the footwell.

Ow!

But no. Pain was good. She blinked and tried to focus on it.

She couldn't let herself pass out. He must have drugged her cranberry juice. Stupid. So freaking stupid! She hadn't let the drink out of her sight. At least she thought she hadn't. But he had taken it from the bartender to hand to her. If he was good at sleight of hand, he could have dosed the drink while passing it.

Tired. *So* tired. She blinked her heavy eyelids closed. Once. Twice.

The car accelerated fast and the jolt had her eyes shooting open again. Shit! Had she almost fallen asleep?

What the hell was she thinking? If she fell asleep, she was dead. She'd be raped and murdered and all the terrible things her mom had warned her about. It was all happening. First with Paul, and now being drugged and kidnapped, oh gods oh gods—

Stop it! Stop freaking panicking.

She forced her eyes open as wide as they could go and she tried to focus. She'd only sipped about a third of the glass of cranberry juice. She had to try to get out of this. The man was taking her somewhere, but they weren't there yet. There was still time.

Rain spattered the windows as the car rolled down the dark streets. They were still in the city. Okay. She had to escape the car the next time it stopped. The man was obviously counting on her being passed out by this point or too incapacitated to try anything.

Probably because you weren't even able to walk on your own back at the club.

But she hadn't been terrified for her life then. Adrenaline surged through her veins, painting her options in stark black and white.

The car turned a corner and her body seemed to flip 360 degrees, everything went so topsy turvy... until she realized she was wedged so tightly in the footwell, she hadn't moved at all, frozen like a rabbit hiding from a wolf.

So maybe her head wasn't *perfectly* clear. Still, no way she was gonna lie here and accept whatever this guy had planned for her.

When the car next slowed, she exploded into action.

Meaning she sluggishly climbed back up onto the seat and

reached for the door handle. Her limbs were concrete. It took her several precious seconds to figure out how to flip the lock, but she pulled the handle right as the car came to a stop.

The door opened and she hurled her body into the night.

"Hey!" she heard the guy shout as she hit the wet pavement. Raindrops smacked her face.

Up. Get up, now, she shouted at herself. Instead, she lay there dazed. The city swirled around her, towering skyscrapers stretching into the endless night. She was small as a raindrop, a wet splat on the blacktop...

Feet hit the ground as the driver side door opened and her kidnapper got out.

She dragged herself off the ground, using her door for leverage. She spared only the quickest, frantic glance around. They were stopped at a red light. Rain beat down on the empty sidewalks. Everywhere she looked, shops were dark and silent.

But far ahead down the sidewalk off to her right, one door was illuminated. *Light.* Light meant people. People who could help her. Or if nothing else, it meant a place to hide.

She ran toward the light. The world narrowed to a dark tunnel, her hope shrinking to the size of the cone of rain-washed light. She ran, bare feet smacking cold puddles. Her heels had fallen off somewhere along the way, thank the Fates. She was much steadier without them. The rain biting at her cheeks sharpened her focus. She ran, adrenaline powering her forward, the man's shouts chasing, but not catching up. Yet.

She tumbled down the steps that cut below street level and slammed into the door. The man's shouts were closer than ever. He was almost on top of her. She yanked at the door handle, managed to drag it open, and rushed inside.

Her refuge was a bar or club of some sort, probably private, judging from the subdued lighting and mahogany wood that filled the place with shadows. Dimly she could make out an empty bar and booths lit by small lamps.

Crap, why was she standing here taking in the décor? Her

kidnapper would be on her any second. Trying to quiet her breathing, she slipped toward the wall on her left, hugging the shadows and dripping as she went. She passed a doorman's stool and a coat room. Where was the bouncer? If this was a private club, would they kick her out?

She looked down at herself. Her little black dress was smeared with mud from the street and she was sure her face didn't look much better.

But she was thinking more clearly. Finally. So there was that.

And there wasn't a bouncer that she could see. When she paused and listened hard, all she heard was the pounding of her heart, and a few subdued voices in the back. The place was closed for the night, or very, very exclusive. If she moved quietly enough, she might be able to find a back door and leave unnoticed.

Her plan held for a few seconds, but the door behind her burst open, slamming into the wall with a loud *bang*. No! She bit back a scream, cringing in the shadows. The arrival of her pursuer caught more than her attention, though.

From the far left came a shout. The bouncer, finally making an appearance.

"Hey, man, you can't come in here."

Persephone blindly felt along the wall until she nearly fell into a corridor. She waited a moment, listening.

"I was with my girl—I need to see if she came in here..."

Scared as she was, everything in Persephone protested: *I'm not his girl; I'd never met him before tonight.* The bouncer was also arguing with him, telling him the place was private.

"If you remain here, Mr. Ubeli ain't gonna be happy with you." The man's voice was unnaturally deep, and Persephone imagined he was a huge man, a brute in a suit. "You need to leave."

"No, I'm telling you, she ran this way..."

The seconds ticked by, and Persephone realized that her pursuer wasn't going to leave.

Thumping footsteps, a shout— "Hey, you can't go in there!"

Persephone backed deeper into the hallway. She turned and grabbed the closest doorknob she could find. Locked. Frantic, she moved down to the next one. The voices were getting closer.

The door opened. Blindly, she rushed through and closed it, cutting off the shouts.

Inside the light was subdued, the room a long dim expanse filled with as many shadows as the club. Persephone stood with her back to the door, and gasped as soon as her eyes adjusted to the light.

In front of her, beyond an expanse of rich red carpet, was a desk.

Behind the desk was a man.

She froze. Her sluggish mind turned to this new problem. The man wore a suit tailored to broad shoulders. His head was bent, his dark hair gleaming, as he worked by desk light in the long, dark room.

He looked important. Interrupting this man with his imposing office in a very private club would probably only lead to trouble. Still, anything was better than the situation she'd escaped. Right?

She stood, barely daring to breathe, water dripping from her hem onto the beautiful rug. For a second Persephone thought that the man hadn't seen her, he was so absorbed in the papers in front of him. In a fluid movement, though, he raised his head and looked straight at her the next moment.

Persephone moved back against the door. He was handsome, but in a terrifying way, like he'd been cut from marble and the sculptor had forgotten to smooth out the edges to soften the features. She could only guess at his age. Early thirties, maybe? Shadows rested on much of his face, especially under his eyes. These he moved over her, taking in her too-short dress, her unshod feet, her wet hair.

Persephone, heart racing painfully, stood like a statue.

Neither of them said anything.

Slowly the man rose, a question forming on his lips. Persephone also stepped forward, mind racing with possible explanations.

But she met the man's eyes, dark gray, accented by the brooding light, and her mind went blank. She wasn't sure if it was the remnants of the drugs in her system or just being near this man. She swallowed hard.

Behind her, a knock sounded sharply against the door. Persephone shot backward, her arms wrapped around herself.

"Mr. Ubeli?" someone called.

"Yes?" the man answered without taking his eyes from her.

The door opened slightly and Persephone shrank back. The speaker didn't enter the room though, and she was completely hidden behind the door.

"We got a guy out here; says he's lost some lamb he's lookin' out for. You hear?"

"I hear, Charon," said the man called Mr. Ubeli. "Get rid of him."

Persephone felt her whole body relax. Her breath escaped silently, even as Charon said, "You got it, boss. Do you want me to dump him?"

"No, turn him away." Mr. Ubeli glanced down at his desk, shifting some papers as he called out orders. "Smack him a bit if he means trouble."

"Yeah, Mr. Ubeli. Will do."

The door closed, leaving Persephone exposed again, alone with Mr. Ubeli. For a moment, he studied her with narrowed eyes.

"Was that guy giving you trouble?" he asked, moving out from behind his desk.

"Yes," Persephone whispered. "Thank you."

Hunching her shoulders, she shivered, and Mr. Ubeli came forward carefully, like she was a wild animal that might run.

She shrank away, but he walked past her, going to the coatrack beside the door and lifting a coat from it. Returning, he held it out, shaking the sleeve toward her arm.

For a second Persephone didn't move. She stared up at the man, into the deep, shadowed eyes. Turning, she put her arm through the sleeve, and let him help her into the coat. Once it was on, she realized it was a suit jacket, gray and too big for her, hanging slightly over her hands.

But as she wrapped it around herself, it felt like a shield against all that had happened tonight. The wave of relief hit her so hard that she all but collapsed into the chair the man guided her to in front of his desk.

She was finally safe.

It was over.

She sank back into the chair. She hoped her wet dress wouldn't ruin the red leather but she couldn't give it more than a moment's thought. It was so warm in here. Warmth and safety felt like everything that mattered in the world.

Stupid, really. She was still out of a job. And since the job had been a live-in nannying gig, she was also out of a place to live. She drew the coat even tighter around herself.

"You were his girl?"

It took a second to register his meaning, but as soon as it did—"No," Persephone said violently, shaking her head and shuddering, "No. I didn't know him before tonight. He put something in my drink. And he—he—"

"Hey," he said softly, his eyebrows furrowed. "I'll make sure he never shows his face around here again."

Who was this man, to make such a promise? But the way he stated it, with such authority, made her believe it. It should have disconcerted her, maybe.

Instead all she felt was relief.

Relief and warmth.

She nuzzled her head into the plush leather of the wing-backed chair. Gods she was tired. More tired than she'd ever been in her whole life.

"What's your name?" he asked.

"Persephone," she said automatically, and then pressed her lips together. Should she have told him her name? *Strangers are dangerous,* her mother's words rang through her head. *The outside world is treacherous. It's only safe here on the farm. I'm the only one you can trust.*

"Nice to meet you, Persephone. I'm Hades. Hades Ubeli."

She nodded sleepily.

"Nice...to meet you...too."

Her eyes kept falling shut. It was rude and she struggled to blink them open. She really did. Well, maybe she'd rest them. But only for a moment.

Only...a...moment.

But the warmth folded her under and she fell asleep.

3

When Persephone woke up, she remembered the drink—the red liquid, shining jewel-like in the glass. She startled awake, her heartbeat racing like a terrified rabbit's.

But she wasn't in the backseat of a car. She sat up and looked around, head swinging back and forth, her messy hair falling about her face.

She was in a hotel room. A really, really fancy hotel room, judging from what she could make out by the light of the single dim lamp.

Was she still dreaming? She scrubbed groggily at her eyes, and slowly, she started to remember the night before. Paul, the club, her so-called friends, the man who'd bought her the drink. The backseat of the car. Wet pavement as she ran away, down the street until she found the basement stairs, and the door, and everything that lay behind it.

That part seemed like a dream, and she would deny it happened, except she was lying between the smooth sheets and the velvety soft pillow of a five-star hotel bed.

And she was still in her dress from last night.

She blew out a sigh of relief.

Good gods, what had she gotten herself into?

Well, you can't stay here in bed all day. Time to go face the mess that is your life.

"But I don't wanna," she groaned and coughed. Gods, her throat was dry.

As she got up, she noticed a glass of water on the bedside table. She almost reached for it but stopped at the last moment. She was done accepting drinks from strangers, no matter that her throat felt drier than the Mojave Desert. She yawned and stuck her tongue out as she stretched.

Ugh, her muscles ached like she'd been run over by a truck. And her head hurt. A lot. She groaned as she stumbled out of bed. She headed toward the bathroom adjacent to the room, clawing back the tangled fall of her wheat-colored hair.

How long had she slept? She'd have to look for a clock when she went back to the bedroom. The cool marble of the bathroom stung her tender feet. Squinting over the two sinks—both made out of a striking black marble—she saw the color had returned to her cheeks. She must have slept for a long time.

She yanked hard on the knobs on the bathroom sink so the water blasted and cupped her hands underneath it, and then she drank swallow after swallow.

She washed her face afterward. The cool water washed her clammy skin clean and by the time she was finished and toweled off her face, she felt marginally better.

Especially when she saw a new toothbrush and tube of toothpaste arranged beside the sink.

"Thank the Fates," she moaned and grabbed both. She brushed long and hard, not caring if she was taking off the topcoat of enamel, she was so determined to wash last night off of her. Especially when she remembered Paul trying to kiss her. *Shudder.*

A shower was up next.

She felt slightly more human after she finished and stepped out. The headache was dissipating with the more water she drank.

As she toweled off her hair and walked back into the bedroom, she found that someone had left a shopping bag on a chair near the door of the hotel room. The skirt and top she found inside were her size. Along with some underthings. She paused, not sure how to feel about that. Was it considerate, or creepy? Probably considerate seeing as the only other clothing she had was the little black dress she'd gotten at a thrift store for ten dollars. And it wasn't like she wanted to put dirty underwear back on after her shower.

Was it the man from last night who'd bought her these things?

Duh, who else? But he'd probably had his secretary get them or something.

Would she ever see him again? Or had he taken pity on her, arranged for her to sleep it off in this nice hotel room, and gotten her clothes so she wouldn't have to do the walk of shame? And that was that, he'd done his good Samaritan act for the year?

She dressed quickly, feeling embarrassed for having taken so long to get out of the hotel. She was probably overstaying her welcome. What was check-out time? Jeez, she didn't want them to charge the guy extra because she'd washed her hair twice. The shampoo had smelled so *good*. And why wasn't there a dang clock in this room? She hadn't bothered pulling back the heavy drapes to see how high the sun was in the sky because she'd been naked and changing and now she was leaving so she didn't bother.

She quickly folded her old clothes before cracking open the bedroom door.

"Oh!" she squeaked in surprise. She'd been expecting the hallway of a hotel but instead, she was met with an even larger room.

She was in a hotel *suite*. A really, really expensive hotel suite by the looks of it. With as big as the room was... was this the *penthouse*? Holy crap.

The long wall of windows was dark—there weren't any city lights visible, so Persephone assumed it was the kind of glass that could be turned dark on command—and there were no lights on in the living room. What time *was* it? She ventured forward, wondering if she should call out *hello* or go knock on some of the other doors in the suite.

"How did you sleep?" a voice snaked from the darkness.

"Oh!" Persephone squeaked again, hand clutching her chest.

There, in an armchair in the sitting area down by the bar, was Hades Ubeli.

"Fine," she said, smiling timidly. "I slept fine."

She moved down toward him, still looking around. The room stretched out in shadow. The penthouse must take up one whole side of the building, she realized. There was a kitchen and bar, sunken areas for lounging, TVs and, in one corner, a baby grand piano. Everything was in grey or black, with touches of cream.

"Do you like the place?" Hades Ubeli stood with his hands in his pockets, the shadows grey on his face and under his eyes as he watched her.

Right. She was probably staring like a country bumpkin. "It's nice," she said and inwardly cringed. *Nice?* "I mean, it's really fancy." Gods, *fancy* was worse than nice. "Elegant, I mean. Really elegantly decorated."

Shoot her now.

To get into the lowered seating area, she passed a statue, a contorted figure in white marble.

"That one's mine," he commented, and she paused politely to stare at it. "The hotel lets me furnish this place to my tastes."

The statue was of a woman, a body and thin cloth all finely sculpted. It looked Greek, and well done, but the figure's face unsettled her—a sweet youth's features twisted as if in some horror or fear. She moved on, descending into the sunken area where her host stood.

"So you live here?" Persephone asked.

Hades Ubeli chuckled. "No, I keep it in case I want to get away."

Of course he did. Drawing in her breath, she nodded as if this was normal. But holy crap, what must a place like this cost? And he kept it as what, a place to crash when he was up late in this part of the city?

Or a place to bring women. Her cheeks heated at the thought.

"Would you like a drink?" He approached, and she shrank away from his tall, dark figure, suddenly imposing. But he only turned and went up the steps to the bar.

"No, thank you." She shook her head, still feeling a little sluggish. At the bar, glass clinked and then he was back. "How long did I sleep?"

Again, a small chuckle. It wasn't unkind, but it made her feel like she missed the joke. "I just watched the sunset."

"What?" She was horrified. "No way." She went to the window. "Can you turn these clear?"

"Of course." He reached for a remote control and with the tap of a button, the dark windows became transparent. Persephone gasped as the view became bright with rows of light that outlined skyscrapers, artificial and multicolored against a black velvet sky. She really had slept for an entire day.

"Oh, no," she said, lifting a hand to her forehead and feeling completely disoriented. She turned back to her host, who was now standing, his figure cut half through with black, half in grey.

"Forgive me," he said, and she was startled again. He didn't look like a man who would apologize. "I let you sleep as long as you could."

Shadow shrouded his face; she couldn't make out any expression beyond what was in his voice. "I made sure you were okay. Someone stayed here, in case you woke. But when I returned you were still asleep." His voice dropped and became softer. "I figured you needed it."

"It's okay," Persephone said, although she felt weak. "I mean, thank you." She'd slept a whole day! And someone had stayed with her—she wondered who, and hoped it wasn't the muscular bouncer she had seen in the club. She had so many questions—who *was* this man? Why was he being so nice?—but she bit them back, feeling his dark gaze on her.

"You hungry?"

She shook her head sharply, remembering the pitch of her stomach during the chase. The memory didn't seem a day old.

Too late, she thought of her manners. This obviously wealthy man had taken time out of his day to check in on her when she was sure he had a million more important things to be doing.

"I'm sorry. I'll get out of your hair. And I really should be getting home."

She didn't even cringe as she said it. Well, not too much. But whatever her problems were, she was done foisting them on this man.

He tilted his head sideways, examining her in a way that made her mouth go dry again. "Last night you said you didn't have a home."

Persephone felt her eyes go wide. "Oh." Shoot her now. She knew she talked sometimes in her sleep. She tried to laugh it off. "Well, I was working as a live-in nanny."

"And?"

Persephone opened her mouth and a helpless little noise came out. How could she even begin to— And it wasn't like it was *his* problem—

But Hades Ubeli arched a dark eyebrow in a way that demanded the truth.

"Well, I sort of quit."

"Sort of quit? Either you did or you didn't."

She let out a breath in a rush of air. "I did quit. But I still need to go back and get my last paycheck and all my stuff."

She couldn't help her frown thinking about what sort of scene that might be. But all the money she'd made in the last six weeks was there, and her backpack full of clothes and the few other things she'd brought from Kansas—

"I'll have your things picked up. You can stay here until you're back on your feet again."

"What?" Persephone's back went stiff. "No!"

Dang it, she was being rude again when this man had only been kind to her. "No, I mean, thank you. That's very nice. But I'm fine. I'll be fine. I'll go by and pick up my things and go to my friend's house."

He didn't have to know she was speaking about a hypothetical friend. Especially since her phone was gone. That creep from last night had kept it after he'd picked it up and she hadn't memorized Europa or Helena's numbers.

But the Donahues paid well. She'd have almost fifteen hundred dollars altogether once they paid the half of this month's paycheck she was owed. Maybe she'd catch a bus and find somewhere cheaper to live. The big city was the best place to hide from her mother, but it was too expensive.

"Sounds like you've got it all worked out," he said. "I'll have my driver drop you wherever you want to go." He pulled his phone out of his pocket and touched a button. "Charon. Yes. Bring the car around. You'll be escorting Miss..." Hades's eyes came Persephone's way.

"Vestian. Persephone Vestian."

"...Miss Vestian wherever she'd like to go."

He hung up the phone and slid it back in his jacket pocket in one fluid gesture. "It's nine p.m. I'd be happy for you to stay here another night and let all your responsibilities rest until daylight. What can you really accomplish tonight?"

Persephone clutched yesterday's dress to her stomach. "Oh, it's fine. I'm a night owl. So are my friends." Lies. All lies. She was usually in bed before the evening news.

If Hades could tell she was lying, he didn't call her on it. He merely inclined his head and held a hand out toward the door. "Charon will be waiting by the time you get to the front of the hotel. May I walk you?"

She blinked, then nodded. She'd never met anyone so... well, so courteous. Courtly, that was the perfect word for Hades Ubeli. He was like some old timey knight with his chivalry, coming to her rescue when she was a damsel in distress.

Books had been the one entertainment her mother allowed and she might have swooned over a knight or two throughout her adolescence.

Hades held out an arm. She shoved her dirty dress behind her back, more glad than ever that she'd balled up her dirty undies and bra inside it, and took his arm with her other hand. Electricity crackled through her body the moment they touched.

Not to mention that the strength that emanated off his body was... wow. Just *wow*. She'd never felt anything like it. Being so near him made her feel a little lightheaded all over again.

He led her smoothly across the living room of the penthouse, out the door and to the elevator. Persephone had never wanted an elevator to come faster and wished it would never show up at the same time.

"So," she said, hating the way her voice came out as little more than a squeak. Gods, she must seem like such a little girl to someone like Hades. "What do you do? Like, I mean, as a job?"

She glanced up at his face.

Bad idea. *Really* bad idea.

She'd only seen him in dim lighting before. The hallway didn't have fluorescents or anything, but it was enough to see that, holy crap, Hades was gorgeous. Freaking stunning from the top of his elegant cheekbones to the strong set of his jaw.

And the way he smiled down at her, still all dark and broody but like she amused him at the same time—it took her breath away. Literally, she was having a hard time remembering how to breathe.

His grin deepened until a dimple popped in his cheek and she jerked back like she'd been struck.

"I own many business and investment properties. You all right?" Hades's brow wrinkled. His eyelashes were black and long, a hint of beauty on a hard, masculine face.

Of course his eyelashes were freakin' perfect.

"Persephone?"

"Yeah. Yes. Yep." She bobbed her head like a fool and got hit with another smile. They say Cupid shoots arrows, but this felt more like a punch, a battering ram, smashing her right in the gut, pushing her insides out and replacing them with a golden glow.

Was this because she'd been completely deprived of male company her whole life and so now she was boy crazy, the first time she got to be this near a man?

No, it couldn't be that. She hadn't felt anything but disgust when Paul tried hitting on her.

She was pretty sure this was all Hades.

He didn't move back. He stared down at her, the smile slowly falling away, replaced by an intensity that pinned her in place like a butterfly to a board.

When the elevator pinged its arrival, she all but jumped out of her skin.

The corner of Hades's mouth tipped up and he let go of her arm. "After you."

Feeling like an idiot, she stepped onto the elevator. She thought he'd leave her there but he stepped on with her. The space shrank and the air heated. Persephone held her arms stiff beside her body. She was an awkward mannequin next to the tall, broad-shouldered god filling the small box.

The hairs on her arms rose where his suit coat brushed against her. The rich fabric felt like the suit coat he'd draped over her last night. She'd never been so *aware* of anyone in her whole life.

She thought that surely it would pass, but nope, the entire ride down, the electric awareness hummed under her skin. She about jumped off the elevator once they got to the lobby.

"Thank you again," she said. "You have no idea how much I appreciate what you did for me. I mean," she shook her head as a shudder worked down her spine, "I can't imagine what would have happened if it hadn't been for—"

She sucked in a deep breath and cut off her word barrage. She looked Hades in the eyes, tried as hard as possible to ignore the way his intense gaze made her stomach go absolutely liquid, and said, "Just, thank you."

"All right, Persephone," he murmured. A flush came over her—she was freakin' lightheaded at the sound of her name on his lips. "You ever need anything, you reach out to me, yeah? I'll take care of you."

Gods, he was so nice. She reached out and gave his hand a quick squeeze.

His nostrils flared at the touch and she immediately let go and spun on her heel, her own eyes wide. Oh gods, why had she touched him? What was she thinking?

Glancing around, she saw all eyes in the lobby were on her and Hades. And here she was, making a fool of herself. She squeezed her eyes shut briefly, horrified at how silly and naïve Hades probably found her.

But she shook it off. Oh well. It was done. For one shining night, okay, two shining nights, she'd been a brief blip on Hades Ubeli's passing radar, and that had been enough.

She bit back the impulse to thank Hades again but instead, kept her back to him and walked across the lobby. It felt like the longest walk of her life. She could feel every eye in the place on her. But was *he* still watching her?

Duh, no, stupid. He probably turned around and went right back up to the penthouse. She'd likely never see him again.

The huge bald-headed bouncer, Charon, was waiting for her as she pushed through the revolving doors.

Persephone stopped short at seeing him. Wow. She hadn't realized quite how... *large* he was. All his proportions were normal, he just came in extra, extra-large. He must be six foot five and could have had a career as a linebacker. He wore a suit that had to have been specifically tailored for his frame and he had a small earpiece in his ear.

He nodded at her and walked around to the back of the sleek, black, expensive-looking car. "Miss Vestian."

"Thank you."

She slid onto the cool leather bench seat and Charon closed the door behind her. She clutched her old dress in her lap nervously.

"Seatbelt," Charon said from the front seat.

"Oh, right." She finally relinquished her clothing to the seat beside her and pulled the seatbelt across her chest, clicking it into place.

"Address?"

She gave him the address and he plugged it into a screen on the dashboard. They pulled out of the hotel's drive and the lights of the city slid over the car. Persephone stared out the window like she always did when she was in a car or on the bus.

Six weeks here and the city still awed her. She'd read books about cities and buildings so tall they scraped the sky, but reading about them and seeing them for herself were two entirely different things.

Persephone had grown up surrounded by corn and sorghum crops. Rows and rows as far as the eye could see. And that was all. The idea of a place so packed with people they had to build upward and stack them on top of each other to fit was something Persephone hadn't really even been able to comprehend before coming here.

The ride was silent. Charon didn't say anything and Persephone was glad because she was too intimidated to talk to the big man. If he didn't talk, that meant she didn't have to either.

And soon enough, she began to recognize the landmarks of the Donahue's neighborhood.

She sat up straighter and looked at the clock on the dashboard screen. Nine twenty. Okay, at least Timmy would be asleep. Her heart squeezed in her chest. She'd miss the little boy. He wouldn't understand why she'd suddenly disappeared. It wasn't fair to him. But there was no way she could stay. Not after what Paul had done.

She took a deep breath as the car came to a stop.

Okay. She'd go in, get her money and belongings, and move on from there. She could get a hotel for the night. She almost laughed thinking about the kind of hotel *she* could afford compared to where she'd stayed last night. She'd have to take the train to the outskirts of the city and look for the cheapest motel she could find, but at least it would get her through the night. Tomorrow she could look for another job and—

"Miss Vestian?" Charon questioned. "If you're having second thoughts, I know Mr. Ubeli wouldn't mind—"

"No." Persephone's attention snapped back to the present moment and she shoved her door open, hiking her feet to the pavement. She cringed, thinking of how the beautiful heels were probably already getting scratched. She'd wanted to return the clothing in perfect order to Mr. Ubeli along with her thanks.

Oh well, she sighed. It wasn't like he could return them to the store after she'd worn them.

"Thank you. And thank Mr. Ubeli again for me." She closed the car door before she could start babbling again.

Charon had gotten out of the car as well and she looked upward at his face, so far above hers. "Mr. Ubeli asked me to give you this." He held out a card. "If you ever have need of him for any reason, any reason at all, you give him a call. You understand?"

She nodded quickly and took the card. She gave a quick smile and turned to hurry down the sidewalk toward the Donahue's brownstone.

She waited until the black car pulled away and drove down the road before knocking on the door. She didn't ring the doorbell because she didn't want to wake Timmy.

It felt weird to knock on the front door rather than letting herself in with her key, but she hadn't even had time to grab those before Paul had accosted her last night.

She shook her head. Had that really only been last night? Because as much as she'd been shocked to find out that it was evening when she woke up today, the events of last night had already begun to feel very distant, like they'd happened to some other girl. A defense mechanism probably, but she didn't have another moment to think about it because the door swung open.

"Mrs. Donahue. Hi. I'm here to pick up my things. I don't know if Paul— If Mr. Donahue told you, but I quit yester—"

"Whore! How dare you show your face back here?"

"Wha—"

But before Persephone could even get the word out, the middle-aged woman stepped out onto the front stoop and slapped Persephone. *Hard.*

Persephone jerked back and lifted a hand to her face.

Ow.

For such a small lady, Mrs. Donahue packed a mean hit.

"Wait," Persephone held up her hands, "there's been some kind of misunderstanding here—"

"Did you or did you not try to fuck my husband?" Mrs. Donahue sneered.

"Of course not! I would never!"

But it was clear by the expression on Diana Donahue's face that she didn't believe a word coming out of Persephone's mouth. And why would she? It was Persephone's word against Paul's.

"You're way out of line," Persephone said, fists clenched, "but you're never going to believe me and I get it. So just pay me the money you owe me and let me get my things and you never have to see me again."

Mrs. Donahue made a disbelieving noise. "You're not stepping one *foot* inside my house, you homewrecking whore. I had to miss *work* today to stay home with Timmy. The gods only know what sort of influence you've had on my baby." She shook her head and went to close the door.

Persephone shoved her foot in the way and pushed on the door. It startled Mrs. Donahue into stumbling several feet back into the foyer. But that only seemed to anger her more.

"I'm calling the police," she shrieked.

"All I'm asking for is what you owe me," Persephone said, barely able to believe what was happening. "You have to pay me. I did the job. And I need my things."

"I *burned* your things. The second Paul told me what you tried to do after you didn't come home last night. I threw them in the trash and set them on *fire*."

Persephone felt her mouth drop open. She'd burned— but that was all Persephone had— all she owned in the whole world—

"But—" Persephone broke off, biting back tears. Paul stalked into the room behind Diana. "Paul, tell her," Persephone appealed. "Tell her what happened. Please. I need the money for the work I did. I don't have anything else. I need that money."

But Paul was stone-faced and when he walked forward, he put an arm around his wife. "You need to go or we will call the police."

"I'm already dialing," Diana said, touching her phone and holding it to her ear. "Yes, hello. There's a psycho intruder in our house. Our former nanny who's stalking my husband."

Persephone stumbled backward and pulled the front door shut

behind her. It wasn't fair! They shouldn't be able to do that to her. She'd been depending on that money.

She heard sirens in the distance. They probably weren't coming for her. Sirens were a normal part of city life but still, it had her running.

She didn't have any ID or even a social security number, thanks to her mom's obsession with living off the grid. It was one of the reasons working for the Donahues was so perfect. They didn't mind paying her under the table in cash.

But now there was no cash.

No job.

No nothing.

She didn't even have her phone thanks to that bastard from last night.

She only slowed down when she turned the corner and ran down the steps to the subway.

She had twenty bucks on her from the night before and that was all. She spent five on a subway ticket and got on the first train that showed up.

Sitting on the grimy subway car, she looked around and the full weight of her situation finally hit her.

She had nowhere to sleep tonight.

Her eyes fell on a dirty, obviously homeless man sleeping in the corner of the train.

Well, that was one option.

Her head dropped backwards against the window behind her and she closed her eyes. Gods, was she seriously contemplating sleeping on the subway car like the homeless bum? Was that how far she'd fallen?

Why are you being so sanctimonious? You are homeless.

She scrubbed her hand down her face.

She thought she was so brave, escaping the farm. She'd done it on the spur of the moment. She'd seen a chance and taken it. Persephone was a terrible liar and no one could read her better than her controlling mother.

Controlling. Ha. Her mother was pathological.

Demeter Vestian watched every single thing her daughter did. She monitored how much food Persephone ate, how much she slept, if she'd done all her chores, if she did her schoolwork and did it perfectly. Most of the time Persephone felt more like a science experiment or a prize show dog than a daughter.

Not that her mother ever showed her off.

No, that was the other singular rule of their lives. They never saw anyone. *Ever.*

If they had to have a vet out to look at the horses, Persephone was locked in the cellar for the duration.

Her mom took the truck into town twice a month for food and supplies, but Persephone was always left behind. Persephone only got to read about other kids in books. She never met any.

Until she was a teenager and got fed up with it.

One time when she was fifteen, she stole the truck and drove down the long road that led away from the farm.

It was stupid and reckless and she only knew the rudiments of how to drive. But the road was flat and straight and it was a bright, sunny afternoon. Within an hour, she'd made it to town.

She pulled the truck to a stop on the side of the road and parked it as soon as she came to a grouping of buildings. She got out and started walking.

She walked from one store to the next, delighted and amazed by everything she saw, but most of all by the people. They seemed as surprised to see her as she was to see them. *Who was she?* they wanted to know. She didn't know how to answer their questions. She felt like it would be betraying her mom to say she lived down the road. No one was supposed to know she existed. She never knew why, but she knew that much.

But someone recognized her. The owner of the general store, a man so old his skin was papery with wrinkles and folds.

"You related to Demeter? You're the spittin' image. The spittin' image, as I live and breathe. You a cousin come to visit? Or her niece?"

Persephone nodded, not daring to speak. She backed out of the general store. Right into a group of teenagers.

One of the boys said she was pretty and he invited her to a party they were all going to. *A party!* Like she'd read about in her Sweet Valley High books.

She got in the back of a truck with the two boys and three girls and they drove out to an empty field. Persephone couldn't stop smiling and laughing even though she started feeling self-conscious after one of the other girls whispered loudly about her, making fun of her worn overalls with the patches on the knees.

But not even that was enough to dampen Persephone's mood. She helped the guys build up the bonfire and she felt a warm glow that had nothing to do with the fire when the boy who'd first called her pretty touched her hair and said it was the color of moonlight.

Persephone had never heard anything so pretty or poetic and when the boy invited her to sit on the hay bale beside him, she giggled but accepted.

They'd started breaking out the beer, which Persephone politely declined, when suddenly the field was lit up by headlights and the blaring noise of sirens.

"Shit, cops!" the boy sitting beside Persephone shouted.

Persephone had jumped up and covered her ears, confused.

The boy who'd called her pretty ran away, along with all his friends, disappearing into the nearby cornfield. They all left her standing there alone as two police cars surrounded her.

Almost the second they came to a stop, Demeter was jumping out of the first police car and running toward Persephone.

Persephone was both relieved and horrified to see her mother. She felt like crying, especially when her mother yanked her by her arm back toward the police car without a word.

She didn't say a single word to her as the police drove them back to her mom's truck where she'd abandoned it outside town.

And her mom didn't say a word after she'd hauled Persephone into the passenger seat of the truck and slammed the side door shut after she was in. Or for the entire forty-five minute drive back to the farm.

As soon as the farm came back into sight, Persephone finally ventured, "Mom, I'm sorry. I just wanted to see how—"

"Do you know what could have happened to you?" her mom yelled, slamming her foot on the brakes and jamming the truck into park. "How could you be so *selfish*?"

Persephone hunched down in her seat.

"After all I do for you." Mom shook her head. "After the years I have sacrificed for you, slaved for you, out here in the middle of *nowhere*. You think I like it out here with no one but you for company? But I do it. For *you*. To protect *you*. And you go and throw it back in my face like this."

"Why?" Persephone sat up, slamming her hands on the seat beside her. "*Why* do we have to live like this? Why can't we live in town? Or a city? Why can't I have friends or go to a normal school?"

But Mom shook her head like Persephone was being ridiculous. "How many times do I have to tell you how dangerous it is out there?"

"It wasn't dangerous today," Persephone disagreed. "Those kids were nice. We were having a nice time."

Mom scoffed. "You're so stupid you don't even know what you don't know. You think those boys were being *nice* to you because they liked you? They wanted what's between your legs. If I hadn't shown up you would have turned out to be a statistic in the morning paper."

Persephone shoved open her door and got out of the truck. "You're wrong." And she'd slammed the door behind her.

All of which was the wrong thing to do.

Because her mother got out of the truck just as quickly and before Persephone could blink, she was around the truck and had Persephone's arm in her iron grip.

She dragged Persephone into the house, ignoring her cries.

"No. No, Mom!" Persephone screeched as soon as she realized where Mom was taking her. "Not the cellar. Please. I'm sorry, okay? I'm sorry!"

But once Mom had made her mind up about something, there

was no changing it. And though Persephone was fifteen, she'd always been small for her age and she was no match for her mom's wiry, compactly muscled body.

Mom had her down the stairs to the damp, chilly cellar before she could even get another plea out. She shoved Persephone to the floor and jogged back up the steps.

"Mom," Persephone called, jumping to her feet. "Mama!" She ran up the stairs right as her mother slammed the cellar door on her.

And no matter how much she banged on the door or begged and pleaded and swore she'd do better, her mom wouldn't open up.

She didn't open the doors for three days and three nights. Not that Persephone knew that until later. At the time, all Persephone knew was that she was in the cold and the dark and that it was never ending. There was a gallon of water and a bucket for her to use the bathroom, and Persephone finally got hungry enough that she opened some of the jam they had stored down there and ate it straight.

And when her mother finally opened the door and Persephone had squinted up at the rectangle of light, things were never the same between them again.

Persephone opened her eyes and looked around the subway car.

She couldn't go home. She'd sworn once she finally escaped that farm, and her mother, that she'd never *ever* go back.

Which meant there was really only one option, no matter how mortifying it might be. Persephone pulled the card Charon had given her out of her skirt pocket.

The subway car was almost empty. A weary-looking woman in business attire sat in the front, the seat furthest away from the homeless man. Persephone stood up, holding onto the poles as she made her way over to the woman.

"Hi, ma'am, I'm sorry to bother you, but could I borrow your phone?"

4

"We have to stop meeting like this," Persephone joked nervously as Hades opened the door to his penthouse hotel suite and gestured for her to come in.

The edge of his mouth quirked up in a half smile. Was he laughing at her joke or at *her*? Not that it mattered either way. He was doing her a huge favor.

"I really appreciate this," she said. "It'll just be for the night." She cringed. "Or maybe a couple of nights? As soon as I get another nannying gig, I'll be out of your hair, I swear."

Hades didn't say anything, he just watched her with that inscrutable look on his face. He tilted his head, indicating she should come in. Well, further in than the foyer where she was babbling like an idiot.

"Charon mentioned you hadn't eaten yet."

"Oh," Persephone said, surprised to see an elaborate table set up in a small dining area. The windows were still not darkened.

She took several more steps forward, awed by the glittering tableau. She'd seen it earlier, but had been too distracted to take it in properly. Now, she swayed as she faced rows and rows of skyscrapers, the entire city laid at her feet.

"I've never been so high up," she whispered. She wanted to go right up to the window but kept back. Looking down on the skyscrapers made her dizzy. "I mean, I knew we must be up this high from how long the elevator ride took, but…" she trailed off, shaking her head.

When she looked back at Hades, his head was tilted, his eyes narrowed at her like she was a particularly peculiar species of zoo animal.

She felt her cheeks heat and lifted her hands to them. Gods, why couldn't she keep her mouth shut? And not let every single thing she was feeling and thinking show on her face?

She moved abruptly to go sit down at the table. "Thank you, I am famished."

Hades moved as she did, getting there right before her and holding her chair for her as she sat down.

His scent enveloped her, his arm brushing hers, and like earlier when he'd escorted her downstairs, the merest touch sent a jolt of electricity through her entire body.

She gasped and sat down, grabbing the seat of the chair and scooting herself in. "Thank you." She ran a hand nervously through her hair as she smiled up at him.

Her plate was covered with a fancy silver plate topper. She lifted it off and steam wafted up. "Oh!" she said, surprised again. Hades chuckled as he sat down across from her.

"I hope you don't mind but I took the liberty of ordering for us. Roasted lamb shank, corn and leek grits, ruby chard, roasted rutabaga, topped with goat cheese."

"Oh," Persephone said yet again, nodding and looking down at her plate, eyes wide. She didn't think she'd ever seen such a large piece of meat. At least not on a plate set in front of her.

"You aren't a vegetarian, are you?"

"No," she said quickly. She and Mom *did* mostly eat vegetarian, but it hadn't been due to any choice on Persephone's part. That was the point of leaving, wasn't it? So that she could finally have *choices* in her life?

Persephone smiled and reached for her fork...only to find there were several forks. She grabbed the one nearest the plate and smiled wider. "Cheers," she said, lifting the fork like it was a wine glass she was toasting with.

Hades chuckled again and she averted her eyes to her plate, digging into the lamb shank. It was so well-cooked and tender, it melted off the big bone. Tentatively, she lifted it to her mouth.

And almost embarrassed herself even more by moaning out loud. She stopped herself at the last second, but holy *crap*.

Her eyes flew to Hades and as soon as she finished chewing and swallowing the bite, she couldn't help saying, "Oh my gods, that's the best thing I've ever eaten in my *entire* life."

He sat back in his chair, brow wrinkled like he'd never seen anything like her before. He hadn't touched his food yet.

"Aren't you going to have yours? It's delicious. Trust me."

"Oh, I don't doubt it," he said. "I'll give your compliments to the chef."

She nodded as she eagerly forked another big bite. "Please do," she said before shoving the forkful into her mouth. Dear gods, *this* was what she'd been missing out on the last nineteen years of her life? Now she had even more to begrudge her mother. It was a crime to have never encountered food this good before.

Her mom was a fan of boiled vegetables. And rice. Plain white rice. Food was fuel, that's what her mom always said. Just fuel.

"Wait till we get to dessert," Hades said, finally taking a bite of his food, his eyes never leaving her.

"What's dessert?"

"Chocolate mousse."

Persephone fought against licking her lips. She adored chocolate.

"So tell me. What made you change your mind and come back?"

"Oh." Obviously, her favorite word for the evening. "Well, I went by my former employers to pick up my, um, paycheck and my belongings, but there was, um..." Persephone looked toward the window. "...a little bit of an issue." She glanced back Hades's way and then down at her plate. "Anyway, I wasn't able to get my paycheck or any of my things. They'd already thrown them out. And I lost my phone last night when that man... So I didn't have anyone's phone number because they were all in the phone and I didn't know where to go without any money..."

She shoved another bite of lamb shank into her mouth if only to cut herself off from saying anything else. She hazarded another glance at Hades. He had his glass of wine in his hand, but he set it abruptly down on the table, frowning. "They didn't give you the money they owed you?"

Persephone swallowed the meat and reached for her cup of water. All of a sudden she felt hot. She fanned herself with her other hand. Did he feel like it was hot in here?

Hades was still staring at her, obviously expecting an answer, so she shook her head, three quick shakes back and forth.

It was embarrassing enough experiencing it the first time around, but now having to tell Hades seemed like adding insult to injury. She didn't know what was worse, him knowing all the details of her pathetic situation or thinking she was a mooch, eager to eat his fancy food and sleep in his fancy penthouse hotel suite.

"That's not acceptable."

The dark look that crossed his face on her behalf both pleased and scared her a little.

She quickly waved a hand. "It's one of those things that happens, I guess. I'll be more careful in the future."

"But surely you have some money in the bank?"

Gods, could she die of embarrassment?

"I don't have a bank account. I kept it all in cash."

She could feel his eyes on her even without looking up. "And, well, I don't exactly have an ID either. Or a social security number. My mom's kind of...intense, I guess is one way to put it. I grew up way out in the middle of nowhere on a farm and my mom homeschooled me and everything. Mom wanted to be off the grid."

Persephone fiddled with her fork in her grits. "Like, *really* off the grid. Apparently she even gave birth to me at home and never, you know, got a birth certificate or social security card or anything for me."

Persephone braced herself and finally looked up at Hades. But she couldn't read a single thing from his features. It wasn't that his face was blank—his eyes were lit with interest, but he didn't look as shocked or appalled as she'd expected. It gave her the courage to go on.

"So when I left home and came to the city, I didn't have any paperwork. I didn't even think about it. I didn't know you needed that kind of thing to get a job. But it turns out it's really important."

"But you still got the nannying job."

She shrugged. "They were fine with paying me cash."

"And they didn't require references?"

"They told me they'd have a nanny cam on me at all times and I got along really well with Timmy during our trial play date. Plus, I wasn't asking for as much money as other nannies, I learned later."

And it had been Paul who'd interviewed her, not Diane. Persephone shuddered. Was that the real reason he'd hired her? Because he found her attractive and had hoped to have an affair with her?

"Well, first of all, we need to start the process for getting you a social security card. You'll be crippled for life without one."

Persephone's mouth dropped open. First by the *we* and second by how confident he sounded that she could actually get a social security card. She'd looked into it on the internet a few times but almost everything that came up was only for how to get documents for babies born at home while they were still babies. Not when they were *nineteen*.

She'd thought about going to the social security office and asking but had gotten afraid. What if she got in trouble for not having the documents? She couldn't actually *prove* she was who she said she was. She couldn't even prove she was a citizen and with how crazy everything had been with immigration lately, what if they tried to deport her to a foreign country? Yes, she was good at thinking in terms of worst-possible-scenarios. After living with her paranoid mom all her life, it was usually her knee jerk reaction.

Besides, she'd gotten the nanny position so it didn't seem so important and definitely not worth the risk.

Feeling stupid even as she asked it, she couldn't help herself. "Doesn't that seem, I don't know...risky? How do I prove that I am who I say I am?"

"I'll have my lawyer look into it, but I imagine it will involve a series of affidavits by your mother and people who knew her while she was preg—"

"No," Persephone said sharply.

Hades's eyebrows went up.

Crap. How to explain this? "My mom and I didn't part on the best of terms, is all."

Hades nodded, looking thoughtful.

Persephone took another bite of her food if only for something to busy her hands with when Hades asked, "Have you ever done any modeling?"

Her eyes bulged and she choked, grabbing for her napkin and dabbing at the red sauce she was sure was all over her mouth.

She hurriedly chewed and laughed. "Ha ha," she said. "Funny joke."

He wasn't laughing, though. His features were set with their stone intensity again. "When I'm telling a joke, you'll know it, Persephone."

She scoffed. "I don't look like a model."

How many times had her mother picked on her appearance? *Why won't you let me cut bangs again? Your forehead is obnoxiously huge. It needs to be covered. And what have you been eating? I'm surprised you can make it through the door with those hips.*

Hades's eyes narrowed. "Don't be one of those girls who pretends she doesn't know she's beautiful."

Persephone's cheeks flamed. Oh gods, did he think she was fishing for compliments? She waved a hand at him but he persisted.

"I have a friend who's a fashion designer, Hermes, and I know he'd love to get his hands on you."

Her mouth dropped open again, the second time in as many minutes. *Get his hands on—*

"Not like that." Hades tilted his head, his grey eyes turning dark. "No one will ever lay hands on you again."

The way he said it had a quality of finality that probably should have disturbed her. And was it just her or did she read an implicit, *"Except me,"* in his eyes in the silence after his statement?

"But it would be work I think you'd enjoy," he went on. "You'd get to meet people your age." He smiled in a way that made her feel every one of the years between them. "And wear pretty clothes."

She rolled her eyes. "I'd feel more comfortable in overalls and flannel. Farm girl, remember?"

Although more than once, she *had* snuck into her mother's closet and tried on the heels hidden in a box at the very back. She'd about broken her ankle the first few times she tried walking in them but had eventually gotten the hang of it. She'd dreamed about the sort of life Hades was describing, but in the same way she dreamed about knights and castles from her books. Not as anything that could ever be *real*.

"You own businesses, right?" she asked. "Why can't I work for you?"

"Out of the question," he snapped and Persephone shrank back from the table.

Hades swiped at his mouth with a napkin. His eyes were on her again. "I own bars. Hotels that aren't in the best parts of town. Not where an angel belongs."

Persephone frowned a little. She wasn't sure she liked being thought of as an angel all that much. The more she got to know Hades, the more she thought she might like to be right down here on the earthly plane with him. For him to see her as a *woman*.

A chair scraped and Hades's shadow fell over her. "Persephone," he took her hand and it happened again, the electricity, but far more intensely this time. Warmth pulsed up her arm, her blood simmering, the flush spreading over her chest and rolling down. Persephone gasped and Hades's forehead crinkled. "Persephone?"

She stared at him as her body throbbed, her lips tingling and breasts swelling. From his touch. One touch. She never even knew that was possible.

"You okay?"

"Yeah. Yes." Her mouth still worked even though her throat had gone suddenly dry. A miracle. "I'm good," she whispered.

Hades narrowed his eyes a moment before his face softened. His thumb stroked over her pulse. Her limbs turned liquid.

"Angel," he said softly, and the way he said it sent thrills through her.

He didn't say anything more, and he didn't have to. Did he... Was he... feeling it too? He had to know how he affected her. And he didn't pull away.

His grey eyes gleamed. Oh gods, he was. He was interested. In *her*.

Very interested, if the way his nostrils flared were any indication.

This was nuts, totally nuts. But it was happening. It was, wasn't it? She wasn't just making things up in her head? She searched his eyes, feeling desperate from all the sensations he was stirring inside her.

"Why are you helping me?" she blurted the question that had plagued her since she'd woken this morning. "I'm no one."

A final squeeze, and his tall, powerful frame moved gracefully back to his seat. She felt breathless, all the nerves in her body still firing from his touch.

He looked down at his plate, his expression shadowed. The silence stretched.

"It's just, you're doing all these things for me. And I'm so grateful, don't get me wrong. But if I could understand *why*—"

"You remind me of someone," he said, eyes still on his plate, and she didn't miss the way his jaw worked. "Let's say helping you is paying a debt I owe."

"Oh." Persephone's stomach sank to the floor, all the lovely feelings dissipating. She was a debt to him? So much for him seeing her as a woman. She felt so foolish. Like a schoolgirl with a crush.

"And this city is a dangerous place. I know better than anyone. I had a sister who was a little younger than you when I lost her."

A sister? And he'd lost her? Persephone immediately felt like a witch for being so self-absorbed. Schoolgirl indeed.

"I'm so sorry. Hades." She reached across the table and laid her hand on his. "What happened? No, gods, I'm sorry. You don't have to tell me." She gave his hand a squeeze and he exhaled a huge breath, finally lifting his grey eyes to hers. She couldn't look away. In front of her was a man, not a boy. He was a man who'd lived through things and survived them, things she couldn't even comprehend. She suddenly wished she was more...well, just *more*, so she might be any sort of comfort to him.

"I want to tell you." His eyebrows were drawn together and she could see a deep grief in his eyes that time obviously hadn't healed. Persephone felt his pain cut straight through her own chest down to her bones. "She was my sister and I loved her more than anything else on earth. When she and my parents were taken from me, brutally, *violently*," his hand shook under Persephone's, "for a long while, I wished I'd died with them."

"Hades," Persephone whispered, barely able to get the word out, her throat was so thick. She reached her other hand out and clasped his, both of her small hands only barely surrounding one of his huge ones.

She didn't know why he'd chosen her to share this with, but from her limited interactions with him, she felt sure this wasn't common for him, that he was a man who rarely if ever wore his heart on his sleeve. He was too in control of himself, too measured in everything he did. Whatever his reasons, she could only feel honored to have this peek beneath the mask to glimpse the genuine man.

"But I *vowed* to do everything I could to take the city they loved under control so that the monsters who killed them would never have free reign again. So you understand why I can't let you go," he said, gaze more direct than ever. "This city is a beast. A beast in a cage. Violent. Brutal. Innocents fall and the criminals go unpunished if left unchecked."

He believed everything he said and he believed it passionately. Absolutely. It sent a shiver down Persephone's spine.

"But what about the cops?"

"What about them?" he sneered. "The police do nothing. They're either corrupt or have no power. There's no law and order, just violence. The strong crush the weak, and death walks the streets. There's a reason they call the part of the city where you were clubbing The Underworld. But it's not just the south side. The whole city balances on a knife's edge. And it's men like me who keep it from going over and falling into chaos."

It's not safe. The world out there isn't safe.

How many times had her mother told her that? She'd repeated it over and over. *Not safe. Not safe. Not safe.*

"I don't want to live my whole life in fear," Persephone whispered.

Hades shook his head. "You won't have to." He flipped his hand and this time it was him squeezing hers.

She felt the strength of his grasp all the way down to her toes.

He leaned in, the burning intensity of his eyes flipping her stomach again as he vowed, "You'll live among the angels where you can't be touched."

5

"Babe, babe, come on, move!" Persephone turned and was blinded by the lights. She'd stepped into the studio and was immediately overwhelmed by the frenetic energy of the place.

"Out of the way! Move it!"

Persephone took a step to the side, disoriented, and then noticed the harried cameraman trying to pass her.

"I beg your pardon," she said, moving out of the way even further. He shook his head at her as he rushed past. She stood unsure, looking this way and that until a short but well-built man came up to her.

"Persephone Vestian?"

"Yes."

The man grinned broadly. "Hermes." He was fresh-faced, dark-haired, and olive-skinned, with sharp cheekbones and flashing black eyes. She wouldn't have thought anyone outside of the seventies could pull off a mustache, but on him it was dashing. Along with his big-framed black glasses, tight jeans, and suspenders over a striped vintage Parisian shirt, he looked incredibly hip in addition to handsome.

Persephone tugged on the hem of her white t-shirt and rubbed her hands on her plain black leggings. Hades had asked her what wardrobe basics she might like and she'd asked for the bare minimum, insisting she would take care of it herself as soon as she had her first paycheck. But maybe she should have worn the blouse and skirt he'd given her the first day.

Hermes held out a hand and when she took it to shake, he pulled it to his lips and kissed her knuckles. "Enchanté. Thanks for helping a chap out in his hour of need. Now, let's get you into hair and makeup." He took her arm and led her to a chair on the far side of the room in front of a row of mirrors, each lined with light bulbs.

"Hermes!" Another man came running up to Hermes, a tablet in hand. "It's a disaster! The zipper ripped on the nymph's maxi dress. Her tits are hanging out. And its Zephoria so there's not enough tape in upper New Olympus to keep those things in without the dress securely zipped."

Hermes lifted a heavy eyebrow and smiled Persephone's way. "A designer's job is never done." Then he looked to a skinny man with a receding hairline who was hovering by Persephone's chair. "Mr. Ubeli said to treat Miss Vestian with the utmost respect. You understand?"

Persephone sensed rather than saw the other man immediately come to attention at Hades's name. "Yes, sir."

To Persephone, Hermes said, "Relax and be yourself." He leaned down and gave her a kiss on the cheek. His cologne was manly and as sophisticated as the rest of him. "You'll do *fabulous* out there, darling, I know it."

With that, he was off and Persephone was left feeling extremely overwhelmed and out of her element.

First came hair, an extensive process of rollers and gels and sprays. While her hair was 'setting,' the makeup artist had his way with her.

He murmured about good bone structure and classic cheekbones but never spoke directly to her for the entire hour he was working on her. Two hours after she'd sat down in the chair, hair and makeup were finally finished.

Persephone looked at herself in the mirror and was stunned. She was covered in violet-shaded white makeup, topped with a powder that gave an iridescent glow to her face, chest, and arms. Striking purple, silver, and black makeup surrounded her eyes, topped off with the longest fake lashes she'd ever seen. It felt funny every time she blinked, when the lashes flapped against her cheeks.

Her hair hung in dark cascading waves down her shoulders, little wisps pinned up here and there that created a wild, ethereal effect.

She looked absolutely nothing like herself.

"Perfect," the artist said, and spun her out of the chair. "Let's get you to costuming."

Costuming. Persephone could only internally shake her head. This certainly felt like playing dress up. Had she really been wiping a toddler's runny nose only three days ago? Though actually, that felt far more real.

This was the dream world. A strange realm full of beautiful, elfin people who were too tall, too thin, and perpetually grouchy. Apart from Hermes, she hadn't seen a single person smile all day.

The assistants who dressed her acted as impersonal as the hair and makeup guys. The dress itself was gorgeous, though. In silver, charcoal and purple tones, it was a draped dress with fabrics sheer as clouds and had the effect of falling like water. With a pleased sound, she turned in them and watched the material float around her. Hermes was a genius.

The assistant was less happy. With a string of curses, he stepped in to pin something, and instead he stuck Persephone's flesh.

Yeouch! Persephone jumped.

"Well, fuck, stand still and I won't accidentally fucking pin you. Fucking amateurs, I fucking swear," he hissed under his breath. "Where the fuck did they find this one?"

Persephone froze and gritted her teeth.

It's a paycheck. Grin and take it for the paycheck.

She waited for him to come at her again, with either more pins or more abuse. But another one of the assistants turned from the rack of clothes and pulled the second man away. He spoke in an urgent whisper.

"Mr. Ubeli," were the only words Persephone caught as she waited, trying to keep a brave face. The first assistant returned and finished his work, silent and stiff. The second disappeared, and reappeared with a bottle of water.

"The lights can be hot," he explained. Persephone noticed none of the other models being given water, but she accepted it. She was directed off to the side to wait her turn.

"But don't sit down," was the assistant's last instruction. "Don't crease the fabric." She gave him a thumbs up but he was already off.

With her clothing draped like a Greek statue and water bottle in hand, she felt like the Statue of Liberty.

She didn't have to wait long though.

"Babe, there you are—" a photographer waved at her, "You're next."

Persephone nodded and hurried forward. Another model, being unpinned from her clothes, turned her head. "Wow," she remarked on Persephone's get up, "you look really cool. Who are you supposed to be?"

"Uh . . . I don't know." Persephone stood aside as two men pushing a huge mirror came through. The thing stood six feet tall, and was still higher on its wheeled mount and gilt frame. They stopped in front of her, cutting off the other model's conversation.

Into the reflected surface, Persephone stared at the striking woman in robes. She'd only been able to see her face in the makeup mirror earlier, but now she was hit with the entire effect.

Kohl-darkened eyes stared back at her. Her hair was big and wild around her but it didn't detract from the luminous, violet sheen of her skin. The tones of the gown only served to highlight the glow of her pale skin even more.

She looked larger than life. *Powerful.* She blinked in surprise at the thought. It wasn't an adjective she'd ever used to describe herself before.

"Well, well, if it isn't the goddess."

Persephone turned around and saw a familiar face, lips quirked up in a half smile.

Hades.

The room around them, chaos only a second ago, cleared out. Stepping back to look beyond the mirror, she could see another model's bare back, the assistant helping her with the bottom half of her costume as they both hurried away. Persephone looked back into the mirror as Hades approached behind her. His smile had dropped and instead his eyes held the intensity of a hunter.

"Hades," she breathed, her stomach feeling strange and swoopy.

He was looking her up and down. With his handsome face and sculpted cheekbones, he looked like a model himself. He wasn't pretty, but the strength and symmetry of his features were powerful. Timeless. Next to him, regular guys were eye-wateringly ugly—until you realized that they weren't, they were normal looking and Hades was a god. Mere mortals couldn't compare.

Her stomach did a sad little spiral. Hades fit in better here than she did.

A few steps and he had crossed the distance between them. She gazed at him in the mirror. When he was right behind her, the two of them looked like a snapshot out of any style magazine. He was wearing a gray button up. He often wore gray or other dark colors. He wasn't wearing a jacket, and the shirt's smoothness couldn't hide the outline of his muscles. He was so *strong*. He didn't have the physique you would expect of a businessman.

Hades's cheek tugged up in one of his signature half smirks. Oh gods, he'd noticed her checking him out.

She felt her cheeks heat, and she looked at her own face in the mirror in alarm, but for once her blush didn't show because of the makeup.

But as she looked in the mirror—oh crap! There was plenty that *was* showing. Her gown might be gorgeous, but all that sheer fabric was practically *see-through*. Had Hades noticed?

She hurriedly crossed her arms in front of her. "I didn't know you were going to be here."

"Do I make you nervous?" he whispered, and she could feel the warmth of his breath on her ear as he skewered her with his gaze in the mirror's reflection.

Even with her arms over her chest, the outline of her body was perfectly clear through the gauziness of the dress. Her hips. The line of her inner thighs.

Hades leaned his face over her shoulder so that their faces were side by side, cheek to cheek.

Persephone felt paralyzed by his gaze.

"You are a goddess," he breathed.

"You shouldn't call me that..."

Hades turned her to him. "Look at me."

She couldn't bear to obey, so she stared at his shirt. He'd undone the top two buttons, giving her a peek of the chiseled line of his pectorals with a faint dusting of hair. It was so...*masculine*.

When he raised her chin to look at him, she was able to follow the sculpted line of his neck up to his jaw and finally, over the strong features of his face.

"Perfect body, perfect skin," he murmured. "How could you not be a goddess?"

"That's very sweet, but you don't have to—" she started.

"No, angel. In a second, you're going to walk out there, and everyone will know how lovely you are."

Her eyes darted away.

"Look at me." He took her in his arms, keeping her still. After a long pause, "Beautiful," he pronounced.

She laughed nervously. Hades smiled and tightened his hold around her, "I'm telling Hermes he owes me big for letting him borrow you. Not one—three or four favors."

Persephone was unsure what to think about that. *Borrow*. Like Hades owned her. The thought should disturb her, but all she could think was *yes, please*. What would it be like to belong to a man like Hades Ubeli?

Persephone looked at herself and Hades in the mirror again, a gorgeous couple out of a magazine. The woman in the mirror's lips were parted slightly, while the man let his eyes browse along her bare shoulders and neck. When he raised his head, his look was cool, but his eyes smoldered. They consumed her.

"Goddess," he whispered again.

"Queen of the Dead, we're ready for you—" a woman with a tablet came out, saw the two of them and took a step back. "Oh, Mr. Ubeli, I didn't mean to interrupt."

"No, no," Hades called back, "she's ready."

Persephone was still feeling paralyzed, but somehow she forced her feet to move forward anyway. Away from him. How, she wasn't sure. But she even managed speech. "Queen of the Dead?" she asked the woman with the tablet. "Do you mean me?"

The woman nodded.

"Come find me at the afterparty," Hades called. "After the show. I'll be waiting."

Without looking back, Persephone crossed through the door, into the lights.

AFTERWARD, her eyes remained dazzled by cameras. She couldn't even remember walking the catwalk. All she could focus on was not tripping in the heels they'd put her in. She'd gotten to the end and posed like an assistant had instructed her, and the explosion of camera flashes had about blinded her. But she'd turned on cue and managed to get backstage without tripping herself or any other models so, *win*.

And now the afterparty. One of the assistants had brought Persephone a dress to change into. The assistant said it was from Hermes, but from the silent looks Persephone got from all the other models, she guessed it was really from Hades.

What are you doing? she asked herself as she walked with the group of models and Hermes's entourage and show attendees one block over to where the afterparty was being held. *Do you really think he's not going to expect something in return for all these so-called gifts?*

Men were pathologically incapable of being trustworthy, her mother always told her. *They always want one thing and one thing only. That's why I keep you here where it's safe.*

But...would it be so bad if Hades wanted her like that? She didn't need gifts. It would be enough if he was interested in her. He didn't need to do anything else.

And oh, the way she felt when he even *looked* at her...

And besides, he hadn't tried anything. Nothing like the 'one thing' men supposedly only wanted. If Hades was a bad man, he could have tried to force himself upon her a hundred times over when he had her alone in his penthouse.

But he hadn't. Because he was honorable. He was a good man. And kind, and generous, and handsome and—

They got to the afterparty and if she thought the show and preparations for it had been overwhelming, she quickly realized it was nothing compared to when New Olympians really got down to *party.*

The party was held on a gorgeous rooftop terrace. The evening was cool, but there were space heaters throughout the terrace keeping it warm and everyone around her seemed to be in a jubilant mood. The show was apparently an unmitigated success according to early reviews and social media.

All around her people laughed and chatted and Persephone smiled, but she never seemed to be in on the jokes about this or that model or actor.

And all they served was champagne and other alcohol. Persephone was parched and dying for a glass of water.

She went in search of one when she heard her name called.

"Persephone! Darling!"

Hermes came over to her and clasped her hand. "Our famous Queen of the Dead, in the flesh. I wondered where you'd gotten off to. Come, come, I have so many people I want to introduce you to."

And for the next thirty minutes, Persephone was whisked around in a whirlwind of introductions, names and faces she knew she'd never remember. She tried to object when Hermes kept introducing her as Hades's girl but to no avail.

Finally, Persephone managed to excuse herself from Hermes's side to go in search of the water she needed even more desperately now.

She'd asked for a cup from the bartender and had taken her first amazing, refreshing, beautiful sip when a shadow loomed in front of her, making her almost choke on her last swallow.

"Hello, goddess."

Hades.

She rolled her eyes and coughed into her elbow, some of the water going down the wrong pipe in her surprise at seeing him.

How did he always sneak up on her like that?

"Not a goddess anymore," she finally managed to say once she got her breathing under control. She snuck another sip of water. "Just regular old me." She lifted her hands, *ta da, here I am*, like a dork.

"I beg to differ."

She shook her head at him. She couldn't even look him in the eye. It had only been hours since she'd last seen him, but she was overwhelmed all over again. Every time. How could she not be? He was the epitome of power and masculine beauty. Plato's form of the perfect man, made flesh.

"Persephone," he called softly. "Look at me."

She obeyed. She couldn't tell him she couldn't look at him directly or his perfection would scorch her like the sun. She met his grey eyes and welcomed the inner flutters, a thousand butterflies throwing a party in her middle.

"How do you like the party?" he asked, eyes crinkling. Like he knew how he affected her and he liked it.

The glittering terrace stretched before them. A jewel-blue pool was illuminated in the center and everywhere beautiful people stood gathered, chatting beautifully.

"Everything's so lovely." Persephone tilted her head to the side.

"But?"

Persephone blinked. She hadn't meant to let any dissatisfaction show through. She knew this was all meant to be a treat. Getting to be a model. Coming here to this fancy afterparty. It was a Cinderella moment and she didn't mean to be ungrateful—especially since she was getting paid on top of all of the rest of it.

"Don't go shy on me now," he said. This was yet another reason she couldn't look at him. His intense, demanding stare always brought out the truth.

She leaned in. "This isn't exactly my scene. I sort of feel like..." She looked out at everyone again. "I don't know, like I'm a scientist and this is a sociological experiment. And I'm in disguise, getting to observe the beautiful people in their natural habitat. I feel like I should be taking notes for a paper or something."

Hades lifted a brow.

"Like her." Persephone nodded her head toward an especially emaciated model who'd been fascinating her for the better part of an hour. "Species modelsapien domesticus, approximately 95 pounds. Never actually eats food, but holds it between her forefinger and thumb and pretends to nibble at it for thirty-eight and a half minutes. Then she casually sets it down on a passing waiter's tray and starts the whole charade again with another item of food. And don't even get me started on the mating rituals."

Hades barked out a laugh, and looked surprised at himself.

And then, to Persephone's surprise, he hooked her around the waist and pulled her away from the bar where she'd been standing and over to the shadowed corner, hidden behind two tall, planted palm trees.

There was just enough light to see the glint in his eyes.

"I like you." He pronounced it so solemnly, Persephone couldn't tell if he was happy about it or not. Persephone was definitely happy to hear it. Exhilarated in fact.

"Really?" she squeaked.

This brought out the half smile she was quickly becoming addicted to. "Really."

He leaned in, his weight shifting to press her back against the wall of the building.

Oh gods, was he really about to—?

His lips were gentle against hers, but only for a moment. Like everything else about him, his lips quickly turned demanding.

And Persephone was helpless to do anything other than obey.

Her lips parted on a gasp and he took the opportunity to plunge his tongue into her mouth.

She'd never been kissed, really kissed, and— She lifted her arms and wrapped them around Hades's broad shoulders if only to have something to hold onto and ground herself. Because she felt like she could float up, up, and away.

He was kissing her senseless. Her stomach somersaulted with every powerful swipe of his tongue. Persephone couldn't help arching her breasts up and into his chest. Oh gods, had she really done that?

She tried to pull back, but Hades wrapped a hand around her waist between her and the wall, securing her even more tightly against his body.

Her eyes flew open. He was— She could feel his—his *hardness*. She gasped for breath in between kisses and when he finally pulled away and cupped her face in his strong hand, she rolled her cheek into his touch, blinking dazedly up at him.

He had a satisfied smile on his face.

Would he take her home now and—and make love to her? That was what happened next, right? Even though he'd put a little bit of space between them, she could still feel him.

She didn't know much about sex, but she knew she wanted it. She wanted everything Hades had to give.

She'd never felt this way before. His presence rolled over her, overwhelming, taking no prisoners. Was this attraction? Or something more? Every molecule in her quivered, standing at attention.

Hades dominated her senses, made her giddy. Alarm bells rang in her head. *Let him in, and he will rule your world.* Hades wasn't a man who did anything by half measures. His control over her would be absolute, but she wouldn't hate it. She'd revel in it.

It was too much. It was happening so fast. She closed her eyes, dizzy.

Now she knew why the poets sang of "falling in love." Because it felt like falling. A wild and free and awful descent. And once you fell, it was over. There was no coming back.

"Persephone, are you all right?"

She nodded, eyes still closed. She couldn't look at him. It was like staring into the sun.

"Persephone. Look at me. Don't hide."

She lifted her chin and blinked at him. "You terrify me," she whispered.

He raised an eyebrow. "Well, you've always struck me as an intelligent girl."

"What happens now?"

He pushed a strand of hair behind her ear and she shuddered in pleasure at the touch. His eyes flared and she immediately wanted to press her breasts into his chest again.

What would it feel like to have his hands on her? She hadn't forgotten the way he'd looked her up and down in the mirror earlier. He was such an intense man. What would it feel like to have all that intensity directed at her? To have nothing between them. No clothes. No pretenses. No years.

"Now," he leaned in and pressed his lips against hers again, the briefest kiss before pulling away, "we get Cinderella back home to sleep before she turns into a pumpkin."

He pulled back and took her arm.

"I don't think that's quite how the fairy tale goes," she murmured as he began to lead her through the crowd. Conversations stopped and eyes turned to them, the crowd parting like the Red Sea as they passed through.

Why did they all treat him that way? She glanced up at Hades but his face was cold as marble. If his arm hadn't been so warm and sure on hers, she might have shivered from seeing it. She glanced around at the faces of some of the crowd.

There was more than respect on their faces. There was fear.

Who was Hades Ubeli besides the man who was turning her life upside down? Did she want to know? Or, a more disturbing question

—did it matter to her, as long as in private she got to see the man beneath the mask?

She was tense-slash-giddy for the entire ride home. Charon drove them and when a window closed between the driver and the back seat, she was sure that Hades would kiss her again. He didn't, though. He put an arm around her and played with her hair absently during the ride home. It was silent other than the Rachmaninoff that echoed throughout the car.

She frowned when the car stopped after only a short ten-minute drive and Charon got out and opened her door.

Hades pulled away from her and she looked at him in confusion. "We aren't to the Crown yet, are we?" It had taken over half an hour to get from the hotel to the venue for the fashion show earlier today. Granted, there had been traffic, but surely they hadn't covered all that distance so quickly, had they?

She looked out the window and no, the historic hotel was nowhere in sight.

"I've arranged an apartment for you," Hades said.

She swung around in her seat to look at him, her mouth dropping open. The penthouse at the Crown was one thing. He apparently always had that on reserve, but another apartment? For *her*?

"Hades, I can't—"

"You can," he put a hand to the small of her back to urge her out of the car, "and you will. Think of it as house-sitting. My secretary is on an extended vacation in Europe for the summer. You'll be a help if you stay here. You can water the plants."

But when Persephone got upstairs, she didn't find any plants. What she did find was a luxurious, fully furnished three-bedroom apartment with a fabulous view of the park.

"This is incredible." She padded through the huge rooms. Her feet sank into the thick carpet. Hades stalked behind her, hands in his pockets, a half smile slanted on his stunning face.

Persephone stopped at a fireplace, running a nervous hand over the marble molding. An apartment like this, in this part of town, had to cost tens of thousands of dollars a month. She felt small in the overwhelming luxury.

"It's too much. I can't—" Her voice died when she met Hades's intent gaze. He'd given her so much already.

"You can and you will. Stay here. Stay safe." He looked like he might say more, but the front door opened. A few moments later Charon appeared. He nodded to her and handed Hades an envelope.

Hades opened it and glanced inside. His smile turned shark-like, satisfied. "One more thing, angel." He held out the envelope. Her hand trembled as she took it.

Inside were bills. Crisp greenbacks packed into the white envelope. The number on the bill made her knees wobble. "What's this?"

"Your pay. You told me your former employer owed you."

"They did, but..." Her fingers fumbled through the thick bundle. She did a quick count. "This is too much, it's way more—"

"They weren't paying you enough. Charon had a little talk with them, and they saw the error of their ways."

Clutching the sheaf of money, more money than she'd ever seen, much less held in her hands, her senses swam.

"A talk with them?" The big man regarded her impassively. From what she knew of Charon, he wasn't much of a talker. Did that mean—?

"You didn't—" She stopped herself before she said, *hurt them.* She couldn't very well ask if he'd beaten Paul up, could she? "They're okay?"

Charon raised his chin. "They send their apologies. Wanted you to know they're getting marriage counseling. Cutting back hours at work, spending more time with their son."

"Oh. Good." Charon did talk to them. Or, at least, they talked to him. Told him all that, and paid out well over her earnings in crisp one hundred dollar bills. She stared at the money in her hand as if it were a snake.

"See, angel?" Hades murmured. "They won't bother you again."

Charon was gone and it was just the two of them. He stepped closer and her world narrowed to his frame, tall and imposing, devastating in a dark suit. Her senses filled with his nearness, the five o'clock shadow edging his jaw, his delicious cologne. Her uncertainty disappeared. "You wanna thank me?"

"Thank you," she breathed, drunk on his nearness. Deep down, a little voice whispered a warning, but the rest of her was too far gone. Her heart fluttered in her chest, wild but happy. Happily trapped.

"No, baby," Hades stopped, so close if she stepped forward, her nipples would brush his suit again. The tiny alarm bell abruptly cut off. "I meant, do you really wanna thank me?"

"Yes?"

"Then stay here. Live in this apartment. Enjoy it. And have dinner with me tomorrow night."

"Tomorrow," she whispered. His dark hair fell over his brow, softening the hard planes of his face. She swayed.

"Tomorrow," he whispered back. And he backed up, breaking her trance. She hoped he'd stay, but he only gave her that damnable half-smile and said, "Goodnight, goddess."

She was left so desperately wanting as he withdrew and closed the front door behind him. After it clicked shut, she slumped against it and lifted her hands to her lips, to her face, through her hair.

All she knew was that something huge had begun tonight with Hades Ubeli, and her life would never be the same.

6

Hades was a perfect gentleman. Persephone stood in the foyer of her beautiful apartment a month later, putting on her earrings in front of the mirror, waiting for Charon to knock on the door.

Occasionally Hades sent his employee to pick her up. Hades got caught up in meetings sometimes, but didn't like to be late for their outings. Charon was a decent stand in, taking her to a restaurant, where they would serve her a glass of wine, and Hades would always arrive soon after, smiling and full of compliments to her beauty.

A perfect gentleman, she thought again. He hadn't kissed her again, but he put his arm around her to keep her warm whenever they went on long drives through the park, or to his favored private club on the edge of the city. And when he took her to more dangerous parts of town in order to show her a friend's restaurant, he would loop her arm through his as they walked from the car into the building, and stay by her side all night. She felt safe with him.

He was generous, too. The roses in the foyer were a gift from him. The dress and necklace she wore were other gifts. She always blushed when she got a gift—it seemed too much. But try telling

Hades that and he just shook his head and got stubborn. And when Hades got stubborn, well...

Once, telling her that he had to miss a date because of business, he told her to go into a shop and try on whatever she liked. Charon had followed, a silent shadow who saw everything and said nothing. Everything she touched, whether she liked it or not, arrived in large shopping bags at her apartment the next day.

She would have been exasperated—she already felt that things were so uneven between them, and every gift he gave her only made her feel that gap all the more. She didn't care about the jewelry or the clothes. Sure, they were nice.

But all she wanted was Hades.

In the end, it was why she accepted all the gifts. Because she knew it made him happy. It meant something to him, she could tell, to be able to drape the woman he cared for in fine things. To help her stand out as *his*. And that was all she ever wanted because she could barely remember a time before Hades.

But could something so beautiful and perfect actually last? For her, Persephone Vestian?

Things were just *so* good. And well...she couldn't help feeling on edge, waiting for the other shoe to drop. She couldn't help it. Her mother had built a lifetime of paranoia in her.

It didn't help that she felt sure she was being watched. Once in a while, returning home from work in the evening, she'd be coming down the street and get the feeling. She'd look over quickly, and there would be the sleek tip of a car turning out of an alley, or parked on the street. The windows were always tinted so she could never see inside.

At first she'd been terrified, sure it was her mother come to steal her back to the farm. But when nothing ever came of it, when the cars continued simply waiting patiently and following her movements... she couldn't help wondering. Was...was Hades having her followed? Or was she just being totally paranoid and no one was following her at all?

It's a coincidence, Persephone thought to herself as she got ready for her evening out. *You're making up something to be worried about.*

Standing in the small room that served as a foyer in front of the door, she faced the mirror one last time.

Tonight was important. Hades had been busy lately, working early and late and all hours in between, so that she barely saw him. Their last date had been three nights ago, at a new restaurant called simply 'Nectar'. His car had met her at the animal shelter where she'd been dropping off a volunteer application and taken her straight to the place, despite her protests that she wasn't dressed for the occasion. The night started with champagne in the car and ended with them both on the rooftop of the building, looking down over the world while the band played softly for the few late customers.

"This is beautiful," she said.

"You're beautiful." Hades wasn't looking at the city. "I think I like you in your work clothes."

She was just wearing jeans and a plain T-shirt. She tugged at the hem of the T-shirt. "You owe me for this, Hades Ubeli."

His mouth quirked and she went on. "Dragging me to this fancy restaurant, plying me with champagne...I'm barely fit to ride on public transport in these clothes."

"I'll make it up to you," he said. "I'll buy you a dress."

She rolled her eyes and blushed like she always did. And his face, usually so serious under his dark and shining hair, had held a little half smile.

"I'd buy you all this if I could." He swept his hand over the city, glittering below them like a box of jewels. Persephone giggled at his teasing. Seeing Hades so at ease and making jokes, while he stood so close to her, she felt euphoric.

"You mean you can't?" she smiled back. "Mr. Ubeli, what will we do with you? You've been working too hard." The moonlight cupped his dark features, the shadows under his eyes evidence of long, long nights. She wanted to reach up and touch his face, but she didn't quite dare.

"I've missed you," he said. Two fingers came to stroke her cheek.

Her heartbeat took flight. He was touching her. Gods, he was touching her. "I can't believe I have someone like you."

She stared at him and he stared back. Had he really just said that? To *her*? She knew she was infatuated with him. Any girl would be. But was it... Was it actually within the realm of possibility that he could actually feel anything back? For *her*?

But as he stared at her, she'd swear he looked just as stunned as she felt. Oh gods, could it be true? Please, please, could it be true? She'd give anything, pay any price for this man to care for her back even half of what she felt for him.

And then she realized she had just been standing there silently. Crap.

She spoke up, haltingly. "You've been great too. You're kind, more than generous. You've treated me like a princess." Gods, she wasn't saying this right. How could she make him understand? "I came to the city with such big dreams, but . . . every girl dreams of a life like this. You've made it come true." She looked up at him, knowing that her cheeks were alive with the heat of the moment and the cold of the wind.

Her words weren't enough. She wanted to tell him how she felt about *him*. It wasn't just gratitude for all he'd done. Even if he'd never given her a single thing, she would feel the same way about him. She saw how he was with everybody else. Cold. Distant. The greatest gift he'd given her was himself. He'd let her in when he never let anyone in besides Charon.

His fingers remained on her cheek, but still as if any movement more than breathing would shatter it all.

"Persephone," he whispered, and she strained to hear. The wind nearly took his words. "I want..."

"What?" she had whispered back, but there was no answer.

In the silence she'd shivered a little, and he was there, folding her into his chest, suit jacket and satin handkerchief pressing into her cheek. And he was warm, so strong, and nothing could take her away from his shelter or his heat.

"I want to keep you safe," he said. "I want to hold you, like this..."

When he didn't go on, she realized he didn't have to. It was okay if he didn't have the words. "Shh..." she whispered and closed her eyes, sinking into him.

They had stayed that way for a long time, till after the band stopped playing, and the waiters swept up, and finally they went back down to where Charon sat in the car with a fist over his mouth to keep from yawning. She had kept her head on Hades's shoulder all the way home, as the light on the car window softened with dawn.

Hades had kept his promise. The dress had arrived that afternoon, with a note: *Wear it, and we'll call it even.* She had grown used to opening gifts in the weeks that he had been preoccupied with work, but this one made her gasp as she lifted it from the tissue—the fabric was luminous gray and covered over with clear beads that glinted like city lights. A small box accompanied it. It opened to showcase a necklace. The setting was shaped like a tear, two diamonds and another stone, a large red one she couldn't recognize.

So now she found herself standing in the dim light of the little foyer, allowing herself one last look in the mirror before her escort knocked on the door and whisked her away to Hades. She couldn't wait to see him, but she wanted to look perfect for him.

The dress was lovely, soft and gray, like the stuff of clouds. The tiny beads twinkled, even though the only light in her dark apartment came from the cityscape outside her windows. She had turned out the lights in preparation to go out, and now saw her reflection in stark shadow and dulled light.

Still, her eyes were shining, and the jewels at her ears and neck flashed in the light of the city. She smiled. A happy, but pale face smiled back. She touched her cheek with cold fingers. So white, as if she'd been frightened. Patting them sharply to give them some color, she breathed in the scent of the roses.

A knock sounded behind her, and she all but jumped out of her skin. She laughed at herself as she put a hand to her chest. Grabbing her clutch, she turned to the door. She almost grabbed for the doorknob but stopped herself and checked through the peephole, as

Hades had instructed her. *City instinct,* he had told her. *Don't trust you know what's beyond your own front door.*

He sounded like her mother. But still, she humored him.

The head outside the door was bent. Frowning, she waited for it to straighten so she could see a face. It certainly wasn't Charon; his head was shaved. The one she was looking at had a full head of hair, brown and a bit tousled, though wet like it had been raining on the streets.

Finally, the head raised. Her mouth dropped open in a silent gasp and she went cold as she recognized the face from that night at the club. The night that ended with her on her back in a car, before she escaped into the streets and the empty club where she had met Hades.

She backed silently away from the door, fright closing her throat.

He didn't see you. He can't see you.

Still, all she wanted was to run to her bedroom and hide under the bed like a little kid. Instead, she retreated to the kitchen, grabbed her phone along with a big kitchen knife, and went into the bathroom. She closed and locked the door behind her.

Shaking, she dialed. It was a number Hades had given her if she needed to reach him. No one ever picked up, but she had never left a message before without Hades or Charon getting the information.

"Hello," she whispered in the bathroom, "this is Persephone." Even though she was speaking as quietly as she could, her voice echoed off the bathroom walls. Was the man still out there? Could he hear her?

"There's a man outside my door," she continued into the phone, both her hand and her voice shaking, but she gave every detail as carefully as she could, speaking slowly, like a small child. She hung up and waited.

Ten minutes later, she thought she could hear another knock on the door. Phone in hand, she didn't move. Again, a knock. The phone rang, breaking the silence and nearly causing her to scream. She answered it with a half-strangled, "Hello?"

Charon was at the door. It took three tries for her shaking hands to unlock it, and when she did, he came in before she asked him, ushering her to a couch with a strong hand, flipping on lights as he did. He poured her a drink and assured her Hades was on his way. Then he went back to the foyer and she heard his deep voice, talking to what she assumed were more of Hades's security team.

Charon was back a few minutes later, a certain look on his face that told her that he was cautiously pleased with something.

"You okay?" he asked. She'd gotten to know Charon a little bit over the past month, well, as much as you could get to know a gruff, silent security guard. But there was genuine concern in his eyes as he looked down at her.

"Yes," she said, smoothing still trembling hands down over her gown. "I think so."

"Two of my men were outside the apartment. They think they may have spotted him, and saw him dive down into city transport. They're still on the trail." There it was again, a look of quiet smugness that suggested Charon was sure he'd have his hands on the man soon. "You'll never see him again."

Persephone frowned. The way Charon said it, it sounded...*final*. Not like if they found the guy, they'd call the cops.

"He didn't do anything," she said. "Just scared me, that's all." What the hell was she doing? Defending her kidnapper? She lifted hands to her temples and rubbed. "How—how did he find me?"

But Charon's face was now impassive, and he was suddenly no longer willing to speak. A few minutes later, Hades arrived, and she was comforted, complimented, and cradled in his strong arms. All the while Charon watched, and Persephone felt the silent, knowing glances between the man and his boss.

"Why don't we stay in tonight, babe. Go order Greek. Charon will pick it up for us."

She left the room reluctantly, feeling the eyes of the two men on her. When she returned, they were standing close to one another, both faces hard and strained, though she had heard no raised voices.

As quiet as she was creeping back, she only heard Hades mutter, "Don't let it happen again," before he turned back to her, a cold but gracious host.

Persephone stood at the threshold of the room. She'd changed out of the beautiful gown into soft jeans and a plum colored cashmere sweater. This was the other side of the man she...the man she cared for. It was easy to let herself get swept away in the Hades he was when they were alone together. Passionate. Tender. Sweet. But there was another side to him. A darkness.

"Give Charon the restaurant name so he can get the food." Before the bald man left the room, Hades added, "I don't want any delivery boy knowing where she lives." The quiet fury on his face made her pause halfway to the couch. He put out his hand to call her to him and she remained where she was.

"Hades," she asked when Charon had gone, "who is this guy?" Would he open up to her?

"I told you, babe. He's some dick off the streets who saw a goddess he can never touch and can't get wise." With a sigh he seated himself on the couch, staring off into nowhere, his face turned to stone.

Finally, though, he relaxed. "Come here," he said, and held out his hand again. Slowly, she moved forward and took it, allowing him to pull her down onto the couch. He cradled her as he had when they had first met, arm around her, her head against his suit jacket.

"I don't want you scared," he whispered, his lips right near her face, "Don't think you aren't safe. Nobody, I mean nobody," she felt him tense up, angry, "touches my girl."

She wanted to soothe him. She wanted *her* Hades back. "I'm fine," she murmured. "Nothing happened."

They sat in silence for a time, and as the clock ticked, the tension left his body. Persephone could feel his breathing soften. She held herself very still, like a moth trapped against a lamp; feeling the danger, unable to break away. But she didn't want to break away.

Let me in, she pleaded silently. She could handle his darkness, if he would let her be his light.

"And nothing ever will. I'll keep you safe," he said. "I won't let you out of my sight."

She remembered the gleam of the black car she spotted sometimes and frowned. "You already don't."

"What?" His voice mixed with the doorbell and she pulled away.

"It's okay," Hades said, his hands steadying her, "it's only Charon with the food." He mistook her anxiety and she let him, body still taut and held away from him, even though she was still so close her hair spilled over his suit.

"Persephone," he repeated, and she relaxed.

"I'm hungry, go get dinner," she said, but she turned her face away from him as he stood up and went to the door.

He *was* having her followed, she knew it now. Charon had all but admitted it when he said men watching her apartment had followed her abductor, and Hades's words just now... This was exactly the kind of thing she'd left her mother to get away from.

She breathed out and squeezed her eyes shut. What had she gotten herself into? Did Hades think she didn't know? Did he think she was an idiot? Was that what he wanted, some dumb, foolish little plaything he could occasionally amuse himself with?

Moving to one corner of the couch and tucking her legs under her, she listened hard. Voices in the foyer—Hades and another, no, two other men. Charon? Or the other two, the ones who had been so conveniently close to her apartment? The question was: *why* was he having her watched? For her safety...or because he didn't trust her?

"You okay?" Hades asked when he returned with a paper sack of food. Persephone smiled and nodded, but it was the fake smile she always used to use with her mother. Gods how she hated to use it with Hades. But she didn't know what else to do. Everything had seemed so sure only an hour before and now...

They set out the food, and before they tucked in, Hades asked again, "You sure you're okay?"

"Yes." The answer was shaky, but sure. She smiled again, the same fake smile. Hades didn't notice anything was amiss, and that broke her heart a little.

"I told you, babe," was all he said, "I'm going to take care of you."

"I HAVE to get off early tonight," Persephone called to the back of the shelter where she'd started volunteering. She hadn't been able to find another job without an ID and social, other than a few other all-cash modeling gigs she'd gotten off of Hermes's show. Volunteering made her feel less stir-crazy in the meantime while she tried to sort something more permanent out.

"Okay," said Hecate, who ran the shelter. "Start at the end and get as far as you can, cleaning. The bucket is in the closet, sponges and soap by the sink."

Persephone passed two hours in silence, cleaning cages. It was hard, dirty work. Somehow, though, she felt cleaner after doing it. Scrubbing reminded her of being a kid on the farm where life was simple and full of honest, hard work. At the age of ten, it had been her job to scrub the floors of the house and to muck out the stables.

Ironic that she should be feeling nostalgia for that place she couldn't wait to get away from.

But things were so confusing here in the city.

Hades continued to court her, taking her to the best restaurants. Sometimes she felt like he was showing her off. But that was ridiculous, he was the glamorous one. Whenever they walked into a place, people sat up and took notice. The restaurant owner would rush out to greet them, give them the best table, and check in during the meal to make sure everything was okay.

Everywhere they went, people kowtowed to Hades, and, in turn, Hades took care of her. He continued with the gifts, no matter how much she continued telling him they weren't necessary. He even insisted his car pick her up from the apartment and drive her to the shelter. She protested but Hades said, "goddess," in his deep voice, amused and superior and sexy all at once, and got his way. He always got his way.

And as for her misgivings from the other night...

She frowned as she scrubbed even harder at the bottom of the cage. What was she really complaining about? That a man considered her so precious he wanted to make sure she was safe at all times?

And if he was having her followed because he didn't trust her, well, he was a wealthy man and she was a nobody. Maybe he'd been burned before. She didn't know just how rich he was, but she knew he owned lots of businesses and was powerful, too. He'd only just met her. It was only smart for him to want to know if she really was who she said she was. Plus, it wasn't like she had anything to hide.

And, the question she'd finally asked herself several nights ago: wasn't he worth it? When she was with Hades she felt like she could fly. And gods, when he touched her, even just the barest brush of his hand against hers...goosebumps pebbled up and down her arms at the mere thought.

She liked him. She really liked him. She was scared to let herself think about how she felt about him, it was so strong. A lot stronger than *like*, if she was honest with herself. And he was giving her everything she'd ever wanted. A new life, a new identity, one in which she could be suave and city-savvy and glamorous. That's why she came to the city, to be free of her mother. Even if Hades helped her, protected her, okay, maybe controlled her a little, did that mean she wasn't free?

A long time later, Hecate found Persephone sitting in one of the cages surrounded by cleaning supplies, one rubber glove on and the other off. Hecate had long red hair threaded with gray that she mostly kept braided. She came to check on Persephone.

"Persephone," she called, and Persephone blinked out of her musings and glanced up. "How are things looking up here? Oh wow, you got through more cages than I thought you would."

Persephone smiled. "I have experience." Cleaning cages wasn't exactly the same as mucking out stables, but the work ethic required was the same.

Persephone yawned and swiped at her forehead with her arm.

"Aw, you look tired. I hope you're taking off early to head home and get some rest."

Persephone shook her head. "Not quite. Hades is taking me out to a friend's restaurant."

Hecate's easy expression dropped and her eyebrows furrowed. "I worry about you, honey. Are you sure things aren't moving too quickly with that man?"

Persephone smiled at the older woman. 'That man' treated her like a queen. He could have anyone, and he looked at Persephone like she was the only woman in the world. She still didn't understand it, why he'd chosen her. But he had and that was all that mattered.

Persephone knew Hecate felt a matronly affection for her but, it wasn't necessary. "I'm a big girl. I know what I'm doing."

Hecate didn't look convinced. "Did you see today's paper?"

Persephone frowned. "No," she said, but Hecate was already holding out the paper she'd had under her arm.

"I was using the paper to line the cages and the headline caught my eye. How well do you really know him?"

Persephone stared down at the New Olympian Times. *Known Crime Boss Surfaces at Club.* The picture was grainy, but she'd recognize Hades anywhere.

Persephone averted her eyes from the paper and scrubbed violently at the corner of the cage for a moment while she tried to gather her thoughts.

Crime boss.

Was it true?

But then she thought of how Hades was treated everywhere they went. The bowed heads, the fearful, surreptitious glances. The power she knew he wielded, even if she hadn't understood why. And the darkness in him. If she was being honest, she'd suspected it was something like this, hadn't she? But being honest with herself wasn't her forte lately.

Because what she was feeling wasn't surprise. It was the queasy uneasiness of confirmation. She'd never asked Hades too closely about his business because she hadn't wanted to know.

But here it was in black and white. Printed on the front page.

She glanced back at the paper Hecate was still holding out and her eyes skimmed the first paragraph. They called Hades the *Lord of the Underworld*. She looked away again but Hecate obviously wasn't going to drop the issue so easily.

"How well do you know him?" she asked again.

Persephone stopped scrubbing and tossed the sponge back into the bucket of soapy water. She scooted out of the cage and pulled off her second glove, then pushed back wisps of hair that had escaped her ponytail.

"He's a good man, Hecate."

She pulled the newspaper out of Hecate's hands and tossed it to the floor of the cage she'd cleaned. She liked Hecate; she really did. They'd hit it off ever since she'd come in to volunteer, but Persephone didn't need another mother trying to tell her what she could and couldn't do.

Still, she respected Hecate. She was nothing like Persephone's real mother. She wasn't pushy or overbearing and it was unfair to lump the two into the same category, so Persephone reached out and squeezed the older woman's hand.

"Trust me," Persephone said. "The paper always sensationalizes things. Hades is a good man." She didn't know what else to say, but of that she was sure. He was *good*.

Hecate looked unconvinced but she nodded and squeezed Persephone's hand in return. "Promise me you won't let yourself get swallowed up in him. You left home to find yourself and be free of your family." Persephone had told Hecate a truncated version of why she'd left home, and she nodded at Hecate's assessment. "So don't let him steamroll over you. There's no need to rush things. And if you ever need help, remember you can always come to me."

Persephone smiled in appreciation at her friend's concern. After months in the city, she did count this woman as a friend, the first she'd made apart from Hades. Did it say something about her that the two people she'd gotten close to were both over a decade her senior, and with Hecate make that two decades? Her mom had always said she had an old soul.

"All right," Persephone dusted off her jeans as she stood up. "I have to go. I'll see you on Thursday."

Hecate nodded and Persephone headed for the bathroom. She changed quickly out of her work clothes and into a clingy black dress with a daring slit up the thigh. She put on some mascara and lip-gloss, and headed to the front, which was a little shop for pet goods.

Charon was waiting. "Miss Vestian," he said, holding open the door for her.

Hades worked so much, she only got to see him every few days. But whenever they were together, it was like no time at all had passed. They picked up right where they'd left off.

Charon drove her to the club where she'd met Hades the very first night. Walking the steps she'd run down so fearfully gave her the oddest sense of déjà vu. She could remember the fear so vividly.

Charon pushed through the door at the bottom of the stairs and held it open for her. She swallowed. It was just the echo of that fear that was giving her goosebumps right now. It had nothing to do with the newspaper article. Right? Right. She took a deep breath and followed Charon through the door.

She walked back to Hades's office, knocked lightly, and pushed the door open. And immediately relaxed upon seeing Hades's familiar and beloved face.

He kept his office so dark his face was as shadowed as it had been the first night she'd met him, all hard lines and harsh angles. But that was the air that Hades liked to project, wasn't it? He was cold and scary to everyone but her.

...or was she just deluding herself? Was she actually special? When it came down to it, how well did she really know Hades? She knew how he made her *feel*, but that wasn't quite the same thing.

"Hi," she said shyly.

His head came up from the papers he was looking over and he paused, obviously taking her in. He did that fairly often, unabashedly checking her out and if the heated look in his eyes was anything to go by, appreciating what he saw.

He pushed his chair back from the desk and held out an arm for her, beckoning her closer.

She went. As she crossed behind his desk and stopped in front of him, she saw how tired he actually looked.

"Long day?" she asked, and he didn't reply, simply put his hands on her hips and pushed her back so that she was leaning on the desk. He gripped her hips and squeezed them, digging his thumbs in and massaging her flesh. The touch was so presumptuous and possessive, all the air fled Persephone's lungs in one great gasp.

Hades looked up at her and she couldn't read what she saw in his storm grey eyes. "Sweet Persephone, so innocent," he whispered. He bowed his forehead against her middle. He wrapped his arms around her waist and pulled her against him, his face still flush with her stomach.

Her hands dropped to his hair. He hugged her with the desperation of a little boy holding onto a blanket for comfort.

Was that what she was for him—a place he could finally relax and find comfort? The thought sent an elated zing down her spine. How she would love to be this complicated man's safe place. She stroked his hair, down to his neck, massaging his shoulders, before her fingers drifted back to his hair, and he clutched her tighter.

The New Olympian Times stuck out from underneath the papers he'd been looking at. Had he been upset by the newspaper? Because maybe they'd gotten it all wrong and it was slander and—

"All right, we need to get going." Hades pulled back and if she'd expected to see his features soft or tender, she was disappointed. He looked as calm and cool as ever.

Persephone frowned, but he was already standing and taking her arm to lead her out to the car.

Hades never liked to talk much when they were in the car. He always had Charon put on classical music and Persephone got the feeling it was the one time in his busy day where he got to just sit peacefully and relax. He rarely pulled out his phone to check emails or take calls. He simply sat, sometimes with his eyes closed, most of the time just watching the city streets going by, often taking her hand like he did today. He rubbed circles back and forth with his thumb and she couldn't deny that the rhythmic motion along with the music *was* relaxing, to the point of being hypnotic.

Persephone was tempted to let the relaxation of the moment and Hades's touch soothe her fears. But she kept hearing Hecate's voice in the back of her head: *How well do you really know him?*

And it erupted out of her: "I saw the paper today. It scared me, Hades."

He immediately went tense and pulled his hand back from hers.

"Please, Hades. Will you tell me what's going on? Is it…is it true?"

"You don't want to know," he said. She took a deep breath and turned to look at him, forcing herself to wait for an answer even though she could see a glint of anger in his eyes. After a moment, something like a smile quirked his lips, though the coldness didn't leave his face.

"But you're my girl, so I'll tell you."

She waited through a long pause for him to continue.

"Couple of weeks back, two friends of mine decided to go in on a club. They bought the old theater, renamed it, set it up real nice. Big project like that, they needed some help. I helped them."

He paused again as if wondering how much he should share with her.

"But rumors were circling—you know, people talk. Someone thinks something's up, and the press hooks on it like it's the only story in town. There were stories going around even before the place opened. Then last night," a large sigh, "the press showed up."

She waited a moment after he stopped. "And?"

"They took pictures and jumped to conclusions. They slandered my friends and tried to shut them down. And, because they can print whatever trash they want," his jaw went hard, "it got smeared on the front page. All my friends wanted to do was open a club. Whose business is it how they run it? And the stuff they said—drugs and dirty money—none of that's been proven. Those accusations belong in court. To slap it on a front page to sell papers—that's what's illegal."

From where she sat, Persephone could feel him getting angrier, though his voice never rose. She could feel it through the small distance between them, waves of cold fury, kept tightly clenched under his suit and silken tie.

"It's one thing to come after me directly. It's another to use my friends." He stared forward at the rearview mirror; his and Charon's eyes met there.

The car glided through the streets. The windows were thick, keeping out sound, so it seemed silent, apart from the brooding classical music. Persephone studied Hades's face, afraid of what she saw there. He was distant, cold.

Without thinking, she shivered, and with a murmur—"You okay, babe?"—he put his arm around her, and they rode on with the heavy weight across her shoulders.

And, though the questions screamed inside her—*who are you? Is that really all there is to it? What do you mean, you 'helped' your friends?*—she found she couldn't say any more.

So deep was the silence, it took them both a moment to realize the car had stopped.

Charon opened the door and she found herself looking up at a tall building, with many stairs leading up to its large doors.

"Go on." Hades pushed her gently, and she dutifully climbed out.

"Is this the restaurant?" she asked, teeth chattering with a sudden cold wind. Hades, having stopped to speak with Charon, came and took her under his arm and coat jacket, ushering her forward.

He gave her an enigmatic smile as they went up the steps. She could barely see beyond his sheltering arms as he pushed open the doors.

As soon as they stepped inside, humid heat rolled over Persephone, lapping at her arms and face like an ocean wave. It was completely dark, though. But Persephone relaxed anyway, walking into the darkness without being afraid. Hades was at her side.

"What is this place?" she breathed.

A flashlight switched on, and the beam danced over palms and ferns, flowers and green—a whole host of growing things, sheltered in the building of glass.

"A greenhouse!" she cried, and Hades chuckled as he came forward to show her around. They traipsed the narrow paths and found their way through the dark with only his single flashlight.

How did he know that this was exactly what she'd needed? As much as she admired the city, sometimes it got to be oppressive—so much concrete, pavement, brick, and steel, block after block in all directions. She missed growing things. She missed being able to walk out her front door and touch the earth, smell the soil, and watch the sun rise in the big open sky.

She held out her arms and laughed as her hands brushed the beckoning soft branches and leaves.

She squinted. "I see something up ahead." She dropped her arms and pressed forward.

Hades obligingly followed with the light, until they pushed past one great frond and found a little table and some wine, lit by a silver candelabra. Going around her, he pulled out one of the chairs.

"Welcome to paradise, goddess."

Speechless, she sat quietly while he poured the champagne, and took a glass.

"A toast," he said, "to our new favorite place."

She couldn't help it; she laughed. His eyes sparkled over the glass as he drank first. She was still waiting, wide eyed, when he finished. He toyed with his glass before placing it down decisively.

"You aren't like any other woman I've dated."

"Oh?" she asked. He came over to her, and she looked up at him, heart beating so rapidly she lifted a hand to her chest like that might slow it down. Would he kiss her again? Every time he did was so overwhelming and exquisite, she thought she might die of the pleasure.

"When I first saw you, angel," he said, "I knew you would be my wife."

Persephone lost her breath for the second time that night. He— He did? His *wife*?

Her mind was racing a million miles a minute as he came near her and cupped her cheek.

"So lovely, so innocent. You are exactly what I've been looking for and didn't even know it." He knelt down before her on one knee. "I need you to be mine, Persephone." He reached into his pocket, keeping his eyes on hers.

What was happening? This couldn't be happening. Oh gods, was this happening?

"Hades?" she started to ask, but he opened the jewelry box, and she found she couldn't speak.

It was a ring. It was a freaking ring!

"Marry me," he said, smiling at her shock.

"Oh, Hades," she mouthed. Her breath was gone; she was mute. Instead, she reached forward to touch the ring. The metal was silver colored, but she knew it would be white gold. There were tiny diamonds, cut to sparkle. But the main gem was red. Mesmerized, she realized he was speaking.

"I almost got you a diamond, a real nice rock. But you look so good in red." He looked at her suddenly in such a way that she blushed. She leaned back in her chair, away from both him and the ring, hoping she could hide the fear that had pierced through her.

There was a darkness in Hades. She still believed what she'd told Hecate earlier this afternoon. Hades was a good man, but there was a darkness in him. Was she really ready to commit her life to a man she knew so little about? He was careful around her, showing her only the parts of himself he wanted her to see.

"So?" he prompted, after a moment of silence.

"What if I'm not ready?" She didn't know where the words came from. Dark fire flashed through Hades's eyes, but otherwise he hid his frustration well. "It's just so soon," she hurried to say. "We've only known each other a couple of months."

"I think you're ready," he said and he stood up, towering over her, until he drew her to her feet. He moved his face close, as if he would kiss her, and she was frozen, watching his lips, "I think you want to say yes."

And then he did kiss her. "Say yes," he murmured while his lips played over her skin, kissing down her throat in the most delicious way. "Say yes."

She closed her eyes, wound her arms around his neck, and like always when it came to Hades, gave in.

"Yes," she whispered in the darkness. "Yes, I'll marry you."

Even as he smiled and kissed her, though, a small, worried voice piped up in the back of her mind. The setting was romantic, yes. The ring was beautiful. He'd expressed more of his feelings tonight than she'd ever heard from him before.

But he hadn't said a single thing about love.

7

"Now that's a nice ring," Hecate said in her quiet, matter-of-fact way when Persephone came to volunteer that week. Hades had frowned when Persephone told him she'd be busy until dinner, but she was adamant to keep to her schedule. Not even planning a rush wedding to one of the wealthiest men in the city would make her bail on Hecate.

"Thank you," Persephone murmured, and removed the 'nice ring,' stringing it on her necklace before donning gloves. An hour cleaning cages wasn't something most people would look forward to, but she jumped right in as if the dirty work would make her clean.

In a few weeks she'd be married. Married. To a man who intimidated and intoxicated her all at once. He came into her life, and now he *was* her life. Every part of her world belonged to Hades.

Except this part. Was that how it would be after the wedding? Everything that was Hades swallowing up everything Persephone had been? Should she be fighting harder to retain some autonomy? But every time she was with Hades, all she wanted was more of him.

Nothing else mattered. The rest of the world dropped away so it didn't seem like a sacrifice. And it wasn't as if he'd *asked* her to give anything up. He just slowly occupied more and more territory in her life, like a slow and not unwelcome invasion.

"Persephone," Hecate called a little while later, and she blinked as if awakening from a trance.

"There's a man out here, looking for you."

Persephone got to her feet so fast the newspaper scattered. The clock above her head read seven o'clock. Charon was already here.

"Oh," a curse sprang to her lips. Hecate's brows flew up. Although Hecate wouldn't take offense at the word, she looked surprised to hear Persephone use it. Persephone knew she usually came off so prim and proper, and she covered her mouth with her right hand. Her other toyed with the ring on the chain.

"You okay?"

"Yes, I'm late, I'd better go."

Hecate hesitated. "Are you sure? He's kinda rough looking; I nearly sent him away. Are you sure you want to see him?"

"Yeah, it's fine," Persephone mumbled, stripping off her apron. She headed out front, smoothing her hair with her fingers. She was in jeans and a t-shirt, but she'd have to change at the club.

She passed through the door that led to the pet store. Rounding the corner past a display of dog food, she stopped dead. The man had brown curly hair. It was him. His back was to her, but she recognized the man who'd roofied and tried to kidnap her.

Run!

Shout for help!

There wasn't a front door between them this time. They were all alone in the small shop.

But... *I'm never alone.* The wild thought comforted her even as her hands shook.

"If I scream, someone will come." Hades still had men watching her. They kept out of sight, and she didn't mention or make a fuss about it because she could pretend everything was normal that way. So how did her former attacker get past them?

That didn't matter. All that mattered was that if she called, they'd come. She knew it. She wasn't a victim anymore. She was soon to be wife of Hades Ubeli, the most powerful man in the city.

She crossed her arms in front of her to hide her tremor. "You need to leave and never come back again."

The man raised his hands, still facing the front. "I'm not here to hurt you. I swear. Just want to talk."

He finally turned and Persephone gasped. Instead of moving back, she stepped forward. *Gods.* "What happened to you?"

The man's face was misshapen, bruises covering his face in multi-colored patchwork. She should run, or speed-dial Hades on the special cell phone he insisted she carry. But the man wasn't making any move to come closer, so she stayed.

"Did Charon do this?" she asked, her heart beating hard.

"Yeah," the man's words were a garbled mouthful of pain, spoken through all the bruises and swelling. "Boss don't like it when a man oversteps his bounds."

Boss?

"What?" she whispered.

"I came to warn you," he said. "Boss won't like it, but you gotta get wise. That way, you'll be ready. I done wrong and I'm tryin' to make it right. Makin' amends is what they call it. So I'm tellin' ya, you gotta be ready."

"Ready for *what*?"

The man shook his head, and groaned as if the movement pained him. It could be a trap. He could be pretending to be hurt worse than he was. She stayed back, the aisle of dog food between them. But she couldn't help asking, "Are you okay? Do you need a doctor?"

"No," the man gasped. "Listen, I'm tryin' to warn you."

"Warn me?" Her attacker was beaten, weakened. The longer she looked at him, the more convinced she was he wasn't faking it. Persephone uncrossed her arms and rested her fists on her hips. "You come here after drugging my drink, trying to kidnap me—"

"It was them. It was all them. The boss and Charon. They planned it. They laid it out. I'm down the chain, didn't hear it straight from them, but they were behind it."

"What?"

"Watching you. Scouting you. That night in the club, I saw a chance and took it. Figured the boss would be happy if I brought you in early. He wasn't happy. He had a plan—"

"The boss..." Her mouth was dry and her heart beating what felt like a thousand times a minute. "...you mean *Hades?*"

"Yes." A car slid past the shop and the man startled, staring with the whites of his eyes.

"No." Persephone shook herself. "No, you're wrong. Hades helped me. He and Charon protect me from...from you!"

The man jerked his head, teeth gritted. "They were watching you. They were planning to pick you up from the start. I was watching you. Those were my orders."

"Orders," Persephone repeated, her head starting to throb.

"I gotta go. I gotta run. They won't like it. Once you're in, you're in forever." He was babbling. He was crazy. He'd had a blow to the head. Multiple blows to the head.

Behind him, a long black car pulled up to the curb. Her ride was here.

She turned, but the man had gone. The door to the back was swinging closed.

Charon found her there, still clutching her arms to her chest among the aisles of dog food. "Ready to go?" he asked, looking her up and down.

"I need to change," she said, fighting the urge to back away. Charon seemed to sense this, and stayed close, hovering, protective.

"You can do that at the club." He turned, stiffening when the back door opened, but it was only Hecate, frowning for some reason.

"You nearly forgot this," she said in her low, no nonsense voice, handing over Persephone's purse. Charon held out a hand for it, and Hecate pulled it out of his reach. The older redhead gave him a level glance. "Excuse me."

"It's okay, Hecate," Persephone said. "I trust him." She blinked suddenly, surprised at how quickly she said those words, wondering if they were lies. Gods, she needed to think.

Hecate looked at her with an unhappy expression, but gave Charon the bag.

"Good night." Persephone's small smile must have helped Hecate hold her thoughts in, but lines still formed on the older woman's forehead.

Persephone survived the drive in silence. *Warn me?* She rubbed her bare arms.

Once you're in, you're in forever.

When Charon guided her down the steps to the club where she had run to that night long ago, she didn't struggle. But the illuminated door that had once seemed like such sanctuary now felt like... Cold shivered down her back as she crossed the threshold.

Her mind felt blank. It was all too much to process. Whenever a panicked thought tried to break through, she reminded herself that that man was crazy. He'd kidnapped her for gods' sake and then had continued *stalking* her. Why should she trust anything he said?

But he'd been so beaten down, literally and figuratively. He'd said he wanted to make amends, like he was in some twelve-step program.

What if he *wasn't* lying?

A minute later Persephone was alone with Hades in his office. Mr. Ubeli. The shadows still cut across his face among the mahogany and rich carpet. Nothing had changed from that first night.

No, everything has.

"Hey, babe," he said, and leaned back in his chair with a sigh. With one hand he scrubbed his hair out of his face; the other reached out, calling her toward him. She had planned to be strong, but something in the way he pushed the dark spikes of his hair away from his eyes reminded her of a little boy, up past his bedtime. She went to him. Gods help her, she went to him.

"Long day?" she asked, and he didn't reply, simply put his hands on her hips and pushed her back so that she was leaning on the desk. His fingers stroked her arms, wrists, and hands, before retreating.

As soon as they left her skin, Persephone wanted them back. She was the one who needed a twelve-step program. She was addicted to Hades.

"Where's your ring?" Hades's voice didn't sound cold, not quite. But his face was blank in a way she knew he wasn't happy.

"Oh," Persephone grabbed the chain around her neck. The diamonds flashed in the light. The garnet was so dark it seemed to drink the light in. "I put it here so it wouldn't get dirty."

Hades's lips pressed together, and she quickly undid the delicate chain, freed the ring, and replaced it on her fourth finger.

She wiggled her fingers in Hades's direction. "All better. Did you think I'd lost it?" Just like always, when she was with him, everything else disappeared. She knew she'd been very upset before coming into the room, that she *still* should be, that there was a chance that man had been telling the truth—

"No." Hades captured her hand and toyed with the slim band. His touch ignited a wildfire, racing up her arm, turning her insides into an inferno. *Oh*—

"Don't worry," she breathed out, fighting to keep her voice normal as her pulse jumped, hammering a million times per minute, "I won't forget I'm engaged to you."

"Not you I'm worried about. It's every guy who looks at you, sees an angel and thinks he can get close."

"Possessive, much?" she joked, but the intensity in Hades's gaze seared her.

"You have no idea."

She closed her eyes as his fingertips grazed her temples, then traced down her cheeks. Her universe expanded, and it was full of Hades. Everywhere Hades, Hades, *Hades.*

And she let him, remaining still, heart now hardly daring to beat, as if even a breath might break the moment.

"I should have done this a long time ago," he murmured.

"What?" she started to say and leaned forward to hear the answer, but at that moment he looked up, and caught her mouth with his. And then it was all over.

Every thought went out of her head, all but Hades, and he was standing now with his arms around her, his body pressing hers against the desk.

"Hades," she gasped when he released her lips.

"It shouldn't have taken me so long. With any other girl it wouldn't have taken me so long."

"So long to do what?" she asked, her thoughts still swirling.

"This," he said, and again his mouth closed over hers. The breath rocketed out of her, her hands flying up and hovering by his face. But she didn't dare touch him, terrified to break the spell. But she needn't have worried.

His whole body got into the kiss, closing in, dominating. His heat and scent surrounded her, flooding her with fire. Her hands gripped his strong shoulders, clutching the bunched muscle, nails digging into the fine Italian fabric as if they would scratch the smooth olive skin underneath.

"That's it, angel. Hold onto me," Hades ordered, propping her on the desk and drawing her head back by her hair as his lips seared a brand onto her skin. His large palm cradled her head as his mouth worked down her neck. Persephone let her head loll back, her body arching as Hades pushed up her shirt and covered her breast with his hot mouth.

"Hades, Hades," she panted. Her body was dry tinder, a field baked in the sun all summer. One spark and everything went up in flame.

His large hand slid down her midriff, skimming over her soft skin into her jeans and panties, touching her where no one had ever touched her before. Her eyes flew open, lips parting. Only to catch Hades's wolfish gaze as he stared hungrily into her eyes.

"So sweet. Such an innocent. Persephone," he groaned against her mouth, his eyes becoming hooded as his finger swirled between her slippery folds. "You like this?"

Her eyelashes fluttered. She— It felt— She'd never— Oh *gods*.

"Answer me."

"Yes," she finally managed to gasp.

"That's it, my goddess," he whispered, his fingers fluttering against the sweetest spot. Her stomach was liquid and she could feel this...this insane amazing pleasurable pressure building. Oh gods she'd never felt anything like it before. How was he—? Oh gods yes, right there, like that, right there—

Her knees knocked and his breath caught. "Go over."

At his command, the tightness cracked and eased and everything poured out. Oh, oh, *ooooooooh!*

Her hand came up to stop him but, no, it simply took the plane of his cheek as if she would hold him to her, and her fingers raked through his hair, her breath coming out in a shudder as his mouth covered hers again. The shocking waves of pleasure, she'd never...*oh*—

She sagged against Hades, breathing in the crisp linen scent as aftershocks stiffened her limbs, stiffening and releasing, stiffening and releasing.

Hades gave her a final stroke, making her entire body shudder again, and withdrew his hand.

I've never done that before, she wanted to tell him. *Everything is new with you. I'm new with you.* The satisfied smirk tucked into the corner of his mouth told her he knew.

She ran her fingers over his perfect lips and the elegant line of his jaw. He was real, flesh and blood. Not a god. Not a statue carved by a master sculptor. He was a man.

He was hers.

Catching her gaze in his grey one, Hades pulled out a handkerchief and wiped his hand. He folded it and pressed it to his nose, inhaling before replacing it in his pocket. Her cheeks burned.

"Beautiful." Hades pulled her close to his body. At her height, sitting on the desk, the position pressed her soft center against his crotch. A hard length pressed there, distorting the tailored slacks. Her eyes rounded.

Hades's thumb skimmed her jaw. "Gorgeous. Tell me you're my girl."

She didn't even hesitate.

"I'm your girl."

"You belong to me." It wasn't a question.

"Yes."

"You gonna give me what I want?"

"Yes." She swallowed, searching his eyes. "What...what do you want?"

"Everything." He took her mouth, pressing close and tipping her off balance, forcing her to hang onto him until he broke the kiss.

"But not tonight." He stroked her porcelain cheek. "You're tired." He held her quietly, her head against his chest. She listened for his heartbeat again, and soon, realized he was speaking, telling his love to her over and over again, maybe in the only way he knew how.

"I'll keep you safe, babe, you know it. You won't ever need a thing. You're my goddess, and I won't let you go—"

"Hades," she sat up. "This is happening so fast." Didn't he realize she wasn't going anywhere? There was plenty that should have scared her off, maybe, okay scratch that—*definitely* should have scared her off. But she still wasn't going anywhere. This thing between them was too strong, too powerful. So powerful it scared her sometimes, on top of everything else. "There's no rush."

"I know you're scared, babe." Of course he knew. His dark grey eyes never left hers. "But you're with me. You're going to be okay. You can't escape, angel... This is your destiny."

Persephone collapsed forward, resting her forehead against his.

"I want you," he said. "But you're so perfect. So innocent. I wanted to do it right." His fingers threaded through hers, rubbing the ring.

She sat up, suddenly understanding. "That's why you want to marry me so quickly."

He dipped his chin. He didn't want to... not until they were married. Her heart clutched at the sweetness of the gesture. She didn't know a lot about these things but she suspected, a man like him, going without couldn't be easy. But he was doing it, for her. Even now she knew he was stifling his need. She'd felt him so hard against her thigh.

"Hades." She slid her arms around his shoulders. "I'm here. I'm not going anywhere."

"I'm not taking any chances." For a moment she clung to him in perfect silence.

He said, "From now on, you have two guards wherever you go."

"But—"

He placed a finger at her lips. "No argument. I know that dick turned up again." His face grew sober. "Charon saw him in the shop."

She straightened. "I didn't— He didn't—" She wasn't sure what she was trying to explain so she stopped.

"I know."

Persephone bit her lip. It was now or never. "He said something. He was trying to warn me."

"About what?" Hades's face was carefully blank.

Did it really matter what that man said? He'd drugged and kidnapped her. He was obviously fixated on her, and he'd had several blows to the head. Was she really going to believe his 'warning' over everything she knew about Hades?

Not that she really knew Hades, but so far he'd been a perfect gentleman. And she did know him, didn't she? The things that mattered anyway.

Her eyes dropped to her lap. "Nothing. He said nothing."

Hades trapped her hand between both of his, squeezing. "Persephone, this...what we have...is new. But it's gonna last."

"I know that." And she did. Because now she couldn't imagine her world without Hades in it.

"You know my work isn't always above the law."

"I don't know much about what you do—" she started shakily.

"You know enough."

"I know who you are, Hades. I know that you have principles. You want good people to be safe... And bad people punished."

"That's right. I do." His grip tightened, almost painful, then it eased and he raised her hand to his lips, kissing her knuckles. "But I promise you, my work will never touch you. I'm gonna put you so high on a pedestal, you'll live in the stars."

"Lock me in an ivory tower?" She tried to smile. "The penthouse?"

"If that's what it takes." His voice was hard but then it turned reassuring. "Persephone, that man won't ever bother you again."

Her stomach plummeted, a jumble of guilt and relief. "He won't?" she whispered. *What will you do to him?* She gulped back the question. Even if Hades told her, she didn't want to know.

"No." His eyes crinkled in a chilling smile. "Don't worry. I told you I'd take care of you."

8

They got married two weeks later in a brief, private ceremony in a small chapel near the Crown hotel.

Well, *private* in that Hades only invited what he called the 'bare minimum' of his friends and business associates who would be offended if they didn't get an invitation. So the chapel was full to bursting with people.

Traditionally his guests would fill one side of the aisle and hers the other, but Persephone only had one person to invite—the only other person in the city she really knew besides Hades—Hecate.

Persephone felt a pang as she hovered at the back of the church thinking about her mother, but it was mainly along the lines of wishing she had a normal mother who could be here, happy and joyful to give her daughter away. Instead it would be Charon walking her down the aisle.

The only other person she even really knew there was Hermes, and he was still technically more Hades's friend than hers, though she did get to enjoy more of his boisterous personality as she had dress fittings with him. He had a line of wedding dresses so it seemed natural to go to him for her dress.

Never one to go completely traditional, Hermes had picked a dress that was white with black straps and black lace at her waist. Persephone wasn't picky. The dress was beautiful and it was clear Hades approved by the look in his eye as she walked down the aisle. She wore white flowers in her hair and she positively floated the last few feet to him.

She couldn't believe she was actually here, about to marry him. He would be hers, forever.

She was so giddy, she couldn't stop grinning throughout the entire ceremony, even though the priest droned on.

And finally, the ancient priest got to the only part Persephone cared about. "I now pronounce you husband and wife. You may kiss the bride."

Hades pulled her close, cradled her head in his large hand and slanted his mouth over hers. It wasn't a chaste kiss. Fireworks exploded as his tongue stroked once, twice, three times before her lips parted and it swept inside. Heat rolled through her, running into her mouth like nectar from Hades's lips, spilling down her neck, chest, and pooling with exquisite weight right between her legs. Her thighs clenched. Wedding bells were ringing, and every cell in her body blasted to life.

He finally released her, the cheers of the guests echoing in her ears. Sparks sizzling in every corner of her body, Persephone reached out and swiped a thumb at the corner of his mouth where her lipstick marked him. Hades gave her a wink and her whole body convulsed.

"Soon," he mouthed and she flushed redder than she already was. He turned to greet the guests, handsome face smooth and polite, but she sensed the tension, the dormant readiness in the lines of his powerful body. He was impatient with the pomp and ceremony too.

First there was the reception, an elegant affair in one of the Crown hotel's ballrooms. Persephone clung to Hades's hand in the receiving line as person after person came by to congratulate them. Some of the faces she recognized. Santonio—or Papa Santa as he liked people to call him. He ran one of the restaurants Hades invested in. And then there was Jimmy Roscoe and his wife and their five children. Persephone didn't know how Hades knew him except that they did business together.

The rest were a blur of names and faces she didn't bother trying to keep up with. She smiled and shook hands and accepted congratulations until finally the line dwindled and they were through.

"Another half hour then we'll cut out of here, I promise," Hades whispered in her ear as he led her out on the dance floor.

That sounded like heaven to her. She relaxed into his body as soon as the band started to play a slow, romantic jazz number. He led her expertly across the floor, smooth as spun honey.

And true to his word, half an hour later, they'd cut the cake and made their goodbyes, encouraging everyone else to stay and enjoy the party and the open bar.

They escaped upstairs.

Persephone was tired after the long day, but adrenaline had her feeling wide awake as they stepped on the elevator to go to the penthouse.

It was officially her wedding night now.

She and Hades hadn't talked about it, but it was obvious that tonight would be *the night*. He'd take her virginity and they'd finally be united in every way possible. She'd truly be his, and him hers.

It was stupid, but she had the romantic notion that her whole life had been leading up to this moment.

"Oh, Hades," she sighed, leaning into his body as the elevator continued to rise. "I never knew happiness like this could even be *real*."

He didn't say anything, he just put his arm around her and pulled her into his chest.

The elevator pinged and he let her go as he strode forward and slid his keycard from his wallet and into the door.

Persephone eagerly followed behind, hurrying into the penthouse suite.

But apparently she wasn't fast enough because Hades pushed her from behind, grabbing frantically for her and shoving the door shut with his foot.

It was like he couldn't get his hands on her quick enough. He kissed her forcefully, hands at her waist pulling her into him.

Persephone opened to him, her adrenaline spiking even higher as pleasure warred with fear over what was about to happen. She'd tried to learn a little bit about sex online using her phone, but the pictures that had come up—suffice to say, she'd quickly closed the browser in horror. Besides, she'd reasoned, she trusted Hades to lead her through whatever she needed to know.

Hades immediately shucked his jacket and yanked at his tie, but then, as if he was impatient, his hands came back to her. His hands slid down her waist and around to her backside. He squeezed her bottom and she couldn't help the groan of surprise and pleasure—gods, having him touch her so intimately was shocking...and amazing.

Next he was tearing at the buttons on his shirt and yanking it off, then pulling his undershirt off over his head.

Persephone's eyes about bugged out of her head at seeing his bare chest.

Her husband was gorgeous.

To die for gorgeous.

She knew he worked out in the mornings but...her mouth went dry the more she looked at his toned chest and the cut of his abdominal muscles, all leading to a sharp V that—

"You like what you see?" he growled and pulled her to him again, kissing her deep.

But only for a moment, because he pulled away and spun her around and pressed her face first into the wall.

She felt his fingers pulling at the laces of her dress the next moment. "Godsdamned Hermes," he hissed, tugging impatiently. "How the hell do I get you out of this thing?"

Persephone giggled and reached back to help him but he batted her hands away. Finally, she felt the dress loosen around her waist and Hades finished by pulling down the zipper. His hands glided over her flesh as he pushed the gown to the ground and helped her step out of it.

She was left in a white strapless bra, thong, and thigh-highs. She lifted her arms to her chest instinctively.

But Hades wasn't having it. He pulled her arms down and stared at her in that way of his, like he was drinking in every inch of her.

He lifted her in his arms and carried her to his bedroom. She squealed and circled his neck with her arms, clinging to him, but he carried her like she weighed nothing at all.

He deposited her smoothly on the bed and followed her down, kissing her and climbing in between her legs.

She groaned as he put pressure right where she needed it. She wrapped her legs around him and ground restlessly against him, seeking what she didn't even know. Oh gods, was this really finally happening? Was she actually here, in her wedding bed with Hades? It was a dream. Things like this never happened to her. Was she really getting the happy ending?

But Hades's lips on her felt real enough. A shudder wracked her body at his touch. Gods, the way he made her *feel*. He still had his pants on but he was kissing her and she was happy to let him take the lead.

As much as she hated to think of him with other women before her, it meant he was the one who knew what he was doing.

And now he's yours. Only yours.

She grinned and dug her hands into his hair. Gods, she loved his hair. It was so thick and dark. Their children would have gorgeous dark hair. Would they get his gray eyes or her blue ones? They hadn't even talked about children other than Hades asking for her to get the birth control shot a month ago. There was so much they still didn't know about each other.

But they had their whole lives to learn. Starting tonight.

Persephone's stomach flipped in joy and pleasure as Hades reached beneath her and unclasped her bra.

When he pulled it off, she waited in anticipation for him to touch her breasts. Her nipples had hardened into little nubs and she was suddenly aching for him to touch them.

Instead, Hades lifted her arms above her head and continued to kiss her.

He climbed off of her and moved up the bed.

"What are you—" she started to ask but he cut her off.

"Do you trust me?" His gaze had never been more solemn and intense. It made Persephone want to cover herself again but she swallowed. She'd be brave. Because yes, she did trust him, and she told him so.

"Yes."

He gave her the half grin she loved as he pulled one of her arms up and outward. Tension rippled through her as he lifted a silk scarf she hadn't seen that was already tied to the bedpost to wind around her wrist.

What was he—? She lay still as he tied first one wrist, and then the other, to the bed. She tugged against one experimentally and even though it was silk, the way he'd knotted it, it didn't give an inch.

"Hades," she said, brow furrowing. "I don't know about this. It's— It's my first time, you know."

"That makes me very happy to hear, goddess," he said, moving back down the bed to kiss her deep again.

His drugging kisses soon had her forgetting all her objections. Especially when he kissed down her neck and kept going. When his mouth closed over her nipple finally, she arched up into him and let out the most embarrassing moan. But gods, she couldn't help it, it felt *so good*.

He wasn't done with teasing her though, apparently, because he continued kissing down her body. Down to her belly button. Lower.

When he got to the hem of her white lace underwear, he dragged them down with his teeth. Persephone gasped and her chest heaved as warring emotions fought for dominance—fear, exhilaration, but above all, desire.

Desire for her husband, the man she loved. Dear gods but she loved him.

It was on the tip of her tongue to confess it as he tugged her underwear and slid it down her legs, baring her to him completely.

She wasn't embarrassed or ashamed.

Because she loved him.

She wanted to whisper it in his ear. She wanted to scream it from the rooftops.

She was in love with this god of a man and she wanted the whole world to know. She grinned at him as he massaged her calf and looked up at her body.

He wasn't smiling. He looked pensive, like he was deep in his head.

"Hades?"

He didn't answer as he pulled off her thigh-highs, then tugged on her ankle and—

Her forehead furrowed when he pulled yet another red scarf from the foot of the bed.

"Wait, Hades." She tried to draw her leg up but he pulled her leg back flat to the bed with his inexorable strength, massaging her calf as he went.

When he looked up at her, his eyes were stormy. "You said you trusted me."

And what could she say to that?

So she let her leg go limp as he tied one ankle and then the other, until she was spread out on the bed like a virgin sacrifice.

She expected Hades to climb up and cover her, to warm her with his body and soothe her discomfort at the position with his drugging kisses.

But instead, he left the bed. Glass clinked. Persephone craned her neck. Hades stood at the sideboard, pouring himself a drink.

"What are you doing?" She tugged at her bonds. Glass in hand, Hades moved to the end of the bed, his face half in shadow. In between sips, his sculpted lips were set in neither a smile nor a frown.

"Hades," she called, breathless. "Please. What—"

"If only Demeter Titan could see her little girl now."

What? How—

Goosebumps pebbled all over Persephone's skin. She'd never told Hades her mother's name. Much less her mother's married name.

Mom had gone back to using her maiden name, Vestian, after they moved to Kansas.

But for Hades to know—

He stepped into the light. His stone expression turned Persephone cold. "Surprise, little wife." He took a long pull of his drink. "You've just married the big bad wolf."

9

No, no, no, no, no. This was all some big mistake. Or she was dreaming. Yes, that had to be it. It was still the night before the wedding and she was having a nightmare. This was pre-wedding jitters and her brain was conjuring the worst thing it could imagine.

"Hey." Hades ran his fingertips up her inner thigh. "Stay with me. This is important. Don't want you to miss a thing." His lips twisted as he leaned over her. "Breathe. You gotta remember to breathe."

She sucked in air, frozen, staring at his face. His strong jaw and hooded grey eyes. The handsome warmth she loved was gone, replaced by a mask. The same hard, menacing mask he gave to everyone else—but now he was using it on *her*.

"Hades, stop it," she jerked against the scarves binding her wrists and ankles. "You're scaring me."

"Good," he rumbled, and it was the first time since he'd tied her up that she'd seen anything resembling emotion enter his eyes. His finger trailed down her bare leg, making it twitch. Reminding her she was bound and naked. Not that she needed a reminder. "You should be scared."

He circled the bed and set his drink on the side table. Hands in his pockets, he studied her. His shadow cut over her body. "My sister was scared—when your father's goons snatched her off the streets, threw her in a dirty room and violated her."

All the oxygen left the room. Persephone's ears rang, her vision dimming, narrowing on Hades's hard face. "What?"

"They tied her up...just like this. She was a good girl. Sweetest soul on the face of this planet. She loved everybody. Never took a step out of line. And he killed her in cold blood. Your father."

Persephone jerked her head and body from side to side. "No. No, you've got me mixed up with someone else. My dad died in a car accident and my mom—"

"Your mom took you into hiding when you were four years old to protect you from *me*," he sneered. "But then after all these years, what do you know, a girl who's the spitting image of Demeter Titan comes waltzing back into *my* city, except instead of brunette, she's got her daddy Titan's blond hair."

Persephone's mouth dropped open. No. What he was saying couldn't be true. But the look in his eye, the cold fury—the *hatred*—he certainly thought it was true.

Persephone's mind raced with all he was telling her. Could it—? Had mom really hidden away for all those years to protect her from—

Persephone's eyes shot to Hades, sitting so smugly above her. Even if what he was saying was true, she couldn't imagine it, but even if it was— "I didn't do anything to you or your sister. This is the first I'm hearing of any of it."

Hades shook his head and took up his drink, swallowing the dregs before setting it down with a thunk. "Do I look like I give a fuck?"

Persephone flinched at his harsh curse. He'd never used such language around her.

"My sister didn't do anything either. I live by a Code." He reached down and cupped Persephone's cheek and she jerked away from his touch. He let her.

"Under my Code, you would have been untouchable. But your

family violated all that is sacred the night they took Chiara. And there's only one way for the scales to be leveled. And before I killed your father, I looked into his eyes and told him that his little baby girl was next."

Persephone felt her eyes go so wide she didn't even dare blink. Her father hadn't died in a car accident. Hades had— Hades had *killed*— And she was—

"Are you going to kill me?" she whispered.

Hades's lip quirked up on the side, the smile she'd loved only a half hour before. "No, angel. What fun would that be?" His fingertips skimmed her cheek. "Why would I kill you when I could keep you?" She fell into his gaze, drowned in it.

"No," he murmured. "You don't get a death sentence. You get a life sentence. Death is quick. But suffering...suffering can go on forever."

The air left her lungs. Persephone panted as her body tightened, turned to concrete.

"Breathe, baby." Hades settled a large hand on her chest. "You gotta breathe."

She inhaled, compelled as she stared into his dark grey eyes. There was something about Hades she had to obey.

"I don't want you to hurt me," she whispered.

"I know, angel." For a second his face softened, conflicted. "I didn't want to hurt you, either."

Persephone's heart leapt with hope. "But why—"

"There's an order to the universe. Everything has its place." He settled beside her, lecturing like a professor. "Everything's weighed on scales." He raised two hands, palms up. "Things gotta balance. Light and dark. Day and night. Good and bad." He dropped his hands. "Crime and punishment."

Persephone's mouth worked but no sound escaped. She met Hades's gaze and drowned in it.

"When your father," his voice vibrated under the weight of his rage, "did what he did, things got out of order. Out of place. There need to be consequences. I've been waiting for this day for a very long time."

"But *I* didn't do anything."

He looked away. "You aren't hearing me. Someone's gotta answer for what they did. I found my sister..." His eyes closed, and Persephone's heart cracked. Because it was still Hades. And the pain on his face was so real. "Her eyes were open. Her body broken. They did things to her. Things that should never be done. Angels wept..."

"I'm sorry," she whispered. It slipped out. Not apologizing for herself, but because it was what you said when you hurt for someone you loved.

He tied you to the bed! He hates you!

But she...she'd spent the last two months loving him. It didn't just disappear. She didn't know how to turn it off.

Hades closed his eyes. He pinched the bridge of his nose, his chest rising and falling rapidly. His jaw was shadowed with stubble. Everything in her strained to go to him, to hold him. For all his power and control, Hades was a man. Just a man. She'd seen him at his best, and at his lowest. He hid nothing from her.

Except, he had, hadn't he? He'd hid his nature in plain sight. And she was the naive prey that had walked right into his trap.

I'm sorry. Her apology lay between them, small and inadequate against the huge debt.

He dropped his hand. He was the Lord of the Underworld once more, his expression carved from stone. Back in control.

"No, beautiful, you're not. But you will be."

He stalked out of the room. Persephone shivered where he left her. Everything had turned around so quickly, she felt dizzy. She closed her eyes until soft footfalls jerked her attention back to Hades.

Despite everything, her pulse fluttered at the sight of him, his huge bare chest dusted with dark hair.

"What's going to happen? What will you do with me?"

"Whatever I want." A shark-like smile. "You're not going to die. You're going to live a long, long time. By my side as my wife. Forever."

How could he be so cold? So ruthless? How could she have been so foolish as to think he loved her? Now her wedding night was a nightmare. So much for happy endings.

She couldn't help the tears that welled up and spilled down her cheeks.

"That's right, gorgeous. Cry for me."

That was when she saw what Hades had picked up—his phone. He'd turned on the camera and was aiming it her way. Red rage bloomed in her head.

"No."

"Yes." Hades backed away, like he was framing the perfect shot. "We've got to have some wedding photos to send your side of the family. It's the least we can do considering your mom and your uncles couldn't make it to the wedding."

Her *uncles*? She didn't even know she *had* uncles.

"Stop." Her begging was muffled as she hid her face in her arm. "Please stop."

"Look at me," he ordered. "Persephone." His footfalls stalked closer. "This is happening."

"No." Think, she had to *think*. This was still Hades. Inside the man, the monster, there was a powerful attraction to her. Maybe she could find an inkling of the Hades who cared.

A hand closed around her wrist like an iron shackle. She resisted.

"Persephone, I'm not going to ask you again."

Her bones melted. She let him pull her hand away. He looked down at her and her body flushed under his scrutiny.

"You're sick," she bit out. Anything to deny her body's pull to him.

"I won't take the pictures if you submit to me."

Her laugh wracked her body. "How? It's not like I can run away."

"I'll drop the camera if you submit to me. And act like a wife."

"You mean like I love you?"

He inclined his head.

The cracks in her heart dripped poison. "I did love you, you know. That wasn't a lie."

"I know."

"Was everything you said to me...was it all an act? Was it never real?"

He didn't answer.

"Fine. I'll do it." she raised her chin. Pretending to be brave. "It's not anything I haven't done before."

He was switching off the camera when he swung back to her, his normally grey eyes going black. "Excuse me?"

"Oh, did you think I was a virgin?"

He came back and covered her knee with his hand. He squeezed and her breath stuttered, betraying her. "I don't think you're a virgin," he told her. "I know you are."

She raised her chin. "I've had guys," she lied. "Lots of them."

He shook his head. "You're a terrible liar."

"It's true."

Hades moved over her, his large body stretching head to toe with hers. His cologne mixed with the crisp linen scent of his white dress shirt. She was naked, he wasn't, but coiled power rippling through him was visible in his taut muscles and the endless depths of his eyes. Heat crackled between them. "Lots of guys, huh? I'll have to make you forget them."

His touch seared her as it always did. Her legs trembled and she blinked at him, searching his face for any semblance of the man who took her in and cared for her.

And then she remembered his callous smile as he'd aimed a camera at her.

"I hate you."

His eyes crinkled in a cold smile that didn't touch his mouth. He tutted. "Is that any way to talk to your husband, wife?"

"Don't call me that."

"Wife? That's what you are."

Her head jerked negative and his expression darkened. "Yes." His hand rested on her tensed chest, sliding up to collar her neck. "My wife. Better or worse." His gaze roved over her, his eyes gunmetal grey. "Rich or poor. Sick or healthy. Till death do us part."

She closed her eyes at his mocking version of their vows. He was going to humiliate her, hurt her, and her body didn't care. It responded to Hades and warmed at his touch. Her heart thrummed and lungs strained. She panted as if she'd run a marathon.

He reached for his belt buckle. Persephone's eyes were wide before, but now they swallowed up her face, flashing white. Her entire body shuddered. Oh gods, why had she let him tie her up? Stupid.

But she'd believed he loved her.

He never said it. So why did you think it?

Because he asked her to marry him! What other reason could he have had? Apparently revenge for crimes committed more than a decade ago that she hadn't even known about.

"You told me you'd take care of me." Her voice was small, plaintive.

"I did." His deep voice dripped promise. "I will."

"Please," she gasped, knowing it was pathetic to beg, but still unable to believe there was nothing of the Hades who'd held and kissed her so tenderly left inside the cruel man sitting before her now. "Don't touch me."

"No?" His lips twisted. "You don't want me to touch you?"

"No." But he was touching her, barely, stroking the side of her breast. It felt so good. She never wanted him to stop. "You want me to stop?" he asked as if reading her mind.

"I—"

"You like it when I touch you."

She whimpered. His fingers never stopped stroking, stroking...

"Admit it," his voice deepened, rolling over her senses. The room fell away.

"I'm going to touch you whenever I want, wife. And you're going to like it."

"But...you hate me." She was ashamed of how her voice cracked. And even more ashamed that she was leaning into his touch. But he was so familiar. And his touch felt like a comfort, even now.

"Hate never stopped anyone from feeling pleasure."

Persephone's eyebrows knitted together. What did that mean?

Hades's dark hair brushed her belly. He dipped down over her body, and as if the last terrible fifteen minutes had never happened, he kissed down her stomach again. His cologne washed over her, smooth and sweet.

Her elbows and knees softened, her stomach flip flopping. Persephone stared at his shining head. His mouth was warm on her cool flesh and then his hands were there, gripping her hips like she loved so much. Oh *gods*.

She couldn't help the noise that escaped her throat and he paused.

"You gonna fight me, angel?"

She should fight. She should shout 'yes' and try to wrench out of her bonds, do whatever it took to escape.

But his tongue touched the smooth plane of her stomach and something inside her snapped. She wasn't prepared for it and her muscles clenched at the sudden shocking rush of pleasure. Golden liquid gushed through her, pouring from her belly and filling up her pulsing center until it overflowed. She felt her own moisture on her legs and her face flamed with embarrassment.

"I guess not," Hades chuckled. He pulled back and she knew he was admiring the wetness flooding the space between her legs. "Shame. I would've enjoyed a fight."

Tears immediately cascaded down Persephone's cheeks.

His fingers trailed over her pale skin, bringing a rosy flush to her chest. They trailed down, over her quivering belly to sink into the wetness. Persephone gasped and tugged at the wrist bands. Hades's eyes narrowed, but he kept stroking her. Her hips rose, jerking in time to his come-hither movement.

"You know, you can stop this at any moment."

What? Was he serious?

He twisted a finger in her virgin hole. Her feet dug into the bed and her abs tensed as she lifted herself into his hand. Her body pulsed around his fingers as he cupped her.

"Just tell me. Say, *stop*."

What was his game? She could stop at any moment? She could—

"Stop," she mouthed but no sound came out.

His fingers stilled but her hips kept rocking. Persephone clenched her teeth. She wanted him to touch her. She wanted...

Hades raised a brow. She whimpered. Her hips tilted in invitation.

"Poor wife. So confused. Do you want me to touch you? Do you want me to kiss it better?"

To Persephone's horror, she nodded.

Hades bent his head to taste her. Her legs spasmed, her body sighing into his mouth.

Stop, she screamed in her head. *Stop.* But when she opened her mouth, still no sound came out. His mouth worked over her mound, detouring to her slick thighs, nuzzling her labia, nipping at them with his teeth. She stayed silent, other than her moans.

What was happening? He'd given her an out. Why hadn't she taken it? He hated her. He'd only married her to get revenge. But his caresses, his kisses, they didn't feel hateful. They felt familiar. They felt like *Hades.* The man she... The man she loved.

That man's not real. He never was.

But for a second, she wanted to pretend. She wanted to pretend that he'd never said all those awful things. She wanted to pretend this was their wedding night as it always should have been, and he was kissing and worshipping her because he adored her.

So when he kissed lower, she let him.

His mouth touched her most intimate place. She squealed in shock and shame and— And *pleasure.*

"Hades," she murmured, meaning to ask him to stop.

But he began to suckle at the top of her sex and his finger dropped to explore, teasing at places she herself had never touched.

She never even used tampons, so to feel someone—and not just someone, to feel *Hades,* oh *gods*—

And the things he was doing with his mouth—

Persephone heaved shocked gasps, in and out, tossing her head back and forth because it was the only part of her body she could actually move. She grasped onto the silk scarves. She needed something to hold onto, something to ground herself as the wild, shocking sensations rose higher and higher—

Oh gods, she didn't know what to do with— If this didn't— Where was this all going—

"*Ohhhhh!*" Her squeal faded to a high-pitched whine as pleasure rocked her body, as suddenly as if she'd been shocked by a jolt of electricity. She felt it to the tips of her toes as her legs went rigid. For two counts of her heartbeat, it was all perfect.

And then it was over and Hades was crawling up her body.

She blinked back to the moment, trying to get her bearings.

Hades. Who wasn't her beloved after all. Who'd only married her for revenge.

But would he still make love to her now?

He was straddling her body and she could see his…his sexual member. He'd pulled it out of his pants. Veins stood out on the long shaft. It was darker than the rest of his body and pulsing.

And it was huge. *Huge.*

Was he going to try to stick that inside her?

Even as horrible as things stood between them, with the way he'd made her feel, would she object?

Yes, her mind said. Her heart on the other hand… It was pathetic, she knew, to want any part of this terrible man. And yet—

But Hades wasn't trying to stick it in her, it looked like.

No, he was taking his long, thick shaft in hand and rubbing it up and down. Ruthlessly. Viciously.

Persephone should look away, she knew.

But she'd never seen one. And to see Hades so naked, not literally but figuratively— She looked up his taut stomach and into his face, only to find him looking down at her.

She couldn't read what she saw in the half-second before he lowered his gaze to her breasts. Persephone didn't look away, though. She continued watching his face as he pleasured himself.

He gave himself over to it, that much was clear. In this one thing, at least, he either didn't bother with keeping up his mask or he simply couldn't. Persephone saw a million things in the vulnerable, longing scrunch of his brow—or at least she thought she did.

It made the pleasure that had barely subsided in her rear up again. Her hips jerked involuntarily, looking for friction. But Hades was too far away, all but straddling her breasts.

He continued to work himself for several more moments and then threw his head back.

Persephone's face jerked down when warm wetness splashed her chest. She looked on in astonishment as spurts of white cream erupted from the head of his huge shaft as he tugged it more mercilessly than ever.

When he'd finally emptied himself, he looked down at her, his chest heaving. He reached down and rubbed his seed all over her breasts, squeezing her nipples as he went.

Persephone shuddered, so turned on and shocked by the entire thing. Did people normally do this in bed or did Hades see this as some sort of punishment? It all felt so good.

Hades climbed off the bed. "You like that, don't you? Then make sure to smile for the camera."

"Wha—?"

But Hades was already snapping pictures with his phone. Pictures of her naked body, smeared with his—with his—

The blood left her face. "You said you wouldn't!"

"Naive little Persephone. All's fair in love and war."

"Really, I don't even need this." He dropped the phone onto the bedside table. With a dark smirk, he pointed to the corner where two walls met the ceiling and held a dark shape of a second camera, its tiny bright eye blinking red. "Video makes so much more impact than photos, don't you think?"

Persephone bit her lip, unwilling to give him anything after how cruel he'd just been to her. He laughed, and it wasn't a nice laugh. This really wasn't *her* Hades. That man had truly never existed.

If she needed any more proof, him leaving her all alone in the room, tied up with his seed drying on her chest certainly did the trick.

10

Hades stood in the small dark closet he used as his security room, sipped his drink, and stared at nothing. On screen, his new bride struggled in her bonds. Her beautiful hair fell over her face, a sheaf of wheat spilling over the pale palette of unmarked skin.

He'd just come, but he was harder than ever, ready to conquer, to plunder. She was right where he wanted her, bound and helpless, a virgin offered up as a sacrifice to appease a monster. Which she was —a virgin and a sacrifice.

And he, the monster.

She didn't deserve this. The second his Shades had spotted her, he'd had them monitor her every move. She didn't so much as sneeze without him knowing. She looked like her mother, but acted nothing like Demeter.

He had to see it to believe it. But at first he couldn't stand to look at her. He sent Charon instead, Charon, whom he regarded as a brother.

"Well?" he'd asked when the big man returned to report. "What's she like?"

"*Kind. Naive, but hopeful. Sweet.*" Charon didn't have to say it, but Hades heard the silent commentary. *Just like Chiara.*

The gods gifted him the perfect revenge, wrapped up in a lovely package. So lovely, he didn't want to destroy it. How the gods must be laughing. He had the means for revenge but, for the first time in sixteen years he didn't want to take it.

Oh, he wanted Persephone. When he laid eyes on her, he was undone. The flick of her eyelashes, the flutter of her fine boned hands, the shy smiles he drank in like a man who'd crossed a desert. She was the oasis he didn't know he craved.

On screen, she tossed her head back and forth, the fragile column of her throat taut as she called out for him. Her skin shimmered like mother-of-pearl where he'd spilled his seed. And gods, when she'd come, the pleasure so obviously foreign to her...

His dick curled up to his belly, aching to take her. When he'd spewed his seed all over her beautiful bare breasts, he hadn't been thinking of revenge. He'd been lost in her. The taste of her sweetness still drugging his senses. Unable to look away from her half-mast eyes hazy with lust even though she'd just come. She wanted more and gods, he'd wanted to stay there all night and give it to her.

He'd barely managed to force himself from the room after smearing his seed all over her chest, marking her as his like a barbarian.

He forced himself to finish his drink, savoring the bitter dregs. Even now, the thought of having her at his mercy, separated only by a wall, absolutely thrilled him. All that innocence at his fingertips. He would've enjoyed corrupting her, keeping her tied to his bed, even if she wasn't his enemy.

These momentary misgivings would fade. A king had to be ruthless in order to maintain control. He'd long ago accepted that he was a necessary evil.

He had her. He would keep her. Time would fade her beauty and warp her innocence.

He'd dreamed of this day for years and he wouldn't let anything ruin it, even a foolish thought of last-minute sentimentality. Revenge was a heady draught, wine made from pomegranates. Sweet with a bitter edge. He'd drink as deeply as he could.

And then he'd pour the rest down Persephone's throat until she choked.

11

"Hades," Persephone shouted for the millionth time. "Hades!"

She dropped her head back to the mattress in frustration and humiliation. He'd just left her here, tied to the bed. She had no idea how long it had been. She'd fallen asleep for a while and she could see morning sunlight peeking through the Venetian blinds on the window. And she had to have been yelling for an hour straight with no response. Gods, was he just going to leave her here?

"Stupid," she hissed, her throat aching and dry as she slammed her head back into the mattress. Her other bodily needs couldn't be ignored for much longer, either.

How had she gotten herself into this mess? But it wasn't like she could claim ignorance. Her mom had warned her about how dangerous the world was.

She's exaggerating, Persephone always told herself. *She's paranoid.*

Or maybe she knew exactly what she was freaking talking about.

You're only in danger because she lied about who she was. About who Dad was.

Persephone looked up at the fancy texture on the ceiling, her eyes searching out patterns. Looking for meaning where there wasn't any. Story of her life.

If Mom had only told Persephone *why* she was keeping her so isolated instead of ordering her around and forbidding her from taking a step off the farm, maybe they could have worked together. But no, Demeter Vestian always knew best and God help anyone who told her different.

And consequently, Persephone had walked right into the lion's den without even knowing it.

"Stupid." But this time it was directed at her mother. Why couldn't she have trusted her own daughter?

Persephone looked up at the hand where she'd been slowly working at her ring. It was difficult to take off a ring with only one hand.

Difficult, but not impossible.

She swore she'd lose her shit if she had to wear this mark of his ownership one more second. She'd fought her whole life to be free and she wasn't giving up now.

She bit her lip as she finally managed to wiggle it past her largest knuckle, and finally off, into her hand. She gave the rope as much slack as possible on that hand by straining all her other limbs, before she flung it as far as possible to the far corner of the room. She smiled as it got lost among the greenery in the corner.

"That was poorly done, wife."

Persephone's head swung toward the door, her mouth going dry. Well, drier than it already was. She was parched.

She yanked at her restraints. "Let me free."

Hades wandered over and propped a hip on the bed. His large hand encircled her ankle and slid upward, leaving a tingling trail in its wake. Persephone fought the response but her body apparently didn't know any better. Her limbs weakened and her stomach flipped, reacting to Hades as she always did.

"Are we ever truly free?" Hades mused, stroking her thighs. She hated the liberties he took with her body. Hated and loved it.

"Freedom..." He looked toward the window. "It's an illusion. From the minute we're born we serve a purpose." His face turned back to her, his eyes cold. "We play a role. The gods design our lives and we are merely pawns."

Persephone fought the urge to roll her eyes. It was such bullshit. "You don't believe that."

Hades's hand trespassed closer to her throbbing core and she jerked her leg as far as it would go—almost a whole inch. She didn't know what she was angrier about, the fact that he was touching her or her own response. No, it was more than anger. She was furious. She couldn't remember ever being more furious in her entire life. He thought she was meek and pliable and that she'd be terrified of him and do whatever he said. Well he had another thing coming.

"You think you are a god," she spat. "Rich, powerful, handsome—"

"Handsome?" he raised a brow.

She ignored him, or tried as hard as she could while his fingers grazed her pussy and her body released a shot of heated serum. She bit back a groan and focused on keeping her voice steady. "You think everyone else is a mere mortal you can toy with."

"Hmmm," he considered this, his fingers tracing arcane symbols on her inner thigh.

She gritted her teeth. "Stop touching me."

Hades seemed amused. "Why? Because you hate it? Or because it makes you feel too good?" He leaned in, his hands taking further liberties. "You belong to me. You know it. Your body knows it."

She hated him. *Hated* him. She didn't belong to anyone but herself.

She spat in his face. He jerked back, mood broken. The only sound was her harsh breathing.

She regretted it immediately. It was stupid. She was letting her anger make her reckless. She should conserve her fight and wait for the most likely chance of escape. But gods, he'd offered her paradise and brought her to hell. And anger felt so much better than letting that hurt in.

He pulled a handkerchief from his suit coat pocket and wiped his face.

"Be careful, wife. I've killed men for lesser offenses."

And there it was. She'd shut her mind to the warnings and fooled herself. She'd defended Hades, insisting he was a good man no matter what the papers said. No matter how Hecate tried to warn her. But now he told her the truth. He had nothing to hide.

She believed it now.

Hades was a murderer. She was married to a monster.

But when she said it out loud he only smiled.

"You're finally beginning to see things clearly."

"It's true, then. All the things they say of you." She ought to be feeling a lot more fear in this moment. But she was so off kilter, all of this so surreal, the fear didn't penetrate.

Hades shrugged. "You'd think they could come up with a more imaginative title than Lord of the Underworld. But rest assured, my Shades and I are the shadows that hold back the chaos in the streets of New Olympus."

"More like you profit off it," Persephone muttered furiously. She knew she should stay silent, she knew it. But for him to stand here and pretend so sanctimoniously that he did what he did for any other reason than money was just—

Hades tilted his head at her and she saw his jaw flex, but he said nothing.

"How long are you going to keep me like this?" When he still didn't reply, she tugged on the scarves. Her wrists would bear red marks for a while. "You can't keep me tied up forever."

"Can't I?"

Persephone furrowed her brow. "I guess you could. But why?"

"Until you learn your place."

"My place? As what, your wife?" She slowly worked it out in her head. "A trophy on display to prove your power over the Titans?"

Hades shook his head as he shrugged out of his coat jacket. "Maybe so."

"You're nuts." He loomed over her, dark and beautiful in the low light, removing his cufflinks and rolling up his sleeves. At the sight of his forearms, sleek and strong and dusted with dark hair, her core clenched. It was almost enough to distract her from her rage.

Almost. "If you think I'm going to forget what you've said, what you've done to me..." She clenched her teeth.

"You know how many women would kill to be in your place?"

"What, tied to your bed?" she scoffed.

He raised an arrogant brow. Gods, why was he so handsome when he was mocking her?

"They can have you. I don't care." She turned her face away, keeping her expression blank.

"I could have them," he agreed. "A different one every night. If I wanted to tie them up, they'd beg me."

"Wow, I'm so impressed by your manly prowess," she deadpanned. "Do you keep notches on the bedpost?" She twisted to look up at the headboard even as her stomach twisted at the images his words conjured, imagining Hades entwined with another woman.

"You'll learn to watch that smart mouth of yours," Hades muttered. "And what was it you said before? Rich, powerful, handsome...most women would settle for one outta three. Lucky you."

His hand dropped to her thigh. "You're the one I want. As soon as I saw you, I knew that I would have you. Here, like this." His voice deepened and despite herself, her inner muscles contracted. Hades trailed his rough fingers over the thin skin of her inner thigh. "I knew I'd be the one to break you. We'll have such fun, angel, you and I."

She fought to hide the way her breath hitched at his touch. Gods, *why?* Why was she still so attracted to him?

"Stop touching me," she gritted out. She couldn't think with his hand between her legs.

The gentle touch became a strong grip, solid and claiming. Her body liked that, too. "You're mine. Bought and paid for."

Every word out of his mouth only made it worse. She wasn't a whore. "That's not how it works," she spat, still fighting the pull of her body toward his with everything she had in her.

"Isn't it? I spilled blood for you, Persephone."

She flinched at that and her body momentarily cooled. "The man who roofied me." The one who'd come to the dog shelter to warn her, his face mottled with bruises. *Don't think about that.* If she went down that trail, she'd start screaming.

There had been so many warnings and red flags. But she wouldn't listen, would she? She'd explained every one of them away, she'd been so blinded by Hades. And now... "That man, he's dead, isn't he?"

"He put his hands on you. No one harms you and lives." The words might as well have been carved in stone.

"No one but you." A wave of tiredness swept through her. "What do you want from me?"

"Your submission."

Never.

She glared at him.

He bent forward and the light cupped his face. His gaze raked her naked flesh. "Your total submission. Instant, utter obedience. Your training starts now."

"Training?"

"You won't act like a wife, fine. You're still my property."

"What does that—"

"If you want off of that bed, you're gonna have to get familiar with crawling."

Her skin prickled and her chest felt hot, the fury burned hotter and hotter. "Go to h—"

"First things first," he cut her off. He pulled an item she couldn't see out of the bedside drawer, something that clinked. "You won't wear my ring, you can wear this." He held up a piece of thick leather attached to a long, glittering chain.

A collar.

"You're out of your mind," Persephone whispered, staring aghast at the collar.

"On the contrary." He leaned close. So close she could smell the aftershave she used to love. But his face? His face was nothing like that of the man she thought she knew. "I've been waiting a very long time to see my enemies crawling at my feet."

She shook her head. What did he—? "I'm not your enemy," she whispered. "I barely know you."

"The sins of the father shall be visited upon the sons. Or daughter in this case. The sins of the father, Persephone."

He caressed his hand down her cheek and she yanked away. Echoes of the fury and the new terrible, terrible sadness warred in her chest. She'd never had a chance with Hades, had she? He'd always see her as her mother when he looked at her. The thought made her want to throw up. Because that meant it really all had been a farce.

How had he managed it? Kissing and touching her all those months? Holding her hand and looking into her eyes when she wore her mother's face that he so despised?

She shut her eyes. This wasn't Hades. The Hades she thought she knew was dead. Or worse, he never existed. She couldn't appeal to this man's humanity. He had none.

"You said you'd take care of me." It escaped anyway, a heartbroken whisper.

"I will. I will take care of you. Submit to the collar, Persephone."

It was no use. She needed to harden herself, like he had. Gathering her reserves, she spat, "Go to hell."

"I see you need more time to consider your predicament. I'll come back when you're ready to assume your place."

He was almost to the door when Persephone called out, "Wait! I'm sorry. Please." Even she could hear the desperation in her own voice. "I... I'm thirsty. And I need to go to the bathroom."

She closed her eyes. *It doesn't matter. They're just words.* Words didn't mean anything. And if groveling meant she could get free of being tied naked, spread-eagled to a bed, certainly she could survive a little indignity.

Because that was the key word to focus on—survive.

She'd been strong enough to survive everything her mother put her through. The years of isolation. The punishments. The emotional manipulation.

She'd survived and come out stronger.

But Hades.

Would she be able to survive Hades?

A shudder went down her spine even as she forced herself to look up at him and lock gazes when he peered down at her in return.

"I hate you." It popped out but this time he didn't pull back, he only chuckled. It was so wrong, hearing the same sound she used to adore, now, here in these awful circumstances, as he lifted her hair and secured the collar around her neck.

"I had this made special for you." Eyes holding hers, he clipped on a chain and tugged. Heat singed Persephone's cheeks. Followed by terror. She had to get out of here. He'd just put a *collar* on her. No sane man did that. He'd *killed* people.

She couldn't stand being here another second. She had to escape.

He untied her wrists.

Steady, she whispered to herself. *Be smart. Think this through.*

But her heartbeat fluttered like a rabbit being chased down by a predator.

Run.

Hades moved to the bottom of the bed, the chain tied to the collar around her neck clinking as he went. It didn't look like he had the best grip on it. He wasn't even looking at her as he untied her ankles.

Run.

The second he had her left ankle untied she exploded off the bed and bolted for the door.

Run!

Only to be jerked painfully backward by the collar around her neck. She choked as she was wrenched off her feet onto her ass. Coughing and gasping for breath, her hands flew to the collar.

"Ah ah ah," Hades walked around front of her, wagging a finger calmly. He wasn't even holding the leash. He'd looped it around the headboard and that was why she'd been yanked backwards so unforgivingly.

"You really do want to be tied to the bed again, don't you? I guess we'll try this again later."

"No, no! I'll be good! I promise."

It had been fight or flight—the impulse was too strong, and she'd known there was no way she could fight Hades. But some monkey part of her brain had thought, maybe, if she was untied, she'd be fast enough to make it to the door—

"No!" she screamed when Hades grabbed her by the wrist and shoved her back down on the bed, landing on top of her with his body.

She thrashed to get him off, but it was no use. He was twice her size and before she knew it, he had tied her collar to the headboard in a way that choked her unless she lay very still.

"Careful," he murmured. "Don't want to damage that pretty neck."

This time he took the time to pull out real, heavy leather cuffs for her wrists and feet. He soon had her wrists bound. Oh gods, no. She bit her lip hard as she fought back tears while he spent a moment stroking the red lines on her skin from her struggle with the scarves. No, he would not see her cry.

She clung to the anger and tried to stoke it again. Like a fire. Like a shield. She tried to let every ounce of hate pour from her eyes and kicked out when he grabbed her ankles. But it was no use.

Within five minutes she was spread-eagled again, this time tied more securely than before to the bed.

"We'll try this again in an hour. You'll learn to play by the rules, little girl. One way or another."

She let out a furious grunt, glaring at Hades.

He only chuckled again as he left the room.

It took long minutes for her head to clear but finally she forced her breaths to even out. Just like she used to when mom would lock her in the cellar.

She would get through this. She'd lived through one indignity after another with her mother, hadn't she? And all because she could taste her future freedom. She'd lived in that imaginary future and let it nourish her for years.

This was just another momentary setback. But she'd escape this bastard—and not by trying to make a run for it the first moment she was free. That had been stupid. No, it would require cunning and planning and maybe even—she swallowed hard—it might even require playing along with Hades's sick little twisted games.

No, next time she wouldn't run. She'd be the sweet little terrified girl he expected. And then when the time was right, she'd make her escape, steal out of town and eventually make Hades Ubeli rue the day he ever thought to trap her in the first place.

12

An hour later, Hades was back sitting at the edge of the bed, holding out a glass of water with a straw in it. He'd already taken Persephone to the restroom and then reattached her collar to the headboard. He'd been prepared for her to make another run for it but she merely followed his instructions with her head bowed.

She was more subdued than she'd been during his last visit. He didn't know why he was disappointed not to see the fire in her eyes. It made his cock rock hard every time she talked back with that smart mouth of hers. And even more determined to get her to submit.

She sucked greedily at the straw.

"Not too fast or you'll get cramps."

She glared up at him. Ah, there it was. He didn't bother hiding his grin. He never imagined how much he'd like having her helpless, completely dependent on him.

Normally women were nothing more than a form of stress relief. Useful for a night's indulgence, but rarely brought back for a repeat performance. If they were, it was only because they were convenient and knew the score. He didn't need the hassle or a possible pressure point his enemies might use against him. He wouldn't make the same mistakes his father had.

But Persephone was something altogether different. And he still wasn't sure how he felt about that.

"Careful," he murmured as she choked on the water. His stomach tightened as she coughed and gasped in a gulp of air, finally regaining her breath.

His entire body had been coiled, ready to turn her around and pound her on the back. What the fuck? He should enjoy the sight of her sputtering, her eyes watering.

Instead, relieved, he wiped her mouth carefully and helped her sit up to drink the rest. She stiffened but let him handle her. The feel of her warm, lithe body in his arms turned his erection painful. He had to take a moment to compose himself under the guise of setting the water glass aside.

It wasn't supposed to be like this. He had her right where he wanted her. But instead of crushing her and teaching her the merciless lesson he'd intended, he was coddling her.

Taking care of her.

It had been a problem from the beginning. Dating and courting her hadn't been as painful as it should have been. He'd taken himself in hand every night, and gotten off imagining Persephone looking up at him, eyes wide and innocent and so very trusting.

Even now, he wanted to unbuckle the collar, check for marks, and soothe her sore skin. And somewhere along the line, he decided to *train* her to obey, being careful to ensure she'd bend and not break.

Because even though she was his enemy, he didn't want her totally broken.

Oh yes, the gods were laughing. And Hades was the butt of no one's joke. He was meant to be ruthless in all things. Especially revenge. So he would turn his heart and flesh to stone, harden himself to her pleas and wide eyes, and take the pound of flesh she owed by virtue of her birthright.

Behind him, Persephone sighed.

Don't ask. You're not supposed to give a damn.

"What?" he bit out.

"I'm just wondering. Do I have a tattoo on my face that says 'victim'?"

His brow wrinkled and he turned around to look at her. "What's that supposed to mean?"

"You're not the first person to take advantage of me. Oh no. There's a pattern here. I came to the city to escape it. But look what a great job I'm doing." She scoffed humorlessly. "The Donahues, then the guy who—"

"You won't ever have to deal with them again," he said before thinking.

"Oh right. You did something to the Donahues, didn't you? Threatened them. Or whatever. Still." She rocked her head back and forth, as far as the collar would let her. She wasn't looking at him. Her derision was reserved for herself. "It's always the same. I thought it was just my mother, but I'm sensing a pattern. And the common denominator is me."

Hades forced his fists to unclench and his forearms to relax. She'd been hurt before. Why did it make him so angry? It shouldn't affect him one way or the other.

"It started with my mother, and now you—"

"What about your mother?" he interrupted.

"—you all think you can control me. And I let you. I'm so weak. I don't want to be weak anymore." The last part came on a whisper, as if she was speaking to herself.

"What did your mother do?" Hades forced himself to remain calm. He didn't know much about Demeter other than that she'd grown up in foster care and had no family to speak of, then she married Karl Titan at 22 and had Persephone a year later, her only child.

Persephone scoffed, eyes to the ceiling. "What didn't she do? She locked me in the basement, held me against my will. Kept me on the farm like it was a prison. She wouldn't let me leave even for school or to socialize. Then there were the times she'd get physical, slapping or punching me if I ever stepped out of line, not to mention all the verbal abuse."

Persephone shook her head. "Gods, I don't even think I've ever said it all out loud. But I was as trapped as...well, as trapped as I am now." Her mouth twisted in a mocking semblance of a smile. "She did it all to *protect* me, of course. That's what she'd tell you, if you were ever on speaking terms."

"She hurt you?" A storm brewed in his chest. The thought of Demeter slapping or beating his Persephone... Because she *was* his. His jaw clenched and his vision narrowed the way it did when he had an enemy in his sights. No one else had the right to put their hands on what was his.

Persephone looked at him a long moment. "I survived it, Hades." She said it so matter of factly. "I'll survive this, too."

He was doing it again. Forgetting she was the enemy. "Of course you'll survive. You'll live a long miserable life, I'll make sure of it." No one would hurt her. No one but him.

She sighed. "Did it ever occur to you that I'm just like your sister? An innocent, caught by circumstance."

"You're nothing like my sister," he bit out again. "She died, and all the good in me died with her."

It felt good to finally tell her the truth. And it was a good reminder of why she was here and the mission he'd devoted himself to since he discovered Chiara's broken and bloodied body. His jaw hardened.

"That's not true." Persephone strained forward. "There is good in you. I told Hecate so because I believe—"

"That's enough." Time to teach her her place.

He unlatched her chain from the headboard and held it firmly. She made no protest when he led her out of the room.

He ought to make her crawl. He'd intended to humiliate her in every possible way. But it just didn't...feel right at the moment.

He still wanted it. Badly. To see her on her knees before him—his cock went steel just at the thought. But there was something about her willing submission, that moment when she finally gave in, the feisty spark still firing in her eyes—gods, he was quickly becoming addicted to it.

In fact, he hoped to see it in just a few moments.

She allowed him to lead her to the table, a heavy wooden piece long enough to seat twenty where they could eat with a view of the city glittering before them.

A table set for one.

A cushion lay beside his chair. He felt the moment she saw it and recognized what it meant.

"No." She tugged away. "Uh uh."

Hades waited, holding her leash firmly, pleasure unfurling in his stomach. It was wrong to be enjoying her training this much but after all these years of self-control, it was the one impulse he couldn't seem to deny himself.

"This is the price," he reminded her. Food already sat on the table, plates covered by silver steam covers. The food smelled delicious and he could only imagine how it tormented her. Her stomach growled, an undeniable argument. She had to eat.

He watched the internal fight play out on her face.

And then finally, beautifully, she went to her knees.

Triumph sang through his chest. "Good girl," he murmured as she settled on the cushion.

She bristled. "I'm not your pet."

"Aren't you?" The chain clinked as he drew her forward. She waited, chin by his knee, as he removed the steam covers, releasing mouthwatering smells in a rush of steam. If he thought about how close her mouth was to his cock, he wasn't going to make it through the meal.

Instead, he tried to concentrate on a small forkful of omelet and lifting it to her mouth. She glared daggers at him. But then she opened her mouth and ate.

"See," he said after a few minutes feeding her. "This can be nice."

"This is fucked up," she muttered after swallowing the last of the omelet.

He patted her mouth with a napkin. "The Persephone I knew wouldn't cuss like that."

She gave a saccharine smile. "Then you shouldn't have killed her."

His cock twitched painfully in his pants.

"Are you done? Full?"

A quiver entered her voice. "Yes." She watched him carefully, like prey would a circling predator. It ought to have disturbed him, how much he liked the image.

Enough waiting.

He rose and pushed the food plates to the floor before drawing her up. He set her on the table and splayed a hand on her chest, pressing her down. "Lie back. I want to look at you."

With a whimper, she tensed, but let him push her to her back. He propped her legs open and reseated himself. He had a full view of her private parts...everything. She was delectable. Her scent intoxicating. His breath puffed over her folds and he saw her shiver. She tried to close her legs, but his shoulders nudged them open.

Her beautiful virgin pussy. Wet and glistening for him. He licked his lips, his erection painful now. More than anything, he wanted to stand up, rip off his buckle and plunge into her wet depths. The thought of how tight she would be tormented him. He could barely sleep last night and he'd had to take himself in hand twice more before finally entering her room again this morning.

He traced her plump labia with his forefinger. "Tell me, do you touch yourself often?"

She looked stubbornly at the ceiling but her cheeks flamed pink and as he began to probe inside, even more heated juice spilled onto his fingers.

"So ready for me," he murmured.

She cursed him under her breath.

His fingers bit into her thighs. "Excuse me? What was that?"

"You heard me." He also heard how her voice quavered.

"I don't think you understand the nature of your situation. This." He covered her pussy with his palm and didn't miss the way she squirmed against him. So responsive. It drove him insane. "This is mine."

"So is this," he shoved two fingers in her mouth. Her eyes widened. "You eat when I tell you, speak when I tell you, kneel when I tell you. And you don't talk back. If you need to learn the lesson, I'm happy to teach you." He removed his fingers, wiping them on her midriff before burying his face in her cunt.

She squealed and her legs went tense around his head before relaxing and flopping open a moment later.

The sounds that came from her throat were fucking indecent. And the way she tasted. Ambrosia. The gods wished they could have feasted on her.

But she was his.

All his. Only his. Forever his.

And he was going to take her and make her his wife in every way possible so she never forgot it.

He thrust his chair back and stood up. "Stay here. Don't move."

His condoms were in the bathroom. She'd gotten a birth control shot before the wedding, but he wasn't taking any chances. The fact that he could even think straight enough to remember was a godsdamned miracle. But he'd sworn never to bring a child into this fucked up world and not even Persephone's magic pussy was enough to make him forget that most basic tenant of his life.

He stormed out of the room, only barely keeping himself from all out running. Finally, he'd sink his cock inside her. Maybe it would finally quiet the insanity she created in him. Yes, once he had her, her siren pull would ease. He'd be able to think clearly again. He could go back to the original plan.

He grabbed a condom from the box in his bathroom, on second thought grabbed two more, then turned to head back toward the dining room.

He'd imagined it a thousand times, what it would feel like to finally sink balls deep into her delectable pussy. And now he was only moments away from—

But Persephone was scrambling toward the front door, chain in hand, all but tripping over her own feet in her haste to get there before he got back.

Hades was across the room in four strides.

She screamed when he locked his arms around her from behind. So tight he probably knocked the breath out of her, but he didn't care.

She thought she could run from *him*? She thought she could escape?

She flailed and slammed her elbow back. Fuck. He couldn't help the "oof" that escaped his mouth. It hurt. But he didn't let her go. He would never fucking let her go. And soon she'd realize it because it was a lesson he wouldn't let her ever forget.

But then she just went insane in his arms.

"Help! Help!" She kicked out and connected with the white column that held the statue she'd admired when he first brought her to the penthouse, a million years ago. The statue hit the ground and shattered. But she didn't stop flailing, kicking and scrambling and thrashing.

"Fuck," Hades cursed. Persephone kept screaming as he carried her to the bedroom.

"Be quiet," he ordered, holding her down with his weight. "Persephone. Be still!"

She froze at his barked command. He lay a hand on her heaving midriff, calming the storm. "Are you hurt?"

She looked at him like he was the crazy one.

"Lie still and let me make sure you didn't get glass in your feet." He released her and examined her bare legs. He wanted to shout at her, *what the hell were you thinking?* But he knew what she was thinking. She was trying to get away from him.

And now a shard of glass had embedded itself in her calf. Who knew what the state of her feet were. A sick feeling twisted through his stomach. He hadn't protected her. Scowling, he pulled it out. "I need to clean this. Will you stay on the bed?"

When she stared at him, he sighed. Without a word, he shackled her leg to the bedpost. It was a much longer chain, but still secured fast.

She wouldn't have gotten hurt if she'd just listened to him. He went to the bathroom and returned with a first aid kit. She jerked a little when he cleaned the tiny wound, but lay quiet and blinking as he bandaged it. He held his breath as he looked at her feet, but there wasn't any more glass. He breathed out a relieved breath.

"You need to stop fighting me. You could have really hurt yourself."

Her jaw hardened and he realized that the words had come out with more bite then he'd intended. Well, she could get over it. Things would only go one way in this marriage. His way.

Her next words only proved she didn't understand though. "If I stop, will you leave me alone?"

"No." He closed the kit with a decisive click. He met her gaze and underneath the stubbornness, he saw her. The her she never had learned how to hide. Vulnerable. Beautiful. Precious. "I told you, Persephone," he finally said more softly. "I'll take care of you."

Persephone's brow furrowed like she didn't know what to make of him. But he could see it in her eyes. She wasn't resisting him, even when she said, "I can't do this." She jerked her foot, testing the shackle's hold.

"You can," he murmured. He knew how strong she was. But he needed to show her there could be strength in submission, too.

"You fight me, but you don't want me to leave you alone." He leaned closer and she closed her eyes, like she was letting his deep voice wash over her. "Let go, Persephone. Just let go, and let yourself be mine."

He slid a hand up her thigh and her breath shuddered out of her. Her leg was tense under his touch, but she didn't move.

"Let me show you," he murmured. "Let me give you a taste of what it'll be like. I can be a kind master."

Emotion rippled through her at the word *master*, her body inadvertently responding to him. Instead of disgust she felt desire. Even with eyes closed, her face betrayed her.

"We can do this the easy way or the hard way. It's up to you." He kept stroking her leg. "Imagine what it would be like. To not fight. To not have to be strong. To let me keep you." His voice deepened, relaxing, hypnotic. "I can keep you safe. No one will touch you."

She stirred a little at that. "No one but you."

"But you like it when I touch you. We've established that. What makes you think you wouldn't like the rest of my rule over you?"

A little sigh. Her body stretched before him, flushed and perfect, made by the gods to be claimed and plundered by him. She was open and compliant as he touched her, clay in his hands. Even though he'd hardened himself, he felt the strangest stirring.

What if—? What if it could be like this? Days with her on his arm, by his side, and nights with her yielding to him?

He wouldn't just *be* the most powerful man in the world. He'd *feel* like it, too. Everything he'd built, everything he'd done, all the shit and grit and sin he'd waded through for years... what if it could all be for her? Innocence put on a pedestal and guarded like the precious thing she was. His wife, his trophy and reward.

He just had to mold her...

Slowly, he shifted and seated himself on the bed where she could still reach him, even with the chain. "Come lie over my lap."

She blinked at him, brow furrowed. Uncertainty warred with curiosity.

"Now, angel," he said, still gentle. "Or it'll be worse for you."

She moved, crawling over the bed to him, and he hid a smile. He'd read the signs right. She wanted to fight, but her instincts told her to submit.

He'd show her she wasn't fighting him as much as herself.

His cock hardened as she draped her lithe body over his legs. *Later.* He'd relieve himself later. Right now, he needed to focus on her.

"What...what are you doing?" Her voice was small and uncertain.

"I'm going to teach you a lesson," he said in a soothing voice, rubbing her pert bottom. She shifted and he squeezed harder, a silent order to be still. She obeyed right away, letting her light weight collapse on his hard thighs. His cock rose in his pants, brushing her belly. Every breath she took, he felt.

Gods, this might kill him.

He focused on massaging her ass and the backs of her thighs, working out knots. Preparing her for punishment.

"That feels good," she mumbled.

"That's right. Be a good girl and I'll make you feel good. There's no need to fight. You won't win."

She gave a little huff, but kept still. He rubbed the place between her legs and she jerked, her shoulders tense.

"Easy," he soothed like she was a wild horse. "Let me make you feel good."

He felt the moment she decided to surrender as she finally relaxed into his touch. She'd pushed the boundaries as far as she could and now, tired of fighting, she could submit. He withdrew his fingers and she gave a gusty sigh.

"I'm gonna spank you now," he told her firmly, "and you're going to take it. You know why you're being punished?" He paused, but she remained silent. "You ran from me. You can't do that, Persephone. You'll only end up hurt. I can't protect you if you don't obey."

"I'm never going to obey you." A defiant whisper. The last of her resistance.

"You will. I'll teach you." He squeezed her right cheek hard enough to press a white patch on her bottom, outlined in red. He smacked her left cheek lightly, enjoying the ripple through her firm flesh.

His palm clapped down harder, one cheek and then the other. She wriggled and he gritted his teeth against the torment of stimulation to his leaking cock. He was in charge. He would not lose control and rut her like he wanted to, so badly. Not until she earned it.

He weighted her legs down with one of his, holding her with a large hand in the small of her back. After a token struggle, she gave up, her body growing loose and languid, accepting of each swat on her bare ass.

As far as spankings went, this was a light one, enough to sting but not enough to bruise. Hades didn't miss the hitch of her breath or the slight shift of her hips as he spanked close to her pussy. He used his leg to split her thighs apart, and saw with satisfaction that her folds were glistening.

"You're doing so well," he purred. "Submitting. Taking your punishment. Such a good girl."

She didn't answer, but he didn't need her to. The slick serum leaking between her legs, dampening his slacks told him how she really felt. But hadn't he known all along? There was an undercurrent to the undeniable attraction they had for each other. He dominated and she obeyed. They'd cleaved together in the easy dance, her yielding power, him taking it, since the first moment they'd met.

If she wasn't the enemy, Hades would say she was his missing half. Only she could make him whole.

But she was the enemy, and he knew better than to succumb to her charms. He'd mold her and master her until she knew her place —at his feet—and his inexorable rule over her. The small voice that told him it would be better if she freely came to him to submit... He shook his head against the thought. That was weakness and had no place in his reasoning.

Persephone whimpered and he palmed her right ass cheek. Her pale skin was flushed, warm to the touch. He'd spanked her with increasing intensity and she'd accepted it.

Part one of the punishment was over. Time for part two.

His hand slipped between her legs, finding the slick furrows on either side of her clit and stroking. She writhed and he weighted her down, his fingers never pausing in their rhythm.

"Stop fighting," he said. "Just enjoy it."

"I shouldn't..." Her words were slurred like she was drunk. Drunk on endorphins. Drunk on him.

"Do you want me to stop?"

An endless pause before she answered in a clearer voice, "No."

Hades allowed himself a satisfied smirk.

He eased his grip on her, giving her freedom to wriggle away if she wanted. She stayed still and he rewarded her, strumming her like an instrument, her gasps and moans a music of his making. He played her to perfection until she stiffened and gasped and came, soaking his hand and his crisp white shirt cuffs.

"Good," he praised her. "So very good."

But he wasn't done. Once wasn't nearly enough to get his point across. And he couldn't keep his hands off her flesh even if it was.

He rubbed her pink bottom and shifted his leg off hers. She didn't move though, and didn't protest when he spanked her again, round after round interspersed with rubbing her needy flesh until she came and came and came.

The third time she forgot herself and moaned loudly and wildly as her orgasm hit, which only drove Hades to demand more of her. By the fifth, she was exhausted and mewling her release but it was all the sweeter, watching her sweat-dampened face, all confusion and fight faded to sweet, sweet surrender.

Her legs splayed open freely and she pressed her bottom against his hand even when he wasn't pleasuring her. In this moment she was his and his completely. And he'd never felt more like a king.

It wasn't until after, when he stood over her limp and sated body, that he realized his mistake. That every gasp and inadvertent squeeze of her cunt on his fingers was a link in a chain, locking him to her as securely as he'd tied her to his bed.

He waited a long time, watching her sleep, too hard to think straight, too tangled up in her to leave.

13

Persephone jerked out of her dream. A nightmare. She'd stood at her wedding, said her vows, and then Hades turned into a monster and carried her off. She'd screamed and reached out to the wedding guests for help but Hermes and all the rest only sipped their drinks and laughed.

She squeezed her eyes shut again and rolled to her side. Something tugged her ankle with a clink. The chain.

It wasn't a dream.

The wedding. The wedding night when he'd filmed the whole thing and had been so cruel... But then he'd changed again. He was so tender after she'd broken the statue. Then the... punishment.

It had been humiliating to be taken over his knee like that, but she told herself she was allowing it because she needed to get underneath his defenses. Trying to make a run for it again had been just as stupid and useless as the first time.

She just needed to outsmart him. To play by his rules for a little while. Give him what he wanted and gain his trust. Already he'd made her leash longer. He couldn't keep her here locked up forever.

He wanted her as a trophy and what fun was a trophy if you couldn't show it off in public? If she played his games, maybe he'd give her more and more leeway, and then she could make her escape once she had a real shot at it.

The problem was, once his 'punishment' had started...

Her eyes all but rolled back in her head as she remembered. At first it was just a confusing mix of pain and pleasure while he spanked her.

But then...it went somewhere else entirely. She didn't even know how to explain it. It was like she'd floated off the ground while still being in her own body. Like a timeout from real life where she didn't have to worry about anything except sensation. And pleasure, oh gods, the *pleasure*. She hadn't even known it was possible to come that many times.

She gave over her body to him, leaping off a cliff and knowing, just absolutely *knowing* that he would catch her.

What the hell was that about?

Her cheeks heated and her stomach went liquid at the memories. Every time he touched her, she melted.

She scrubbed her hands down her face and looked out the window. She didn't know how long she'd napped. It looked like it might be nearing sunset.

She slipped off the bed, testing her new, longer leash. The chain let her go to the bathroom, if she sat with her foot outstretched. How generous.

The shackle around her ankle didn't have a lock to pick, as far as she could tell. Same with the collar.

You won't act like a wife, fine. You're still my property.

She clenched her teeth, shaking off memories of the confusing pleasure. Fuck that. Just because he could play her body like a violin didn't change anything.

"Yeah, I said 'fuck,'" she said, looking around the room. "Get used to it." Her mother taught her good girls didn't swear, but where had being good gotten her?

Tied to her bed on her wedding night.

She spent long minutes testing the strength of the chain and the bedpost securing it before giving up.

She glared up again at the camera in the corner, red light still blinking at her. "I'm hungry," she announced. She was only a little bit hungry after the filling breakfast earlier, but she had the feeling it was a request Hades wouldn't ignore. He seemed to have a thing about taking care of her physical needs. She'd bet that in a minute, Hades would enter and tell her whatever humiliating task she had to perform for food. And she'd do it.

Submit. Survive. Escape.

"Any day now," she muttered, flopping back on the bed. She was still naked. Her new husband seemed to like her like this. Helpless. Naked. Chained. The sick fuck.

She ran her hands over her arms and then her chest. She'd gotten through her first day of marriage. What would tonight bring?

More of the same, no doubt. He would come for her and she would bend, bow, and scrape. She couldn't help it. Something in her responded to him. He held all the cards, but she'd do anything to stay in the game. So yes, she'd bend. But she wouldn't break. She'd remain her own no matter what he did.

No matter how many times he called her, *"Mine."*

Long minutes passed and he didn't come. Was it because he knew she was trying to exert some small control over the situation? She crossed her arms over her chest but she couldn't help her thoughts from straying where they always did. His body strong and beautiful as a god's, powerful, all consuming. Thinking about it, her breath came faster and her nipples pebbled.

How could she resist his power over her?

Stroking her right arm absently, her wrist brushed her nipple. Heat shot from the tight bud to her awakened core. Whenever Hades walked into a room, her body came alive.

Maybe she could… No, she shouldn't…

But what if she did?

She bit her lip. And then, easing back, she opened her legs. The first graze of her fingers was like the coming of spring, warmth breathing over the land. The heat unfurled and bloomed with a thousand petals bursting open. She'd never dared touch herself before. Her body was a secret garden and only one man held the key.

Fuck that. Her finger dipped into her wet channel, spreading silky slick over her inner folds.

Why had she waited so long to do this? This wasn't shameful or indecent. It felt—

"Oh gods," she groaned, her legs tightening, her eyelids fluttering closed. The pad of her finger found a spot that sent electric sparks through her.

Forget Hades, she could please herself.

On second thought, *Hades...* His hard face filled her vision, silver eyes flashing, the points of his cheeks tinged red with anger and arousal. *Mmmm*, yes, right there.

Her back arched as her finger circled her clit. So good.

She blinked languorously—

"Hades!" she yelped and scooted back, giving herself room to sit up.

Her husband loomed over her.

"Enjoying yourself, wife?" There was a world of tension in the word 'wife.'

"Actually, I am." Her voice came out an airy squeak, with nothing of the defiance she intended.

He followed her, a storm cloud dark with barely controlled violence. He gripped her wrist, brought it to his lips. He held her gaze as he sucked her fingers into his mouth.

She whimpered, pressing her thighs together. Who was she kidding? The pleasure brewing between her legs was a volcano now compared to the flickering flame of her earlier arousal. Hades cleaned her essence off her fingers, tongue curling around each delicate digit until she closed her eyes, dizzy with pleasure.

His left hand cupped the place between her legs. "This belongs to me. You feel pain and pleasure only at my command." For a beautiful moment, the heel of his hand grazed her clitoris. A shockwave rolled through her.

He released her and it was gone. Persephone bit back a moan. Her body throbbed, mourning the loss.

"Well, excuse me, lord and master." There was her defiance. Apparently losing out on an orgasm made her cranky and unhinged her brain from all survival instinct, because she kept snarking. "I didn't realize you were going to take over all my body functions."

"Everything, Persephone. All of you belongs to me."

She swung her legs over the side of the bed. "Well, in that case, *your* stomach is hungry. Feed me."

He moved to the bedpost and crouched next to the chain. His body blocked her view, so she didn't see how the mechanism worked.

Next time. He had to slip up at some point.

He returned with the chain in hand and gave it a thoughtful tug. "I'll feed you. But you'll still be punished for touching what belongs to me."

"How are you going to punish me this time? Tie me up? Humiliate me? Spank me? Oh wait, you've already done all that."

"You think this is the worst that could happen?" He wound the chain around his wrist, tugging her upward.

She came to her feet, quivering at his closeness. She wanted to rage at him, to beat his chest and scream and rip out his heart like he'd ripped out hers. The rest of her wanted him to touch her, strong and sure and gentle, satisfying the hunger that beat inside her.

He drew her up on tiptoes. She gave him her best glare, but she was caught and at his mercy, a fish on a line.

He opened his mouth to say something and her stomach growled loud enough to echo through the room.

Hades closed his mouth, amusement glimmering in his silver eyes. "Hungry?"

"Already told you I was." She could fight him better with a full belly.

Dinner was much the same as breakfast. Her on the cushion at his feet. Him feeding her filet mignon bite by delicious bite. Sometimes he didn't use the fork. He made her suck the juices off his fingers.

And she did it, becoming wetter and wetter each time, especially when his thumb lingered in her mouth, caressing her bottom lip and dragging down her throat to her chest where he plucked at her nipples.

She moaned helplessly, so riled up she was sure that he could make her come with only a few swipes of his fingers. Or better yet, his tongue.

When dinner was finished, he didn't lift her up on the table like before. And when he took her back to the room, he merely reattached her chain to the bed.

And then.

He.

Left.

"Wait," Persephone said, "where you going?"

He turned at the threshold and looked back at her. "Miss me already? Do you want me to stay?" There was a hungry wolf in his eyes as he asked it.

"No," Persephone said automatically. "I hate you."

"Well, your wish is my command," he said, completely solicitous. The next second, though, the wolf was back, all predator. "But if I so much as see your hand brush that pussy that belongs to me without my say-so, believe me, you will not like the consequences. You'll wish for the days when you were merely tied to the bed." The ice in his voice sent a shiver down Persephone's spine.

She lifted her chin and glared at him. "Get out if you're going to go. I can't stand to look at you another second."

His mouth lifted in a half smile. "Beware what you wish for, little girl."

And then he was gone.

14

Persephone rested on the heavy cushion, leaning against her husband's leg. Above her head, on the desk, the keyboard crackled as Hades typed.

This wasn't what she thought her honeymoon would be.

Walking around naked, posing for her husband, letting him lead her with a collar and chain like a pet? Curling up on a cushion at his feet and dozing the day away. At night she slept with a chain leashing her to the bed. She didn't dare complain in case he decided to tie her up completely again.

She didn't even know what day it was. Maybe five days since the wedding? Six?

Several times a day, sometimes after a meal, sometimes out of the blue, he'd press her to the floor or lift her onto his office or dining room table or the floor. And then he'd toy with her and lick her and tease and torture her...all the way until she was *riiiiiiiiiiight* on the edge of coming.

And then he'd stop and go back to whatever he'd been doing as if nothing at all was the matter. Always with the threat of tying her to the bed again if she dared touch herself to finish off what he'd started.

She was so damn stir-crazy and horny and on edge, sometimes she wondered if it might be worth it. Just once. Gods, if only she could come just *once*.

She didn't know how he'd done it. Sex wasn't anything that had even been on her radar until Hades.

But ever since she'd felt his hands on her body and experienced the kind of pleasure he could wring out of her...it was like those drugs they said you only had to try once or twice to become addicted.

Well, she felt addicted to sex now...and she was still a virgin! Gods, what would it be like if they finally...?

She swallowed and glanced up at Hades. Even worse, she had a horrible suspicion that her addiction was Hades-specific.

Above her head his fingers flew on the keyboard. He wanted her next to him, kneeling on the cushion while he worked. Curled up at his feet like she really was a pet.

The second day he chained her to his desk, she got vocal. "How long are you going to keep this up for? You can't just chain me like a dog wherever you go. I'm a person, godsdamn you."

No response.

"Hey, I'm talking to you." She'd shoved his legs underneath the table.

He responded then, all right. He gagged her and cuffed her hands behind her back and that was how she spent all of day two until bedtime. Other than the three times he'd driven her to the brink of orgasm and pulled back at the last possible second, leaving her so wanting she was glad for the gag because in that moment she would have begged and pleaded and promised him anything if only he'd please, *please* finish what he'd started.

Thankfully, she'd gotten herself under control by the time he released the gag before bed, and all she wanted to do was scream in his face. Scream and kick and punch and scream some more. But she bit her damn lip because after a day going out of her mind with boredom and the devastating bouts of pleasure stopped just short of orgasm, she was beginning to get the picture.

This was about power.

And him letting her know that she didn't have any.

Day three was little better. She spoke up a few times. "Can I at least have a book to read? Paper to draw on?" She wasn't an artist by any means but even doodling would feel like extreme intellectual stimulation at this point.

She'd already examined every inch of his penthouse office by this point, counted every one of the 113 books on his bookshelf—most of them dry looking business and accounting books with a small section of Stephen King novels—and spent hours looking for faces and shapes in the artfully spackled drywall.

Unsurprisingly, there had been, shocker, *no response.*

The daytime chain he allowed her was slightly longer than the nighttime one. She could sit up at his feet while he worked at his desk. Another thing she was grateful for and furious at her own gratitude.

One thing was clear, Hades Ubeli was a master manipulator. He had been from the beginning.

Today she sat at his feet, her mind stewing.

She was angry, bored, frustrated, and so, so horny.

She sighed and ducked her head, examining the fraying edges of her manicure. She thought she was so fancy, going to the spa, getting ready for her wedding. If she could send herself a note, she would've told herself to ditch everything and run.

Not that the old Persephone would believe her. She'd believed in fairy tales, in a handsome businessman meeting a beautiful, young woman and falling in love. Sweeping the girl off her feet. A wedding of her dreams and life of wedded bliss.

She should write the authors of those fairy tales and tell them they were full of shit.

She wiggled to get into a different folded position. Her legs kept falling asleep. Hades didn't speak, but rested a hand on her collar in silent warning to be still.

"This sucks," she blurted.

The keyboard went silent. Oops. Hades was scarier when he was still, a shark sensing blood in the water. She'd poked the bear. Oh well, too late now.

"I'm bored."

"You expect to be entertained?" Grown men would go mad with fear if Hades spoke to them like that. She stared at the carpet and said nothing. Because he'd spoken to her. Finally, after days of silence, he'd finally spoken again. She thought she'd exaggerated the low sinful timbre of his voice in her head, but gods, no, every syllable was a rasp that went straight to her sex.

A click and Hades pushed the closed laptop away. Then she was up, tugged and lifted onto the desk, facing those scary grey eyes. Hades ran his hands over her arms, studying her bare breasts.

He didn't look angry or annoyed. More, thoughtful. He stroked her hair back from the collar, sifting a corn silk lock between his fingers. Heat bloomed in her, rising to her cheeks, making her dizzy. A few simple touches and her body primed itself for him.

From the smirk etched around his mouth, Hades knew it.

"Time for your punishment," he told her, and pushed her legs apart.

"Hades—"

He propped a finger at her lips. "Quiet, angel."

Her eyes widened. He hadn't called her angel in a while. Well, he hadn't called her anything considering he hadn't been speaking to her, but *angel* hit her in her solar plexus. Which was so, so, stupid.

But then he was touching her and the world went hazy. He took his time, palming her knee and positioning her thighs wider, treating them to tiny strokes that seared her core. He inspected her often like this, and she submitted. She was always wet, and when he stopped, she always undeniably wanted more.

She shook her head, unable to reconcile the ugliness of her situation with the beautiful things he made her feel.

"Poor neglected pussy," he mocked, swiping his thumb over her folds gently. She objected to the tone, but didn't want him to stop. Maybe, since he was talking to her again, it meant he'd finally stop torturing her. But she didn't dare ask out loud. No, her begging was all silent.

Don't stop. Keep touching. Right there—

"Close?" His long eyelashes flicked up to her face. Her hips danced and his left hand steadied her. He leaned in, pinning her left leg under his elbow as he bent his head close—so close— He was— Oh *gods—*

His tongue swirled over her slick skin, finding the needy points, soothing them, increasing the ache. Her hips bucked and he chuckled, hot breath puffing over her sensitive flesh.

"Hades," she wanted to grab his silky hair and tug him close but didn't dare. "Please—"

A few more licks and she was so close. So close—

Hades scooted back in his chair.

No!

And lifted her back to the cushion at his feet.

NO!

He meant to leave her unsatisfied *again*.

She glared at his shiny black shoes underneath the desk. Her jaw locked. He pulled the laptop to the middle of the desk and started typing again, like nothing at all had just happened.

Persephone's fists clenched. He could toss her away so easily. He made her mad with want but he was Mr. Unaffected.

Hades saw her family as strong. These uncles Persephone had never known about.

But Hades saw her as weak, merely a pawn to play against them.

It didn't matter that she didn't even know her uncles. Or her father. Her father who had killed an innocent *girl*.

That was the blood running through her veins. A murderous father and mother so overprotective, it bordered on abusive.

Persephone scoffed. Who was she kidding? It had gone over the border on more than one occasion. All the time, in fact. She hadn't even known how abnormal it was until she got out into the world and learned how other people lived.

And now here Persephone was, falling back into her same old

patterns. Head down, yes ma'am, yes ma'am, whatever you say, Mom. Except replacing her mother with Hades. Better to follow the rules than endure the punishment.

Persephone shook her head and looked down at herself.

The chains might be new but the slavery wasn't.

She thought she could change. She'd sworn she *was* changing. Had changed.

But here she was again with her head bowed down, waiting for someone else to decide her fate.

And then she got a crazy idea.

An absolutely fucking absurd idea.

She looked toward Hades's legs underneath the tall desk and felt like giggling hysterically. Well, he certainly wouldn't be able to ignore her existence if she...

Images flashed in her head of Hades walking around the bedroom each night after he'd showered. He liked putting his body on display for her. She thought back to the past few days and the hungry way he'd lapped at her sex. He hadn't been indifferent then. It wasn't just to 'punish' her. Even now, she could see his cock straining against his dress pants.

Persephone's insides tingled thinking about it all.

Thinking, that was the problem. Or rather, *over*thinking.

So she decided to stop. Thinking. Overthinking. All of it.

It was time to take action.

She crawled underneath the table.

Between Hades's legs.

She'd been married for over a week and hadn't even gotten to touch him. To touch *it*. So she reached for his belt buckle.

He jolted in his chair when she made contact and began to undo the buckle. But that was all. He didn't say a word or move to stop her.

Was this a game of chicken? Who would flinch first?

It wouldn't be her. Not because she had nothing to lose. She had plenty to lose still. She wouldn't flinch, though, because she was actually curious to see this through.

Curious and afraid, but that was nothing new.

So when she finished with the belt, she quickly moved to unbutton and unzip his pants.

The audible hiss he expelled above her? Now *that* was gratifying.

Here was power. Was it a fucked up way of getting some back? No doubt. Wasn't stopping her.

She reached into his pants and slid her hand between the slit in his boxers.

In a sudden motion, his strong hand came down and clenched around her wrist.

She took a page from his book and ignored him, saying not one word.

He was thick and round and firm in her grasp. Soft over steel. It was dim underneath the desk but she could still make out the basic shape of him.

And her eyes went wide.

It wasn't the first time she'd seen it. But seeing and touching were two different things. And the way it hardened and grew in her grasp—

Her gasp escaped before she could muffle it.

As quickly as his hand had taken hold of her wrist, he released her. Interesting. He was going to allow her to continue her explorations.

Was it because he was male and it was true what they said, that no man would turn down sex? But he'd had her at his mercy for a while now and other than that first night, she hadn't even seen him take himself in hand.

Because sex was about power to him. Did he still think he had the power in the situation just because she was the one on her knees?

Even the thought infuriated her.

She would show him. She was not a pawn in somebody else's game. She was a motherfucking player.

So, pushing all other thoughts out of her mind, she went up on her knees and took the bulbous tip of his sex into her mouth.

"Gods," he choked.

Persephone smiled and licked all around the tip. It was curiously salty and a little bit bitter. She grasped the bottom of his shaft with both her hands—he was large enough it took both—and took more of him into her mouth.

He leaned back in his chair and widened his legs further. She saw his stomach flatten and heave as she started to work him, in and out, in and out, just the head.

She'd never done it before, but she'd read. She'd read a lot. First in her romance books and then, as her wedding day neared, everything else she could get her hands on, well, apart from the Internet which still scared her. But plenty of women's magazines had lengthy articles on the art of giving your man the perfect BJ and Persephone employed every tactic she'd ever read about.

Spelling out the alphabet on the very tip of his...his *cock*, right where she felt the tiniest slit. Bobbing up and down with her lips over her teeth, making sure to pay special attention to the ridge of his crown while still rolling the flesh of his shaft up and down. And every so often, taking him deep, as deep as she could manage without choking.

When she decided to employ yet another tip, reaching down and tugging on his balls, he shoved his chair back and pulled himself out of her mouth.

Persephone fell forward onto her hands, looking up for the first time into his face since she'd begun. She wasn't sure what she expected to find there but it was better than she could've hoped for.

He did not look cold. He did not look distant.

There were two spots of color high up on his cheekbones, accentuating the sharp cut of them even more. His eyes were wide and his nostrils flared with every heaved breath. His heavy cock jutted out from the front of his unzipped pants and Persephone couldn't help but stare. She'd just had that in her *mouth*?

Dear gods, what the hell had she been thinking?

She swiped at her mouth with her forearm and above her, Hades let out a low growl like an animal might.

Definitely not disinterested. Or indifferent.

Oh shit.

Hades reached for her and she scrambled back but he shoved the table out of the way. Shoved. The. Table.

The next thing she knew, he was bent over and unlocking the chain attached to her collar. He gathered her up in his arms and he was carrying her.

Okaaaaaaaay, so this was unexpected.

"Hades," she whispered.

He didn't respond. What he *did* do was carry her to his bedroom.

He laid her out in the center of his bed and he followed after.

For the first time in days, he looked her in the eyes. It was stupid, but her breath caught. His gorgeous, intense, demanding eyes. He still didn't say anything, but he held her gaze as he slid his hand down her stomach.

He caught her chin and her eyes searched his. She had no idea what he was thinking. What was he thinking?

"Undress me," he hissed.

She swallowed and nodded. Her fingers found the buttons of his expensive Italian shirt. *Steady, steady. Just breathe.* Ignore the solid plane of his chest. Ignore the tiny jolts of electricity zapping her every time her knuckles brushed him. Ignore the stutter in his indrawn breath, the demanding length poking her bare thigh, promising pleasure and pain when the time came to tear her open.

This was it. She knew it was. There was no more waiting, no more teasing, no more half measures.

The white shirt fell away, revealing strong forearms. He helped her peel off his undershirt and then—

Dear gods above. Faced with a wall of smooth, firm muscle, olive skin dusted with a little dark hair, she swayed on her knees. She knew Hades was strong, but hadn't contemplated the acres of muscle under his tailored suits. Now, half naked before her, he was just so… big. His head towered over hers. Her hands couldn't fit around his upper arm.

He caught her wrists, drawing her close. His head ducked, his lips caught hers for a hard, claiming kiss. His erection dug into her thigh until she swiveled her hips, pushing her throbbing parts into the satisfying length of him. She was a virgin, never had anything inside her, but she wanted it. Oh gods, she wanted it...

When Hades broke the kiss, her lips were throbbing, swollen.

"This," his big hand slid over her bottom and squeezed, "is mine."

She nodded frantically, tears pooling in the corners of her eyes. She wanted him to take, to own her. She needed it.

Hades let out a groan that told her he was as undone as she felt.

"No one but me, Persephone. No one touches you but me."

He laid her down, hands catching her hips. "Spread for me, baby."

She propped her legs apart. He dove between them, dark head working.

No. Her head flew back. No, no, no.

The gleam in his eyes did it. *YES*. She flew apart. Finally, after so many days of teasing. But gods, it wasn't enough, there and then gone too soon. She needed more. She needed so much more.

And there he was, still watching her, so focused, so single-minded. Her hands lifted to his shoulders as he moved over her body. She couldn't look away as she felt him reach down and position himself.

He was preparing to enter her.

To *enter her,* enter her.

She swallowed and unwittingly, her fingertips dug into his shoulders.

But he paused, his voice strained and gravelly. "You say *no* right now and I stop."

His eyes searched hers back and forth.

Say something. Tell him no. Hell fucking no. What was she even doing?

Earlier... Sucking his... That was about taking her power back. But this? Letting him... Who had the power now?

But the look on his face, gods damn him, she was right back where she'd been the moment she was walking down the aisle toward the man she loved with all her heart. His features were gentled and there was something raw in his usually hardened face.

Another manipulation.

But damn it to hell, instead of saying no, she nodded her head yes.

And he was there, pressing in at her most intimate place. Fear struck. She remembered how huge he was. He'd split her in two.

But he shook his head ever so slightly like he could sense her fear. And while he didn't stop, no, she could see he wouldn't, couldn't stop now that he had begun, he pushed forward slowly, carefully.

Persephone felt it the moment he came up against her barrier and so did he. Persephone could see it in his eyes. He didn't stop, though, and she didn't want him to. She nodded again and he pushed forward. Her hip twitched and there was a sharp pinch before her flesh gave way. He sank deeper. She closed her eyes and clutched his shoulders.

"Look at me," he demanded.

Why? *Why?* He knew what she was giving. She'd been a fool to think she could ever wrest any power away from this man. He was an unstoppable force and to him she was nothing but a wildflower, here today and paved over tomorrow.

"Persephone, give me your eyes."

Her throat stung as she opened her eyes. She felt the tears as they rolled down her temples and into her hair.

Hades's sharp eyebrows were drawn together, his huge body looming over her small one, as he worked himself inside her, inch by inch.

Her breath caught as he probed the tight fist of her inner muscles. "Easy. Open...open for me."

Her hands clawed his back, caught his strong shoulders, and hung on.

"That's it," his breath tickled her ear. "Hold tight to me."

The pressure grew. She gritted her teeth, ducking her head to hide in the curve of Hades's throat. He was a rock, immovable. She was the ocean, ebbing, moving around him.

Slowly her body opened, her legs softening even as the pain swam through her.

"Yes. Yes, that's it, beautiful. Give yourself to me."

"Hades," she rasped. Tremors ran through her head to toe. His hips melded with hers as he invaded her. When he stopped, fully rooted, thrills ran down her sides. Her chest rose and fell, nipples hardened to diamond points.

Hades held himself over her, his arms taut by her face. His head was bowed, dark lashes casting shadows on his cheeks. His lips moved slightly.

If she didn't know different, she'd guess he was praying. She felt like praying too. They were fully merged, his body towering over hers, protecting and claiming her.

This was what heaven felt like.

She'd never felt more connected to another human being.

The pain ebbed and he began to move. Slow rocks at first, nudging further into her inner sanctum, trespassing boldly. The strong ridge of his manhood rubbed a delicious part of her and Persephone raised her hips, seeking more.

"Persephone," he rasped, and there was a world of possibility in her name. Her fingers passed over his face as if she were blind and wanted to memorize the cut of his features. In this room, this dark womb, she would forget all the hurt he'd done her.

"Hades," she turned her face up to his. He dragged his lips over her mouth, her cheek, the corner of her eye, giving her silent, bruising promises as his body reaped pleasure from hers. He made a prolonged, male sound, pushing deeper. His eyes were closed, his face intent as if he'd found something important, something beautiful he'd longed for, but never hoped to experience.

Yes, she prayed. *Hades, come back to me.* He groaned again, the muscles in his back turning to steel under her stroking hands.

She felt it. For the first time, she understood how the entire act worked in harmony, every part of his body so perfectly made to bring pleasure to every part of hers.

He was made for her.

"Oh gods," she cried out. "Oh...oh...*oh! Hades!*"

Her chest thrust up and out and she clung to him, her fingers in his hair as the climax hit, bright and beautiful, and so, so right. Yes, *yes*. This. *Him*.

A thrust, two, three, and he rooted himself deep and stayed there. She held on and hoped she read the signs right.

After an eternity, he pulled out. She hissed, her insides protesting.

"You all right?" he searched her face.

"I'm good." Her legs were noodles, her muscles overstretched. She'd be sore tomorrow.

"That was...thank you." She shouldn't thank her captor. But this was Hades. He'd come back to her for a moment and for a moment, it was beautiful.

"Yes. You did well." He parted her legs and studied the stains on the sheets. Watery blossoms, evidence of her virginity. She covered her cheeks. She shouldn't be embarrassed, but it seemed more intimate. She'd bled for him. Her blood mingled with his seed.

But then something seemed to come over his face and he turned away from her. Long seconds ticked by. Finally, his back stiffened and then he looked over his shoulder.

"Not bad, for a virgin." She flinched and met his mercurial stare, horror rising in her as he said, "I know I'll watch the recording of this many times. And I think your uncles will really appreciate Part II of the wedding video, especially when you screamed my name and came all over my cock."

With a dark smirk, he nodded toward the corner camera.

The blood left her face. No. Not after all this. They couldn't be back to where they'd started. She'd seen the way he'd looked at her when he was deep inside her. She'd seen it in his *eyes*...hadn't she?

The pain twisting her guts felt like that first night all over again when he'd first betrayed her.

But she didn't say a word or speak up for herself as, without another word, he left the room.

15

Well, that had not gone according to plan.

Not the sex and not his cruel comments afterward. It was a lie about the cameras recording. He always turned the cameras off whenever he was with her.

And gods knew he thought about taking her virginity. Thought about it all damn week and for the months before. But this last week, fuck, every time he teased and tasted her, every time his cock grew painful in his pants, all he could think about was finally taking her and making her *his*.

But he was training her and training meant discipline. Patience. Making her crave him and pleasing him above all else.

He just hadn't expected— He never could have prepared himself for—

He hadn't even worn a condom. And if he had it to do again, he would have done it the same way. She'd gotten the shot almost a month ago and gods, feeling her virgin pussy, nothing between them, with how she clenched like a vise around him—

He scrubbed a hand down his face and watched her on the monitor even though he was disgusted at himself for doing it. Every second he wasn't in her presence, he found himself glued to this damn screen. She was supposed to be obsessed with him, not the other way around.

He was about to shove his laptop screen shut when he saw her back start to shake.

Fuck. She was crying.

She looked so tiny in the big bed.

He dragged a hand through his hair, remembering every moment of when she'd taken him into her body, so hot and tight—gods, she'd gripped him like a vise—eyes wide, without guile—

Like an innocent. She was a virgin. He'd known she was, but knowing and experiencing were two different things.

And when her orgasm had hit, milking his climax out of him at the same time, she'd looked at him like he was a god himself, like she'd worship at his feet forever and give him her submission along with her whole self and her soul, too.

The problem was, he was terrified he might have been looking at her the same way.

So he'd shut it down and reminded them both of who they were.

And now she was crying.

Hades wanted to hit something. She wasn't playing by the rules. This wasn't how it was meant to go. None of this was going according to plan.

His phone rang once, loudly in the otherwise silent room. Hades snatched it out of his pocket, never more glad for the distraction.

"What?" Hades barked.

"We got a situation," Charon's voice rumbled.

"Don't tell me I gotta come down."

"You gotta come down." Charon confirmed.

He gave a sharp nod even though Charon couldn't see him. Maybe getting out of here was exactly what he needed. He needed to get his head together, that was for damn sure.

"Be there in twenty." Hades hung up and stood. He went to his bedroom and dressed in quick, practiced movements.

He meant to leave right then and there. But, without fully intending to, his feet took him to Persephone's door.

Leave. You only did what had to be done. She's the enemy.

He stood frozen for several more moments. And then he quietly opened the door.

Persephone was lying down now and he walked to the bed. He didn't know what he meant to say when he got close, but then he saw it didn't matter. She'd cried herself to sleep.

She was beautiful in repose, but then she was beautiful no matter what she was doing. Sleep didn't erase the furrow of distress on her brow. Was she dreaming of him?

His eyes squeezed shut. *Sentimental idiot.*

Still, he couldn't leave without giving her something. She'd be sore when she woke. Even though it had been her first time, he hadn't taken it easy on her. The least he could do was give her the means to take a bath in peace.

He ran a hand gently down her calf and when she didn't wake, he undid the ankle cuff and freed her from the bed post.

"Sleep well, wife," he murmured. She didn't so much as twitch.

Without another word, he turned and flipped the lock he'd had installed outside her door as he left. Then he strode for the front door and soon he was in his Bentley, his driver speeding toward the Styx.

No, tonight had not gone according to plan.

But nothing with Persephone ever had. She was never supposed to show up in his office that night, bedraggled and beautiful. She was never supposed to flash him that trusting, adoring smile afterward, day after day after day.

He'd made a new plan, of course. Marrying Demeter's daughter had struck him as an even better means of revenge than the simple kidnap and ransom he'd initially intended.

It all served the same purpose: to draw the Titans out into the open and make them pay for their crimes. Persephone's father had been the one holding the knife, but his brothers had been there, too.

Hades had waited a long time for his vengeance, but he would have it now.

None of the remaining Titan brothers had children. Persephone was the only heir. Demeter would go to the brothers. She had no choice, no power on her own.

And if he could make her suffer in the meantime, imagining the horrors he'd visit upon her daughter? All the better.

But there was still no sign or word from any of them.

And today he'd crossed a line he didn't know how to come back from.

Innocents ought to be spared.

Hades lived his life by a code and that was its bedrock. He mired himself neck deep in shit doing what had to be done because at least when he was in charge, he could make sure that only the guilty paid.

But it was never meant to touch the innocent.

Like his sister.

Chiara was beautiful. Delicate and pale, her head in the clouds all the time, she'd never seemed to fully inhabit the same grimy reality as the rest of the world.

And that was as it ought to have been.

What should never have been was finding her bleeding out on a dirty mattress in a filthy crack house where the Titan brothers had taken and discarded her.

His parent's death, he'd understood. His father had started as a lowly immigrant shopkeeper, and built an empire. Vito Ubeli had faced injustices and fought in the face of it, and built an army to protect the weak. That didn't mean he wasn't brutal, and one day found death at the hands of an enemy he'd crushed. And when he'd died, his son Hades was meant to assume control.

But Hades was only fifteen at the time and he'd waited, thinking someone more qualified would take the lead in his stead. In another year's time, his sister was dead. He'd never forgotten the lesson: strike first and strike fast, and seize any power to be had.

He was a necessary evil to hold back the chaos.

He watched the city lights fly by as they drove. East of the city, the streets grew narrow together. Hades had his driver stop at an alleyway too small to fit a car into.

"Cover me," Hades said, after scanning every corner of the intersection.

"You sure?" The man in black also looked suspiciously down the alley.

A door opened in the side of one building and Charon's unmistakable silhouette stepped into the pool of light.

"Wait for me. Should be under an hour," Hades told his soldier, and got out of the car.

"Picked one of our men up tonight, late to a drop," Charon said. "Went looking for him and found him in a bar on the *Westside*."

Charon emphasized the name of the territory between New Olympus and their sister city, Metropolis. Like Hades ran the Underworld of New Olympus, the Titans ran Metropolis. And the Westside was currently a no man's land where Hades still battled for the same control he enjoyed over the rest of New Olympus.

"Said someone stopped him and took his shipment, so he was hiding out, trying to figure out how to tell us."

"You believe his story?"

As usual, Charon's face held no expression. Lesser men cracked after an hour staring into the mask of rich, midnight skin and fathomless eyes. *Like staring into the fucking abyss,* Roscoe, one of the capos, would say.

"His story doesn't add up. And there's been suspicious activity on his route before, which is why we had eyes on him. We think he handed over the goods to our old friends out West, but got them to cash him out and make it look like a hold up."

"If it's our old friends," Hades used the euphemism for the Titans, his blood heating, "then this driver isn't just passing on goods. He's feeding them information."

The two men walked through the warehouse, passing by rows and racks of garments, until they reached the stairs to the basement. The air reeked from the stench of the fabric dyes and detergents. The chemical smells did a good job of masking the scent of blood.

Charon paused at the foot of the stairs. "Got the boys to soften him up a bit. He doesn't know I'm here."

"Alright," Hades said. "We play it like we did with that last switch—what was his name? The Frenchman."

"Le Mouchard," Charon pronounced perfectly, and stood aside, letting Hades lead the way between the dye vats to the cleared space where they'd tied the snitch up.

A few men all in black stood around a wretched figure blindfolded and hanging from the ceiling so that his feet barely brushed the floor.

The Shades were Hades's soldiers, loyal enforcers who ran his massive empire. They were recruited young off the streets, trained in a central facility, and given every opportunity to rise through the ranks. *You can tell a leader by the men who follow him,* Hades's father had told him time and time again.

The Shades all nodded to acknowledge their leader and Hades let himself almost grin, before slipping into character.

"What the fuck?" he shouted, and his voice rang out in the empty space. The snitch, a doughy man in a stained wife beater and khaki shorts that had seen better days, started shivering. Sweat ran down under his blindfold, into his sparse beard. Hades knew the Shades had worked him over a little bit, but left nothing more than painful bruises. His blood had yet to flow.

Hades directed his false anger around the circle of Shades. "I ask you to bring him in for questions and this is what you do?"

"Fuck, sorry, boss."

"Cut him down. For fuck's sake. Now."

The men scrambled to bring a chair and loosen the ropes that held the man suspended from a few exposed ceiling pipes.

"Give him some water."

Hades sat in the chair that was provided for him and continued to study the traitor.

"Take that fucking thing off." He nodded at the blindfold. "Gods, this isn't an interrogation. This how you treat my employees?"

A Shade handed Hades a bottle of water and the boss waited until the blindfold was cut away.

The man before him was breathing heavily, trembling with relief. As soon as the filthy scrap of cloth was gone, Hades leaned forward, filling the snitch's vision.

"Here." Hades handed over the water bottle, and rested his forearms on his knees, studying the snitch.

"T–t-thank you," the traitor said. "I thought I was a dead man."

"Marty, right?"

The man nodded.

"I'm Hades Ubeli."

"Yessir, I know you, Mr. Ubeli." The man took a sloppy swig of water, holding the bottle with shaking hands.

Hades smiled. "I remember you. You took that gun shipment up to Eyrie, when the suits were putting in checkpoints at the weigh-in stations up and down 95."

"Yeah, yeah, that was me."

"You took back roads around all the points, and when a local cop stopped you at two am, you told him you were looking for a place that was open so you could take a dump."

"Right, that's it," the man guffawed half-heartedly, his beady eyes darting around the room at the silent circle of Shades.

"That was good thinking." Hades raised a finger and shook it at Marty. "Real good."

"Thank you, sir. Can I ask—"

"No muss, no fuss, no questions asked," Hades cut him off, and the man fell silent. *Bingo,* Hades thought. "So what happened to my shipment?"

"Your shipment?"

"Yes, Marty, all the goods that go in the back of your truck belong to me. I'm ultimately responsible for them, so if there's a break in the chain, I need to know about it."

"Uh...I told them, sir, and they didn't believe me. Someone took it."

"Someone? Do you know who?"

"No, fuck, I'd tell you if I could," the man's voice strained with sincerity, and he never broke eye contact. A sure sign he was lying. "They wore masks."

"Of course," Hades motioned toward his water bottle. "You need another of those?"

"What?" the man stared at it like it had sprouted from his hand, then took another swig. "No, I'm good. Thank you."

"Marty, I hope you don't mind if I keep you here, talk to you some more. See, I have to figure out where this shipment got to, so I can go and retrieve it. I need your help to do that. You willing to help me?"

"Of course, yeah." The man wiped his mouth, but couldn't stop his eyes shifting around the stone-faced enforcers surrounding him and Hades.

"It may take a while. You want me to get a message to someone who's waiting up for you? A woman or something?"

"Uh, no, my wife, she's used to my late hours."

"Alright." Hades glanced around the circle of waiting men. One Shade, looming over Marty's right shoulder, cracked his knuckles, massaging his beefy hands. With a subtle shake of Hades's head, the thug backed down.

Interrogation of a suspect couldn't be done with force. The man would give false information, would say anything to stop the pain. Manipulation led to much more reliable information. Befriend someone, and they will tell you what you want.

Every time.

"Thanks for helping me out, Marty. I appreciate it. And I have a beautiful woman waiting for me in my bed, so I'm sufficiently motivated to finish this."

A chuckle ran around the circle and even Marty's features relaxed.

"So here's the thing that I don't understand," Hades leaned forward in his chair. "Why didn't they kill you? I mean, that's what I would do. Shoot the driver, take the goods, dump the body."

Marty mopped the sweat from his forehead. "Uh, I don't know."

"You don't know. Lucky break for you, though. Seeing as you're breathing and not dead in a ditch."

"Look, I ran over something, drove a mile and the rig, she was pulling weird, so I stopped to check it out. The car came out of nowhere and these men jumped out waving guns. They had me outnumbered."

"Of course." Hades closed his eyes. "How many men?"

"Don't know how many, saw two waving guns, another on the other side, maybe two in the back. They got me out and on my knees and told me not to move. Thank the gods your guys were looking out for me."

"Why were you on the back road and not the Ape?" Hades mentioned the Appian Way, the main artery out of New Olympus.

"Thought I knew a quicker route."

"Even though your orders were to meet up at the abandoned rest stop on the Ape? I'm told you went ten miles out of your way for this shortcut."

The man licked his lips. "Listen, I know it looks bad. I know it looks like I was headed to Metropolis."

Hades's eyes narrowed but he didn't interrupt.

"But I ran over something and I didn't want the load at risk. If I had an accident, fuck, the suits would be all over it. I didn't want that to happen so I took a shorter route. I mean, it's been years and the Titans ain't done nothing—"

"The Titans? I thought you said you didn't know who jumped you."

"I don't, I mean, I just guessed. They're your enemies."

"That's also a little out of their way to pick up a shipment, but the road you chose was wooded, secluded. Not a bad place for a meet."

"Or an ambush." Marty corrected.

Hades let the silence stretch. Marty nailed his story airtight, maybe was briefed by the Metropolis gang. The Titans were nasty fuckers. If Marty was dealing with them, maybe there were balls of steel under his worn khakis.

Time for a crowbar.

"Listen, Marty, it's getting late. I'm a man who values my time; I'm sure you're the same way. So I'm going to tell you: I already sent someone to your house. Charon, you know him? Big guy. Doesn't say much. His fists do the talking, although he's a keen hand with a wet saw."

"Oh gods." The man's pasty skin went white.

"They call him the Undertaker. Kinda cliché, I know, but it gets the point across."

Marty's mouth flapped open like a dying fish, but no sound came out. Hades kept talking.

"Anyway, Charon's not a big fan of waiting, either, and he's standing in your wife's bedroom now, watching her sleep. In a minute I'm going to text him instructions, and what I tell him depends on what you say."

"Oh gods, no. Not my Sadie." The man fell forward out of the chair, onto his knees. "Please, please, don't hurt her. I'll tell you."

Hades nodded. "You have two minutes. Start talking."

TEN MINUTES LATER, Hades walked back out to the stairwell where Charon was waiting.

"Fucking Titans," Charon growled.

"Send out a patrol. Shipment's long gone, but maybe we can still track it, be ready next time."

"Already done. We're bugging up the rest of the goods. If another trucker flips, we'll have ears inside."

Hades rubbed his stubbled jaw as if he could wipe away the night. "This is the second incursion into our territory this month," he said. A man's broken cry echoed out from the metal dye vats behind him. "After all these years, they're finally making their play. It's got to be because of her."

Persephone's mother. She must have gone to the Titans and pleaded her case just like Hades had known she would.

Charon nodded.

"They're not gonna stop. Not until we end it." Charon's midnight skin shone even in the shadows.

"It's about time." Marty's screams rang out again, and Hades headed for the stairs. "Tell them to turn the fans on. Drown out the noise."

16

When Persephone woke up, her head felt thick, her eyes swollen. What time was it? It was dark out. The last thing she remembered was giving in to the tears half an hour or so after Hades left. She'd swiped them away as fast as they fell, furious at herself. How had she let herself feel anything for that selfish, monstrous, unfeeling—

Wait, something was wrong. It was the middle of the night and she wasn't sure what had woken her. She frowned as she swung her feet over the side of the bed.

But then it hit.

The weight around her ankle. It was gone.

She frantically turned on the bedside lamp.

Holy shit! She lifted up her ankle. And then laughed in disbelief.

The weight around her ankle was gone, along with the chain leading to the bedpost.

She'd done it. She'd earned his trust. Or was this another test?

She waited ten minutes, occasionally calling out Hades's name, but got no response. Biting her lip, she got on the bed, spread her legs, and touched herself, knowing that if he was in the apartment and watching, that would definitely bring him running.

Still, nothing. He wasn't home.

It was now or never.

She scrambled to the door. It was locked.

But after her mother locked her up, she'd vowed never to be stopped by a locked door again. She'd practiced for hours and hours after studying online videos—it was one of the first things she'd done as soon as she got free of the farm.

She went to the bathroom and grabbed a few hairpins. A few minutes scratching at the lock and it clicked. She backed up, barely daring to believe.

But when she turned the knob, the door opened.

Think, she had to think. She grabbed a plain t-shirt and jeans from the closet. Clothes Hades had never let her wear the whole time she'd been here. And shoes. She needed shoes. The fabric scratched her skin. She'd grown used to being naked.

How long had she been in here? A week? More?

She pulled her hair into a ponytail and let the door creak open. Maybe he posted a guard, anticipating her escape.

But no. There was no one in the penthouse. She crept into the open room, barely daring to believe it. Hades never left her alone for long. The gods were smiling on her, giving her a perfect chance to escape.

Too perfect, the little voice said, and she hushed it. Hades expected the locked door to hold her. She'd outwitted him for once.

Before racing out the door, she grabbed a coat and buttoned it to cover the collar and leash she still wore. She didn't have time to figure out how to undo it.

She put her hand on the doorknob and paused. Someone had cleaned up the statue she'd broken. A giant bouquet of flowers sat on the column instead.

She preferred the statue.

Not that it mattered. She was never coming back here.

She pulled open the door and escaped into the night.

17

"Are you okay?" asked a female officer two hours later, checking in on Persephone where she waited in a windowless room inside the police station.

Persephone was huddled on a chair with her knees to her chest, arms wrapped around them. She looked up at the sympathetic looking woman. "I asked for someone to come cut this thing off of me an hour ago."

Persephone held out the chain connected to the collar around her neck. Her voice sounded slightly hysterical even to her own ears but she couldn't help it.

After sneaking out of the hotel, she realized she didn't have a place to go or anyone to help her. Hades had confiscated her phone that had Hecate's number programmed into it, but even if Persephone still had it, she wouldn't have wanted to bring the older woman into this. People were scared of Hades for a reason.

So Persephone had found a cop and asked to be taken to the station. They were the only ones she could think of who actually could help her.

It was over now. She was free. So why was she still so on edge?

The woman's eyes went wide. "Oh my gosh, of course. I'll be right back with some cutters."

The door shut behind the woman and Persephone couldn't help immediately getting up and going to check the doorknob. It wasn't locked. Persephone pressed a hand to her heart, willing it to slow.

You're being paranoid. These are the good guys.

But she was still on Hades's turf. As soon as she'd blurted out everything that had happened ever since her wedding day to the policeman at the front desk, he brought her to this room. Fifteen minutes later, a superior officer, Captain Martin, had come and she'd reiterated her story more slowly.

"Please," she begged. "Hades is a powerful man. You need to transfer me to a station that's further away. We are still on his turf. He has soldiers, I don't know how many. You probably know more than I do. What if he attacks the police station—?"

"It's all going to be okay now," said the kindly police captain, a man in his mid-50s with more salt than pepper in his hair, as he patted her hand. "You're safe now and we won't let anything happen to you. Ubeli isn't foolish enough to attack a police station. That's not how his kind works. Now you just rest up while I make some calls and we'll see about a more permanent situation for you."

But Persephone hadn't been able to do anything other than pace back and forth in the small room and then finally curl up into a ball on the chair while waiting for any news. Whenever she shifted on the chair, she was reminded of last night. Of what it felt like when Hades had finally...

Taken the last of your innocence.

She still felt it now, the bowling ball tearing through her guts when she realized it had meant nothing to him. That he still only saw her as a means of revenge. She would only ever be her father's daughter to him. So she'd run.

By now Hades would have come home to the apartment. He'd have found her gone. The cameras in the room would have shown her picking the lock and escaping. He'd also probably deduced that she couldn't have gotten far, especially if she'd been caught on any street camera footage.

It was probably only a matter of time before he tracked her to the police station.

She pressed her fingers to her face. Oh gods, oh gods, oh gods, what was she going to do? What if the cops couldn't—

She jumped out of her skin when the door banged open again. But it was the female policewoman with what looked like bolt cutters.

"This might be overkill," the woman said apologetically, "but I know it will get the job done."

"Fine by me," Persephone said. "I want this thing off my neck."

The woman nodded. "I'll be careful."

She slid the cutters between Persephone's neck and the leather and with one firm snip, the leather collar came free and with it, the chains clanked to the floor. Persephone cupped her neck. The bare skin felt strange. Not that she wanted the collar back, she just—

The cop was watching her.

Persephone forced a smile. "Thank you. Just...thank you."

The woman put a hand on Persephone's shoulder and squeezed. She bent over and picked up the chains attached to the severed collar. "I'll get these out of your sight." With that, she left the room.

And Persephone was back to waiting, waiting for she didn't know what. Her new life to begin, she supposed.

It wasn't five minutes before the police captain entered again, carrying a folder. Captain Martin sat at the table across from her. Persephone forced herself to drop her knees so that her feet were on the ground. She'd taken off the voluminous coat but now she shivered even though it wasn't especially cold. It was Captain Martin's face. He didn't look like he had good news.

"What is it? Is something wrong?"

"I don't think I have to tell you that Hades Ubeli is a dangerous man."

Was this guy kidding? "Yeah, I figured that out when he locked me in a room for over a week with a collar around my neck. You don't have to convince me that he's a bad guy. Preaching to the choir."

"Good, good," the police captain said. "Then you'll be happy to testify against him in a court of law."

"What?" Persephone shoved back from the table and stood, holding her hands up. "What are you talking about?"

"Well, you've come in here with a pretty fantastic story," Captain Martin said. "We've been trying to nail Ubeli for years on racketeering, drug trafficking, money laundering, you name it. But kidnapping and captivity will make for one hell of a story, especially if you have any insights into the rest of his business dealings."

Persephone was shaking her head the entire time he spoke. "I don't have anything to do with that. I want to get out of here. Right now. I want one of your guys to drive me as far west as you can take me and I'll disappear." She held her hands up again. "I don't want anything to do with Hades Ubeli. I want to forget he even exists."

"Well, that's not likely to happen, seeing as how you're married to him. But if you work with us—"

"I'm not going to testify!" Was this guy nuts?

The captain's eyebrows scrunched together. "So maybe your so-called captivity wasn't as unwanted as you're calling it. You know, lying to the police carries a penalty of—"

What the fuck? "I didn't lie to you! I wasn't lying about being kidnapped. Well, I mean, at the beginning, I thought it was the start to our honeymoon. But it all changed when he—when he— How dare you even suggest that I wanted what he was—" She pressed her hands to her head. "I didn't want to be there with him. Not like that. But I don't want to testify..."

"If you're worried that he'll get to you, punish you for talking to us—"

She flinched at the captain's choice of words. *Punish.* That's exactly what Hades would do. Punish her in the most delicious way possible. Make her submit to his will and make her like it. "I'm not afraid of that..." Okay, she was. Because if she stayed to testify, there was no way Hades wouldn't find a way to get her back.

She jumped to her feet. "I want to get out of here."

"Mrs. Ubeli—"

"Don't call me that," she snapped.

The captain's face hardened. "You want to see what sort of monster you married?" He opened the file and photos spilled out. Bodies splayed and bloody, eyes open, faces contorted in fear, frozen in the moment they realized their oncoming death.

She recognized one face. The curly haired man who'd roofied her. He'd said he was following orders. He'd tried to warn her.

Now he was dead.

I'm gonna take care of you.

"This is what your husband does," the captain ranted. "This is how he conducts his business."

"Do you have proof?"

"No. That's why we need you."

Light dawned. Persephone scraped the photos up with her fingernails and stacked them into a pile. "You want me to testify against him somehow. Say he did these things and confessed to me."

Excitement flickered in the captain's eyes. "Yes."

"You want me to lie."

He said nothing.

This city is a beast, Hades told her once. *Innocents fall and the criminals go unpunished.*

"My husband doesn't think he's a criminal," she told the captain quietly. "He thinks he's dispensing justice." Even when he didn't want to. There were moments when they were together, where he hesitated. He could've destroyed her for what her family did to his sister. Instead, he'd...

"That's what the cops and courts are for."

The police do nothing. They're either corrupt, or have no power. And here was proof. The captain wanted her to lie on the stand. She wasn't about to give her freedom up in order to satisfy some police captain's wet dreams of glory in capturing a notorious crime boss.

She just wanted to get the hell out of here.

"If you testify for the DA, we could get you what you want. Set you up with a new life. New identity. Ubeli would never be able to touch you. You'd be safe. Free."

"You mean witness protection?"

He nodded. "Federal marshals would have your back. You could live somewhere nice and sunny, all year round. Pick your paradise."

Persephone's eyes wandered to the mirror that covered one wall. She looked tiny. Pale with shadows under her eyes, her long hair snarled. Who was she to try to stand up against the Lord of the Underworld?

She closed her eyes, not able to bear looking at herself anymore. There were no good choices. She wasn't a little girl anymore, shielded in her mother's controlling arms. The world wasn't a pretty place and she had to face it.

"No. I won't testify."

Captain Martin didn't say another word. He simply picked up the folder he brought in with him and strode from the room. The door shut behind him with a heavy *clang*.

Persephone laid her head in her arms on the table. What now? Would they not even help her if she wasn't willing to testify against Mar—

But she hadn't even finished the thought before the door was pushing open again.

And there stood Hades himself. "I must say, wife, choosing not to testify against me is the first smart thing you've done all day."

18

"Hades," Persephone sucked in a breath, her heart hammering like a bird in a trap. She backed away, putting the table between her and Hades. Her mouth opened to scream, but she thought better of it.

"What are you doing here?" she croaked. Did the police know he was here?

Hades tilted his head to the side, a cold smile curling his perfect lips. Despite everything, the sight of him hit her in the ovaries.

They were back in this cruel game where he was the hunter and she was the prey. She retreated as he paced forward, stopping when her back hit the wall. Cornered.

"Did you think the good officers of this precinct wouldn't notify me of my missing wife's appearance? Persephone," he put a hand over his heart in mock concern. "I was so worried."

Ice trickled through Persephone's veins. The police? He even had the *police* in his pocket? Was it just this local department, or how high up in the city did it go?

Hades put his hand to her neck and she closed her eyes, preparing for him to squeeze.

But all he did was rub his thumb across her collarbone. "What have you done with my adornment, wife? It was a wedding present, after all."

"What are you going to do to me?" She licked her lips, and heat flared in Hades's gaze.

"What I'm going to do now is take my wife home." Her nipples hardened at his proximity and the look in his eye. Her crazy body responded to him as always.

Nothing stopped Hades from getting what he wanted, and he wanted her.

He took her wrist in an unflinching grasp and pulled her toward the door. She tugged at him, more out of habit than outright defiance, and he paused.

"If you make a fuss, you won't be the only one who pays." He didn't look back at her and didn't have to. He wouldn't just punish her. He'd punish the cops in the precinct who helped her. Maybe the captain deserved it, but the lady cop who'd been kind to her didn't.

Persephone didn't protest as he pushed open the door and pulled her firmly out. His presence rolled over her senses and everything else receded.

Oh gods. He was taking her back with him. And she was letting him. Before, submitting to him was a game she'd played in her head. She always swore to herself that sure, she'd submit—in order to get his guard down. And if she enjoyed it sometimes, well, that was all the better, because she'd be more convincing to Hades that she was harmless.

Escape had always been the ultimate plan.

But there was no escaping Hades. Today had made that more than clear. There was no place to run and nowhere to hide where he wouldn't find her. At least not in this city.

So what did it mean that she went with him now without even trying to fight? As they walked through the police precinct, the halls were eerily quiet. Was she supposed to just accept this as her fate? To give up all her dreams of freedom?

While the precinct had bustled with people on her arrival, now there was no one to be seen as he walked her down the hallway.

Seeing the abandoned desks made it all sink in—just how powerful her husband was. She'd never had a chance.

She swallowed hard against the choking emotion as Hades pushed through a set of doors Persephone hadn't seen before, that led to a side alley.

Charon stood waiting by the car. If he was surprised to see Persephone, his face didn't show it. He merely opened the back door like always. Hades didn't acknowledge him. No, his focus seemed to be all on Persephone as he marched her directly to the backseat and urged her none too gently into the car.

She wrapped her arms around herself and scooted to the opposite end of the bench seat the second he let her go. His presence affected her no matter what. It filled the car, like the subtle scent of his cologne. A sweet ambrosia, drugging her, dragging her under.

She wanted to try the other door, to open it and run as fast as she could. But no doubt it was locked, and even if it wasn't, Charon would be able to easily chase her down. She wasn't in the mood to lose the last ounce of dignity she had remaining.

Hades was silent on the short ride back to the Crown hotel. Again he grasped her wrist instead of her hand as they exited the car and made their way through the lobby. Persephone felt all eyes on her. The way he was dragging her after him, no doubt she looked like a chastised schoolchild.

She hung her head so that her hair obscured her face. But only for a moment because what the hell did she have to be ashamed of? She lifted her head and squared her shoulders, glaring down anyone who looked their way. It wasn't her who ought to be ashamed, it was everyone else who allowed themselves to be under Hades's thumb.

If she shouted that Hades was keeping her against her will, would any of these people even bat an eye?

What could they do even if they did, though? Call the police? A lot of good that would do.

They were in the elevator now, Hades and her, ascending to the top of the building. It felt like only seconds later that the *ping* sounded and the elevator doors opened again. She was right back where she started. And everything was worse. So much worse. Her heartbeat began to race.

She wanted to ask Hades again what he had planned for her punishment, but no. She kept her back straight and her head up. She'd handled everything he'd thrown at her so far.

And if he ties you to the bed again? Fucks you slowly? How long before you break down and beg?

In spite of herself, Persephone's entire body trembled as Hades pulled her over the threshold into the penthouse.

She'd submitted before because she could justify it as a means of eventually gaining the upper hand and escaping. But now? Now if her enemy made her cry out his name in ecstasy, there was no excuse. There'd be no way to rationalize her actions in her head next time.

No, if she submitted to Hades again, it would mean facing the truth she'd long been denying—that some part of her liked it. Craved his touch and his dominance.

Her mind immediately tried to reject it. No. Never. She'd never—

"Welcome home," Hades said sardonically, letting the door slam shut behind them. Persephone jumped at the noise. Hades didn't let go of her wrist.

"Hades, I—"

"I don't want to hear it."

"But—"

"Silence." The barked word was like the crack of a whip.

He tugged her to the living room and pointed to the couch. She sat on the very edge of the cushion, body tense and feet not quite touching the ground, waiting like a student called into the principal's office. But the seconds stretched to minutes and judgement never came.

Hades paced away, pulling off his jacket and removing his cufflinks. He looked back once as he rolled up his sleeves, exposing his forearms, lean and hard and dusted with dark hair. Persephone's breath caught, but he only strolled to the side bar. Glass clinked and he returned with a glass half full of amber liquid. He offered it and she shook her head, but when he didn't move she finally accepted it.

He strolled back and poured another glass for himself. He took his drink to the window and stood sipping, his profile outlined in shadow.

In the silence, her nerves were screaming. *What would he do to her?* The waiting might kill her.

Persephone raised her own glass but stopped when she breathed in the alcohol's cloying scent.

"Just get it over with." Her voice broke the airless quiet.

Hades turned and regarded her. She set her glass down on a side table with a solid click.

"Punish me, yell at me, whatever you're going to do." She folded her arms around her middle. *Don't let him in. No matter what.* He wanted to enslave her just like Mom had for all those years. She said it out loud to remind herself he was no different. "My mother locked me in the cellar. I guess getting tied up in a bedroom is an upgrade."

Hades's gaze darkened. He ambled over, his casual stroll at odds with the fierce intensity on his face. The focus of a hunter intent on his prey.

She couldn't move, trapped in his regard. Not even when he stepped so close her knee brushed his.

No. You want to be free. It's all you've ever wanted.

His hand went around her neck, collaring her with warm, hard fingers.

Her pulse hammered under his palm. She closed her eyes against his gorgeous face. But she couldn't shut out the warmth of his hand or the way her body completely relaxed at his commanding touch. Why? Why did he affect her like this? She was so confused; she didn't know which way was up.

"I had to try," she blurted when silence became too heavy to bear.

"I know." His thumb stroked her chin in a semblance of tenderness.

"So do it." She tried to sound strong but her voice wavered. "Whatever you plan to do with me. Do your worst." And she looked him straight in the eye. His eyes were dark, almost black.

He dropped his hand and took a seat opposite her.

Her breath stuttered out of her. He savored his drink and observed her like she was a piece of art he owned. "Do you know why I'm training you?"

Because you're a controlling madman? she wanted to bite out. But he'd told her the first night why he was doing all this. "Because you delight in torturing me."

"Yes." He swished the dregs of his drink. "There is that. But ultimately, Persephone, I keep you so you're safe."

She laughed. She couldn't help it. "You really believe that, don't you?"

She shook her head, rubbing her tired face. "You do all these awful things in the name of peace. You tell yourself Olympus is dangerous and that you're the only one who can hold back the violence."

"It's true. No one else is strong enough."

"You think you're the city's savior."

"Not a savior. An emperor."

Of course. She could totally see him standing on the Senate steps. Handing out laurels. Sending out troops. Conquering nations, torching cities, enslaving the enemy and sowing their fields with salt.

"It's better to be feared than loved," she quoted Machiavelli. Hades in a nutshell.

"Do you, Persephone? Do you fear me?"

"Yes." Her answer was barely a puff of air.

He cocked his head, looking pleased. "And what about love?"

"What about it?"

"You said you loved me."

"That was before. Now I know the real you."

He stood and pulled her to her feet. "I've been too lenient with you. I let you off the leash and you betrayed my trust."

Had he really thought she wouldn't run if given half a chance?

"You'll never be free. But now you know the boundaries of your cage." He leaned close, his scent washing over her, a mix of subtle cologne and scotch. "There's nowhere to run to, Persephone. I will hunt you down. You belong here, at my side. Forever."

Her breath hitched but he wasn't done. "So why not stop fighting it? Let yourself go. Let yourself be mine." He backed up and she wobbled. His presence was a force and when it was gone she felt the loss.

"Now, strip." With that order, he left her.

Submit. Obey. Escape. That still was her ultimate plan.

But that required submission, didn't it? And Hades wouldn't be satisfied with anything less than total control of her body and command over her mind. She was losing herself and the scary thing was—she liked it.

It's okay. A small voice told her. *He's bigger, faster, stronger than you. You may as well enjoy it.*

And if she didn't obey, no doubt he'd strip her himself. So she shucked off the jeans and shirt along with any sense of normalcy. Her skin pebbled in the cool room.

When she was down to her bra and panties, Hades returned, box in hand. He set it down and put his hands in his pockets, nodding at her to carry on the show. Face tight, she stripped out of the rest. It wasn't like she had anything to hide. Today was the first time she'd put on clothes since the wedding.

But still, she waited, chest heaving, as he studied her. Eventually he came to her side, running a hand down her back and sides like he was examining a horse he wanted to buy. She couldn't help a shiver of desire when he cupped her ass. She remembered her last punishment all too well.

"Are you going to punish me?"

Bent halfway through his examination of her quivering thighs, he tilted his head up. "Do you want me to?"

Her answer stuck in her throat. What would she do to ease the weight of anticipation?

His words rang in her ears. *Let yourself go. Let yourself be mine.*

She didn't trust him. *Couldn't* trust him. At least not with her heart.

But her body? Gods, the thought about what it might be like if he took her back to that perfect, ecstatic place where she could finally,

finally escape her own head and all the confusion and noise. Where she could just...*be*.

"Yes," she said, suddenly decisive. "I want you to punish me."

Something flashed in his eyes, gone in an instant. He raised his chin. "I think, wife, I may have underestimated you."

Her heartbeat pounded in her ears. Was it possible to surprise him? To challenge him and make him regard her as an equal?

Hades opened the box he'd brought and lifted out a heavy collar. Metal, silver, stainless steel and linked to a leash. So much for being his equal.

Smirking, he drew her before a giant mirror with a heavy gilt frame. He positioned her in front of it and held her still with hands on her hips.

His lips found her ears. "What do you see?"

"You, me. Us."

"I see a submissive."

A ripple went through her body. He held her up with an iron arm around her waist when her legs would buckle.

"Such a shame we have to be enemies. Circling each other, round after round, fight after fight. We were made for each other."

"Don't," she whispered, feeling close to tears. She was raw, wrung dry. His tender words were arrows. She could withstand his cruelty, but not his soft, soothing voice, spinning a story of destiny. After all, who could fight the Fates? Why even try?

It's just your body. It doesn't mean you're giving him your mind. Or your heart. And he can do such lovely things to your body.

"Give yourself to me, Persephone." He raised the stainless-steel collar. She closed her eyes just before the click.

"Mine," he breathed, then he tugged on the leash, forcing her head back, forcing her to look him in the eyes.

At the same time he dipped a finger inside her. She gasped, her walls clenching in pleasure at the invasion. She was already wet. She had been from the moment she stepped back inside the penthouse.

His strong fingers twisted, probed, and tested her inner walls, the whole time his thumb teasing circles around her clit. Her body sprung to life for him as it always did.

"You're beautiful."

His gaze swallowed her whole. Everything was Hades. His thumbs chafed her nipples lightly. She let her head drop in surrender as he worked her body to the peak.

"That's it. That's my good girl. Give yourself over to me and I will give you everything."

As her hips began to rock and pleasure bloomed, she stood again on the precipice—the devil whispering in her ear and the whole world spread at her feet.

His palm ground into her sex and her orgasm rose, brilliant and devastatingly beautiful, a bright sunset unfurling through each limb, rosy and tinged with gold.

At the last moment, though, he took his hand away. She cried out but didn't move. It was right there. *So* close.

"You want to come?"

"Yes." More than that, she needed it.

"Then crawl, Persephone. Crawl for me."

He moved to crouch several feet back, holding her leash out of the way. She was a needy knot of limbs.

"Come, Persephone," he beckoned. "Crawl to me."

For a long moment, she froze. Here it was. The crawling. But as she watched him, she saw it for what it really was: a choice.

To do it meant to submit to him completely. Voluntarily. To crawl not because he'd shoved her forcefully to her knees but because she wanted all he had to give her.

And in the end, the choice felt so simple.

She sank to her knees. Because this final decision meant she didn't have to do any more deciding or worrying or justifying. Life shrank down and became so simple.

"Yes, beautiful. Gods, you've never been more beautiful. Come to me now."

All tension left her, body and mind, as she gave herself over to him. The storm in her head finally quieted.

She wanted it and she didn't have to be ashamed anymore. She wanted his eyes on her slinking form, her swaying hips. She wanted to seduce and delight him. And the way he looked at her...like she was the most beautiful thing he'd ever seen, his face the picture of a man obsessed. Yes, gods, *yes*. Nothing had ever been more right.

She crawled eagerly.

"There," he murmured when she reached him, positioning her so her chin was high and back arched, pushing her bottom in the air. Her body shuddered at the touch of his hand as it ghosted across her backside. "All the way to the bedroom, goddess."

So she crawled, ass swaying, eyes lifting occasionally to see Hades's glowing gaze tracking her progress, all the way to the bed.

She'd barely gotten there when he was reaching down and tugging her to her feet.

"It's time for your reward." His voice sounded strained like he could barely manage to get the words out.

But the next second he was back in control of himself, always in control. He loosened his tie, stripping with smooth movements. He shucked his shoes, shirt, pants, and boxers and paused, unwittingly posing in the half light. He was naked and she was lost because here was a god in human form.

Wide shoulders, strong chest tapering to lean hips, powerful thighs. Either he worked out every morning or performed some magic to make his muscles strong and sleek, even and well formed. He could've been a statue carved by a master, but at the sight of him a sculptor would lay down his tools and weep at the perfection that defied reality.

Yet for all his otherworldly beauty, he looked like a man, coarse hair dusting his hard thighs and chest. He looked like a ruler of old. He only needed a crown. If the people wouldn't give him one, he'd take it.

And he was hers. He said she belonged to him, but it went both ways, right? He could've handed her over to an underling, or made Charon punish her. But he would never allow another man to touch her. He wanted her for himself. She'd wanted a sign that she meant something to him—was it here all along, inherent in his possessive nature?

She could only hope. Because she was becoming lost to him.

"Lie back and spread your legs."

She wanted him inside her now. She wanted to throw her arms and legs around him and grind their bodies together. She wanted him frantic with need for her, to know for certain that he was as lost as she was.

But instead she did as he said, lying back on the bed and opening eagerly to him.

He took his time arranging her, pulling her to the edge of the bed, angling her legs just right. Gods damn his control. But it was all worth it when he finally climbed over her.

"Hands above your head."

She lifted her hands. Anything to move him along. But she should have known that nothing could hurry Hades. That was the point, wasn't it? For her to give in to him completely. His way. In his time.

And when he finally, finally entered her, the first slow drag of his cock had her right at the edge again, her previously denied orgasm revving right back up.

He pushed into her and she held her breath, her body tightening. Everything in her focused on the slow, fluid glide of his cock entering her, easing the ache and stoking it at the same time. She lay there quivering, an empty vessel waiting to be filled.

Her legs and back tensed, nipples hardening and toes curling as Hades's thrusts drove her toward orgasm. He moved over her, the snap of his hips driving her further up the bed. She caught his shoulders, gripping and petting the bunching muscle, such magnificent power under her palms.

He paused and slipped his hands under her bottom, large palms cupping her back cheeks and drawing her close. The new angle made his pubic bone graze her clit and she bit back a moan. Fuck, she was close, her climax like a freight train, rushing toward her, an inexorable force about to hit—

He stopped. Pulled out. Stepped back and surveyed her heaving flesh like a piece of furniture.

"Hades. Please."

He took himself in hand, fisting his cock with her own slick as lubricant. He watched her with hooded eyes. "Touch yourself. Pull your nipples."

She plucked at her breasts, obeying instantly. Anything to bring him back. Anything.

Pleasure surged through her, but it wasn't enough. Without Hades, it would never be enough.

"Punishment," he reminded her, and horror bloomed over her. He was taunting her, touching her, teasing her. He'd fuck her forever and never let her come. He knew her body and mastered it.

"Please," she whispered. "I need it." He didn't chastise her so she continued. "I need you. Hades, please."

"All fours."

He'd barely given the command before she scrambled into place. Head up, back arched, bottom upturned, just like he'd taught her. The bed creaked under his weight and then—

He slammed into her.

Yes!

His hips drove into her in delicious rhythm. A tug on her throat told her he'd taken hold of her leash. He was being gentle, but reminding her she was owned.

"My beautiful darling, how well you beg." Another beautiful stroke. And another.

Her orgasm blew up like a bomb, a silent explosion, a billowing mushroom cloud against a sunset. Her limbs weakened, body wracked with aftershocks of the orgasm she'd been dying for.

She ended up bowed, head resting on her forearms and bottom in the air as he battered her from behind. At last he growled and finished.

When he tugged her up and led her to the bathroom, she clung to him with her arms around his waist. She stood as if in a dream. A trance, a reality that mirrored the life she wanted, as if her world had turned upside down but she found she could live in the reflection. In fact in this moment, she wanted to live there forever.

Hades took her into the shower and turned on the heated spray that soothed every part of her.

"You did so well, goddess," he murmured as he washed her body, slowly, inch by glistening inch. His own cock jutted out from his body, hard again, but he didn't make a move to satisfy himself, or make her do it. He cleaned every inch of her, even shaved her legs and mons. Meanwhile she felt like she was floating, like she'd never step foot back on the ground while he cared for her like she was a precious treasure. Precious to him.

When he dried her off and propelled her toward the bedroom, she felt drowsy. Her body was languid, her thoughts sluggish. He'd put her under a trance and she didn't want to wake. So it was good when he took her back to bed and tucked her in. He sat beside her and then leaned down, pressing the sweetest kiss to her forehead. He lingered there long moments, his head bowed over hers like he was in prayer.

As she sank off to sleep, the image remained in her head, him bowing like a supplicant even though she was the one who'd just given her submission.

19

So this was...different.

Persephone sat at the table with Hades for breakfast later that week. Yes, *at* the table, not under or beside the table at Hades's feet.

She shook her head and took another bite of her eggs.

Hades was reading the paper, apparently completely oblivious to her. He hadn't said a word to her this morning, not even when he'd set her plate on the table opposite his instead of on the floor.

It was a first. The last few days, even after he'd put away the chain, the plate had still gone on the ground.

She hadn't known how to feel about that. Was he rewarding her for her submission in the bedroom? Or had he just finally realized that, duh, there was no point in chaining her if she'd be scooped up if she tried to leave the penthouse anyway?

But that would've been true all along, so the chain had been more about humiliation and subjugation than actually keeping her trapped. So, did he consider her appropriately cowed after the police station and the...the crawling?

Her face heated even at the memory.

Or maybe *this* was the fucking point, to have her constantly questioning and second-guessing, and even third-guessing herself so she never knew which way was up. Because while every time he took her to bed, dominant and demanding, so often he took her to that place of ecstasy beyond thoughts, just *feeling*...in the morning she woke to find her brain firmly in command again.

And her brain didn't know how to deal with what her body so welcomed. Hades. In control. His will ruling every single minute of her life.

She dropped her fork to her plate with a loud clatter and sat back in her chair, crossing her arms over her chest.

Hades finally dipped his paper to look at her, but only for the shortest moment.

"We are going out tonight. So shower and shave."

What?

"What?"

He lowered the paper enough to look at her again, his expression unreadable. "If you don't, I'll do it for you."

"Fine," she snapped.

"A stylist will be here at four. Be ready by then."

"I don't have anything to wear."

"She'll bring the dress."

"Where are we—"

"Enough," he cut her off impatiently.

She clenched her teeth mutinously. But if he was telling the truth... And he was actually going to take her out of the penthouse... Well, it wouldn't kill her to play by his rules for another day.

SHE SHOWERED. She shaved. And at 4 o'clock, a knock sounded on the door. Hades opened it to a thin, fashionable man pulling a suitcase and a rack of what Persephone assumed were dresses in black hanging garment bags.

"Don't speak to her," Hades ordered abruptly. "I'll choose the dress."

Persephone glared at him, feeling her cheeks heat. Was this what it would be like all night? Him humiliating her in front of whoever it was they might see, wherever it was they were going?

She took a deep breath in and let it out slowly. It didn't matter. Her pride didn't matter. She could *behave*. And she wouldn't be stupid like last time.

She wouldn't run down the street on her first opportunity out of the penthouse crying for help. No, she had to play this game smart. If Hades wanted her to be a puppet on a string, she had to pretend to dance.

But that didn't mean that she couldn't still use tonight to learn all she could and to seek allies and opportunity.

So later, she smiled sweetly at the stylist who nodded at Hades, obviously intimidated if not outright afraid, and gestured toward the master bathroom. "If you come this way, we can get started."

Three hours later, she was made up, her hair teased and curled and sprayed into a sleek updo with curls cascading over one shoulder.

Hades had chosen a red dress, far more daring than anything she would have ever chosen for herself. The front was modest, but it draped daringly over her shoulder, exposing her back so that the stylist had to use tape to make sure none of her derrière would be exposed.

She stared at herself in the full-length mirror, even more bewildered feeling than when she'd looked at herself on her wedding day.

She looked sophisticated and worldly. Far more than she felt. She was a farm girl from Kansas.

She shook her head. No, that wasn't true. Not anymore. She wasn't the wide-eyed girl who'd first ridden the bus into the city three months ago. Not after Hades.

Still, she wasn't... She turned and looked at the daring dip of the back of the dress in the mirror, and saw Hades coming up behind her.

Her breath caught at the sight of him.

Hades in a tux was... Terrifying. Formidable. Drop dead gorgeous.

He came right up behind her. She gasped when his hands came

swiftly to her neck and watched with bated breath in the mirror as he used the small, oddly shaped key to unlock the collar around her neck.

She could only guess at what the stylist had thought of it. The clunky stainless steel had obviously not gone with the elegant look, but per Hades's instructions, the stylist hadn't said a word.

Hades tossed the collar to the bed behind him and produced a large, square velvet box from his suit coat jacket. He sat it on the dresser beside the mirror and opened it, still silent.

What was he—?

"Are those dia—"

"Yes."

Persephone's eyes went wide as he lifted the delicate diamond studded choker to her neck. Chill bumps raced down her body as he lifted her hair. His fingertips graced her skin as he fastened it at the back of her neck.

The one-inch thick interlaced diamond necklace sparkled, even in the dim light of the room. It was made of what looked like hundreds of smaller diamonds along with larger diamonds studded in a central pattern.

It must have cost a fortune.

Persephone couldn't help her hand lifting to touch the spectacular piece of jewelry, but she stopped herself at the last second from actually making contact, dropping her hand again. She swallowed hard and the diamonds glittered with the movement.

"Why?"

"So everyone will know you are mine."

Persephone nodded. Finally an answer that made sense.

"What if I lose it somehow? Or the clasp breaks and I don't notice it fall off, or—"

"It won't fall off. Now, I trust you won't manage to lose this again, either."

He pulled out another box, this one smaller and familiar, and opened it.

It was her engagement ring and her wedding ring that she'd

thrown across the room that first night. Had it only been two weeks ago? It felt like a century.

Her eyes flew to Hades's in the mirror but his face was stone. Impassive.

She took the rings out of the box and slid them on the fourth finger of her left hand.

After she had, Hades put his large, cool hands on her bare shoulders, eyes meeting hers in the mirror.

"You will not embarrass me tonight. You will act like a proper wife."

"Because gods forbid anything sully your sterling reputation?" The barb was out of her mouth before she could help it.

Hades was not amused.

He slid his hand from her bare shoulder over to her throat and for the first time all day, she saw a fire stoked in his eyes.

He put no pressure on her throat around the choker, but kept his hand there.

And in demonstration of how much Persephone was not the simple farm girl from Kansas anymore, the sight in the mirror and the feel of his commanding hand there had her tingling in all sorts of ways, none of which were fearful.

She might not be an innocent anymore, but she was assuredly just as foolish. Because her heart squeezed at his touch, too.

She turned away from the mirror and strode for the door. "I assume our chariot awaits."

So yes, the stylist and the dress and the necklace should have tipped her off. But Persephone still wasn't prepared when Charon let them off in front of a red carpet. It was a gala with an Actual. Red. Carpet.

It was a charity gala, Persephone would learn over the course of the next hour as Hades took her arm and she was blinded by camera flashes as they walked the aforementioned red carpet into the

Elysium hotel ballroom, the only hotel in New Olympus fancier than the Crown.

Persephone tried to keep her eyes from bugging out of her head when she saw famous actors, actresses, musicians, and politicians mingling all around them.

Hades strode through the crowd without batting an eye and Persephone did her best to keep up with him. He'd stop occasionally and make small talk. And he was charming. Charismatic even. He introduced her around, his hand always at the small of her back.

Persephone had officially entered the twilight zone. Hades was smiling. It was obviously a show he could put on at will, but still, she'd forgotten what his full smile looked like. The dimple. She'd forgotten about the devastating dimple.

Was this what he had been like when they were 'dating'? But no, after twenty minutes of watching him, she realized it wasn't. She didn't know if she felt better or worse that he hadn't taken the energy to be this full, false self to draw her in, or if it meant she'd been able to see slightly more of the real him from the beginning.

Or maybe she still had no idea who the hell the *real* him truly was.

After he'd met whatever quota of social engagement he felt was appropriate, he led her to view the auction items that had been donated for the charity gala. All sorts of things were up for bid: Paintings. Box seats for popular sports teams. Dinner with the mayor. A helicopter tour of the city. Theater tickets.

The theater tickets were the only thing to tempt Persephone. She promised herself as soon as she had any disposable income, she'd go see a show.

"Anything catching your eye?" Hades asked. "Maybe a handbag or two?"

She rolled her eyes and set the flyer down about the hottest show on Theater Row. "Nobody's around now. You don't have to keep up the act."

"Did you just roll your eyes at me?" The question was quiet and slightly incredulous.

Persephone gulped as she looked up at him and her tongue snuck out to lick her lips. That zinging sensation was back in her belly at the intensity she saw on his face. Stupid girl. Stupid girl.

A gong sounded and everyone around them started to move out of the auction area, but Hades kept staring at her.

Persephone's hand went to the necklace around her throat, stroking the glittering gems. She pointed her chin at the retreating crowd. "I think that means dinner is about to begin."

Hades stood unmoving for another long moment before giving a sharp nod, taking her arm, and walking so stridently to join the flow of people that she had to lift her skirts in order not to trip as she followed him.

They were seated at a large round table with ten other people. Hades glanced at their seating cards and at those beside them. His face went dark, and he promptly switched them with two from another table.

Persephone wasn't sure he was allowed to do that, but who was going to stop Hades Ubeli?

Persephone sat down and smiled awkwardly at those already seated at the table but Hades didn't sit beside her.

"I'll be right back," he murmured before stalking off to the side of the room to talk to someone. Persephone watched him go and get into a discussion with a man. That man called over another man. Hades pulled out his phone and quickly texted someone.

Why was she staring at Hades? She had her own agenda.

She looked around the table and smiled at the two other couples seated there. "Hi, I'm Persephone. It's so nice to meet you."

The two women at the table exchanged a glance before looking back to her. "You're married to Hades Ubeli?" asked the one a couple of seats away from her, a pretty redhead whose male companion had to be at least forty years older than her.

Persephone tried to keep her smile genuine. "Yes, two weeks now. Still in the honeymoon stage."

"How nice," said the redhead in a tone so patronizing, Persephone gritted her teeth.

She glanced back at Hades and saw that he was now talking with three people. Two men and a woman, a blonde who had her hand possessively on his arm, her body angled into his in a way that brought Persephone's breath up short.

It was an intimate touch. An invasion of space unless... Unless you knew the person very well. Intimately so.

"Persephone, darling!"

Persephone swung her head around in time to see Hermes heading her way. He leaned down and gave her two kisses, one on either side of her cheek. He stepped back, beaming at her.

"Look at you. Absolutely stunning, my love. I must talk Hades into letting you model the dress I'm working on. No one else could do justice to the signature piece. I designed it with you in mind."

Persephone flushed as Hermes plucked the two seating arrangement cards beside her, handed them to an assistant who was trailing him and sat down beside Persephone.

"So what do you think of your first gala?" he asked, raising his arms flamboyantly. "Does it live up to expectations?"

"I didn't really have time to make any expectations," Persephone said, "I didn't know we were coming here until we arrived."

"That beast," Hermes said. "You look stunning."

Persephone glanced over at Hades again. The woman was still there and she'd moved closer, if such a thing was even possible.

"Ugh, that woman is a witch."

Persephone jerked her head back at Hermes who'd obviously noticed her looking at Hades.

"You know her?"

"Unfortunately."

When Persephone stayed silent, Hermes obviously took pity on her.

"She's an executive at one of the big telecom companies in New Olympus."

"They dated?"

Hermes lifted a hand and waved it in a so-so gesture. "I'm not sure I would call it that."

"For how long?"

"Off and on for maybe a year or two."

"Then what happened?"

"The rumor mills said she wanted more. Apparently he didn't." Hermes raised his eyebrows significantly.

"How long ago was it?"

"I guess they broke things off maybe two months before you got to the city."

Persephone reached for her glass of water. After a long swallow, she thumped her glass down, almost sloshing water onto the tablecloth.

"She's old news, honey. He's only got eyes for you. I've seen the way that man looks at you."

Persephone barely stopped herself from scoffing. If Hermes only knew.

And what the hell was she doing wasting energy thinking about this anyway? Persephone turned to Hermes, angling her back away from Hades. Tonight was about developing relationships. And yes, Hermes was Hades's friend... Or maybe they had some business together? Persephone didn't know what a crime lord and a fashion designer might have in common but still, Hermes was a start. The more information she had, the better.

"So, tell me how you've been. How is the line doing? And the spas? You've opened a chain of upmarket spas, right?"

"Ugh, they've been running me ragged. I thought being an entrepreneur and being my own boss meant I got to set my own hours and sleep in. Ha! I work from dawn till dusk and still never get to half the things on my to do list." He leaned in. "Probably doesn't help that I party from dusk till dawn." He winked.

Persephone barked out a laugh, startling herself. How long had it been since she'd genuinely laughed? It felt good. It felt really good.

Persephone reached out and gave Hermes's forearm a squeeze, letting go almost as quickly as she touched him. But her smile was genuine when she said, "It's good to see you, Hermes. Really good to see you."

"Hermes," Hades's deep voice came from behind Persephone. She jumped in her chair and craned her neck to look up at him. He set a hand possessively on her shoulder before sitting down beside her.

"How's business?" Hades asked and Hermes transferred his attention to him.

Persephone watched Hades. Had he seen her touch Hermes? Was he mad at her about it?

But Hades seemed at ease. More at ease than he'd been all night, relaxed back in his seat and sipping from a glass of bourbon he'd picked up from somewhere as he and Hermes chatted about the newest spa Hermes had opened. Unlike with other people Hades had chatted with tonight, he and Hermes seemed genuinely friendly.

Waitstaff came around and collected cards asking which entrée they'd like, and Persephone excused herself to the restroom.

Hades stood up at the same time she did and his eyes skewered her. She heard his unasked question.

She leaned up on tiptoe and whispered in his ear. "Let me guess, you have thugs guarding the ballroom and I'll be snatched up and taken back to the penthouse if I take a step out of line?"

Hades wound a hand around her waist and pulled her up tight against him. His breath was hot on her ear as he answered, "Something like that. I expect you back within ten minutes. If you don't, I will come looking for you. Or one of my...thugs will." When he pulled back, the corner of his mouth twitched.

He gave her waist one last squeeze and let her go. But Persephone could still feel his touch long after she'd walked away from the table toward the restroom.

She went to the bathroom, relaxing only when she closed the door to the stall. What was she doing? Had she actually felt *jealous* of that woman out there? When what she was meant to be doing here was trying to find a way to escape?

She dropped her face into her hands but lifted it again quickly. She couldn't afford to muss her makeup. She rolled her eyes at the ridiculousness of her situation.

Talk about a gilded cage.

But sitting on the toilet wasn't going to get her anywhere. So she flushed and opened the stall, heading for the sink. She was so in her own head, she didn't even really notice the woman who'd opened the door as she began to wash her hands.

"So, you and Hades Ubeli."

Persephone looked up and her eyes widened at seeing the elegant blonde had stepped in the door. The same woman Hades had been talking to earlier.

"I have to say, bravo. I thought that man would be a bachelor for life. He always did like his fuck toys young, but I never imagined he'd go and marry one."

The woman advanced and stood at the mirror beside Persephone. She settled her clutch on the bathroom counter and pulled out a tube of lipstick. Her dress was black, the lipstick fire engine red. She looked to be in her mid-30s. She was stunning, refined, sophisticated. The kind of sophistication that came from experience and not a fancy dress.

Persephone couldn't help staring at her as she began touching up her lipstick that already looked perfect.

The woman's eyes slid back to Persephone. "Well, aren't you a quiet little mouse." She put the top back on the tube of lipstick and closed her clutch with a *snap*.

Persephone still didn't say anything. It wasn't like she could defend her relationship with Hades or would even want to. He didn't mean anything to her. She hated him.

"Really? Nothing to say? You know he and I have been lovers for years? I was supposed to be seated beside you but you saw how upset he became. It's still so raw between us. We fight like cats and dogs and then we make up passionately, that's how it's always been. But trust me, he always comes back to me."

The woman looked Persephone up and down, eyes narrowing, obviously waiting for a response to her cattiness.

And it wasn't that her words didn't make Persephone feel small and little. They did. This was not her world. She didn't know the rules to the games these people played, Hades least of all.

And suddenly she had the strongest longing to be back at the farm where everything was simple.

If only she could go back in time. Her mom wasn't really *that* bad. And it was nothing Persephone couldn't handle now. She wasn't a child anymore. She could stand up for herself now.

After a day like today... And everything with Hades...

If only she could go back to a life of rising when the sun came up, spending her days on the land, and sleeping after a hard day's work.

Gods, she'd do anything to go back to that.

The woman looked like she was going to make another snide comment before dismissing Persephone completely, when Persephone reached out a hand. "Can I borrow your phone?"

"What?"

"Can I borrow your phone? I forgot mine at home and there's someone I need to make a call to."

The woman's eyes narrowed in confusion but she opened her clutch and slid out her phone. "If you use it to text something to Hades pretending to be me, he'll see right through it."

Gods, the petty games these people played. "I'm not texting or calling Hades." Persephone snatched the phone out of her hand and stared at her. "Do you mind waiting outside?"

The woman snorted an amused laugh and sashayed to the door. She looked over her shoulder once as she grabbed the door handle. "I'll be waiting right outside when you're finished."

Persephone nodded distractedly, already dialing.

She glanced underneath the stalls, but the restroom was empty apart from her.

"Hello?"

Persephone closed her eyes and leaned back against the counter at hearing her mother's voice.

"Mom."

"Persephone!" A clatter sounded over the phone. "Persephone, where are you? Where is he keeping you? Are you okay? Tell me where you are and we'll be right there. We'll kill that son of a bitch."

"No, mom," Persephone frowned. "I'm fine. It's okay. I thought maybe we could—"

"Where are you? I swear that bastard will never hurt you again. We'll make him pay. I'll cut his heart out of his chest and we'll go back home where no one can ever hurt you again—"

"Mom!" Persephone spun around and slapped a hand on the counter. "Listen to me for a second. I'm fine."

"Tell me where you are," her mom all but shouted.

"Right now, at a gala at the Elysium hotel. And the rest of the time he's keeping me at the Crown. Why didn't you tell me about dad? And what he did?" She hadn't meant to ask it, but it popped out.

"Because you were never supposed to be part of this world. It was always supposed to be you and me. Just you and me. And that's how it will be again. We'll kill that son of a bitch and—"

"No," Persephone said, irritated and angry. "I don't want you or my uncles to hurt him." As soon as the words were out of her mouth, she realized they were true.

"What?"

Persephone stared at the floor and lifted a hand to her forehead.

Gods, she was fucked up. Because it was true. She didn't want Hades hurt. And what that woman had said earlier, it had bothered her. She *had* been jealous.

And as nice as farm life sounded…she couldn't go back. It was too late for that. What she'd begun with Hades, whatever this was, she had to either see it through or get out of it on her own.

She looked at herself in the mirror. And now the woman reflected back didn't look like as much of a stranger anymore. She looked pale but striking. The jewel tone red of the dress made her skin look luminous.

"He's gotten into your head." Her mom stated it icily.

Persephone couldn't deny it. Why wouldn't she want all the retribution her mother was promising otherwise?

"We haven't been able to get into the city but we're working on it, baby. We're coming." Her mother's voice was so ice cold that it sent a chill down Persephone's spine.

Persephone had heard it like that before, usually before a punishment, one of the bad ones.

"I have to go, Mom. I can figure this out on my own. I just wanted you to know I'm okay."

Persephone hung up the phone before her mom could say anything else. And she strode to the door, opened it and all but slammed the phone down into the beautiful blonde's hand.

It had been stupid to take it and stupider to call her mother. Even hearing her voice brought it all back.

The slaps if she burned the bacon at breakfast. Being shoved to the ground and locked out of the house if her mind wandered off and she was late returning from the fields. Denying her meals if Demeter thought she was getting too thick around the middle. The daily barrage of demeaning words and name-calling.

Yes, Hades had put a collar on her. But he'd never once hit her. He didn't call her names and if he continued allowing her freedoms like this, getting out of the penthouse, maybe even going back to volunteer at the shelter—

So because he's the lesser of two evils, suddenly he's your knight in shining armor?

"You know," the woman whose name Persephone still hadn't learned, lifted an eyebrow at her coyly. "Hades can be adventuresome in the bedroom. The next time he and I get together, it could be fun to have you as the third in our ménage à trois."

Persephone glared at her. "You can go fuck yourself."

She strode back toward the table where Hades was sitting. Hades stood like he meant to pull her chair out for her but she jerked it out roughly before he could and sat down hard, keeping her eyes firmly forward at the auctioneer and not looking his way.

Champagne had been served around the table and Persephone grabbed her glass and tipped it backward. It was bubbly and cool and in spite of the bite, she drank it all the way down. She reached for the untouched glass in front of Hades but he swiftly put his hand out and stopped her.

She glared his way. His eyes darkened and locked with hers in response. He did not look happy.

Well, fuck him too. She gave him a saccharine sweet smile. "Oh darling, I'm so thirsty," she said loud enough for everyone else at the table to hear.

"Have my water, sweetheart," he replied, handing her his water goblet.

She narrowed her eyes at him but accepted the water. She'd get her hands on more champagne later. If there was ever a night to get drunk, this was it. She didn't care that she was only nineteen.

Suddenly, Hades lifted an auction paddle she hadn't even realized he had in his lap and called out, "$50,000."

There were gasps from all around them and Persephone sat up straighter, suddenly looking back and forth from the auctioneer at the front of the room to Hades.

"Well folks, that's one expensive set of theater tickets. Do I have any other bids? Didn't think so. Sold, to number forty-six."

Persephone's mouth dropped open. Did he just—? Her head swiveled back to Hades.

"What did you do?"

He gave her his characteristic mouth twitch. "Donated to charity."

She stared at him as the auctioneer went on to rattle off the next item.

She was left to stew in her own head about the evening, her mother, the woman in the black dress, and most of all, Hades. She came to few conclusions about any of it other than the fact that she was very confused and probably couldn't trust her own judgment.

The auction finally finished and dinner was served. Hermes chattered in her ear about city gossip and others around the table made polite conversation. When the subject of Hades's donation came up, a reckless hair struck Persephone.

"I'm not surprised," Persephone said, smiling at Hades. "Hades supports all sorts of charities. It's one of the reasons we fell in love. He loves the fact that I spend so much time at a dog rescue shelter down on 35th and Thebes." She turned her smile toward Hades. "Isn't that right, honey?"

His eyes narrowed but he nodded. "Yes, I've always admired your generous spirit."

"Oh really?" said a man from across the table, leaning in in obvious interest. "I don't know if I said, but I work for the New Olympian Post. Everyone is always curious about the elusive Mr. and now Mrs. Ubeli. I'd love to get a story on the charity."

"No," Hades said at the same time Persephone clapped in apparent delight and said, "Yes! That'd be wonderful."

Hades's head swung her way and she continued smiling at him. "Oh, come on, darling. You're such a respected businessman about town." She lifted a hand to straighten his tie even though it was already perfectly straight. "It's natural that there's curiosity about you."

Persephone looked back to the reporter. "Come by this Tuesday. I'll be volunteering then."

Underneath the table, Hades's hand clapped on Persephone's thigh. She turned back to him and gave him a glittering smile. "Hecate will be so delighted to share the shelter's story."

Hades smiled coolly, his eyes hard, before changing the topic. His hand, however, was still very much engaged, as it slid under the slit in the side of her gown up her inner thigh.

Persephone had to hide her gasp by taking a quick sip of water.

Hades's hand didn't stop there, though. With one hand he ate his smoked salmon and with the other, he continued his path up her thigh until he was nudging her panties aside and then, *oh*—

Persephone's fingers went white knuckled around her fork as he thrust a finger inside her. Right there at the dinner table. In a room with hundreds of people. While she was wearing a designer gown and Hades chatted with another man about the current state of the stock market.

How dare he—

Oh. *Oh*—

The pleasure quickened her stomach, sharp and surprising. She sank back in her chair and opened her legs as wide as the dress would allow.

No. What the hell was she doing? She couldn't—

Oh! Two of his long, thick fingers explored her now, in and out, stroking through her folds and up to her clit before pushing inexorably inside her again.

It was wrong. So, so wrong for her to be enjoying this.

Her chest rose and fell sharply as pleasure radiated throughout her body, warm lapping waves. She clutched her water glass and bit her bottom lip to keep herself from crying out. Oh gods. Oh yes. Oh *yes*. Right there. Just like that.

It was coming— *Oh!* She wanted to throw her head back and close her eyes. But none of them could know what he was doing to her. She didn't even want to admit what he was doing to her. His fingers worked her even more furiously.

The climax hit soft at first but it spread, wave after wave, radiating out from her center. A lightness so pure and freeing she wanted to hold onto it forever. The things Hades made her feel, oh gods. The things he made her feel—

He kept stroking her through it, more languidly now as she rode the crest, riding it and riding it and riding it—

He clutched her entire pussy in his large hand and massaged it as the waves subsided. A tremor rocked her body that she couldn't help and her eyes flew open. Shit, she hadn't even realized they dropped closed but the pleasure had been all-consuming.

His hand retreated. She almost gasped at the loss.

Hades pushed his chair back from the table. "If you'll excuse us," he said crisply. He held out a hand to Persephone. "Darling?"

It was not a request; Persephone could tell by the fire burning in his eyes. Her hand trembling, she lifted it and took his. He pulled her up from the table, his fingers interlocking with hers. Persephone briefly shot a wobbly smile in the direction of everyone at the table. Hermes looked back knowingly. Oh God, had everyone at the table realized what was happening?

Hades didn't say anything as he pulled her through the crowded tables and Persephone didn't dare either.

Out of the ballroom, they went. All the way to the coat check.

"Your ticket number, sir?" asked the attendant.

"Do you know who I am?" Hades asked.

The attendant's eyes widened and he swallowed. "Yes sir, Mr. Ubeli, sir."

"Give us the room," Hades demanded. "Twenty minutes."

The attendant pushed open the half door he stood behind and scurried out without another question.

Persephone shook her head at Hades's heavy handedness but the next second, he was dragging her into the room and closing both the bottom and top half of the door as well as locking it.

Then he pushed her up against the rack of coats.

"I don't appreciate being contradicted in public," he growled, his eyes dark. "By anyone, but especially not by my wife."

His wife? Persephone couldn't help scoffing. "Let's not pretend I'm anything more than a convenient...what did that despicable woman call me? A fuck toy? And every time you fuck me, you're getting revenge on my father, so I guess I'm a two-for-one special."

If it was possible, Hades's gaze got even darker. His voice was dangerous when he said, "What woman?"

"I didn't catch her name and she wasn't wearing a collar, but apparently you like to have threesomes with her, so I hope you at least know her name."

"Lucinda."

Stupidly, hearing her name on his lips hurt. Because Persephone was a stupid, stupid girl.

But apparently Hades was moving on without any more comment on his former or perhaps still current fuck toy. "If you think telling that reporter that I'm keeping you against your will will help you—"

Persephone laughed bitterly. "If you have the New Olympian Police Department under your thumb, I'm pretty sure you'd handle the third most popular newspaper in the city without much effort." She leveled her gaze with his, which unfortunately meant she was still looking up to him, a disadvantage not even her three-inch heels could help.

"I want to see my friend, Hecate. She's got to be worried about me since I haven't even spoken to her since the wedding."

Even talking about the wedding hurt, remembering how hopeful and excited she'd been on that day.

Persephone lifted her chin defiantly. "Besides, surely a mobster like you will take any good press he can get because that's how it works, right? The hypocrisy of this city? Everyone knows what's actually going on but you all come to parties like this and rub elbows and smile at each other and pretend you care about charities when it's all a smokescreen for the terrible reality?"

"Careful," Hades barked and his hand came to her throat.

Persephone kept glaring at him. "Lock me back up. Starve me. Hit me if you want to. It's nothing I haven't had before. I told you, I survived before and I'll survive you."

Something flickered in his eyes but before she could try to figure out what, Hades grabbed her by her waist and twirled her so she was facing away from him. He dragged up the skirt of her dress and the next second, had her panties down.

There was the noise of a zipper and he pulled her back against himself. She felt the heat of his long shaft against her buttocks and her sex clenched in anticipation.

Such a stupid girl.

He bent his head over her shoulder so that his five o'clock shadow bristled against her ear.

"You will never disrespect me in public like that again. You'll do as I say. When I say."

He thrust inside her drenched sex. Her eyes all but rolled back in her head at the fullness of him. His fingers had felt good but this, oh gods, *this*—

"Sorry if I'm not your usual mindless bimbo fuck."

His arm circled around her chest and curved up until his hand was at her throat again. "Language," he growled.

And as if for good measure, he gave her ass a sound *smack*.

Persephone let out a hiss of outrage even as her sex clenched around him. His other arm that was a bar around her waist dropped until his fingers were strumming her clit and immediately the pleasure started to rise again. It was always like this, she'd noticed. After having one orgasm, the second was easier and quicker to rise, as well as often being harder and more fulfilling.

"This doesn't change anything," she panted even as her hips bucked back against him in pleasure. Oh gods. "I still," gasp, "hate," gasp, "you."

"It's time to shut that pretty mouth of yours," he barked.

When he'd taken her virginity, he'd been gentle and patient.

It appeared that patience was at an end. He clutched her to him with both arms and he thrust deep and wild and violently.

Persephone stopped thinking. She only felt with all her senses.

The wet sound and feel of his thick cock sawing in and out of her. The harsh noise of his breath in her ear. The smell of his sweat mixed with cologne. Looking down and seeing his strong, manly hands clutching and working her.

He was usually so in control. So studied and cold. But his thrusts were wild and his noises animal as he took her. He couldn't hold himself back any more than she could. This thing was bigger than the both of them.

Persephone couldn't help the cry of pleasure that escaped her mouth when the climax hit this time and Hades's hand moved from her throat to her mouth to muffle her noises. Somehow that made it even sexier, him fucking her so hard in this coat closet, hand over her mouth to keep her quiet. She clenched on him as the spasms rolled through her, involuntarily at first and then voluntarily as he swore in her ear and pumped even harder still.

He crushed his face into the hollow of her neck and thrust the deepest he ever had yet as she felt him, the heat of him as he spilled inside her and she felt a high beyond that of climax, of womanly triumph.

He pulled out and thrust in again, and again and he stilled, like he was unwilling to let go of the moment. He stayed there a long time, his breathing ragged and Persephone clutched around him with every ounce of strength she had.

She didn't let the thoughts back in yet. Not yet. Not yet.

There was only Hades and her in this moment, so perfectly connected.

She didn't know how long they stayed like that. A full minute? Two?

Before he finally pulled out and she felt his seed begin to slide out and down her inner thighs. Her sex clenched again, involuntarily, as if to keep him inside her.

She was glad she was faced away from him because she didn't know what he would have seen on her face in that moment.

She was only sure of one thing as she stared forward at the rack of coats, exhilarated and horrified by all that had just happened.

That had *so* not been part of the plan.

20

Three days later, Persephone entered the dog shelter. A pause and she ran, flinging herself into Hecate's arms.

Hecate squeezed her close but only for a little bit before pulling back and holding Persephone's shoulders. "Let me get a look at you." She'd been grinning, but her smile dimmed at looking Persephone up and down. "Sweetie, are you all right?"

Persephone's bottom lip trembled and she fought back tears as she nodded. She hugged Hecate again, hard.

"Oh, sweetie," Hecate said, rubbing Persephone's back soothingly.

Persephone closed her eyes and sank into her friend. Gods. She hadn't realized how much she'd needed a friendly face. Tears crested and fell down her cheeks but she didn't make a noise. She clung to Hecate. For a long time.

When she finally let go, she swiped at her eyes and gave a short, somewhat false laugh. "I don't know what's come over me. So much has happened since I've seen you." She reached out and grabbed Hecate's hands, giving them a squeeze. "I'm sorry I didn't reach out sooner."

Hecate squeezed her hands back. "It's okay, I understand. I

remember what it was like being a newlywed." Then her eyebrows furrowed. "But honey, seriously, are you okay?"

Persephone swallowed hard and nodded.

Hades had made it more than clear at breakfast that she wasn't to disclose any of the truth of their situation to her friend. He hadn't gone so far as to threaten Hecate's safety should she not comply, but Persephone wasn't about to put her in that position. Maybe it was selfish to even come back here. Hades was dangerous. Putting Hecate anywhere on his or his Shades' radar wasn't doing her any favors.

But things between her and Hades had continued to thaw even more since the gala. He was still letting her move freely throughout the apartment and they discussed letting her volunteer again at the shelter on a temporary basis, once a week. Today was the trial run.

Well, by *discussed*, she meant Hades had decreed it, with a long list of conditions, including having his Shades guarding the front and back of the building and Charon escorting her at all times.

Hades worked all day and sometimes nights, but they had meals together at least once a day, though they never did much in the way of talking. Sometimes he read to her, though. First from the newspaper. And without discussion, he'd plucked a book from the bookshelf and started reading it aloud. It was a Thomas Hardy novel and it was very beautiful and very sad.

And every night, without fail, he came to her room. He took his time with her. Sometimes it got a little rough, but it was never quick and, as much as she hated to admit it, it was never unwanted.

She'd begun to look forward to him coming home with an excitement that disturbed her.

He was the enemy. Wasn't he?

She. Was. So. Confused.

All that to say, Persephone could use a friend now more than ever.

"I'm all right," Persephone said and her smile was a little less tremulous this time. "I mean it."

The bell over the door jingled and the man from the gala walked in, the reporter, this time not in a tux but in jeans and an attractive gray Henley. He smiled as soon as he saw Persephone and she waved.

"Hecate, this is the reporter I called you about, who wants to do a story on the shelter."

Hecate looked briefly at the man but her eyes came back to Persephone. "We'll talk more later, okay?" Her eyes searched Persephone's and Persephone nodded.

"Definitely," Persephone said.

Persephone showed the reporter, Joe Garcia, around the shelter and explained how things worked as she went from cage to cage, feeding the dogs.

"We accept any and all strays and drop-offs, no matter what. Hecate has committed to this being a no-kill shelter, which means that other than the dogs that are simply too old or too ill for us to care for, no animals are euthanized here. But that puts a huge burden on us to get these animals adopted and to continue caring and housing the ones that remain. We depend on donations and volunteers to stay afloat."

Joe nodded and made a couple of notes on the small pad he had with him. "And how long have you been volunteering here?"

"For about two and a half months, ever since I came to the city."

"Where did you live before that?"

Persephone stopped in front of Puggles' cage as she opened his door and scooped in his food. "Out West," Persephone said noncommittally. "We work hard to walk the dogs at least once a day, depending on how many volunteers come in. And when we can, we advertise our adoptive services. The more we're able to get the word out about this place, the more dogs we can save."

"Have you always had a love for animals?"

Persephone saw what he was doing. He obviously wanted this to be an article more about her than the shelter, and no doubt any reporter worth his salt would try to dig to get what scoop he could.

Persephone smiled sweetly at him. "This is Boris," she introduced him to a large German Shepherd. She opened the cage and poured in his dog food, giving him a belly scratch before closing it again. "Now, I have a soft spot for him. He's big and intimidating looking, but once you get to know him, he's really a sweetheart." She leaned in. "A little like my husband."

Joe's eyebrows went up at that. "Oh really? Are you saying that Hades Ubeli has a soft underbelly?"

Persephone laughed. "Oh, I wouldn't go that far. Hades is many, many things, but I wouldn't call him soft. Let's say he can be a perfect gentleman when he's of a mind to be."

Joe scribbled furiously at his pad, no doubt trying to record the quote.

Persephone moved on. "A lot of people think adopting a dog from an animal shelter means getting an older animal, but that's a misconception. We have a lot of puppies, as you can see. It's unfortunate, but too many people take on animals they simply aren't ready for."

"But we work hard here to match potential owners to pets that are compatible with exactly what they're looking for. We don't want to see a dog back here in several weeks any more than an owner wants to bring them back. So we talk to people and have them fill out questionnaires. We spend time with the dogs to learn their quirks and habits, all so that we can make the best and most long-lasting matches."

Joe nodded and made a few notes, but with not nearly as much enthusiasm. "So how did you and Mr. Ubeli meet? Obviously, you had a short engagement if you only came to the city two and a half months ago."

Persephone gave a slight, enigmatic smile. "Something like that."

"Oh, come on," Joe said. "Give me something for my readers. Hades Ubeli, consummate bachelor, suddenly ties the knot after knowing you only a few months? The news set New Olympus buzzing. Surely you can give our readers some insight into your whirlwind romance. Did your families know one another?"

Persephone stopped at that and turned her back to him. Did he know something? Did he know she was a Titan?

She worked to suck in an even breath as she took another scoop of dog food from the plate and poured it into the bowl of a stray border collie Jack Russell mix. No, there was no way he could know about who her parents were, otherwise the news would've been splashed all over the headlines long before now. She'd seen unpleasant headlines about Hades before, and news *that* big... Even Hades with all his power and influence might not be able to suppress it.

But most likely, Joe Garcia was shooting into the dark, hoping something would land.

Persephone dragged the bucket over to the next cage and felt Joe follow behind.

Still not looking at him, she said, "I don't really know how to explain Hades and me." Ha. That was the understatement of the century. "It was raining one night and I ran into his club to get out of the storm."

She finally looked back at Joe. "He dazzled me." More truth, even though the pang in her chest was more like an ax blade.

"And I guess I made an impression on him too. Have you ever experienced a moment and known, with everything inside you, that it was going to change the rest of your life? That's what meeting Hades was like. There was my life before meeting him and my life after. And that's the way it'll be defined until the day I die. Before and after."

Joe had stopped scribbling. He stared at Persephone, absorbed, as she told him the simple truth.

"I'm starting to see why Mr. Ubeli might have been dazzled in return," he said.

Persephone tilted her head and smiled at him. "Flattery will get you everywhere, Mr. Garcia. Now come this way, I want to show you the puppies."

"THAT WENT WELL, I THINK," Hecate said, looking at Persephone over her steaming cup of tea. Hecate always said there was nothing that couldn't be solved over a good cup of tea. But Hecate had only met Hades once, and briefly, at the wedding.

"Hopefully, the publicity will bring in more people to the shelter looking to adopt," Persephone said.

"I was eavesdropping," Hecate admitted, making Persephone smile.

"I would expect nothing less."

Hecate's face went serious. "But how are you really?"

She reached out and squeezed Persephone's knee. They were sitting in the back of the shelter in Hecate's cramped office on stools beside the tiny break area where a microwave, coffee, and tea station had been set up in a corner.

Persephone tipped her head back and let out a heavy sigh.

"That bad?"

Persephone looked back at her friend. "Not bad, necessarily," Persephone said. She wondered how much she could say without revealing the true extent of it.

"Marriage is... Well, marriage to a man like Hades is...more complex and intense than I was maybe prepared for."

"Honey, you're only what, nineteen? I'd be shocked if it wasn't, though I wish the honeymoon phase would've lasted a little longer."

Persephone smiled. "Hades works long hours and he's not always the best communicator." That was putting it mildly. "And I guess I worry that..." How to put this? "I came to the city to try to find myself. To be free of my controlling mother and now..."

"Now you're married to a controlling man?"

Persephone nodded. Again, an understatement.

"It's not that surprising, honey," Hecate said gently. "It was what you were used to all your life. And it's true what they say, unfortunately. We are attracted to partners like our parents because it's all we know."

Persephone dropped her face into her hand. "Gods, don't say that," she moaned. "The last person I want to be married to is someone like my mother."

Hecate laughed. But then she got serious again. "Is he good to you? Is he kind?"

Persephone stared at the floor for a long moment before finally admitting, "Yes."

She looked up at Hecate. "He's not like my mom. He's not petty or mean for meanness' sake." Then she wondered if that was true. "I don't know, it's still early. What if he really *is* like my mom?"

"Honey, you listen to me. You ever want to get away from that man, if he ever lifts a hand to you or starts being abusive with his words, you tell me. I don't care who he is, we'll get you away from here."

There it was. Everything she'd wanted to hear ever since Hades had flipped the script on their wedding night. Someone willing to help her escape him.

But Persephone shook her head and reached out to give Hecate's hand a squeeze. She told herself it was because she didn't want to bring down the world of trouble Hecate's words might incite from Hades.

But she was afraid she believed her next words more. "I think I could be happy with him. It's been an adjustment and we're still learning to communicate but... I think I could be happy..."

She looked around her at the dogs in cages. Were the dogs happy there? They were well fed, taken out for walks once a day, and some of them in far better situations here than the abusive homes they'd been in before.

The dogs were grateful every time she poured food in their bowls or gave them a belly rub or took them outdoors for a walk.

But always they came back to the cage.

"Do you think they're happy?" Persephone asked suddenly. "Spending their whole life waiting in these cages until someone thinks they're worthy enough to adopt them?"

"It seems to me," Hecate said quietly after a moment, "happiness starts in here." She leaned forward on her stool and pressed her fist to Persephone's chest, right over her heart.

Persephone looked up at her and her eyes stung again like when she'd first gotten to the shelter. She swallowed hard. "It's not that simple. All I ever wanted was freedom."

Hecate gave the slightest shake of her head. "You are already free, baby. You always were. Where it counted."

She lifted her fist and pressed it to Persephone's chest again. "I want the best for you, girl, whether you want to leave or stay, and I'll help you whatever you choose. But till you demand your freedom here," she opened her palm over Persephone's heart, "it won't matter who you're with or what rules they or their lifestyle put on you."

"I don't understand," Persephone said.

Hecate smiled. "You will."

21

Hades sat at a table in the back of Paulie's with Charon and several of his lieutenants. They did not have good news for him.

Angelo, a junior lieutenant, was animated as he spoke. "They hit us in the Westside, all at different parts of our business. One dealer was hit, two men approached him to take over his corner. He got away. A truck was targeted; we found it empty and abandoned on the Ape."

The Ape, or Appian Way, was the main highway that linked New Olympus to Metropolis.

"Obviously, it was the Titans," Hades said. "But you got anything more specific for me?"

"We're looking for the driver now. Could be that fucker defected. But the worst hit was Santonio's girls' incall house."

Shit. The incall house—as opposed to when the girls met clients at a hotel or on an *out*call—was usually filled with muscle to protect them. "What happened?"

"Two guys came in separately and booked overnights. Drugged the girls and then snuck out of the rooms and set the house on fire."

Hades got very still. "Casualties?"

Angelo shook his head. "Guys downstairs smelled the smoke and got everybody out in time, but the two girls are in the hospital for smoke inhalation. And one of the guys did some things to the girl while she was out. We're still waiting for her to wake up."

Prostitutes worked illegally but they lived in the Underworld and were therefore under Hades's protection.

"Santonio's putting double protection on his stable."

"They weren't after the girls," Charon spoke up, moving forward from the side of the room. His gaze met Hades's across the table.

Hades nodded. Charon slept at the incall house a few times a week. Always with different girls. If he wasn't there, he was at a different incall house, but this one was his favorite.

He didn't even have a place of his own. If the man liked sleeping next to a warm body at night, who was Hades to judge? But the fact that the Titans were targeting Hades's right hand man?

"They're getting bolder," Hades said.

Angelo nodded, eyes locked with Hades. "They hit us, we gotta hit back ten times as hard." He smacked his fist into his hand.

"How we gonna strike, boss?" asked Carlo.

Hades could feel the energy from his lieutenants all around the room. This was a war they'd all been waiting for.

Hades most of all.

But now that it was here?

Hades felt uneasy. Those girls who'd ended up in the hospital tonight? They were just the beginning.

And while they might not be innocents in the eyes of the public, they were to him.

How much collateral damage would an all-out street war cause? How many innocents would have to die?

And for what?

All because he'd had to have his revenge and capture Persephone. They'd been at an uneasy détente with the Titans for almost a decade now. He'd been the one to turn a Cold War hot again.

He hadn't even considered any other options at the time. He got the report that Demeter Titan was back in the city and he had to see for himself.

But of course it wasn't her. It was her daughter. And as soon as Hades had seen her, he'd had to have her.

Chiara would finally be avenged.

It was all he could see. Only now, months later after having gotten to know Persephone, had he started for the first time in years to remember Chiara's life and not just her death.

He thought he'd been honoring her memory by avenging her death, but all of this... More war? More death? It was the last thing she would've wanted.

"It's time to make our play," Angelo said when Hades stayed quiet. "We send them the video Hades took on his wedding night. We put the bitch up for ransom to draw the leadership out. Ambush those motherfuckers and kill every last one of them."

Only years of discipline stopped Hades from throwing himself on Angelo and beating his face in for calling his wife a bitch.

Noises of assent came from all around the circle at Angelo's words. Clearly it was a popular idea.

It had been Hades's idea in the first place and he'd shared it with his lieutenants when he first began courting her.

"Can't," Hades said sharply. "I fucked it up when I tried to transfer the video to my computer. The file got corrupted."

Angelo stared at him, obviously confused. "So make another one."

But the place he and Persephone were at now, Hades couldn't imagine doing anything that would make her cry like she had after he'd said that stupid shit.

And he'd lied to his lieutenants just now. The file hadn't gotten corrupted. He'd deleted it.

He'd been watching it, about to email it, and it made him sick to his stomach. For the first time in years, he heard Chiara's voice in his head. *Hades, what are you doing? Do you think this is what I want?*

Before he could think better of it, he'd trashed it and emptied the trash.

"Hades?"

Hades glared at Angelo. This little shit was getting too big for his britches. He was only a junior lieutenant and he had a lot of nerve, questioning Hades and throwing his balls around like he had any say.

"I'll think on it and get back to you."

Angela looked at him like he'd grown a third head.

"But, boss—"

Hades had had enough. He jerked Angelo up from his seat and shoved him back until he was flat against the wall, his hand against Angelo's throat. "It would behoove you to respect your elders. You've been in the organization what? Eight years? Everyone else at the table has fifteen years on you. So don't speak unless you're spoken to. And Persephone might be a Titan but she's also my wife and as such she deserves respect. Do you hear me?"

Hades pulled out his weapon and put it to Angelo's forehead. "Tell me you hear me."

Angelo's body started to tremble underneath Hades's hand at his throat. "I hear you," he whispered shakily.

"Good," Hades said with one last shove.

He turned back to the table and holstered his side arm. "The Titans will be dealt with. Their violence will not go unanswered. But we do it smart. Tiny, Fats, find out who their major supplier in Metropolis is. Double up the Shades' presence on the Westside. No more Titans get in our city that we don't know about. No more surprises. And find that godsdamned driver, see what he knows. Meeting adjourned."

There were nods all around and the guys stood up and hurried off. Smart. Most people knew not to mess with him when he was in a mood. Angelo skittered off with his tail between his legs. Hades would have to watch that. Angelo had a big ego and he was ambitious. That could be a dangerous combination.

Marco glanced at his watch. He knew he was old school, not

staring at his phone every godsdamn second, but people were on those things too much.

He looked to Charon. "Everything considered, it might make sense for you to lay low for the time being."

Charon nodded and left without another word.

Probably why the big man was his closest friend, if the term applied to anyone. He knew when it was best to keep his mouth shut.

22

It was a different driver than Charon who picked Persephone up at the shelter. She'd changed into a dress and heels as per Hades's request and she fiddled with her purse strap. It felt strange to be driving in the car without Hades. Strange to be anywhere without Hades. And yet, Persephone found herself doing the exact same thing she'd be doing if Hades was in the car anyway.

She stared out the window, silent, hand on the glass as she watched the beautiful glittering lights of the city.

"Um, sir, can you put on some classical music? I think it's preset one?"

The strains of Rachmaninoff filling the Bentley made Persephone relax back against the chair. Between the gentle lull of the music and the soft leather seats, Persephone felt her eyes drifting closed.

She'd watched a TV show while Hades was gone at work yesterday about these beekeepers who used smoke to daze the bees, lulling them into a false sense of security while the beekeepers emptied their hives of honey.

Was that what was happening to her? Being lulled into a false sense of security by routines and little gifts after periods of hardship her husband himself had inflicted?

Was she being manipulated by a master?

She rolled her eyes at herself. Gods, what was with the animal metaphors today? But maybe it was natural that she couldn't help thinking about traps and cages on the one day she was free.

The driver pulled in front of Paulie's, where apparently Hades was already waiting. Several Shades shadowed Persephone as she stepped out of the backseat and, looking both ways, they ushered her out of the car and hurried her into the restaurant.

She'd been here a couple of times, before they were married when Hades had stopped in briefly for business and she'd drunk coffee in a front booth while he was in the back. Today though, Hades was in the booth in a little room separated off from the rest of the restaurant. He was alone, not meeting anyone, as if he was waiting for her.

The waitress took Persephone directly back to him and Hades waved for her to take the opposite booth seat.

Persephone nervously fingered her purse and sat down, scooting over until she was in front of him, the narrow table between them.

"How was your time with your friend?"

"It was good. Thank you for letting me go." The words were a little hard to get out. She shouldn't have to ask *permission* to go see her own friend. But she kept her temper in check because she really wanted him to award her more and more freedoms like this afternoon.

Hades tilted his head at her and she wondered what he was thinking. Seemed like she was always wondering what he was thinking lately. His face was so unreadable and his actions often inexplicable. He'd eased up so much from the wedding night but she didn't know why or what was coming next. She was back to constantly waiting for the next shoe to drop.

"I don't suppose we could talk like real people?" she asked with a sigh.

Hades's eyebrows went up in surprise. "By all means."

But that was all he said. She sighed again. He'd never make anything easy, would he?

"How was your day?" she asked.

He continued studying her, and shrugged. "I dealt with business."

Persephone rolled her eyes. "Fine, don't tell me about your day. I'll tell you about mine. It was great to see Hecate again. And the dogs. The reporter was nosy but I kind of expected that." Her eyes had been wandering the restaurant but they came back to Hades. "Don't worry, I didn't tell him anything."

"I wasn't worried that you would."

This time it was her looking at him in surprise.

"I give you more credit than that. You're smart. It's one of the things I like about you."

It was one of the things he liked about her?

"Though I might have let it slip how grumpy you are in the morning before you get your first cup of coffee." The teasing comment slipped out but she couldn't deny the way her chest warmed when she saw his lips twitch.

No. Stop it. No smiling at the sadistic captor. Getting on better terms with Hades so he gave her more freedoms was one thing, but... liking it?

So she just started babbling so she wouldn't have to think about it anymore. "One of the golden retrievers was a little too eager to meet Joe when we took him out for his walk and started humping his leg. Hecate got him under control, though. She's trying to train him in some of the basics because she thinks he'll make a great family dog. We were hoping Joe would feature him in the article but *that* plan went a bit awry, what with the whole humping incident."

"Joe?" Was Persephone crazy or was there an edge to Hades's voice?

"You know, the reporter from the other night. Joe Garcia," she said, dismissing the thought. "Anyway, I think the whole thing went off pretty well. Hopefully, it will bring some recognition and publicity to the shelter and will get more people in, wanting to adopt."

Her eyes lifted over Hades's shoulder. "And it was good to see the dogs again..." Wait, she'd already said that. She bit her lip as she watched the waitress, Maria, approach with their food. Persephone hadn't ordered anything or even seen menus.

"I took the liberty of ordering for us when the driver messaged that you were on your way."

"Oh," she said. She didn't like his high handedness, but it was Hades. And when she leaned over her plate of pasta and took a deep inhale, she smiled. "Thanks. I'm famished."

"Enjoy," Hades said, eyes still on her, not his food.

Feeling a little self-conscious, she dug in anyway. The meatballs and marinara were delicious. Simple fare but excellently executed. "Oh my gosh, this is amazing," Persephone said as she finished chewing a large bite.

Hades watched her with what looked like amusement as he ate his meal. She was embarrassed when she looked down and realized she'd polished off almost her whole plate and he was only halfway done.

"I'll give your compliments to the cook."

Persephone felt her cheeks heat but decided, screw it. Good food was good food and she wouldn't be embarrassed about enjoying it.

Hadn't Hecate impressed on her the point that happiness and freedom started with her? She wasn't sure she fully understood what Hecate had meant but she could guess that it had something to do with attitude and outlook. She could sit here and sulk about her situation and pick at her food.

Or, she could enjoy the fuck out of this amazing pasta, be satisfied that she'd had a great day at the shelter with her good friend, and tonight, if the pattern of the last week was anything to go by, she'd probably end the day with at least one earth-shattering orgasm.

Was it really that easy?

Be happy in her cage and move on with life?

"What are you thinking about so solemnly over there?"

Her eyes jerked back to Hades. She didn't know how long she'd zoned out for, but he looked almost done with his pasta now. He gazed at her over his glass of red wine.

"Nothing," was her knee-jerk response, but then she took a deep breath. She was the one who said she wanted to talk about real things, right?

"I guess I was wondering...well, I'm always wondering...what it is you want."

Hades looked surprised again. "What do you mean?"

Was she really doing this? Maybe it was the afternoon with Hecate, maybe it was the fact that Hades had been relatively nice to her lately, but she decided to take the plunge.

"Well," she started slowly, "I can't help but notice that things have been...different lately."

He didn't say anything, so she went on.

"...And I guess I was wondering if you are still determined, um, for me to be...well, miserable."

Her eyes dropped to her plate but she glanced up briefly at him. Pointlessly, because his features gave no indication of what he was thinking.

So determinedly, she went on. "Because I was thinking, um, if you're out for revenge on my dad, us being together, whether I'm happy or miserable still does that job. Because I'm guessing you're the last person on earth he would want me with."

Time to get the rest of it out quick. "I've never known the guy so I don't necessarily feel any loyalty to him and things were never that great with my mom. Anyway, what I'm trying to say is that maybe a life here in New Olympus, a life with *you*, could be good. I mean, I could be contented if you were okay with me doing things like I did today, going out and not being locked in the apartment all day."

"And I could make it a good home for you," she hurried on to say. "I could cook and clean—"

"That's what the maid is for," Hades said sharply.

Persephone jumped at his voice, but hurried on. "Well, I could do other things. Um, wifely things." Persephone couldn't help but look down at her plate again. "The gods know we're compatible in that department."

She took a quick breath in and forced herself to look back up at him. "I guess what I'm proposing is a cease-fire between you and me."

"A cease-fire," he repeated.

She nodded, forcing herself to keep his gaze even though like always, the intensity of his gaze made doing so a difficult feat.

He was quiet a moment but then he moved swiftly, standing and moving around the booth until he stood at her side, hand held down to her. "I accept."

Persephone felt her mouth drop open. He accepted? Just like that?

"Okey-dokey," she whispered. She reached up her hand and he clasped it firmly.

"Tomorrow I'll have another stylist come in," he said as he swiftly walked to the front door, dragging her along with him.

Well, he was full of surprises today. "Where are we going?"

"To the theater. But right now we're going home."

23

The driver turned off the boulevard of respectable brownstones into a private drive and radioed ahead for the caretaker to open the iron gates. A twenty-foot-tall railing ran all around the property perimeter, along with a thick evergreen hedge. It hid the grounds from the view of the street, and in the forested areas, delineated the property woods from the rest of the park.

Maybe Hades hadn't liked her cease-fire idea after all and he'd brought her out here to kill her and bury her in the woods.

But no, the step forward they'd seemed to take back at Paulie's had felt real enough.

Even now, while Hades wasn't talking, just listening to music like normal, his hand was still outstretched toward hers, their fingers interlocking.

So she dared to ask, "Where exactly are we going? I thought you said we were going home."

"We are. To the Estate."

When he didn't say anything else, Persephone pressed. "The Estate?"

Hades let out a sigh, but it wasn't like she'd ever seen this place before and curiosity was natural. "The Estate is the last holdover from the old Ubeli family wealth. Twenty acres of prime real estate, still within city limits. It backs up to the larger Park, which spans many more blocks."

"An oasis in the center of the city."

Hades nodded.

"But hardly a welcoming place, as you can see." He gestured a hand toward the window.

And Persephone got what he meant. As the car crept down the winding drive, she tried to picture a young Hades running around the manicured lawns of the Estate. Even during the day, the shadows lay long under the ancient trees.

No wonder Hades now preferred a modern penthouse to the dark Estate.

The Estate house itself loomed three stories over a paved forecourt. Built of stone, she'd bet the house could host twenty guests at a time overnight, and entertain a few hundred in the long ballroom. Tonight someone left the light on in one room upstairs. The rest of the windows were cold and grey, staring at the surrounding forest.

It all had a very Gothic feel. And taking a second glance at the Estate architecture itself, she finally saw it for what it was: a fortress, built by the elder Ubeli to protect his family during a war.

Two more cars pulled into the drive. Persephone glanced out the cold windows nervously as Charon and a few other men she recognized as Shades exited the black sedans in the drive.

"Why did we come here?" Persephone asked as Charon approached the house and opened the lock. Several Shades from the car behind him went inside first, no doubt to double check the house for security purposes. Hades had seemed particularly on edge lately and Persephone had noticed more Shades around than usual.

"You said you wanted a cease-fire. And as my wife, you should be familiar with my family Estate. This is where I usually stay, especially on the weekends when I need a break from city life."

He was bringing her in. Letting her see all of him.

"My childhood was a very happy one here. Until it wasn't."

"Your sister," Persephone whispered. "How old were you when she died?"

"Sixteen."

Persephone watched the way the vein in his throat flexed as he swallowed and she'd bet anything in the world he blamed himself for his sister's death. But still, *sixteen*? He'd been a boy who'd already lost his parents, all alone in the world.

"I bet she was wonderful."

Hades jerked his head once up and down and then turned away. "Come on, I'm tired. It's been a long day."

It was only about nine o'clock and while yes, the day had come with a certain amount of exhaustion, being in Hades's most intimate space had adrenaline shooting like crazy through Persephone.

Did he bring his girls here often? To impress them with his family's wealth? Somehow, she doubted that.

Why hadn't he ever brought her here before?

No doubt tying up a captive and tossing her in the basement here would incur less risk than doing it at the top of one of the most in demand downtown hotels.

What if everything he said in the restaurant was just a lie to get her out here for exactly that purpose?

Persephone's hands trembled as she reached for the seat handle, but the driver was already there, opening it from the other side. Hades came around as well, offering a hand down to her. There was nothing else to do other than take it. The sharp points of her heels dug into the grass as she stood.

"Maybe I should have changed back into my sneakers I wore at the shelter," she murmured quietly.

"Don't worry. There's a stone path right up here."

"Oh. Okay," Persephone said.

Hades held her arm as they walked the narrow flagstone path from the driveway to the door where Charon was already waiting for them. Apparently, the Shades' security check of the house had shown nothing awry and Charon gestured them inside.

"We'd like the residence to ourselves for the evening," Hades said and Charon nodded.

"I'll let the Shades know. Only perimeter patrol."

Hades raised his chin and then he and Persephone were over the threshold and inside.

Hades didn't seem to be in the mood to show her around, either.

No, he carried her straight up the central staircase, in spite of her repeated squeals that she could walk, she could walk! All the way down a short hall to the master bedroom, where he deposited her in the center of the bed.

He followed her down, sliding his knee between her thighs.

Oh, so they were going to start this portion of the evening early tonight, was that it?

He rarely came to her bed before midnight. Sometimes hearing him open the door woke her up, other times she managed to stay awake in anticipation. But it was barely nine o'clock, twilight still hung outside, and when Hades leaned over, he hit a button that turned on two table lamps to a soft muted glow. So apparently, they wouldn't be doing this in the darkness either, as was per their usual.

Persephone trembled underneath him.

He planted his elbows beside her head on the bed and dipped his hips, dragging his erection against her most sensitive place. His greedy hands were on her thighs, reaching underneath the skirt of her dress.

His hands on her body felt so familiar.

Too familiar.

She'd gotten used to fucking this way.

But after all they'd said, if he really meant for it to be a cease-fire...

His lips kissed down her collarbone and the next thing she knew he had latched onto a nipple.

It wasn't that things had become routine in bed. Far from it. Hades was always showing her new positions and ways to feel him inside her and to get her off.

But apart from the first time, he rarely sought eye contact. His kisses weren't often on the lips, and he took his pleasure and left to return to his own bedroom.

And Persephone didn't think she could keep giving herself to him if that was the way it was going to continue.

She wasn't sure if Hades felt her tense up beneath him, but his head came up and, as if he could sense the very thing she was thinking, his gaze caught hers.

If true inner freedom came with taking action and claiming it, well, here went nothing.

Persephone grabbed Hades's face with both hands and drew him down to her face. To her mouth.

She didn't know what she was doing. So she smashed her lips against his. It was awkward. She never initiated kisses and she was terrible at it—

But then his lips gentled on hers and his clever tongue began to tease at her lips until she couldn't help but relax in response. And when his hands on her sex over her dress did something that felt especially good, she gasped.

Hades used the opportunity to slip his tongue in her mouth and oh—*oh*—

Her tongue moved tentatively to meet his and holy *shit*! The second the tips of their tongues touched, it was like connecting a live wire straight to her clit.

She moaned shamelessly and lifted her pelvis up against his hand.

"That's right," he growled. "That's how it should be. Give it to me."

At this point, Persephone couldn't *not* give it to him.

He shoved her skirt up and her panties down, not even bothering to get them all the way off, just to her ankles.

She kicked at them but only halfheartedly because Hades had shifted his weight above her. She hadn't even heard him undo his zipper, but the heat and length of him was undeniably at her center, the fat head of his cock pressing and teasing for entrance.

Persephone let out the highest pitched cry yet. She wanted him.

She wanted him more than anything she'd ever wanted in her entire life.

Now she knew her answer. She didn't care if she was caged or free. As long as she came home to this man every night, she would be happy. Deliriously so.

She loved him.

She grinned at the revelation, wanting to tell him so that he could feel her joy.

But the next second it dimmed. Because there was no way he felt the same. And what the hell was she doing, loving him? She was still the naïve girl imagining she was a princess and he was the prince and that there was still a way this could end in anything other than tragedy.

"What?" Hades wrapped his arms around her and pulled her close. So close their chests were cemented together like...like he couldn't bear to lose her. "What has you looking so sad?"

She forced a smile. Dammit, she wouldn't ruin this. Caged or not, tonight she wanted to fly completely free. She wanted to let it all go. To surrender absolutely to the bliss of being in his arms.

She tried to kiss him and distract him but he shook his head.

"Persephone," he demanded, balls deep inside her, invading her everywhere.

There was no getting away from Hades Ubeli. There never had been.

"You were here, with me. But then you went away."

He was supposed to be some dangerous crime Lord. He wasn't supposed to see shit like that. But maybe reading people had made him so good at what he did.

Persephone wanted to hide her face against his cheek. But she doubted he'd let her get away with that either.

So she looked up at him, and meeting his eyes this time was one of the bravest things she'd ever done in her life.

"Hades," she whispered. "I still feel it. It never went away. Not fully. I still feel it, Hades. And more."

Hades's eyes got dark at that but he didn't make her explain further.

This time it was his lips crashing on hers and the way he kissed her, it was like he was devouring her. Did that mean that he, too—? Had he finally developed feelings—?

But there was no time to analyze things because it was moving quickly now.

Hades fiddled with the zip at the back of her dress, managed to get it halfway down, whereupon it got stuck. And Hades ripped the rest of the dress in half to get it off of her.

Persephone screeched in protest but Hades only grinned. It wasn't a twitch of his mouth, either. It was a full, all out Hades grin accompanied by the dimple and it took Persephone's breath away.

Which was unfair because then, when Hades rolled them and flipped them, Persephone was unprepared. Especially when she ended up on top.

"Wanna see you ride me, gorgeous."

Persephone's mouth dropped open but the way his gaze glittered, Persephone wasn't in a mood to deny him. So she undid the clasp of her bra and took it off, shaking her hair out of its pins while straddling him. It had the intended effect of making her tits jiggle back and forth.

Hades groaned, "Stop with the torture. Get that hot little cunt on my cock again."

"So crude," Persephone pretended to chastise, leaning over and wagging a finger in his face. This had the bonus benefit of allowing her nipples to brush the hair on his chest and pebble up.

A sight which was not lost on Hades. "Fuck," he whispered harshly before reaching for her breasts.

He caught the entire weight of them in his large hands and he immediately began to roll them and gently pinch at her nipples.

She couldn't help the immediate whimpered gasps that came from his actions. "Yes, yes. Like that. Just like that."

She didn't want him to stop for even a second, so it was her who reached down to align his member with her entrance again.

And with him torturing her nipples and filling her again with his thick, long shaft, she was right on the edge and yet it felt like they'd only barely begun.

She rolled her hips and ground down against him. She didn't care that they'd only begun. She needed it. She fucking needed it. *Now*.

So she rolled and ground down hard and dirty. She grasped Hades's hair and crashed their mouths together as the orgasm hit her. She screamed it into his mouth and clenched around him as tight as she could. His thrusts started getting more frantic and she hoped he finished soon because she didn't think the orgasm would last for much longer.

Ohhhhhhhhhhhhh. Oh! One last little aftershock and it was done.

Hades had slowed down his thrusts and she frowned. Did he—?

A gentle chuckle from Hades rumbling beneath her was her answer.

"No, honey, I didn't come yet. That was the first of many for you and when I come, you'll know it."

He rolled her yet again, this time so that she was on her stomach and he was coming at her from behind. He lifted her hips up and sank into her.

SMACK, he spanked her ass.

"Hey!"

Hades chuckled deeper. "I may have let you be on top for a minute, but don't forget who's in charge."

Chill bumps raced up and down Persephone's body. And not out of fear.

So Persephone curved her head over her shoulder to look at him and she blinked her pretty lashes and she said, "Yes, Sir."

If she thought his eyes had been bright before, they were nothing to the way his entire face came alive at her words.

He landed another smack to her opposite ass cheek.

And afterward he soothed the skin he just smacked, sliding a finger down and around his shaft to gather some of her cream and rub it all around her ass, including her asshole.

Where, as he began to fuck her again, she felt one of his fingers start to probe.

That sent her into a full-bodied shudder. What was he— That was so *dirty*—

So why did it feel so damn *good*?

He stroked forcefully in and out of her sex, one hand at her clit, the other at her ass. And it was so much stimulation, all Hades, everywhere Hades—

Persephone unabashedly howled her second release, squeezing on Hades as he hit that glorious spot inside her with his every thrust, clenching and releasing around him, and clenching and releasing and *clenching*—

Hades was right behind her, leaning over her shoulder to kiss her as he stilled, violently jerked back once and shoved back home.

Persephone clenched and squeezed around him, wanting to hold onto him forever.

But as the moments always did, this one too came to an end.

Persephone felt tears immediately flood her eyes. Dear gods, what was she thinking? How would amazing, soul shattering sex help anything when it came to her confusion over Hades?

Hades climbed off her and Persephone immediately rolled to the edge of the bed, reaching for tissues from the nightstand to clean herself up.

"Where's my bedroom?" she asked, proud of herself that she managed an even somewhat steady tone of voice.

Hades didn't say anything, but right as she'd tossed the tissues in the trashcan, an arm hooked around her waist from behind.

"Hades, what—?"

But she was already being dragged back down into bed. Hades climbed beside her, or rather behind her, spooning her. He threw the sheet and comforter over them.

He turned off the lamp on the side table with his other hand and settled into bed as if nothing was wrong or out of the ordinary.

Hades had never *once* cuddled after sex.

Usually the man treated the bed like it was a hot potato he

couldn't wait to get away from fast enough after they were finished. So what gave?

Hades slid his hand around her waist. It crept upward until he was cupping one of her boobs. He slung a leg over hers, all but pinning her to the bed.

Did he think she'd go wandering off throughout his grand Estate and find some family secret?

But as his breathing quickly eased behind her and he began to gently snore she was hit by an even more stunning thought: he'd really meant the cease-fire. The truce.

This was what life could be like with Hades, as his wife.

Everything she'd said this evening to him over dinner… A big part of her never thought anything like that was possible with Hades Ubeli. She thought she'd make her big speech and he'd keep on being his normal asshole self and at least she wouldn't feel as bad about running when the time came.

But now?

She sank her head into the pillow beside Hades, while his arms wrapped around her, making her feel more safe, beloved, and cherished than she ever had in her life.

And what, exactly, was she supposed to do with *that*?

24

Persephone was exquisite in the red velvet dress that hugged her curves in all the right places. Hades stopped in her doorway and watched as she put on her earrings. She was so beautiful, it almost hurt to look at her. She smoothed down the skirt of the dress, eyeing herself in the mirror and touching her earrings, double checking they were fastened correctly.

From the slight crinkle in her brow, Hades could tell that she wasn't seeing what he was seeing. At first, he thought it was an affectation—her pretending not to know the effect of her beauty. But he'd slowly realized she genuinely didn't see it. She considered herself plain. Ordinary. Her mom had really done a number on her. She didn't know how special she truly was.

Hades wasn't sure if he looked forward to the day she finally realized it or not. With enough time, would she be spoiled and corrupted like everything else in this city?

No, the answer came to him almost as swiftly as the question had.

Persephone wasn't like anyone else he'd ever known. She wasn't afraid of him and she didn't want anything from him, apart from the obvious, to be rid of him. He couldn't help the smile quirking his lips at the thought.

And now?

Now that he'd felt her soften and go pliant underneath his touch, even knowing all she did about him? Could he ever let her go?

Again the answer came swiftly.

Never.

He cleared his throat and Persephone jolted, spinning around to look his way.

"The driver is waiting with the car."

Persephone nodded. "Of course. Let me get my shawl."

Hades had it over his forearm and he held it out to her. It was a luxurious mink shawl and he draped it around her shoulders.

He wrapped it around her and captured her arms with it, pulling her back against his chest and dropping his nose to the back of her neck. Her hair was done up, exposing the area.

He inhaled deeply and dropped a kiss right behind her ear. "You look exquisite tonight," he breathed.

"T-thank you," she stuttered.

Hades smiled against the back of her neck, held her captive another moment, and finally let her go.

"Come," he said, finally pulling back. "We don't want to miss the opening act."

She nodded but Hades didn't miss the way her breath hitched.

She turned and he took her arm, guiding her out of the penthouse and to where the driver was waiting outside the lobby with the Bentley.

Neither of them said a word until Hades had her tucked safely in the back of the car.

When Hades spoke, Persephone looked over at him in surprise. "Persephone, I want you to know..." He was usually quiet in the car. It was one of the few places where all the noise and people wanting his time and attention stopped.

But right now, he was more interested in Persephone. He wanted to make her understand.

"I wasn't always like this."

Persephone's eyebrows knit together and she didn't say anything, but he definitely had her attention.

"Growing up, my father always wanted the best for his family. He would've done anything for my mother and us kids. But he was an immigrant and powerless to stand up to the Titan family. They used to run the streets."

Now he definitely had Persephone's attention.

"The so-called 'protection tax' the Titans asked for ate up almost all my father's income. Everyone else's too. So my father decided to do something. He hadn't come to this land only to be poor and starving like in the old country."

Persephone hadn't taken her eyes off him.

"And Gino Ubeli was a natural leader. He built the outfit up from nothing and within five years, he was challenging the Titans for territory. It was all out war. The Titans had held a monopoly over New Olympus for decades by that point, but their supremacy had made them lax in enforcement."

"It was Karl, Ian, and Alexander's father who had created the Titan Empire, they were just the heirs. They'd never fought for territory before and they were laughably bad at holding onto it."

Persephone swallowed hard but she didn't avert her gaze, not even when he said her father's name. *Karl.*

"They thought to crack down by becoming more vicious in their collection endeavors. They went after not only the men who owed them, but their families. It had the opposite effect they intended. Because my father promised people that he lived by a Code. No one would suffer but the sinners themselves. The innocent would be left out of it."

Hades's eyes drifted to the window as he thought of Chiara. "My father held fast to his Code until the day he died."

Hades shifted his gaze back to Persephone. "The Titans, however, lived by no such Code."

"Chiara," Persephone said.

Hades nodded but he couldn't say more about his sister. Not tonight. Maybe not ever. "Anyway, that's how it began. I took over for my father and I tried to enforce his Code. It might not be anything you could ever believe, but I do what I do to keep those like Chiara safe." Even as he said it, though, he felt his own hypocrisy. Because no one was more like Chiara than the woman sitting on the seat beside him.

Persephone's small hand found his.

He pulled away. What was wrong with her? How could she look at him like that, with eyes brimming full of sympathy? Her family and his were natural enemies from the day both of them had been born.

She had no business looking at him with understanding. Especially after what he'd done to her.

He didn't even know why he was saying all this. Why was he trying to pretend that he was anything other than what he was?

"Forget about it."

"No. No, Hades, no."

She grabbed his hand again. "You look at me this time." He looked at her if only because nobody else had the balls to try to order him around like that.

"I'm so sorry for what happened to your sister, Hades. I'm so sorry that any of this happened. We should have met in a different world where you were just a man and I was just a woman."

He shook his head, but he couldn't help reaching out and caressing a thumb down her face and over the apple of her cheek. So much of his life dedicated to protecting it and he'd almost forgotten what it looked like—true innocence.

"You're a marvel," he murmured.

He continued tracing with his thumb, over to her mouth and across her plump bottom lip. She sucked in a sharp gasp at his touch.

He smiled. She was so affected by him. Even when she'd professed to hate him, she'd always been so affected.

The devil in him drove him to thrust his thumb between those sweet lips. This was *her* effect on him. It was impossible to see her innocence without wanting to have it all to himself.

Her tongue darted forward to lick the pad of his thumb in her mouth and immediately his dress slacks became uncomfortably tight.

He only pulled back with reluctance. As much as he'd like to shove that fancy dress up and pull her into his lap, he didn't trust that he wouldn't rip the damn thing off considering the things he felt like doing to her. And he wanted to give her this night.

She loved the theater. She lit up reading the stupid brochure the night of the auction. The desire to put her needs first was a strange impulse he felt himself giving into more and more.

He was glad when they arrived on Theater Row and the driver pulled to a stop. Sometimes the train of his own thoughts around Persephone unsettled him.

Several of his Shades approached the car as he helped Persephone out. He raised his chin to each of them, all men he trusted. They would be on guard at all times tonight, both in and outside the theater. Charon was still lying low.

Hades took Persephone's arm as they headed into the theater. It was the largest and grandest theater on the Row, with a huge marquee all lit up with flashing bulbs. Hades wanted to hustle Persephone inside but she'd stopped, staring up at it all, her eyes wide, perfect lips parted, glowing like a goddess.

Hades stood there drinking her in for a moment. Too long a moment. It wasn't safe here out on the street. Hades frowned and grabbed her arm more firmly.

"Let's go," he ordered gruffly.

Persephone huffed, obviously annoyed at him but he ignored her. She never understood even the basics of what it took to stay safe in a city like this. Obviously. She'd walked right into his waiting clutches when he was so obviously a lion and she a lamb.

Well, she might not have any instinct for self-preservation, but he did, and he'd keep her safe no matter what. Safe from everyone but him.

He led her up the grand, red carpeted staircase and down the secluded hallway to the balcony of the box seats. Ushers looked at them as if to ask about their tickets but as soon as they got close enough and recognized Hades's face, they simply dropped their heads and scurried away again.

Box seats weren't always the best seats in the house but they were in this theater. Hades helped Persephone settle into the front row of the box seat that provided a perfect, unimpeded view of the entire stage and orchestra.

Even though nothing was happening yet, Persephone seemed mesmerized, using the tiny binoculars to look at all the people who were arriving.

"Everyone looks so fancy," she whispered, breathless.

Hades smiled at her. Her neck was long and elegant with her hair done up like that. He followed the lines down to her creamy chest and the smallest peek of cleavage afforded by the elegant gown. He could barely wait until later tonight. He could imagine it, what the buttery soft velvet would feel like under his skin as he grabbed her around the waist and slowly, slowly slid down the zipper at the back, unwrapping his prize.

"Oh, sorry," Persephone said, dropping the little bronze binoculars and holding them out to him. "Did you want to look?"

"Everything I want to look at I see just fine," he murmured, taking another slow perusal of her body up and down.

Her cheeks flushed such a pretty pink in contrast to the pale of the rest of her face. She was so young and fresh, like an unplucked petal.

"What am I going to do with you?"

Her eyebrows wrinkled the tiniest bit and Hades could have sworn he saw a quiver to her lip. Her features were full of unchecked emotion and vulnerability. As if a word from him could make or break her.

Foolish girl. Foolish, foolish girl.

But how could he berate her for it when it was what he lo—

He shook his head—when it was what he *appreciated* about her most?

But he was disturbed enough by his almost mental slip up to turn away from her. Luckily, the lights around the theater began to dim at the same time.

"The show is about to start," he said unnecessarily, lifting a hand and running it through the back of his hair.

He was glad when darkness settled completely over the box and lights focused down on the stage.

The play was a modern retelling of *Romeo and Juliet*. Hades had sat through it before but not paid much attention to the narrative. The theater was a nice, respectable place to meet up with contacts who didn't feel comfortable coming to visit the Underworld.

He couldn't say he was getting much more out of the show this time around, either. It was much more fascinating to watch the play of emotions on Persephone's face instead.

Her hands clutched the wooden railing of the box seat as she bent over, mesmerized for the entire production. At the end, copious tears poured down her cheeks and she jumped to her feet, clapping furiously.

She wasn't shy about sharing her thoughts, either. As soon as the lights came back up, she was talking a mile a minute.

"If she'd just woken up a minute sooner," she gushed, tears still wet on her cheeks. "Or if he hadn't been so stupid and rash in killing himself like that. And nobody should rely on a stupid bike messenger when it's about life and death! What were they thinking?!"

Hades nodded to his Shades as they exited the theater, putting his hand to the small of Persephone's back and leading her to the car that was waiting at the curb.

"How did you not even tear up?" Persephone exclaimed, pausing on the sidewalk. "Did you not just watch the same play that I did?"

Did she know how kissable she looked when she was in a pique?

Hades smiled down at her. "In the car," was all he said.

Persephone shook her head at him but scooted into the car after he held open the door for her.

He got in and instructed the driver, "Take us back to the Estate." The driver's head dipped, formal as always with his round chauffeur's cap firmly in place.

"I mean Juliet was so sweet and smart, Romeo should've known she would've found another way to be with him. If only he would've trusted her—"

Hades silenced her with a kiss. He'd wanted to do it since midway through the first act when she'd begun biting that luscious bottom lip in anxiety over the lovers on stage.

He sucked her bottom lip into his mouth and nipped at it with his teeth until a petite little groan escaped her throat. Fuck, yes. It was so easy to lose himself in her. In the feel of her soft body molded to his as he laid her down across the backseat. In the taste of her on his lips.

She was so innocent. Good. Pure...

Except for the ways he alone could defile her. No other man would ever hear those little breathy aroused noises she made. No one else would ever revel in her delighted giggle as they ran their stubbled cheek along her neck.

He would never let her go. She was his, for always.

She'd come into his life like the sun bursting through the clouds after a long, frozen winter. He'd tried to deny it. He hadn't wanted to admit how precious she was to him. He'd been so blinded by his agenda and his thirst for revenge, but now...

He looked down at the face that brought him so much... He shook his head as he pulled back and brushed a wisp of hair behind her ear.

"Persephone, these last couple of months with you... I never thought that I..."

Her eyes searched back and forth between his. "You never thought that you...?"

She looked like her life depended on what he was about to say next.

But something had caught his eye out the window—First Athens Bank? Why were they on Athena Boulevard? They were supposed to be heading east out of the city to get back to the Estate.

Hades frowned and looked in the rearview to try to catch the driver's eye. As if feeling his gaze, the driver glanced back at him.

The eyes were feminine and he didn't have any female Shades.

Shi—

It all happened so fast. The driver stomped on the brakes and the car wheels screeched, Hades barely had time to wrap his arms around Persephone, and they were both thrown forward against the seat in front of them. At least Persephone always put her seatbelt on and the driver's seat stopped Hades from flying too far forward, although it hurt like a son of a bitch when he rammed into it. Persephone's terrified scream filled the car.

Hades didn't bother shouting. There was no time. He had to focus. He had to get Persephone out of there. As soon as the car stopped—

The car finally came to a stop and Hades struggled with Persephone's seatbelt to get it undone.

"Take your hands off her. Hands up."

"*Mom?* What are you doing?!"

Hades turned and there she was. Demeter Titan, pulling off the chauffeur's hat that had hidden all her dark brown hair and tossing it to the side.

She held a sizable pistol, the barrel pointed straight at Hades's chest.

"Persephone, get out of the car," Demeter ordered.

"Mom, put the gun down!"

Demeter never took her eyes off of Hades even as her voice got sharper with her daughter. "Get out of the car now or the gods help me, Persephone, you won't like the consequences."

Hades already had reason to hate this woman but her treatment of Persephone only cemented it. If he moved quick enough, he could jam the gun upward and even if she got a round off, it would land harmlessly in the—

"Tell your sister I send my fondest regards," Demeter said. "Poetic justice, if you think about it. Mine was the last face she ever saw, too."

Wait, what? *She'd* killed Chiara—

"Mama! No! I love—"

Two things happened at once, simultaneously, really. It was a moment Hades would live and relive over and over again in his memory. Why hadn't he seen what Persephone had? Why hadn't he realized that Demeter was done eulogizing?

Because there was the explosion of a gun firing right at the same time as Persephone's body slammed into Hades's.

Demeter's agonized scream only reinforced what his brain refused to process.

No.

Persephone hadn't really just jumped in front of a bullet for him.

She wasn't *that* foolish.

But when he pushed her back onto the seat, her face was ghostly pale and, though not immediately visible against the red velvet of her dress, his hand came away slick with her blood when he touched the left side of her chest.

Demeter had thrown away the gun and was screaming and reaching back to try to get to her daughter, but Hades shoved her away.

"Drive! She's going into shock, get us to New Olympian General. We're five minutes out."

Blood streamed down Persephone's bare arm now and pooled on the leather seat underneath her.

Hades put pressure on the wound. "Stay with me. Persephone, do you hear me?" he barked. "Stay with me, dammit!"

Persephone's dazed eyes drifted toward him but he wasn't sure she heard him at all. Fuck!

"Drive faster," he shouted to the front.

Demeter didn't say anything but she did run the next red light, barely skirting past an oncoming car. Hades didn't care. Persephone's breath was labored and her eyes were erratic.

"Stay with me. Stay with me, Persephone." It was all he could say. He kept chanting it until it was a prayer.

She couldn't leave him. She couldn't fucking leave him now that he'd found her. He couldn't go back to—to— There was no life for him without her in it.

"We're here," Demeter called and Hades looked up to see that they were indeed at the hospital, at the emergency room entrance.

Demeter pulled the car all the way up to the entrance and several emergency room techs ran out.

Hades shoved open the back door. "Bullet wound, upper left chest. She's losing a lot of blood."

Several more techs had brought a gurney and together they expertly lifted Persephone out of the car and up onto the gurney.

Hades followed behind as they wheeled her into the hospital. He only spared one glance back for Demeter, standing beside the driver side door, watching her daughter be wheeled away.

He should have texted his lieutenants right then and there to grab the woman before she could sneak out of the city.

Instead, he kept running beside the gurney. Blood, there was so much blood. It was even more apparent against the white of the gurney sheets. So much blood. Just like Chiara. It was just like Chiara, and what if he lost Persephone, too?

More people joined the procession running beside Persephone as they flew down the hall with her. Nurses, doctors, all of them calling out questions and medical jargon that Hades could only half follow.

He clasped Persephone's hand and kept up his mantra, interspersing, "Stay with me," with "I won't ever let you go."

But as they finally wheeled Persephone into a room for surgery, an orderly pushed Hades back. "You can't come in here, sir."

Hades glowered at the man and got right in his face. "She's my wife," he growled. "And she just got shot. You do not want to try to get between me and her right now."

The orderly looked like he was about to shit himself but with a wobbling chin, he repeated, "No loved ones allowed in during surgery, sir."

"Do we have a problem here?" asked a second man, a nurse who had moved from Persephone's side to join the orderly, blocking the door.

"Get back to my wife's side," Hades all but shouted. "What the fuck are you doing over here? She needs you over there." He pointed back to where four people hovered around his wife, all of them working on her. He wanted to be beside her as well, holding her hand, promising her he'd make everything okay again.

But that was a crock of shit.

There was every chance that nothing would be okay. That she would *die*.

The orderly put his hand on Hades's arm to try to guide him out of the room and Hades shoved him off. But he turned of his own accord, not wanting to distract them all from the far more important work of focusing on Persephone. He stormed down the hallway several paces as they shut the door to Persephone's room.

For a second, he was completely at a loss.

What was he supposed to—

How could he—

He turned to the hallway wall and banged both fists against it, letting out an enraged roar.

What the *fuck* had she been thinking?

Throwing her body in front of a *bullet* for him?

Why would she do that?

Why the fuck would she do something so fucking idiotic?

He'd effectively kidnapped her for gods' sake. He'd seduced and married her under false pretenses. Put a collar around her neck and chained her to the bed. Who in their right mind would take a bullet for someone like that?

If she wasn't dying in the other room, he would go and fucking strangle her for her stupidity.

He wanted to strangle someone, that was for damn sure. Someone needed to pay. Blood for blood.

He whipped his phone out of his pocket finally and dialed Angelo before even calling Charon.

"Yeah, boss?"

"You've got your war. Hit the vulnerable targets you've talked about in Metropolis. I want blood. I want the streets to rain with fucking blood."

25

The war with the Titans was begun. And Persephone was in a coma.

It was a medically-induced coma, the doctors kept reminding Hades, as if that was supposed to make him feel better.

They said she would wake up any time now. But they'd been saying that for days. And she still hadn't woken up.

The bullet had entered her chest and gone down into her gut, which was better than if it had traveled toward her heart or lungs, but still—fucking *coma*.

Hades sat by her hospital bed, her cold little hand lifeless in his. When he wasn't conferring with his lieutenants, he was here. Sitting on this hard, plastic chair, holding her hand.

Oh, what the great Hades Ubeli had been reduced to. He squeezed his stinging eyes with his thumb and forefinger.

"The doctor said it's good to talk to you. That hearing familiar voices might help you, I don't know." He shook his head, looking out the window at the cold, dreary, rainy day. "Might make you wake up faster. Or that you might still be able to hear my voice or some bullsh—"

"Anyway," he leaned forward, giving her hand a squeeze. "I'm not sure if my voice is one you'd be excited to wake up for, all things considered... But I'm all you've got."

None of his Shades had been able to get a beat on Demeter before she slipped out of the city. Which was probably a good thing. Hades didn't trust himself with her if he ever got his hands on the woman. She put Persephone in this bed. But not only that.

Tell your sister I send my fondest regards. Mine was the last face she ever saw, too.

If Demeter was telling the truth, it hadn't been Persephone's father after all who'd killed his sister. And why would she lie? She'd thought it was Hades's last moment on earth. No, she was telling the truth.

And the more Hades thought about it, the more it made sense.

The Titans had been a smart outfit back in the day. They hadn't just been brawn, there'd been brains behind the operation as well.

Except that after they got kicked out of New Olympus and retreated to Metropolis, they devolved to being just brawn.

Because Demeter had taken off with her small daughter. And she'd been the brains all along. It was only because she was back that the Titans were able to do the scheming and machinations it took to even attempt to retake their territory in New Olympus.

It had been right under Hades's nose the entire time and he hadn't seen it. Demeter was a woman in a traditionally man's game and she'd used that fact to make everyone underestimate her. Including Hades.

It wasn't a mistake he'd be making again.

So many mistakes.

"This wasn't supposed to happen." Hades let go of Persephone's hand and shoved his chair back, standing up. "None of this was supposed to happen." He kicked the chair for good measure.

"I had a plan. I had a plan and you weren't supposed to be— I was never supposed to..."

He shook his head, then he walked back to her bed and put a finger in her face. "I didn't ask for this. I'm a simple man. I want simple things. To keep a lid on this city when every godsdamned day some new idiot thinks they are gonna try being a big shot and steal somebody else's territory. I keep the drug running to a minimum, I see that it stays out of the schools, I make sure Santino treats his girls okay, and gods knows no gun goes in or out of the city without my say-so."

He got further in Persephone's face. "And do I do it for the money?" He laughed, pulling back. "What the hell would I do with more money? You see how I live. Money is only good because it gets you power. That's the only currency I ever cared about. Without me calling the shots, this whole place would go to shit. I know because I tried once, letting someone else take the lead. But I already told you that."

Hades collapsed on the side of Persephone's bed. Her slim body was so small, there was plenty of room. "What I didn't tell you was that it was *me* that got my sister killed. I should've claimed my birthright the day my mother and father were gunned down. But I didn't." His voice almost broke on the last word. His deepest fucking shame.

"I let them down and I let Chiara down." He bent over Persephone's body and whispered his confession with his forehead to hers. "It's my fault she died. We hid. For an entire year, we hid away at the Estate. I *didn't* continue the work my father had started. I let the Titans run rampant in the city, naïvely thinking they'd leave us alone."

He shook his head, his voice a bleak whisper. "We were both kids. Teenagers. I thought they'd leave us alone."

But it hadn't mattered to Persephone's mother. Hades should have known any Ubeli would be considered a threat as long as they drew breath.

Hades hadn't even considered it, though. Because his father lived by a Code. Women and children were left out of it, kept separate from the business. It was Gino Ubeli's most sacred law.

But he should have known that the Titans had no such scruples. He should have known and, even though he was young, he should have taken up the mantle his father had left behind. He knew the business. His father had begun schooling him from the time he was eleven. All the players knew him well.

They certainly hadn't minded taking orders from him a year later when he was sixteen. Then again, he hadn't been a normal sixteen-year-old. After Chiara's death...

Mom had always said he was a sensitive child. But he'd numbed any sensitive parts he had left and made himself a robot.

He executed men without even the blink of an eye. He felt nothing. And he'd gone on feeling nothing. For so long that it became normal. It was good for business. He could make the ruthless calls without emotion.

"Until you, Persephone," he whispered, lifting his head and looking up at her. "Please come back to me. Come back to me, Persephone." He cupped her face roughly. "You have to come back to me. You've made me feel again and it scares the shit out of me. I was never supposed to feel this deep ever again. I was never supposed to love anyone—"

He pressed his lips to hers but they were cold and unmoving underneath his.

"Wake up," he commanded. "Wake up!" She was always so good at obeying before. Why the fuck not now?

He shook her shoulders in frustration. With great effort, he stopped. What the hell was he doing? He let her go and stood up again, taking a step back. Jesus Christ. He turned his back on her and scraped his hands through his hair.

What the hell was he doing? He was acting crazy.

And he didn't love her.

He couldn't.

What was he doing here day after day, hovering over her bed like a lovesick schoolboy? It was because of her that he hadn't taken action sooner against the Titans.

Again. He'd been lulled into thinking that there was a path forward that could actually lead to peace, when long experience had taught him that brute force and violence was the only language the world understood.

He turned for the door. No, softness had no place in his life.

He opened the door only to find Charon on the other side, his fist raised like he was about to knock.

"What is it?" Hades barked.

Charon looked him up and down. "Brother, are you all right?"

Hades glared at the bigger man even though Charon towered over him. Things had really gone to shit if his second in command thought to question him so intimately. That was not how their relationship worked. Hades gave commands and Charon enacted them. Charon offered wise counsel at times and could play devil's advocate with the best of them. But never did they ask one another about their personal lives or their fucking feelings.

"Report," Hades demanded.

Apparently Charon wasn't giving in that easily, though. "It's okay to take a minute," Charon rumbled. "You care for the girl. I see how you are around her and I like what I see."

Well, now Charon was really starting to piss him off.

"You saw me playing a part," Hades snapped. "Persephone was always a chess piece for me to play against the Titans. And she served her purpose. She drew Demeter out and now we know who's the real brains behind the operation. And as an added bonus, wifey dearest made herself a shield and took a bullet for me. I'd say that's mission accomplished as far as she's concerned, better than I ever could've hoped for. Plus, she's a great lay, so—"

"That's enough," Charon cut him off, stepping up and getting right in his face. "I know you're hurting and that's the only reason I'm not—"

But then Charon's head jerked up as something behind Hades's shoulder caught his eye and he pushed Hades to the side.

"Bella, you're awake!"

26

Ten Minutes Earlier

EVERYTHING WAS DARK. So dark and cold.

Persephone had never felt colder in her entire life, or more alone. It was like being locked in the cellar but a million times worse. In the cellar, at least she'd been able to feel the floor beneath her feet. She could count the steps up to the door, nine steps up and nine steps back down. There were the brick walls. How many hours had she spent feeling along the contours of each one, memorizing them?

But here in the void, there was nothing. She tried to scream but no noise came out. She tried to flail her arms but they wouldn't move. She couldn't even feel them. She heard voices, muted, coming from very far away through the dark fog.

I'm here! I'm right here. Come and find me!

But no one ever heard her. No one lifted a hand down into the darkness.

The voices moved away.

But they'd come back. Closer. She concentrated so hard. *Please*, she begged.

And she heard it. Clear as a ringing bell.

His voice. Calling her name.

"Persephone."

Everything within her, all of her soul, recognized him.

Yes, I'm here!

"Come back to me, Persephone."

I'm here. I'm here, can't you see me?

He was commanding her to wake up and for the first time after wandering for so long in the darkness, in that terrible, terrible void, she felt something. Actually *felt* it.

His hands on her face.

She was back in her body. She could feel her limbs, her arms and legs and face and fingers and her nose.

Her lips. Her lips that he was kissing.

But he was gone, pulling away right as sensation came back to her body in lapping waves, a little more each second.

And with it came a terrible heaviness. She was back in her body again, but it felt like she'd gained five hundred pounds. She tried to lift her hand to signal Hades but it was a lead weight. It wouldn't budge.

Her eyelids felt the same but she cracked them determinedly open.

Blinding light split the darkness and everything tumbled together, the void and the light and Hades. Persephone wanted to cry and she wanted Hades to hold her again. She wanted his hand in hers. She remembered that, how he would hold her hand sometimes.

Was he even still here?

She dropped her eyes closed again and listened. *Yes.* There was his voice. And Charon. They were both here.

She had to let them know she was awake. What if they left her because they didn't know she was here? She couldn't let them leave, she couldn't let them—

So, even though it took everything she had, she forced her eyelids open again, but she wasn't any better prepared for the blinding light.

She focused on the voices to help steady her and forced her eyes open even wider.

And that's when she heard his voice again. His precious voice.

But... The things he was saying...

Persephone was a chess piece... served her purpose... mission accomplished... a great lay.

Persephone blinked. Once and then again. No. Someone was playing a trick on her. Or her mind was. She wasn't awake yet after all. This was a horrible dream because her Hades would never say things so cold and callous. She meant something to Hades. Didn't she?

Liar. How many lies had she told herself to make her situation more palatable? She'd done it back when she lived with her mother and all over again with Hades. Telling herself they loved her. A thousand times even when all the evidence was to the contrary.

Pathetic.

"Bella, you're awake." Charon at least sounded genuine in his excitement at seeing her awake.

The light was still painful but Persephone dragged tired eyes over toward the large man as he hurried to her bedside. Her vision was a bit blurry but she didn't miss Hades in the background keeping his distance.

Charon took her hand and, focusing, she managed to give a wan squeeze.

She let her eyes close again.

Now she knew the truth. She and Hades weren't star-crossed lovers or any of the rest of the romantic bullshit she'd made up in her head.

She was still the puppet and everyone else still thought they were pulling the strings.

"I'm gonna take you home," Hades told her as he walked over, and she bowed her head in agreement.

One thing was sure, though.

She'd never let herself be taken in by Hades Ubeli again. She'd escape New Olympus and his clutches as well as her mother's. She'd find someplace she could truly be free.

And in the meantime, she imagined lifting her leaden fist to her chest, she'd be free where it mattered most—the part of her that none of them could ever touch.

***

Read several extra scenes from Hades' perspective: sign up at https://geni.us/Hadesextras

PART II
AWAKENING

"The god of Love has conquered me..."
Orpheus, Ovid's Metamorphoses Book X

27

Persephone leaned against the giant window in the expansive living room of the most expensive penthouse in the most expensive hotel in New Olympus.

Far, far below, people scurried like ants down the narrow sidewalks. Cars crawled through rush hour traffic.

If Persephone waited long enough with her face pressed against the glass, would she see a woman, young and beautiful with stars in her eyes, step off the bus and spin in a slow circle, mouth parted in awe at the magnificent cityscape? Maybe the young woman would look up and imagine someone like Persephone, diamonds in her ears and hair sleekly coiffed away from her made-up face.

Would the young woman be wistful, wondering what it'd be like to live in the penthouse and float in the beautiful world above the streets? If she could hear Persephone whisper, *Get back on the bus, run away,* would the young woman escape before the darkness swallowed her whole?

Persephone backed away from the window, chest heaving. Only months ago, she'd been that young woman. The city had been beautiful, overwhelming and alien, a far cry from the blue skies and waving wheat of the farm she'd grown up on back in Kansas.

She'd been full of so much hope. She'd ascended the heights and now she lived in her husband's penthouse, with everything she could desire. Diamonds and dresses, fine art decorating the elegant apartment.

Every morning someone delivered fresh flowers to a giant vase on a pedestal by the door. The blooms filled the open space with their delicate floral scent. The lilies of the field, plucked and cut and perfectly arranged to live one day at the height of their beauty. And tomorrow? Tomorrow they'd be gone. Thrown away.

Persephone crossed to the front door and ran a finger over the silky petals. Here was a rosebud, tightly furled. She could pull it out and place it in a cup of water. It wouldn't look as grand, but it would still be here tomorrow. She could save one flower. It might be enough...

Crossing the room, she caught a glimpse of herself in a giant gilt mirror. A young face stared back at her, pale and lovely under layers of artful makeup. She'd spent all day at Hermes's spa and every inch of her skin was plucked, smoothed, and polished. Her hair had been cut and styled as well.

When she'd lived on her mother's farm, she'd wear old overalls, t-shirts, a farmer's tan and freckles were her only adornment, and go months without examining herself closely in a mirror.

These days, every inch of her was scrutinized, first by her stylists, then by society when she went out on Hades's arm. The wife of a wealthy businessman must look the part.

Especially if that man's business had deep ties to the city's criminal underworld.

Hades Ubeli, the ruler of New Olympus' underworld. Her husband.

When *he* stood by the window, he only saw his kingdom. His abject subjects scurrying far below. They saw only what he wanted them to see, an elegant businessman, handsome and shrewd, with a new and pretty wife.

They applauded his philanthropy and patronized his legit businesses—and only half listened to the whispers about his dark dealings. Only the rich and ultra-powerful knew the truth about Hades Ubeli. He had a representative on every shadowy street corner. Cops, judges and juries were in his pocket. Even the mayor owed him favors.

By the time you learned the truth about Hades Ubeli, it was too late. He owned you, too.

And Persephone was his most prized possession.

Yes, she lived a grand life, far above the masses. Weekly spa visits, shopping sprees, meals in the finest restaurants, entry into the glittering nightlife of New Olympus high society. Beautiful clothes, a magnificent penthouse with its amazing view.

She preferred volunteering at the animal shelter downtown and curling up on a couch with a book, but it didn't matter. She was a cut flower in a gorgeous vase, beautiful and elegant and dying a little more each day.

Oh yes, she played her part perfectly in exchange for this new life her husband had given her. Because that's all it was: an even exchange.

Four months ago, she'd thrown herself in front of a bullet for him and saved his life. So now he'd given her all the freedoms she desired, even those that he himself had once denied her... She thought back to those days, miserable but also sort of wonderful through the haze of recollection. Because back then she'd been naïve enough to believe her husband could one day love her.

He'd disabused her of those notions while she lay on her hospital bed after being shot, just coming out of a coma. He didn't know she'd overheard him, which made it all the worse because it meant he'd been telling the truth.

Persephone was always a chess piece for me to play against the Titans. And she served her purpose... As an added bonus, wifey dearest made herself a shield and took a bullet for me. I'd say that's mission accomplished as far as she's concerned, better than I ever could've hoped for. Plus, she's a great lay, so...

She was just a possession. That was all she'd ever be to him. He'd never loved her. He'd seen her as a commodity and a tool to use against his enemies. And as someone convenient to warm his bed at night. It was all she would ever be to him. He simply wasn't capable of feeling anything more. At least not for her, a Titan.

Not after finding out that her mom, Demeter, had murdered his sister in cold blood. And come back fifteen years later to finish the job on Hades himself, no matter the fact that Persephone had begged her not to do it, to put the gun down, to *stop*.

Persephone had chosen Hades.

And taken the bullet meant for him.

She still had the four-inch scar on her stomach from where they'd had to operate to take the bullet out.

But after her recovery, what had there been to come back to? This life, stuck in the no man's land between two rival gangs, shunned by one because of who she loved but never fully embraced by the other.

"Persephone." Hades's deep voice rolled across the room.

She jerked her head up in surprise.

Her husband stood next to the floral bouquet. When had he come in? She hadn't even heard the front door open, she'd been so deep in her own head.

Hades was as handsome as ever, the most gorgeous man she'd ever seen, if she was being honest. His hands were in his pockets and his face was tilted into the shadows enough that she couldn't read his expression. Not that she'd be able to read him even if the room were lit with a hundred blinding light bulbs. She didn't even try anymore.

She knew who he was and what was in his heart. She'd heard him loud and clear. In the days and weeks following the coma, his coldness toward her only reconfirmed everything he'd said that day.

He was solicitous towards her. He provided the best medical care money could buy. He continued giving her countless gifts but he never delivered them himself. His driver, Charon, drove her to rehab every day for two months as she regained her strength.

But Hades worked dawn till dusk and she could go entire days, once an entire week, without seeing him. He was awake before dawn and back long after she fell asleep. Often he'd sleep in the guest bedroom, saying he didn't want to wake her with his erratic hours.

He never came to any doctor's appointments yet still seemed to know every last detail of her care regimen. When he did talk to her it was to remind her to take her supplements or to ask if she'd eaten enough. And the day the doctor pronounced her well enough to resume physical activity, he came to their bed at night and made love to her in the dark.

The sex was as intense as ever. Their chemistry in bed was undeniable. Some nights his kisses felt frantic as he wrapped his arms around her and pulled her against him so tightly it was like he was afraid she'd disappear.

Sometimes it was fast, his mouth or hands on her working to bring her to a desperate, wild release, and then he'd bury himself inside her and spill within minutes. Only to wake her up hours later in the middle of the night with his need pressing against her backside, and then he'd take her slowly, so achingly slowly that she thought she might die.

But always in the dark. And when morning came, he was gone as if the night had never been.

Tonight he wore his signature suit, and he looked just as fresh and unwrinkled as he had when he first put it on the day before. His effortless, controlled perfection was as much a mystery to her as on their first day of marriage. His black hair fell across his brow as he looked her up and down.

She stared back out the window, unmoving. "You're home early."

"We're going out tonight—remember? I thought you'd be ready."

She had on makeup, high heels, and a coiffed updo fresh from the spa, but the rest of her was still wrapped in a robe.

She hadn't forgotten but still she said, "We're going out?"

"The concert at Elysium. New act. A big one."

She looked Hades's way again as he shrugged and she watched his face carefully. She found herself doing this more and more lately —poking the bear to see if she could get some reaction out of him, some proof that he was really human and could show genuine human emotion. As usual, though, his poker face gave nothing away.

"I always give a photo op on opening night," he continued.

"I didn't forget," she said, turning fully towards him and letting the light christen her hair. He had to squint to try to see her. "In fact, I went shopping for just the right outfit."

"Did you now?" He rubbed the dark shadow around his jaw, the only evidence of his long work day.

She undid her robe and let it fall in a rustle of silk. As she moved closer, she watched her husband's eyes grow hot as they took in her body. A black lace camisole with built in bra cupped her breasts. A sexy garter belt was slung low around her waist, holding her sheer black stockings up.

Persephone felt satisfaction at the intense look on his face. "What do you think?"

This was all they had between them.

Sex. Fucking. That was how Persephone thought of it now—as fucking. Or at least how she tried to think of it.

Hades liked fucking her.

She was a good lay, after all, right?

Her teeth ground together at the memory. It was just another reason she'd chosen her outfit so carefully. Sex was a weapon that plenty of women used to control the men in their lives, right? No one would ever control Hades but if she could even get the slightest edge up on him, it would be something. She was determined that the next time they had sex, it would be on her terms. In the light where he'd be forced to see her face.

Hades studied her carefully, letting the silence lengthen between them. He smirked, the barest upward quirk of his lips.

"I think the paparazzi will eat it up."

He prowled forward, put a commanding hand to the back of her neck, and drew her head to his.

She told herself not to open to him, to play hard to get—after all, what would entice the man who had everything more than being denied the one thing he seemed to crave?—but the second his lips touched hers, her body went liquid. Such was his power over her. Damn it all to hell.

How did he always manage to do that? To get the upper hand? She'd been so determined to master *him* for once.

But when Hades pulled back for a moment, his dark eyes catching hers, a jolt of pleasure shot through her.

"I like finding you like this," he whispered. "Waiting so eagerly. Wanting."

He lifted her up and settled her on the small makeup bureau. Kneeling, he parted her legs and leaned forward to inhale deeply, his teeth catching at the top of her lace panties. "I like smelling how much you want me."

Persephone felt her face flame. For as calm, cold, and professional as Hades was on the outside to everyone else she'd ever seen him interact with, it was still shocking how crass and brutish he could sometimes be in bed. Or on the makeup bureau, as it were.

She rubbed her legs together but he wasn't having it. He shoved her thighs open wide and stepped between them as he rose back up, the front of his fancy suit pants jutting obscenely. He made quick work of unbuckling and unzipping them. And all her plans went out the window. She just wanted him inside her now, whatever way she could have him.

She thought he might shove into her quick and harsh, like he often did in the dark. No matter how many times she told herself, *not again*, she always ended up welcoming him into her arms, clinging to him, and spending all day living for the half hour at night when his hands would reach for her in the darkness.

In those moments, it was so easy to let herself forget the truth of their situation. That to him, she was only a trophy of his latest victory. Because he *had* been victorious in quelling the brief insurgency the Titans had attempted on New Olympus. It had been months and there was no word from the gang her mother now apparently ran.

Hades had triumphed, as he always did. There was no point resisting him. He had a will unlike anyone she had ever met and that was saying something, considering that she'd been raised by Demeter Titan.

And yet still Persephone had to cling to her sense of self. She couldn't let herself be obliterated by Hades completely. It was why she continued her futile campaign to gain the upper hand in this marriage. She might never escape him but it didn't mean she had to be tormented forever by her unrequited love for him.

But wait, no, she *didn't* love him. It had merely been infatuation.

And it was an infatuation she would cure herself of, one way or another... But she'd been trying for months with no success.

In the meantime, she meant to gain more of an even footing with him. It was why she'd thrown herself so violently into society life. She was determined to have a life apart from him. And maybe, if she asserted herself more in their bed play, then she wouldn't feel so completely overwhelmed by him each time and so shattered in the aftermath.

She could only piece herself back together so many times.

Because while she knew in her head that to Hades it was only fucking, to her stupid heart it often felt like making love.

Which was why she'd put on her armor today and surprised him in a full-frontal assault.

But five minutes later, he had her on her back and one hand splayed ever so gently across her throat.

His dark eyes searched hers for a quick moment and her breath caught. He was so gorgeous, his face sculpted with sharp lines and commanding angles. Even through the tux she could feel the power of his large body, muscles bulging against the expensive tailored fabric.

She lifted a hand, reaching toward his cheek. How long since she'd seen him like this in the light of day?

But he grabbed her wrist before she could make contact and slammed her wrist to the bed above her head, pinning it there. She couldn't help the whimper that escaped her at the commanding move. Everything he did turned her on. Everything he was.

She thought he would pull himself out and take her right there. She was only a few seconds away from begging for it.

Instead, though, he pulled back and flipped her over so that she was on her hands and knees. He didn't make her wait long, though.

He dragged her lace underwear down and immediately stroked inside her. She was drenched and his passage was smooth.

Apparently he wasn't looking for smooth.

He pulled out and rammed into her roughly and gods, it felt so good. Like he was claiming her. Like she'd actually managed to rile him up for once.

She shifted her backside needily against him and he swore, clutching her hips in a punishing grip as he continued to pound into her.

She tried to look over her shoulder at him but he wasn't having it. He put a hand on her neck urging her down to the bed, ass up.

He followed, his body dominating hers as his relentless thrusting continued. "Next time you think to tempt me with such slinky little underthings, goddess," he hissed in her ear, "remember to be careful what you wish for. You only make me want to remind you who you belong to."

She'd been on the edge since he first thrust into her but his words sent her over. He was hitting that perfect spot deep inside. Yes, oh gods, *yes*.

In order to stop herself from howling Hades's name as she came, she thrust her face into the pillow.

But he knew her too well. He pulled back and stopped thrusting right as the first astounding bloom of her orgasm hit.

She cried out with the loss of it and he wrapped his arms around her, holding her still. "Say my name," he commanded in a low, guttural voice. "Say who you belong to."

She shook her head in an attempted denial but he just gripped her tighter and gave her a slight shake. "Say who you belong to."

His cock teased at the edge of her entrance, tormenting her, her pleasure was so close and yet so far away.

"Hades," she finally wailed and he slammed back into her, immediately lighting her back up. She screamed his name again as her pleasure ramped higher and higher and then exploded like a night full of firecrackers.

Hades thrust himself to the root right as she clenched and spasmed around him, his grip on her body never lessening an iota.

Together, they came, as the light of sunset streamed through the window.

As the pop and sparkle of her orgasm finally dissipated, she panted, short of breath, her entire body alive but languid with satisfied pleasure. And Hades still held her from behind, though he rolled them so that they lay on their side. Him spooning her, his cock still hard inside her and every few moments he'd thrust again, like he wasn't ready to let go no matter the fact that he'd already spent.

His fingers trailed the back of her neck. "I missed this."

Her heart was heavy, full to bursting with the things she wished she could say. "You can have it anytime you want." *You can have me.*

"Oh, I know." She could hear his arrogant smile in his words.

She was glad she was faced away from him. It made her braver somehow, so she continued. "You've been so busy lately."

"Miss me?" She thought he sounded pleased.

"As much as you missed me." She rocked against his hardness. His cock shifted and swelled. His fingers found the back of her neck, no longer stroking but clamping down on the sensitive points.

"I have a weakness when it comes to you." He pulled out of her and left her side to clean up. When he returned, she was still huddled on the bed, back to him.

He came around the bed and his fingers lifted her chin. "What's wrong?"

She was done bottling her frustration. "Only you would describe it as weakness."

"What would you call it?" No sarcasm, just curiosity.

"I don't know…" His honest expression made her bold. "Affection?"

Her heart pounded through the silent seconds. His hungry gaze dropped to her lips and she felt it like a kiss.

His hands cupped her cheeks, and then he kissed her for real.

"Affection," he agreed. He stroked her hair, petting her like she was an adorable kitten he allowed to sleep on his bed. And her stupid, stupid heart leaped up like he'd declared his love from the rooftops.

"What if we…" Persephone's breath hitched but she continued, "what if we just stayed in tonight?" She felt her vulnerability stretched raw, right out there for anyone to see as she asked it. But she didn't take it back. "I— I could make it worth your while." She reached out and placed a hand on the front of his pants, where his cock stirred.

His hand shot down and firmly clasped around her wrist, though, stopping her. She felt her heart sink as he stepped back. He was about to reject her. Again.

"Orpheus is the hottest music act on the East Coast. The press will be there to catch the celebrities attending the concert, and I want them to see you with me. I need you there by my side."

Aha. Of course. He needed Mrs. Ubeli on his arm for a photo op, a distraction to the cameras. Tonight she'd be her husband's arm candy, dressed to dazzle, drawing the camera's eye to the scandalous slit of her dress or her long bare leg exiting the car.

She squeezed her eyes shut to stop a stupid tear from escaping. She legitimized his business, she knew, with her innocent looks and role as the dutiful wife. Like the magician's assistant, she took the focus off him and left him free to whatever quiet business he had in the background.

It was their unspoken arrangement, as contractual as the rest of his business dealings were. She played the role of Mrs. Ubeli and in return he did her the great honor of not killing her and to the best of his ability, pretending she was not a Titan.

But she would never truly be family and she would certainly never be anyone he could ever love. Men like Hades didn't understand that emotion. They understood power, and in this relationship, he had it and she didn't.

She'd been an idiot yet again, showing even an ounce of weakness by asking him to stay in tonight.

She turned away from him and forced her voice to be steady and cool. "I'll be ready in an hour."

28

The sidewalks around the Elysium club and concert hall were packed with excited concert goers. Hades's black sedan slid to a stop in front of the back doors, where the crush of people was thicker than at the front entrance.

Persephone peered out at the throng. "Hades," she said nervously.

"It's all right." Hades leaned forward and gave an order to the driver.

Outside, a few muscled men dressed all in black threaded through the crowd. His Shades. In a matter of seconds, they lined the entryway and were holding back the throng, though it looked like a near thing. Persephone had never seen a crowd so big.

Still, amidst the chaos, the paparazzi sensed something was happening as they pulled close and swiveled the cameras' eyes onto the black sedan.

Persephone shrank back into the dark cocoon of the car. This was her least favorite part: being stripped and exposed for the cameras. She smoothed her ice blue sheath dress and touched her coifed hair to check it.

"Hey." Hades cupped her chin and gently turned her head. "You're perfect."

For a moment, his dark eyes held her transfixed. All the thoughts about the noise and mess outside melted away. He frowned slightly and for a second, Persephone thought she saw the flicker of something more than obligation and duty in his eyes.

Something thumped the side of the car and she jumped. A roar erupted in the otherwise quiet car as the door on her side opened. Turning with her heart in her throat, she saw Charon, Hades's right-hand man, leaning over the car. His large black head filled the window for a moment while he signaled to his boss.

"Stay by my side for a few pictures," Hades said, his jaw working as he eyed the people swarming around them. "Then go with Charon. He can handle the crowd and get you safely inside." He pulled out his phone.

The car door opened with another blast of sound. Persephone slid out, fighting to keep her dress modest and trying not to flinch at the sudden bright lights. She stepped close to Charon, whose large body buffered her as much as possible from the light and noise.

Hades slid out after her and posed for a moment next to the car, six feet of male perfection. Something about his height, his dark eyes and perfect cheekbones under the thick fall of black hair gave him a beautiful intensity. Add in some rumors of a criminal empire, and papers fell over themselves to report on the *Lord of the Underworld*'s fascinating mystique.

Persephone took her husband's arm, falling into her role of eye candy. Smiling down at her, Hades barely seemed to notice the flashing lights or people calling to him. His mask of affable billionaire was firmly in place. She wondered when she'd next see the real Hades.

"Mr. Ubeli!" a reporter called. "How does it feel to have landed the hottest musical act in an exclusive contract?"

Hades turned and offered a charming grin, squeezing Persephone gently to him. She knew what a great picture the two of them cut, with Hades's dark good looks and her light hair and pale skin.

"We're very grateful," Hades was answering. "We want Elysium to showcase only the best."

He'd completely remodeled the venue, inside and out, since they'd come here for the charity ball and auction all those months ago when he'd purchased the fateful theater tickets that would lead to the night ending with a bullet in her guts. Now instead of a venue for conferences and parties, it was one of the hippest clubs and concerts spaces in New Olympus.

A few more questions from the media and Persephone felt her fluttering heart calm. Hades made it look so easy, whether in public or private, he always looked poised and perfect. She was the only one who ever got to see him lose a bit of that perfect control, like she had earlier in the bedroom tonight. A pleasurable tingle skittered down her back even at the memory and she let her lips curve into a satisfied smile. Cameras flashed.

She wasn't as practiced as Hades at deception and the few times she'd offered fake smiles, the press had commented on it. So she'd taught herself to think of happy things when in front of cameras, even if it meant thinking of Hades and the memories came with a vicious afterbite.

Hades looked down as if reading her mind and gave her his own heated version. His hand slid a little lower than her waist.

Persephone forced herself to keep her smile but reminded herself it was just for the cameras. Hades was so drop dead gorgeous when he smiled, but he rarely did it anywhere else other than when there were cameras around.

They were turning as one to go when another person called, "What about reports that Orpheus has connections to the mob in Metropolis?"

Hades barely let his grin flicker but Persephone felt his body tense. He waved for a second and pushed Persephone forward. Charon was immediately at their side, along with several of Hades's other hand-selected bodyguards. The Shades protected the Ubelis and would die on Hades's command. Or so the rumors went. Dressed all in black, muscles bunched under their suits, they cut menacing figures on the red carpet.

Usually Persephone felt uncomfortable with them hanging

around, but, as they stepped forward and formed a phalanx around her and Hades, she was grateful for their protection.

Charon hovered close, a mountain in a tux. "We need to talk."

"Later. Get her inside," Hades ordered, and the group moved in perfect formation, Charon at the back.

"See you at the concert," Hades told Persephone, and handed her off to his trusted second in command.

She glanced back once, right before she went inside, to see her husband standing solid against the mad rush of reporters trying to interview Elysium's owner. Then she—and her black clad corps—were inside.

Charon's large hand ghosted over her spine as they went down the back hallways, up to the second story to the private lounge.

Persephone wondered if she'd see Hades for the rest of the night. That's how it went sometimes. She was good for pretty pictures but once he had no more need of her... Persephone bit her lip and stiffened her back. No. He didn't have the power to hurt her anymore because she knew the score now.

Still, once they entered the bar area, Persephone breathed a sigh of relief. No more false smiles required for a while. There were no cameras up here; Elysium's elite patrons didn't like attention. The ones who paid for access to this private lounge were all business associates of Hades's.

A few of them were at the bar or in booths, enjoying a quiet drink. Persephone recognized a few right away. Santonio, who ran a high-end prostitution ring—he preferred to call them *escorts*—stood talking to Poseidon, who controlled all of the distribution business in the Styx, a territory south of the city, near the docks. Another two, Joey and Andy DePetri, were at the bar, arms around women at least ten years younger than them.

It was looking more and more like the concert was a perfect cover for Hades to gather his capos and discuss business.

Persephone ducked into the first booth she came to, hoping they wouldn't notice her. If they saw her, they'd want to pay their respects, and she didn't want to talk to them.

Charon paused for a moment at the end of her table, surveying the room. The rest of her bodyguards seemed to melt away, although she could see them discreetly stationed near the gold fringed theater curtains that decorated the lounge.

"Charon," Persephone leaned forward. The big man didn't turn but she knew he was listening. He noticed everything. "Was all of that madness for the band tonight?"

The crowd outside had really been something, unlike anything she'd ever seen before. Elysium might be one of the top clubs in the city but still.

Charon shrugged. But she didn't expect him to answer. He rarely spoke to her, even though he was Hades's right hand man.

She relaxed back into her booth, studying him. A wire wrapped around his large bald head, and he wore an expensive platinum watch around one wrist. Like Hades, he looked flawless and in control even after the mad rush at the door. His tux was perfect; she wondered where he bought it to fit his large frame.

"Nice suit," she said to his back. "You look good."

In answer, he twisted slowly and gazed down at her. Touching his crackling headpiece, he turned and walked away.

Persephone sighed. "I need to make friends," she muttered to herself.

Real friends, not the kind who socialized with her out of ambition or fear of her husband's position. Her only real friend was Hecate, two decades her senior, who owned the dog shelter where she volunteered. But it would be great to have more people she felt comfortable around at things like this.

"Mrs. Ubeli," a perky cocktail waitress came by. "The usual?"

"Thank you, Janice." Persephone watched the young woman dart away, thinking that the waitress was probably around her age. And how hard would it be to strike up a conversation? And meet her for drinks later? Or go out for a mani/pedi?

Persephone tried to imagine asking Hades if she could have a girl's movie night up at the penthouse. Nope, couldn't picture it.

Meanwhile, the waitress had returned with her glass of wine.

"Are you excited about the concert?"

"Yes." Persephone met the young woman's enthusiasm with her own. "Do you know the band?"

"Orpheus?" the waitress practically squealed. "Everyone knows him. He's amazing. Look—" The girl plucked a newspaper off of a nearby stand and showed Persephone the Arts Section.

"Rock God packs Elysium," it read.

Persephone smiled. Hades would be pleased with the free publicity.

"His songs are amazing," Janice kept gushing.

Glancing up, Persephone saw a few of the men around the club looking their way, attracted by the girl's excitement. Persephone put her hand on the paper and looked pointedly at Janice.

"Thanks," Persephone said quietly. "Can I keep this?"

As the waitress left, Persephone scanned the article. It was short, just talking about Orpheus's top hits and incipient fame around the country.

Persephone buried her head in the paper, hiding her face from the rest of the club to read until the concert started.

"Mayor Pledges Reform as Elections Draw Near" splashed across the front page, with a picture of a handsome blond waving to the crowd. Zeus Sturm. The Op/Ed scoffed at the pre-election speeches, citing broken promises of previous terms. Meanwhile the Style pages were dedicated to articles on the mayor's reign as "most eligible bachelor" with an emphasis on his suave wardrobe. The Gossip pages spun the tale of his latest lover, with a byline listing all his famous liaisons on the side.

"Mayor or Player?" Persephone read the title and rolled her eyes. She tossed the paper onto the table, ready to donate it to the shelter so it could line the bottom of the dog cages. At least the election would be over soon.

"Hey, sweetheart. You're looking beautiful tonight."

Persephone frowned up at a tall, stout, balding man in a floor-length fur coat staring straight at her chest. His fat fingers bore a gold ring on each hand.

"Uh, thank you." She glanced around for a bodyguard, but couldn't see one. They probably were out handling the crowd; it looked like they needed all hands on deck. Besides, wasn't she always telling Hades she would be fine by herself? Well, it was true he let her go wherever she wanted in the city, but his Shades were always in the shadows following.

Realizing she had her hand up by her neck in a vulnerable pose, she touched her diamonds lightly and then forced her hand down.

She made herself smile at the man. Was he one of Hades's business partners? Maybe partner to Santonio or Poseidon? If he was, there were too many politics involved for her to tell him to get lost. She would play nice until she was sure.

The man smiled back down at Persephone, but it wasn't a nice smile. A lot of Hades's associates looked at women like that, although they always acted like perfect gentlemen to her when she was on Hades's arm. They wouldn't dare disrespect her husband like that.

Maybe this gentleman needed a reminder of who she was. "Are you enjoying yourself in our club?" She kept her tone cool and confident.

"Oh, yes, absolutely, toots. In fact," he slapped down a business card in front of her, "I was going to invite you to visit mine."

Persephone glanced down at the card and read the purple lettering out loud, "The Orchid House."

"Finest establishment in town." The man grinned and a gold tooth flashed. "In fact, I recommend you visit sometime this week. Preferably around eleven. We're holding auditions."

"Auditions?"

"That's right. Body like yours, you'd make a killing. Guys love the skinny no-tits look nowadays."

Persephone stiffened.

"I'm not saying I don't," the man continued, chuckling a little. "Especially with that baby doll face you got."

As he spoke, a skinny redhead wearing a scary amount of eye makeup sauntered up.

"Am I right, Ashley?" The man slid his hand over Ashley's rump and squeezed. In response, the redhead put her arms around him. Her long nails looked vicious as they stroked and smoothed the man's fur coat. She scowled at Persephone.

"Anyway, tell the boys Ajax sent you. They'll put you to the front of the line." The man winked. Ashley looked like she'd seen a pile of dog vomit in the booth right where Persephone was sitting.

Persephone could feel her cheeks flushing with embarrassment and anger. Who did this man think he was?

But Ajax still smiled at her, eyes narrowed as he waited for her reaction. Persephone took a deep breath and channeled her Inner Ice Queen.

"Excuse me—" she started to say—she still couldn't help being polite, even in Ice Queen mode—when Hypnos, in a tux and bright blue hair, ran up to the booth. Together with his twin brother Thanatos, he managed Elysium, and he more than lived up to his name. Thanatos did the books and took care of the back office while Hypnos stage managed and, on nights Elysium wasn't booked for a show, played as the House DJ.

"Mrs. Ubeli?" Hypnos gasped. His blue eyes were wide and frantic under his shocking hair. Both Persephone's unwanted visitors stepped aside as Hypnos leaned in. "Have you seen your husband?"

"No, Hypnos, why, is something wrong?" Persephone rose, relieved to have a familiar face in her corner.

"It's Orpheus. The singer for tonight—he's refusing to play."

"What?" Persephone and Ashley said at the same time. The latter immediately looked disgusted that she shared the same thought with Persephone.

Meanwhile, Ajax was studying Persephone with a shrewd look on his face. Persephone felt his gaze, and, even though red burned on her cheeks, she refused to look at him.

"He just stopped tuning his guitar and started freaking out. Thanatos sent me to find help." At this, Hypnos turned to Ajax. "Has he ever done this before?"

Ajax shrugged. "He's an artist. He's temperamental."

"You're his manager, for gods' sake." As the blue-haired man's voice got louder, it cracked. "Why aren't you in the green room with him?"

Persephone's eyes shot back to Ajax. He was Orpheus's *manager*?

"Thought I'd meet the locals," Ajax said. "Look, I discovered him. I got him here for you. If he doesn't sing, it's on him. Not my problem." Ajax reached down to a bowl of bar nuts the waitress had left on Persephone's table, took a handful and slapped them into his mouth. His jaws shook a little as he chewed. Persephone looked away in disgust.

Hypnos looked like he was about to explode and Persephone took pity on him.

"Ok, calm down," Persephone said. "Let's go see Thanatos." She put a hand on his arm. "We'll figure something out."

Relieved to have a reason to escape, Persephone started walking away.

"Nice to meet you, Mrs. Ubeli," Ajax called after them, spraying pieces of food onto the carpet.

"What an ass," Hypnos muttered.

"Who is he, and why is he here?" Persephone couldn't keep the anger out of her voice. "A simple band manager wouldn't have dared take the liberties he did. And the things he said—"

Hypnos glanced at her. "What'd he say to you?"

"He, uh, told me he admired my body." She shook her head in revulsion. "He offered me a job."

"What, really?" Hypnos looked ill. "Don't tell Mr. U that."

"Why, what does he do?"

"He produces pornos."

"What?" Persephone cried out.

"Don't worry," Hypnos said drily. "Once Hades finds out he's here, he's going to kill him."

"What? Why?"

"Those two go way back. Before Hades was—" Hypnos lowered his voice and intoned solemnly, "Lord of the Underworld."

"Don't let him catch you calling him that." Persephone grimaced, but she knew what Hypnos meant. Before the age of thirty her husband had become a juggernaut in the city of New Olympus, with business on both sides of the law. She knew firsthand how impossible it was to cross him. "So why is Ajax here?"

"Ajax is like a cockroach; disgusting and indestructible. Careful around him...he's smarter than he looks. Makes good money off his porn business and his club. Hustles on the side. One of his boys had a bloke who owed him a debt, and turns out the bloke was just about to discover the world's newest hot rock star."

"Orpheus."

Hypnos nodded. "Ajax took over the debt and signed Orpheus. We booked the show and *then* found out it came with Ajax. Hades doesn't want him around."

Persephone considered this. She couldn't imagine Hades not getting his way. Although, given the boost Orpheus would give to Elysium, she understood why Hades compromised.

Persephone bit her lip. "I think he may have been...testing me." She remembered the intent look in his beady little eyes.

"Testing for Mr. U's weaknesses," Hypnos nodded. "Ajax looks like a slob, but don't underestimate him."

Persephone shook her head like she could shake off the encounter. "His companion certainly didn't think much of me."

"Please. I own shirts longer than that skank's dress," Hypnos cracked.

Persephone smiled. Of all Hades's employees, the blue-haired Hypnos was her favorite. Even when he was acting jittery—which he was about half the time she saw him. The other half he seemed almost too mellow.

Hypnos slowed abruptly as they turned down a new hall and saw two large men guarding a nondescript door.

The door opened before he could address the guards and Thanatos, Hypnos's brother, faced them, solemn faced. Thanatos wore a grey suit and a pale violet tie, and, other than his clothes and plain brown hair, he looked exactly like his blue haired brother.

Just like the first time she met them, she marveled at how one twin looked like an accountant and the other looked ready for a rave.

The two men stared at each other like they were looking into a mirror at a fun house. Hypnos seemed even more agitated when juxtaposed with his dignified brother.

"He won't play," Thanatos stated and Hypnos started up a fit of cursing.

"What can we do?" Persephone interjected.

"Get Mr. Ubeli. Or Charon—Charon can threaten to beat his head in."

"Brilliant," said Hypnos at the same time Persephone said, "No!"

She frowned at both brothers. "Can I see him? Maybe I could talk to him."

Thanatos and Hypnos exchanged glances that might as well have said, *Couldn't hurt.* Thanatos led them into the room.

The green room was, in fact, green. Stage hands in black rushed around and more bodyguards in suits stood like statues around the room. Brightly lit mirrors lined one wall; two makeup artists stood at the counters fussing over their supplies. A knot of people were in the corner beside them, looking bored and drinking designer water.

"He's over there." Thanatos nodded toward the corner.

Persephone hesitated, suddenly nervous. "I don't know if I should do this. He has ties to Ajax, right? Hades might not want me to meddle."

Thanatos blinked. "You met Ajax?"

"Back in the lounge. He cornered her," Hypnos explained. "I practically rescued her. That man never misses an opportunity to make a bad impression."

"I'm just saying, if he's one of Hades's enemies then maybe I should lay low," Persephone said.

Thanatos scowled at his brother. "You've been talking too much."

"What?" Hypnos threw his hands up. "You want this concert to happen, right?"

Thanatos looked at Persephone. "We need him to do this, for PR. There's a lot of support in the lounge."

Persephone nodded, catching his meaning. Business support.

People who came out to see Orpheus in private before the show. People who would owe her husband a favor.

She took a deep breath, because though her husband might always see her as only her mother's daughter, she was determined to make a life for herself here. She would prove herself indispensable and she would start by somehow pulling this off. "Ok. I'll do it."

Smoothing her dress, Persephone practiced her model glide all the way to the huddle of people in the corner of the room.

Thanatos fell into step with her. "Look, he may be rude. He may just ignore us. We've been trying not to strong arm him and risk offending his...artistic sensitivity."

"Thanatos, I can handle sensitivity. I'm a model, remember? And a woman." She stopped on the edge of the huddle and looked for a way to break through the throng of bodyguards, managers, assistants and groupies.

Thanatos cleared his throat. "Excuse me, Mrs. Ubeli would like to meet Orpheus."

All eyes turned to her. The groupies looked annoyed. Persephone blushed a little, realizing they thought she was just another rich man's escort, in her expensive sheath dress and diamonds.

A path cleared and Persephone found herself approaching a young man sitting on a stool in the corner, hunched over a guitar. His blondish hair had fallen into his eyes, his head bent towards his fingers. Other than his extreme concentration, he looked almost normal. He wore jeans and a plain white button-down shirt, and with his unruly hair he looked like a kid made to wear church clothes. Not like a rock god at all.

"Orpheus?" Persephone made her voice as soft and dulcet as possible. She felt awkward but apparently it didn't matter how strange she found the situation because he didn't move or look up either way.

"It's nice to meet you." She searched for something to say. Orpheus still hadn't looked at her, instead remaining focused on his instrument. His fingers moved, ghosting across the neck of the guitar, forming chords, playing soundlessly.

Persephone waited a minute, watching him play silently, in his own world. A lock of hair fell away from his face and she tried again. "Is there anything you might need? Some water maybe?"

One of the groupies stepped forward, offering a water bottle. Orpheus ignored it. Persephone could hear whispers start to circulate around her.

"Mob boss's wife," she heard someone say, but when she turned all she saw was a circle of blank faces, staring at her. Persephone felt her own face stiffen, become a mask. She had to remember she was playing a role, typecast by their judgment.

She always hated being surrounded by people like this—fake, judgmental hangers-on who hoped a little fame or power would rub off on them simply by being in proximity to it. Maybe Orpheus hated it too, maybe not. Judging by his closed off body language, she'd say he didn't *love* it... Or maybe he was just really into his music.

Either way, there was no way she could talk to him like this.

"Clear the room." When no one moved, she squared her shoulders and said it in a far louder, no nonsense, do-not-fuck-with-me voice. "*Clear. The. Room.*"

And people started to move. Slowly at first but Persephone said to Hypnos, "Should I go get my husband?" and everyone started scurrying at a much quicker clip after that until just she, Hypnos, Thanatos, and Orpheus were alone in the room. She waved out Hypnos and Thanatos.

Orpheus finally looked over at her. "You're the club owner's wife, right?"

She nodded.

"You look a lot younger than him," he said thoughtfully.

"He just looks older sometimes," she smiled.

"How old are you?"

"You and I are the same age, I think. Nineteen, right?" She blushed a little under Orpheus's intense scrutiny. He was a good-looking boy.

"You look about sixteen," he laughed and sang a little phrase from a song she recognized, *Sixteen Summers*.

Persephone stilled and listened until Orpheus was done. "That's one of your songs?"

He nodded, a genuine smile lighting up his face.

"Wow, I didn't realize you wrote that. They play it all the time on the radio."

"I wrote the lyrics and they bought it for a female artist to sing. That was before I was discovered."

"You sold your song?"

He shrugged. "Practically gave it away, so I could eat and keep on. I just want to make music." He started humming the song again, eyes closed reverently. His fingers flew in a riff on an air guitar and didn't stop until he sang the last chorus.

When he opened his eyes, Persephone clapped. She couldn't help it. He looked so charming.

He was oblivious to it, she realized, this light that shone from him. His gift. When he accessed it and shared it freely, he shone like the sun.

"That was amazing."

"Thanks. Wrote it for Eurydice." His brow furrowed. "I'm waiting for her. I can't go on until she's here. It's a big night."

"She's your girlfriend?"

Orpheus lit up again, smiling impishly. "I have a secret. I'm hoping she'll be my fiancée. I'm gonna propose after the show tonight." His brow pinched. "But don't tell anyone. Ajax wouldn't like it."

Persephone shook her head. "Your secret is safe with me." She wanted to ask him more about Ajax and why he'd taken the sleazy man on as a manager but the door pushed open.

"Orpheus?" A tall, lovely young woman pushed forward. Her dark curls were a halo around her head, emphasizing her full lips and beautiful mocha skin. So he had a real name after all.

"Eurydice," Orpheus said in the gravelly voice of a hipster singer. He swung his guitar down and the young woman stepped straight into his arms.

Her height put her perfectly face to face with him still on the stool.

"You okay, babe?" Orpheus searched her eyes, worried lines etching his brow.

Eurydice nodded. "Always. I'm so sorry I'm late." She wound her arms behind his neck. "I missed you."

"Nothing's right until you're here," he whispered. "It's you and me against the world."

They gazed into each other's eyes with a look of such love and longing...

Persephone's breath caught and a pain she couldn't explain clenched her chest. She wanted to look away, to give them privacy, but most of all to shield her eyes from the aching sweetness of their love.

They kissed gently, and Persephone did look away but not before seeing the naked intimacy on their faces.

"Ma'am?" the young woman called. Persephone glanced back; Orpheus and Eurydice were still in a clinch, and Eurydice was looking back at her. "Can we go backstage now?"

"Yes," Persephone managed to say, her throat suddenly dry. "I mean, I think so. I'll check...if you're ready."

"We're ready," Orpheus said, face lit up. He hadn't taken his eyes off of the lovely Eurydice, whose smile bloomed easily on her lips.

Persephone backed away, signaling Thanatos, who stepped in.

"That went well." Hypnos appeared at her elbow, looking way more mellow than when she last saw him. She suspected he'd stepped out and taken something; his blue eyes looked a little glazed. "He'll play?"

"Yes, he was just waiting for—" Persephone broke off when the crowd jostled her to the side. Orpheus's entourage moved towards the door.

"Good work, toots." A rough voice made both Persephone and Hypnos turn. Ajax stood there smoking a cigar.

"You can't smoke in here. It's a fire hazard," Hypnos sputtered.

"Beat it, freak." Ajax stared the shorter man down. Ajax was as broad as he was tall, but his bulk only added to his menace. "I'm here to talk to the lady."

"Mr. Ubeli won't like it."

"Mr. Ubeli doesn't like a lot of stuff I do." Ajax gestured with his cigar holding hand, sprinkling bits of ash on the floor. He turned to Persephone and she shrank back. He was the last person she felt like dealing with right now. "I'd like to continue our earlier conversation."

"I'd rather not." Persephone tried to keep the quiver out of her voice. He was just a man and they were in public. She didn't have to be such a coward. This was her life, she tried to remind herself.

"Oh, I think you do." And Ajax slung his arm around her shoulders, steering her towards the door. Persephone tried to step away, but he was built like a bear and easily blocked her. She felt panic rising as he bullied her forward.

She could see Hypnos's wide blue eyes following her worriedly and she tried to halt in her tracks, but Ajax's arm caught her and pushed her towards the door with him. *What the—*

She tried to twist away from him but his hands gripped even tighter, hard enough to leave bruises. She was on the verge of freaking out when a voice rolled across the room.

"Get your hands off my wife."

Hades stood in the doorway, glowering at Ajax. As always, Persephone felt his presence like a physical thing, a storm front moving into the room. Everyone, including Ajax, froze.

"Hades, man of the hour." Ajax grinned at the new arrival. His arm fell away and Persephone scuttled to the side.

Hades put his hand out for her and, gods help her, she went to him. He pulled her close and she sank against his side, "Are you ok?"

"Yes," she lied. She could feel the heat of his anger, but he kept it controlled. She wished she hadn't had to be rescued, least of all by him. She needed to pull away from him if she was ever going to keep her sanity.

But Hades only put his arm around her shoulder and tucked her more firmly to his side before facing Ajax. And it felt so good, so safe in his arms.

The room had mostly cleared. Hypnos had retreated near the makeup tables and was instructing the people there to take a break and move out. Two of Orpheus's bodyguards stood hulking around; Persephone guessed they were Ajax's men.

The mobster faced Hades and she realized that if his shoulders weren't so stooped, he'd almost be as tall as her husband. Ajax was larger than Hades, too, and although Hades had the frame of an athlete, the older man struck an intimidating figure. She felt a little better about not standing up to him. Even now Ajax smoked his cigar casually, acting unfazed as he studied Hades.

"Ajax," Hades finally acknowledged him. "I see you met my wife."

"Beautiful girl you have there, Hades. Real sweet too." He winked at Persephone and she stiffened in shock. Was he trying to imply she'd been flirting with him?

She shuddered in disgust and Hades's arm around her tightened.

"We'll have to forgive Ajax for being so rude," Hades said to Persephone, although he kept his eyes on Ajax. "He hasn't been to New Olympus in a while."

Ajax lost all interest in Persephone as he narrowed his eyes at Hades. "That's right. A bunch of riffraff showed up. Didn't like the way the neighborhood was going."

"A bunch of your friends moved out at the same time, as I recall. One particular family with two brothers."

"Used to have three brothers." Ajax's eyes glittered with anger, but he controlled it like Hades. He stuck the cigar in the side of his mouth and spoke around it. "Actually only two moved to Metropolis."

"Ah yes," Hades's voice held a note of cool satisfaction. "One of the three disappeared during his time here. The one with a twin—what were their names?"

"Karl and Alexander." Ajax puffed angrily.

"Karl and Alex. Forgive me, I always get them mixed up." Hades chuckled. "I don't even remember which one disappeared."

"Karl. Missing, presumed dead."

Dear gods, they were talking about her father. Like she wasn't even here. Like she had nothing at stake in the conversation.

Ajax had forgotten his cigar for the moment and Persephone stared at its lengthening ash. Ajax snatched it out of his mouth. "His brothers, Alexander and Ivan, send their regards."

Hades's face split into a scary smile. "They do? How considerate. His widow, too, I assume? How is Demeter? Our last meeting was far too short. And you're such a good little errand boy—tell me, when the brothers sent you to spy on me, did they also tell you to bring me my take of your little club? Because that would definitely soften me up. Probably not enough to let my control of the city slip, but your time in exile hasn't made you any smarter."

The mobster flushed so red Persephone wondered if he'd explode with anger. The room was empty except for the Ubelis, Hypnos, and Ajax with his two thugs. Persephone felt nervous watching the showdown, but Hades seemed as calm and in control as ever, so she took her cues from him. She was sure her husband's men were just outside the room.

In the meantime, Ajax had gotten himself under control as well. "What, I deliver a musician to you, a show that everyone in the nation is dying for, and I give him to *you*, in an exclusive two week run—and this is how you repay me?" He forced a laugh as if he'd heard a weak attempt at a joke. "You accuse me of spying, of plotting? Hades, I knew you when you were a boy! I knew your father."

"Don't mention my father in my presence again," Hades snapped. The two thugs behind Ajax shifted and pressed their hands against their weapons as if Hades's words were actual weapons pointed at them.

Persephone held herself perfectly still, recognizing the tension in the room. For a long moment everyone waited for the Lord of the Underworld to break the silence.

"Your bosses have a long memory. So do I," Hades said softly. "This is my city. I own it. My power is still absolute. You can take that message back."

"I'm here to protect my investment. I'm not leaving—" Ajax sputtered.

Hades held up a hand and Ajax fell silent. Hades spoke in a low voice, but everyone in the room felt its menace.

"I respect the deal we made. You can stay in my city for two weeks. But once Orpheus is gone, you will no longer be welcome in New Olympus."

Ajax licked his lips, his hatred for Hades plain on his face.

"Make your arrangements, Ajax," Hades commanded. "Two weeks and you're out." Hades started for the door with Persephone still on his arm. He guided her forward then looked back over his shoulder at his enemy. "And your club still owes me tribute."

Hypnos was at the door, opening it for them. Persephone and Hades swept out and Hypnos followed them, unnaturally quiet. Persephone didn't know what to think, but her legs felt a little weak from the entire confrontation.

Outside in the hall, Charon stood with a knot of black-clad Shades, awaiting their leader.

"You hear that?" Hades asked Charon.

The large man nodded. "Two weeks and then kick him out. That really how we're gonna play it?"

"Let him look around before he reports back to Metropolis. Then he can tell Demeter and the brothers we're not afraid of them."

"You sure they're behind this?" Charon asked quietly.

Persephone was surprised they were talking so freely in front of her but she was glad, too. She'd been relying on whispers and snatches of conversations she overheard here and there to know what was happening in the war between her family's criminal dynasty and Hades's.

"It hasn't been so long that they've forgotten what it was like to rule."

Hades jerked his head at the Shades. "Get in there and check on him."

The soldiers immediately left the hall for the green room, to watch over Ajax. "Orpheus is a Trojan horse. To get our guard down while Ajax looks around. But if we move too early, we'll look nervous. We can't afford to look weak."

"Better play this perfectly," Charon murmured in a voice deep as a grave. "We've managed to keep it to a few skirmishes between us and the Titans so far. But if this goes bad, it means war." The big man turned and stalked away, pictures on the wall trembling in his wake.

Persephone finally took a deep, shuddering breath.

"You okay?" Hades turned to her. "You shouldn't have had to see that," he murmured.

She was confused when he held her close for a moment, rubbing a soothing hand up her back. Did he mean she shouldn't have had to see it because he was sorry that it might upset her hearing about the ongoing fight between him and her family? Or that she shouldn't have seen it because he didn't think it was any of her business?

"I'm alright."

"I made you late for the concert." He looked concerned, and in his arms, Persephone felt all her tension drain away. She was tempted, so tempted, to pretend that Hades was just a handsome businessman who owned a nightclub and concert hall, and she was his wife. To pretend they were a normal couple.

But she was done with all that. She'd glimpsed real love a moment before, on Orpheus and Eurydice's faces. When Hades gazed at her fondly, she was a beautiful possession. A toy he didn't have to share. It hurt so much, knowing real love wasn't something she could have. Not love like Orpheus and Eurydice shared—sweet and fragile and innocent. Hades didn't understand that sort of sentiment, and if she tried to explain it, he would laugh at her.

She pulled away and crossed her arms over her chest.

A small frown furrowed Hades's brow but he only said, "Hypnos will get you to your private box. I'll be there for the second half, after I finish talking to some people."

He didn't wait for a response before handing her over to Hypnos and leaving in a square of bodyguards. And he didn't look back even once.

29

Persephone sat in the beautiful box, looking down on the polished wood floor of the stage, waiting for Orpheus's New Olympus debut.

She glanced over at the empty box seat beside her. For a second, she wished Hades were here with her to see the entire show. But then she shook her head at herself.

It's better this way. Hades might eventually show, but this was not a date. They weren't that kind of couple and Persephone needed every reminder she could get if she was going to get over her ridiculous infatuation with her own husband.

She was distracted from her thoughts as Orpheus came on stage. The crowd immediately started going insane.

Security strained to hold them back from the stage. Orpheus had only just walked out, but already the front of the stage had a mound of roses and lacy underthings.

Orpheus sat on the stool provided, much like his posture backstage. He leaned forward towards the mic. The stage went dark except for a single spotlight shining down over his head.

"This is for Eurydice," he said in his raspy voice, and the fans started crying out in ecstasy. Persephone watched one faint, falling against a security guard who struggled to keep a barrier between the pressing fans and the stage.

Then Orpheus started playing.

And Persephone forgot about everything. The concert hall, her complicated relationship with Hades, even the intermittent cries of fans.

The music.

His *voice*.

It was haunting, full of such longing and...*love*.

He held nothing back. He ripped himself open, right there on the stage for all to see and share. But no, it wasn't for everyone. He didn't look out over the crowd like normal singers did.

It was for her. *Eurydice*. Every time he looked up, his eyes focused only on one place, and Persephone knew it must be where Eurydice was sitting.

When he sang about stars in her hair and how she was melody made flesh and how Cupid's arrow had pierced his blood and bones—

Persephone held herself still even as tears poured down her cheeks. Her body was alive with goosebumps but it was so much more than that. His music transported. It was ecstatic. Transcendent. Soul-shattering.

And it didn't stop until the last guitar chord was struck.

Persephone inhaled on a sob, her fingers clenched on the railing, the echo of his voice still ringing through the club.

And then reality crashed down.

The fans, mostly women, were screaming their pleasure. The noise was painful, piercing, and yet Persephone still couldn't hear anything but Orpheus's last song ringing in her ears.

AND IF YOU *die before I wake,*
I'll give my soul; it's theirs to take,
I'll come up to the river gates,
I'll come and sing the gods to sleep,

And steal you home for keeps.
Forever mine.
Forever love.
Forever.

Persephone sat back with a sigh, feeling as tense and coiled as a guitar string. She wasn't sure she'd be able to stand if she tried.

Orpheus didn't move from his spot in the center of the stage. He looked perfectly ordinary again.

Until he began playing the encore. Then he transformed again somehow. It was as if his voice transported around the place, making him seem larger than the simply dressed man standing before them.

His voice promised things and caressed the words of the songs. With every passing minute the energy in the room grew higher and higher, until the aching need was a tension no one could ignore.

He finished up another song and the women went mad again. Persephone watched one of them start to climb and claw at a security guard, desperate to get on stage.

"I love you," she was screaming. "Please, I need you."

Disturbed, Persephone stood up. Her heartbeat was racing. She excused herself past the few of Hades's associates who shared the box. If they thought anything of her tear-stained face and ruined make-up, they were wise enough not to stare. Her bodyguards were parked in the back, also mesmerized by the song. She slipped past them into the hall.

In the bathroom, Persephone breathed deeply, finally letting herself sob outright. The music ran like a current through her and she thought again of how Orpheus and Eurydice had looked at one another backstage.

His music was love personified. Every chord he played, every word he sang…

Why couldn't Hades love her back?

Love her even a *tenth* of that?

Again she lost her breath because she couldn't believe she'd just admitted it, even in the quiet of her mind. Oh gods, but it was all she wanted.

Still. *Still*, all she wanted was for Hades to love her back.

He could drape her in all the diamonds from all the world and give her power and freedom and position and a million spa trips—none of it mattered. None of it was what she truly wanted.

All she wanted was the simplest gift. But it was the one that Hades would never give.

His love.

"Stupid girl," Persephone said to her reflection, shuddering with emotion. She hadn't learned a damned thing in all this time.

Hades used her. Maybe he was nicer to her now than he'd first intended or envisioned. And after saving his life, maybe he felt a little bit indebted to her. But she was still just another cog in the machine of his business. A pretty face for the press.

Only in the privacy of their penthouse did she even get a glimpse of the man behind the mask but she was probably just deluding herself about that, too. What she pretended to herself was intimacy was likely him just using her to meet another of his needs.

He used to fuck that horrible Lucinda woman on the regular, but now Persephone was more convenient. She was already always around, so he fucked her instead. But gods, she didn't even know if he was faithful. They'd never made any promises of the sort to one another. And the way he always kept her apart from himself…

He never let her in and he never intended to.

She dropped her head in defeat and for once, allowed the grief in. It was like a death, finally abandoning her hope of ever being loved back.

Long minutes later, she shook her head and looked up at her face in the mirror. Ugh, she was a mess. She couldn't let anybody see her like this. It felt more important than ever to learn the game of pretending to be fine even though nothing was.

She began the arduous process of using endless scraps of tissue to clean up her mascara and was just finishing up when—

One of the stall doors banged open.

What the—? Persephone jumped. She hadn't realized there was anyone else in the bathroom. Had they been in the stall the whole time she'd been having her meltdown?

"Hello?" Persephone called out, stepping around the corner.

A figure was slumped on the floor just inside the furthest stall.

Persephone gasped and ran forward. "Are you okay?"

When there wasn't any response, she moved the door slightly so she could see.

Inside the stall, half sprawled in front of the toilet seat, was a woman. Her dress was black and red, and her long, wicked looking nails were painted to match. It was Ashley, Ajax's girl from earlier.

"Oh my—" Persephone whispered.

Feeling sick, Persephone kneeled down to look at the woman's face. Under the mess of hair, the muscles were slack. Her eyes were open, staring, glazed. She wasn't moving.

Someone in the hall knocked sharply on the door and Persephone jumped. Suddenly every detail seemed sharper, clearer. She saw the needle lying on the floor beside the woman's arm.

"Everything ok in there?"

"Charon," Persephone cried out, recognizing the voice. "Help...please."

Seconds later the underboss barged through the door. Persephone still crouched, frozen, next to the stall door.

"She's not moving," Persephone whimpered. She backed away as the big man approached.

Charon peered inside the stall and uttered one sharp curse. "Did you touch her?"

"No." Persephone couldn't stop staring at Ashley's face. The vacant eyes seemed to follow her, accusing.

Then Charon stepped in front of Persephone, blocking her view. "We need to go." He rumbled and took her arm. His large body pressed forward, herding her bodily toward the door.

"Wait— What about her—? Is she—?"

"She's dead," Charon growled and guided Persephone firmly out of the bathroom and down the hall. Persephone stumbled a little on shaky heels and Charon almost picked her up, righting her while still moving. "And you can't be seen in there."

A crackle came over Charon's earpiece and Persephone knew he was no longer listening to her. "I've got Mrs. Ubeli. South bathrooms. Yes, sir. Right away."

"What?" she asked. What else could possibly go wrong tonight?

"The fans rushed the stage and the green room. Orpheus barely made it out. I've got to get you out of here, now."

30

"What the hell were you thinking wandering away all alone in a crowd like that?" Hades had managed to hold his tongue until they got back to the penthouse but not for a moment longer.

He'd been dealing with cleanup from the mobbing incident on the car ride back anyway—one woman had been injured in the stampede and when Orpheus caught wind of it, he said he refused to play any more gigs. Thanatos and Hypnos were freaking out about it.

But right now Hades couldn't give a shit about anything other than the beautiful, disobedient woman standing in front of him.

Persephone's mouth dropped open as she turned to look back at him right as he closed the front door. "I didn't wander away. I went to the bathroom. And—" Her eyes flashed. "—And I wouldn't have been alone if you'd joined me like you said you would." Her chin went up like part of her wanted to take it back but then she decided not to.

"On. Your. Knees," Hades ground out through clenched teeth.

Persephone looked at Hades in disbelief. "You've got to be kidding m—"

"Don't make me repeat myself, wife." His voice was so cold it could have iced the North Pole.

But he kept reliving that moment—getting to the balcony where she was supposed to be sitting right as the crowd mobbed the stage.

And he'd had no clue where his own wife was as the violent scene unfolded below him. He'd shouted over his earpiece to all of his Shades but none of them had eyes on her. How the fuck did none of them have eyes on her after the earlier incident with Ajax?

How the fuck could you have left her side after what happened with Ajax? He'd been meeting with his capos about the big shipment due to arrive later this month. It was imperative that they secure the goods and manage distribution instead of the Titans.

But none of it fucking mattered if he lost her.

It had been six torturous minutes before Charon located her. And when he had, he found her with a dead girl.

Hades's hands clenched. He needed to regain control and he needed it now.

But Persephone only crossed her arms over her chest stubbornly and glared at him.

He didn't miss how her chin quivered the next second, though. He wasn't the only one who'd been shaken by tonight's events. Persephone had been the one to discover the girl who'd overdosed—Ajax's girl. Because of that asshole, his wife had to look death in the face.

She needed this as much as he did. And he would always give her what she needed. He could quiet her mind and make it all go away—if she would just give herself over to him.

"Bedroom," he ordered.

Her lips tightened but she marched to the bedroom. Good girl. If she'd protested, he'd have turned her over his knee right in the foyer, then made her crawl.

As soon as she stepped into the bedroom, his hands were on her. He stripped her quickly, his cock pressing against his pants as her slender form was revealed. He stepped away to gain some control.

Control. Right. That's what this was about.

He crooked his finger and pointed to the floor. She stepped out of the dress, naked but for her heels and diamonds, but didn't obey any further.

"Knees. Now." It wasn't a request.

Persephone tested him for another long moment. But then finally, lips pursed, she sank to her knees in front of him.

The furious rushing noise in his ears quieted, replaced by a different sort of adrenaline. Yes. Hell yes. He'd needed this very badly and he hadn't even realized it.

He regularly claimed his wife's body in the middle of the night. At first he'd tried to stay away and deny his need for her. He couldn't afford any weaknesses and she made him weak. She made him soft when he had to be more ruthless than ever now.

The Titans had pulled back from an all-out street war but now Demeter was trying to undercut him with all of his suppliers, willing to take massive losses if it meant driving him out of business. Some were loyal but others, especially foreign players, were loyal only to the dollar.

And the customer didn't care. Why buy product in New Olympus if they could make the hour and a half drive to Metropolis and get it for half the price?

Some even brought it back and tried to resell it in his streets. Ruthless enforcement only went so far when suddenly everyone thought they could make a buck and undercut Hades's outfit completely. And just like happened every time, when rogue elements tried to step up and seize power, violence ensued.

The Titans didn't have to step one foot in the city and they'd already created chaos.

Controlling supply was the only answer, plus showing people the consequences of fucking with Hades Ubeli. He'd bring peace and stability back to his city and stomp the Titans out for good this time. But at the moment, he was barely holding his city together.

Which meant he couldn't afford any distractions.

And Persephone? He'd never known a greater distraction in his life.

If he could just get control of her, though, and himself too, then maybe everything else would fall into place. Maybe he'd had it all backwards. Maybe true control started at home and worked its way outward, like the concentric circles from a stone tossed in a pond.

Yes, if he could only master control here...

He put his hand on Persephone's head, her hair silk soft underneath his fingers.

"You know what to do," he told her. He could and would order her, but this first act would prove her compliance.

Biting her lip, she opened his pants and took him out. Her breath quickened imperceptibly, but he noticed, as he noticed everything about her. He noticed her nipples hardening in her dress. The dreamy cast to her gaze. How she raised her chin, bringing her face alongside his cock, and how she took a deep breath. She swayed a little on her knees as if the scent of him intoxicated her.

His cock throbbed just watching her and she'd barely touched him.

"Kiss it, angel. Show me how much you love this."

A tremor went through her at the word "love" and he hid a smile even knowing it made him a bastard.

She loved him, he knew it. He also knew she wished she didn't. Her love satisfied him in a deep place, even though he didn't love her back. He couldn't. Not if he was going to be the King of the Underworld, the Scourge of the City. They had many names for him. But if there was the one thing the Lord of Night could not afford, it was love.

It was unfair to his sweet Persephone. It always had been. If he loved her, he would let her go and tell her to run as far away from him as she could get. Alas, it was just another proof of his black heart.

He would *never* let her go.

She was *his*. Something he would prove again to both of them tonight.

He needed to break apart his lover and remake her into a new creation, a creature born of savage lovemaking, a creature belonging only to him.

Her lips brushed the dark head of his cock, her eyes closed like she was in prayer.

Fitting, because here he was her god.

His hand left her head and cupped her soft cheek. "That's it. That's right. Good girl."

Persephone shivered again and put her mouth on him, running her tongue over his turgid length. Slowly savoring.

Her hand came up to stroke his balls. His groin tightened at the sight of her delicate, perfectly manicured fingernails lightly scratching his scrotum.

Her lips worked over him just as he liked it, popping his head into her mouth and tonguing and sucking the most sensitive spots.

He let her worship, stroking her head and whispering "good girl" over and over. This was a perfect moment, meant to wash the fear and anger of the night away. And it worked. He could rule the world as long as he owned this beautiful woman.

As long as he could have her like this, on her knees.

Looking down at her innocent face taking his cock almost brought him to his. He gathered the hair at the base of her neck and used it like a leash to turn her head this way and that.

He tugged her off his cock and then dragged her up one side of his length and down the other. She nibbled on the head when she came back to it and he pushed her lower so she'd suck on his balls. And suck she did, rolling them one by one in her mouth.

A curse escaped him and Persephone's eyes, blue as a summer sky, opened lazily. She gave him a small smile that made his heart soar.

"Suck me," he told her gruffly to hide his reaction. He tugged her hair and she obeyed, letting him slide deep in her mouth, stretching her lips and hitting the back of her throat. Was there any better feeling?

Only one, he decided. The feeling of her cumming around his cock. He might allow that tonight, after he dominated her. After he reminded her of her place.

His hips surged and she gasped around him. He drew out, letting her cough and sputter. Her eyes watered.

"Too much?"

With a little shake of her head, she pushed back onto his cock, determined and straining to take him deeper. *Fuck, that's it.* Her mascara streamed in rivulets with her tears and it was fucking beautiful. Innocence sullied, but only for *him*.

She kept swallowing him down until her nose nearly pressed to the base of his cock. Her tongue fluttered underneath and he lost control.

"Persephone," he moaned. Folding, he grabbed her head and kept her there as he sent his cum shooting down her throat and into her belly. He released her as quickly as he could, but she remained on her knees, chest heaving as she sucked in air.

She'd submitted to him fully and pleased him beyond measure. Then why did it feel like she was the one in control?

In a rare moment of weakness, he murmured, "*Sei bellissima. Sono pazzo di te.*" *You're so beautiful. I'm crazy for you.* Her brow wrinkled but he didn't translate. It was bad enough that he'd whispered it aloud in the first place.

Mustering himself, he straightened. With his handkerchief, he gently wiped the mascara stains from her face. "You did well tonight. I never should've left you alone."

She blinked as if shocked by the admission that was close to an apology. "It's fine. I survived."

"You'll never be alone like that again." He'd have Charon stick to her side if he couldn't escort her personally.

"You don't have to worry about me."

"I do. You're my responsibility. My most treasured possession."

She closed her eyes at that, an expression crossing her face. Not hurt or anger, but longing. Persephone might fight, might protest, but deep down she understood his possessiveness. She craved it, even. She was his perfect mate. And she'd been in danger tonight. True danger.

He brushed his fingers over her face. "Were you afraid?"

"A little."

"My business won't touch you." Sudden memories of Chiara gripped him. Finding her body bloodied and broken. No. He would *never* let that happen to Persephone. He gripped her chin. "It will never touch you."

"Hades." She looked up at him, lips shiny, gaze soft and submissive. "You touch me."

He bent, lifted her to the bed, and lay her down. She spread out before him, a sacrifice on an altar.

The diamonds glittered at her ears and wrists and the hollow of her throat. He touched the right earring, enjoying her needy shudder as he fingered her earlobe. The bright jewels winked at him as she moved. She couldn't wear his chains out in public, but she could wear these. She was his and everyone would know it.

"Yes, I touch you. I'm the only one who can. The only one who ever will." He bent over her, rough hands grasping and claiming. He wished he could touch every inch of her at once, hold her in the palm of his hand.

As his fingers penetrated her, he sucked on the tender juncture between her neck and shoulder. Her hands slid up his shoulders and into his hair until he caught her wrists and pinned her.

She quivered under him, eyes wide and pupils blown. He transferred her wrists to one hand and held them above her head. His right hand splayed between her breasts.

"All of this. All of you belongs to me." He needed to know she understood, and that she understood it deep in her bones.

She gave a slight nod. He rewarded her with two fingers in her pussy, working deep, brushing against the sensitive spot inside her until her hips rose off the bed. Her chest flushed as he watched her orgasm bloom in her. Her eyes went wide, almost shocked, as it peaked, going on and on as he crooked his fingers inside her and tugged. Her feet dug into the bed and her whole body went taut as aftershocks rolled through her.

When it was done, she sagged to the bed. He removed his fingers and thrust them into her mouth. Her mouth softened, accepting him even though he wasn't gentle. Her tongue curled around his wet fingers, licking and lapping, tasting herself.

His cock curled up to the sky, his own orgasm threatening to boil out of him. He'd already cum once and hard, but his cock had forgotten. It throbbed as if her very presence could set him off.

He pulled his fingers out of her mouth.

She was submissive to him. Only to him. And he would keep her safe.

He crawled onto the bed and rose up over her, cock in hand. "Touch your breasts," he ordered. "Cup them. Show them to me."

Persephone's slender fingers did as he commanded and he stroked himself faster.

"Your nipples. Pinch them. Harder," he demanded.

She was already rolling her nipples, ripe berries between her fingertips, obeying him like she read his mind. Like they were one—

His climax blasted through him, sending semen spurting over her naked flesh. Growling in pleasure, he marked her with his seed. Without being ordered, Persephone stroked her stomach, rubbing the silky essence into her flawless skin. Accepting him.

Her hair spread around her head like a halo. Her body shimmered, pale and beautiful in the low light.

"Angel," he breathed.

It seemed only natural to kneel down at the end of the bed, slide his hands under her shapely thighs to draw her close, and dip his head to her sex to drink of her essence.

After she came once or twice or fifteen times, he rose again and finally fucked her. He fucked her like he owned her because tonight he'd proven again that he did, both to her and to himself.

And he knew that her writhing cries would nourish him through the night and into tomorrow, when he would don his suit like armor and go forth to do battle in the boardroom, in the clubs and street corners he owned—shoring up defenses and strengthening borders until the constant attack from the Titans broke against the unseen walls like a tide.

Tonight though, there was only Persephone, the daughter of his enemies, now his in every way.

"*Tu mi appartieni. Per sempre.*" *You belong to me. Forever.*

She sighed as he spoke into her skin. She didn't understand the words of the incantation but the spell still wound around her body nonetheless, binding her to him.

He couldn't tie her to the bed forever, but he could tie her to him with pleasure. With dresses and diamonds, and nights drenched with passion. He couldn't tell her he loved her, but he could keep her safe, locked in a high tower, and give her his body without reserve.

It would be enough. It had to be.

31

Two days after the concert, Persephone sat sipping designer bottled water in a robe and watched people backstage at the fashion show. Hades's friend, Hermes, had just come out with a new line of resort wear, and Persephone had been roped into modeling it.

Hair and makeup done, she sat backstage bored out of her mind and half listened to the models' gossip.

"I met Orpheus last night," one of the women was smiling smugly into the mirror. Stunningly beautiful with sky high cheekbones and pouty lips, she was playing with her blonde hair. Her friend, an equally lovely brunette with wide eyes, leaned closer.

"What? Where?"

"At an after party, duh. He was luscious."

"So did you talk to him? What did he say?"

Persephone leaned forward too, curious.

"Well, he didn't say much. You know he's refusing to play the rest of his nights? He said he thought it was too dangerous." The model shook her head at the mirror. "I told him he was being silly, and that his art needed to be shared. I think I inspired him."

Persephone swigged her water bottle and wondered if she should comment.

"We had a more private conversation after that." Model number one smirked.

"Oh, my, gods," the brunette squealed. Persephone rolled her eyes.

"I definitely gave him a few more reasons to stay and fulfill his contract."

Persephone decided she'd had enough. "What about his fiancée?" she broke in. Orpheus would have proposed by now and she knew Eurydice would say yes. The way those two had looked at each other…

The two models stared at Persephone like she was speaking Greek. "You know, the one he writes all the songs to," Persephone persisted. "Did he mention her at all?"

"Sweetie, most men don't mention their significant others around me. I guess, around me, they're less significant." The beauty flipped her hair over her shoulder and her eyes went back to the mirror, preening.

Persephone wanted to bitch slap the model until the woman made proper eye contact during a conversation. Instead, she jumped up. "I need more water. Do you want anything?" Without waiting for a response, she strode off toward craft services.

She heard the women gossiping about her as she left. They didn't bother to lower their voices.

"I don't know how she got this job at all. I mean, she's fat."

"Her husband landed it for her. He's a crime boss and probably killed someone to get her in."

"Probably."

Persephone walked with head held high, her posture perfect, focused straight ahead. She had to stop to let three young fashionistas rush by with a rack of clothes. Another young hair stylist, his hair in a mohawk, caught her eye from his place behind a model's chair. He smiled sympathetically and she grinned back. She recognized him from Hermes's spa, Metamorphoses, where she was a regular.

The spread of food at craft services mocked her queasy stomach. She grabbed a bottle of coconut water instead and found a place to sit near the sound system on the outskirts of the activity.

Try as she might, Persephone couldn't keep the model's words from bothering her. She didn't care what people called her; it was Hades she was worried about.

He hadn't come home last night. Since Orpheus debacle at the club several days ago, Persephone hadn't seen her husband. She was used to his long business hours. Hades often went for a late-night swim in the penthouse pool, but at least he'd come home and lie down for a few hours before donning his suit again at dawn.

This morning she woke up beside his untouched pillow. And the papers reported the rumor that Orpheus's concerts would be canceled. Thanatos officially denied the report but she knew it wasn't making Hades's job easier.

The night after the concert had been... Persephone lifted a hand to her neck just at the memory of it. They hadn't done anything like that for a long time and then two sessions in one night... She felt her face flush.

Out of the corner of her eye, Persephone noticed she wasn't sitting alone on the outskirts anymore. A woman all in black had strutted over and slouched against the wall nearby. Her black hair fell around her face in a short, blunt cut. With her faded jeans and her scuffed boots, she looked like a photographer, except she didn't have a camera. Persephone wondered for a second whether she was a model; she was pretty enough, though she didn't look happy about it.

Arms crossed and wearing a frown, she surveyed the scene with Persephone and moved close enough to comment, "I'm so over these bitches. Cat walk, more like catty-walk."

"Are you a model?" Persephone asked politely.

"Please," the woman huffed. "I'm not one of those brainless bimbos. Like I'd be seen trotting my bare ass down a runway. Do I look like an idiot?"

Persephone's lips quirked into a smile and then flattened out as she waited for the woman to notice who she was talking to.

"Oh, shit, I'm sorry." The woman realized Persephone's catwalk-ready hair and makeup. "Blast, I'm always putting my foot in my mouth." She turned and stuck out her hand. "I'm Athena."

"Persephone." Persephone shook Athena's hand. "Pleased to meet you. So, if you're not modeling, what are you doing here?"

"Favor to Hermes. The pretty, bronzed dick head. I did his whole web platform and he wanted me here to make sure I got the vibe right." Athena went off cursing, calling Hermes several more colorful terms while Persephone sat silent in shock.

"Are you mad at him?" Persephone finally asked.

"Mad at Hermes?" Now Athena seemed shocked. "Not at all. I'm here, aren't I? And I'm going to his party tomorrow. Are you coming?"

"To his party? I don't think I'm invited."

"Ah, of course you are. I'll ask Manny."

"Manny?"

"My pet name for Hermes."

Persephone reigned in her laugh.

"Oh, I nickname anyone I like. Yours would be easy. Persephone Bora."

"So you're a website designer," Persephone changed the subject desperately.

"Programmer, hacker. Website design is something I only do for close friends and ex-lovers." Athena hopped up on the heavy cases for the sound equipment and swung her legs.

"I see." Feeling mischievous, Persephone asked, "Which one is Hermes?"

"Huh?"

"Which one is Hermes—a close friend or ex-lover? Or does a lady not kiss and tell?"

Athena barked out a laugh. "Oh, honey, I'm no lady. Truth is, he's both."

"Oh?" Persephone let her eyebrows rise at this tantalizing gossip.

Athena shrugged. "It was late, I was working. He called me a genius." A hint of red tinged her cheeks. "That always gets me," Athena muttered. She shook her head forward so her hair fell over her face.

"Are you blushing?" Persephone teased, amused to find a chink in the gruff woman's armor.

"He's a slut, though. Everybody's had him. And we weren't good for each other. We're better as friends."

As if on cue, Hermes went by, looking harried yet suave in a grey suit.

"Manny!" Athena shouted. Everyone backstage paused to stare at her. "Is Persephone invited to the party tomorrow?"

"Of course, Athena. My love. Now please shut up. Makeup!" And he rushed off into the lights.

Athena chuckled, shaking her head so her short hair fell around her face.

"See, told you. You're invited. Come to the party."

Persephone's mouth was gaping open at this point.

"Oh, come on. Do you want me to beg? Ok, I will. Please, come to Hermes's party. I need someone there to talk to. No one understands me." Athena fake pouted.

Persephone couldn't help it, she laughed.

Athena looked slyly out from under her black helmet of hair. "Oh, so the perfect facade does crack."

"You're funny," Persephone told her. "I like it."

"Glad to be of service. Are you coming to the party?"

Persephone sighed. "I'll ask my husband if we have anything going on."

"Good, clear your schedule. Besides there's a hottie or two there I want you to meet."

"Athena," Persephone gasped. "I'm married."

"Not for you! For me, dumbass." Athena huffed and blew her hair out of her face. "You can give me tips on how to woo him." She grinned and wiggled her eyebrows.

32

Hades prowled through the penthouse, looking for his wife. They'd lost another shipment to the Titans tonight. Guns this time. Demeter was trying to flood his streets with semi-automatics.

Just last week he had to put down a gang that thought to fight his men for territory. Others had the same idea now that the Titans were challenging him so outright, thinking they could take advantage of his distracted focus.

They were wrong. He'd put every last one of them six feet under. But an influx of weapons like this would only further embolden new enemies.

It was just eight at night and he should still be at the office discussing blockades into the city.

Instead he was standing here in the doorway of his master bath. Watching his wife as she toweled off, humming to herself, obviously oblivious to his presence. Steam still filled the air. She must have only just stepped out of the shower.

As she raised her head, she shrieked, seeing his steam-blurred reflection in the mirror.

"Hush, it's just me." Hades stepped into the room as she wrapped the towel around herself.

"You shocked me," she said, eyes still wide. "I didn't expect you home this early."

"It's almost eight."

"You didn't come home last night. And isn't there a concert at Elysium?"

"Not tonight." Hades leaned against the sink and watched her, his eyes running up and down her toweled form.

But soon looking wasn't enough. He stepped closer and then his hands closed over her shoulders, sliding down her bare skin and taking the towel with them.

"This is why I come home," he whispered into her ear. "You make me forget all my troubles." It was more than he meant to say but true all the same.

They didn't play today. No, his need was too urgent. He had to be inside his wife so he boosted her up onto the counter, unbuckled and shoved his pants down and then—

He threw his head back as he sank inside her. She was wet for him. Always wet. He reached up and pinched her nipple. Her sharp gasp made him even harder, though he wouldn't have thought that was possible.

This was all he'd been able to think about, all day long. He'd been pissed about the shipment, it was true. He wanted to strangle Demeter Titan.

But more than that, he'd wanted to get in his car and break every traffic law to get home and fuck his wife.

He pulled out and then stroked back in and she clenched around him so fucking deliciously. Her body was made for his. There was no other way to describe it. Sex had never been like this before. Like something that felt as necessary as breathing. Every hour of the day he went without being inside her he wanted to make up with two more buried balls deep in her pussy.

Some of his lieutenants were grumbling about his disappearing acts. Charon had reported that little shit, Angelo, trying to stir the guys up by saying Hades was pussy whipped by a Titan. Charon had given the boy a beating he wasn't likely to soon forget for his disrespect. But times were tense and the less time Hades spent at home, the better.

Frankly, he'd thought it would get better with time. That he'd work his wife out of his system. But like feeding an addiction, it only got worse. Sometimes he fucked her three times a night and then again in the morning…and yet all day he could think only about coming back home and doing this—

He thrust in again, clutching her ass to get the best angle possible, to go deep and also grind against her to make her mewl in pleasure. Her little noises that he was fucking addicted to as well if he was being honest with himself.

"*Tesoro mio. Mia moglie.*" My treasure. My wife.

Her breathy squeaks got higher and higher as he drove her to the edge and everything else fell away. There was only this. Her body. Her nails clawing his scalp and her hips thrusting against his in desperation, she was so close.

Some nights he loved to torture her. To pull back and make her beg. To remind her who exactly was in control.

But right now he just wanted to make her fly and to feel her milking him so he kept pounding away. And when she screamed her orgasm and it echoed off the bathroom tiles, he let go and spilled into her, a king conquering his queen and marking her as his in the most primal way possible.

When it was done, she bowed her head over his shoulder, breath heaving. He ran his fingers down the small bumps of her spine and she shivered. He was still planted inside her and he pulled out and gave another small thrust, groaning at the pleasure she still brought him.

The steam from the mirror had mostly disappeared and he could see their reflections, the beautiful expanse of creamy skin tapering down to the tiniest little petite waste before flaring out again at her womanly hips. And him behind her, dark to her light, brute to her petite beauty.

She looked so tiny. So unbearably breakable. The world would snap her like a twig if he didn't protect her.

He wrapped his arms around her and held her to him, tight. Something in his chest squeezed uncomfortably.

He looked away from the mirror and let go of her, finally sliding out. "I'll let you clean up," he murmured.

For a brief second, she looked up, her huge blue eyes locking on his. Whatever she was thinking, he couldn't read it in her gaze. Except that maybe she wanted something from him. Something he couldn't give.

"Hermes is having a party," she said tentatively.

Hades's brow furrowed. Whatever he'd expected her to say, that wasn't it. "When?"

"Tomorrow night."

"You can't go." He was busy tomorrow night.

Her mouth dropped open and then her eyes flashed. "I wasn't asking for your permission."

"Well you should have been." The city was on the edge of fucking implosion and she wanted to go to a party? Who knew what kind of security would be there and who might sneak in? The wife of Hades Ubeli would be more than an attractive target for countless enemies.

"I was trying to ask if you wanted to go with me but now I rescind the invitation." She hopped off the vanity and strode out of the bathroom.

Oh-no-she-didn't.

"Don't you walk away from me." He grabbed her elbow and spun her around.

"And don't you fucking touch me without my permission." Her eyes blazed and Hades's groin tightened. Oh he would have fun teaching her this lesson. She thought she would defy him, on today of all days?

But before he could even begin to chastise her, his damned phone rang. He couldn't afford to miss a single call. Not after all that had been happening.

"What?" he barked after pulling his phone out of his pocket.

"Boss, you gotta come down here," Charon said. "We already got a lead on a buyer for the semis. Shouldn't talk over the phone, but I'll tell you everything when you get here."

Fuck. He felt like throwing the phone against the wall. But no. Control in all things. Control always. Otherwise people got hurt.

He pointed a finger in Persephone's face. "You and I will talk later."

She just crossed her arms over her chest and got an even more obstinate expression on her face. Oh yes, he'd enjoy teaching her this lesson very much. It would give him something to look forward to the rest of the very long night he had no doubt was ahead.

But his business kept him out all that night, and the next day, too.

33

Hermes's party was in an enormous brownstone on the corner of two streets. Persephone got out of the car, feeling a bit strange walking around in her little purple dress and stilettos without Hades on her arm.

Her nightlife usually entailed a trip to one of Hades's restaurants for drinks and greeting her husband's business associates. She felt giddy to be doing something for herself, by herself. And then immediately guilty because Hades had told her explicitly not to come.

Well, he'd never come home to finish the argument, so she'd decided that meant his point was forfeited.

"Ms. Ubeli, slow down." Her assigned bodyguard exited the car behind her. Persephone rolled her eyes.

She'd tried to give him the slip earlier but no such luck. That was fine. She knew security was important and that Hades also likely already had word of her disobedience...and she couldn't deny the fizzle of excitement that thought sent through her. Which was probably more than a little screwed up. But she'd decided she wasn't thinking about it anymore.

She was here to have fun.

But she slowed when she saw the bouncers at the door.

"Invitation?" one of them rumbled.

"Um, I don't have one. Hermes invited me."

The man just stared down at her. "Name?"

"Persephone Ubeli," her bodyguard supplied. "Hades Ubeli's wife."

The bouncer's eyes widened and he stepped aside immediately. Persephone ducked her head, waving her hand at his apologies.

Once inside she hissed at the bodyguard, "Can I just keep a low profile for once?"

"Sorry Mrs. Ubeli, just trying to help." The man didn't sound sorry at all.

Persephone wished that, for one night, she could just be Persephone, country girl from the Midwest, alone in the big city. Of course, that had gotten her in trouble all those months ago. Right around the time she met Hades.

She sighed. "Just stay over there. I know you have to do your job but everyone here is safe."

A young man with crazy curly hair ran by, holding a smoking bottle of something and screaming, "I've got a bomb!" He bowled into a knot of models who shrieked angrily and swatted at him. The bottle boiled over into a harmless puddle.

Persephone closed her eyes. "Ok, that was just poor timing."

The bodyguard grimaced as three guys in suits and large pink wigs went by. "Go have fun." His tone doubted that she would.

Straightening her dress nervously, she turned back to the party. She recognized a bunch of bored-looking models from the fashion show the day before, and made a note to avoid them.

A cheerful shout caught Persephone's attention, "Hey, bitch!" Athena, looking slightly less scruffy in a black spangly top and the same black jeans and scuffed boots, waved her over with a beer in hand. "Come get a drink."

Persephone started over and her bodyguard shadowed her. She stopped and addressed him again. "Um, do you mind just waiting over by the wall? I think I'll be safe with her. She's a friend."

The stonewall face was her answer. She sighed and headed over to Athena, determined to ignore her bodyguard. Halfway there he caught her arm and stopped her.

"Look, Mrs. Ubeli, I want you to have a good time. But I work for your husband. And I answer to him. He's not particularly happy that you're here and ordered me to keep eyes on you at all times."

So he *had* already called Hades. Persephone stared the man down, furious. Hades thought she needed a babysitter. Even after all this time, Hades would only allow her the illusion of freedom. He still thought he could tell her where to go and when she could go there. And gods forbid she go anywhere without these ridiculous Shades, who always wore sunglasses, even though right now they were inside a house. At night.

Still, she'd catch more flies with honey. She smiled sweetly at the man. "I'll stay out of trouble. I don't want to make your job any harder." She pulled her arm from his grip and joined her friend, shaking her head.

"What's with the entourage?"

"My husband couldn't come. He wanted to make sure I'm safe."

Athena raised her eyebrows. "You know, while you were strutting your bare ass down the catwalk, I had a chance to look into you. I didn't think Ubeli would ever be an old married guy. And to someone like you."

Persephone felt her cheeks tinge, with embarrassment or anger she wasn't sure which. "What do you mean?"

"Oh, Persephone Bora, I just put my foot in my mouth again. Ignore it." Athena handed her a drink with a paper umbrella in it. "Drink up."

Hermes flitted by, a model on each arm, one male, one female, both wearing bunny ears. Hermes himself had lost the suit jacket and was now in tight grey jeans and a sleeveless purple top. The tips of a black tattoo peeked out on his muscled shoulders.

With his dark eyes and swarthy skin, he could almost be Hades's younger brother.

"Hey, look, Manny, you match." Athena sloshed her drink as she pointed towards Persephone's purple dress. "Oops."

"Oh, Persephone, you gorgeous, gorgeous creature," Hermes faced her. "Great work yesterday."

Persephone flushed prettily. "Thanks, Hermes."

The two models on either side of Hermes looked sour.

"I'll be back in a bit, must make the rounds. Come on, bunnies." His entourage turned as one, and Persephone could see more of Hermes's tattoo across his back. Someday she'd ask to see it all.

"Lucky bastard." Athena swigged her drink.

"Why do you say that?"

"Hermes's amazing." Athena pointed with her drink again, this time toward the retreating trio. "Dropped out of school to start his own spa. Now he owns twelve, ships product all around the world and has a budding fashion line."

Persephone took a tentative sip of her cocktail. "How do you know all this?"

"Wikipedia." Athena winked over her beer.

"You liar. You know everything."

Athena shrugged. "Everything interesting."

"What sort of products?"

"Huh?"

"What sort of products does he ship?"

"How the hell should I know? Hair goop of some sort. Do I look like I go to a spa?"

Persephone turned towards her. "You could come with me sometime."

"To their mothership?" Athena watched three models glide by and narrowed her eyes. "I'd sooner die."

"Ok, it's not going to turn you into a bimbo. Unless you want to become one." Persephone giggled at the image and then soothed Athena, "I'm kidding. Just come and get your hair layered." Persephone looked at Athena's silky black locks. "You'd look amazing with a new cut."

"You think so?" Athena touched her hair uncertainly.

"I know so. My dream job would be giving people makeovers—from hair to shoes."

"Would you go shopping with me?" Athena asked. "I hate clothes. Seriously, I'd love some help."

"No problem." Persephone smiled and clinked her glass against Athena's. "Just let me know when."

"I'd like everyone's attention, please!" Hermes stood on a table next to the drinks, now completely topless except for a furry vest with a tortoiseshell pattern.

"Just don't make me look like that," Athena motioned towards the man. Persephone nodded.

"A toast to a successful new fashion line!"

"To Fortune!" someone else cried, and everyone chimed in. "To Fortune!"

"These are Fortune jeans," Athena told Persephone. "One of the first he designed."

"I'm sure," Persephone said, eyeing the faded pair.

"Oh, holy shit, there he is." Athena grabbed Persephone. "See him?"

Persephone looked in the direction she was pointing, but all she saw were a few guys in pink wigs laughing with some models. "Where?"

"Right there, dummy! In the corner."

Looking past the more vibrant partygoers, Persephone saw two guys standing in the corner, one dressed in a preppy polo shirt and the other in scuffed jeans and a faded t-shirt. Neither looked like they fit in but several models stood around flirting with the one in the polo shirt. Both guys were handsome, but they looked young, like they couldn't be any older than Persephone herself.

"Ok, I see two guys. Which one do you mean?"

"Well..." Athena bit her thumbnail, eyes flicking between the two boys. "That's the thing, I can't decide. They're college roommates, both these wunderkinds working together on some crazy exciting research in medical technology. Save the world kind of shit."

She glanced back at Persephone. "I might not look like it but I'm totally a sucker for a hero."

Persephone smiled. "So why don't you ask one of them out?"

Athena's face scrunched. "Well, every time I see them out, they're surrounded by..." She gestured rudely at the flock of bobble-headed women giggling and flicking their hair around the boys.

"The one on the right, Adam Archer," Athena indicated the blond in the polo shirt, "is the heir to Archer Industries."

Persephone let out a low whistle. "Whoa." Archer Industries was one of the wealthiest companies in the *nation*, not just New Olympus. They were even regularly listed among the top ten wealthiest companies in the world.

"And the one on the left?" Persephone asked.

"Logan Wulfe. Boy genius. No one knows anything about his family, but who needs to? He's crazy smart and just look at him. Mmm mmm mmm. All dark and broody."

Persephone laughed. "So why don't you ask *him* out?"

As they looked on, one of the models who'd been talking to Adam only moments before threw herself against Logan, arching her back and flipping her blonde hair, pushing her breasts up into his face. Logan's brow wrinkled, his hands hovering in midair as if reluctant to touch what was freely offered.

Again Athena's face scrunched in amusement. "I dunno. I like the idea of him but I think...he's a little bit...unseasoned for my tastes. These med school types. No time for relationships, but they can name all my body parts...in Latin. I prefer a man with more finesse."

"A better bedside manner?" Persephone deadpanned.

"Look at you, making jokes!" Athena swatted her arm. Persephone's pink drink splashed everywhere, mostly right into a redheaded model's path.

"Watch what you're doing! Stupid bitch," the model hissed. Out of the corner of her eye, Persephone saw her bodyguard start forward, and she shook her head sternly.

He stopped and leaned back against the wall.

In the meantime, Athena had jumped up and shouted, "Piss off!"

Everyone at the party turned to stare. Athena tossed her head, proud to be the center of attention. "Hermes! We need music."

"Coming soon, delightful Athena," Hermes called back from the entryway. "In fact, we have a special guest I'd like to introduce to everyone."

A familiar figure stood next to Hermes holding a guitar. Persephone recognized Orpheus with just enough time to cover her ears. The excited screams of the women around her immediately followed as the fans rushed Orpheus immediately.

"Ladies, ladies," Hermes tried to fend them off. "He's going to sing for you if you'll let him."

In the crush of bodies, Persephone's bodyguard looked distracted. But then, the riots Orpheus seemed to generate would be more than any single protector could handle. The room was filled with shrieking, girly chaos, the sort that would strike terror into a man's heart.

Persephone jumped up, ready for her opportunity. She waited until the poor bodyguard was pushed into the wall by some rabid models.

"Come on." She grabbed Athena and dragged her new friend out of the great room, back to where she saw some people disappear. The large kitchen was almost deserted except for some extra bottles of champagne and gorgeous young people in bunny ears opening them or lining serving trays with glasses.

Persephone grabbed a filled glass and sipped it. The screams had died down and there were guitar sounds coming from the room they just left. Her bodyguard was probably sifting through the room now, looking for her.

"What's wrong? You don't like his music?"

I like it too much, Persephone wanted to say. "We'll never hear it over the screaming."

"I don't know how Hermes got him here. He's the hottest thing in this city right now."

"I know. He plays at my husband's club."

"I've been meaning to ask you about that." Athena swigged champagne straight from the bottle. "How did you meet Mr. Lord of the Underworld?"

Persephone winced at the reference to a newspaper article

printed two years ago. "Please don't call him that." She set down her empty glass. "It's a long story."

"Cliff notes, please." Athena's dark eyes glittered over the neck of the bottle.

Persephone ran a hand through her hair. How to sum up her intense courtship? "He swept me off my feet. Gave me everything I could ever imagine. It was amazing."

Athena pressed a new glass into Persephone's hand. "Did you know about what he did for a living?"

Persephone shook her head. "I didn't find out until later."

"So you didn't target him?"

"What?"

"You didn't find out he was wealthy and seek him out?"

Now the blood rushed to Persephone's face as she realized her new friend was accusing her of being a fortune hunter. "No, I didn't know anything about him. He...helped me out of a situation. I knew he was wealthy, but that wasn't why I—" Persephone halted.

"Wasn't why you?" Athena prompted.

"Wasn't why I fell in love with him."

"You love him."

Persephone nodded, unable to speak. It was the first time she'd said it out loud after admitting it to herself at the concert the other night. Athena seemed to accept her further silence on the topic, and gave up her interrogation. In the other room, the song had stopped or was drowned out by clapping and cheers.

"Champagne for everyone!" Hermes shouted from the other room, and the bunny ears dutifully exited the kitchen carrying trays.

Athena pulled Persephone back to the party. The room had cleared out a little; Orpheus was getting a tour of the house with his shrieking entourage. A few models and revelers in pink wigs lounged on the couch, too drunk to sit upright. Persephone's assigned bodyguard was nowhere to be seen. He was probably searching the house for his missing charge.

Athena pushed Persephone onto an empty couch and pressed another glass of champagne into her hands.

"Didn't mean to grill you back there." Athena sat next to her. "I just wanted to know what sort of person you are."

"I understand," Persephone said. She realized the woman was apologizing to her.

Athena shook her short hair and frowned. "I'm too blunt sometimes. But I find it saves time." She turned towards Persephone, who was sitting stiffly on the couch. "Here's the deal, Persephone. I like you. And I want to be your friend. But I want to know who you are first."

"Okay." Persephone nodded. "Do you have any more questions for me?" Persephone had wanted a friend, badly, and if Athena was going to just drop in her lap like this, well, she didn't mind jumping through a few hoops.

"Not right now. And if I ever pry too much, you can tell me to piss off, you know."

Persephone grinned.

"Like if I ask you whether you and Hades would consider a threesome—"

"Athena! Piss off."

Athena smiled into her champagne.

"I'm not sure if I should drink this." Persephone looked doubtfully at her third glass. "After two glasses I'm pretty much gone."

"Well then bottoms up, babe," Athena ordered, and then shouted to Hermes, who was walking by. "Oi! Persephone's a lightweight."

Hermes waltzed over, smiling enchantingly. "I'll take good care of you, sweetness."

Persephone giggled. "That's what I'm afraid of." She sipped and hiccupped.

"Oo la la," Hermes laughed. "Persephone, you've stolen my heart."

Athena kicked Hermes to get his attention. "So how'd you swing Orpheus? I thought he was sworn off of performing anywhere."

"Oh, for that we must thank Mrs. Ubeli," Hermes grinned. "Or, rather, her intimidating husband." Two servers in bunny ears approached him and pulled him away.

"Well done, Ubeli." Athena gave Persephone a wicked smile. "What do you give your husband when he's good?"

"Athena," Persephone smacked her new friend with a pillow.

Athena giggled. "Aw, let's make love not war." Athena leaned in, pretending to try to kiss Persephone.

"Oh, my gods, my dreams have come true." Hermes was back standing over them, grinning ear to ear. He'd lost his two gorgeous escorts, as well as his faux vest.

Athena's lips detoured at the last minute and smacked Persephone on the cheek. Gods, she'd even used a little tongue!

"Gross," Persephone sputtered, swiping at her cheek, and Athena laughed.

"Later, bitch, I'm going to get more booze." Athena stalked off towards the kitchen again.

"Just you and me, kid." Hermes spread his arms, showing off his not unimpressive chest.

Maybe it was the drink. Maybe it was the freedom she felt that night. Persephone took a chance because she'd always been curious about his tattoo. "Hermes, turn around."

Grinning ear to ear, he did.

The tattoo spread over his shoulders—white, angelic feathers, with the tips dripping black ink. The muscles of his back bunched at his shoulders and tapered to his waist. He lifted his arms and his pair of wings seemed to move.

"Oh, wow," Persephone reached out but pulled back just short of tracing the edge of a feather. It was so beautifully done. But then he turned and grabbed her hands, pulling her from her seat.

"Come with me, Persephone, darling. You must see the view."

She went eagerly. The alcohol had made her warm and the whole night felt like an adventure. And friends. Was she actually starting to have some genuine friendships? With people nearer her own age?

Hermes led her through the hall and up an impressive staircase. She could hear people hollering up ahead as they toured the second floor.

"The house was built a century ago. The balcony overlooks the park—you can see all the way to one of the fountains."

"Who lives here?" Persephone carefully jogged up the stairs in her stilettos, scurrying to keep up with the fleet-footed Hermes.

"A friend," Hermes said lightly. They came onto a landing and walked down a long hall, then through a room that led to gigantic French doors. Hermes scampered ahead and pushed the doors open with a flourish, revealing a balcony.

"Oh, wow," Persephone breathed. The whole city glowed golden before her, spreading beyond the black forest of the park.

"See the fountain?" Hermes stepped closer to her and pointed. Persephone stood on tiptoe and craned her neck to see. Sure enough, there were lit geysers beyond the trees.

"It's beautiful."

"Yes, it is."

Persephone realized that Hermes was hovering close to her, and stepped away. Oh. He didn't think— "Thank you for the invite to the party. Maybe next time Hades can come."

He smiled down at her. "It's good to see you out without him. You two seem stuck together."

"Yes, well, we're married now." She waved her left hand to show off her ring finger. "And I like having quiet nights in." It was true. She'd very much liked last night. Before the arguing, anyway.

"Boring." Hermes rolled his eyes. His fingers were busy in his hair, tousling the sexy dark locks, making them stand up as he struck a magazine model pose.

"What's wrong with boring? Maybe I like boring." She shoved him playfully. "I can be boring if I want."

"I didn't mean that. You're anything but boring." Hermes's dark eyes caressed her face.

"Whatever." She turned back to look out at the view. "I'm planning on getting out more anyway. Having more fun."

"Good for you. And I'm glad you came out tonight, princess, even if it took Athena to finally get you past the ogre and out of your tower."

Persephone frowned but Hermes just babbled on.

"I mean, whenever you come into Double M, all the stylists fight to work on you. You're funny. And you actually have a brain."

"Thanks," Persephone laughed. "I think."

Hermes waved his hand. "You know what I mean. You're more than just a dumb trophy wife."

"Is that what people think of me?"

"Look, it's no secret what your husband does for a living. A lot of people think it's better him than the family that used to run things." Hermes came close to her again, but she was too distracted thinking to notice. *Dumb trophy wife.*

"No one saw Hades date, much less thought he'd marry. He has too much to hide. And then you show up, all naïve and innocent, a tasty little morsel for the big bad wolf. And he gobbled you right up."

Hermes chuckled, right in her face. "But you're smart enough to know what's going on. I mean, you can't just stick your head in the sand, with the big shipment coming in and everything."

Too late Persephone tried to hide the question on her face.

Hermes leaned over her, his eyes gentle. "He didn't tell you." His hand reached out and stroked her hair back from her face. "Oh, Persephone. Naïve, innocent little Persephone."

She frowned and grasped him by the wrist. "Don't touch me like that," she glared. The alcohol in her wore away some of her softness. "I don't know what you're trying to say, but—"

"I'm sorry," Hermes also drew back from her, his dark hair falling in his face. He seemed to sober up, as if he had shown her more than what he meant to. "I think, I just was drinking and didn't mean it." He darted towards the French doors. "Stay up here as long as you want— I have guests to attend to."

He scuttled down the stairs, leaving Persephone rubbing her suddenly aching head. What the hell was that all about? Hermes had never acted like that when she visited his spa, Double M, or Metamorphosis. He'd always been nice, if a little clingy, but she thought that was just his style. Tonight, she would've thought he was hitting on her except for the backhanded compliments.

She shivered in the cool night air. Weird night. First Athena and then Hermes. Maybe they were on something? Maybe she shouldn't come to more parties, just stay home and ask her husband about his mysterious business. Big shipment coming in. It made sense, he was always headed to the area of town called the Styx, southeast near the docks.

So what if her husband didn't share his business with her? She was a commodity to him, not a partner. Besides, maybe she really didn't want to know.

Somewhere in the big house, a crowd of people were whooping loudly. Persephone wondered absently where her bodyguard was. Probably searching the corners of this big, dark house.

"Mrs. Ubeli?"

Persephone jerked up, arranging her features to be properly contrite. She turned, expecting to see the bodyguard.

Orpheus stood just inside the doors to the balcony. He wore his usual outfit of jeans and a white shirt. His head was bent and his hair was tousled, falling over his eyes.

"Orpheus? Where is everybody?"

The singer gestured harshly, as if to hush her. "They're in the movie room. It was dark and I slipped out."

"What are you doing here?"

"Please." He approached her, stumbling a little. Persephone backed away, wondering if he was drunk. "You have to help me. No one else will."

Goosebumps ran up her arms. "What's wrong?"

"They took her." His eyes were wild. "Eurydice. My fiancée. She went to pack up her apartment and get everything ready. We were going to elope."

"And then she left and didn't come back?" Persephone guessed. "Did you have a fight?"

"No. We've fought before, but not...not about this. They took her, so I'd keep playing." He paced a little in front of the French doors, squeezing his hands together.

"Who do you think took her, Orpheus?" Persephone asked, even though she could guess the answer.

"Ajax. He wants me to play. He won't let us go. I can't play without her. He's going to kill us both." His voice raised a little.

"Shh, ok. Let me think." Persephone shivered as she glanced back at the city. The night suddenly seemed big and terrible. "Can you go to the police?"

"I have to wait forty-eight hours. Besides, they won't let me go anywhere. The only reason I'm at this party is for some publicity thing." Orpheus started pacing again. "They're acting like it's all normal, saying she'll be back soon, that I just need to finish the concert series...but she's not answering her cell phone. She always answers when I call. Or texts back if she can't talk. They took her, I know it."

"I can talk to my husband—"

"No." Orpheus came towards her and Persephone took a step back towards the balcony railing. "Please don't. Ajax will kill her if he knew Ubeli was involved."

"Orpheus, then, I'm sorry. I don't know how to help." Persephone held up her hands, feeling useless. "Where would I even look?"

Orpheus fumbled in his pocket for something. "The last text she sent me...she was stopping by The Orchid House. She used to work there."

"The Orchid House?" Persephone cast about trying to remember where she'd heard the name. *Finest establishment in town,* Ajax had said.

"That's Ajax's club. I can't go there," she whispered harshly.

"Persephone?" a man's voice called up the stairs. Both Persephone and Orpheus's heads jerked in the direction. It was Hades. Dammit, she thought she'd have a little more time. He'd said he was busy tonight.

"I have to go," she whispered.

"Please." Orpheus held out a worn picture, old, taken in a photo booth. It was of Orpheus and beside him, Eurydice, beautiful with flawless mocha skin and pretty eyes. Eurydice was laughing. Persephone stared at the image. So much happiness waving in front of her. Out of reach.

"She needs help. And I have no one else to go to."

Persephone took the picture. Persephone had been all alone in the city once, powerless with no one to save her. And then a white knight had come to her rescue. Or so she had thought.

Persephone's eyes fell closed and she took a fortifying breath. She wasn't powerless anymore.

"Persephone, are you upstairs?" Hades's deep voice rumbled. Persephone looked over her shoulder as he continued to bellow. "Don't make me come up there."

When Persephone looked up, Orpheus had disappeared.

"Wait," she glanced around frantically, holding out the picture, but she was all alone. Stuffing it into her bra, she turned to wind her way back through the rooms and down the stairs, but it was too late.

Hades stood in the doorway. And he did not look pleased.

34

"Hades, I—" Persephone started.

"Not another word." His broad shoulders blocked the light. The shadows loomed around him and became part of him, flooding over her and casting her into darkness.

"But I—"

Hades stalked across the space between them in two strides and then his hand was on her jaw. "Open."

Eyes captured by the dark intensity of his gaze, she obeyed and dropped her mouth open.

He pulled something out of his pocket and then popped two cool little metallic balls with a small thread tying them together into her mouth. Each ball was about an inch in circumference.

"Now suck," he growled darkly into her ear. Obediently she ran her tongue around the gum-ball like metal pieces. Her eyes asked questions but she was too well-trained.

"If memory serves me correctly, I believe I told you that you could not come to this party tonight."

Persephone tried to reply in her defense but her response was garbled because of the balls.

"Hush." Hades lifted a finger to her lips. "Not a single word." And then he held out his hand in front of her mouth.

She let the balls fall onto his palm.

"Hades, what—"

"I said not a word," he chastised, and by the dark look in his eye, she could tell he meant it. "Turn around. Pull up your dress and lean forward. That's it. Tug your panties down and put your hands on the wall."

As gracefully as she could, she got into position. This is how it always went. He commanded, she obeyed.

The picture of the happy couple burned against her breast as she waited with her bare ass sticking out. She and Hades played some kinky games, for sure, but never in a strange house with a party raging a floor below. *Was he going to fuck her? Here?*

"So pretty and obedient." Hades cupped her right ass cheek, fondling it and giving it a light slap. He did the same with the left, landing a slightly harder spank. "At least when I'm here with my hands on you. But you've been a naughty girl, haven't you?"

"I don't look kindly when you put what is mine in danger." His voice dropped lower. Persephone shivered, but not in fear. "Spread your legs, angel. I'm going to remind this pussy who it belongs to."

Persephone rocked her legs apart. *Oh gods oh gods, he was going to—*

A long finger slid into her slick pussy, slowly probing. She arched her back, already desperate for him. So much for fighting for her independence.

"So wet, baby. Is this for me?" His voice went dark as night. "Or someone else?"

"You," she moaned, pressing her forehead into the wall. "Only you."

His finger continued dipping in and out of her. "Is that so? What were you doing up here all alone, then?"

Persephone closed her eyes. *Alone.* He hadn't seen Orpheus. He didn't think she was sneaking away for a private assignation.

"I wanted to see Hermes's place. I needed a second alone. The party, all the people, it was just..." Hades added a finger and her voice caught. "A-a lot."

"My sweet, sheltered innocent. My man called me to tell me you ran off. I told him my loving wife wouldn't make so much trouble on purpose. Or put herself so foolishly at risk."

"Please don't punish him. It wasn't his fault."

"I'll punish whomever I wish. And right now...that's you." A gust of air blew against her bare haunches. Persephone looked back to see what he was doing but with a stern shake of his head, Hades ordered her to face front. She didn't have to wait long.

With strong fingers, Hades pushed the metallic balls up inside her. Persephone went to her toes with an indrawn breath. Her pussy clenched automatically, and a ripple went through her as the balls' weight pressed on delicious points inside her.

"There," Hades said. "These are called Ben Wa balls. You'll keep them in." He pulled her panties up, her dress down, and he smacked her bottom again. Persephone cried out as the balls rocked inside her.

"Careful," Hades warned with what sounded like dark amusement. "You don't want them to fall out."

Slowly, Persephone straightened. Her legs tightened, wanting to press together. The balls moved in her wet channel, sending taut waves of pleasure through her. Turning around took an eternity.

With a wicked smirk, Hades stretched out his hand. "Shall we?" His murmur was all innocence.

"Hades," she whimpered, grabbing his hand as her knees threatened to give out. "You're not going to make me walk like this... I can't..."

He drew her close, his large body looming over her. His face turned gentle. "It's okay, goddess. I'll be with you every step of the way. You want to please me, don't you?"

Her insides turned liquid, golden honey simmering in her veins. She couldn't resist him like this, the kind and loving husband she wanted. "Yes." Her voice wobbled like her legs.

"Then walk and show me you're learning your lesson," his smile turned cruel along the edges, even as the next moment he added gently, "I got you."

Gripping his hand in both of hers, Persephone made her way down the stairs. The balls clanked inside her, but she grew used to their weight. Her panties were soaked.

At the foot of the stairs, a phalanx of bodyguards waited. None of the faces were familiar. Persephone raised her chin and ignored them, hoping they wouldn't think too much of her mincing steps and the blush staining her cheeks.

"Easy now," Hades murmured, wrapping an arm around her as if she was unsteady because she was drunk. He led her through the rooms, slightly emptier of bodies than before. From the sounds of things, the party had moved to the back of the house. Models and servers scattered, quieting and hugging the walls when the Shades entered.

"Mr. Ubeli." Hermes pushed through a knot of people by the door, Athena at his side. Persephone made herself smile, praying her body would behave.

"Excellent party," Hades said to Hermes. "Excuse us, we can't stay. My wife isn't feeling well."

Athena's eyes widened. Hermes nodded knowingly. To reassure them, Persephone gave a little wave. "Later," she mouthed to Athena as Hades steered her towards the door.

Her husband was a perfect gentleman, helping her down the steps and guiding her to the waiting car. As soon as they grew close, however, he pushed her forward and the motion made the balls rock inside her.

"*Oh*," she gasped.

"Easy. We're almost to the car."

She scrambled into the backseat and collapsed, panting. If the balls moved any more inside her, she'd come close to orgasm.

Hades followed, sitting across from her. He rapped the closed divider to signal to the driver, and leaned back as if to take in a show.

"Sit," he demanded. "Legs apart. Pull up your dress."

Biting back a needy noise, she bared her legs to the thigh.

"Panties off."

"Hades, I don't think—"

"Do it."

She stripped off the sodden scrap of white lace and spread her knees. Hades took her in, gaze hooded. He looked at her like a piece of art, an object he owned.

"Rock back and forth on the seat."

She did, and oh— *oh!* The balls rolled inside her. Millimeters that felt like miles. The weight of the balls pressed on all the right spots.

"Hades, please," she panted. "I'm going to—"

"Stop," he snapped. "You don't cum without permission."

"Do I have permission?"

"No. You deliberately ditched your bodyguard and snuck away into a crowded house full of strangers doing all manner of stupid things. I could kill Hermes for inviting Orpheus." He shook his head, his glare dark. "What if there was another riot? What if someone grabbed you?"

"Don't blame Hermes."

Hades leveled his stormy gaze, pinning her to the seat. "I *will* keep you safe, Persephone, even if I have to chain you to my side."

And here it was. He protected her, but he didn't love her. He wanted her, yes, but only as an object he could control.

"Chaining me to you won't keep me safe," she blurted. "Remember last time? She put her hand over her stomach, right over the place where she took a bullet. "By your side is a dangerous place to be." She said it under her breath but he heard.

His jaw clenched. The heat of his anger rolled over her, blowing up like a bomb in the car. She could barely breathe.

And then, just like that it disappeared, stuffed away into the fearsome man before her.

"For that outburst," he said in measured tones, his jaw tight, "you won't be cumming for a long time."

He made her rock on the seat and stop whenever she got close. By the end she was gripping the seat edge and keening. Her and her stupid big mouth. Why had she said anything? It wasn't like it changed things. Except now she could cry from being so close to satisfaction but being denied from paradise over and over and over again.

Her head hung down and she panted as the car rolled to a stop.

"We're here."

Here was another high-rise, with a fancy facade and a red carpet lined with camera toting paparazzi. Wait, what?

"Where are we?"

"Donation dinner. I'm introducing the headline speaker."

"What?" Her mouth dropped open. He couldn't be serious. She was a breathless mess and he expected her to face a red carpet?

"Last minute decision. The mayor requested my presence. Of course, I need you by my side."

She gaped at him.

"Dress down," he ordered, sounding almost bored. "Cover yourself."

She reached for her panties but he beat her to them. "I'll keep these." He brought them to his face to sniff before stuffing them in his pocket.

Now there was nothing between her pussy and the air. No safety net if the balls fell out.

"Hades!"

"You can do it," he said in that gentle, encouraging tone. As if he were a doting husband and not her torturer. "If you're good, I'll let you climax later."

He *was* serious. "But," she gasped, hand going to her hair. "Hades, I'm all..." She was a sweaty wreck, that's what she was.

Large, gentle hands pulled her worried ones away. Hades knelt before her, stroking back the flyaways.

"You look beautiful," he told her firmly. He ran a finger along the edge of her dress and her nipples rose in response. "*Perfetto.* Remember, you are mine." And with a kiss that seared her lips, he tugged her out of the car.

In the blinding flashes of the camera, Hades posed with his arm around her shoulders. He kept holding her as he guided her up the red carpet, playing the doting husband.

Okay, okay, she could do this. *Keep it together. Don't let the vultures see anything is amiss.* And really, it wasn't like anything was. Her husband was screwing with her mind and body, just like always.

Except, oh yeah, if these damn balls fell out on the red carpet, she was pretty sure she'd die from mortification. *Clench.* She squeezed her inner walls even tighter and held her thighs together, all the while trying to put on a natural-looking smile for the cameras.

She leaned into Hades, keeping her stroll smooth and controlled. If she looked stiffer and more flushed than usual, she could blame her awkwardness on the overwhelming paparazzi.

Thankfully, she and Hades were a few minutes late so the dinner had already begun. Other than a few nods to people he knew, Hades didn't leave her or let her go until they found their table. He pulled out her chair and she sank down gratefully. Thank the Fates, the damn balls had stayed in. Hades patted her shoulder and headed to the front.

Watching him walk away, Persephone felt a pang of desire in spite of herself as her husband ascended the stage. If only he weren't so handsome, his presence so commanding, then maybe she'd have half a chance of withstanding his charms. His dark head bent for a moment to speak to the much shorter man who announced him.

But as it was, when he straightened and surveyed the crowd with a casual authority, he took her breath away. He really was beyond gorgeous, damn him.

"Good evening," his deep voice rolled over the crowd. A few ladies sat up straighter, faces brightening under their thick makeup. Persephone felt an undeniable stab of jealousy. *Hands off, he's mine.* She should want him to move on from her, from their marriage bed, but the thought broke her. As much as she loved to hate him, if Hades left her for another woman... Nausea struck even at the thought.

Hades's gaze swept the crowd and settled on her. She went still. "I prepared a long and glorious speech to introduce the next speaker, but my wife asked me to keep it short. And I live to keep her happy."

He smiled at her, dimple appearing, and her insides went molten. A blush burned through her cheeks as light laughter swept the room and people turned to look at her. She kept her eyes on Hades. Like if she just looked long enough, she could figure out why, *why*, he had the effect he did on her. Gods, what would it take to rid him from her heart? Because as much as games like tonight might get her off, what was it worth if at the end of the day he still didn't love her—*and never would*?

"Without further ado, it's my great honor to introduce the man of the hour. Our illustrious mayor, ready for a new term: Zeus Sturm!"

Persephone craned her neck to see the familiar blond head as the mayor incumbent ascended the stage. The man was as handsome as his picture, with a boyish grin that endeared him to everyone so well. He waved to all the cheering people. In the hubbub, Hades slipped from the stage without shaking the mayor's hand.

Zeus Sturm approached the podium like he owned it. Persephone tried to distract herself from her maudlin thoughts by focusing on him, intentionally *not* watching Hades as he walked back to the table.

"Friends, welcome, welcome!" He grinned his handsome smile and told a warm-up joke that immediately had the crowd roaring. Over the course of his speech, the winsome politician continued making them laugh, until they all were eating out of his hand. Even Persephone cracked a reluctant smile.

Zeus covered education, economics, and at one point, crime.

"When I took office, this city was in the grip of the crime families. With the support of the commissioner and our boys in blue, we've made our streets safe."

"Miss me?" Hades murmured as he took his seat next to Persephone. A few people close to their table spared a second to study the two of them. Time to play the part. It was familiar and far easier than dealing with her real emotions. She fixed her face in an adoring expression and fluttered her eyelashes at her husband.

But then, when attention was off them, she hissed, "You didn't have to mention me in front of everyone."

Hades took her hand and kissed her knuckles. Persephone could almost hear the older women in the audience sighing over his chivalry. Still pressing her hand to his mouth, he gave her a wicked smile. "I almost said you preferred Zeus over me, but I figured that was too close to the truth."

Persephone pulled her hand back and faced the stage. "I don't even know the mayor. The only reason I'd prefer him is because he doesn't torture me like you do."

She quivered as Hades tucked her into his side. His fingers ran up and down her arm, stroking lightly, so lightly. She felt the touch right in her ever-tightening core.

"But you love it, don't you? All this torture...you enjoy it."

"I enjoy when it's over," she snapped.

"So will I." The smug promise made her womb convulse. "Now be a good girl and pay attention. The mayor is telling the city how much safer and prosperous it is under his rule. Lies, of course. The only reason New Olympus is still standing and not a smoking hole of ruin is because of *my* rule."

"You should've put that in your speech."

"Next time I will. I'll have you introduce me."

"I'll tell everyone the truth."

"What truth? That I dote on my wife. And give her everything?"

"No." Persephone smiled sweetly at nothing, suppressing a shiver as Hades traced the curve of her ear. "That you're the devil." She almost cringed as she said it. Why was she goading him? Sometimes he liked her to stand up to him, a kitten scratching him with ineffectual claws.

Apparently, tonight was one of those times. He chuckled and stopped his slow, tormenting touch. She was both relieved and disappointed. "I am a devil. I'm not the only one in this city." He nodded to a passing pair of men. "But I am the most powerful. Everyone wants to deal with me. Just like the devil, they come to bargain with me, and leave with everything they desire."

"Except their soul."

"Except that." He smirked.

The mayor finished and Hades made a show of standing and

applauding, slow golf claps that echoed above the rest. The night would continue with entertainment and gentle calls for donations.

Hades put his hand on Persephone's shoulder. "What about you, Persephone? Do I own your soul?"

"No," she denied vehemently, praying it wasn't a lie. "Just every other part of me. As you well know."

She waited as Hades spoke to a few people, mostly men who greeted him loudly and then leaned in to conduct their business in lower tones. Hades stood beside her chair as he spoke to them. He kept his hand on the back of her neck.

Persephone sipped her wine, resting, grateful for the reprieve. Grateful, and anxious. Hades had only begun and she had a feeling tonight would test her limits. He wouldn't be satisfied until he proved his total domination over her body and senses. Maybe even her soul, like he'd just talked about. He'd leave her with nothing.

And yet...there was a big part of her that couldn't wait to get home. As much as she craved his love, she'd take his dominance. What did that make her?

Leaning forward as if to fix her shoe, she let her hair fall over her breast and slipped the picture Orpheus had given her out of her bra and into her clutch. She didn't need to glance at it again; she had it memorized.

Eurydice had the love Persephone wished for, but Persephone had Hades. Arrogant, powerful, frustrating and sexy Hades. Her husband. She wouldn't trade him for anything, even the remains of her heart. Her dignity. Her soul. He was the devil, indeed.

As if sensing her thoughts on him, Hades glanced down with a lazy smile. His thumb brushed her cheek. "A few more minutes, Angel."

The people he was talking to spared her a smile. *How lucky*, the women were thinking. *What a doting husband.*

Persephone reached up and captured Hades's rough hand. He squeezed hers and didn't let go. She studied the dark hair dusting his olive skin.

Hades didn't feel love for her, only obsession, but if she couldn't have one, she'd take the other. Maybe it could be enough to sustain her?

Her breath quickened when Hades made his goodbyes and helped her out of her chair. He offered his arm with a sardonic arch of his brow. "Tired?"

"Not really." It would be just like him to take her home and put her to bed without relieving the desire he'd stoked. If he did that, she'd scream. Not that she wouldn't scream if he fucked her. She always lost control when he claimed her. And after the night of tumultuous thinking, she wanted that most of all. She wanted the bliss of being lost in him. For time and space to disappear in only the way that he could provide.

"Good," he purred in her ear. "Because the night isn't over yet." His hand covered hers where it rested on his strong forearm.

"Excuse us," he announced to the cluster of businessmen he'd been speaking to. "I promised my wife a tour of the art gallery."

"I hear it's stunning," a man with silver hair said. "Closed this time of night, though."

"I arranged a late-night viewing. We prefer...privacy."

The men laughed at that, and Hades led Persephone to an elevator. A Shade stepped out of the shadows to hand him something. Hades muttered something that sounded like, "keep the area secure" before inserting a keycard into a slot above the elevator buttons.

"Where is the art gallery?" Persephone asked, her voice calm even as her heart fluttered.

"Upstairs." Her husband straightened, his wide shoulders filling the space. It wasn't just his height and powerful body, but his very presence that dominated the vicinity. "It's a new installation, part of the remodel."

"Let me guess, your businesses had something to do with it."

"Art is a good investment," he said.

"And it's beautiful."

"That too." He turned to her and took her in fully. She pretended to ignore him, facing front, but her body hummed, knowing he was inspecting her as if she was a Degas "little dancer" painting he wanted to purchase.

He hit the emergency button. The elevator stopped with an angry buzz.

And so it begins.

"Hades," she said breathlessly. His hand came to her neck, thumb stroking a sensitive point. "How's your pussy?" he asked and she closed her eyes. "That bad? Or that good?"

Her pulse pounded under his palm.

"Poor wife. What can I do to make you feel better? Hmmm?" He leaned closer. "Are you wet for me? Let me check."

He sank to his knees, pulling up her dress. Persephone gave in and leaned against the elevator wall. She reached for him.

"Hands behind your back," he ordered sharply and leaned forward after she obeyed. Her fingers scrabbled desperately against the metal railing behind her.

"Poor, sweet neglected pussy. I'm here," he crooned, his lips brushing her labia. Persephone nearly came then and there. Her head swam as she began to float, her body becoming alight with sensation.

"Hades...please..."

"You have permission. In fact, I expect you to come. Multiple times. If you don't, I will be very displeased." He punctuated this with a kiss to her sopping slit.

Persephone's hands scrabbled on the rail, dying to grab his shoulders and hang on. But no, he'd said to keep her hands behind her back. Obedience equaled pleasure. It was all so simple when they were together like this.

Hades lifted her right leg and propped it over his shoulder.

"Feel free to scream," he remarked, before diving in. He feasted on her with gusto, nibbling on her lower lips and probing them apart with his tongue.

Her body convulsed and she fought to stay standing on her left leg. Hades fit his shoulder under her right as he settled himself in and laved up and down her seam.

"Oh— *Oh*— Hades!" she couldn't help crying out.

Her propped leg opened her further to him, and he used his fingers to part and probe her sex as his tongue fluttered next to her clit.

That was— It was so incredible, she couldn't even—

With a growl, he sank his fingers deep, rubbing her inner wall. Persephone went up on tiptoe. *Oh.* The balls inside her pushed further up her channel. Their weight combined with his crooked fingers send shockwaves reverberating through her.

"Cum for me," he commanded, and she did, her legs collapsing as she melted down the wall. Only Hades's hand on her hip and his shoulder steadied her and kept her upright.

"My wife." He moved up and kissed her. She tasted salt, she tasted herself, and underneath was Hades. Always Hades, dominating her lips and mouth while her body pulsed with aftershocks.

His thumb caressed the edge of her jaw and their gazes locked. It was moments like these, when her body and heart were wide open, that she wondered if she'd fallen into a dream. That sweet peace. Like Orpheus and Eurydice had, the kind of forever love that inspired his haunting songs.

Then Hades shoved his fingers into her mouth.

"I knew when I saw you that you were submissive. You just needed a firm hand."

He pulled his fingers out and wiped them on her dress. The casual degradation made her cheeks burn. So much for sweetness.

"You did well. You've pleased me."

She gritted her teeth.

"What do you say?"

"Thank you."

"Good girl."

Good girl. He was always saying that. Good girl, good girl, good girl. So fucking patronizing. It wasn't something you said to an equal.

But then she wasn't an equal, was she? Not to him. She was a *good lay.* Of course he'd never love her. How could he love his 'good girl', his sex object that got him off when she wasn't being paraded around as his trophy wife.

Earlier tonight she told herself this was enough. That she could be satisfied as long as she had this.

But dammit, didn't she deserve more? Didn't she deserve to be loved? Truly loved? Why was she putting up with these half-measures? Did she really think so little of herself?

She ducked her head away from Hades. "I...need a moment."

He backed away and hit the elevator button. The smooth ascent began, but Persephone's heart remained a few stories down, with the mirage of the caring man her husband could be.

"You all right?" he asked, casually. Not as if he cared. So much wealth and privilege and he couldn't afford to care.

When she remained silent, he called her name. "Persephone, answer me."

He wanted her to speak? She'd give him words. "You know, I could've loved you."

He didn't react. His face showed no sign that she'd fired the first shot. "You don't love me?"

"As if I could, after what you've done to me."

"Is that a no?" A hint of a smirk before his expression smoothed. He was calm as a lawyer questioning a witness.

Fucking arrogant man. "No, Hades, I don't love you. Not anymore. Not like before."

She remembered everything, how much hope she had right up until the wedding night. How he'd held all her happiness in the palm of his hand. How he'd let it fall and then shatter.

"You could've married me, given me the honeymoon of my dreams. You could have told me about your sister. I would've grieved with you. If you had told me the truth and opened up to me, we could've..." Her voice choked off with all the could-have-beens.

Hades still watched her with no expression.

"But you chose to punish me." Her voice cracked and she fought for control. "To *break* me."

He reached for her and she wrenched herself away. She wouldn't let tears fall. She wouldn't. "You can have love or you can have revenge. We both know what you chose."

HADES LOOKED DOWN at his bride, quivering with the force of her anger and pain.

Blue eyes, the color of a summer sky. Hair a dark blonde, like wheat fields. Her complexion was pure, peaches and cream, her scent fresh as the country air.

He'd never seen anything like her, not in his city. She stepped off the bus into his world, and he'd known if he didn't take her, claim her for his own, the city would eat her alive.

All that innocence ready to be sullied. He saved her from a long hard fall. He *saved* her.

She should be grateful.

But instead she glared at him, her expression as close to hate as he'd ever seen it.

He loomed over her. "This isn't story time. I'm not a handsome prince. Fairy tales aren't real."

She raised her chin. That vibrant inner strength, the core he couldn't touch. Couldn't break.

"Love is."

"If you believe that you're not truly broken."

She started to shake her head and he grabbed her chin, forcing her to face him. "I will risk everything, even your hate, to keep you safe. To let you live in a world where you believe love is real."

Her expression softened. See, she couldn't hate him. She was too full of goodness. The light in her saved him from the darkness, even when he deserved her hate and earned her loathing, over and over.

"Oh Hades," she whispered. "What have you become?"

For a moment he wavered. He would tell her he didn't want revenge. That having her was enough, if she would just give herself fully to him—

But no. That was too close to groveling. And he didn't grovel. The facts didn't change whether his face was in her pussy or she was on her knees with his cock down her throat. He owned her.

Body, mind, soul. Heart. End of story.

They were almost to the top floor, but not quite. Good enough. He needed to teach his bride, his *wife*, a lesson.

He stabbed a button. "On second thought, I think we'll take the stairs."

The doors opened and he swept a hand out. "After you."

She took a few trembling steps into the darkness. He'd left the balls inside her. She'd have to tighten her muscles and accept another round of growing arousal. The motion sensor lights blinked on. A museum of white walls and shining wood floors stretched before them, full of statues.

"Run," he ordered her coldly. He could all but hear her heart stutter to a stop.

"Wh-what?"

"Run," Hades repeated, shrugging out of his jacket. He hung it on a nearby statue and started rolling up his sleeves. "I'm going to chase you. If you reach the other side without dropping the balls..." He arched an eyebrow. "...you get a reward." Then he dropped his voice. "But if you let them fall—"

Her eyelashes fluttered, her breath coming faster. "What if you catch me?"

"If I catch you, I get the reward."

"What's the reward?"

He stared intently into her eyes, which were flitting this way and that before finally settling and focusing on his. "Anything I want."

She gulped.

He'd lied earlier. Some parts of fairy tales *were* real. Like the big bad wolf hunting down an innocent girl. He was the hunter. She was his prey.

And now she would understand that she would never, ever escape him.

She kicked off her shoes and then took off up the stairs. He leaned on the rail, watching her go. She couldn't quite run. Her ass wiggled back and forth in her attempt to keep her thighs together so the heavy balls would stay inside her. Hades pulled her panties out from his coat pocket and took a long inhale before finally starting up the stairs himself.

She hazarded a glance over her shoulder and let out a small *yip* when she saw he was following and how quickly and easily he was gaining on her.

Oh he liked this game very much.

She scurried ahead, darting around installations and statue laden pedestals. He paced behind her, a hunter who knew his prey. She left the scent of arousal in her wake.

She reached the end of the room and slipped through the door. He was gaining on her even with his steady, even tread. His legs were longer and she had to take small, mincing steps or risk punishment for losing the balls.

Either that, or she wanted him to catch her. He grinned at the thought. For all her protests, her body recognized its master.

He paused just outside the door, staying in the shadows as he peeked inside. The second room held only a giant staircase, spiraling up several stories to the sky.

A massive chandelier blazed above with each of its crystals twisting slowly so shining patterns danced on the white-gold marble.

There she was, starting up the staircase. She was going slower, gliding from step to step, her face turned to the light. The brilliant waterfall turned her hair into a glowing halo. Bright and fiercely perfect.

A fist clenched Hades's heart until he gritted his teeth against the pain. She was so fucking beautiful it hurt.

She is mine, and mine alone. Possessing her completely was the only thing that eased the ache.

He finally came into the room and followed her up the stairs, taking them leisurely two at a time, not rushing but not waiting either.

When he'd closed the distance to less than twenty steps, Persephone glanced back and gasped. Her legs slammed together and she grabbed the railing, pausing to regain her control a second before she fled again. Hades's chuckle echoed around them.

Head bowed, she scurried higher, her steps jerky and panicked. Her fear was so delicious. Especially because he saw her arousal glistening on the pristine stairs.

Near the top floor, he closed the distance to ten steps. In her rush, she must have forgotten to mind the balls. They fell, bouncing and spinning with wet drops flying.

They both froze to listen to them clatter over the white-gold marble, down one step and then another and another, echoing like tinny music around the large chamber. When the noise stopped, Hades met his wife's wide blue eyes and smiled.

She turned and raced up the final steps, but too late. Hades sprang and tackled her, his weight driving her to her hands and knees, even as his arm caught her middle and broke her fall.

He eased her down the last inch. Her hands slapped the marble and he tossed up her dress, ripping it in his haste.

He was the victor and he wouldn't waste time in devouring his prize. Her legs parted automatically and he thrust three fingers into her wet center, hooking to find her G spot.

"Scream for me," he ordered and she did, her torso writhing and cunt milking his fingers. "Again." His fingers probed, finishing what the balls started. She was wet, so wet. If he hadn't rolled up his cuffs they'd be soaked.

When she'd convulsed with a second climax, he pushed on her back with his free hand, so her body bowed and her ass propped up right where he wanted it. He knelt a step behind her as she half lay on the landing, legs spread and hindquarters bare, ripe and ready for him.

He almost broke his pants zipper getting it open. His cock throbbed, pointing straight towards the wet heat waiting for it.

The cry she made when he slid into her almost set him off. His balls were tight and ready with a massive amount of cum. He gritted his teeth and took a moment to smooth his hands down her shuddering back.

Then he drove into her, sending her body rocking forward with each thrust. She sobbed and begged for more, her back arched so her ass ground into him. He wound a hand in her hair and made her bow backwards even further. He rode her that way for a while before hooking a hard arm under her helpless body and drawing her up against him, so he could growl in her ear,

"Enough. Enough of fighting me. You'll do what I say because I keep you safe. You'll do what I say because *it is what I say*. You stay pure. Untouched except by me."

His hips slammed into her so hard her body jerked, to make the point. "You are mine and no others. Not even your own."

He wound one of his arms around her until his fingers were at her throat. He squeezed only hard enough that she felt him there. "Your life is in my hands and I have sworn to protect you. And you will fucking *let me*. Do you understand?"

When she didn't say anything except for her moans of pleasure, he shook her again. "Do you understand?"

"Yes!" she cried. "Yes, oh, *Hades*."

Then she came apart in his arms again, softly keening.

Gods, he needed this woman. His arms clamped around her, holding her tight as if he could merge them into one. When his climax came, it blinded him.

He let them both sink to the floor, one arm around her middle and the other propping them up slightly. Persephone lay safe in his arms, her hair spilled over the gleaming stone. They were both bathed in softly spinning light.

He wanted to lie here forever. The fields of paradise couldn't be better than this. Persephone's warmth soaked into him, warming him down to his bones. For one long, perfect moment, he closed his eyes and let himself bask in her sunlight.

...

...

...

But...*no*. He couldn't. His place was in the darkness. In the cold. In shadow.

So he gathered himself, drew down her dress, and used a ripped piece to sop up the dripping mess between her legs. He had to help her down the first few steps, until she regained her equilibrium. Halfway down he stopped and pointed to the abandoned Ben Wa balls.

His body still buzzing, he wanted to whisper a sonnet to her.

Instead, he made his voice icy. "Clean up your arousal."

He handed her a handkerchief. Cheeks an adorable shade of pink, Persephone wiped the steps and collected the balls as he towered over her. When he held out his hand for the bundle, she didn't look at him but bit her lip. The sight sent another shot of arousal stabbing through him.

With a hand on her back, he escorted her to the elevator, steadying her when she wobbled. Her dress was torn in the back, the straps slipping down her shoulders, but she was too dazed to notice. She couldn't do anything but lean on him.

If he could keep her in this state, freshly fucked with his cum spilling out of her puffy pussy, gaze hazy and cheeks tinged pleasure-pink, he would. He'd be tempted to sell his businesses, buy the whole Crown Hotel, and take her in a different room night after night after night.

Catching her in his arms, he gave her a kiss.

"Angel," he murmured and she melted into him.

Fuck it. Hades gave into what he ached to do all night.

He wrapped her in his jacket and carried her the rest of the way, down the elevator, through the building empty of all but his Shades, and out to the car where he held her all the way home.

35

"Orpheus seemed desperate," Persephone told Hecate early the next morning, as they were taking inventory at the shelter's store. Hecate had initially asked about how things were with Hades—

But Persephone just couldn't. Last night... Last night was... She'd thought if she finally got it all out and stopped pretending to be the good little wife...

But her rebellious actions and words had seemed to fire Hades up even more, if that was possible. She wouldn't have thought so. But that race up the stairwell, and when he caught her— Her entire body flushed hot.

Last night had only proved that nothing had changed. She was just as far under Hades's thrall as ever.

She'd loved every single thing he did...but that had always been the problem, hadn't it? She *loved*... Whereas Hades only...what? Amused himself with her? Enjoyed taking his possession out to play with?

And when he tires of you?

No, it was far better to think about other people and *their* problems if she wanted to stay sane. Hence throwing herself into the Eurydice mystery as soon as she'd gotten to the shelter this morning.

Plus, Orpheus and Eurydice really did need her help. And Hades was wrong. Real love *did* exist. These two proved it was still possible, even in this corrupt, ugly world. It didn't matter that that kind of love would never be Persephone's.

"I didn't know what to say when he asked me for help, though. But the more I think about it, the more I know I have to do something."

"A lot of people would say it's not your problem." Hecate swung her red hair over her shoulder, out of the way of her clipboard.

Persephone moved down the aisle, counting the bags of dog food and the chic chew toys the shelter sold to raise money for their non-profit. She looked forward to her volunteer time even though it was only two days a week. Though the dogs barked in the back, to her the place seemed peaceful. But any bit of peace was a mirage in the city. She was starting to see that. Hades had always talked about how this city was barely held back chaos…

Hecate let her work in silence until she came to the end of the aisle and faced Hecate again. Persephone thought of the photo booth picture that even now she had in her pocket. Their bright smiles, full of such hope. And love.

"Orpheus is right. I'm in a position to help. If I don't do it, who else will?" Persephone said with sudden certainty.

This city was a bad place to be friendless. And even though Orpheus was worshiped and adored, *Orpheus*, the man behind the persona, didn't have any true friends. No one else who could help him. He didn't have anyone else in the world on his side, other than the woman he loved.

Hecate didn't look surprised. "So where do you start looking?"

Persephone bit her lip as she thought about it. But she always came back to the same conclusion, no matter how distasteful it might be. "The club where Eurydice worked. I think I'll drop by there today."

Hecate raised an eyebrow. "And what does Hades say about all of this?"

"I can't tell him." Persephone looked away. She was pretty sure Hades would just tell her to stay out of it and that it was none of her concern. And there was a possibility that... "It's complicated. And anyway, he's busy."

She looked at Hecate for validation. "I was just going to slip away and check around. See if anyone's heard anything. Maybe no one but us needs to know."

Hecate reached out and tugged away Persephone's clipboard. "You're done here. Get going, but be safe."

Persephone nodded, feeling scared and relieved at the same time. She couldn't even fully explain to herself why she had to do this. Maybe because after last night, she had to show herself Hades hadn't swallowed up all of her yet—that there would be something left of *her* once he tired of her. She hoped her motives were better than that. She genuinely did want to help Eurydice and Orpheus.

Either way, she was doing this. She pulled her apron off over her head and strode toward the back of the shop.

Besides, what Hades didn't know wouldn't hurt him.

Persephone slipped out the back door of the animal shelter, pulling her hair up in a ponytail and tugging a knit hat over it. She never went out this way. The dumpster was out in the parking lot off to the side, so she never had need to use this door.

Still, before she stepped onto the street, she glanced this way and that to make sure Hades's men weren't around. Usually they dropped her off at the shelter and left, with the unspoken understanding that she stay in the building.

Even if they were hanging around—which they likely were with how twitchy Hades had been lately—they'd probably be out front. As long as she was back before they came inside to get her at the end of the day, she'd never be missed.

As she loped down the alleyway, she felt a private triumph. This would be her first excursion out in the city all on her own since...she couldn't even remember when. Since before Hades and that seemed like an eternity now, like a different life.

She cut across to a side street, then took the bus part of the way and walked the last bit down a street lined with shops. Finally she came to a nice covered entryway with black pillars. "The Orchid House" was inscribed in purple letters over the door. It looked like a restaurant.

She bit her lip and glanced around. The chances of her running into Ajax were high. He owned the club. But if she stood here for much longer, she'd definitely look out of place. But she'd forgotten—until now—that Ajax had told her to attend auditions at eleven.

A glance at her phone showed that it was around ten now.

She took a deep breath. It would be fine. She'd be in and out before anyone noticed. Well, she *hoped* she would be.

Or she could be smart and get the hell out of here right now.

She pulled the old picture out of her pocket. Eurydice smiled back at her, so innocent and carefree.

"This is the dumbest thing I've ever done," she hissed under her breath to Eurydice's picture before pocketing it and pushing into the club.

A dark narrow hallway led to a coat check area. From there the room opened up into a lushly decorated restaurant, with a bar on one side and leather armchairs facing a stage. And she couldn't miss the two poles going from ceiling to floor on the stage.

She gulped, hard. If she was caught, how exactly was she going to explain to Hades why she had showed up to a strip club at ten in the morning on a Tuesday?

She almost turned around and left. At least she'd tried.

"Hey, honey," a friendly voice called.

Busted, Persephone peered into the gloom.

A young man stood behind the bar, wiping glasses dry. "You're too early. Auditions don't start until eleven."

"Sorry. Um, I'm looking for someone who works here?" Persephone called.

The man leaned against the bar. He was gangly but good-looking, with longish blond hair ending in curls around his face. "What's your friend's name, honey?"

"Eurydice."

"Is that her real name or stage name?"

Uhhhhh...good question? Persephone's mouth was suddenly as dry as dirt. She swallowed several times. The young man cocked his head and gave her a dazzling smile. He seemed amused by her discomfort.

Fumbling inside her pockets, Persephone approached and laid the picture of Eurydice and Orpheus down on the polished surface.

The young man studied it, then shook his head. "I don't know her. You sure she used to work here?"

Persephone tried to recall what Orpheus had said. "I think so. She's missing and I'm looking for her, for a friend." She stopped abruptly, wondering how much to share.

"If you wait a minute, Aphrodite might be able to help you. She's worked here longer. She might recognize your friend."

Persephone nodded her gratitude.

"You can sit if you want. Aphrodite should be right out."

"Uh, I don't know." Persephone turned and stopped, distracted by the posters on the far wall. Most were of women in provocative poses, poorly disguised as gaudy art. "I don't have much time."

"You sure you're not going to audition?" The bar boy was still smiling at her, now overtly appraising her body. When Persephone caught his eye again, he winked.

"Don't be shy, sugar. Everyone's nervous their first time." He nodded towards the stage and Persephone turned back, walking slowly to one of the chairs to sit.

She saw smoke curling out from the corner of the stage.

"Um." She glanced over at the bartender. He was watching it too and seemed unconcerned. For a second Persephone listened hard, until she could hear the click of a fog machine in the background. She relaxed and turned back to face front.

The mist kept creeping over the black stage, thickening until it was at least a foot deep.

Then a song started playing, violins plucking on beat.

A figure slowly appeared in the mist. The arms appeared first and then the face of a young woman, her big brown eyes staring right into Persephone's. She was petite and curvy, her figure clad only in black hot pants and a white skintight top. She came out of the fog, moving swiftly to grab a pole.

She twirled slowly, her feet swishing through the smoke. She landed and twisted, spinning gracefully and then soaring around the pole again, somehow hooking her legs so her hands were free.

She peeled the white shirt off provocatively, baring a sexy midriff. Then she smiled at her audience of two. She turned her back to them, then glanced back over one sexy shoulder as her booty swayed wildly. She reached up and loosened her long, glossy hair, letting it pour over her.

The song ended and wow. Just...wow. Persephone had never seen anybody move like that, so unconsciously raw and feminine and sexy. A clapping sound from the left caught her attention; the bar boy was grinning as he gave a standing ovation.

The dancer disappeared and the smoke machines sputtered to a stop. In a minute the woman reappeared, hair tied back again, shirt tucked into wide legged black pants. She looked perfectly normal, like the girl next door.

"Bravo," the youth at the bar clapped his approval. "Looks great, Aphrodite."

"Thanks, Paul." The woman had a high-pitched, breathy voice. "Everything's working perfectly. This is going to be my best show ever." She giggled, a gorgeous, delighted sound.

"Hey, this lady's here to see you." Paul waved to Persephone.

Aphrodite kept her sweet smile as she approached Persephone. "Can I help you?"

As she came closer, Persephone caught her breath. Aphrodite was beautiful. Wide brown eyes surrounded by thick black lashes and perfectly bronzed skin—the woman wasn't wearing a touch of makeup and she was lovelier than any model Persephone had ever seen.

"Are you here to apply for a job?" Aphrodite asked, smiling broadly. She was several inches shorter than Persephone, if more curvy. Even her plain clothes couldn't hide her sexy figure.

Persephone realized she'd been staring. "Um, no, sorry." She shook herself. "I'm looking for a friend who works here. Her name is Eurydice."

Aphrodite's smile switched off. Her dark brown eyes became assessing. She obviously knew something about Eurydice.

"I just need to talk to her," Persephone pleaded, lowering her voice. "She's missing and her fiancé is worried."

"I haven't seen Eurydice in a while," Aphrodite said. "She used to work here but I think she left when she got engaged." She hesitated, glancing at the bar hand as if she didn't want to say more in front of him. "Paul? I'm going to head out for a bit and then I'll be back."

"You're on at two. Though I might need a dance or two before because the others are always late."

"I'm sure it will all work out." Aphrodite smiled enchantingly.

"Did you get everything you needed?" Paul asked Persephone.

Persephone blinked and nodded. "Um, I need to go actually."

"I'll walk you out," Aphrodite added in her breathy voice. "Just let me grab my purse."

The petite woman ran behind the bar and grabbed her things. She came back, sliding on large dark sunglasses that swallowed up her face. The hoodie pulled over her hair took care of hiding the rest.

"Come on." Aphrodite grabbed Persephone's hand and pulled her out of the club.

They ended up on the street. Which was where Aphrodite rounded on her, her voice sounding more normally pitched and less sex kitten.

"Look, I'm going to ask this once," Aphrodite demanded, "and I want the truth. Are you one of Ajax's girls?"

Persephone blinked in the bright light, surprised by this turn of events. "Um, no."

Aphrodite put her sunglasses up so she could gaze straight into Persephone's eyes. "Are you working for him?"

"N-no," Persephone blurted as the shorter woman got in her face.

"Then how do you know Eurydice?"

"I know her fiancé. Orpheus. He's a singer and doing a show at—" She stopped when she realized she shouldn't say 'My husband's club.'

"I know who Orpheus is. Everybody does."

Faced with those striking brown eyes, Persephone wanted to tell the truth. "I met him backstage and then later at a party. Eurydice is his fiancée and she's been missing since yesterday. He wanted me to help ask around until the police can get involved."

Aphrodite's eyes narrowed, weighing Persephone in the balance.

"Orpheus asked me to come look for her. He's not allowed to leave to look himself. Something about his contract. The guys he's working with aren't the best types..." Persephone trailed off.

She couldn't imagine how that sounded. Right, a famous guy she'd met a couple times at a party had asked her to look into his missing fiancée. She probably sounded nuts.

For a moment Aphrodite just studied her face. Persephone shifted from foot to foot, ducking her head nervously when someone drove past. Ajax could walk up at any moment. They were still far too close to the club for Persephone's comfort. But crazy or not, she couldn't just let this go. Aphrodite obviously knew something about Eurydice.

"Look, I'm not here to pry. Or cause trouble. I can give you my number, and if you find anything out, just call me, ok?" Persephone fumbled in her pocket and took out the little notebook she carried. She handed Aphrodite a slip with her number scribbled on it.

Aphrodite took it, and Persephone started to walk away. If the woman didn't trust her enough to talk to her, there was nothing Persephone could do.

"Wait," Aphrodite called. Persephone stopped and looked back.

Huddled in the hoodie and sunglasses too large for her face, Aphrodite seemed almost childlike. "Why would you help Eurydice?"

Persephone took a deep breath. She'd wondered that herself, all the way from the shelter to The Orchid House.

You and me against the world, Orpheus had said. The lovers in the green room, gazing into each other's eyes like they were the only people alive.

"She and Orpheus were going to elope." Persephone took out the picture again and held it up so Aphrodite could see it. "I want to help them. It means something, to have a love like they have. It's special and precious. But it's not..." Persephone shook her head as she tried to find the words. "It's not just that. It's... I could *be* her."

She met Aphrodite's eyes, trying to be as honest as possible. "When I first came to the city, I needed someone to watch out for me." She paused again. Hades's face flashed in her mind but she shook it away. He'd been her savior all right. With a vengeance. "Right now, I think Eurydice needs help, too. Sometimes that's all it takes, one person willing to help. It can change everything." Not always for the better, but that was neither here nor there.

The dancer's eyes bored into her, piercing her skin. Persephone wished she hadn't said so much, so awkwardly. She was ready to bolt, leave the area and find another way, when Aphrodite spoke.

"I can tell you about Eurydice," Aphrodite said. "But not here."

36

Aphrodite led Persephone to a shop around the corner.

Part coffee shop and part bookstore, the restaurant had nice private booths with high backs. Aphrodite slid into one. "This is my favorite place to get a Buddha bowl. And they do a nice vegan lasagna. Plus espresso to die for."

"I'll have what you're having." Persephone smiled at her, glad she was letting her guard down.

Aphrodite ordered without looking at the menu. After the waitress got them waters and a pot of green tea, Aphrodite settled in and studied Persephone's face.

"I recognize you from somewhere."

"I sometimes work as a model," Persephone admitted. She was nervous about giving too much of her identity away but thought it was best. She wanted this beautiful woman to trust her, but revealing she was the wife of Hades Ubeli... Some things were better left unsaid. "You may have seen me in a magazine."

"Maybe," Aphrodite said softly. She poured the tea and cupped her hands around her mug, eyes still on Persephone.

"How long have you worked at The Orchid House?"

Aphrodite smiled absently. "Awhile."

Persephone paused. "Should I not ask questions about it? Is that rude?"

Aphrodite laughed her delightful laugh. "It's not rude, not unless you're going to be rude."

"Why would I be rude?"

"Most people like to judge."

"Well, I don't. I mean, I won't. I don't like looking down on people." Persephone felt her cheeks heat. Why did she always get so tongue-tied around people she admired? "Anyway, your dance was amazing."

A smile curved Aphrodite's lips. "Well, thank you. I don't mind talking about my dancing. I've been doing it about four years now."

"Wow."

"Yeah." Aphrodite gazed into her mug, a fond look on her face. "I love it, actually."

"I'd love to see your act." It was the truth. Persephone had never seen anyone move with such sensuous grace. An image of Hades, naked and prowling toward her, popped into her head. Okay, she'd never seen a *woman* move with such sensuous grace.

"You should come back, then. Don't come alone. Come with a man. And I'll make sure to mark you two, so none of the other girls fight over you. Although not many of them approach couples; they don't know how to market to them."

Persephone could never go back to Ajax's club, as nice as it would be to see Aphrodite's act, and she certainly couldn't imagine asking Hades to go with her. Still, she was curious. "Market to them?" she asked after the waitress had put down their meals and coffees and walked away.

Aphrodite pulled off her glasses and unzipped her hoodie to expose a fair bit of cleavage, then she grabbed her coffee and pulled out her phone. She smiled sinfully at the camera, the coffee at her lips and snapped a selfie.

Then she zipped the hoodie back up and shoved a forkful in her mouth before her fingers were dancing over the buttons on her phone. She spoke around a mouthful. "It's all about marketing yourself these days. Online and in person. It's a business. If I dance, I get tips. If I dance well, people want more. And then I upsell. Champagne room. VIP section. Private lap dances."

Persephone digested this, picking at her food. The Buddha Bowl was a meal in a giant bowl. The turquoise ceramic dish held spinach, kale, chunks of avocado, and some brown grain Persephone couldn't identify.

"Quinoa," Aphrodite explained. "It's good for you. Try it."

Persephone did and found it was good. "So," she continued after a few bites, "Eurydice worked with you?"

Aphrodite chewed for a bit before answering. "Eurydice was a dancer. She did parties, too, and another side business. That's probably where she met Orpheus."

"What side business?"

"She was an escort."

Persephone thought back to some of the events she'd been on Hades's arm, surrounded by other couples. Some of the men had women with them that looked out of place. Too young and gorgeous for their partners. "Like, going out and being a date at parties?"

"Sometimes. I've done the arm-candy-for-hire thing. But there's also a side of it that happens in private, in a hotel room."

"Oh." Persephone blinked.

"It's alright," Aphrodite laughed, "It's a pretty good gig. You can work for an agency or on your own."

"So have you ever...?"

Aphrodite just smiled in answer. Persephone was torn between wanting to apologize for prying and wanting to ask a million more questions. She blurted out the most pressing one. "Why are you telling me all this? I mean, you just met me."

"You're honest. And you seem like someone who wants to help. Which is kinda rare. And you don't seem like a creeper. I mean, you're my age and you could easily be working alongside me. And, I guess, I don't know, I like the idea of someone looking out for one of us."

Persephone nodded. "So any ideas on how to find Eurydice?"

"Eurydice and I worked for the same agency. They aren't the

problem here. They were fine. They screened clients and I felt safer working with them than anyone else. But Eurydice was caught up in much deeper stuff. She hung out with a bad crowd."

Persephone fell silent, trying to piece things together.

Aphrodite put her elbows on the table and leaned in. "A few months ago, Eurydice stopped dancing. But she was still caught up in the life—she came to the club a couple of times. I thought for a second that she was a sugar baby—"

"What's that?"

"A lady who gets an allowance from a man to regularly escort him, or be with him."

"Her sugar daddy."

"Exactly. So Eurydice was hanging around one of the guys who came to the club a lot. I thought she was getting an allowance, maybe good enough to keep her from dancing or being with any other men."

Aphrodite's voice dropped to a whisper. "But I don't think that's what happened. I think Eurydice was in trouble, and this man was holding something over her. And then suddenly she was with Orpheus." Aphrodite shrugged. "I saw her once. She seemed happy with him. She told me she was out of the life."

The waitress took their bowls away, and Persephone realized how long they'd been sitting there.

"Thank you for telling me all this."

"Happy to help," Aphrodite said.

They stood up to go but had only walked a few steps when Aphrodite pulled out her phone again, this time aiming it not at herself, but at an artful bit of stained glass in one of the windows nearby. She frowned and moved the phone around to different positions before finally snapping the shot.

"But be careful," she looked back Persephone's way. "The guy Eurydice was with before Orpheus, he's bad news. I've seen girls get caught up with him before and then disappear. I think he runs a ring or something."

"A ring?"

"Trafficking. Really scary stuff. Maybe guns and drugs, too. His name's Ajax."

"Ajax?" Persephone said his name slowly. "Are you sure?"

Aphrodite paused as several people passed by, then leaned in. "Have you heard of him?"

Persephone thought of the concert, Hades's tense standoff with Ajax, and the girl, Ashley, dead on the bathroom floor.

"I met him. At a concert." She shivered. "He gave me the creeps."

"He's definitely creepy."

"I heard he owns The Orchid House."

Aphrodite nodded, grimacing. "He's involved somehow. He hasn't been around for a long time. I wish he'd stayed away. If he hangs around much more I'll probably end up quitting."

"You thought I was one of his girls."

"You're his type. Well, one of his types. I don't know, I just try to avoid him." Aphrodite re-donned her large sunglasses and put the hood up over her hair. "He wants me to star in a porno. I mean, I wouldn't mind it, but not with him producing."

Persephone followed her new friend out of the restaurant, wondering at Aphrodite's incognito look. Right outside, Aphrodite pulled out her camera phone again. Before Persephone realized exactly what she was doing, Aphrodite had lifted her phone and snapped a picture of Persephone herself.

"Please don't put that up on social media," Persephone said. Hades might freak out.

But Aphrodite just dropped the phone with a smile. "Don't worry, I won't. That one's just for me. I like taking pictures of beautiful things."

Oh. Persephone felt her cheeks redden but Aphrodite was already walking, so Persephone hurried to catch up with her.

They rounded the corner and a man came out of an alley and fell into stride beside Aphrodite.

"Hey, Annie," he said.

Persephone gripped her purse tighter and looked around. They were on the sidewalk of a wide thoroughfare but for once, there were no Shades to call for if this guy made trouble. She hadn't realized until now how much she'd begun to rely on them. And take them for granted.

Aphrodite didn't seem fussed or worried, though, but she did pick up her pace. Persephone kept up with her, ready to run if the situation called for it.

"Pete." Her voice lost all of its sultry qualities. "Don't call me that."

The man grinned and rubbed his chin where a three-o-clock shadow was already appearing. His stubble was grey and matched his closely shaven head. "Call you what, Aphrodite Banana?"

Aphrodite growled and looked over at Persephone. "Don't talk to him. Ignore him and he'll go away."

"I'm really a nice guy. Here to help. Protect the weak." He flashed a badge. He was a *cop*? "Gather little orchids up and take them back to their house."

"Well, we're no shrinking violets, so get lost."

"Huh," he guffawed, shoving his hands back into his pockets. He looked around her towards Persephone. "Who are you? You look familiar." The cop frowned, and Persephone wished she had large sunglasses and a hoodie to hide behind, too.

"She's a friend, Pete. Back off. You'll get the info."

"Get it to me and I won't crash your little party tonight. I know what goes on in the back rooms of that place."

"Legal lap dances." Aphrodite almost sounded bored. "You have nothing."

"Oh, and the side business in the hotel room afterwards?"

"Time spent between consenting adults. Don't be a dick, Peter. I know my rights."

"Careful, tiny dancer. And lovely friend, if you ever need to call on the boys in blue..." He shoved a card towards Persephone and, for lack of knowing what else to do, she took it and dropped it in her purse.

The man stopped abruptly at the corner of the block facing The Orchid House. Aphrodite and Persephone continued walking briskly. He seemed like he wanted to say more but simply watched them go.

"Oh my gods," Persephone breathed in relief once they were on the steps of The Orchid House.

"I know. He's a dick but he's harmless."

"What was he talking about?"

Aphrodite shrugged. "Just something I'm helping him with." She rolled her eyes towards the door as if to say, *Anyone could be listening.* "Hey, I'll dig around and let you know. Come visit me again?"

Oh. Persephone glanced behind Aphrodite at The Orchid House. She'd gotten lucky today but did she really dare push it? If Aphrodite called with news about Eurydice, they could meet somewhere else again, like at the little restaurant. All she said though, was, "Sure."

Persephone had actually really enjoyed spending time with Aphrodite and adding her to her fledgling group of friends would be kind of great.

"Ok, come soon."

Persephone waved and started to walk away when a thought struck her. "Aphrodite," she called. "What's your stage name?"

Aphrodite's smile this time was mysterious, enticing. "Come to the show and find out."

PERSEPHONE WALKED BACK to the shelter slowly. She'd seen Ajax's club and met the charming Aphrodite. Talk about beauty and beast. She wondered if she should've warned Aphrodite, telling her to get away from Ajax.

He had to be behind Eurydice's kidnapping. He was acting as Orpheus's manager. He needed the singer so he could do his business in New Olympus.

Hecate took one look at her and sat her on the couch in the office with a mug of steaming tea.

"How did it go?"

The whole story came out. The older woman listened without moving a muscle.

"I don't like this. I don't like that you were there alone. Take someone next time."

"I don't intend on there being a next time. Aphrodite's great but Ajax's too dangerous."

"And Aphrodite? Do you trust her?"

"What do you mean?" Persephone frowned.

"It's possible she was throwing you off the scent."

Persephone thought for a moment and conjured up Aphrodite's sweet, honest face. "I don't think she was lying."

"She was very quick to open up to someone she'd just met."

"I think she recognized that I didn't have an agenda. She was friendly, sure…but she's friendly as part of her profession. And maybe she does have an agenda of her own, but she's still worried about her co-worker. She told me she was glad that someone cared about Eurydice."

Hecate's mouth moved into a small smile. "Well, you state your case for your new friend quite well. I think this excursion was good for you."

"How do you mean?"

"You seem to have a lot of strength to tap into when you're working on behalf of others. But what about for yourself?"

Persephone jerked her head in a quick little no. "I just—"

"You have more energy now talking about helping these women than in the past few months combined. It's like you've come alive." Hecate frowned. "I've been worried about you."

Persephone was about to start babbling about how she was fine, how everything was *fine*, when Hecate continued.

"And I want to ask something else, but I'm afraid you'll get upset at me."

Persephone shook her head. "I'd never get upset with you for asking a question. You're my closest friend." It was the truth, age difference be damned.

Still Hecate hesitated a moment, but then she finally asked, "Why are you coming to me with all of this instead of going to your husband?"

The question hit Persephone like a load of concrete, but Hecate didn't notice. "Is it possibly because you think he might be involved? In the girl's kidnapping?"

Persephone shot off the couch and paced away. An immediate denial was on her lips but she didn't voice it. She couldn't. Because... Hecate had just said out loud one of her deepest fears.

Nobody knew better than her just how ruthless Hades could be. Especially when he felt like he needed to be in control. Having Ajax, an obvious enemy, as Orpheus's manager might have thrown him. So he could have sought out the upper hand to regain control over his investment by pinching Orpheus's pressure point—Eurydice.

It didn't fit with the Code he supposedly lived by... But then again, that had been his *father's* Code. Hades had made it very clear that everything had changed the moment the Titans killed his sister, Chiara.

"I've upset you. I'm sorry," Hecate said.

"No, no. It's fine." Persephone flashed a smile that both of them knew was fake. "It's okay." Her phone beeped with an incoming text and she pulled it from her purse.

It was from Hades and had all of two words: Home. Now.

What had crawled up his ass now? Then she bit her lip. Had he somehow found out about her excursion to The Orchid House? "I have to get going anyway." She walked over and gave Hecate a long hug.

Hecate rose too, and started walking her out.

"Good, get some fresh air. The next hour of my life is going to be giving this puppy a bath. Meet Cerberus. I'll need a few hours at the spa afterwards." Hecate pointed to a large grey dog lying in a cage. Persephone stopped to stare.

"That's a *puppy*?"

Hecate chuckled. "Few months old. His mother was a Great Dane and got out when she was in heat. Breeder dumped the pup on a family that couldn't keep him when they realized how big he was going to get."

"What did the mom breed with, a horse? Look at his paws—he's going to be huge." Persephone dropped to her knees and reached her hand through the bar to pet the puppy. He immediately raised his paw up as if to "shake."

"Is he trained?" Persephone shook the gigantic paw.

"I've been working on it." Hecate smiled as she watched the two. "He just seems to like you. Want to help?"

"I'd love to." The mutt was rolling over now, ears flopping. Persephone laughed. Her phone buzzed again and she stood reluctantly. "I've gotta run."

On the way out, she checked her texts. She had some older ones she hadn't seen yet. One from Hermes, thanking her for doing the show and coming to the party. One was under a name she didn't remember programming in: 'Goldwringer': Hey, bitch! It's Athena. Let me know when you want to party again.

Persephone smiled and texted back polite replies. While she did, two more texts came in.

She scrolled down; they were from Hades.

Are you on your way yet?

Don't ignore me unless you want the consequences.

It was wrong, so very wrong that she thought about not texting back just to see what these *consequences* might be.

But then she thought of Hecate's words and her fingers were flying over her phone screen. Leaving now.

Charon was waiting outside with the car.

37

"What the hell is taking so long?" Hades barked into his phone.

Charon's cool voice responded back. "The fans are mobbing the bottom of the building. Security and cops are trying to hold them back from the lobby. I've arranged with Marco, Stan, and Lorenzo to head the team guiding Mrs. Ubeli into the building from the southeast entrance. We are approaching now."

"I'll meet you there," Hades said, thumbing the phone closed and jamming it in his pocket. His jaw clenched. How did the fucking vultures even learn Orpheus was here? But no, he knew the answer the second he asked it.

Ajax. He was trying to put pressure on them and see how they'd react. Force their connections out into the open. The sooner that bastard was six feet under, the better. But keeping Orpheus playing shows was important, too, and not just because of ticket sales. Mobs needed appeasement. Even the ancient Romans knew that.

It was the off-season for the Spartans, the New Olympians favorite sports team, and Hades needed the people distracted.

Look over here at the shiny, sparkling attraction—instead of seeing what I'm actually doing under the table in the dark. Keeping the people amused and happy was one of the first lessons Hades had learned as unofficial king. He could keep them safe and drugs mostly off their streets and the gambling halls and prostitution rings regulated.

But it was a mistake to forget that people always wanted a little bit of sin.

Try to clean up the drugs completely and the city became combustible. The one and only time he'd tried, he'd nearly lost his crown to an upstart gang who took it as an opportunity to try to usurp him. He'd taken the little shit down easily enough and learned the lesson. He eased up on the drug trade, deciding it was enough to keep it out of schools. Consenting adults could do whatever the fuck they wanted.

But with Orpheus had come Ajax, and that was one nasty surprise Hades could do without. He was handling the situation, but he didn't like it. Not one damn bit.

The elevator opened to chaos on the lobby floor. Cops were everywhere, questioning people and checking their IDs before letting them up to their hotel rooms. Outside, the blues and reds of police lights flashed. And the roar of the crowd outside. Hades's hands unconsciously closed into fists.

Ajax had set the mob on his home by moving Orpheus here, to a private floor. The fans found out, no doubt tipped off by Ajax himself. And now he and his wife would be stuck in this mess any time they wanted to come or go.

Hades turned on his heel and headed for the Southeast entrance. It was around the back of the building, near the gym and should be less crowded. By the time he got there, Lorenzo and Stan were already ushering Persephone through the doors. She looked harried but not scared. His strong, beautiful wife. For a moment, all he could see was her. So fucking beautiful even after working with smelly animals all day.

"What's going on?" she asked.

Her question immediately brought back Hades's sour mood. "Orpheus moved in," he snapped.

"He's here? Don't they have to ask you before they do that sort of thing? Move in such a high-profile client?"

Hades's eyebrows went up. "I'm flattered you think my sway extends so far, but no." He glared as they rounded the corner to the main lobby. "If I had any say, this debacle would never have happened."

Persephone looked confused. "But don't you own the hotel?"

Hades laughed out loud at that. "What gave you that idea?"

Her mouth dropped open. "I don't know, I just assumed... Since you live in the penthouse suite permanently. After a while I guess I thought this was just another of your businesses."

"No, I don't own the Crown."

Her brow furrowed. "Then why do you live here? You own so much real estate in the city."

Hades smiled at that because this was one of his favorite triumphs. "A man owed my father a favor; I called it in. He owns the hotel, but the penthouse is mine for as long as I want. And as long as I live here, he'll never forget what he owed my family."

He chuckled grimly. "He hates me. Wishes he could throw me out, but he can't without everyone knowing he went back on his word. But whenever he thinks of his pride and joy of a hotel, he grinds his teeth because he thinks of me, living in the penthouse he designed for himself."

Persephone looked appalled but Hades would never apologize for who he was. Like everything in his life, Hades's residence sent a message.

And now his castle was under siege. His bad mood came thundering back. Especially when two police officers came toward him like they intended to question *his* credentials.

Hades immediately locked eyes with his man, who came forward and cut the other two off at the pass. Good.

When he looked back to Persephone, he saw her watching the whole exchange with curious eyes.

"Upstairs," he commanded her. He'd intended another long, slow night of reminding his wife exactly where her place was in their marriage—underneath him—but dammit, he was letting her get underneath his skin again.

He'd been spending time with her when he needed to be focused on the business at hand.

The shipment.

Nothing could go wrong this time. The mob would be appeased for only so long by side shows. If everything went as planned, then he would have the monopoly on the next hottest commodity the crowd would be slathering over. Which meant crushing the Titans and bleeding them dry of every tyrant's greatest source of power—money.

"Lorenzo will keep watch outside the door while I'm gone until they get this mess settled. I have to go out." Hades's features hardened as he looked around. No more distractions, not until the shipment had been delivered and distribution was going smoothly.

He turned away from his wife. "I've got business to attend to tonight."

38

The next morning after a restless night, Persephone met Athena for a shopping excursion.

Persephone had almost cancelled their plans, except her new friend had been so excited when she'd promised. And Hades wasn't home when she woke up. He'd stayed out all night again. Doing his *business*, whatever that was. Or whomever. The thought was acid in Persephone's brain.

And it wasn't like she had any more leads on Eurydice. She thought about calling the police. "Excuse me, I'd like to report a missing person. I have a picture of her but we've never met. Oh, and please don't tell my husband I'm asking; his men might have abducted her."

Sure. That would go over well.

Persephone was waiting on the curb, deep in thought, when a latte appeared in front of her face. Athena stood grinning at her.

"Oh, you're an angel." Persephone took the proffered cup and sipped it. Perfect. "Thank you."

"Least I could do, considering the Herculean task before us."

"Shopping?"

Athena grimaced. "I hate clothes. If I ever move somewhere warm, I'm not going to wear them."

Persephone sputtered a little. "That should go over well at work."

"It's my company." Athena sipped a coffee of her own. "They'll get over it."

Persephone paused. "Wait, you own your own company?"

"Aurum? Yeah, it's mine."

"Aurum? Like the mobile apps and devices?"

"Yep."

"Holy crap." Persephone stared at the shorter woman drinking coffee in faded black jeans and a turtleneck.

"What?"

"I've read about you, in the papers. You're like a super genius." Aurum was one of the fastest growing companies in New Olympus.

"Told you," Athena said smugly.

"You were at Hermes's show, doing his website?"

"I like to get out among the commoners once and awhile." Athena shrugged. "Besides, I love Fortune jeans. They're pretty much all I wear."

"Well, we're going to change that."

"Bring it on."

As they started walking, Athena's eyes immediately shot to Charon, large and hulking in a black suit, who'd started following them. Persephone's shadow for the day.

"Ignore him," Persephone whispered.

Athena just raised an eyebrow. "Not sure I want to. That man is one hunk of gorgeous beefsteak."

Persephone laughed out loud at Charon being described that way, then shook her head.

Persephone started with the shop she used to always walk on by her first weeks in the city. Back then she could only gaze longingly but it had become one of her favorite haunts after marrying Hades. Athena followed her around obediently, only fussing when the shop manager approached. "Back off. I'm with her."

Persephone's head flew up to see the manager's startled face. She always helped Persephone and she was actually really nice. "Sorry," Persephone mouthed and hurried to get Athena into a dressing room.

In the next few hours, Persephone kept Athena busy trying on new outfits. Athena didn't want anything but black, and the color suited her all right so Persephone went with it, picking out different fabrics to lend a little richness to Athena's monochromatic look.

"This looks like crap," Athena announced, pointing at a display of dresses. The shop manager's eyebrows shot up to her hairline.

"Time for the dressing room," Persephone sang, pushing her friend inside the room and shutting the door behind her. Persephone continued looking and flipped a few clothes over the door, ignoring Athena's muffled curses from inside.

"She's...prickly," Persephone told the manager. "I'll take care of her."

As the clothes mounded up beside the register in a "To Buy" pile, the manager's expression changed.

"She owns a really successful company," Persephone told the manager and cashier. "The tech company working on the phone you can fold in half."

"Oh wow," the cashier breathed.

"Perhaps you'd like to open a personal shopper's account? That way you can conduct in-office sessions for your client."

"That's a great idea," Persephone said as Athena's voice rang out in the back of the store—"This is crap!"—accompanied by gasps from the store personnel.

"Ring up everything," Persephone instructed, and ran to rescue the poor saleswomen from Athena's blunt barrage.

In the end Athena paid without comment, and the entire store's staff sighed in relief when Persephone pushed her friend out the door.

They lunched at a popular curry house.

"Well, that wasn't as bad as I thought it would be."

Persephone smiled quietly into her mango lassi.

"Seriously, after the fashion show and party, I'm surprised I didn't wind up getting fitted for bunny ears."

Persephone nearly choked, remembering Hermes's arm candy at the party. "Oh, that's the next stop," she teased. "I'm just giving you a break before more torture."

"That's what you think. All I have to do is call that giant you call a bodyguard over and he'll be ready to carry you away if you push me."

Persephone stilled. "You mean Charon?" He was sitting in the corner far enough away to give them their privacy but he was far too big to be unobtrusive in the busy restaurant.

Athena shrugged. "Is that his name? Who is he anyway?"

"Just one of my husband's colleagues," Persephone said, gnawing on her lip.

"He doesn't look like a colleague, looks more like a... I don't know. A wise guy or something." Athena laughed and for once Persephone wished her new friend wasn't so blunt.

Persephone honestly didn't know what to say, and it seemed impossible to talk about her husband's business here, in a restaurant, in broad daylight. This was why she didn't have friends. She hadn't realized it until now. They'd ask uncomfortable questions and she'd retreat into the safety of her husband's penthouse.

Athena pushed around her rice, obviously noting Persephone's silence. "So, what's the deal—I can't imagine you get into too much trouble." Athena was studying her; Persephone could almost see her calculating how much to pry.

Time for a topic change. And, considering what Athena did for a living...

Persephone hesitated, then put her drink down. "Athena, if you suspected someone was missing, and you needed to look for them without anyone else knowing, how would you do it?"

"Ping their phone," Athena answered immediately, her eyes lighting up. "There's technology that allows you to pinpoint a device. Like a trace."

"Is it legal?"

"Not really. But where's the fun in that?"

The rest of the lunch turned into a technology lesson. Athena showed Persephone some of her hacks and some of her company's apps. Persephone's phone got an update and a few new downloads, with Athena's promise to show Persephone how to use them.

"Thanks for all the help, I really appreciate it." If Persephone could get a hold of Eurydice's phone number, then maybe she could figure out this phone pinging thing and get another lead. Once she found out where Eurydice was being held, she could send the cops in. Hades never had to know she was involved and Eurydice would be safe.

"No problem." The bill came by and Persephone reached for it, but Athena grabbed her hand. "Persephone, you'd tell me if you were in trouble?"

Persephone nodded.

"I know we just met but...I'd like to help."

Persephone bit her lip but then took a chance. Like Aphrodite, Athena seemed genuine. "I may need to take you up on that."

"Anytime, bitch," Athena said affectionately. "Except for the shopping part."

Persephone laughed. "I guess I can't convince you to visit one more shop, then, for shoes?"

"Hell, no. I'm more interested in your other...project."

"I'll keep you posted," Persephone promised. "And will hopefully have something to you soon."

An idea was budding, but first Persephone needed to get home. Persephone hugged Athena goodbye and then signaled Charon she was ready to leave.

39

Back at the Crown, Persephone pressed the up button to the private floor on the elevator and punched in the code. The police had the horde of fans well in control outside, finally, and once Charon saw her get in the elevator, he didn't follow. He'd gotten a call right before, so she guessed that Hades needed him more than she did.

She'd gotten used to living in the high-end hotel, in the section that was more of a palace of suites. Who owned the hotel? Who had owed Hades's father the favor?

She shook her head. She had more important fish to fry. Like getting Eurydice's phone number.

She had to go see Orpheus. And he now stayed in a suite one floor below where she lived. A private floor that required a key, just like her floor. The same key worked for the top floor with the pool...so maybe she'd luck out?

Persephone held her breath until the door slid open to the requested floor. *Yes.* Her intuition had been right. The key worked for Orpheus's floor, too.

The door to the private floor opened and she walked in. A

hallway held a series of doors that must lead to suites. Two thugs lounged on either side of the nearest doors.

Surprisingly low security, considering the night before. Something was up. Was Hades involved? He'd been so upset about the invasion into their privacy last night. He might not own the Crown but his power and influence everywhere throughout the city was undeniable.

The men stood up and came to attention as she approached. Ajax's men. Gods, Persephone hoped their boss wasn't anywhere nearby.

"Hey, lady, you need to leave." One of the men held out a meaty hand to stop her from going further down the hall.

Taking a deep breath, she channeled her inner Ice Queen. She wore nice jeans and a sweater along with a string of pearls around her neck. They probably thought she was just another hotel guest. Maybe some rabid fan.

Persephone looked at them coolly, her chin notched up. "Do you recognize me?"

"Woman, you could be the queen of England, you can't be here."

"I'm Mrs. Ubeli. As in, Hades Ubeli's wife."

The two men didn't budge.

"I'm here to see Orpheus. My husband wants me to make sure he's comfortable."

"No one gets in. Boss's orders." The larger one folded his arms across his chest.

"Just go tell him I'm here to see him." Persephone tried to channel Hades's authority. "If he doesn't want to see me, I'll leave."

The one with his arms folded leaned forward, getting into her space. "We don't take orders from you."

Persephone didn't back down, she just lifted an eyebrow as if to say, *oh really*? A classic Hades move.

"Wait," the other said, looking a little nervous. "Let me check something." He went inside the room, closing the door behind him.

The other stared hard at her. She ignored him. The types Hades associated with usually studied her like she was a threat or a piece of meat. When he finally looked away and leaned against the wall, she memorized his face, from the blunt features to the little gold ring in his ear.

Meanwhile, the other guard came back out, holding his phone like he'd just taken a call. "He wants to talk to you. Says he knows ya."

Persephone started forward and the thug with the earring put his arm out to stop her. "Wait," he started but she cut him off.

"Touch me and my husband will hear about it." The two men stiffened. "You two have been nothing but perfect gentlemen so far," she continued, with a sweeter tone. "I'll only be a minute."

She flashed a smile. The first guard settled back on his heels. The one with the earring looked like he wanted to kill her.

"Only a minute," she sang as she entered the apartment. And stopped.

The room was trashed. A room service cart lay on its side at her feet. The food from the tray was all over the ground. In the suite itself, a chair lay on its side, leading her eye to the brocade curtains hanging askew on their rod.

Across from the bedroom, lovely white and gold wallpaper was stained with ribbons of red liquid, as if someone had picked up wine delivered on the cart and thrown it. The rest of the room's décor, with Victorian chairs, was largely untouched, but it was shocking, this scene of obvious violence.

Persephone was about to call out Orpheus's name to ask if he was all right when the guard with the little earring stuck his head in and laughed, not a nice sound. "He's temperamental."

Persephone swallowed, and didn't let them see her flinch. She wouldn't show weakness to them.

She turned and stepped carefully, hearing broken glass under her boots. The doorway to the bedroom gaped.

"Orpheus?" she finally called. "It's Persephone. Hades Ubeli's wife."

A slight noise drew her to investigate. Once her eyes adjusted to the dim light, she saw Orpheus's curly head jutting over the bedcovers.

"Orpheus, are you ok? Did something happen?"

"It was me." The rock star's voice came weakly. "I did it."

"You did this?" She picked her way carefully into the room, stopping at the foot of the bed. Gods, he looked terrible. His hair was dirty. The room stank. She didn't know when he'd last showered but it couldn't have been recently.

He drew a raspy breath. "She left me. She didn't love me anymore. They showed me a note she wrote. I sort of freaked out and...trashed the place."

Persephone squinted at him. "They showed you a note? What did they say?"

"They said they went to look for her." He stretched a hand over to the bedside table, knocking another bottle onto the floor. Persephone darted forward to help him. Grunting softly, as if the movements were painful, he handed her his phone.

Persephone turned it to see the picture. A woman lay sleeping, her face wan on the dirty pillow. Eurydice. Even Persephone understood what the needle in her arm meant.

"She's using again. She doesn't want me anymore."

"This is your proof?" She held it up. "Who took this picture?"

"One of Ajax's men."

"Men like the assholes outside?" Persephone could feel the rage welling up inside her. An innocent woman, drawn into this net. She worked over the phone, forwarding herself the picture, then going to Eurydice's contact information and forwarding that too.

Something had to be done. It couldn't be a coincidence that a woman disappeared when her fiancé was threatening to break a multi-million-dollar contract.

After seeing that picture... This wasn't Hades. Maybe he would have kidnapped Eurydice to put pressure on Orpheus, but he never would have put her in a dank hellhole or pumped her full of drugs. No, this was all Ajax.

"Orpheus, it's been long enough. We need to go to the police. She's in trouble."

"I threatened and they told me to try it. They said she'll end up in jail, or worse." He stared up at the ceiling, eyes bloodshot. "I can't do anything. I can't help her."

Drawing in a harsh breath, Persephone let the phone fall. She turned, went to the window, and drew back the curtains in a violent move.

Orpheus cried out but she felt no sympathy for him.

"Enough. Get up. If you ever loved her, get out of bed and start acting like an adult."

"She left me—"

"I don't care! She's in trouble and someone needs to find her." Persephone took another deep breath and said firmly, "I've already started looking and have some leads."

"You won't find anything. If they took her and got her using again, she'll never be back."

"Then I'm going to find her and give her that option. If you could, would you help her? Get her to rehab or whatever?"

Orpheus was sitting up now. He nodded. "Of course. I love her."

"Then get up out of bed and start acting like it. Practice or something. Your job is to play." She drew herself up, trying to show confidence she didn't feel. "I'll take care of the rest."

The two guards outside Orpheus's room jumped when the door swung open. Persephone stalked out.

"Call the maid." She looked them in the eye. "This place needs to be cleaned up, even if you take Orpheus to another room while they do it. And order him a decent meal."

With that, she swept out into the hall.

40

Back in the penthouse, the afternoon sun slanted thickly over the living room. Persephone dropped her purse and worked busily over her cell, sending Eurydice's phone info to Athena to trace.

Goldwringer replied: Cool! Give me five.

Relaxing back on the couch, Persephone allowed herself a satisfied smile. They were one step closer to finding Eurydice.

She raised her head when she heard the front door open. Strange. Hades was never home this early, not lately anyway. But this was good. He wasn't the one who took Eurydice. Maybe it was time to talk to him, to lay it all out on the table and ask for his help.

Standing, she squared her shoulders. Even if Hades had business reasons he shouldn't cross Ajax, she was going to convince him. What was a business matter against a person's life?

"Hades? I thought you were out on business tonight..." she started to say, then gasped.

Ajax's frame filled the doorway. The man looked larger than when she saw him at the club; his bald head shone in the sunlight. The rest of him was dressed simply in a long trench coat, a grey shadow on his unshaven face. His beady black eyes were fixed on her, assessing.

Shit, what should she do? How had he even gotten in? She must've left the penthouse unlocked when she returned from seeing Orpheus. The only people who could even access their home needed a special key to work the elevator. But duh, she'd just proved the same key worked on all the private floors. And as Orpheus's manager, obviously Ajax would have access to the same key.

"What are you doing here?" Fear made her voice sharp.

Ajax sauntered into the room, looking around like an investor surveying a potential property. Persephone stiffened her spine so she wouldn't shrink away. One thing the Underworld taught her: if you cowered, they thought you were prey.

Still, she was glad there was a couch between her and the approaching gangster.

"You shouldn't be here. Hades won't like it."

"Nice place." Ajax strolled forward, taking in the view. His stoop took inches off his height, but also gave his movements a predatory look. Like a bear, sniffing outside its lair.

Ajax stopped to study a white statue of a bearded man capturing a fleeing woman. Walking around it to view it, he rubbed his jaw. "You pick this out?" He squinted at her, then at a small but exquisite replica of a statue, a copy of the first one.

"My husband." Persephone's voice was clipped. "And he'll be home any minute."

Ajax turned from the statue to face her. The deep lines around his mouth bent into a smile. "You know, for a woman stepping out on her man, you sure invoke his name a lot."

What the hell was he— "What are you talking about?"

"You think I wouldn't find out about your little visit to my pet singer?" The man started walking towards her. "I thought I'd hide him here, keep him from the fucking fans. Freaky rabid bitches."

Ajax smiled. He kept walking forward, closing in on her. Persephone backed up despite herself. "Well, now we have a new story for the paparazzi: Ubeli's wife doing Orpheus. Little Miss Innocent spreads her legs."

"How dare you?" Persephone snapped. She'd had enough. She

stood up to him, not backing down any more. Her five feet eight inches put her almost at his grizzled chin. "When I tell Hades—"

"You were in his bedroom," Ajax spit back at her. His breath was foul on her face. "There are cameras in the hall."

Persephone froze as what he said sunk in.

Ajax watched her face closely. "Tell me, little girl. What's Hades going to think?"

What *would* Hades think? There was no trust between them, not now. Still, she refused to give this disgusting man an inch.

But Ajax took advantage of her momentary silence to reach out and capture a lock of her light hair.

"So, gorgeous," he twisted the strands between two fat fingers. "What will you give me to keep your little tryst from your husband?"

Persephone jerked back. Ajax let her move away, watching her go with glittering eyes.

"That's right, baby, think about it. Then think of how to convince me." His eyes swept up and down her figure.

She felt dirty just being in the same room as him.

"You can't threaten me," she said, trying again to channel some of Hades's authority. It came out sounding petulant. A child refusing to go to her room.

She cleared her throat and tried again. "I know what you did. I'm telling Hades—you kidnapped an innocent woman to threaten her fiancé."

Ajax stared at her, then his shoulders started to move. A strange, heaving sound came from his barrel chest. Persephone watched nervously, thinking he was having a fit.

Then she realized the man was laughing at her.

Ajax's mouth gaped, showing his gold tooth. "Are you kidding me? That's your threat?" The man's jowls shook with mirth. "I'm going to tell," he mocked her voice. "Pretty, stupid slut. You think your husband doesn't know I took Eurydice? Ubeli ordered it."

Persephone felt his words like a blow. "No," she whispered.

"That's right, little girl. And if you ever push me, I'll tell him exactly where you were this afternoon. And what do you think he'll want me to do with his cheating whore of a wife?"

Squeezing her fists, Persephone let his words wash over her. She was still stuck on the thought that Hades ordered Eurydice's kidnapping. But he hated Ajax. Didn't he? He'd never work with him...

But he already was, wasn't he? To book Orpheus. If Hades had wanted Eurydice gone and ordered Ajax to do it, he wouldn't have had control over Ajax's methods. But Hades was all about control. So did that mean Ajax was ly—

"Maybe I'll be the one who gets to punish you," Ajax continued, smirking. "You might even like it."

Fighting back furious tears, Persephone watched the man move to the liquor cabinet. "Hell, half of Ubeli's men must be gagging for you. We'll get a movie camera; make it a bestseller. The black giant would be first in line. I know I'd pay to watch you choke on him." He chuckled as he poured himself a drink.

A rushing sound filled Persephone's ears; she couldn't find her voice to talk or scream.

"I'm just saying, if Daddy ever don't satisfy—Uncle Ajax is here."

"Get out." Persephone's voice came out strangled.

He raised the glass to her and then downed it. She watched him, fists balled. She'd never hated anyone so much in her life. "Get the *fuck* out of my house right this second."

Ajax took his sweet time moving to the door. "Pleasure visiting you, *Mrs. Ubeli.*" He spoke her name with a sneer. "Hope to do it again real soon."

Persephone shivered with anger and fear.

He was almost outside when he turned. "Oh, and we're moving your boy, so no more little visits. Although, if you do come down—" His hand slipped down to his crotch crudely. "Uncle Ajax will be ready."

Persephone wanted to kick him where he was so rudely gesturing. With her pointiest heels.

"It'll be our secret." He winked at her.

Persephone waited until she was sure he was gone before

collapsing on the couch, still shaking with fury. *Ubeli ordered it.* She mopped her face with a hand, ordering herself to get it together.

He was lying about Hades. Right?

One thing she was sure about, she was going to free Eurydice from Ajax. Then she would find a way to make him pay. *Pretty, stupid slut.*

Her phone buzzed. She looked down and opened Athena's text, then clicked on the highlighted address. The link took her into a map, where a light blinked, signaling the location of Eurydice's phone.

Persephone took a deep breath. She knew exactly where Eurydice was. Or, at least where her phone was. And it was time to finally do something about it.

41

Midafternoon the next day, Persephone took a little walk into the park. No bodyguards with her. She'd given them the slip again after they dropped her off at the shelter earlier that day. She'd been worried about what she would say to Hades or how to act with him once he got home last night...but he never came home.

Whatever Hades was up to had him working day and night. Either that or he was avoiding her. Which was probably for the best right now, all things considered.

She flopped down on a bench and checked her messages. Nothing.

A shadow fell over her, and she squinted at Pete the cop. He took a seat next to her on the far side of the bench. His posture was relaxed, but his eyes swept the path and park area around them.

"I have to say, you're the last person I expected to hear from." Pete looked her over. "I nearly dropped my phone when I got your message last night. I looked into you. Married to the biggest crime lord in the city." He let out a low whistle.

Persephone spoke without looking at him. Anyone watching

would see a young woman resting from her jog and a man on lunch break. "I want to be clear. I'm not ratting on my husband."

"Oh, you made that clear." Pete sat up and rummaged in his pocket, taking out a cigarette and lighter. "I heard about your little visit down to the station two weeks after the wedding. Wouldn't flip even though the feds were offering you witness protection." He lit the cigarette and puffed on it.

"The offer wasn't real," Persephone said stiffly. "It was a test." And if it hadn't been, she'd still have made the same decisions. There was no point dwelling on the past.

"Well, you passed anyway. Not sure what that says about you. The type of woman you are." He squinted at her through his smoke.

She waved the cloud away. "I'm loyal. And anyway, I'm not here to talk about my husband."

"No? Then why the hell did you call me?" He glanced around warily. "You playing some sort of game?"

At the cop's raised voice, a grey shadow lying on the ground next to Persephone raised its large head. Cerberus, the Great Dane *puppy*, got to his feet, coming around the bench to stand in front of Persephone, between her and the cop.

"Gods, what is that thing?" Peter coughed and scooted further down the bench.

Persephone reached out a hand and scratched the dog's ears. "Great Dane mixed with something. I took him from the shelter to stretch his legs." She raised her hand and the dog leaned happily toward her, begging for more.

"I thought he was a boulder." He watched as she praised the Dane, and got him to lie back down to chew a toy. "So Ubeli lets you wander around alone?"

"My husband's men are too busy to be babysitting me." The lie fell easily from her lips. But she realized it was the wrong one when Peter's eyes lit up.

"Busy, huh? What has their attention?"

Persephone took a deep breath. "That's not why we're here. I'm actually trying to find a missing person. The singer at my husband's club—Orpheus. His fiancée disappeared late Saturday."

Pete shrugged. "So have him go to the station, file a report."

"It's more complicated than that." Persephone rushed to fill in the details about the tragic couple and her and Athena's search. She pulled out Eurydice's picture and laid it on the bench for him to see, along with the shot she'd forwarded from Orpheus's phone of Eurydice. "We think a man named Ajax is behind it. We tracked her phone. She's in his club, or well at least her phone is. And she's in trouble."

Glancing down at the picture, Pete grunted. "Yeah, I heard of Ajax. Used to run a few corners in this city. Got flushed out with the old crowd. Now he's back."

"The old crowd?"

"Gods, your husband don't tell you anything. The Titan brothers. There were three of them, or maybe it used to be three? I think one of them got axed back in the day?" He frowned as he thought. "They owned this town before your husband did. Some think they're trying to get back in. They say that this Ajax is the first advance."

The wind picked up, and Persephone wished she'd worn something other than a cashmere sweater. Even in the sun, she felt the chill. "So, can you help find Eurydice?"

Pete snubbed out his cigarette on the concrete by his feet. "Look, miss, this just isn't my line of work. Find a missing junkie? You don't even know if she wants to be found. Maybe she wanted to leave this Orpheus fellow and go back to scoring."

"She didn't want to leave him. And Ajax's a snake. He—"

Pete cut her off. "But I guess I *could* tail this Ajax guy a little. But I'm not doing anything without getting a favor back. This is small time stuff you're asking here. I'm going to need something in return. Something juicy. And I wanna know why you're not taking this to your husband."

Persephone didn't answer, staring down at the picture of Eurydice.

"You think Ubeli's involved," Pete deduced. "That's why you're sneaking around."

"I'm not—"

"You called up a cop and asked for a meet. How's that going to look to your husband? Or anyone who runs with him?"

This sounded too close to what Ajax had said to her. "Hades knows I'm loyal."

The cop rubbed his head and jaw again, not listening. "Hell, I'm probably a marked man just for meeting with you."

Something inside her snapped. "Then why'd you chase me down and give me your card?" Persephone rounded on him. "You know what—forget it. I thought you had a pair. An innocent woman is in trouble."

She snatched up Eurydice's picture and waved it in his surprised face. "You're supposed to be a—I don't know—a protector of the city. Instead you just want a big bust to make your career. And use whoever you can to make it."

She turned away from the cop's surprised face and stuffed the picture back in her purse. "Look for someone else to hand you my husband's head on a silver platter. And anyway, he's done more to protect people in this city than you ever will—"

"You really think that, you pampered princess?" Pete rose to his feet, towering over her. She tugged at Cerberus's leash and the big dog leapt up, pushing between them.

The cop retreated, but kept talking, his face twisted with anger. He shouted after Persephone as she hurried away, Cerberus in tow. "You're just like the rest of them, with your money and your secrets. You people think you're gods and goddesses, better than us. Untouchable by us mere mortals. Well, you know what? We're going to bring you down."

She strode away, head down, as his rant hit her back like ineffective bullets.

And when she got home, her fingers flew to open her contacts. She hesitated a moment, then dialed.

Hermes answered the phone. "Persephone?" Surprise was in his tone.

"Hey," she said lightly. "Are you busy?"

"Just about to leave the spa—why?"

"I need a favor." She bit her lip and remembered how the designer had hovered over her at the party. If she'd read his body language right, he'd be up for helping her. She only hoped she wasn't opening herself up to too much trouble.

"Sure—you ok?"

"I'm fine. I just—I promised a friend of mine I'd help her out and go see her show tonight. Hades is working late and I wondered if you'd go with me."

"Uh, sure. If it's cool with your husband, I'm free. What's the show?"

"Well, that's why I'm asking you to go. It's a tiny bit out of my norm." She rose and pulled Ajax's card from her purse. "I need you to take me to a strip club."

42

Two hours later, Hermes glanced out of the taxi cab in front of The Orchid House and frowned at the sign.

"Persephone, as happy as I am to visit this fine establishment, are you sure this is a good idea?"

"Relax. It's just to help out a friend." It wasn't even a lie. Persephone grabbed her purse and made to get out of the cab but Hermes caught her arm.

"I don't think Hades is going to like this."

"What he doesn't know won't hurt him. Besides, he'll just think it's cute."

"He thinks you're cute. He'll just kill me," Hermes muttered.

"He's not going to kill you." Persephone shook his hand off.

"You're right, he'll get the big guy to do it."

"Charon's not going to hurt you, either. I won't let him. Now come on."

She swung her legs out of the car and immediately regretted wearing a miniskirt. She'd gone for maximum vamp style, hoping to lower the chances of her being recognized. Black mini skirt, black spangly top, and black high heels: she looked a little like a goth princess. Add to that thick smoky eye makeup and a black wig she convinced Hermes to loan her (and help affix to her head) and she was sure she'd be totally under the radar.

"This is insane." Hermes checked his hair in the cab's rear-view mirror one last time and then exited the cab. He wore a grey suit and white shirt with a skinny black tie. With his mussed hair and her thin black clad figure, they looked like two kids playing dress up.

"Just follow my lead and I won't let you do anything dumb. I mean, other than this entire venture." Hermes stuck out his arm to escort Persephone in. "I haven't been this reluctant to visit a strip club since...ever."

Persephone looked around as they walked in. The Orchid House looked much classier at night. The bar had cool purple lighting, and there were actual flowers placed on pedestals near the walls.

As soon as they were inside, Hermes seemed to relax. He charmed the hostess and kept his hand on Persephone's back as they took a booth near the stage. He flirted with the waitress when she came to take their order, batting his long black eyelashes almost as much as the woman batted her mascara-laden ones.

"What are you doing?" Persephone asked once the waitress left, walking on air.

"Just chillin.'" Hermes smiled when the waitress returned with a bottle of champagne. "Be cool."

Persephone sat back in the deep chair but she couldn't relax. She couldn't stop scanning the room, glancing at the faces all around them to make sure she didn't see anyone she knew. Especially Ajax. But mostly all she saw was men in suits, and a few couples.

Hermes handed her a glass of champagne and leaned close. "Don't look around so much. Some people here don't want to be recognized, either."

"You seem pretty comfortable," she whispered back.

Hermes shrugged. "I'd like it better if you'd tell me what's really going on."

Persephone paused with her champagne glass halfway to her lips. "What do you mean?"

"You're acting funny. For one, you called me and asked me out. To a strip club. Without your husband. Are you two doing ok?"

Did he think she'd asked him here because she— Unable to find her voice, Persephone just stared into Hermes's dark eyes.

He sighed. "Look, Persephone, I'm happy to help. That's what friends do. But it'd be nice to know what I'm getting into."

"It's not what you think," she blurted. "That is, I don't know what you're thinking exactly, but Hades and I are fine." Okay, that was a giant lie, but she wasn't going to even start getting into that with Hermes. That wasn't why they were here. "I just need to help...a friend."

"And Hades isn't involved?"

She hesitated.

"Right, well when we get out of here, we're going to talk about it. Like I said, I want to help you, but I don't want trouble."

Crap. Maybe it wasn't fair to ask him to help her. She'd never fully understood the nature of Hades's and Hermes's business relationship. The last thing she wanted was for Hermes to end up getting burned because of her.

"I understand." Persephone said softly.

Hermes turned to her and took her hand. "It's not only that we're friends. Hades and I are business partners. Without him, I never could've gotten Double M off the ground."

Persephone nodded, thinking about Metamorphoses, Hermes's spa. It was opening its third location soon.

Okay, if she was going to keep asking him to help her, he deserved an explanation. She leaned in and was about to explain when she noticed the fog starting to roll over the stage.

"Ladies and gentleman," a voice came over the loud speaker, "We are proud to present: *Venus*."

A trance-like humming filled the room, a woman's breathy voice. The fog piled up on the stage as the music intensified, building with drums. Subtle lights revealed a pool of water shimmering under the mist.

Aphrodite emerged slowly from the water, a wet cloth clinging to her body, leaving it covered and at the same time fully on display. Rising from the mist, she looked like a primordial goddess; her curves evoking a millennia of raw, potent desire.

"Wow," Hermes breathed.

The music went low until there were only drums beating. Beating deep into the brain. Aphrodite smiled at the crowd, pirouetted slowly, and let the cloth peel away.

Underneath she wore a gold bikini, stretched tight over her flawless figure. The audience murmured their appreciation as Aphrodite floated to the pole for her dance routine.

Persephone glanced over at Hermes; he had his mouth open and was almost drooling.

Aphrodite's dance was less acrobatic this time and much more sensual. Her hips made love to the air, and every man in the room felt it right in their groin. Aphrodite gyrated slowly and Persephone couldn't help mentally filing the move away for later. She needed all the help she could get to manage Hades.

People were throwing money but Aphrodite danced over it like she didn't notice.

The stage went dark and the cheering went on for a while. When the lights came up, Aphrodite stood there transformed, now wearing a glittering red dress with a plunging neckline. As an old tune came on, she started to sing in her sweet baby voice.

The crowd went crazy.

"That's my friend," Persephone whispered to Hermes. The svelte young designer looked so mesmerized; it was almost comical. He took a gulp of champagne and poured some on himself without even noticing.

"Hermes," Persephone called, and he blinked. She looked pointedly at his suit. "I didn't know you had a drinking problem."

Grabbing a napkin, he hurriedly blotted the liquid, then gulped more champagne.

"Oh my gods," he said hoarsely, then cleared his throat. "Uh, she's incredible. How did you meet?"

"Long story." Persephone smiled up at Aphrodite as she vamped with the mike. "She's helping me with some charity work."

The song ended and other ladies came on stage.

Aphrodite descended to dance and flirt with her patrons.

Persephone wasn't sure if Aphrodite recognized her until Aphrodite winked at her. She came slowly over and leaned over Persephone as if she might kiss her.

"We need to talk," Persephone whispered, then indicated Hermes with a slight jerk of her head. "Alone."

Aphrodite nodded, looking deep into Persephone's eyes as part of the act. "Just follow my lead."

Aphrodite moved to Hermes, swaying over him. He held his hands over her hips like he wanted to touch her, but she gathered them, and pulled until he came up out of his chair. He followed her obediently on stage as the announcer spoke again. "Please welcome onstage a special guest, here on his birthday!"

Persephone sat up, wondering what was going on. The women had set a chair onstage; they tied Hermes to it and took turns grinding on him. The crowd whooped.

Hermes's face held a look of goofy pleasure and he didn't even protest that it wasn't his birthday.

Then two of the dancers climbed up, straddled his head as they faced one another and started rocking back and forth.

Eyes fixed to the debauchery on stage, Persephone almost didn't notice Aphrodite signaling her to come around the stage to a side door.

Grabbing her purse, Persephone rose and loped to Aphrodite. The audience was transfixed on Hermes's plight onstage. The women had climbed off of Hermes and now were untying him and forcing him down onto his hands and knees. One of them was unfastening his belt.

"Time for his birthday spanking—"

Aphrodite pulled Persephone into the hall and shut the door, cutting off the raucous laughter.

"Um," Persephone began.

"Can't talk here," Aphrodite whispered and drew her through gauzy curtains and then a door marked *VIP*.

"Is that your boyfriend? He's a handsome one." Aphrodite motioned Persephone inside the dimly lit room.

"No, just a friend." Persephone entered and stood in the center of the lush surroundings. "And, uh, I'm just curious. What are they going to do with him?"

"Oh, don't worry, he'll love it. It's part of the fun."

Persephone wondered how much the fun had to do with Hermes getting lashed with his own belt. "Ok."

"They won't hurt him." Aphrodite giggled. "Much. So, what have you found out about Eurydice?"

Persephone caught her up to date, explaining Athena's cellphone trick. "Eurydice has to be here—or was here at some point, and left her phone. Have you seen or heard anything about her?"

Aphrodite shook her head. "Maybe one of Ajax's guys has it. They've been crawling around here lately." She shuddered. "Although, it's possible she was here…"

Aphrodite broke off when they heard voices in the hall. The sounds grew louder as people stopped just outside the door.

"Shoot—someone has a customer."

Aphrodite rushed to the back of the champagne room and Persephone hurried after. Crap. The last thing she needed was to get caught here. Aphrodite had just said that Ajax's guys were crawling the place. And she couldn't tell where on earth Aphrodite was taking her.

But as the voices grew louder Aphrodite drew back one of the curtains covering the wall to reveal…a wall. But then Aphrodite leaned down and pushed on the crown molding and with a slight *creeeeeeak*, a panel of the wall slid aside. A hidden door. Thank the Fates.

As Persephone crowded behind her, Aphrodite stepped into the dark passageway beyond. It was totally black. No lights at all.

Persephone couldn't help hesitating on the threshold, but Aphrodite pushed her into the hidden corridor and tugged the door shut after them. It clicked back into place just in time, too, because the next moment they could hear voices muffled in the champagne room.

"Where are we?" Persephone breathed, the barest whisper. She fumbled in her purse and fired up her cellphone flashlight, raising it so she could see more of the narrow hall. It stretched in both directions, just barely wide enough for the two of them. Persephone put her hand to the opposite wall and felt the cold brick.

"This place used to be a speakeasy," Aphrodite whispered. "I think this leads to a secret room in the back. I haven't explored it much. Too creepy. And with Ajax's guys everywhere the past few days, I haven't really been able to sneak away."

"You think they could be keeping Eurydice here?"

"We could look." Aphrodite's voice was quiet but held an undercurrent of excitement.

Persephone kept the light high. "Which way?"

43

A few minutes later, Persephone's arm ached from holding up her cellphone light. And she was battling claustrophobia. It was *really* tight in here.

The passage had narrowed even further and she couldn't be sure because her sense of direction was a bit turned around, but she felt like the floor was sloping down. Like they were headed to a basement or lower floor.

"Are you sure you don't need to be back onstage?" Persephone called quietly to Aphrodite. Aphrodite plunged ahead confidently, almost like she was enjoying this.

"Don't worry," Aphrodite waved a hand. "They'll think I'm back in the VIP room with a customer. If we happen to get caught, I'll tell them you wanted a lap dance and we got carried away."

"Yeah, snooping around in dark creepy basements always turns me on," Persephone joked feebly.

"You'd be surprised what people like." Aphrodite stopped in her tracks as the narrow passageway broke out into a larger room. Persephone huddled close to her.

"What now?" Persephone's voice wavered a little. The place was spooky, with a low ceiling that was barely six feet tall. At five feet eight inches, Persephone felt like stooping. Dust and cobwebs hung from the beams. Real cheery place. Persephone shivered.

"Over there." Aphrodite pointed out a small door. They crept forward together, huddling in the small pool of light. Persephone's eyes kept skittering all around the room. Her phone better not run out of battery, that was all she was saying. She didn't dare check, though. Eurydice could be only a room away and she couldn't let her fears stop her now. Just please, gods, no rats. Please no rats.

They made it across the room but the door was stuck. Aphrodite took the cellphone and Persephone pushed at it. The thought of being stuck down here in the old air gave her a burst of strength, and she forced it open with her shoulder, staggering forward when it opened suddenly.

The room was tiny. Little more than a closet.

And it was empty.

"Damn," Aphrodite cursed softly. "I really hoped we would find her."

"But look, is that a bed?" Persephone pushed through the door and stepped into the small room, nose twitching at the stale air. Aphrodite followed and pointed the cell phone flashlight at the floor. They both looked at the pallet and ratty blanket stuffed inside the tiny space.

"Do you think..." Aphrodite began but then trailed off as Persephone knelt down and pushed her hand up between the wall and the pallet.

Holy shit, was that a—

Persephone came away holding a cellphone in a bright pink case. "It's Eurydice's. I'll bet anything. They kept her down there, I'm sure of it." But Eurydice herself was long gone. Still, this was one more clue.

When Aphrodite said, "Let's get out of here," Persephone was only too happy to agree.

They were back in the dark passageway when Persephone caught Aphrodite's hand. "Wait, slow down."

Persephone held the pink phone between them and tried turning it on. It was dead. Persephone cursed and took her purse back from Aphrodite, sliding the new phone in there.

"Do you think—" Aphrodite started, her voice grim.

Persephone shook her head and cut her off before she could voice it out loud. "I don't think Ajax would harm her, yet." Other than a needle in her arm. "He still needs her as leverage over her fiancé." She said it for Aphrodite as much as for herself.

Aphrodite nodded and threaded her fingers with Persephone's again. "Come on."

They started back through the tight space, holding hands. It seemed like it took forever. But gods, all Persephone could see was that tiny closet and the pathetic pallet on the ground. Eurydice must've been so scared. And if they locked her in there without light? A shiver went through Persephone that shook her down to her bones. She clutched tighter onto her phone.

But no, Ajax still needed Eurydice. They could still save her. How much had they missed her by? A day? Hours?

When they reached the secret door to the VIP room, Aphrodite's fingers gave her a squeeze before pulling a latch and pushing the door open slowly.

They both waited a beat, listening. For a moment there was nothing but silence. Persephone's shoulders sagged in relief. She might just get away with this after all.

Then someone inside moaned and both Aphrodite and Persephone froze, hearing the sounds of two people kissing and panting. Aphrodite looked at Persephone and Persephone made a face.

Someone was having a good time in the VIP room.

"Come on," Aphrodite mouthed, and Persephone shook her head. Since they were stuck anyway, Persephone picked a few more spider webs out of Aphrodite's hair. Aphrodite held still and after a minute Persephone had gotten them all. Persephone felt like a nervous wreck but Aphrodite looked completely composed, barely a hair out of place.

Persephone looked down at her own cobweb-streaked dress and

grimaced. She swiped at them and held still as Aphrodite checked her wig.

After they were both set aright, Aphrodite mouthed, "*Ready?*"

Not hardly, but she still let Aphrodite tug her into the room and close the door behind them. They were behind the curtain and the champagne room lovers hadn't yet noticed them. Granted, they were otherwise engaged, the man moaning a little.

"You like that, baby?" a woman's voice purred. "Takes the edge right off."

Aphrodite peeped out from behind the curtain.

Persephone pulled on her shoulder. "*No*," she mouthed, but Aphrodite shook her off and stepped into the room. What was she *doing*? Did she not get how dangerous this all was?

Persephone peered out after her. A dancer was moving over a male client, wearing nothing but a thong, as she giggled and let his hands roam all over her curvy body.

Aphrodite strode confidently past them to the champagne bucket on its stand. She popped open a bottle and started pouring glasses.

"Oh, Aphrodite, I didn't hear you come in," the other dancer said, glancing up. "He was looking for you."

"I'll take over." Aphrodite nodded and the other dancer immediately vacated her spot.

"Come join us, baby." The man sounded woozy, reaching for the retreating dancer.

Wait, Persephone recognize that voice.

Hermes?

She yanked the curtain aside more abruptly to get a better look. And yep, it was Hermes. He was lounging on the plush loveseat, his hair messy and his shirt half unbuttoned. His belt was gone.

"I'm coming," Aphrodite said sweetly, pouring champagne.

Persephone came out from the curtain and put her hands on her hips, frowning down at Hermes. He looked totally wasted.

"Persephone?" His eyes blinked lazily. "Where'd you come from?"

Persephone rolled her eyes, accepting a glass of champagne from

Aphrodite and taking a gulp to steady her nerves. She was officially ready for this night to be over.

Aphrodite's wide eyes over the glass said it all.

Reaching in her purse, Persephone pulled out the pink cellphone. "It's definitely dead," she said, still pressing buttons.

"It's a clue." Aphrodite came over with wet wipes, and started cleaning up Persephone's dress better. In the light of the room, the dust smudges were still apparent.

Hermes hiccupped on the couch.

Persephone ignored him and tried to piece together what had happened. "So her cellphone died but she figured Orpheus would know about this place and would look for her here. So she leaves it behind. But that means she was alert enough to leave it."

Persephone paced a few steps and stopped and spun back to Aphrodite. "And there must be a message on it, or something. Otherwise why would she leave it behind?"

"You guys wanna play?" Hermes interrupted. They both looked down at him. Gods, his eyes were glazed and his pupils were huge. What the hell had he taken?

Aphrodite shifted her gaze back to Persephone. "What are you going to do now?"

"Get him out of here." Persephone frowned at her drunken friend. "Regroup. See if I can get anything off this phone."

"What do you want me to do?"

Persephone started to answer, when she heard a raised voice in the corridor. A very angry voice.

Persephone's eyes shot to Aphrodite's. They both recognized it.

Ajax. It sounded like Ajax.

Aphrodite darted to the door. Persephone ran to Hermes.

"Come on, we have to go," Persephone hissed, pulling at his arms.

"Don't wanna." He grinned up at her, catching her hands playfully. Persephone squawked in surprise as he pulled her down on top of him.

"Persephone, you always smell so nice." He nuzzled her neck until she pushed herself away. "You're my dream girl."

Behind them, Aphrodite was standing at the door. It opened and Aphrodite shoved her body into the crack, posing provocatively in her sexy red dress.

"Looking for some fun?" she purred.

"Get out here; they want you on stage again."

Persephone stiffened. Definitely Ajax's voice.

"Sounds great, big boy." Aphrodite arched her back and slid her arm up the door frame so she was blocking the room from Ajax's view. "I'll just help these two finish up, then—"

Aphrodite's body jerked forward and she let out a soft cry. Someone had manhandled her into the hall.

Persephone jerked her face away from the door to hide it. She hurriedly slipped her purse off her shoulder and stuffed it behind a cushion.

"I said now," Ajax was growling. Aphrodite didn't reply. Persephone could hear the door swing open.

Whirling back to Hermes, Persephone straddled him. She tugged down her shirt until her bra covered breasts popped out. Hermes's face fell forward into her chest and she let her hair fall across her cheeks.

She could hear Ajax's heavy breathing as he stood in the door watching them. Hermes moaned suddenly and Persephone, afraid he'd call out her name, drew his head back and smashed her lips against his.

Hermes's eyes popped wide open. Persephone stared back into his, trying to communicate her panic to him.

"Make sure you get the money, sweetheart, before you go all the way," Ajax muttered from the door before closing it.

Persephone heard the knob click and she sagged, then scrambled back.

Hermes was breathing heavily. "Uhh, Pers—"

She leaped forward, plastering both her hands over his mouth. "Just shut up for a minute," she whispered harshly and listened for sounds of Ajax bursting back in.

When nothing happened, she relaxed the pressure on Hermes's

face, but kept her hands against his mouth. His bushy eyebrows were raised in surprise, his eyes shifting wildly.

"I'll explain everything later," she whispered. "Right now we have to get out of here."

"Ok." Hermes's words were muffled under her hands. She snatched them away and wiped them off on her skirt.

Ok, think, *think*. Ajax was outside; he wouldn't expect them to be done anytime soon. Not if he thought she was one of his girls. She could wait a while but he might come back any minute to check on them.

Someone banged into their door as they moved down the hall and she jumped.

"We're going out a different way," she said, grabbing her purse and pulling Hermes to his feet. He stumbled forward and it was enough for her to drag him behind the curtain.

She opened the door and took a left, moving forward in the dark, the opposite direction she and Aphrodite had gone earlier. Aphrodite said this way led to an exit and they just had to find it.

Persephone didn't care about the dark this time. Ajax was far more terrifying than some stupid rats. If he caught her, she'd be at his mercy, on his turf, and neither Hades nor any of his men even knew where she was.

"What the hell?" Hermes mumbled at her back.

"Keep moving," she whispered hurriedly. She finally turned on her phone's flashlight again. The long narrow hallway stretched out in front of them, and there were a couple of doors ahead. She headed toward the one at the very end. They'd go out the back way and hope no one was watching that exit. If they were, she didn't know what she'd do.

They came to a doorway and Persephone listened at the heavy wood. She didn't hear anything. Ok, this had to be the back exit.

She turned the doorknob and pushed the door open.

"Hey! Who's there?"

Oh shit! Not an exit, not an exit!

Persephone nearly climbed onto Hermes's back, she pushed him back so forcefully down the narrow passage.

"Go, go, go," she hissed. Hermes lost his footing and bounced a little off the brick wall. Persephone almost got tangled up in him, but somehow, they managed to move forward.

"Hey, you can't be in here!" The lights hit on her back as the door behind them opened before adrenaline kicked in and gave her some speed and Hermes some focus back. They surged forward, running into the darkness of the hall, Persephone continuously pushing Hermes forward.

"Where are we going?" Hermes asked, sounding more sober as they turned a corner.

"Just keep moving," Persephone bit out frantically. "The door should be up here."

Tiny lights from around the crack of a door up ahead gave her hope. The hall had widened enough for her to move past Hermes, and she nearly clawed at the next door handle they saw.

It had to be this one. It was really stuck, though, like it was rarely used. She backed up and charged it wildly, only barely hearing Hermes protest feebly behind her, "Wait. I think that's the—"

The door burst open and Persephone staggered forward, out from behind a curtain and right onto The Orchid stage.

Aphrodite had slipped off the dress and was in the gold bikini, gyrating with her ass towards the audience. Her head flew up and she stared at Persephone in shock.

Whirling back the way she'd come, Persephone only managed to slam her body into Hermes. He toppled over and she went down under him.

"Well, if it isn't the birthday boy, back for more," she heard Aphrodite adlib. Persephone pressed her face into Hermes's shoulder to hide it and think of what to do.

"And it looks like he got lucky," Aphrodite announced.

A few appreciative whoops rose up from the crowd. Persephone wrapped her arms around Hermes and desperately hooked a bare leg around his waist.

Hermes looked completely dazed. "Persephone, what the *hell* is going on?"

"Just go with it," Persephone pleaded. "We need to get out of here."

∽

"So then what happened?" Athena demanded. She sat at her computer desk, sorting through chargers that would match Eurydice's phone.

Persephone shook her head, causing the faded black sweatshirt she'd borrowed from Athena to slide off one pale shoulder. "Then Aphrodite got the lights to go down and got us off stage. We left out the front." She flopped backwards on Athena's couch, still unable to believe they'd all gotten out in one piece.

Athena shook her head. "A night at a strip club and you don't take me. I thought we were friends!"

"Keep it down," Hermes groaned.

Persephone glanced at him where he lay on the couch, an ice pack held to his head. On the taxi ride to Athena's, he'd admitted to taking some pills from the first dancer they'd found him with—something to help with the pain of his rump. Mixed with champagne, they'd messed him up and then given him a big ol' headache.

Persephone felt little sympathy.

"So, you still have no idea where this Eurydice girl is?" Athena had found a charger and was now working on one of her many computers. She had a whole wall of her tiny loft dedicated to electronics.

"No, and I'm out of leads besides the phone. Well, except for Ajax. But I can't just follow him around."

"Think maybe it's time to get your husband involved?" Hermes asked.

She closed her eyes and tried to envision it. What would Hades say if she took it all to him? What would he *do*?

He'd definitely put Persephone on lockdown for defying him and going places without his bodyguards.

But would he do anything to help Eurydice? That was the question. There was still a chance he had a part in the kidnapping. Persephone didn't want to believe it, but she hadn't wanted to believe things of Hades in the past and they'd turned out to be true.

Persephone shook her head. She couldn't risk putting her belief in Hades again and not just because she didn't think her heart could bear another disappointment. If he locked her away again, then who was there to help Eurydice? She'd be just another disappeared girl in a city that didn't care. "No, I'm not taking this to him. I need to figure it out myself." She yanked on her braids, unravelling them roughly.

She noticed Hermes and Athena were both staring at her.

But then Hermes was nodding. "She's right," he said. "Hades has other things to take care of right now."

"Right, he's busy," Persephone agreed, filing away Hermes's insight for later. What did he know about Hades's late nights and the business that kept him away all hours lately?

"How do we even know Eurydice had her phone with her when she was supposedly abducted?" Hermes asked Persephone.

"She's a twenty something year old woman. We sleep with our phones."

"Especially when they're on vibrate," Athena muttered, clicking her mouse.

Hermes perked up.

Persephone cleared her throat. "Anything on the cellphone yet?"

"Well, it's charging. I'll work on it tonight and as soon as I hack it, I'll let you know." Athena's fingers flew over her keyboard.

"I'm staying here." Hermes sagged back onto the cushions. "Let me know if I can help any more. Especially if your friend Aphrodite is involved."

Athena and Persephone both rolled their eyes.

"Well, my ride's here." Persephone stood the moment after her ride service app pinged. "I gotta go. Let me know as soon as you get anything."

Charon had sounded grouchy over the phone earlier when she told him she was staying late at the shelter to help Hecate take inventory. Persephone had been surprised at how easily the lie rolled off her tongue. She was getting better at it.

"You're not really going to try to tail Ajax, are you?" Athena asked, pulling out a drawer and rummaging in it.

"Let me sleep on it."

Persephone might be determined, but she liked to think she wasn't stupid. Today's activities aside. But tailing Ajax? That might tread into TSTL territory. Persephone was still unconsciously playing with her hair, letting it pouf out in a corn silk cloud.

"Wait," Athena held out a hand. "Give me your phone."

Persephone's brow wrinkled as Athena clipped a black case over her device. "What is that?"

"It's called a Wasp. It's a stun gun that looks like a cellphone case. New prototype. The next one will be smaller, but this works pretty well." Athena grimaced as she fitted her hand around the bulky thing. "Here, watch."

She showed Persephone how to uncover the two tiny metal teeth that delivered the shock, then slid a button to activate the stun gun. It was all but invisible against the casing of the phone.

"Holy crap, Athena, are you sure?"

"Absolutely. It's still in beta testing, so you'd be doing me a favor if you use it and let me know how it works."

Feeling bad ass, Persephone took her phone and pressed the case's "on" button. A buzzing sound filled the apartment.

"Six hundred and fifty volts. It'll knock a grown man on his ass." Athena grinned at the thought. "Come here, Hermes, let's try it out."

"Pass," he called from the couch. "I've been beaten enough by beautiful women tonight."

44

Persephone rounded the corner to arrive at the shelter and saw Charon standing on the curb, glaring at the door. She halted in her tracks. Well crap.

Persephone eyed her husband's second in command. Well, no point putting off the inevitable. She straightened and moved forward towards Charon, who had spotted her.

"Where have you been?" Charon asked as she approached. She didn't answer, but stepped through the door he opened for her.

Inside Hecate came forward, hands outstretched apologetically. "Persephone, I'm sorry, I told him you were just on a quick walk..."

"It's ok." Persephone turned back to Charon, who was still by the door.

"Get in the car."

Shrugging her purse higher on her arm, she obeyed.

"Where's Hades?" she asked, once they both had slid in, her in the back, Charon up with the driver.

"Mr. Ubeli has been tied up in a business deal. It's important. He sent me to check on you when you didn't return his message."

Persephone pulled out her phone and checked her voicemail. A new one was there. She sighed.

"I didn't hear it ring. It was an accident." She'd put it on silent before entering the club earlier. She put it away, shaking her head. "You don't have to babysit me, Charon. I'm a grown woman. I can take care of myself."

"Stop the car," Charon told the driver. Persephone's heart thumped faster as the car slowed to a stop and the big man turned around in his seat to address her.

"You were out walking the streets. Alone. You don't need Hades to tell you how fucking stupid that is."

Persephone cringed. Usually Hades and his men kept the language clean around her.

"There's trouble coming and we've been dealing with it." From Persephone's family. Charon didn't have to say it. "But until it's blown over, you're going to need to act like a fucking adult and use some common sense."

Something flared inside Persephone, a little spark of anger. She was sick of people talking to her like she was a little girl.

"Charon, I was fine, I was just walking—"

"It's fine until one of our enemies pulls up, kidnaps you, and rapes you with a knife until you bleed out for us to find you. You think being a Titan will save you?" He gave an ugly scoff. "I've seen what these animals can do. In their minds, you've chosen the enemy's bed. They won't take mercy on you."

Persephone's breath left her. Her spine pressed deep to the car seat as she met Charon's angry gaze. How many men had seen this face just before dying?

"If you don't want to be treated like a naïve little girl, stop acting like one," Charon growled. "I'm going to get you to the penthouse, and you're going to sit tight until Hades comes home and takes you to dinner. Because he's been neck deep in shit all week and he wants a nice night out with his wife."

Unable to find her voice, Persephone jerked her head *yes*.

Stone-faced, Charon turned around and the car moved on.

Persephone sat quiet, but somewhere, deep inside, her anger started to boil. *Stay on the farm, Persephone. Don't talk back. Mother knows best.* Then Hades. Now even Charon. Meanwhile the Eurydices and Ashleys of the world were disposable. Throw them out with last week's trash. Who would fight for them if not another woman? Who would even fucking *care*?

She got it, okay? The world was ugly and dark and people were only looking to use one another. But she wanted to believe in something more. She wanted to believe in a world where love meant something and good was real, even if it didn't always triumph like the storybooks said. It was still worth fighting for.

It was still worth fighting for, dammit.

Hours later, Persephone stepped off the elevator, dressed for dinner. Her bodyguard stood off to her left, a constant shadow. Hades was in a meeting already at the restaurant and was sending his car to pick her up. Following orders, she was to wait for his driver in the lobby.

"Can I wait at the bar?" she asked her bodyguard. He nodded and she stalked towards it. Two guys in designer polo shirts watched her pass, taking in her long legs, put on display perfectly by her short peach-colored cocktail dress. She'd let her hair down and curled the ends so it bounced around her face like a movie star's. Her makeup played up both her blue eyes and red, red lips.

Charon wanted her to grow up, she'd show him. Hades, too.

She paused as she entered the posh hotel restaurant and pulled out her phone to check it.

Any luck? she texted Athena.

No answer. She'd called Aphrodite and Hermes back too, but gotten only voicemail. The phone would turn up something. It had to.

"White wine, please," she ordered at the bar. She was about to hop on the bar stool when a familiar snigger caught her ear.

She turned to see a couple sitting at the bar. And her breath caught.

There was Ajax in his long fur coat, gulping down oysters. One of his thugs stood nearby. The man and her own bodyguard exchanged nods.

Persephone felt cold chills up and down her spine as she stared at the mobster. He sat there, so smug and carefree while he caused all this misery.

Persephone's chest went hot with sudden rage. Probably in part because when she'd seen him earlier today, she'd been so terrified. She hated that he had that power over her, over any of them. She put her hand to her chest to steady herself.

"Ah, Mrs. Ubeli. Looking lovely tonight." The bastard raised his drink to toast her. His eyes glittered. "Going out? Your husband's a lucky man."

Persephone ignored his gold-toothed grin. "Say, Persephone, have you met my little friend? She's about your age." He turned and touched the arm of a woman who sat beside him, very straight and stiff, staring ahead.

Her face was hidden behind her brunette hair but her red dress left little to the imagination, cut short on her thighs and even then, open on one side almost up to her waist.

Persephone recognized that tight dancer's body poured into an hourglass shape. *But no. No, it can't be. Please—*

Ajax turned to grab the woman's arm and she turned, her hair swinging back from her sculpted face.

Aphrodite.

Before she could stop herself, Persephone was up and moving in their direction. Out of the corner of her eye she saw her bodyguard following and halted. "Where's the ladies' room?" she asked a passing server.

By the time Persephone had gotten directions, she was sure Aphrodite would notice her trajectory towards the back of the room and follow. Her mind was racing. What the hell was Aphrodite doing there with Ajax?

Persephone paced for several minutes in the fancy bathroom

seating area, waiting for her new friend. Had Ajax figured out they'd been snooping around at the strip club? How much did he know?

Persephone whirled around as the doors opened and Aphrodite finally walked in.

"Aphrodite, what's going on? Why are you here with Ajax?" Persephone's voice cut off when she saw the furious look on Aphrodite's face.

"How dare you," Aphrodite said. "Like you even care."

Whatever words Persephone had been about to say died on her lips.

"Persephone *Ubeli*," Aphrodite ground out her last name. "You think I wouldn't find out? Your husband is the biggest mobster in Olympus."

Under all her makeup, Aphrodite looked tired, but her brown eyes flashed. Persephone wasn't the only one who was fed up. "I should've guessed it when you showed up at The Orchid House. You weren't there to help. You just needed more soldiers in your war."

"Aphrodite, no, I—"

"Don't." Aphrodite held up her hand. "I trusted you. I needed to get away from Ajax, not sucked into a vendetta between him and his biggest enemy—your husband."

Gods, no, that was the last thing Persephone wanted. But how could she even begin to explain—

"Don't worry, he didn't recognize you. It was your friend you brought with you—the designer. You think Ajax doesn't know his whole business is a front for your husband's drug trade?"

Persephone drew in a shocked breath. *That* was why Hermes and Hades were so close?

Persephone shook her head. "Aphrodite, I swear I didn't know Ajax would recognize Hermes. You have to believe me."

"Ajax hates your husband," Aphrodite hissed. "He knows everything about him. And now he thinks I have an in with Hermes somehow. He's looking for weakness. I should point him straight to you."

All of Persephone's air left her lungs.

"Don't worry," Aphrodite said bitterly. "I won't sell you out. I have standards."

"Gods, Aphrodite, I never wanted to drag you into this. I'm sorry. I'll get you out of it, I swear—"

"You've done enough." Then Aphrodite's face fell, her expression going bleak. "You should know, Ajax will do whatever it takes to hurt your husband. We're both just collateral damage." Aphrodite took a step back. "Ajax says he'll be taking me back to Metropolis to star in some movies. He owns me now."

"I'm sorry. I'll figure something out," Persephone babbled. She didn't know how, but she had to fix this. "I'll come for you."

Tears glistening in her eyes, Aphrodite shook her head. "They call me a whore. But you spread your legs for a monster. I never want to see you again." And with that, she left.

Persephone let herself sag into a chair. Aphrodite's words had hurt, but worse than the accusation of betrayal was the look of terror in her eyes.

He owns me now.

Lowering her head into her hands, Persephone tried to think it through. Had she just made everything worse?

The question was, was Ajax *still* working for the Titans (aka her mom)? Or was he branching out on his own now that there was unrest among the power players?

Either way, it amounted to the same thing. Ajax was just a power-hungry pimp. And he wanted to expand his borders beyond Metropolis. He'd needed an in to New Olympus.

Her mind worked through it, clinging to the facts and trying to work out the bigger picture now that she had even more puzzle pieces.

Ajax was looking for Hades's weaknesses when he came to town, that was for sure.

He found Orpheus and Orpheus's weakness—Eurydice. So he kidnapped her to control Orpheus. Then he could use Orpheus to dick around with Hades. But what did that really get Ajax besides giving Hades a headache and a publicity hit when Orpheus refused to play Hades's club?

No, it had to be about something bigger.

What about that mysterious shipment she kept hearing about? The way people whispered about it, it sounded like a game changer.

It was drugs. It had to be. And now that she knew that Hermes's businesses were a front for Hades... Ajax wanted a way to get access, so he took Aphrodite.

So what now?

"Come on, think," she whispered furiously. *Pretty, stupid slut.*

At least all this meant Hades couldn't be behind Eurydice's disappearance. Ajax had thrown that out there to manipulate her, just like he was using Eurydice, and now Aphrodite.

What would he do when Aphrodite and Eurydice no longer helped him get what he wanted?

Persephone felt cold, very cold inside.

A rap on the door startled her. "You okay in there, Mrs. Ubeli?" Persephone's bodyguard called.

"Coming," she said, rising.

Enough was enough. The cops wouldn't help. She couldn't tail Ajax; she'd only get herself hurt.

No matter the consequences to herself, Hades was Eurydice's and now Aphrodite's only hope. He had the resources to take on someone like Ajax. His Shades could find out where Ajax was holding Eurydice.

Persephone checked the mirror and straightened her dress, making sure she looked perfect.

Yes, it was time to talk to her husband.

He would hear her out or he wouldn't. He'd lock her up again for breaking his rules and going out on her own or he wouldn't. He'd either help Eurydice and Aphrodite or...

She turned for the door.

Looked like she was still a stupid girl after all because even after everything, hope pulsed in her heart like a beacon that Hades would listen, that Hades would care, and that Hades would be willing to help.

Otherwise, she didn't know what options Aphrodite or Eurydice might have left.

The place was full, but only a few of the tables at the front held normal couples. Towards the back, a line of his Shades sat hulking at the little tables. Hades had taken all precautions to make sure the meet went off smoothly, including surrounding himself with his soldiers.

The restaurant had old world charm with mahogany-paneled wainscoting and dark leather booths. Hades slid into the booth seat across from his wife.

Her wide eyes blinked up at him, and even though he'd been about to immediately rip into her for ditching her guard, for a moment he was frozen, mesmerized by her beauty. Red lipstick highlighted her kissable lips and as always, her blue eyes entranced.

"Hey," she said softly, then swallowed like she was just as affected by him as he was by her. Good. She better be. It was his one comfort in all of this.

And suddenly he couldn't stand not having his hands on her. "Come here," he commanded.

Her eyebrows went up. "Where?"

He gestured to the booth seat beside him.

Her eyes narrowed. "Why?"

"Now."

She let out a small huff but scooted off her side of the bench and moved over to his side. She left about two feet between herself and Hades and he let out a small growl of impatience.

Then he moved over, hooked an arm around her shoulders, and cemented her body tight against his. And the fist that had been clenched around his lungs ever since Charon called earlier finally released. He hadn't even realized until this moment that he carried the tension around for all these hours. And it pissed him off that she could still affect him this way.

He squeezed her shoulder. "I hear you've been a bad girl."

Her head swung towards him. "Let me guess. You're going to punish me for it." Her eyes held a challenge. Like she dared him.

The wolf inside Hades growled. "You'd like that, wouldn't you? I haven't played with you for a while so you decided to get my attention, is that it?"

With a gasp of disgust, she pulled away, or at least tried to. Hades wasn't letting her go anywhere.

Her eyes flashed at him. "I'm not a toy you can take off the shelf and play with whenever you feel bored. I'm more than that." She yanked harder and finally squirmed out of his grasp. "And to think, I wanted to talk to you about something real. Something that's actually important."

She'd pulled her body away from his and he didn't like it. He didn't like it at all.

"Being reckless and putting yourself in danger is something I have to address," he spoke through his teeth. "But yes, wife, we are going to talk about it and deal with it." He scooted close to her, halving the distance between them. "And then you're going to tell me everything going through that head of yours."

"Because you own me?" She glared up at him.

His pants tightened as he went rock hard. Just like he always did when she challenged him. He caught her cheek and chin with his hand, forcing her gaze to lock with his. "Yes. Because you belong to me."

Her mouth dropped open but no words came out. That delectable little fucking mouth. He wanted to do a thousand debauched and filthy things to that mouth.

Right now, though, a mere kiss would have to suffice because he couldn't stand another moment without devouring her.

As he dropped his lips to hers, though, the room erupted with gunfire.

46

Hades wrenched Persephone to the floor. She moved in slow motion, in shock, not realizing what was going on. As glass smashed and people screamed over the deafening reports, they hunkered down under the table, his body sheltering hers as the gunfire continued.

Persephone didn't know when the sharp racket stopped. Her ears rang.

Hades already had his phone out and was speaking into it. "Shots fired at Giuseppe's. Tony should've been out front. We need backup." He crouched beside the table, barely a hair out of place.

Persephone pushed up from the floor as her husband pocketed his cellphone. His other hand was fitted around a gun.

The weapon brought the world into focus.

"You ok?" he was asking. She read his lips and nodded. A minute ago they'd been sitting at the table. He was about to kiss her and then — And then—

"Sit tight. I'll be right back."

Slowly, she started to hear the sounds in the restaurant: the dazed, pained din of shocked patrons. Some crying, a few screams.

Weirdly, Persephone's teeth started chattering, but her body became light and loose, untethered from the moment.

Her thoughts swirled. *I've never been shot at before.* No, wait, that wasn't right. Her mom had shot at her. Well, at Hades, but the bullet had hit her. Still, she didn't remember that gunshot being as loud as these were. So loud. Was this what Hades's life was usually like? But... It would be his enemies shooting. So that meant... Her own family, right? Did her mom know she was here? Did they want her dead, too?

Before the whole world started to crash down again, Hades returned. "Come on." His face was cold and chiseled even as he held out his left hand to help her up.

They left through the back kitchen, hurrying past a shrieking Giuseppe and his panicking workers to escape into an alley. A black sedan rolled up and Hades opened the door, climbing in behind Persephone.

"What do we know?" he barked at the driver.

"All other Shades were out of range but Tony's on their tail. He saw them pull in and called for backup. They took off right after firing the warning shots."

"Firing into a restaurant where I'm eating with my wife—that's more than a warning. That's asking for war," Hades bit out. "Get Charon on the phone."

War. She'd known somewhere in the back of her head that things were escalating between her family and Hades. But war? She was being naïve and stupid again. Really, it was shocking that it had been put off for this long.

It had been easier to dig her head in the sand, though, and fight for something tangible. To fight for Eurydice.

But here it was. Her husband sat across from her, calling out orders with a gun in his hand. Rocco, Santonio, Joey and Andy DePetri—they weren't just rough-looking men who were nice to her when Hades met with them at the Chariot. They were warriors and her husband was their general.

People *died* at their hands. Just like people had probably died tonight, simply for being in the wrong place at the wrong time:

standing between the gunmen and their target: Hades and her, the Ubelis, rulers of the Underworld.

We're just collateral damage.

The adrenaline hit Persephone's stomach. She doubled over and retched onto the car floor.

And then Hades's hands were there, holding back her hair and offering her his handkerchief to wipe her mouth.

"You're ok, baby," his voice was clipped but his hand was soothing on her back.

The driver talked over his shoulder. "Charon's online, says Tony lost the trail. But it's looking like it isn't Poseidon."

She heard all the words but barely registered them. The voices sounded muted and far away, like she was underwater and separate from everything that was happening.

"Put him on," Hades ordered, sitting forward, one hand still on Persephone's back even as she curled up into the car seat, trying to make herself as small as possible.

"Where the fuck is Poseidon?"

"Back to the ship," came Charon's voice over the speakers. "He's not coming back."

"If he crossed us, I swear to the gods—"

"Not him. I was with him the whole time. You think this is Metropolis?"

Hades breathed hard out his nose. "Has to be. And they know about the shipment. Must be an inside man."

"Ajax." Even over the phone, Charon's menace was clear, a tangible hate. Persephone couldn't believe she'd ever thought for a minute Ajax was their associate.

"We move on him now, it's all-out war," Hades said. "The Titans will move in to protect him. We'll lose Poseidon, the shipment, the deal, everything."

"What do you want to do?" Charon asked.

Persephone watched her husband control himself and take his emotions in hand, shutting them down. Always so controlled. How did he do that? She wanted it so desperately right now, to not be able to feel anything.

"Ignore Ajax," Hades fired orders into the phone. "We'll deal with him later. Meet can't happen tonight. We prep the street, tell Poseidon we need more time."

"Needs to be soon," Charon answered. "Poseidon wants the deal, but he's not a patient man."

"Tomorrow then. I'll tell our man with the force and he'll keep the docks swept."

"We get this done and then we start making plans to visit our friends in Metropolis." Her husband's voice hardened, and Persephone could feel cold rage rolling off him.

"Any word from Tony on the scum who did this?"

"He lost them. But they fired on sacred ground. We'll make them pay."

Oh gods. Persephone leaned forward then, whispering, "Giuseppe and the people there—are they ok?"

Hades's eyes cut to her.

"Yeah, Charon, you hear that? Make sure the Shades are standing by to see how we can help these people, ok?"

Persephone sagged back. She didn't have anything left. Nothing left. She was used up. Wrung dry. *Collateral damage.*

Hades hung up the phone.

"Never again," he said, staring at the road in front of them. "Never again."

"Where to, Mr. Ubeli?" the driver asked quietly.

"Take us to the Estate," Hades ordered.

47

Persephone was trembling as Hades led her inside the Estate. Fucking shaking so hard, he could all but hear her teeth clacking. And it wasn't from the cold.

She was scared. Scared out of her wits. They'd shot at her. Opened fire with no care for who might be nearby—

Hades clenched his jaw as it all flashed again before his eyes. The eruption of gunfire, a sound you never forgot after you heard it once. Shoving Persephone down under the table, not knowing whether she'd been hit or not—fuck, he needed a drink. Or to shoot something. But no, dammit, both of those things would take him away from his wife's side and he wasn't letting her out of his sight.

"We're going upstairs," he barked as soon as they were inside. Useless to say, really, since he was all but dragging Persephone up the stairs already. His men had already checked the residence when they first arrived and he'd ordered them to stay outside on perimeter duty for the night.

Persephone didn't say anything or talk back. That wasn't like her. Neither was passively letting Hades move her around like a doll as they got to the master suite. But she didn't give a moment's protest when he led her straight into the bathroom.

And she washed her face like he instructed and brushed her teeth without a single word. What the fuck? Where had his spitfire gone?

"Persephone, look at me." He grabbed both her cheeks once they were done in the bathroom and tried to force her to look at him. She stared at the floor.

"Look at me," he demanded again.

When her eyes finally moved sluggishly up to meet his, they lacked their usual shine.

"Stop it or I'm going to take you over my knee."

No response. Not the usual flare of her nostrils or widening of her eyes. Her face was as blank as a painted doll's.

"Persephone. Persephone." He wanted to shake her but he didn't trust himself. He was feeling too many things. He'd gone so long without feeling anything and then now for everything to rain down on him all at once, coming at him from all directions—

He gripped Persephone's hair at the nape of her neck and wrapped his arm around her waist, crushing her body to his. Willing her to wake the fuck up.

He crashed his lips down on hers.

She was still unresponsive. Limp in his arms. Pale and cold and lifeless like some dead thing.

"Gods damn it! Persephone." He pushed her up against the wall and pressed his lips to hers again. But for once in his life, he didn't demand. He didn't force his way in.

He coaxed.

He teased.

He prayed at the altar of her lips.

He closed his eyes and kissed her. *Come back to me. Come back to me. Please.* He didn't know if he was entreating Persephone or the gods.

Because what he was really begging for was forgiveness.

None of this was ever supposed to touch her. He promised to keep her safe.

He'd promised and he'd failed her. Just like Chiara.

No. He shook his head. No. Not his Persephone. He wouldn't lose her. He fucking refused. He'd never let her go. The gods and Fates be damned.

He pressed his body more firmly against her so that she was pressed tight, trapped between him and the wall. He'd shield her until the day she died. Which would be a long fucking time from now.

And yes, he was hard. He was hard whenever she was near. Even now. If he thought it would bring her back to him, he'd bury himself balls deep right this second. But he couldn't be sure it wouldn't do more damage.

So instead, he took her wrists and pinned them to the wall above her head. He stepped even closer into her, crouching slightly so that his face was beside hers.

"Do you feel that?" he demanded. "Your heartbeat is right next to mine. Because we're both fucking alive. People died back at that diner but it wasn't you and it wasn't me."

Her brow scrunched, the first sign of life he'd seen since before the shooting began.

He brought a hand between them and clutched her cheek roughly. "That's right. You are alive and I'm not letting you go anywhere."

"Because you own me?" Finally, a spark lit in her eyes. "Tell the truth. I'm just as expendable as any of those people back there. Except, I forgot. I'm still of use to you. Or maybe not so much anymore. I can't be much of a pawn to hold over the Titans if they were willing to kill me tonight just to get to you."

He let her talk only because she was finally showing signs of life again, but every single word out of her mouth only pissed him off more.

"Expendable?" He couldn't keep the incredulity out of his voice.

But either she didn't hear it or she pretended not to. "Collateral damage," she said. "We're all just collateral damage to you. Nothing matters but your agenda. You don't care about anyone or anything."

His hips thrust forward at her insolence, his rock-hard cock jutting rudely against her thigh. Her body shifted to cradle him between her hips. His cock snug against her sex.

Her eyes flew open, apparently just realizing what she'd done at the same time he did.

He smirked down at her. "Your body knows who you belong to."

Fury lit up her eyes but his head was already descending, taking that lush mouth. Taming it.

Or at least he tried. She bit his lip and yanked her arms down from where he held them above her head and started pummeling him with them. Well, as much as a kitten could pummel a lion.

He easily caught her wrists again and pinned them above her head. She screamed out a roar of such fury and frustration, the Shades outside would surely hear and wonder what the hell was going on in here.

But Hades didn't care if they heard. He didn't care about anything except the furious, bright, and shining goddess in his arms.

He could have lost her. He'd barely found her and he could have fucking *lost* her.

It was just like four months ago when she'd been on that gurney being wheeled into surgery except worse. Because now he'd had four more months of knowing her, four more months of coming home to find her sweet body in his bed, always so hot and receptive to him. Four more months of her whip smart intelligent eyes on him, challenging him, not letting him get away with any of his shit, and he—

"I love you."

It was out of his mouth before he even registered what he was saying.

Persephone froze and stopped struggling, blinking up at him in confusion.

But Hades wasn't confused, not anymore. "I love you, goddess."

He felt like laughing, it was such a weight off his chest, finally admitting what he'd struggled for so long to deny. He'd loved her a long time now. So long he couldn't remember what not loving her felt like.

Persephone shook her head back and forth, her brow scrunching.

"No. You just want to use me. I heard you. The night I woke up from the coma. I heard you and Charon."

Fuck.

He let go of her arms and instead cupped her cheeks again. Gently this time. "I'm an ass. I don't know what all you heard that night but I've been a coward. For a long time now. Ever since I met you, you've made me feel—"

He shook his head. "You're different from anyone I've ever met. *I'm* different when I'm with you. I thought it was weakness."

Her huge blue eyes searched his back and forth like she was terrified to believe what he was saying. He'd fucked this up so badly but he'd make it up to her.

"But it's not weakness." He narrowed his eyes and brought his forehead close to hers, needing her to understand. It was all so clear now. "You're my strength. You wash me clean. Without you, I'm nothing. None of this means *anything* without you. I *love* you."

"Stop saying that," Persephone whispered.

Hades shook his head. "Never. I love you."

Fat tears rolled down Persephone's cheeks. "Don't say it unless you mean it. Please. Don't—" her voice choked off, head shaking back and forth. "Don't—"

"I love you. I love you. I love—"

His words cut off when Persephone threw her arms around his neck and smashed her mouth against his.

Drinking in her kiss, he scooped her up and strode into the bedroom. He lay her down on the bed and draped himself over her. "Goddess," he smiled against her mouth.

"Now," she panted breathlessly, squirming under him, tugging up her dress. He helped, tearing the fabric and palming her sweet pussy. Gods, she was wet.

"This is mine," he reminded her. She nodded so frantically he chuckled. "As long as you remember who you belong to." With his thumb, he rubbed her favorite spot, to the upper left of her clit and her body spasmed, her gaze going hazy.

"That's my girl," he murmured, brushing the sweet spot over and over until she trembled. "Let it come, let go for me, that's it—"

Her breath rushed out and pink flared in her cheeks as a soft climax took her. Her hands grabbed his shoulders and pulled him in for an eager kiss.

He indulged her, rubbing his face against hers, leaving her cheeks red from his rough stubble. He loved marking her. Later, he'd rub his face between her thighs and leave her chafed and aching so tomorrow, she'd remember him.

Now he had to be inside her. His fingers fumbled with his zipper.

They both moaned as he breached her soft entrance. Her inner walls kissed along his cock. When his thumb found her clit again, teasing another climax, her pussy squeezed him so tight he grew light-headed.

Persephone twined her arms around his shoulders, tugging him close. "Say it again," she whispered as if afraid the moment would shatter.

"I love you."

Her happy gasp nearly sent him over the edge. He rose up to one elbow, hitching her long leg over his hip so he could drive deep. Her head flew back but her own hips rose up to meet each thrust.

Hades growled, pulling his cock almost all the way out to slam into her slick wetness again. As he bottomed out, he ground against her entire pelvic cradle until her juices coated his lower stomach. Then he pulled out and slammed home again.

"*Ooooh*," Persephone moaned, her face scrunching. He stilled.

"Did I hurt you?" Each thrust went so deep, his cock bumped her cervix.

She shook her head and wound her legs tighter around his back. "More."

Fingers clawed into the bed, Hades drove in his wife's welcoming body, pounding her into the bed. Persephone's nails raked his shoulders, her feet digging into the muscles of his back.

"Hades, I'm—"

"Come for me, baby." She detonated with a series of soft cries, her cheeks and chest blooming pink roses. He nuzzled her a moment before pistoning his hips faster, driving towards his own climax. His limbs and torso tightened, a bow ready to let loose the arrows of his seed.

When he came, his world shook apart, focused on the sweet, smiling face of his beautiful wife.

"Angel," he brushed his lips over hers, kissing every inch of her mouth. Gods, he wanted to live inside her. He could tie her up forever and fuck her every hour and it wouldn't be enough. Never enough.

With a groan, he separated from her. Her pussy was as pink and swollen as her well-kissed mouth.

"I meant to be gentle," he muttered.

"It's all right." Her fingers trailed along his shoulders, soothing the scratches her nails had left. "I'll take you as you are."

"Because you love me." He rolled to his side so he could cup her cheek.

"Yes." Her breath hitched.

"Even when you didn't want to." He smiled as he traced her lips. He didn't deny the swell of pride. She'd given her love even when he hadn't deserved it.

"Yes." Her eyes grew shadowed and he leaned in to taste her.

"Never again. I won't hurt you. I'm gonna take care of you."

She winced and he cursed himself. He'd made that promise before. "It'll be different this time. I'm gonna keep you safe, protect you from everything—"

"Even yourself?" she added with a wry smile. She was too smart. She saw right through him, to the monster he was.

She loved him anyway. The depth of his feeling made his heart thud to a stop. He'd do anything for this woman. Even die for her.

"Yes. I won't let the darkness touch you, Persephone."

With a small, hesitant hand, she reached up to stroke the dark hair from his brow. "You can't keep it away," she murmured. "It's a part of you." She sighed, her gaze slipping away. "It's a part of me now, too."

"You're made of light, angel. Summertime and everything good."

He buried his nose in her hair. She even smelled like sunshine. "Your light will drive the darkness away."

"Maybe." She pulled back and palmed his cheek, her blue eyes searching his. "Just love me. It'll be enough."

In response, he turned her away from him so he could hold her to his chest. Her head rested over his heartbeat.

Later, he'd clean her up and go down on her. Go slowly, make her scream. But right now, he wanted to hold her. His dick was hard again, straining, but he'd wait. He had the rest of the night to be inside her.

The rest of the night, and the rest of their lives.

48

Hours later, Persephone awoke with the sounds of gunshots ringing in her ears. She sat up in bed, gripping the empty sheets beside her until her dream—of bullets crashing into the restaurant—faded away.

Persephone looked around, confused for a second not to be in her bed at the penthouse. But then the rest of it came crashing in.

I love you.

Three little words with the power to break her. Or remake her. She pulled the silk sheet up to her chest and crossed her arms over her knees.

He loved her. He loved her back.

She smiled silly and looked around, but Hades wasn't anywhere in the large master suite and she didn't hear him in the ensuite bathroom either. And then her chest tightened with fear. Would he take it back? What if it was just another cruel game to him?

All of a sudden, she could barely breathe. She threw the sheet back and jumped to her feet, grabbing a robe and all but running out of the room. She had to find him. She had to know if it was real or not.

She'd just pulled open the bedroom door when she heard angry voices coming from somewhere in the house.

Frowning, she followed the sounds down the hall. She and Hades always stayed in the master suite on the second floor. Most of the house had been closed up for over a decade, the furniture under blankets like ghosts from another time.

The voice was coming from somewhere near the front door. She paused at the landing above the stairwell, pulling her robe more tightly around her and listening hard.

"We had a deal." The words echoed around the foyer's cathedral ceiling and came right to her ears. It was a man and she'd swear she recognized the voice from somewhere. "I've done my part. Given you land rights, re-zoned the docks. Turned a blind eye to the scum building up on every corner in the Styx."

Holding her breath, Persephone crept around the corner. Hades's dark head came into view. He stood with Charon at his back, facing two other men who'd come with the noisy guest, a handsome blond man who looked familiar. Persephone couldn't put her finger on where she'd seen him before. He was shorter than Hades, but he stood in the center of the foyer with a posture that said he was used to dominating conversations.

"I kept you clean," the blond said. "You've stayed in power. But everything you've built on is mine. I laid the foundation. I control it. I can take it away."

Who dared talk to Hades this way?

Beside Hades, Charon shifted slowly. Persephone's breath caught. Charon was large enough to take all three of them down. And here, on twenty acres of private land, who would ever find out what happened? Was she actually afraid for the blond man and his two bodyguards? She couldn't tell. So much had happened today, she could barely sort through one thing before another was being thrown her way.

"I understand your concern." Hades's voice came low and level. "At the same time, I can't help but be offended by what you imply."

"I'm not implying," the blond man said, taking a step forward and getting right in Hades's face. Gods, did the man have a death wish? "I'm telling you. I've done my part. I expect you to deliver. I don't expect a restaurant to be shot up the very night I'm pointing out my strong stance on crime."

Persephone's eyes flew open and her hand shot to her mouth to cover her gasp. It was the mayor. Storm or Strum or something. No, *Sturm*. Zeus Sturm, she remembered now. She'd seen him talk at the charity dinner. He and Hades worked together? The golden boy mayor and the city's biggest crime lord?

"It's being handled," Charon rumbled.

"My ex-wife's hairdresser could handle this better," Zeus snapped right back. "We're looking at war. Now? On the eve of the election?"

Persephone backed further into the shadows, wanting to know more about how he was connected to Hades.

"What I want to know is if you'll make good on the promises you've made over the years." The mayor jabbed a finger towards Hades. Persephone sucked in a breath. She'd never seen anyone talk to Hades like that.

"The reporter vultures are circling. They'll say I look soft on crime. The vote is in less than a week. You move on your enemies now, this whole election goes down in a hail of gunfire. You say you control the streets? Then control them."

"Mr. Sturm, you're upset. You're not seeing the big picture." Persephone recognized that voice. The quieter and more still Hades became, the more dangerous and calculating he was.

"Big picture, my ass. Here's the big picture: Tuesday, I lose, and the Titan brothers are back in town with the circus. Then we can stand around and talk about the picture, because we'll both be out of it."

Hades paused before answering, using silence to his effect. It worked. By the time he spoke, Zeus looked a little less sure of himself. "Because of your status, and our partnership, I am going to overlook your disrespect. But I will tell you. This is the last time you come to my house and make demands of me."

"Believe me, Ubeli, I don't intend to be seen with you ever again,"

Zeus returned. "Our partnership works because you run your thing and I run mine. But I'm a man who does what it takes to prove to people I intend to return on their investment. And to do that, I need votes."

"You'll have them. Tuesday," Hades said in the deep, final tones of an executioner. "Charon will see you out."

Zeus opened his mouth, but seemed to have run out of words. Instead he glared up at Hades.

"We'll be in touch," Hades said, and his voice held a note of finality.

Charon moved forward then, herding the three towards the door.

Before Persephone could move back towards the bedroom, her husband turned his head and pinned her with his eyes.

Persephone saw many things in that gaze.

A very dangerous man.

A predator.

Her husband who loved her.

It *had* been real. She could see it even now in his eyes, though the meeting with Zeus had obviously angered him.

He looked at her like he wanted to eat her up but also like...like he loved her.

Her breath caught. And maybe her heart skipped a beat or two as he started up the stairs towards her.

All she knew was that if he loved her, if he *really* loved her, then she would give him the world. She would be his world.

And she would start by soothing the beast. She smiled saucily down at him and let her robe hang open.

He growled in reaction and started taking the stairs two at a time. "I won't take it easy on you."

She arched an eyebrow. "Who says I want you to?"

But as he closed the distance between them, she retreated up the steps.

"You should run," he warned and she whirled, her robe flying behind her. She made it down the hall and almost to the bedroom before he slammed into her, his weight carrying her forward to trap her between him and the door. She struggled and he caught her arms behind her, pushing her against the unyielding wood.

"Got you," he growled in her ear. "You didn't run fast enough."

Her heart pounded against the door. "I wanted you to catch me."

He turned her roughly. She looked straight in his eyes, full of feral possession, and she smiled.

"Oh, goddess. You were made for me." His mouth slammed onto hers, lips hard enough to bruise.

She pushed up to her tiptoes and hooked an arm behind his head, meeting his kiss. His hand found the doorknob. They stumbled together into the bedroom, Hades recovering first. His hand clamped on the back of her neck, marching her to the bed.

"You've been a naughty girl." He shoved her down, face first and held her there, cheek to coverlet.

"Yes," she breathed as he shucked off her robe. "Punish me?"

"Oh, I will." He slapped her ass hard enough to shock the breath from her. "Floating through the house wearing almost nothing, flaunting that body just out of reach…"

"Do you think your guest saw?"

"You better hope he didn't. Not him, not the Shades. No one gets to see this but me." His fingers swept over her pussy and she quivered, yelping when he followed the gentle touch with a sharp smack.

"Not even Charon?"

Hades growled. "You have a thing for Charon?"

"No…he's just so…big." She bit her lip at her brazenness. Her nipples pressed into the bed.

"I'll show you big." Twining his hand in her hair, Hades wrenched her up and forced her to her knees. His cock bobbed in her face. "Suck."

She reached for him and he grabbed her hands, shackling them with his. "Just your mouth. You know better than that."

"I'm naughty," she whispered, eyelashes fluttering. "Remember?"

"I'll teach you to be good."

"Teach me, Daddy," she mouthed over his head, and his eyes turned black.

Gripping her hair, he slid into her mouth. He thrust his hips, each time pushing a little deeper. His cock bumped the entrance to her throat and she coughed, eyes watering. He eased out only a moment before doing it again. He choked her on his cock over and over but the hand on her head turned gentle.

"That's it, good girl. There's a good girl." He no longer held back her hands. When she cupped her breasts and rolled her nipples between a thumb and forefinger, he murmured his approval. "Touch yourself. Show Daddy what you like."

She shivered, rivulets of pleasure running through her. Tears streamed down her cheeks as he invaded her mouth, but she loved every second. The taste and the smell of him. His wiry hair scratching her face as he made her throat him. Her pussy throbbed like a second heart.

She gasped when he pulled her off and tugged her to her feet. "Up. Onto the bed."

She scurried to her hands and knees with her ass upturned, just the way he liked. Since their first night together, he'd trained her and now she didn't dare disobey. Especially since she didn't want to.

"So precious." His fingers penetrated her, teasing her slippery folds, finding the mind-melting spots inside her pussy that made her weak. He pressed between her shoulder blades and she folded, head down, ass up, back bent to offer her glistening center. If she was lucky, he'd only tease her a moment before he made her cum…

A gust of air told her he'd walked away. *Noooooo*. But she knew better than to move. She didn't ease the strain of her back, or slip a hand between her thighs. He'd punish her for sure and she might never earn her release.

"Good girl." Hades was back, palming her ass, squeezing the cheeks, holding her open. She held still, knowing better than to squirm underneath his gaze. She didn't protest as he parted her most secret places and examined her. She hoped he liked what he saw…

A condescending smack on the side of her thigh, a small chuckle. "You're so ready for me. Needy. Does my pretty pussy miss me?"

"Always," she whispered against the coverlet.

"Does it want me to touch it, make it feel good?"

"Yes...please... Hades, I need..."

Another smack. "I'm not talking about you. I'm talking about your pussy."

Persephone clenched her teeth, holding back a whimper. He knew just what to say to humiliate her, to make her burn...

"What about the other parts of you, hmm? Do they feel neglected?"

What was he talking about? His finger left a wet trail up between her ass cheeks and she knew.

"No," she moaned, catching herself too late.

"Yes," Hades said, pressing a firm finger to her clenching asshole. "It's time." He stroked her bottom a moment. "You belong to me. All of you. It's time I claim this."

"Will it hurt?"

"It might. I'll go slowly but it will be uncomfortable. At first. But you want this, right?" His voice deepened, as hypnotic as his slow stroking touch over her backside. "You want to please me? Make me feel good?"

"Yes," she admitted. His thumb came to her asshole and her cheeks tightened.

"No," Hades turned stern. "Don't tense up. Open for me."

She forced herself to relax. Hades's thumb pressed rough circles over her sensitive rosebud.

"Good girl." His stubbled cheek rubbed over her ass. She stilled as his tongue swept between her cheeks, probing her virgin hole, tickling the crease. His free hand cupped her pussy, keeping her from wriggling and escaping his insistent tongue.

Persephone didn't want to like it. But she did. Gods, she *did*. Tingles spread over her back and a shot of hot, slick serum leaked from her pussy onto Hades's hand.

He bit her ass lightly before straightening.

"You...you licked me."

"And you got wet." He sounded so smug. "I think you want this more than you're letting on."

"I want you."

"You'll take me. All of me." Something cool and slippery slopped over her asshole. Lubricant of some kind? Then he probed one finger deep, pushing past the tight ring of muscle.

She gasped. It felt intense. His free hand stroked her pussy and the sensation flipped. It felt good and so fucking dirty.

"Fuck." The swear word slipped out before she could muffle it. She pressed her face into the bed.

"Naughty wife. Shall I spank you? Punish you so the first time I claim your ass it's bright red and sore?"

"Oh gods." Now he was probing her with two fingers. Her tiny asshole was going to be so stretched by the end of the night.

The fingers of his left hand still circled her clit. To her dismay the pleasure rose hotter and higher because of the intrusion in her ass.

"No." She wiggled, trying to escape and earning that spanking he'd mentioned. A few sharp slaps on her rear and she quieted. The subtle sting from his hard hand helped her accept the fingers in her ass.

Hades got up to three before he stopped and focused on making her cum. Her climax built in every corner of her body, spurred by the light strokes of his thumb around her clit.

When he added a finger in her pussy, her brain shot sparks. Her pussy clenched, begging for more stimulation while her ass did the same, protesting the stretch of three hard fingers.

Persephone put her head down and let the climax roll up her spine. Her legs shook, out of her control. Her body was no longer her own.

It belonged to Hades.

His dick probed the back of her thigh as he pulled his fingers out of her ass. She relaxed even though she knew what was coming. He kept his finger in her pussy as he added more lube to her crease.

A wet squelching sound told her he was lubing his cock as well. Her breath quickened and she rocked forward a little, resisting the urge to scramble away. It wouldn't work. Hades would catch her and make her pay.

So she waited on all fours for him to claim her ass—

"You ready?"

She almost snorted. Did it matter? "Yes."

She was done waiting. A small part of her was curious how it would feel. An even smaller, secret part of her wanted it... "Do it."

A slap to her thigh. "I give the orders around here."

He did and she loved it. But the wait was killing her, so she put her head down and pushed her ass up, presenting the target as best she could.

His half growl told her that was a good choice.

"I'm going to fuck this ass," he told her. "You're going to make me feel good."

Her pussy juiced in response. Something hard probed her asshole. She spread her knees wider. But Hades wasn't done.

"Beg me for it. Beg me to fuck your ass. To let you make me feel good."

Shit. She couldn't do that.

"I'm waiting, Persephone."

"Please..."

"Please, what?"

"Please put your cock in my ass. I'll be good for you. I'll make you feel so good."

"Fuck." The desperation in his voice made the humiliation worth it. Persephone smiled to herself...until he started to push his very big thing into her very small hole.

"Fuck." He backed up, added more lube. This time when he pressed, his cock head stretched her. She squeezed but he didn't back out. He pushed forward, millimeter by aching millimeter.

"It's too big."

"Relax, sweetheart." He pulled out. More lube. He swirled the head of his cock around her back hole, stimulating the thin skin. "Breathe, Persephone. Remember to breathe."

Right. Her lungs filled on his order. Relief rolled through her and relaxed her enough to let him pop inside. He slid the rest of the way easily.

She waited for him to stop before gasping for air.

"You doin' okay?"

She tossed her head, a half shake, half nod.

"You're doing so good." His free hand stroked her back. She opened to him further and he gave a shallow thrust.

"Oh gods." He was splitting her open.

"Be good and take it." Fuck if the order didn't make her hotter. His actions belied his words, though; he stroked her back with a gentle hand. His cock moved in tiny increments back and forth, letting her adjust. The discomfort eased, and when he reached down to play with her clit, a flush of pleasure spread over her.

"*Ohhh*," she moaned into the bed. Her limbs went liquid. Golden honey simmered in her veins.

He started rocking, slow at first, increasing in force as he penetrated her bowels. Her cunt tightened, welcoming the intrusion. She felt full, stimulated and satisfied. "Oh yeah, baby. You're going to cum with me deep in your ass."

"No," she squeaked as her thighs began to shake. She couldn't come with him balls deep inside her ass. It was too embarrassing.

"Yes, you are. I can feel it. Fuck, you're so tight, I can feel you milking me..."

Biting off a string of curses, Hades braced her hips and sawed in and out of her faster. A few passes later, his dick tripped some switch deep inside her.

Pleasure bloomed, warm and golden, delicious sensations spreading through her limbs. Her body juddered under Hades's. Her throaty cries filled the room, mingled with her husband's cussing.

"You like that? You love taking me in your ass?"

"Yes," she moaned. Her cheeks burned. Another climax built in her, low and deep, forbidden pleasure rising from secret, shameful parts. Only Hades could take her to the brink like this. He gripped her throat and held her over the abyss. She might fight him but in the end, she surrendered and embraced the fall—

"My turn, baby." She thought he'd fucked her hard before but no. Now he gripped her sides and rode her, using her body for his pleasure. Climax after climax bubbled through her. She didn't know where one ended and the other began.

Finally, after forever, Hades seized her tight enough to bruise and brought it home. Hot cum filled her. When he pulled out, it slid out of her, running down her leg, staining the bed. She covered her face as he held her bottom open and inspected her. She knew he loved the sight of her marked with his seed. He was such an animal. She was lucky he didn't pee on her.

When she gave an embarrassed groan, Hades chuckled and tugged her up. She gave token resistance, more embarrassed than unwilling to have him hold her. Gods, she was a mess. Sweaty, sticky, dripping with cum, face slick from when he fucked her mouth, her makeup smeared—

"You're so beautiful." Hades looked at her like she was the only woman in the world. He kissed her forehead and tucked her into his chest, holding her tight. Gods, yes, she loved this, it was all she'd ever wanted...

They lay together in the dark and quiet bedroom. Persephone forgot her mussy hair and the cum leaking out of her. Hades nuzzled her face, brushing his lips over her forehead, cheeks and chin, even eyebrows, before finding her lips. He drew back and breathed her in. Against her leg, his dick stirred.

"Fuck. I can't get enough," he muttered. "I could take you every other minute and it wouldn't be enough."

A smile curved deep inside her. "I know how you feel," she told him softly.

"Do you, baby?" He tucked her close again, draping his heavy thigh over her legs to draw her as near as humanly possible.

"I do." She sighed and lay her head on his chest, ear over his heart. His heartbeat matched hers. "I know how you feel...because I feel the same way."

"Almost missed this," he whispered, almost too soft for her to hear.

She raised her head. "What?"

His thumb traced her cheek. "This. Love. Us."

Oh. Her heart squeezed. She couldn't take it. "Hades, I've always loved you."

"I know. You give and give, and I only take." She shook her head but he stilled her with his thumb at her lips. "It's true. But that's gonna end. Now you take as much as you give. And I give as much as I take."

"It's not a competition. You've had a hard life, I understand if—"

"Not an option, Persephone. You take what I give you." His gaze heated as she ran her tongue over his thumb. "I've been looking for this all my life, not even knowing what I was looking for. Dropped right into my lap. Beauty, innocent. Pure. You're every good deed I've never done. Every pure thought I never had."

"Hades, I—"

But he shushed her. "You're the balance, Persephone. I'm darkness, but you're light. You fill the room with your presence, and the shadows disappear. Understand?"

She understood. In his own way, Hades was telling her she had as much power as he did. More. Because didn't darkness always leave before the light?

"I'm here for you, Hades." Her heart swelled with everything she'd felt for him but never been able to express. "I will always be your light."

49

When Persephone woke the next morning, paper crackled under her hand. Hades was gone but his pillow still bore his crisp scent. He'd left a note.

Angel, I have business tonight. Don't wait up. When I return, I'll make it up to you. —Hades

She pressed her lips to the bold strokes that made the 'M'. He didn't sign it *love,* but she felt it all the same.

Persephone flopped dramatically back onto the bed, her hair floofing all around her. Her hands came to her face. She wasn't sure she actually believed last night really happened. He loved her? But when she shifted, the aches in her body confirmed that yes, the night before had indeed not been just her imagination.

She'd never seen so much in his storm grey eyes before as when he told her he loved her. She'd always seen Hades as the epitome of control before. To the point of stoic and unfeeling.

But she saw the truth now. He felt *so* much. He was a hurricane in a bottle. Leashed chaos. Just like the city he held so tightly in his fist. Only in their lovemaking did she get a glimpse of it. For a moment, the lid came uncapped and she saw what he couldn't hide—at his core, he was a singularly emotional being.

When he hated, he hated so virulently he'd tear whole cities apart to exact his revenge. And when he loved...

She grinned, happiness hanging over her with the hazy morning light. Well, noon light, because when she looked at the clock, she saw it was almost twelve. She was tempted to stay in bed, lounging and reliving the delicious moments of last night, but the joy singing through her pulled her to the closet where she tossed on jeans and a t-shirt, then applied minimal makeup. She'd take it easy today, to be ready when Hades returned. *I'll make it up to you.*

But then she frowned. She had other things to talk to Hades about when he got back, though. There was still so much she needed to tell him. About Eurydice. About Aphrodite. He'd help her find them, she knew he would. Ajax was no match for her husband.

She sat up and reached for her phone. Only to find it was dead. A few minutes of scrounging around in her purse and she found the charger, then plugged it in.

She pressed the buttons to wake it up but it took a while to be able to use once it was completely dead. And she wouldn't be able to do anything until Hades got back later anyway, so she decided to go for a walk.

Not that the Shades guarding the doors downstairs looked happy about it when she tried to leave. When she arched an imperious brow at them and asked, "Shall I tell my husband you're trying to imprison me in my own house?" they were quick enough to move out of the way.

They didn't look happy, but they parted to let her through.

"Stay away from the perimeter," they warned.

"I will," she promised. Easy enough. The grounds were extensive and well-kept, with giant oaks and neatly trimmed green grass. A dark forest surrounding the Estate hid its occupants from the busy world outside.

Persephone couldn't imagine Hades growing up here, a little boy playing with wooden toys or a rubber ball. Well, she couldn't imagine Hades as a little boy at all. He seemed so solemn and powerful, sprung fully formed from his father's head. Born to run Gino Ubeli's business and grow it to the point where he owned everyone in the city, and through them, everything.

She was too light and happy to dwell on gloomy thoughts for long, though, so she forgot them and browsed around a cluster of rhododendrons. The grounds were quiet, even for the Estate. She found a path and walked leisurely along it as light filtered through the tall oak trees overhead.

About fifteen minutes later, she frowned when she saw a roof peeking out from the huge trunks ahead. The path did twist and turn. Was she already coming back around to the house?

She continued forward curiously. Oh! It wasn't the house at all. The building was large, though, square and fronted with high columns and stone lions. It was like a structure from Roman antiquity had been transported here.

What was this place? With hushed reverence, she tiptoed to the open door. A few dried leaves had blown in but the marble was cool and gleaming, without a trace of mold or dirt. Someone kept this place clean.

As soon as her eyes adjusted to the gloom, she gasped. Three stone coffins stood in a row. Heart thudding softly, she crept close enough to read the names carved into the marble slabs. *Ambrogino Ubeli. Domenica Ubeli.* Hades's father, Gino. And his mother.

She knew the name on the final coffin before she read it. *Chiara Ubeli.* A weeping angel stood above the tomb, its hands covering its stone face. Forever mourning the atrocities wrought on the girl buried here. By Persephone's own family—her uncles and mother.

"I'm sorry," Persephone whispered. She wished she had better words, some sort of prayer. Prayers should be the only words spoken here. She retreated, taking in the three sarcophagi.

Her heart ached, but not for them. No, they were at peace. She hurt for her husband, who'd buried them here and grieved them. He'd only been a teen when he lost them but he grieved them still. Some losses you never got over.

For the first time, she realized just how alone Hades was. He had no one but Charon and his Shades. And now her. No wonder he was so possessive. She'd hang on desperately to those she cared about, too, if everyone who loved her had died.

As she drifted closer to Chiara's coffin, she frowned at smudges on the edge of the stone lid. The pattern made her glance at the floor, but no, there were no marks there.

Of course not. There was no reason for any marks on the floor, which was well scrubbed and polished until gleaming. The marks on the coffin must have been missed when whoever cleaned this place last came through.

But it nagged at the back of her mind, because the marks almost looked like...like fingerprints—desperate, grabbing fingers along with the spatter on the dark wall. *It couldn't be.* But the faded rust color couldn't be mistaken for anything but what it was.

Blood.

She took a step back.

"You can't be around here, Mrs. Ubeli," a Shade's voice echoed behind her, making her shriek.

"Gods," she gasped, clutching her chest. She backed away, trembling.

The Shade was young, almost as young as she was, and he looked dreadfully uncomfortable. "I'm sorry, Mrs. Ubeli, but you need to come away now. Your husband wouldn't like you here."

Head bowed, she hurried out.

There was plenty of space in the mausoleum for more stone coffins. At least two more. One for Hades...and one for her.

She shivered and shook her head to dispel the morbid thought. *Not for a long time,* she told herself firmly. *After a good, long lifetime of love.*

But she hurried across the lawn and didn't stop until she reached her room. No wonder Hades wanted to keep her here, safe.

When she got back to her room, she immediately went for her phone.

There was a missed call from Hermes. Several new text messages from a few numbers. Hermes's texts popped up first, in shouty caps: OH MY GODS ARE U OK? WHERE ARE U?

Cradling her phone, she texted rapidly. I'm fine. At the Ubeli Estate.

Her phone blipped immediately with his reply. I was so worried. News reported shooting! What happened?

We're fine. We were in the back. Didn't see anything. She paused, deliberating on what to say next. Hades is handling.

After a pause, Persephone watched the dots indicating Hermes was typing. They just kept flashing and flashing until finally Hermes returned: So much going on, but wanna say I'm so fucking sorry for the other day. I woke up remembering everything. I was messed up. Didn't know what I was doing.

Persephone shook her head as her thumbs flew over the keyboard. Don't even think about that. It was just an act. To keep Ajax from discovering me. And I'm sorry. It was wrong of me to put you in that position.

Maybe. But I'm glad you didn't go alone. And then: Have you talked to Hades about it? Wanting to help the girl? You can't keep it from him.

Persephone's chest tightened. But no, it would be fine. Hades would understand. He had to. Soon. I'm going to.

Nothing for a second, and then the dots came back and finally Hermes's next text. Ok. Really glad you're okay. I'm about to go into a meeting but talk more soon? Come have a spa day with that gorgeous friend of yours?

Persephone typed back a laughing face emoji and: For sure.

Then Persephone moved on to the next message. She didn't recognize the number but it was a picture message and curious, she clicked on it.

And then screeched and dropped the phone on the bed.

"Aphrodite," she gasped and reached for the phone again. Persephone brought it close to her face and looked at the picture of her friend.

Aphrodite had been beaten, that was clear. Her face, her beautiful heart shaped face was beaten black and blue. Her left eye was swollen shut and blood from her temple poured down the side of her face. Her head hung back, slack, and Persephone didn't even know if she was conscious. If she was alive.

There was a message underneath the picture. Call me. If you tell your husband, she dies.

Persephone's hands were trembling so hard she could barely manage to keep hold as she dialed the number and lifted the phone to her ear.

The phone rang three times before he picked it up. Ajax's smarmy, self-satisfied voice came over the line. "Are you alone?"

"Yes." Persephone tried to make her voice cold but she couldn't quite shake her tremors. "Let me talk to Aphrodite."

"Oh, so you *do* know this little cunt. And here she was swearing up and down she had no clue who you were or how that picture of you got on her phone camera. Even after I had my boys work her over."

Persephone's eyes sank closed and her body curled in on itself. The picture Aphrodite had taken of her outside the restaurant the first day they met. Of course Ajax had taken Aphrodite's phone. Persephone put a hand to her forehead.

"What do you want?"

"Five million dollars. Delivered by you personally."

Persephone let out a strangled noise. "You're crazy. Where am I supposed to get my hands on—"

"Well you better figure it out. Aphrodite's already endured a beating for you. I'd hate to see what would happen next if I really let my men have their way with her. But if you don't care about her, then I guess—"

"Stop!" Persephone jumped to her feet and paced the length of the room, looking out the windows as she went. "Fine. I'll get it but it will take some time. Maybe a few days—"

"Tonight."

"Tonight?" Persephone squeaked, her voice going high-pitched. "You can't be serious. That's impossible!"

"Then I guess your friend doesn't mean very much to you after all. She's dead if you don't get me that money personally. It's tonight or never. I'll see you around, Mrs. Ubeli."

"Tonight then. What time? Where?" Gods, what was she doing?

"Eight o'clock on the dot. Underneath the statue of Atlas in the park."

"I need proof that they're alive. Let me talk to Aphrodite."

"I'll be seeing you, Persephone."

The line went dead. Son of a—

Persephone looked around frantically, needing to do something but not knowing where to start. Hades. She needed Hades. He would know what to do.

She reached for her phone but then froze.

She couldn't call Hades, even if he had his phone on, which he probably didn't. He'd been lining up everything for the shipment for months. She couldn't screw that up.

And if she told Charon, he wouldn't help her, he'd only try to get in touch with Hades. And he definitely wouldn't let her go to the meet.

She huffed out a breath. Because she couldn't do *nothing*.

Aphrodite was only in this mess because of her. She'd screwed everything up and she had to try to fix it.

"Think. Think." She looked back down at her phone. Which was when she noticed the other message she hadn't yet opened. It was from Athena. Quickly, she tapped her thumb on the message so that it popped up.

It was just two words but Persephone knew immediately Athena was talking about Eurydice's phone: "Cracked it."

Persephone immediately dialed her.

"Good work. Anything useful?"

"Holding your applause to the end, hmmm? Let me see here...the last thing here is a text to Orpheus. Saying she's almost done with moving out. Then a text from a person named Ashley."

"Ashley? Are you sure?" Persephone thought of the redhead in the concert hall.

"That's the name. The text reads, Need to meet you. Orchid House, 1 pm. That's it."

Ashley couldn't have texted her that. She was dead by then. Persephone explained this to Athena.

"Then whoever has Ashley's phone knew her well enough to unlock the password and send it. Or this is the first case of ghost texting ever."

"Ajax."

"All roads lead to this guy. It's kinda getting boring." Persephone could hear Athena reach into a bag and eat a handful of chips.

"Athena, listen. Ajax has Aphrodite...my friend."

"The dancer that Hermes won't shut up about?"

"Yes. She's probably with Eurydice. We need to get them out. But first I have to find them."

There was a short silence on the other end. "Well, I might be able to help with that."

"What? What did you find?" Hope rose in Persephone. "You know where they are?"

"Not completely. I got a partial address." Athena gave her the cross streets. "It's somewhere close to that intersection.

"Thank you, thank you."

Now that Persephone knew where Ajax was holding the girls, she didn't have to wait for the meet up in the park where he would undoubtedly try to double-cross her. He had no incentive to actually bring the girls and she knew it was a trap.

But if she could surprise him...

"What are you thinking about doing?" Athena's voice came over the phone. Persephone had forgotten she was still on the line. "Because you better not even think about leaving me behind," Athena continued.

Persephone's eyes fell shut. Was she really considering doing this? By herself? Or well, with Athena, but it wasn't like either of them were master spies. Or trained mobsters. Ajax was ruthless and he'd surrounded himself with the sort of men who'd happily beat up a woman, and worse.

It would be dangerous and Hades would be furious with her. But he'd be gone all night and Aphrodite and Eurydice didn't have that kind of time.

So Persephone made the decision that needed to be made. "Okay, Athena, I need you to pick me up. The park by Roman road—as soon as you can. I'll be waiting."

"Ok. Oh my gosh, I can't believe we're doing this! It's so exciting!" That was one word for it. But Athena hung up before Persephone could caution her about her enthusiasm.

Then Persephone laid back down on the bed. There was one last phone call to make.

She reached underneath the mattress and pulled out the card that she'd thought about throwing away so many times. She still wasn't sure if she was glad she still had it or not.

Dialing the number, even now she didn't know if she was making a mistake. She prayed she wasn't. She prayed her gambles tonight would pay off and when Hades eventually learned all she'd done… some part of him would be proud, even if he'd be furious at her for how she went about it.

"Yeah," answered Pete the cop, sounding supremely bored.

Persephone bristled. "You're only interested if there's a big bust to be made, right? Well, listen up because I've got one that will make headlines. But you need to do exactly what I say."

50

"This is so freaking exciting," Athena said. They were parked in the street around the corner from Ajax's safehouse.

Persephone had a hell of a time sneaking off the Estate, but the guards were far more interested about people trying to break in than one small slip of a woman sneaking out through the back kitchen exit. There had been fewer guards on duty, too. Most of them were with Hades to deal with the mysterious shipment.

Persephone had waited for Benito, the guard on outer perimeter duty to turn the corner and then she'd fled toward the woods and past the fence into the public park beyond. She hadn't stopped running until she reached the meet up point with Athena.

"The cops are ready, too?" Athena asked. "Is there like some signal?" It had taken hours to set everything up, for Pete to get the SWAT team in place, and the sun was low in the sky now.

Persephone's racing heart felt like it was about to leap out of her chest but she managed to keep her voice somewhat calm as she answered.

"I'll give a verbal signal, and yes, they're here, they're just hidden." She didn't know where they were either. Pete said his team would be waiting nearby, and for once she trusted him—only because it was in his self-interest to work with her. Him looking out for number one, that she could rely on.

"And the wire, you're sure it's hidden?"

Persephone swallowed and nodded.

That had been Pete's stipulation. He still wasn't impressed with her 'so-called detective work'—his words—so the only way he'd agree to help was if she wore a wire and either caught something damning on tape or saw something inside the safehouse she was sure would let them throw the book at the notorious mobster and rumored human trafficker, Ajax Wagner.

Luckily the technology had gotten far better than what was usually shown on TV. When Persephone and Athena met with Pete half an hour ago, he'd easily attached a button camera to the button of her jeans and slid a barrette into her hair that doubled as a microphone. No clumsy wires necessary.

And now here they were.

A big part of Persephone wanted to turn tail and run away but she wouldn't give into it. Everything was in place. She had back up. And she was far too valuable an asset for Ajax to hurt her...at least that was what she was counting on. She'd planned as much as she could.

Now there was nothing left to do but jump.

She got out of the car before Athena could say anything else. She quickly turned the corner and started towards Ajax's safe house. She imagined the house had been cute once, before age and uncaring owners took their toll. Beyond an old iron gate, a concrete walk led to the door. Pieces of the siding hung askew. The windows stared like huge, empty eyes.

She phoned Ajax as she approached, arms up. She kept her distance, though. She was sure she was in range of their guns, but she also knew she was far more valuable to Ajax alive than dead. At least she really, *really* hoped so.

Ajax picked up right away. "What the fuck do you think you're doing?"

"New rules. You send Aphrodite and Eurydice out, and in exchange, you get me as a hostage."

Silence.

Persephone was impatient now that it had come down to it. "Stop with the bullshit because we both know it's what you were planning all along—to snatch me. What's five million compared to having collateral against the infamous Hades Ubeli? Now send them out or I'm in the wind. There's an SUV parked around the corner, one block down. Once Aphrodite and Eurydice are both safe in the SUV, I'll come inside."

"You think I'm a fool? That I'm just going to give up my bargaining chips?" He gave an ugly laugh.

Persephone ground her teeth together. They were *people*, not bargaining chips.

"If you don't send them out, how do I even know you have them? I'm not going to stand out here exposed like this for long. Either you take the deal or I walk." Persephone channeled Hades and made her voice ice.

There was some shuffling on the other end of the phone, then Ajax's voice again. "Fine. I'll send out one. As a show of good faith." His voice was mocking. "But I don't release the other one until you come in."

Persephone's heart hammered. It wasn't a good deal. Persephone wanted both girls safe and out of that house before she stepped in. Who knew what would happen when the SWAT team stormed the house? Bullets might fly. Persephone would be expecting it but whoever was left inside wouldn't.

But Persephone knew it was all she'd get out of Ajax.

"Send her out," she commanded, "and have the second girl ready to send right when I come in." She hung up the phone before he could reply and stood, back straight, shoulders out, staring down the front door.

Nothing happened.

For long, long minutes, nothing happened.

Shit. Oh shit, what if he called her bluff? What if she'd miscalculated and—

The door opened and Aphrodite stumbled out.

Persephone hurried forward. Aphrodite rushed to meet her with big unsteady steps and frantic eyes.

"Persephone, what are you doing—"

but Persephone just shook her head. Aphrodite looked terrible. Her eye was so swollen and bloodied and her clothes were ripped and—

Persephone couldn't think about all that it meant. She just grabbed Aphrodite by the forearms so she'd look her in the eye. "There's a car around the corner. Over there." Persephone gestured with her eyes and Aphrodite's gaze followed. "Get in and tell Athena to drive. Don't look back."

Aphrodite was shaking her head, fat tears falling down her cheeks. "Persephone, you can't go in there. You can't—"

Persephone dropped Aphrodite's arms and ordered, "Go," in her harshest voice.

Then she turned back to the house and strode straight for the door. Behind her, she heard Aphrodite's footsteps running away. Good girl.

Ajax met Persephone at the door. His potbelly was barely contained by the sweat-stained wife beater undershirt he had on.

"Where's Eurydice?" Persephone demanded. "The deal was for both of them."

The mobster smirked. "Eurydice is going to need a little help getting out of bed." He stuck his cigar in his mouth and spoke around it. "She's...not well. Come on in." He moved back from the door to make space for her.

Persephone took a deep breath and then wished she hadn't—Ajax's cigar plus the inside of the house altogether smelled rancid and turned her stomach. But still, she stepped into the house, turning in a 360 as she did so to give the cops a view of the place after she was in. She didn't immediately see anything incriminating but she was only standing in the foyer.

"Check her," Ajax said and two guys came forward.

She gritted her teeth as the two meat-handed thugs frisked her, lingering far longer than was necessary between her thighs and squeezing as they brushed down her chest.

"That's enough." She yanked back when the shorter, squat one went for another pass. "I don't have anything on me." She went to slide her phone into her pocket but Ajax shook his head at her.

"Ah ah," he said. "Hand it over."

Persephone's jaw locked but she handed the phone to him, eyes tracking it as he slid it into the front pocket of his black slacks.

"Now, where's Eurydice?"

Ajax smiled. "Like I said, she's indisposed at the moment."

Persephone stepped forward but the two thugs grabbed her by her arms. She fought against them. "Where is she?"

Because she'd just had a terrible thought. Ajax trafficked in women. What if he wasn't using Eurydice for leverage against Orpheus at all? What if the reason he wasn't producing her was because she wasn't here? He'd considered Eurydice his girl and she tried to get away, to get out, by marrying Orpheus. Just how angry had that made him?

"I swear, if you've done something to her or shipped her off somewhere—"

"So dramatic," Ajax laughed. "You want to see her, fine."

He motioned the men holding Persephone to lead her upstairs. The squat one kept hold of her as the other released her. Squatty dragged her up the stairs but he needn't have bothered. Maybe it was foolish to hurry deeper into this filthy den but she needed to see Eurydice with her own two eyes. After everything, she needed to see that the girl was okay.

And Pete should still be listening. They'd agreed on a safe word. No matter what, if Persephone mentioned the *Fates*, his team was supposed to come in with guns blazing.

It stank even worse upstairs but when they passed one of the bedrooms, Persephone looked inside and saw a skinny man with greasy hair hunched over a computer that was connected to several screens. Whatever was on that hard drive could be useful to Pete. Persephone made sure to pause with her button camera pointed in the man's direction before Squatty yanked her forward again.

Now she just needed to find Eurydice and get them both the hell out of here.

"Do you know what the little birdies have been talking about all month?" Ajax's voice startled Persephone, it came from so close behind her. Persephone stepped forward to get away from him, continuing down the hallway and looking in each room she passed.

Ajax went on as if she was an active participant in the conversation.

"The shipment. A very special shipment. One of a kind."

Persephone forced herself not to react.

"And my guys, we caught a few of them birdies yesterday, locked 'em in a cage and made 'em sing." A short pause. His man had grabbed hold of her and was holding her still while footsteps sounded on the grimy hardwood behind her, no doubt Ajax huffing up the stairs. "And you wanna know what they said?"

Ajax came around her and spoke, his foul breath right in her face. "They said the delivery was going down *tonight*."

Persephone jerked back from his oily face and bad breath. She glared him down icily. "Where's Eurydice? How long have you had her?"

To her surprise, Ajax answered. "Since Orpheus's little hissy fit that nearly cost me the concert deal."

Persephone just stared at him. "You wouldn't have been out the money."

"You heard Hades. I'd lose access. Access to Elysium, access to his home, access to his whole little world."

"Why do you hate him so much?"

"He took everything from me." Ajax stopped at a door and pushed it open. Dim light spilled out into the hall.

Persephone held her sleeve in front of her face to block the smell as she entered the room. It must have once been a child's room, painted a cheery yellow.

Now the walls were faded and stained, covered in shadows cast by a small lamp by a bed. Trash had collected in the corners of the room. The room seemed cold, and empty, except for a young woman lying on a thin mattress.

"Eurydice," Persephone breathed as she ran over to her. The woman had shadows under her eyes and lank, dirty hair. Her high classic cheekbones now looked skeletal and her beautiful skin had turned grey and sallow. Her eyes fluttered open, then closed again weakly.

"Oh gods." Persephone sank beside the bed to feel the woman's forehead. It was cold to the touch. She checked Eurydice's pulse next, noting the fresh track marks on the woman's arm.

Persephone turned accusing eyes to Ajax. "What did you do to her?"

"Gave her a little hit." He shrugged. "Then a little more. After that, she did it to herself."

Persephone noted the restraints hanging off the bed. They'd tied her down and forced the poison into her veins. Persephone felt sick to her stomach. Had they even fed her? "We need to get her out of here. She could be dying."

"First you deliver."

Persephone looked up in confusion but saw him holding out her phone.

"Call him," Ajax ordered.

Well past fear, she felt surprisingly calm. "The Fates curse you for what you've done," she spat. This evil bastard would rot for all his sins. He'd admitted on tape to kidnapping Eurydice and Persephone felt sure the computer would give even more evidence against him. Plus Aphrodite's testimony.

Any second the SWAT team would come breaking down the door.

"Oh, on the contrary. I think the Fates are smiling on me. After all, they brought you to my door. And you are going to lead me straight to your husband and the cargo ship full of product that's going to shift the tide of this war."

Persephone glared at him, letting all of her hatred shine through. *Just you wait. You'll get everything that's coming to you.*

Any minute now.

Any minute...

Persephone glanced around and listened hard.

Silence.

What the hell was taking them so long? Did Pete not hear her? Or was the mic not working? They'd checked and rechecked it. She fought the rising panic clawing up her throat

But only Ajax's chuckle filled the silence. "What, nothing to say for once? That's fine."

He reached over and grabbed her hand, wrenching her forefinger to cover the fingerprint lock that unlocked her phone. "All I really need you to do is scream."

Ajax pulled the phone back and search through her contacts once it was unlocked. He pushed Hades's phone number and it dialed.

No! It was never supposed to go this far. No matter what had happened last night, that shipment meant everything to Hades—

Hades didn't pick up though and it went to voicemail. Persephone felt a jolt of emotion go through her as she heard Hades's gravelly voice start, "This is Hades Ubeli—"

Ajax hung up and dialed again impatiently. It went to voicemail and he beeped past the voice message.

"Ubeli. Call me now," he intoned, looking at Persephone. "I have something you want." He hung up, still looking at her. "You're an idiot, you know? Giving yourself up for this druggie."

Then he slammed the door on his way out and left Persephone standing beside the bed.

"The Fates help us," she whispered, and then said it louder, over and over, "Fates, help us. Please, *Fates*, we need you now," as she crouched to check on Eurydice.

When Persephone touched her clammy skin, Eurydice opened cracked lips and whimpered.

"Eurydice, shh. Orpheus sent me. We're going to get you out." She squeezed the woman's hand gently. "I'm going to get you out."

"O-Orpheus?" Eurydice rasped out, crusted and unfocused eyes dragging down to meet Persephone's.

Persephone nodded even as tears squeezed out of her own eyes. "Yes. Orpheus loves you. He sent me to help you. We're going to get you out of here."

Behind her, the door knob turned; she jumped but it was only Ajax coming back.

He held the phone out. Hades's voice came from far away.

"Persephone. Persephone! Are you ok?"

Persephone couldn't help but feel a surge of hope at hearing his voice even though she knew it meant she'd screwed up everything so terribly. For whatever reason, the SWAT team wasn't coming. "Hades, I'm here. I'm ok," Persephone barely answered before Ajax put the phone back to his ear.

"Proof of life, as requested. We'll meet you at the docks. I know Poseidon is delivering the shipment tonight. Tell your men to sit tight. My own will take over the heavy lifting. The drugs for your wife, that's the deal."

Persephone heard her husband's voice raised in anger just before Ajax bellowed, "I'm in charge here." He pulled out a gun. With a shriek, Persephone ducked her head as he pointed it towards the bed and fired.

What had he—? Her head snapped up and she looked at Eurydice.

"No!" Persephone sobbed. "*No.*"

Blood soaked slowly through Eurydice's thin shirt. Persephone pressed her hands to Eurydice's chest, moaning. "Please, no."

"One hour, capisce? No tricks." Ajax shut the door hard enough to make the lamp rattle.

Persephone almost didn't hear him. She pressed down as the blood ran faster, watching Eurydice's breathing slow.

The beautiful girl choked once and was still. Her eyes were glassy, staring just like Ashley's. Lifeless.

"I'm so sorry," Persephone whispered. "I'm so sorry."

Ajax's thugs came for her a few minutes later, pulling her bodily up from the floor. They marched her to the door. One of them stopped to take a picture of the dead woman. He followed Persephone and his fellow thug into the hall, cackling. "Sent it to Orpheus. Let's see how well he plays now, the little prick."

Persephone let out an animal, guttural cry of fury. How could they be so callous? Her hair had come undone and hung messily over her face. She pushed it back, then realized her hands were sticky with blood from the wrists down, and all she was doing was smearing Eurydice's blood around her temples.

"Stop dawdling," Ajax barked.

He'd put on a shirt and coat like he was a civilized man but Persephone knew better now. He was a monster. He glanced once more at her phone, then dropped it into his coat pocket.

"We've got a date with the docks. Time to make a trade."

51

The docks looked like a black extension of the street until Ajax's thugs pulled Persephone out of the car. Then she could see the pier drop off into the water, a pit of blackness. She shivered in the chilly night air, wearing nothing but jeans and a soft sweater, now spattered with blood. One of the thugs kept his grip tight on her arm as they walked forward.

Persephone felt...blank. The whole drive here she'd tried to think of what she'd say to Hades, how she'd try to explain it. But then all she could see was Eurydice's face. Her eyes and that second when the life went out of them. Persephone had watched her go. One second she was there and the next she was just...gone.

It didn't make sense. It wasn't fair. Good was supposed to win in the end. Even Hades, eventually, he loved her. At least he had before he'd known what she'd done.

"See, what'd I tell you," Ajax said to his driver, a tall man with a gold earring. "They're using a smaller ship to bring in the goods. Nothing fancy. Poseidon always was smart."

Persephone let them lead her down the sidewalk, into a warehouse where a bunch of crates were piled on a vast stretch of concrete floor.

Three men waited for them in the moonlight, three to match Ajax's three. Persephone's chest clenched. Hades, Charon, and another Shade. Ajax approached them confidently.

The thug who held Persephone twisted her arm up behind her as he jammed the gun into her back and she couldn't help whimpering.

Even in the moonlight she could see the cold fury in Hades's face. *Oh, Hades. Forgive me.*

"Let me check this out first," Ajax said. He nodded to Gold Earring guy, who took out a crowbar and headed for a crate. After prying it open the man held up a nondescript bottle. "Metamorphoses Spa," the thug read, then looked up at his leader, confused. "It's hair gunk."

"Give it here," Ajax ordered. He unscrewed the cap, and shook out a small white pill. He held it up, sniffed it. "Pure," he said with triumphant satisfaction. "The Brothers are going to love this."

"Let's get this over with," Hades ordered from the shadows.

"Oh, no, Ubeli. You don't get to make demands anymore." Ajax waved a hand and Persephone was pushed forward, forced to walk to Ajax so he could hook her under his arm. His other hand raised the gun to her temple.

"You know why I only shot up the front of that restaurant even though I knew you were in the back? Because I want to see the look on Ivan Titan's face when I tell him Hades Ubeli's legs are cut from under him, he's got no goods, and his own men are turning on him."

Ajax's gold tooth flashed as he grinned. "What are your guys going to do when the shipment's gone and they ain't got nothing to push, no way of getting paid? We'll sell it back to them in Metropolis. And Poseidon, what's he going to think?"

"Hand over my wife." The vein in Hades's temple pulsed; Persephone could see it from twelve feet away.

"Let me tell you how this goes," Ajax continued as if Hades hadn't spoken. "You get out of here, all of your men, all of you. Then I turn the girl loose and you leave, forever. This is mine."

Persephone couldn't stop her trembling anymore. Ajax wrapped his arm tighter around her body and rammed the gun into the side of her head. She kept her eyes on Hades, letting her body go limp. She became a ragdoll. A weak thing. A victim.

But while everyone was watching Charon and her husband, Persephone's fingers slipped between the folds of Ajax's coat and found his pocket.

And her phone.

"Stand down," Ajax was saying. "I'm not a patient man."

Jerking suddenly in his arms, Persephone reached up and stuck the edge of her phone—along with the Wasp that Athena had attached all those weeks ago—right into Ajax's neck.

The voltage hit him a second later, jolting through him with enough force to knock him back. He bellowed in surprise and pain, stumbling backwards and almost falling to the pavement.

Persephone staggered too, letting the phone drop. She'd barely regained her feet before someone hit her and brought her down to the concrete, cradling her body against his.

"I got you," Charon rumbled, and spread his large body over hers. She cringed as she heard bullets flying past them.

Then they were both up and Charon was running, carrying her out of the warehouse and into the cold night.

Persephone couldn't see anything, could barely hear anything, but she clung to Charon's shoulders. Then they were in an alleyway and the sound of bullets seemed farther away.

A black car pulled in front of them and the door opened. Charon ducked inside, sliding Persephone in before him.

Charon barely had tucked his feet into the car before he barked to the driver. "Go."

"Wait! Hades—" Persephone shrieked, before she was thrown back into the seat by the car's sudden acceleration. It pulled out of the alley and around to the front of the warehouse, where the Shades were fighting Ajax's men.

A dark figure burst out of the warehouse and Charon threw open the door. *Hades.* He dove into the car and the driver screeched off from the curb, letting the door slam shut on its own.

"Got 'em," Hades reported, and checked his gun before turning and taking Persephone from Charon. She threw her arms around Hades.

A second later, though, he was pulling back from her.

"You ok?" He touched her cheeks and gripped her arms, grabbing her wrists and turning them frantically to inspect her hands.

Oh gods, he must think— "It's not my blood," she said hurriedly.

He pulled her to him, hugging her close.

"Never again," he muttered. "Never again."

Persephone sagged into her husband, letting her shaking subside in his strong arms. He was here. He was safe. They were both safe and Ajax was gone. It was going to be okay. It was all going to be okay.

That was when she heard the police sirens.

Close.

Too close.

Hades's muscles tensed. "What the—" he started. Persephone looked up to see him glaring at Charon over her head.

Charon was already taking a headpiece from the driver and tuning in.

"Police band says an unmarked beige car was followed to the docks. Shots fired."

Hades cursed. "Ajax. Stupid to the last. He must've been tailed here."

Oh. *Shit.*

It hit her all at once. There hadn't been any interference with her mic or the button camera. Pete had seen and heard every single thing that had gone on in Ajax's safe house.

And he'd decided he wanted a bigger bust after overhearing Ajax talk about the drug shipment. No matter that Persephone had said the safe word and tried to get her and Eurydice out *before*—

Persephone squeezed her eyes shut. The cops had betrayed her. And Eurydice had *died* because of it.

Blue and red police lights were already washing over the brick walls as the car slunk away down a back alley.

Persephone nestled closer to Hades, feeling sick even as she did it. Because Pete's wasn't the only betrayal of the night.

She'd betrayed Hades. She lied to him. Conspired with his enemies. Brought the cops to his very doorstep.

"Sir, another report. This one from the club, Elysium," the driver spoke up.

At Hades's nod, the man continued. "Rioting started right after intermission. Orpheus came on and told everyone he was only going to play one more song. A song for the dead."

The man paused, touching his headpiece as if he wasn't sure if what he was hearing was true. "Cops tried to settle everybody but they revolted, rushed the stage. The cops were overwhelmed. They got the mayor out first, and helped the people who were getting trampled."

The man grimaced. "But they didn't get to the stage on time. Orpheus was...torn apart. They say there's no other word for it... He's dead."

Persephone jerked then, feeling horror jolt through her just when she'd been sure she didn't have any more capacity for grief.

Hades's arms flexed briefly, as if he was trying to comfort her. *Her.* When she was the one who'd brought this all down on their heads.

52

Persephone had fallen asleep in his arms, curled against his chest, his shirt squeezed in her blood-covered fists even in sleep. Like she was terrified he'd disappear.

Hades tried to keep his arms soft and gentle around her but it was hard when every muscle in his body was tense with fury. What the hell had happened tonight? How had Ajax gotten his hands on her—

Hades wanted reports from every single one of his lieutenants but he didn't even reach for his phone. He didn't dare dislodge his wife. Whatever she had been through tonight—

The car slowed and she roused, lifting her head from his chest and slowly blinking, looking around. They were at the Estate. She frowned when she recognized where they were.

"Do we have to stay here?" she said in a small voice. "It's so...dark here."

"The penthouse was bugged," Charon said. "We had it swept."

It was Hades she turned her head towards, though. "Ajax?"

Hades didn't answer. He didn't trust himself to speak. When the car stopped, he helped her inside.

She gasped when she caught a glance of herself in a mirror in the foyer. Blood garishly streaked her light hair. And it was all over her hands... Hades grimaced. He'd hoped to get her in the shower before she saw herself. Her gaze darted away and she started up the stairs.

Hades wanted to follow her but there were things that had to be attended to.

"I'll be right up, babe."

She nodded, not even looking over her shoulder at him. Hades's jaw set, but then he turned to Charon.

"You order clean up?" Hades asked.

He could feel Persephone hovering on the landing, paused just out of sight. For whatever reason, she wanted to hear what he had to say. Fine. He had nothing to hide. He'd tried to protect her from all of this and it had only—it had only—

"What about Poseidon?" he demanded, glaring at Charon.

"He's been alerted, but that was before the shipment was confiscated. He'll know now; it's been on the police scanners."

Hades nodded slowly. "What about our contacts?"

"MIA. Still dealing with the fallout."

"Get them on the phone. I've got to make sure—" Hades glanced up the stairs, all but feeling Persephone shrink back into the shadows.

Charon said, "Do you have any idea how he snatched her?"

"No," Hades whispered under his breath. "I'll wait before I ask her."

He heard the softest scuffle on the stairs above. Persephone was continuing on to their room. And again the question plagued him: what the hell had happened to put her in Ajax's path? The Estate was the most fortified place in the city. Had she gone somewhere? Tried to go see a friend or to visit that damn shelter because of some so-called 'emergency'?

A few minutes later, he finished up with Charon and took the stairs two at a time. When he got to their bedroom, he found Persephone on the bed, head bent over her lap. She hadn't turned any lights on so the room was dark and gloomy apart from the tiniest sliver of moonlight coming in through the blinds.

He went to the bed side table and turned on a lamp, then moved around to view her blood-spattered front.

"Let's get you clean."

She nodded and walked into the bathroom, but froze in front of the sink.

Hades followed her.

"My hands." She held them out, palms up. "I don't want to get blood on everything."

She retreated as he came to the sink and turned on both taps. He tested the water then stepped away so she could approach. They still weren't touching each other.

He ached to hold her, but her face was blank, still and hollow as a doll's. She might need him or she might need space. He'd wait and see which.

With robotic movements she thrust her hands under the tap, wetting them almost to mid-arm. The water ran red and she jerked her hands out of the flow.

Hades's throat got thick but he stood behind her then, his arms along hers. He put her hands back in the water and helped her lather with soap and scrub them gently, until the water ran clean. Her bowed head hung as if she was somewhere else, unattached from her hands.

She was still in the bloodied clothes, though, and that wouldn't do. With gentle hands, Hades pulled her shirt off over her head.

She let him do it, like a limp rag doll. When he reached for the button of her jeans, she suddenly jerked away and unbuttoned them herself, sliding them down her thighs along with her underwear and stepping towards the shower.

But Hades wasn't letting go of her that fast. She might have needed to cling to him in the Bentley on the way over here but he— Seeing that gun pointed to her temple—

He yanked his own clothes off and then stepped in behind her right as the spray turned warm.

"Hades," Persephone whispered and in that one word he heard a thousand heartbreaks. She turned toward him, arms folded to her chest, and fell against him. He wrapped a firm arm around her and pulled her to his chest, his other hand pushing her hair back from her eyes.

"Shh, it's all right. It's all right."

She just kept shaking her head. "It's not, though. It's not."

"Yes it is. You were brave. I watched you." He walked her back a little into the spray to wet her hair. Then he lifted her shampoo bottle and squeezed some into his hand.

He talked softly as he began to work the shampoo through her hair, cleaning out the blood. "You couldn't have done more, Persephone."

At her name, she shut her eyes and her entire body shook. Like she was reliving whatever Ajax had put her through. Hades had examined her hands in the car and knew the blood wasn't hers, but still. His jaw flexed.

Ajax would pay and he would pay dearly. But Hades couldn't think about that right now. He had to stay in control for her sake. Always in control.

So, with supreme effort, he managed to keep his voice calm as he continued, "He thought you were weak. He underestimated you. Tonight was tough. I don't know what you went through and you don't have to tell me until you're ready. But you're stronger than you know."

He worked his fingers through her hair, washing all the suds out. She leaned her forehead against his chest as he rinsed her hair. Once it was clean, he dropped his lips to the top of her head. "Don't make the same mistake. Know your own strength. You'll get through this."

He waited, but she didn't say anything. That was all right. He would help her through, one day at a time. He would protect her.

Just like you did tonight? He gritted his teeth. She *should* have been safe here. He'd find out what had gone wrong and punish whoever had put his wife in danger. Starting with that motherfucking bastard, Ajax. He'd make the man wish he'd never set eyes on Hades's wife. Hades would make him wish he'd never been born. He'd —

Persephone stirred in his arms and all of his attention came back to her. Large blue eyes blinked up at him, so full of sorrow. And then she shocked him with her next words. "Will you fuck me? I don't want to think any more."

Hades had been angling his hips away from her for the whole shower. Any time he was around his wife but especially when she was naked, he couldn't help his body's reaction to her. Now wasn't the time though—

But she reached down and grasped him so firmly he couldn't help the groan that slid from his throat. And when she lifted a leg around his waist and positioned him at her entrance, gods, the way her heat tempted and teased the head of his cock—

"Please," she breathed out.

In one swift movement, he turned them around so that her back was to the wall and then he pushed inside her. Usually, he would thrust all the way in, taking and claiming what was his.

But she felt so fragile in this moment. He cupped her cheeks and entered her slowly, so slowly, his eyes tracking her every breath, her every twitch, every flutter of her fingers against his shoulders.

She tried to look away but he guided her face back to his. She might have wanted to fuck but it wasn't what she *needed*.

In this at least, he would not fail her. And as he sank, inch by inch into the sweetest pussy the gods had ever created, he realized he'd needed it, too. When he heard Ajax's voice coming from her contact number and then heard her screaming—

He wrapped his arms around her and held her tighter than he'd ever held anything. She squeezed around him like she too was holding on for dear life. Because that's what she was to him. His whole fucking life.

How could he have been so fucking stupid? Lying to himself for all those months and trying to pretend that she meant nothing to him? She meant everything. He didn't deserve her.

Slowly, tortuously, he slid out and then pushed back in again. A shudder went down his spine as pleasure threatened even though he'd just begun. It was easy to hold back, though. He had only to remember the image of Ajax holding the gun to her head and her terrified eyes pleading with him for help. But in the end, he'd done nothing. She'd helped herself.

No, he didn't fucking deserve her. He clutched her closer still. But he would.

He'd devote the rest of his life to earning this woman. To earning her trust and love and devotion. He'd give her a world that was beautiful and safe and perfect. He'd give her everything he'd never had. He swore it, now, in this moment. He'd wipe the sorrow from her eyes. He'd make her happy, no matter what it fucking took.

He reached down and grasped her ass, angling her just right so that when he pushed in again, he hit that perfect spot inside her and her mouth dropped open in a silent scream of pleasure.

He pulled out and thrust in again, out and in, grinding against her clit until she was shuddering with her climax and squeezing around him so tight he couldn't hold back anymore. His spine lit up and then he thrust and spilled into his wife and for a moment, everything was as it was meant to be. Her, sated and limp in his arms and him, her conqueror and protector.

But then her legs wobbled and he could tell she was so weak, she almost collapsed right there in the shower where she stood.

Fuck.

He turned off the shower and helped her out, wrapping a towel around her and urging her to sit down on the closed toilet seat while he toweled her off. Her eyes were closed and her face, unreadable. Hades frowned. Usually after sex her features were soft and she was more pliable than ever. Right now, though…

"Let's get you to bed," he said gently, helping her up off of the seat and taking her to the bedroom. She stumbled along after him. Gods, when was the last time she'd eaten anything? "I'll have one of the men bring something up for dinner," he started but she cut him off with a wave of her hand.

"No," she said, curling up to the pillow drowsily as he pulled the blankets over her. "Just want to sleep."

It must have been true because only moments later, her soft, delicate little snores filled the otherwise silent room. Hades didn't move from where he sat on the bed beside her, frowning.

Time. It would just take time for her to share all she'd been through so they could work through it together.

And in the meantime... Hades's eyes shot to the window. He stood abruptly and then looked back down at Persephone.

She hadn't moved, not even stirred at his sudden motion. She'd be out for a while. And though he'd managed to block everything out while he was with her, his business couldn't be ignored for much longer. It was a mess now that they'd lost the shipment.

He needed to do major damage control, so, reluctantly, after a lingering stare at his wife from the doorway to make sure she didn't stir, he walked out and closed the door quietly behind himself.

He took a deep breath and held it, letting the mask of Hades Ubeli settle over himself like a Greek player of old. The part of himself he shared with Persephone was sacred. But the world must never see anything other than strength and a leader who crushed his enemies underneath his heel.

He strode down the stairs and straight to the kitchen where he knew Charon would be waiting. Charon was indeed there and he handed Hades a cup of coffee as he came in.

"They have him?" he barked.

Charon nodded. "It's being arranged. They're estimating three hours, maybe four."

Hades grabbed the cup and drink it all down without a word. The liquid burned his throat but it was a good burn and Hades needed the caffeine.

It was going to be a long night.

53

Persephone woke and even without looking at the clock knew it was still hours before dawn. The way the light fell over her hands—they were red-stained. She jerked and stared but they were clean. The blood on them had been washed away, but her guilt went more than skin deep. She'd never get clean.

Hades's side of the bed lay empty. He was probably downstairs, cleaning up the mess she'd made of his business. At the thought, she whimpered. Eurydice and Orpheus dead, a shipment seized, and all the Shades brought under police spotlight.

When her husband found out—and he would find out, of that she had no doubt—what happened then? Would he forgive her? She turned her face into the pillow. Gods, she wasn't sure she'd ever be able to forgive herself, so why should he?

She squeezed her eyes shut and thought of how tenderly he'd held her in the shower. How gentle he'd been with her. How he'd caressed her and washed her hair and...made love to her. She'd asked him to fuck her but he hadn't. After all this time she'd gotten the only thing she'd wanted but it was too late. It was too late for them. She'd ruined it all.

She sat up and swiped angrily at the tears falling down her

cheeks. Hades wouldn't look at her that way ever again, not once he knew. Or... She bit down on her lip. Maybe if she could just explain it... How she'd started with good intentions but it had all gotten out of hand so quickly... And then in the end she'd tried— She'd tried—

A sob gulped its way out of her and she threw her hand over her mouth. But there was no stopping it once it started.

And suddenly, she couldn't be here anymore. She couldn't face Hades when he came back from dealing with the disaster that she'd caused. She couldn't lie to him and she couldn't tell him the truth.

A green light blinking on the dresser caught her eye. Her cellphone.

Hades or Charon must have gotten it from one of the Shades, who'd have found it where she dropped it on the warehouse floor. She just needed a little space. She just needed to breathe and figure out her next move. To figure out how to tell Hades.

She fired off a quick text, then got dressed. Jeans and a tee, under a sweatshirt. By the time she was done, a message was waiting for her.

Hecate: Pick you up now?

She texted back. Yes.

THERE WOULDN'T BE any sneaking out the kitchen exit, not this time. Hades would have Shades on every door.

So she used a tree to escape the house—one she had found on her earlier walk. Persephone padded through the house until she found the room, unlocked the window and looked out. The tree branch that scraped along the side of the house didn't look so sturdy, but she tested it and then swung her legs out to balance on it. It held.

She froze for a moment. *What are you doing, Persephone? Are you really running away? Are you really going to do that to Hades on top of everything else you put him through today?*

But when she closed her eyes, all she saw was Eurydice's lifeless face. And the blood. She could still feel it sticky on her hands, no matter that Hades had washed it away. It would never come off. Never. *Never.*

Her breathing got erratic the more she thought about it and she shook her head, like that could shake the memories away. The only thing that was clear was that she couldn't face Hades again. Not right now. So she scooted down, grabbed the branch, and then dropped onto the wet grass below.

The darkness grabbed her, and she ran. She didn't stop to hear if she was being followed or if someone in the house had spotted her. She headed towards the path she'd found earlier.

She'd been running for a little while, maybe five or ten minutes when suddenly she heard voices and saw some car lights flashing through the trees behind her. Shit! Did they already figure out she was gone?

Immediately she made for the mausoleum, darting behind a lion statue just before the high beams hit the stone structure above her head.

Flattening herself to the ground, she listened and tried to control her breathing. A car was coming towards the crypt, creeping over the grass.

Persephone pressed herself into the little ditch that was just large enough for her. A couple of bushes helped obscure her. She could just see the marble platform before the steps up to the sepulcher.

As she watched, two Shades dressed all in black got out of the front seats. They left the beams of the car on for light so Persephone could see them coming forward to the steps of the mausoleum. One of them was carrying some sort of tool kit. He paused as his partner followed, carrying a chair he must've gotten from the trunk of the car.

"Leave it there," the first one ordered, and the chair was placed in the center on the marble dais, right in Persephone's line of site. He opened the tool kit and drew out a coil of rope, placing it on the chair. The other took the tool kit up the steps beyond where she could see.

What on earth was going on?

Persephone ducked her head, hoping her hood stayed over her light hair. Her heart pounded against the cold ground as she heard them moving around more. What were Hades's men doing out here in the middle of the night? Did Hades know they were here?

She didn't want to know what would happen to her if they found her hiding behind the lion statue.

Slipping her hand into her pocket, she turned off her cellphone, making sure it wouldn't give her away. She hoped whatever the Shades were doing, they'd get it over quickly so she could escape unseen while it was still dark. Hecate was probably already waiting.

More lights flashed and Persephone looked up, squinting past the high beams. What now?

"They're coming," one of the Shades called. Persephone peered just over her arm as another pair of headlights hit the crypt, high beams casting shadows until someone inside the car cut them off.

That was when Hades stepped out of the mausoleum.

Persephone's breath caught in her chest and she slapped her hand over her mouth to stop her gasp of surprise. What on earth? Charon was right behind Hades and just like earlier that night, the two wore long black overcoats. She caught a brief glimpse of her husband's grim expression before Charon stood in front of her and blocked most of her line of site.

"Took them long enough," Hades said. He and Charon stood there facing the lawn, waiting for the oncoming car.

Hades drew a cigar out of his pocket and lit it. He said something too low for Persephone to hear, because Charon leaned down. She heard Charon chuckle and shifted her head so she could see Hades's face better. He looked as he always did when he had a situation under control: confident, an almost-smile on his handsome face.

Suppressing a shiver, Persephone wiggled a little bit closer under the bushes. Hades and Charon looked for all the world like two buddies hanging out at a tailgate, chatting casually. They barely turned to acknowledge a second car's arrival, even when its doors opened and slammed, signaling a visitor's approach.

A man in a taupe trench coat approached the two men; Persephone could see his older face clearly as she looked up now that her eyes had adjusted to the car's low beams.

"Mr. Ubeli," he greeted her husband politely.

In answer, Hades nodded to him and took a casual drag on his cigar. Charon's hands were still in his pockets.

The visitor kept a respectful distance. Something in the slope of his head as he nodded to her husband made Persephone remember back to the day at the Crown hotel, when the cops were there to guard Orpheus. She recognized the man then; he was the police higher up whom Hades had acknowledged in the lobby.

What was he doing here?

Meanwhile, Hades's two men had joined them on the dais. They stood in deceptively casual poses, but the hulk of muscles in their shoulders made Persephone think they weren't just there for show. The Shades were weapons, dark and deadly.

The man in the taupe coat cleared his throat. "Mr. Sturm sends his regards. He's grateful for your support."

What did the mayor have to do with this middle of the night meeting?

While the man in the taupe coat spoke, two more men got out of the second car and opened the trunk to get something. Persephone couldn't quite see what.

"He asks that you accept this gift as a token of his gratitude. But after this, he requests no more contact."

Hades removed his cigar and studied it before responding. "Tell him I respect his request, and thank him for his gift."

The messenger nodded curtly from where he stood on the ground before stepping back to allow his two helpers to carry forward their 'gift'.

Persephone was about to crane her neck to make out what it was when movement on the steps frightened her and she ducked her head. She trembled for a moment, thinking she was caught.

But then she realized it was only Charon. He had moved closer to Persephone's hiding place, taking a position behind the chair the two Shades had set up earlier.

Then her eyes widened. It was a body. Zeus's men were carrying a body.

It hung limp and heavy between the two of them. A hood covered its head, although the build and size told Persephone it was a man.

They sat him in the chair, and Charon knelt to tie his hands to it with the rope.

When the body was secure, Charon stepped forward and whipped off the black hood. Oh gods— Persephone drew in a breath and pushed a fist to her mouth to keep herself quiet.

It was Ajax.

His head lolled a little on his thick neck. His hair was matted down and his coat was gone. His shirt was halfway unbuttoned and he looked the worse for wear. Tied to a chair in the middle of the night, the monster looked smaller, somehow.

"Tell Zeus he has our vote," Hades said coolly. "And we won't be contacting him, as long as certain...property is returned to us."

The man in the taupe coat nodded. "It's being processed. Give it a week. You'll get your shipment back."

Persephone's mind raced. The shipment—returned? And Ajax delivered to Hades's front door as a gift, like a holiday ham.

The man in the taupe coat must be Hades's man on the inside, a connection to Zeus and the force. Of course, the mayor was higher up than anyone.

Mind whirling, she barely heard Zeus's men get in their second car and creep away, leaving only Hades, his men, and Ajax behind. And her, of course.

For a moment, no one in front of the mausoleum moved or spoke. Above them, the clouds rolled away from the moon and caused shadows to flicker over their faces. It looked like something out of a horror movie, ghouls gathering around the crypt.

And Hades? He looked like the Grim Reaper himself. She saw nothing of the man who'd held her so tenderly and washed her hair in the shower earlier that night. A shiver skittered down her spine that had nothing to do with the cold.

"Alright," Hades broke the silence. "They're gone."

One of the Shades stepped forward, handing Charon a water

bottle. The big man unscrewed the cap and splashed it into Ajax's face. Hades's men waited patiently until he woke, sputtering.

"Where am I?" Ajax groaned. His hands, bound behind him on the chair, flexed uselessly.

Pulling the cigar out of his mouth, Hades answered him. "Hello, Ajax. Welcome to hell."

"What the—" Ajax's voice was cut off as Charon gagged him. Charon stepped back, squeezing his fist to crack his knuckles, his eyes on the back of Ajax's head.

Ajax looked around wildly.

"I want to congratulate you on your good work tonight, Ajax," Hades said softly. "You helped the mayor look strong on crime. He'll get elected. My campaign dollars will be well spent."

Hades flicked a little ash onto the ground. "Of course, the outcome isn't quite what you wanted. Jail, and now being brought here to the house of your enemy. It's amazing how quickly you can get a man out on bail when you have friends in high places."

Ajax made a small noise, barely a whimper.

"Do you recognize the family crypt?" Hades motioned and Charon turned the chair to face the intimidating structure.

"My father used to hold meetings here, remember? You were just a young man then."

Ajax whimpered again. Persephone could see his face clearly, his hair and face dirty and matted with sweat. He looked terrified and Persephone blinked, confused. Did she really feel pity for this man?

Then she remembered Eurydice's dead face. He deserved everything Hades might do to him. Right?

"I thought I'd bring you here, refresh your memory of old times," Hades continued. "And also show you where my family lies. You can pay your respects to Old Ubeli. There's even a grave there waiting for me and my wife, when our time comes."

Persephone winced automatically at the mention of her. How could this ice cold, unfeeling Hades even speak of her while he was here, doing what he was about to do? She had no illusions. Ajax wouldn't walk out of here alive. And even though she should cheer the fact...watching Hades...watching him when he was like this...

"Not that it'll come soon." Hades's voice now held deadly malice. "No thanks to you."

He shook the ash of his cigar over Ajax's face and the man squirmed in the chair. Charon stepped closer to hold it steady.

Hades took a pull off the cigar and let the smoke curl out of his mouth, savoring it. Then he smiled at Ajax. It was a smile that had another shiver rocking through Persephone, all the way down to her bones.

"I know you're a man who appreciates cigars." He held the smoking roll up by Ajax's face. "You want some?" Hades's hand dropped carelessly and pressed the burning tip into Ajax's chest until the man writhed and bucked, screaming behind the gag.

Persephone bit down on her fist again to keep from crying out. But she forced herself not to look away. This was the man she'd married. This was the man she...she loved.

Charon and the Shades stood watching silently, still as statues. Meanwhile, Hades had discarded the cigar and paced a little, waiting for the sobbing man to quiet.

"I wanted you to bring back a message to your masters. The ones who sent you here to see how I rule my city. See, I knew the Titan brothers would need more convincing that their rule here is over. That the bitch who leads them around by their little pencil dicks would need more. And I want them to understand something."

Hades stopped in front of Ajax, right in Persephone's line of sight. His face was a cold mask, black eyes boring into the man who'd crossed him. She didn't recognize him as her husband anymore.

"I want you to understand something. I own this city. I own the streets. I own the shops, I own the air. You breathe," Hades pointed to Ajax, "with my permission. And now that your singer is dead—"

Ajax jerked and so did Persephone. It was business to Hades. Just business. But Orpheus was a *person*.

"—it's time for you to leave New Olympus. Permanently."

Ajax made muffled sounds behind his gag like he was trying to plead his case, then it quieted. Persephone could hear him sobbing. Charon, who had bent over him, leapt back.

"Pissed himself," the big man muttered.

Hades's face twisted in disgust. "Face your death like a man."

Ajax shook his head wildly, pleading.

And that was when Hades lost any and all semblance of calm. His features twisted with rage.

"You came to *my* city. Abducted *my* wife. Disrupted *my* business. How did you think this would end? You think you can disrespect me?"

Persephone's heart pounded as she watched her husband snarl at his enemy. She pressed her body into the cold ground.

Abruptly Hades whirled and strode to the car. A third Shade stood there, holding a black case. Hades threw the case open and then pulled something out. Persephone frowned at first and then her eyes widened when he made a fist. He'd put on brass knuckles.

And then before she could even take another breath, he was back on Ajax. "You dared," he landed a heavy blow to Ajax's face, "to touch," another blow, "my wife."

Blood poured down Ajax's face until he was choking on it but Hades didn't stop.

Over and over again, he pounded Ajax's face with a wild madness until the wet, squelching noise of his fist and the brass knuckles on Ajax's head and bones and gristle and brain were all that could be heard.

Persephone turned away and bent over the grass, throwing up.

Still Hades didn't stop.

No one said a word until finally, heaving for breath, Hades stepped back.

"I've decided," Hades gulped in a breath, standing over the bloody mess that used to be Ajax, "how to send a message to the Titans. You'll be that message."

Persephone choked her tears down.

"Prep the body," Hades said, his chest still rising and falling heavily. "Get it to Metropolis."

"Yes, boss." The men answered in unison and scurried forward to carry the chair and dead man into the mausoleum.

"You on clean up?" Hades asked, and Persephone raised her head to see him speaking to Charon.

The big man shrugged. "Just the tricky stuff. These guys don't know how to get off a fingerprint without taking the hand." His tone was casual, as if he and Hades were talking about something totally normal, like taking out the garbage. As if they hadn't all just stood around and watched Hades bludgeon a man's head in.

"If you need help, call the gardener."

Charon nodded. "Yeah, I learned from him. He was the master."

Charon handed Hades a handkerchief and Persephone watched her husband calmly wipe off his hands, sliding the brass knuckles off as he did so. He looked beautiful in the moonlight. Even after what she'd just seen him do. Beautiful and so, so cold.

His lips had a satisfied smile, as if he relished the duty of judge, jury, and executioner.

Persephone sucked in a breath and saw him, really saw him.

She saw Death.

"He's on standby. He'll sod over everything in the morning, if you can get it done by dawn," Hades was telling Charon.

"Will do, boss." Charon turned and started going up the steps. He paused to ask one more thing. "The message to the Brothers—you want me to write a note?" His back was to Persephone but she could hear a joking tone in his voice.

Hades stared at the ground a moment. His profile was cut clean from the car's headlights. Persephone held her breath.

Then he raised his head and his dark hair fell across his face. "Just send the pieces."

Persephone waited until the car crept backwards across the lawn. All the men were in the vault; she could hear them joking about their grisly work.

She rose stiffly and hugged the mausoleum walls. Her body felt frozen so she waited at the back of the building, listening to see if she was found out.

No one came to find her though. There were no shouts signaling they'd spotted her. She was about to breathe a sigh of relief when she heard a strange whine start up.

Someone was using a wet saw.

She was going to be sick again. She bolted before she could be seen and didn't slow until she was in the trees, continuing on the path she'd taken earlier that night.

A car waited alongside the road. She approached and rapped on the glass. Hecate woke suddenly. For a moment her friend stared in surprise, but then she motioned for Persephone to get in the back.

As Persephone opened the door, a large doggy head greeted her. Cerberus, the giant puppy.

"He wanted to come," Hecate said apologetically. "Persephone, are you ok? I've been waiting..."

"Yes, sorry. My phone died." Persephone sat in the backseat and buckled herself in. The large puppy settled down, his head hovering near Persephone's.

Hecate was still looking back at her and Persephone couldn't imagine what she saw on her face. "You sure about this?"

"Yes," Persephone said. *Please don't ask me anything more.* Hecate must have sensed her silent plea, though, because she just pursed her lips and didn't say anything, although it was clear she wanted to. She turned and put the car into drive, then they crept away.

In the backseat, Persephone bent over the puppy's head, clutching him tightly. He seemed to know she needed him and held his body still. A few tears spotted the top of his head.

When she'd left tonight, she'd only meant to clear her head. But what she'd seen... She covered her mouth again and struggled to fight back the bile that threatened to rise up.

She could never go back.

"It's just you and me, Cerberus," she whispered. "You and me, against the world."

. . .

***

Read several extra scenes from Hades' perspective: sign up at https://geni.us/Hadesextras

PART III

QUEEN OF THE UNDERWORLD

"Both her mind and her appearance quickly were transformed..."
Ovid's Metamorphoses, Book V

54

Persephone knew the moment her husband came through the grand doors. His power rolled forward, enveloping her.

Standing in the midst of the party, with her back to the entrance, she felt rather than saw him cross the threshold into the ballroom. Her hands immediately started shaking.

Not now. Gods, please, not now.

Along the edges of the gorgeous room, men in black suits took their places quietly, blending in with her serving staff. Hades's personal cadre of bodyguards. She recognized them because they'd once guarded her.

The guests mingling near the entrance all turned, the men bowing and women fluttering as they greeted the man who secretly ruled the Underworld of New Olympus. Hades Ubeli.

It had been two months since she'd seen or spoken to him, beyond the text she'd sent telling him she was leaving him as she fled his Estate. Of course she'd known that wouldn't be the end of it. This was Hades Ubeli they were talking about.

She'd spent the last two months laying low, knowing he could come for her at any moment. He hadn't, though. He'd respected her wishes...

Or it had been some sort of game to him. One she didn't want to play. She was tired of games. Done with them. Done with *him* and his world of shadows and violence.

Hades's dark head was still barely in the ballroom. He was surrounded by people, couples in tuxes and ballgowns who would pay homage to the King of the Underworld, men with solemn faces who wanted to shake his hand and whisper in his ear. Same as always.

Of course she'd known that eventually they'd run into each other. It was inevitable. She'd tried to brace herself for this moment. She'd gone over it a hundred times in her head. A thousand times.

She thought she'd be ready.

She'd been wrong. So, so wrong.

Hades raised his head. His storm colored eyes swept over the crowded room. He was still surrounded by people, but he hadn't forgotten her.

He'd never forget. He was on the hunt.

Goosebumps rose all over her skin and her heart raced. He was more gorgeous than ever and even a ballroom away, she could feel the wash of power that always preceded his intimidating presence.

Get out. She had to get out of here now.

She glanced around, feeling frantic as she looked for an escape. But she was surrounded on all sides by beautiful, glittering people who were all but caging her in between the giant bouquets of peacock feathers and tables laden with crab and puff pastries.

Hermes had opened another spa, and, to celebrate, talked one of his many admirers into opening their house for the extravaganza. The party was totally lush. He'd told Persephone to spare no expense and she hadn't. But now the excess was completely screwing with her need for a quick escape.

There was the staircase on the far side of the ballroom; she could probably wind her way through the partiers to get there…but it would leave her exposed. Hades might be able to approach her before she could get away. Still, she had to try. She couldn't stand here like a lamb waiting for the slaughter.

She looked up at the tall guest in a white tux who'd been talking to her. "I'm sorry," she interrupted him, having no idea what he'd been saying.

She'd passed off the behind-the-scenes responsibilities to Sasha, her assistant, about an hour ago and had been out among the guests ever since, at Hermes's insistence.

The tall black man smiled, showing perfect white teeth. He was bald and cut an unusual figure in the party. He reminded her of Charon, the dangerous underboss in her husband's business.

"No apologies necessary," the man said in a light tenor voice that belied his height. "I've been babbling far too long. I was excited to meet the woman who made all this happen." He frowned down at her in concern. "Are you cold?"

"No." Persephone wanted to rub her arms to quell the goosebumps but instead lifted her hand self-consciously to her hair. Did she look as harried as she felt? Her hair was a shade lighter than it had been two months ago, worked into an intricate braid around her head. Would Hades like it? She wanted to kick herself the second she had the thought, but still couldn't shake it.

Tendrils were already escaping around her face. Her fingers smoothed them back and drifted to her ears. She was wearing the diamond earrings Hades had given her. The studs hadn't seen the light of day for two months, but Hermes had given her the dress and she'd wanted something to match.

Of course, she'd picked the one night Hades showed up and would see her wearing his gift. Sighing, she pressed her hand to her temple. At least she wasn't still wearing her wedding ring.

"You sure you're alright?" the guest in white asked.

On the far side of the ballroom, the DJ on the dais started a song the crowd recognized. A flock of the younger crowd rushed past, knocking Persephone into the giant man. His large dark hands reached out to steady her.

Persephone smiled weakly as she looked up into the guest's concerned eyes and tried to remember his name.

"Poseidon!" Hermes swooped in, looking dashing in a black velvet tux that contrasted nicely with his dancing black eyes and swarthy skin. "So glad you could come to our party." The boyish designer and spa owner threw his arm around Persephone, cutting off her escape. "Are you enjoying it?"

"I am, thank you," Poseidon rumbled. "It's been awhile since I've been to a party off ship."

"Well, you've come to the right one. Persephone helped pull it off." Hermes squeezed her. "Have you heard of her new event planning company? She just started it. It's called Perceptions. A lovely name, if I say so myself."

Persephone resisted rolling her eyes. Hermes had thought up the name. He'd also called her up weeks ago and strong-armed her into starting the business, helping her file the right paperwork, and loaning her a generous amount of start-up capital.

"Tonight's her inaugural event," Hermes was telling Poseidon.

"Is it?" Poseidon rumbled, his eyes crinkling as he looked down at her. "Congratulations."

"Thank you." Persephone forced a smile. She was happy, she really was.

Or maybe not happy. Content. Happiness was a lie. It seemed to her that everyone was simply trying to get by the best they could. So she did, too. And she stayed busy. That was key. When she was busy, she didn't have time to think. Which was why this event had been perfect.

She barely slept the past week and had almost had a heart attack when the caterers tried to change the menu on her at the last moment. But she'd called around to every fish market in the area and gotten them enough fresh salmon to make their piccata bites right in time. And then she had to fight with the florists to get the arrangements she wanted even though they'd agreed a week ago—

Persephone shook her head to clear her thoughts. "I should probably check on the buffet..."

She started to pull away but Hermes shook his head. "Persephone, darling, the buffet is fine. Quit acting like Cinderella and enjoy the ball. Champagne!"

A waitress wearing little more than a purple bikini and headdress of peacock feathers sashayed by and offered her tray out to them. Persephone had a glass pressed into her hand before she could protest.

"A toast—" Hermes hesitated.

"To the hostess," Poseidon supplied.

"To the hostess with the mostess. To Persephone," Hermes whooped. Persephone tried to shush him; if Hades didn't know she was here before he certainly did now. She was about to extricate herself from Hermes's embrace when Athena broke into their circle.

"Hey guys, what are we toasting to?"

"Athena!" Hermes greeted her. "We're toasting Persephone."

"Roger that." Athena was a hacker Persephone had befriended in the past few months and her friendship had turned out to be a lifesaver. Especially now since they were roommates after Persephone had moved out of Hades's penthouse. Athena relieved Persephone of her glass and downed the rest of the champagne.

Persephone craned her head slightly and tried to scan the room to see if her husband was circling closer. Hermes still had his arm around her shoulders and was doing introductions. If she moved now, she'd appear rude. At least Hades hadn't approached them yet. Maybe there was still time for her to escape?

"Poseidon, this is Athena, resident tech genius who owns Aurum, the tech company. Athena, Poseidon runs a shipping business and owns—"

"A bunch of toys that can only be run on water," Poseidon interrupted, capturing Athena's hand and kissing it.

"Awesome," Athena said, looking down her sharp nose. Athena's face wasn't unattractive but Persephone didn't care for the way she wore her hair parted down the middle, black sheets falling to a blunt cut jaw. The whole hairstyle resembled a helmet. After two months of advising her friend to get her hair cut in softer layers, Persephone had given up, suspecting that Athena preferred to look striking rather than pretty.

Of course, that theory didn't jive with the way Athena flirted.

Right now Athena was fluttering her dark lashes at the shipping mogul. "Do you share your toys?"

"I'll share mine if you share yours." Poseidon smiled.

"Right on. I'm heading out of here soon, but I'll look you up." Athena looked Poseidon over, from his bald head all the way down to his wing tip shoes. "You're what, six one?"

"Six two." Again, Poseidon's smile showed two rows of very white teeth.

"Nice. You know what they say about tall men." Athena looked pointedly at the guest's crotch.

"Athena," Persephone choked out, but wasn't sure why she was even surprised anymore. Athena was smart enough to realize her rudeness—she simply didn't care. "Poseidon was commenting on how nice this party is."

Even as she said it, her eyes were darting around. Where had Hades gone? Had he seen her?

"Oh, for sure. Great party," Athena agreed.

Hermes, now hanging on Persephone, had somehow grabbed a second champagne. He pointed with his new glass, dangerously close to slopping liquid onto Persephone. "See that guy in the corner? That's Max Mars, the movie star."

They all studied the handsome blond holding court in front of the staircase, surrounded by an adoring audience five people deep.

"Hot. I'd fuck him," Athena pronounced. Hermes snorted in Persephone's ear, leaning more heavily on her until she was surrounded by the scent of his cologne. It smelled good but was a little overpowering for her taste. Poseidon's lips jerked briefly into what looked suspiciously like the start of a smile.

Persephone closed her eyes as Athena went on. "Didn't Aphrodite say she was auditioning for a movie that he's starring in? That would be, like, a huge break for her."

"Yes," Persephone said, focusing back in on the conversation at hand. "And she's perfect for the part."

"Where is that bitch anyway?" Athena frowned, looking back towards the entrance. "Aphrodite is another one of our roommates," she told Poseidon, and then winked at him. "There's only one bed, though. Good thing we're such close friends."

Persephone all but choked on a sip of champagne. "How about another toast?" she said desperately. Poseidon's grin was now ear to ear.

"To friends!" Hermes started to toast again, but the hand that held the full glass was still around Persephone's neck.

Athena grabbed the tipsy designer and helped untangle him. "Gods, Hermes, watch her dress."

Persephone was almost free when Hermes caught her arm.

"Do you like the dress?" he asked. "It's one of my creations."

"I actually need to go fix it real quick," Persephone stammered, tugging at Hermes's grip. She'd officially reached maximum stimulus overload. She needed a breath.

"Stop, it looks perfect," Hermes scolded.

"Very lovely. You're like a mermaid." Poseidon smiled down at her.

Persephone glanced down. The blue sheath was strapless, hugging her sleek form until her waist, where it shimmered into turquoise and then down into a sea-foam green train.

"Turn around," Athena requested and Hermes's hand pulled her into a spin that Persephone had no choice but to continue.

Of course, as soon as she twirled, her gaze swept over the crowded party, and Persephone looked straight into the eyes of her husband, Hades Ubeli.

Like in the movies, it felt like everything around them muted and became hazy. Eight weeks hadn't changed much—for him anyway. Hades wore his signature suit. Everything about him spoke of power, from the set of his broad shoulders to his piercing gaze. He stood in a crowd and rose above it, a man among boys.

He stood a little inside the doorway, flanked by two men dressed all in black. Shades, they were called on the street.

One glance, and Persephone stopped mid-twirl, letting her dress continue without her. She stared at her husband, the sight of him hitting her with earth-tilting force. His eyes locked with hers and there was a fire burning in their depths. Searing her to the core.

With time and space, she had convinced herself that she'd imagined the potency of his effect on her. Surely she'd exaggerated how, with a look, he could pin her in place and have her begging.

A half whirl later and she had her back to him, but no relief. She knew his eyes were on her and she could all but feel the ghost of his hands on her body.

More than that, a million other memories were flooding in. Him holding her at night, his body spooned behind hers. Him finally saying the words that she had waited so long to hear, whispering over and over that he loved her.

And that last night before she'd left him. The terrifying sight of him letting the leash off of his control and watching him brutally bash a man's head in. Over and over and over again, even after the man was dead. Hades hadn't known she was there, hiding in the shadows, but she'd seen. She'd seen and she'd never forget.

Persephone stumbled backwards. "I have to go."

Athena frowned and Hermes's head whipped around. They both realized the cause of her panic at the same time. For the past two months, Persephone had been Athena's roommate, and Hermes was a frequent visitor to their tiny loft. They'd listened to her rant, hugged her when she cried, and plied her with ice cream when she moped around for days. She'd never told them the extent of it, though. She'd never told a soul about that last night and she never would.

"Oh darling—" Hermes began, his Adam's apple bobbing as he swallowed convulsively.

Athena was more blunt. "Go."

Poseidon straightened to his considerable height. His eyes narrowed and Persephone froze at the mask of hate that settled over his regal features.

Persephone didn't want to know the reasons why the man in white despised her husband. Hades's whole world was filled with darkness and vendetta. She wanted nothing to do with any of it. And she certainly had no interest in confronting Hades tonight.

Lifting her dress so she wouldn't trip on the mini-train, Persephone fled. Damn it, why had she let Hermes talk her into wearing these five-inch heels? She couldn't go too quickly or she'd break her neck.

"I'm sorry." Hermes caught up with her, sounding sober again.

"You told me he wouldn't be here," she said through gritted teeth.

"I know," Hermes sighed, and she almost stumbled.

He steadied her, then held her back as she snapped at him. "You knew? You knew he was coming, and you told me..."

"Look, I didn't know he was actually going to show up. I may have let it slip that you were working on this event with me. I didn't invite him."

"You dangled me like bait in front of him! That's an open invitation to a man like him."

She glanced back, and, sure enough, Hades was on his way towards the ballroom, moving closer to them. People seemed to magically clear out of his way. *Shit.*

"It's been two months, Persephone belle. Don't you think you should at least talk to him?"

"I *have* talked to him." Okay, she'd texted. She couldn't bear to hear his voice, although she'd saved his voicemails.

"I mean face to face." Hermes sighed again. Persephone felt a twinge of guilt. Her friends hadn't been anything but supportive, although they did point out, gently, that talking *to* her husband might be a teensy bit better than just ranting behind his back.

They didn't understand, though. And they never would because she'd never tell them about that night.

Keeping busy was the only alternative to curling up in the fetal position underneath her bedspread. Over and over, waking and sleeping, she heard the *BANG* of Ajax's gun going off and the endless images assaulted her—the blood, those brief moments between life and death when she'd bowed over Eurydice's prone body and begged her to hang on, still believing that true love conquered all.

But it didn't. True love and happy endings were a lie. Eurydice's eyes had gone glassy and that was only the beginning of that night's violence and bloodshed.

So yes, Persephone had run.

And in the last two months, she tried to build a life for herself. One she could actually call her own for the first time, not dictated by her mother or her husband. She was finally doing what she dreamed of all her life—she was living independently and starting to make her own way in the world. But gods, none of that mattered because Hades was here. She couldn't avoid thinking about him anymore. He'd force a confrontation. It was his way.

"I can't," she said, pushing Hermes away and rising up onto the first step of the staircase. He frowned but let her go.

"It's too much tonight. I can't. I won't." She was now talking to herself, climbing the stairs carefully because of the damn heels.

Halfway up, though, she made a mistake. She looked down.

Hades was standing amid the crowd, looking right at her. Was there sadness in the beautiful hollows of his face, in the shadows under his eyes? She'd expected anger.

Too late, Persephone realized she'd been staring. Hades saw her hesitation, and it was enough. Oh shit. He made his living among the criminals of the underworld, where the slightest weakness could be exploited. So of course he read hers. And, like a siren's call, it moved him.

Holding onto the banister with both hands, Persephone watched him prowl through the glittering masses. He kept his eyes on her, and she read in them a promise. He was the hunter; she was the prey. And Hades Ubeli always got what he wanted.

Under her beautiful dress, her knees wobbled. With what—fear, desire, anticipation?—she didn't know. All she knew was that she was glad she had the banister to steady herself.

Run. Get the hell out of here.

But she stayed rooted in place. Because maybe, secretly, she wanted him to get what he wanted.

A wild card saved her. A curvy young woman walked in, her golden skin glowing against her outfit of pure white. Aphrodite. The people around her formed an admiring circle and Aphrodite smiled, basking in the light of their attention. But behind her, a server lifted a full tray of drinks and staggered under their weight. Persephone gasped as she saw what would happen.

The server stumbled and the glasses crashed down, sending liquid in a shining arc, splashing all over Aphrodite's white clad form. Aphrodite paused for a brief moment, looking down as the yellow stain spread all over her white outfit.

But Persephone should have known Aphrodite could roll with any situation.

Further in the ballroom, the DJ had taken a break and the music was quiet, so people were turning to see this new entertainment. No one else would be able to pull this off, but Aphrodite was a performer, and now she had an audience. She threw back her head and laughed.

With a practiced movement, she let the bolero slide off her shoulders, and tossed the garment onto the surprised server's tray. Every movement was part of the dance, and it was hard to look away. Her undershirt, a complicated camisole done up her front with little hooks was next. With quick flicks of Aphrodite's fingers, her top started to split down the middle as the audience held their breath.

She sashayed her hips, stepping forward. The people around her cleared away as she moved towards a buffet table. Her hands busy with her top, she still managed to step lightly up onto the table.

Now most of the room was watching. Aphrodite remained mostly in place, moving her hips to a silent song.

The DJ filled the room with a throbbing beat. Now some of the younger and rowdier crowd came around the table, and Aphrodite worked with them, blowing a kiss to her new admirers. A few fans started to holler.

Her top came off slowly, teasingly, until Aphrodite dropped it and revealed a pale bra holding up an amazing pair of breasts. If the crowd hadn't been excited before, they certainly were now, and someone clued the DJ in. He turned up the music, bellowing into the mike, "Ladies and gentleman, please welcome—*Venus!*"

Aphrodite was down to her heels, a sexy thong, and a half slip made of tulle that had underwired the poofy skirt she'd been wearing. Not much more than she wore to work at the strip club where she had her show. Even half-naked, she looked elegant, the mesh skirt around her hips flaring out like a ballerina's.

On the edge of the ballroom, Max Mars left his throng of admirers and glided across the parquet to the stage where Aphrodite was dancing. He stepped up, the spotlight gilding his famous profile.

He held out his hand. Aphrodite took it.

Persephone sucked in a breath. Her roommate was laughing, holding hands with the biggest star in New Olympus, and blowing kisses over her shoulder to her adoring fans as Max Mars stole her away.

Taking advantage of the distraction, Persephone's staff cleaned the champagne and wet clothes away. Crisis averted.

Not quite. All that commotion, and Hades was still looking at her. Persephone staggered backwards, nearly falling on the steps under the weight of his stare. The promise in the stormy depths of his eyes.

Fate had one more ace up his sleeve. While his eyes had been locked with hers, Hades had forgotten to survey the crowd. The DJ's music ended and the crowd crush forward to cheer. And amid the waves of people, as if pulled by some magic tide, Poseidon washed into Hades's path.

From her vantage point, Persephone could see her husband's sober expression falter as he looked up at the man who blocked his progression to her. She waited long enough to see the recognition flicker across Hades's features as he stared at the giant in white.

Another second and surprise left Hades's face and hatred flooded in.

Persephone didn't wait to see what happened next. Slipping out of her shoes, she whirled and ran up the stairs.

55

The house was a mini palace, big as a hotel. At the top of the stairs, Persephone slipped past the sign marking the hall beyond as "Private."

Oh well, she'd ask Hermes later who owned the palace so she could beg forgiveness for trespassing. Escape was more important at the moment. She hurried down the hall, testing a few of the doors to see if one could lead to a safe hiding place.

None of the doorknobs turned. Persephone ran barefoot from one to another, imagining Hades stalking up the stairs, the victor (of course) of whatever faceoff he might have had with Poseidon. He'd pause at the top of the stairs, order his Shades to wait, and come for her.

Finally, the door at the end of the hallway opened and Persephone walked out onto a balcony. The air was cold and crisp but did little to cool her overheated skin. Hurrying to the balustrade, she leaned over and looked out over the garden, heaving in a deep breath.

Second floor. No way down. Nowhere else to run.

She blinked rapidly as her heart raced, looking over her shoulder. Maybe he wouldn't find her? But there'd been that look in his eye. He was done waiting.

Two months ago, riding in Hecate's car away from the Ubeli Estate, she'd texted him: I've left you. I'm somewhere safe. Please don't come after me.

She'd turned her phone off, and Hecate had dropped her off at Athena's apartment. After kissing Cerberus goodbye (and getting a doggy lick in return), Persephone had gone inside to Athena and Aphrodite, to hug and cry. Hermes had shown up an hour later bearing wine. Hermes hadn't chastised her, but hugged her until tears came to her eyes. They drank until dawn.

The next day, she turned on her phone and stared at the six voicemails Hades left her. And one text: We need to talk.

After saving the voicemails without listening to them, she'd texted him back. She was a coward, but she was resigned to being one.

I can't right now but we will soon. I promise. I need time.

She'd left out what she really wanted to say. His reply said it for her. I'll wait. I love you.

He'd kept his word. He hadn't sought her out for two months. Oh, Persephone knew he checked up on her, and every week flowers were delivered to Athena's apartment that Aphrodite and Athena swore weren't from any of their admirers. But no phone calls, no texts. No showing up on her doorstep. Nothing until tonight. His patience had run out.

Persephone took her now freezing hands away from the stone and rubbed them together. The truth was, as much as she'd been dreading this day, she knew it needed to happen. Closure, right? Everyone said it was important. If only she was strong enough.

She and Hades were wrong for each other. From the beginning they'd sparked like fire but what was it worth if it burned the whole world down?

She'd told herself that she needed the past two months to think. But the truth was, sticking her head in the sand was the only way she knew to become deaf and blind to his charms. Seeing him again now, she knew the truth.

She wanted him. She...liked succumbing to the pull he had over her. If she was being honest with herself, and this was very, very hard to admit...she always had. She wanted his overwhelming strength to roll over her and fill her with desire. She wanted him too much.

And she hated herself for that. Her desire for him, her weakness. She wanted to be able to stand up to him and prove she was strong enough to live her own life.

She had to break the cycle. It was up to her.

Footsteps sounded behind her.

And now was her chance.

56

Finally, she was here in front of him. Hades stepped through the grand doors and out onto the balcony with her. His wife. They were reunited at last.

The last two months had been hell. Ask anyone who'd been around Hades. Charon, the Shades. They'd all learned to steer clear of him other than when absolutely necessary.

Persephone's back was to Hades but he knew she felt him. She always could. They were connected, no matter the miles that might separate them. Nothing could sever their bond.

So he'd given her the time she asked for. She'd been scared. Everything that had gone down...it was bad. She thought she needed space, so okay. Every single day he'd wanted to drive over, tear down the door to her friend's apartment, and drag her back to the Estate where she belonged. At his side.

For her, though, he'd fought his less evolved nature and let her be.

But enough was enough. She was his wife and it was time for her to come home.

"Persephone." Her name was a sensuous caress on his tongue. He'd never wanted anything as much as he wanted her.

She turned and the string of connection between them pulled taut.

She was so fucking gorgeous, he almost lost his breath. She was statuesque and beautiful, delicate, with pale skin that glowed in the moonlight. The dress she wore molded to her curves but it also highlighted the fact that she'd lost weight.

A hundred disjointed thoughts ran through Hades's head. He wanted to punish her for leaving him. He wanted to fall at her feet and beg her forgiveness. He wanted to grab her, flip her against the wall, and fuck all the frustration of the past two months out between her quivering thighs.

Her hands fisted at her sides as if she could read his thoughts and was forcing herself not to reach for him. He all but growled in satisfaction at the sight. He affected her as much as she did him.

Her eyes narrowed and she squared her bare shoulders, lifting her chin. Whatever statement she hoped to make by the posture was undercut by the fact that her nipples had clearly hardened, completely visible through the tight fabric that clung to her breasts. It was a good thing she'd retreated here for their reunion to take place because now Hades could enjoy the sight all for himself instead of concerning himself with blinding any fucker who dared to stare at what was his.

"Leaving the party so soon?" he finally fired the first volley.

Her eyes flared and she crossed her arms over her chest. More was the pity. "I'm not much of a party person."

He couldn't help smiling at that. "I remember."

He lifted his hand, holding out her ridiculous shoes that she'd abandoned midflight.

"You left these on the stairs."

Her eyes went wide for a moment and little pink spots appeared on her cheeks. "Yes, well. I've had a long night."

He stalked forward, his eyes capturing and keeping hers. She backed up until her legs hit the balustrade. He knelt. So it was to be bowing at her feet after all. He lifted up the silky material of her dress and exposed her perfect ankle. Gods, to touch her skin again...

"Hades," she breathed, and he looked up the length of her. Her chest was heaving and he grinned. She seemed to lose track of whatever she'd been about to say. Oh yes, her body remembered his command over it and soon the rest of her would too. He'd make sure of it.

But even as he thought it, he knew he wanted more. He didn't want unthinking obedience. Not from her. No, what he wanted from her was so much more complex.

Lifting her foot, he slipped the first shoe on and fastened it, caressing her ankle and her calf. The chance to get his hands on her again was too tempting to pass up.

He worked on the other one while Persephone leaned on the balustrade. She was silent, but by the occasional hitch in her breath, his touch was affecting her.

When he finally straightened and stood, she swallowed hard before finally managing a tremulous, "Thank you."

"My pleasure." Their eyes caught and held a moment before she dropped hers and took a small step back from him. As if any amount of distance could stop the blazing furnace of their chemistry.

"Hermes tells me you helped him with most of the preparations," he said. She was like a skittish bird and she'd flee if he wasn't careful. "He says you're indispensable. Your company is taking off."

"Well," she croaked before clearing her throat and trying again. "I've been working hard."

"Not too hard, I hope. You need to remember to sleep and eat."

Persephone let out a brittle chuckle. "You should take your own advice. I learned my business habits from you."

"I want to apologize." It was suddenly out of his mouth and she looked taken aback.

He might not be on his knees anymore but hell, he realized only now that this was what he'd come here to say. This and more, but it had to begin here. He had so much to atone for where his wife was concerned.

"I need to ask forgiveness for the violence at the restaurant."

Her eyebrow raised, maybe at the bare description of the shooting that had blown out the windows and terrorized at least a dozen guests, killing three and wounding another handful.

"I never thought Ajax would be so bold. I underestimated him and put you in a dangerous position. I'm sorry."

"It wasn't your fault." Her eyebrows were drawn together. "But, if it makes you feel better, I forgive you. I never thought you were to blame."

"Then I apologize for leaving you alone at the Estate the next day."

She looked down at the fabric pooling around her feet. "It's alright. You would've stayed if you could've." She took a deep breath. "I accept your apology."

Did she? Did she really?

He still didn't know how Ajax had gotten to her the night everything had gone to shit, but in the end it didn't matter. The responsibility was Hades's. If he hadn't left her alone, she never would've been taken. She was his wife and his business was never meant to touch her.

He wouldn't say more on the subject, though. He would never put her in that position again. He would protect her and keep her safe. Something he could only do when she was by his side where she belonged.

"Good." He couldn't help looking her up and down again in admiration. "You look beautiful."

"So do you," she said, and Hades grinned outright. "Hades—"

"Persephone, we need to talk things out. I've given you time."

"Almost two months," she said softly.

"Have you been keeping track? Counting the days?"

"No," she lied. He didn't need her words, just her expression, to know the truth.

Their gaze locked. She looked both a little lost and a little like she hoped she'd been finally found. So much was said, and unsaid, in one simple look. She was his and she always would be.

"I've given you space, as you requested," Hades said again.

Persephone crossed her arms. Almost as soon as she made the

move, she dropped her arms again as if aware of her every vulnerable gesture. "You admitted to getting my friend to spy on me. And I'm sure you've had your men trail me."

"Or I could've bugged your apartment."

"You didn't. Did you?" Then her brows came together angrily. "The flowers."

Hades rolled his eyes. "Persephone, I was kidding. I didn't bug the apartment. Have the programmer check."

Persephone glared at him, clearly unamused.

"Listen." He ran his hand through his hair. This wasn't going how he'd envisioned. He wanted to be straight with her for once. No games. No bullshit. "I want to talk to you. To get everything out in the open."

"Everything?"

He thought about it. "Okay, no, not everything. You know some of my secrets are better off kept. It's not just about me, it's about my business—"

"Your business is the thing that's keeping us apart."

"Is that why you left?"

She clammed up, shaking her head and looking down again, hiding her eyes from him.

He took a step forward. She stepped back automatically and he stopped in his tracks. "Tell me why you ran. Talk to me." It was infuriating not knowing what was going on in her head.

"Still giving orders." She shook her head but didn't look at him.

"I remember you liking when I gave orders."

When she didn't take the bait, he sighed. "What are you afraid of?"

The silence rose again between them.

"Is it Ajax? Because he's gone."

"Gods." She turned her back to him, shoulders suddenly tense.

"I know you felt threatened." If Hades could kill Ajax all over again, he would. And he'd draw it out this time. "But I can keep you safe."

Persephone stared across the garden. The wind whipped the tops of the trees; the leaves shivered below them. She leaned forward onto the stone balustrade and Hades couldn't read her body language. He didn't like it.

He came and leaned on the railing next to her. "When Ajax called and said he had you, nothing else mattered anymore. You mean so much. You know that, right? You know you're everything to me."

Her eyes closed like his words pained her.

His arm brushed hers and she flinched away. Hades pulled back, chest cinching tight.

"Don't ever be afraid of me, Persephone." His voice came out more rough than he intended, but hell. "I'd never hurt you. I was angry, but mostly I was worried about you. I tried so hard to keep the ugliness of my world far away from you."

"You failed," she choked out, finally looking at him and there was such pain in her eyes. It sliced him to the bone.

"I'm sorry. I never wanted to put you in the middle of things. And when Ajax took you..." He broke off, shaking his head, not able to continue. He still didn't know everything she'd endured that day. She'd come to him covered in blood.

His hands shook, thinking about it. Ajax had done something to her, made her witness something—not only brought her into their world but drenched her in it. And of course she'd run. If Hades were any kind of good man, he'd send her away instead of luring her back.

"It's ok," Persephone whispered. The wind blew hard enough that even though she wrapped her arms around herself, chill bumps were still visible on her skin.

Hades frowned. So much for taking care of her. "Let's go back in. Get you out of the cold."

She made a noise that could be interpreted as negative, so he took off his coat and came towards her instead. At the last minute, she turned around and let him place it on her shoulders.

"I swear to you, Persephone, I'm not a monster." Standing so close and breathing in her familiar scent, he could almost believe it.

He'd done great and terrible things to ensure the stability of his city and they'd rightly named him King of the Underworld. He'd soullessly embodied the title for years, holding the wicked in his iron grip so the weak didn't suffer unduly. It was purpose enough, he'd told himself. It was atonement for failing to protect his sister all those years ago.

But Persephone had burst into his black and white world in an explosion of vibrant color. She'd thawed the ice in his heart and he couldn't go back. Not once he knew what it was like to love her and feel her love in return.

He felt her body tremble at his closeness. "Come back to me," he breathed in the shell of her ear.

When she shook her head, he could feel her hair catch on the rough stubble of his chin.

"You're not safe on your own. Without me."

"People don't think I'm safe with you." She squeezed her eyes shut like if she closed them long enough, he'd go away.

Instead, he turned her gently towards him, and tipped her face to his.

"Who?"

"My friends," she replied, a little breathless.

"Athena Jandali?" Hades gritted out. He'd looked into both her roommates. "Or the stripper? Your so-called friends who left you with Ajax? I don't need to tell you what I think of their judgment."

Persephone stiffened. He felt it, and his hands fell away.

"I want you back. I need you close to me, where I know I can keep you safe. I know we can work things out, if we just talk—"

She whirled to face him. "This is why I left, Hades. You try to control me. You can't let me be."

"I haven't called or spoken to you in months."

"And you corner me and ask—no—*tell* me to come back to you. I left because I'd had enough of that. You can't control me."

She wrenched off the suit jacket and thrust it back at him. When he didn't take it, she spun around and draped it over the parapet before leaning against the cool stone again. She gazed into the garden, stubbornly angling her body away from him.

Pushing her more tonight wasn't going to get him anywhere. But she needed to know he wasn't giving up. Not even remotely. She'd given him a taste of paradise, him who'd lived so long in hell. He wouldn't live without her. He couldn't.

"You can't run forever," he said finally. "We'll talk again in a few days." Before she could say anything else to contradict him, he turned on his heel and went back through the double doors into the mansion.

He'd allow her the illusion of choice for a little while longer.

57

The party was over; the last guest had gone home along with most of the staff. Persephone sat in a sea of blue green feathers, packing the decorations away into their proper boxes and trying not to think about Hades. She felt buzzed, exhaustion pushing her to the point where she didn't feel tired anymore. Sparring with Hades hadn't helped.

It wasn't only him, though. Ever since that night, she hadn't been sleeping. Work wore her down enough she'd been able to get a few hours of sleep sometimes; today she'd gotten two hours in as a midday nap before coming back to attend the party and she considered that a win.

Hermes strolled up, hands in pockets, a leather satchel over one shoulder. Like her, he'd changed out of his formal clothes.

"Still cleaning up?" He smiled down at her, watching her wrap the feathers in tissue paper.

"Trying to get as much packed for the movers tomorrow." She looked up at him, trying to gauge his mood. Standing there, hair mussed and deep circles under his eyes, he looked like a hardworking spa owner, not a devilish flirt.

"You mean today. It's almost dawn."

She nodded.

"I'm surprised you're not scrubbing the floor, Cinderella." Hermes jerked his head to indicate the spot where Aphrodite had given an impromptu performance earlier. Then his eyes got a little glossy. "Your friend is really something."

Persephone smiled at him. "Yes, she most definitely is. Don't worry, my staff cleaned the floor. If the hosts complain, my company will pay for the damages."

"It'll be fine, Persephone." Hermes squatted down near her, putting his satchel to the side.

She smirked at him. "Nice purse."

"Thanks. It's not a purse though, too manly."

"Right. It's a man purse. A murse." She stopped and scrubbed a hand over her face as a wave of sleepiness hit her.

"When was the last time you slept?"

"I got a few hours earlier today." Persephone closed the box she was working on and started filling the next one. Hermes scooted closer to help.

"And before that? Are you getting enough rest?"

"I'm sleeping. At least a few hours a night. Usually."

"Insomnia is a symptom of another condition. Probably mental."

"It's definitely mental. I've been getting these crazy dreams." Persephone tried to laugh it off but the sound came out pathetic.

"You going to go see someone about it?"

"Maybe." By which she meant no.

Hermes sighed. He lifted a peacock feather and stroked down it's spine with a long finger before Persephone reached over and plucked it away.

"I'm still mad at you." She pointed at him with the feather. "You colluded with the enemy."

Hermes leveled her with his gaze. "Your husband is not your enemy. He only wanted to see you." He grabbed at the feather and Persephone danced the frond away. "It was long overdue. You two talk things out?"

"Not really. We're supposed to talk in a few days." Persephone lay the feather down and folded it in tissue paper.

"Well, that's progress, I guess." Hermes crossed his legs and settled down on the floor facing her. "What did you two do up there, anyway?" He waggled his thick eyebrows at her.

"Stop it, or I'll beat you with your murse," she threatened. "We just talked. Why, were you hoping we went somewhere and he made wild, wild love to me?"

"Yes, exactly."

"Well, all the bedroom doors were locked. Which reminds me. Who owns this place?"

"This old palace?" Hermes shrugged. "Belongs to my family."

Persephone's mouth dropped open, looking across the acre of finely polished wood squares leading to the plush red and gold staircase. "Are you kidding me?"

"This, my lady, is the original Merche family home." He raised his hand and swiped it as if to dismiss the vast ballroom.

"Merche? Like the company?" She mentally scrolled through the last things she'd read about the telecom company and the family that still controlled it. "As in Louis Merche? The head of the telecom company by the same name." Her eyes widened as she realized something. "Full name Louis Hermes Merche."

"The fourth." Hermes cocked his head at her. "At your service."

"Oh my gods. You're like—"

"One of the richest families in the world? Pretty much. At least, until the antitrust trials broke the monopoly. But now Merche Ltd. is split into so many companies, you can be sure my family has private controlling interest in all of them. No one really knows how wealthy my family is."

"I can't believe..." she stuttered. "You're wealthy. I mean, really, really wealthy."

"Not me," Hermes corrected. "My family. I've been disowned. The only reason I was able to get this place for the night is through my cousin. If my father found out who this party was really for...well, the only reason he wouldn't kill me is because, to him, I may as well already be dead."

"What? Why?"

"My father didn't like my choice of prom date." Hermes lay back a little, leaning on one arm still facing her. "Papa thought I should date a nice white girl who came from a wealthy family. My mother bought a corsage for me to pin on her dress."

"What happened?"

Hermes smiled ruefully. "My date was white, and came from a wealthy family. But he brought me a corsage, not the other way around."

"Your date was a boy."

"Yep. Papa didn't like confirmation that his only son is gay. Well, bi, to be more specific." He picked up another feather. "Not that my father uses either of those terms."

"Hermes, I'm so sorry."

"I came home that night and my mother was crying. But she and the servants wouldn't let me in the door." His head sagged a bit; his brow furrowed as he studied the feather.

Persephone waited quietly, her hands in her lap.

"I spent the night with my date, hiding out in his room. A very different prom night than I had hoped for. He let me stay for a week at his place and then couldn't smuggle me past his parents anymore. So, I was homeless."

Persephone sucked in a breath, feeling pain all through her. "Homeless? In high school?"

Hermes nodded, his black hair wafting over his face.

"How old were you?"

"Sixteen."

She stared in horror, imagining the beautiful young man alone on the streets. "I'm so sorry."

Hermes lifted his head, his eyes meeting hers. "I'm not. If I hadn't gotten out, I never would've gotten on my feet. Would've never gotten double M or Fortune off the ground. I would be someone else."

"And your family?"

"What about them?" He blew out a breath and his silky black hair wafted away from his forehead. "You want to feel sorry for someone, feel sorry for them. They threw away something good. They missed out. And they don't know the best thing about life."

"What's that?"

"It's never wrong to love," he whispered. He shifted, coming to his knees across from her, taking her hands. She let him; it was a rare moment when he seemed his full twenty-seven years. "Let me tell you something about your husband. I lived for two years on the kindness of strangers, and as soon as I was old enough, I started a business."

She couldn't tear her eyes away from his. "Your salon. Metamorphoses."

"I rented a small place and cut hair for ten hours a day. I'd just hired my first employee when some thugs came by and shook us down. That's when I first heard of Mr. Ubeli. I went to him for protection."

Hermes shifted back, letting her hands go after a small squeeze. "I'll never forget the first time I met him. I'd heard of all the things he'd done: restoring his father's restaurants, building his own empire. He seemed so powerful for someone barely thirty." Hermes looked out over the ballroom as if seeing the moment unfold again before his eyes.

"He's amazing," Persephone agreed quietly.

"Yes." Hermes rubbed his face with his long fingers. "I wanted more than anything to be him. He gave me protection, and for some reason he asked me what I wanted to do. I told him my vision of the spa, and, after a year of working together, he came and told me he'd be a silent partner. And we've been in business together ever since."

She sat silent for a moment. "Thank you for sharing."

Hermes's black eyes were intense. "Your husband is a good man. Hades plays by his own rules, but he's loyal, especially to those he's sworn to protect. When someone puts their trust in him, he'd rather die than break it. His word is his bond."

Reaching out, he took her hand and gripped it. "Talk to him, Persephone. He deserves at least that much. And so do you."

She nodded, swallowing hard.

"Alright." Hermes dropped the serious expression, and his features relaxed into the playful flirtiness she was used to. "Let's get you home. I'll give you a ride."

"What about the movers?" Persephone looked around at the pile of feathers still left to pack away.

"I'll take care of things tomorrow. I think I want to keep some of these feathers—take them home. My housemate loves peacock colors. Come on." He helped her up, and rummaged in his satchel, drawing out a small plastic baggie that held five white pills. "Here."

"What's this?" She eyed the baggie but didn't take it.

"Crack," he said and laughed at her expression. "I'm kidding. They're sleeping pills. Completely harmless. Come on, Persephone, they're barely over the counter," he insisted when she still hesitated. "You need to sleep. Take one when you really, really need it."

"Fine." She took the bag and followed him to a small side door. He paused in the exit, smiling down at her.

"Trust me Persephone...you did a fantastic job tonight. Your business is coming together. Model placement, party planning, image consulting—Perceptions is going to be hot."

Persephone laughed. "I need to settle into one niche."

"That'll come. You keep working hard and let me know what you need. I'm glad to help, like Hades helped me." The look in his eye was fond, like an older brother's.

She grinned in answer, but let her smile drop the moment he turned away. Her mind was still churning with the words he'd spoken earlier.

Hades plays by his own rules, but he's loyal, especially to those he's sworn to protect. When someone puts their trust in him, he'd rather die than break it. His word is his bond.

Her heart squeezed painfully. Hades valued trust and loyalty above everything else. So what would he do once he realized she had betrayed him?

58

Dawn was breaking by the time Hermes dropped Persephone off at Athena's apartment. She wasn't tired anymore, but wired and on edge. On one hand, her head was spinning with thoughts of the party's success, her new business, and finally moving into her own apartment. On the other, the future held some hard conversations with her husband. Anxiety and elation flooded her with adrenaline.

Pushing into Athena's apartment, Persephone walked into a gale of laughter. Athena, black hair hanging wet around her face, sat on the kitchen counter. Aphrodite was squeezed beside her in the tiny space, holding up the long black tamper for her serious commercial-grade blender. Despite being at the party only a few hours ago, the two women looked energetic and well-rested, both wearing comfy, casual clothes. Persephone tried not to resent them.

"Hey guys." Persephone let her purse and bag fall to the oak floor, and started to pull off her boots. "What are you doing?"

"Making breakfast," Aphrodite said in her light yet sultry voice. Persephone and Athena sat around once discussing their sexy roommate, wondering if her voice was really that high or if she was putting it on. After six weeks, they figured it really was her voice.

"She says it's chocolate pudding," Athena said, "but don't believe her. She's a lying liar who lies."

Aphrodite stuck the black tamper back into the blender's top and turned on the noisy thing.

"Geez, Aphrodite, you might want to wait until people are awake," Athena shouted over the noise.

Aphrodite stopped the blender. "What time is it?"

"It's like six a.m. Did you guys just wake up?" Persephone dropped her bag. For two months, she and Aphrodite had been staying with Athena in the programmer's miniscule loft. After all the trouble with her former boss, Ajax, Aphrodite was laying low, working her escort business, and going to movie auditions. The apartment was a tight fit for three people, but they made it work.

"I just woke up. Somebody forgot their keys again." Athena rolled her eyes at Aphrodite.

Aphrodite shrugged and smiled a million dollar smile. "I put them somewhere safe; I just don't remember where."

"You're lucky you're cute and can get away with this crap. Did you check one of your client's bedrooms?" Athena snarked. "Or Max Mars's place? I saw how he singled you out tonight."

Aphrodite shook her head, winking at Persephone. Last week Aphrodite had cut her hair and now she had big silky brown curls around her face. With her flawless caramel skin and hourglass figure, she looked as glamorous in jeans and a t-shirt as she did in a ball gown.

In the aftermath of their ordeal, the three of them had bonded. Aphrodite and Persephone needed somewhere safe to lay low, and Athena had offered the apartment for as long as they needed it. Aphrodite took over the cooking, Persephone cleaned, and Athena bitched constantly even though it was apparent she enjoyed having her friends around.

Because of the long hours they all worked, they could go days without seeing each other for more than a few minutes, which probably made the arrangement work so well.

Persephone had never made close friends so easily, but she

needed them. And she got the feeling they felt the same way. It had been the first time in her life Persephone had been truly on her own and free, and the two of them had kept it from being terrifying or lonely.

"What are you making?" Persephone moved past the large couch and leather chair into the kitchen, which took all of ten steps. A tiny bathroom and bedroom the size of a closet were to the left of the living room and entrance. Athena had moved her computer lab to her office, otherwise there would have been no room to move.

"Chocolate pudding."

"It isn't chocolate pudding, it's sacrilege," Athena muttered.

"It's raw vegan chocolate pudding," Aphrodite explained. "Raw coconut butter, stevia, raw cocoa powder and an avocado. Sugar free, dairy free, gluten free—"

"Flavor free," Athena put in.

Aphrodite stuck her tongue out at her black-haired housemate.

"Interesting," Persephone offered neutrally.

Aphrodite offered the spatula. "Taste. It's good."

Persephone did as ordered, and to her surprise it wasn't bad. "Chocolatey," she said.

"Ha!" Aphrodite looked triumphantly in Athena's direction.

"Don't let the devil woman fool you," Athena said, then slid off the counter. "Alright, kids, I got to get to the office and see if Pig is still working." Pig was another tech genius who co-founded Aurum with Athena and no, Persephone had no idea how he'd gotten the name. "We've been pulling these crazy all-nighters lately. Last time I left him alone he fell asleep on his laptop keyboard and his drool short-circuited the network."

"Want to get coffee first?" Aphrodite was licking chocolate off her fingers.

"Didn't you just get home?" Athena asked.

"I went to bed right after I left the party."

"But did you sleep?" Athena narrowed her eyes.

"A little," Aphrodite mouth curved into a private smile.

"Ooh, was it good? Was his dick really big?"

"Like the Empire state building," Aphrodite mock whispered. "Unfortunately he has an ego to match."

"Wait, is this Max Mars you're talking about?" Athena leaned in.

"A lady doesn't kiss and tell."

"Oh, yes, a lady does. Coffee and gossip, now." Athena jumped off the counter top and ran to put on her boots.

"Let me change." Aphrodite finished putting the last of her concoction away and headed for the bedroom.

"You coming?" Athena asked Persephone.

Persephone shrugged. Watching her roommates banter had given her a little burst of energy. "Might as well. I'm not tired right now."

Athena frowned. "Still not sleeping?"

"I'm going to the spa in a few hours," Aphrodite said as she stepped out of the bedroom, wearing a little black dress that fit her curves like a dream. "I'll sleep there. You could come with me, if you want. Get a massage. That might relax you enough to get some shut-eye."

Anything sounded better than lying in bed for endless hours replaying every second of her encounter with Hades. Persephone nodded.

AT THE COFFEE SHOP, Athena pestered Aphrodite for details of her love life while they all waited in line. Letting her friends bicker, Persephone looked over the stacks of mugs and bags of coffee beans for sale, and unwittingly, her mind wandered back to last night.

Hades had looked so good. In their time apart, she'd tried to tell herself that she'd exaggerated his effect on her. She told herself they *weren't* meant for each other. That her body *didn't* light up with recognition of its perfect mate every time he was near.

You're a lying liar who lies.

"Hello, Earth to Persephone." Athena waved a hand in her face and Persephone jerked her head up. It was her turn to give her order. Once she gave it, Athena pushed her gently toward Aphrodite.

"Go grab the couch," Athena ordered. "Persephone looks dead on her feet."

"Come on, honey." Aphrodite took her hand and led her to the back of the coffee shop. Every man's head in the shop turned to watch them go.

They all settled onto the couch and Aphrodite looked Persephone directly in the eye. "Talk to me. Why aren't you sleeping?"

"Insomnia, I guess." Persephone sagged back onto the couch cushions. "I don't know, I lay awake for hours. And when I do sleep..." She trailed off, shivering at the thought of her last few nightmares—the impression of darkness and blood, always so much blood, and the horrible feeling of responsibility and guilt that lingered long after she woke up.

"Nightmares?"

Persephone swallowed. "The worst."

"I've been having them, too." Aphrodite reached out and took her hand.

Persephone stared. "You have?"

"Oh yes. The one where there's something awful chasing you and you're scared but can't get away. I've had it a few times since Ajax took me." She leaned forward and squeezed Persephone's hand, her lovely face serious. "Because the scary thing really did happen, and my mind needs to process it. So I get the dreams."

"What do you do about them?"

"Let them come. Allow yourself to feel scared and to process what happened. The dreams help us sweat it out. If that's what my mind and body need, I'm okay with that." She shrugged. "Anyway, the most important thing is it's over now. He can't get to us anymore. No one's seen him since."

Persephone tried not to flinch. No one had seen him because he was dead. She remembered the nightmare scene on the dark lawn of the Estate all too well. Her husband raising his arm and bashing Ajax's head in, over and over and over again.

Her memory wasn't a dream. That was real.

I'm not the monster, Hades had said.

Your husband is a good man, Hermes told her.

"You're going to be ok, chica." Aphrodite's smile was warm.

"One tea, one latte, and my five-shot espresso." Athena set the drinks down and plopped down between her two friends. "Scoot over, you guys. So, Persephone how'd the rest of the party go?"

Persephone sat back and tried to smile. Her memories were her burden alone. "Fine. I mean, I got no complaints." Persephone uncovered her tea to let it cool.

Athena eyed her over the latte. "Did you tell that husband of yours to fuck off?"

"Athena!" Persephone gasped.

Aphrodite leaned in. "Wait, Hades was there?"

"Hermes invited him and didn't tell Persephone. Get this: Ubeli walks in all gangster and he practically threw her over his shoulder and carried her upstairs. Totally hot."

"Oh my gods," Aphrodite said.

"It didn't go that way," Persephone broke in.

"You telling me after two months he didn't get you alone and give you the business? He made his thugs wait at the bottom of the stairs and everything. And when he came back he looked smug..."

"Athena." Persephone had her hand over her face.

"Looked to me like Mr. Big Mob Boss Man got some. Just sayin'."

"Okay, first of all," Persephone started, so loud half the café would be able to hear her. She lowered her voice. "You can't talk about Hades like that."

"What's he going to do? Waste me?" Athena gave a sassy little head shake. Obviously she saw the whole thing as a big joke. "If he wanted to do that, he could've done it the first week when he nearly gave me a heart attack standing right outside the apartment when I opened the door."

"What?" Persephone all but shrieked. The entire coffee shop turned to look their way but Persephone didn't care. Athena glared at them until they looked away again.

"Yeah, bitch. Like, the second day you were there laying low."

"He came to the apartment?" Persephone asked.

"Yeah, he's the one who dropped off your clothes. I told him you were out and didn't want to see him anyway. He actually smiled and said that you were lucky to have such loyal friends. He gave me his information in case something happened and I needed to contact him."

Persephone's mouth hung open but she couldn't speak. She could feel anger creeping up her neck, flushing her skin red. She'd say he couldn't help himself but that was no excuse.

"Why didn't you tell her?" Aphrodite asked for her.

"Shit, girl, you said you needed to deal, I let you deal. You didn't want to talk about him so I never brought it up." Athena shrugged and looked at Aphrodite, who'd raised a brow. "What?"

"Nothing. I can't believe you kept a secret for that long, that's all. I didn't know that was possible for you."

"Just because I want to know everything doesn't mean I can't shut up." Athena went back to sipping her espresso.

"Breathe, Persephone." Aphrodite reached behind Athena to touch Persephone's shoulder. "It's going to be alright."

"No, it's not. I'm going to kill him. He said he gave me space. He lied to me."

"About time you wanted to do something about Ubeli," said Athena. "Hermes and I are ready to lock you in a room with him, and see who comes out alive. Or pregnant."

Persephone smacked Athena's arm hard enough for her drink to slosh a bit. "That's it, I'm not speaking to either of you anymore."

"Oooh, silent treatment. So mean," Athena said as she got up and moved to the other side of Aphrodite, away from Persephone. "That's going to be difficult, seeing as we're helping you move in a few days."

"You got the apartment?" Aphrodite chirped, obviously trying to change the subject.

"She did. She's leaving us," Athena answered for Persephone. "And her business is taking off. My little bird is leaving the nest!"

"Oh hush, Athena," Persephone said.

"I thought you weren't talking to me."

"I tried. I can't be mean for long."

Athena looked knowingly at Aphrodite. "Fifty bucks says next time she and Hades meet, she winds up pregnant."

Aphrodite pursed her red lips and ignored their blunt friend. She turned to Persephone. "I'm going to miss you."

"Me too." Persephone hugged her.

"All right, bitches, enough of this mushy stuff or you're gonna ruin my makeup." Aphrodite swiped at her eyes and smiled a dazzling smile. "Who's ready for the spa?"

59

"Come in," Hades barked after a knock at his office door.

Charon, his second in command, peeked his head in. "You called, boss?"

"Get in here."

Charon lumbered his large body through the door and shut it behind him. He stood with his arms behind his back until Hades bit out in frustration, "For fucks sake, sit down. Don't just stand there looming over my desk like the damned grim reaper."

Charon didn't say anything. He merely sat, one eyebrow raised the slightest bit. Hades wasn't in the mood for his silent judgment. Nothing was going his way lately and he was sick of it. He ran a tight ship. But there were too many elements that were out of his control and it was threatening everything he'd ever worked for.

"We've got to get that shipment back. I can't believe Zeus Sturm of all people has finally grown a set after all these years. But if he thinks getting re-elected mayor suddenly means he's above the laws of the Underworld, he's got another think coming."

"We don't know what he's thinking," Charon finally commented. "We can't get a meeting with him."

Another frustrating fact. Zeus's security kept the man all but sequestered. It had been two months, but since he'd secured re-election, he'd only been to three public venues—a gala, a play, and a restaurant opening—none of which Hades had been able to corner him at to get alone time so he could ask where the *hell* his shipment was.

The police had seized the huge shipment at the docks two months ago after tailing that rat bastard Ajax there, but Zeus had promised Hades he'd return the shipment within a week. But then a week had gone by. Then two. Then three. And no word from Zeus.

No shipment got to New Olympus that didn't come through Poseidon. He owned the seas. At first Poseidon had been understanding and hadn't demanded payment for the lost shipment, once it became apparent it was going to stay in police custody. Things like this happened and the Ubeli's have been long and loyal customers.

But then suddenly Poseidon had pulled a one-eighty and said he wouldn't sell any more product to Hades until he paid for the first shipment after all.

Hades didn't know why suddenly everybody thought they could fuck him up the ass, but it was high time he reminded them exactly why people used to be afraid to even say his name out loud.

"It's time to put the fear of the gods into Zeus and anybody else who thinks they can take advantage of me," Hades growled through clenched teeth. "I run this city. No one else."

Charon didn't say anything for a long moment. And when he did, Hades wished he hadn't, because it only made him want to deck his longtime friend: "Did you talk to her?"

Hades glowered at him. It would have silenced any lesser man. But Charon only sat forward.

"Did you apologize? I know it's not in your nature but women like to hear the words—"

"Of course I apologized," Hades cut him off irritably. "She's not ready to hear it. But she will be. I'll make sure of it. Anyway, I'm not having this conversation with you."

Charon frowned. "You can't go in and start ordering her around. You have to be delicate—"

"I'm not taking dating advice from a man who only sleeps with prostitutes."

Charon stood up, turned his back and headed for the door. Shit.

"Wait," Hades called. Charon paused, hand on the doorknob. "I'm sorry. That was uncalled for."

Charon inclined his head once but didn't turn to look back at Hades. "She's the best thing that's ever happened to you."

"Don't you think I know that?" Hades all but shouted. And then, because Charon was the one person Hades could genuinely call a friend and so he deserved it, Hades gave him more, in a quiet, tempered tone. "I'm doing everything I can to get her back. Everything and anything. None of it means anything without her."

Charon gave another simple nod and then exited through the door. It closed softly behind him.

Hades looked at his laptop but soon pushed back from his desk in frustration. He wasn't going to get any more work done tonight.

He paused for a moment, though, looking towards the door, remembering the first time he'd seen Persephone up close. She'd pushed through that very door frantically and shut it again, wet and disheveled, on the run and thinking she'd found a safe place in his office.

Even then he'd been enchanted by her beauty and sweetness. She'd fallen asleep in that chair right there, across the desk from him. He'd lingered longer than he should have, watching her. His beautiful enemy. And then, instead of destroying her like he'd meant to, he'd gone and fallen in love with her. And she'd changed everything.

Life without her was unfeasible. Untenable. He wouldn't go back. He was only getting through each day on the promise to himself that she'd soon be back in his arms. In his bed. Forever.

But standing here mooning like a lovesick teenager was beneath him. So he grabbed his jacket and called his driver to bring the car around front.

He busied himself with emails and phone calls on his way home. It wasn't his normal way, but now riding in cars listening to music only reminded him of when he'd done so with her beside him. So he filled the void with distraction.

At least until he opened the door to his silent penthouse. The place had never felt more empty. He took several echoing steps inside the marble foyer, letting the door shut behind him.

Everywhere he looked, he saw her ghost. In the kitchen cutting vegetables for the salads she was always trying to get him to eat. Lounging in the sunken living area, curled up like a cat on the plush sofa while she read a book.

She'd get so lost in what she was reading, she wouldn't ever noticed him at the edge of the room so he could drink in his fill of her. The delicate curve of her neck. Her plump, pillowy lips and the way the top one was ever so slightly fuller than the bottom. That lip of hers drove him mad, the way she'd bite and worry at it when she was thinking about something. He grew stiff just remembering it.

He frowned and dropped his suitcase by the door. He needed a fucking drink.

But instead of going to the bar at the far end of the room, he found his feet heading towards his bedroom. Because no matter how he tried, he couldn't rid himself of thoughts of her. And she'd never been more present than when she'd given herself to him completely in his bedroom.

He pushed open the door slowly intending to linger in the memories.

But then he threw it open with a bang. "What the *fuck*?"

He pulled out his gun from the holster beneath his jacket and swung around, looking for intruders. After confirming the bedroom and ensuite were clear, he closed the door and called Charon.

"Yes, boss?"

"Security team to the penthouse. Now."

"Sending them." Charon was immediately at attention. "What's happening?"

"Intruders. They may or may not be still on premises," Hades said, keeping his voice low.

"Team is on their way. What tipped you off? Did they ransack the place?"

Hades looked at his bed again and the gruesome tableau that had been laid out there. Three bloody, severed dog heads were arranged as if all belonging to a three-headed dog, a likely reference to Cerberus, guard-dog to the Underworld.

"Looks like the Titans have finally decided to respond to our message from a couple months ago. Either that or Poseidon has decided to up the stakes."

60

Persephone sat in the balcony seat while Orpheus's voice rang out in the hall. It was beautiful. Pure. Perfect. At the same time, everything was wrong. So wrong.

She clutched the railing, shaking her head. No, she had to stop it. She looked around frantically for someone to help but there was no one.

"If you die before I wake," Orpheus sang, "I'll give my soul; it's theirs to take—"

"No!" Persephone screamed but her voice made no sound even as a monstrous darkness rose behind Orpheus. "Run!"

Eurydice stumbled out from the other side of the stage, looking dazed and confused. She was clutching her stomach and when she brought her hands away, they were covered in blood.

"Eurydice," Orpheus shouted, throwing his guitar to the ground and sprinting towards her.

But the darkness, the monster behind him, it was faster. Persephone screamed as it swallowed him up, a title wave of blood drenching Eurydice as she fell to her knees and—

Persephone sat up in bed, hand flying to her mouth to stifle her scream as sweat poured down her temples and her heart raced.

On the side table, her phone was buzzing insistently. It must have woken her. Thank the Fates. Sometimes she was stuck in the nightmare world for what felt like an eternity.

Persephone wiped her forehead with her forearm and reached for the phone, fumbling for the angry little device.

Missed call...four thirty-two pm. She groaned. She'd gotten only an hour of sleep after getting back from the spa.

Her fingers hit the button to listen to the voicemail.

"Mrs. Ubeli," said a familiar voice, and she started at hearing her married name. "This is Poseidon; Mr. Merche gave me your number. Please call me when you get a chance." He gave his number.

She blinked in confusion for a moment but then remembered her earlier conversation with Hermes.

He'd come in while she and Aphrodite were at Metamorphosis, before they'd gone in to get their massages. "Don't mean to interrupt girl's day out. I wanted to let you know I gave Perceptions a referral. You remember the big black guy in the white tux?"

She remembered the intense stare down between the tall man and her husband. "Poseidon...uh, yes."

"Well, Poseidon called trying to get in touch with you. Persephone, he is raving about how great the party was last night. I sent him to your website but I'll send you his number, too. This is huge! He owns a huge company—I bet he wants you to do something corporate. That's big money right there. I'll help you, of course. We'll get some sub-contractors." Hermes's voice had buzzed with excitement but Persephone had been beyond exhausted at that point. She'd hoped she'd fall asleep during the massage, but no such luck.

Saving the voicemail, she dropped her phone on the bedside table with a groan. How long could a person go without sleep before they went crazy?

Hauling herself out of bed, she went tiredly to the bedroom door to stare at the rest of the apartment. No one was home. Athena would probably work through the night with Pig. Where Athena was a devil, stubborn and driven, Pig—Persephone didn't know his real name—was an angel, sweet and talented. His ideas were cutting edge, Athena had told her once, but he'd give them away if it wasn't for her push to get them patented, designed, and distributed properly. Athena was a fiend when it came to business.

Aphrodite was probably getting a private tour of the studio by her new boy toy, Max Mars.

Meanwhile, Persephone thought, *I'm slowly going mad.* Grabbing a laundry basket, she started picking up the place.

When she went to clean her purse, the baggie of white pills Hermes had given her fell out, and she paused, considering. She hated taking medicine for anything. Even when she was little, her mother would let the fever burn out or feed her chicken soup for a cold. She frowned. Her mom was scarcely a role model, though, considering she was a murderous crime lord. Then Persephone laughed humorously. She had a lot of those in her life.

She pulled out one of the little pills. It weighed heavily in her palm, a fair trade for a night's rest.

After swallowing it with a glass of water, she waited a few minutes, then kept packing for her upcoming move.

She was rummaging around in her suitcase when she heard a clink. Checking the small pockets, she pulled out her wedding rings, the plain white gold band and matching engagement ring, unique with both diamonds and red stones. She slid it on her finger, watching the diamonds and garnets catch the light.

She remembered the night Hades had first put it on her finger. That had been another lifetime. She'd been another woman. A girl, really. She hadn't even known who or what Hades was yet. She'd been so naïve. And if she could go back in time and warn her former self? She flopped back on the couch and stared at the ceiling fan. If she could do it all differently...would she?

A knock at the door startled her out of her thoughts.

She glided across the small apartment and opened it, expecting Hermes or even one of her roommates who'd forgotten their keys. She didn't expect the familiar dark-haired form, with tall, broad shoulders filling the narrow frame.

"Hades," she whispered numbly.

The next second he was on her, his large hands cradling her face with infinite care as his mouth closed over hers. Firm lips pressing, pulling, dominating hers until they parted.

She closed her eyes, her breath leaving her in a rush. What was she doing? She couldn't just let him— Hades's hands caressed her cheeks, her shoulders, her hips, guiding her backwards. And she let him. His scent washed over her.

She clutched his shoulders for balance at first, then harder, her fingers digging in and grabbing him. *Yes.* She missed him. She needed him.

He swung her up and her legs locked around his waist. Then they were in her bedroom. On the bed.

Her hips arched upwards, juddering, begging, as Hades braced his big body over hers. His mouth, his hands, were everywhere. His stubble scraped the inner curve of her breast and she cried out in shock at the abrasive pleasure.

Fabric tore and she kicked free of her ruined sleep shorts. Her hands turned to claws, digging into the solid muscle of her husband's back.

Please, I need—

He reared up, a massive shadow over her. In a moment he'd fill her and all would be well. Everything in the world swirled away. It was only Hades, Hades, *Hades*. She couldn't see his face, but as her body convulsed in painful pleasure, the light silhouetted the curve of his cheek, cruel and confident and everything she'd longed for in the eternity they'd been apart...

Persephone woke up with her body shuddering in the throes of her orgasm. Her hand flew to her naked chest as if she could still her pounding heart.

She looked around in confusion even as she checked the sum of her naked limbs. In the cool bedroom light she couldn't tell whether it was night or day. Hades was nowhere to be seen. Had it been...a *dream*?

What the hell? She pushed her hair back from her face and tentatively felt herself down *there*. No, she hadn't had sex. Sex with Hades, especially after going so long without—she'd definitely feel it afterwards.

She flopped backwards on her pillow. She wasn't sure which was more unsettling, the sex dream or the nightmares.

Her phone chirped at her from an unruly pile of pillows on the floor. 7:56 a.m., the glowing light told her, over twelve hours since she'd taken the sleeping pill. She didn't remember anything—taking off her clothes, climbing into bed—nothing except for the dream.

It *had* been a dream, right? Though she didn't feel sore, it had still felt so *real*.

Blushing hard, she gathered the bedspread around her naked form and peeked out of the bedroom. No one was in the apartment, and there was no way to tell whether or not someone had been there.

Except that the air in the bedroom held the heady smell of sex.

Okay. Enough. Persephone jumped off the bed and ripped off all the sheets, throwing them in a pile for laundry before taking the coldest shower of her life.

61

Gods, she was beautiful. No, it went beyond simple beauty, Hades thought as he stared at his wife sitting in one of her favorite coffee shops. She often came here to work on her laptop. Considering the state of things, Hades had a Shade assigned to her at all times. He didn't care if she found it stifling. Her safety was nonnegotiable.

She looked to be working through her receipts, and each of her movements was so graceful, it was like an unrehearsed dance. Her fingertips glided along the laptop keys and her arms were fluid as she moved receipts from one pile to another. Her intelligent eyes were so focused, she seemed lost to the world. It was like that with everything she did. Even when she only volunteered at an animal shelter, she gave it her all. In friendships, she never held back.

And when she loved, she loved so effusively that being on the receiving end was the most incredible and addictive thing in the world.

Hades was just about to head her way when a young man, maybe college-aged, approached her and put his hand on the chair opposite. "Is this seat taken?" He flashed a smile that Hades wanted to shove down his throat.

"It's mine," Hades growled, covering the distance between them in only a few strides. The little prick turned and stiffened. He took one look up at Hades and showed he had an ounce of brains in his head by taking off without a word.

Hades sat down across from Persephone. A deep sense of relief and rightness washed through him at being so near her again.

"What are you doing here?" she hissed. Her flashing eyes had him smiling. He loved it when she was feisty.

"We need to talk." Hades gave a gesture with his hand. Behind him in the coffee shop, his Shades moved, escorting customers out and even going behind the counter to send the green-aproned baristas into their own storeroom.

"What the—" Persephone watched his men clear the coffee shop and then snapped her gaze back to Hades "I told you I'd call."

"This isn't a social call." His tone went grim as he remembered the not so subtle message that had been left in his bed. No one had been found in the apartment but his men also hadn't discovered how anyone had been able to break in in the first place. The lock hadn't been jimmied and nothing was broken. If they were able to get in like that, why not wait and try to assassinate him? Too many questions without answers. He didn't like it.

"It's business, not pleasure." He tossed a black phone onto her bag. "When you do call me, make sure you use this."

Persephone stared at the burner phone. "Is this really necessary?"

"I'm receiving death threats. Not the usual ones I get, either. These messages are...targeted. Serious. The kind that let me know the people sending them are knowledgeable enough to carry them out."

Her eyes went wide. "Death threats?"

"I'm handling it. But you need to be aware." He nodded toward the phone. "And take precautions."

She stared at him for a moment. Her eyes dropped in the most beautiful submission as she reached for the phone. Hades couldn't deny the triumph roaring through his chest.

"I got it," she murmured as she slid the burner into her purse. "If I call you, I'll use this."

"When," he corrected. If she thought she could retreat now, she was out of her mind. Not after giving that little taste reminding him of how delicious it was when she submitted.

"What?"

"*When* you call me."

She glared at him and he couldn't help his smile. "After this display I may not want to call you."

He genuinely had no idea what she was talking about. "What display?"

"This." She waved her hand around.

"Neutral ground." He shrugged. "I chose a place where you'd feel comfortable."

"Normally people come in and order drinks. But you come in and get your ninjas or whatever to scare off the barista and block the door with your bodyguards to keep out all the customers."

Hades just looked at her. She threw up her hands, her voice rising. "You did a hostile takeover of this coffee shop."

"You understand I'm here on your turf for your sake. But I also need to feel comfortable. My enemies won't hesitate to target me."

"I got that when we got shot up at the restaurant where we were having dinner."

"We're not speaking of that here." Hades's jaw went stiff. If he thought of that day, he'd need to break something.

"I thought you were here to speak to me. This is me talking." She threw open her arms. "I'd hate for you to clear out a coffee shop for nothing."

He bit back a smile. Gods, she was spectacular. She'd grown so much from the naïve ingénue he'd first met. Now she was a firecracker. Bold. Explosive.

He wanted to toss her laptop to the floor and lay her out over the table right here. One thing that had never changed, and Hades hoped never would, was the fact that her every emotion played out on her face.

And like always, he felt his desire reciprocated in the crackling electricity between them. She wanted him as much as he wanted her. So why was she denying it?

He leaned in. "I have to disappear for a while." He registered the surprise on her face but kept going. "Come with me. A week of lying low. We'd be able to talk, see if we can work things out."

Emotions darted one after the other across her face and she sputtered, "What? You can't just...you're asking me to..."

"I have no reason to believe you're in danger. That's why you have a choice. But I would like us to talk. Persephone, I want you back. I want us to be together."

"Hades," she began, and sighed. "I've started a life. I know it sounds stupid. It's only been two months, but..."

She bit her lip in the way that drove him crazy. And she kept talking instead of shutting him out, which was progress. "I've started a business and I think it'll work. Perceptions is more than a model placement service. I want to be an advocate for these young women. I know what this industry can do to them."

"You know predators exist."

She nodded and leaned forward. "I help get these women legitimate jobs. Maybe not the most glamorous or highest paying jobs, yet," she admitted. "But it's starting to come together. Young women come to make it in the big city and get sucked down and destroyed. Perceptions could be a life line."

Of course she would make something like this her life's work. And this was only the beginning, he had no doubt. Her heart had no bounds.

"And now I've got clients lining up," she continued excitedly. "Hermes already gave one of the guests my number; he said the man was so impressed with what I'd done and Hermes told him about my business."

"I'm proud of you."

Her breath caught. She flushed and looked away.

"Which guest?"

She paused and for a moment he thought she wouldn't tell him but she arched an eyebrow. "The big man in the white suit. Poseidon."

What?

"Poseidon is asking about you?" Hades didn't try to hide his fury. That bastard knew the Code. Families were left out of business.

"Um, yeah," Persephone said, sounding less sure of herself. "He met me at the party and got my number from Hermes. He called me for a consultation—"

Hades picked her phone up off the table and started scrolling. He saw Poseidon's number and that he'd left a voicemail. Feeling even more pissed than when he'd found the dog's heads in his bed, he pressed the button to listen to the message.

"Hey!" Persephone cried as he raised the phone to his ear. Frowning, he listened to Poseidon putting on a friendly voice as he asked for a consultation, as Persephone said. Hades swore.

"What are you doing?" she asked as he pressed more buttons. She made a move to reach for it and he halted her with a gesture.

"Blocked him." Hades tossed the phone onto her bag. "If he tries to call again or finds another way, use the burner and contact the emergency number. It comes straight to me or Charon. You remember the emergency number?"

Persephone was still staring open mouthed at her phone. "I can't believe you did that. You blocked my first real client."

"Persephone, run from everything I've said today but understand this—" Hades reached forward and grasped her hand, ensuring that she was looking him in the eye. "You need to stay away from Poseidon. I'll talk to Hermes, let him know the deal."

But Persephone only looked pissed. "Oh, no," she said, shaking her head and pushing her chair back from the table. "You don't get to order me around anymore."

She was cute. He smiled. "Don't I?" But he stood up and sobered, coming around the table. This wasn't something to be taken lightly. "I mean it, Persephone. I'm talking about bad shit."

Persephone jerked her head back in surprise, probably at hearing him swear. He almost never did around her. His father had raised him better than to swear around women. But he had to get it through her head about Poseidon.

Hades moved around the table to where she stood. "He's dangerous."

"I can handle dangerous."

Did she mean that as a challenge?

"Can you, Mrs. Ubeli?" He moved forward.

"Don't call me that."

"No, Persephone? Why not?"

"We're separated right now. I don't know if I want to be Mrs. Ubeli right now."

Hades stepped into her space, only inches between them. Her breathing grew shorter, her bosom rising and falling in response to him.

"If you don't want to be Mrs. Ubeli," he said in a voice dangerously low. "Why are you still wearing your wedding ring?"

She blinked, but before she could tear her eyes away from his gray ones, he took her left hand, and raised it slowly to his lips and kissed her cold fingers, without taking his eyes from hers. The diamonds sparkled between them, the more subtle garnets flashing red.

She tried to snatch her hand back, but he gripped it harder. Her breath caught and she swallowed hard. "I was cleaning last night...I don't remember."

A visible shiver went through her and gods, her response drove him crazy. He wanted her. He wanted her so badly that sometimes he couldn't sleep at night but for the wanting and the memory of her body beside his in the bed.

"I've decided I want a divorce," she whispered, finally taking a step back from him.

He laughed.

"It's not funny."

"All right." He shrugged. "I can grant you a divorce."

She stared, obviously not believing.

"You want a divorce, I'll give it to you."

"Just like that?"

"Whatever you want, on one condition." He held up a finger. "You talk to me, *really* talk. And we try to make it work first."

"Hades..." She lifted a hand to her head like he was making her dizzy.

"Persephone, you're still running. You wanted space, I gave it to you. You want my money? I'll give every cent and work harder for more." He closed the distance she'd put between them.

"What are you doing? Hades." She backed up as he came forward, crowding her into the wall beside the coffee bar. All his Shades had wisely disappeared and taken up an outside perimeter. It was just the two of them in the entire shop.

He stopped her with a finger to her lips. "Whatever you want, I can get it. All I want is you."

"You can't have me." She shook her head but her eyes were full of confusion and, if he wasn't wrong, longing. "I don't want to lose myself in you. You're too...powerful."

"Is that what you want? To be powerful?" The small space between them was magnetic, drawing her closer to him. He hoped his gaze seared her the way hers did him. It was his only saving grace—that the obsession wasn't his alone. As much as she tried to deny it, he knew she felt it too.

"What you didn't understand was that you had the power. All along." He lifted her hand. "Together we could be more." He kissed her palm.

Her breaths grew even shorter and finally she whispered, "I'm afraid of you."

He quirked an eyebrow at her.

"I'm afraid of how you make me feel. I'm afraid of us. You swallow me up." And then she leaned in as if she couldn't stop herself from breathing him in. She halted only an inch away and when she shook her head ever so slightly, their noses brushed.

"My feelings," she murmured, "my attraction to you, they overwhelm me."

He nuzzled his nose against hers. Even this simplest touch felt life-giving. "Isn't that just life? Being afraid and acting anyway?"

She closed her eyes as if to ward him off even as their foreheads touched.

"You can't manipulate me, Hades. Not anymore. Not after everything I've proven to you. Proven to myself."

"Why do you have to prove yourself to me? Who told you that you're not enough?"

She pulled away from him, pain welling up in her eyes.

"There it is," Hades said. "That's why you push me away, even though we have something good. Something amazing. You don't think you deserve it."

Tears spilled, sliding down her cheeks. She was hurting and hurting deeply. Why wouldn't she talk to him?

"Come with me," he tried one last time.

She shook her head and swiped at her cheeks. "I can't."

Hades offered her his handkerchief.

"Thank you." She used the white square of fabric to dry her eyes but didn't look at him.

As much as it killed him and as much as he wanted to throw her over his shoulder, pushing her right now wasn't going to get him anywhere. A little longer. He could give her a little longer.

But he wasn't giving up either. "This isn't over."

"So bossy," she sniffed, and laughed.

"That's right, Mrs. Ubeli." He leaned in and kissed her temple. She closed her eyes, her entire body relaxing into him.

He slid a finger along her jaw and stepped away, breaking her trance.

"My men will be tailing you from now on. Don't try to slip away."

62

For the next couple of weeks, Persephone ran around New Olympus. By day she worked in Athena's office, keeping tabs on the brilliant but hopeless Pig (Saturday morning she found him asleep at his desk, still clutching a Sugar Juice can), wrapping up things with Hermes's party and linking her model clients with gigs. By night she first packed up her stuff for the move and unpacked herself at her new apartment before falling into an exhausted sleep.

She thought constantly of Hades. Their talk at the coffee shop had shaken her. She was alone with her thoughts, too, since all her friends were busy—Athena had headed off to the west coast "to shake down a supplier," her words, and Aphrodite had been offered a role in Max Mars's newest feature film, so she was never around. Hermes was off the table because he was in cahoots with Hades, and Hecate was busy opening a second shelter location downtown.

And what else was there to say, really, even if Persephone did have someone to talk to?

When she'd come to the big city, she'd been running from her abusive mother and the smallness of farmhouse life. The move had been her chance to establish herself. Instead, she'd run straight into

Hades's arms and allowed herself to be absorbed into his already perfectly ordered life. Hades lived in a dangerous world, one that forced him to maintain a high level of control just to survive. It was natural for him to order her the way he liked, too. On some level, she'd even liked him controlling her.

But he'd never truly let her be a part of his world. He wanted to lock her up like a princess in a tower. It didn't work like that, though. Being anywhere in his sphere meant you were swallowed in the darkness too.

And when she tried to help an innocent girl escape it... She shook her head as she unpacked her last box. She'd been fighting forces she didn't understand and had only made everything worse. So much worse.

So she'd run again, to give herself a second chance to order her own life the way she pleased. To live in the light, or try to.

Even though, after the confrontation in the coffee shop, she had the feeling that her reprieve was over, and her husband was going to start taking over her life again.

She couldn't let him. She would have to prove to him how strong she was, even living on her own.

It didn't matter that being near him was the only time she'd felt alive in months. It didn't matter that even now, her hand tingled with the memory of his touch. She ran her fingers over her palm.

All I want is you.

A shudder rocked her body at the memory of the burning intensity of his eyes... Gah! She shoved the box of toiletries away from her and stood up.

What was she doing? She moved out of the bathroom and into the living room of her new loft apartment. A low *woof* greeted her and Cerberus, the huge Great Dane mix puppy she'd adopted from the shelter after getting her apartment, all but bowled her over as he rushed over to meet her.

She laughed and scratched his head, crouching down. "Who's a good boy?"

Another happy woof.

She sighed, looking around her sparsely furnished apartment. She'd gotten most of her furniture off of BuyStuff.com and filled in the rest with thrift store finds. But she needed to get some rugs before it really felt cozy and like a home.

"Wanna go for a walk?"

Woof.

Persephone smiled. "Okay, give me a second. I want to check my bank balance. We'll go by an ATM and stop by the farmer's market on the way home."

She grabbed Cerberus's leash and opened up her laptop on the kitchen table. "Come here, boy," she patted her leg as she sat down and logged into her bank account to make sure her most recent paycheck had hit.

Cerberus trotted towards her and she was busy attaching his leash, so at first she didn't see the balance. And when she glanced over back to the screen, she was sure she'd seen it wrong. But when she choked and dragged the laptop closer, nope, she saw that the huge number *was* her balance, even though it was larger than it ought to have been. Off by two numbers and a comma... She clicked to see more details.

Reading through the deposit history, she found her paycheck, looking pathetic sandwiched between two large sums transferred directly into her account.

From her husband's account.

She shot out of her chair so suddenly that Cerberus barked twice. How dare Hades? She was going to kill him. But a reaction was exactly what he was looking for. She paced back and forth, Cerberus following at her heels. Of course he was, she was holding his leash.

She cringed. "Sorry, boy. Let's go for that walk."

She was still steamed half an hour later when they got back from the park. Especially since there had been two of Hades's men shadowing them the entire time when normally there was only one.

And when she returned to the building, she noticed two more stern-faced men in black waiting outside her apartment. One of them had no neck.

"Really?" she sighed, shoving the keys in the lock.

One of them followed her in. "Mr. Ubeli would like you to stay close to us at all times. If you need to go somewhere, a car will be available for you."

"I don't care what Mr. Ubeli told you. I don't like being tailed. I want to feel normal. And I'm fine taking the bus."

She'd slammed the door in their face.

She fed Cerberus and was getting herself some rice and vegetables when her phone rang. What now? To her surprise, though, she saw it was Aphrodite.

"Hey, what's up?"

"Persephone! I feel like I haven't talked to you in forever. Everything's been so crazy with the movie and Mars. But tomorrow is my first official day on set—and I was hoping for some moral support. I'm allowed to have an assistant. Will you come?"

"Let me check." Persephone checked tomorrow's schedule on her phone. Nothing on the agenda. "Sure thing. I can come."

"Okay, great!" Aphrodite squealed and gave her the details of when and where to meet her in the morning.

Persephone heard a man's voice in the background and Aphrodite giggled. "Okay, I gotta go. Mars is here. But we'll talk tomorrow?"

"See you then." But Persephone had barely gotten the words out before Aphrodite hung up. Persephone shook her head. *Young love.*

Then she laughed at herself. When had she gotten so old and jaded? She'd only recently turned twenty.

It was chilly so she lit a fire in the fireplace. She grabbed her laptop and worked in bed, already feeling it was going to be one of those nights when sleep wouldn't come.

THE FIRE HAD BURNED DOWN, leaving only the moon's cool glow. Persephone kissed down her husband's bare chest, loving how the smooth muscles clenched under her lips. Hades drew her back up and took her mouth while his fingers fucked her, sliding easily in and out of her wetness.

She hovered over him, eyelids fluttering with ecstasy. Hades smiled his shark's grin. And then he took his hand from her and replaced it with his cock, slamming up into her. Her breath caught as she felt herself stretch around him.

"Say my name," Hades whispered.

There was no other choice but to obey. There never had been.

"Hades!" she cried, and shattered.

The orgasm woke her. Persephone was still panting and clenching, her hands fisting the sheets even as her eyes popped open and she came back to consciousness.

Not real. It wasn't real.

She whimpered and clenched her thighs together, feeling terribly, terribly empty. She'd come but she'd never experienced a more unsatisfying climax in her life.

The ghost of Hades was nothing compared to the real thing, no matter how genuine it felt in the dream. She wanted to cry in frustration. Maybe she should buy a vibrator. She rolled her eyes towards the ceiling. She had a feeling that nothing would satisfy her other than the real thing, though.

Ugh! She threw her sheets off and swung her legs out of bed.

At least she had going to see Aphrodite to look forward to today. Persephone could seriously use a distraction.

She dressed in what she hoped was an appropriate backstage outfit—comfortable low-heeled boots, tights, a skirt and a nerdy tee that Athena had given her. She took Cerberus out, immediately irritated when Hades's men shadowed them far closer than normal. And after she brought Cerberus back and fed both him and herself, there was a car waiting when she exited the building.

No Neck stood waiting patiently. "We're happy to take you wherever you need to go today, Mrs. Ubeli."

Normally she would take the bus. Normal people took the bus.

Whatever. If Hades wanted his men to tail her, at least it meant she could provide car service for her friend.

She called Aphrodite. "Don't worry about getting to work. I'll be by to pick you up in fifteen."

They picked up Aphrodite outside Athena's apartment building.

"Persephone, it's amazing," Aphrodite gushed. She was glowing. "Everything's falling into place. Just like I remember it."

"You used to act?"

"Small commercials and a few indie movies. My mom wanted me to be a famous actress."

"She'd be proud."

"Yeah." Aphrodite looked out the window, quieting, her face sad. Feeling a little guilty, Persephone reached out and squeezed her knee. Aphrodite turned, her smile springing back into place. Persephone felt the familiar rush of friendship.

As they approached the movie studio, a guard station slowed them.

"Aphrodite Flores and my friend Persephone." Aphrodite rolled her own window down to show the paperwork. "I have passes for both of us."

"And these men?" The two guards at the station frowned at the two men in black sitting in the front seat.

Aphrodite looked at Persephone, who shrugged.

"I'm sorry," the guard said. "But they'll have to remain here."

"Mrs. Ubeli—" No Neck started but Persephone had already opened her door and was stepping out.

"You heard the man, you can't go further," Persephone sing-songed as she pulled Aphrodite after her. Besides, it was a closed movie set. It wasn't like anyone could get at her here. She and Aphrodite escaped the car and trotted quickly past the gate.

The Shades both opened the door to follow, but the movie set guards started yelling at them to stop. Persephone glanced back. Her bodyguards weren't following, but No Neck had a frustrated look on his face. His phone was already out, and probably speed dialing her husband.

"Still fighting with Hades?" Aphrodite murmured.

"Irreconcilable differences."

Aphrodite lifted an eyebrow as they walked through one warehouse and another, passing people carrying lumber and tools.

"It's great that the set is so close to home and not on the west coast." Persephone saw two men struggling to move a giant ornate staircase on wheels.

'I'll probably end up finishing the film there, but they want some outdoor action scenes with the natural background. And they got a huge tax credit for doing it here."

As they entered the next warehouse, Persephone felt her purse start to vibrate angrily. Probably Hades. No doubt that No Neck had tattled on her. She pulled out the burner phone and silenced it without answering.

People bustled all around them. The craft services table was filled with pastries, fruit trays and coffee. Persephone and Aphrodite helped themselves to hot drinks and wandered out into the activity.

"There he is." Aphrodite nodded towards Max Mars. He was handsome, tall, and well-built, but too...well, *pretty* for Persephone's tastes. He matched Aphrodite perfectly, though. He flashed a smile and headed right for them.

"Hey," he said in his signature sexy voice.

"Hola, Papi." Aphrodite's smile curved her red lips as she went right up to him and hugged him. Holy crap, Aphrodite was hugging one of the biggest movie stars on the planet! He might not be Persephone's type but that didn't mean she wasn't still starstruck.

Mars smiled down at Aphrodite, the suppressed desire obvious between them. Persephone could almost see the sparks flying, their desire for each other was so obvious. But they didn't kiss, just wound one arm around each other's waist, as if posing for a picture of the most perfect couple ever.

"This is my friend, Persephone," Aphrodite said and Max Mars turned his mega-watt smile on her. His infamous dimple popped out, leaving Persephone totally dazzled. She opened her mouth, then closed it, speechless at seeing the beautiful man up close. He had adorably tousled hair and wore a t-shirt that read, "I do all my own stunts."

Still a little dazed by being so close to a celebrity, she said the first thing that popped into her head, "Do you really?" She motioned to the shirt, "Do all your own stunts?"

She expected a facetious answer in response, but instead Max Mars puffed out his already impressive chest. "Yeah," he said his voice deepening a little. "I do all my own stunts. Like, all of them."

Tucked into Max Mar's side, Aphrodite shook her head slightly and mouthed, "No."

Persephone looked back and forth between them, not sure who to believe.

"Alright, I gotta rehearse." Mars looked down at Aphrodite and gave her a squeeze.

"Okay, baby," Aphrodite said almost too softly for anyone else to hear. Persephone looked away; the way the two looked at each other, she wanted to give them privacy. Averting her eyes, she waited until Aphrodite cleared her throat. They both watched Mars leave, a real treat considering the way his pants hugged his perfect backside.

"He's really..."

"Full of himself?" Aphrodite finished. "Yeah. But he's a big star. And one of his upcoming films will probably get him nominated for a Golden Idol."

"I was going to say you guys look great together."

Aphrodite beamed. "Oh we do. Should be great for the press conferences."

"So, wait, are you seeing him or is it a publicity stunt?"

"Both." Aphrodite led her to some seats on the side of the set.

Hours later, Persephone concluded that film sets were incredibly boring. Aphrodite sat upright and totally focused on everything in front of her, as if the camera man moving for the billionth time was the most fascinating thing ever.

Persephone was almost relieved when a production assistant came up to Aphrodite. "Max Mars would like to see you in his trailer."

Persephone took her cue. "You go ahead," she told her friend. "I'm going to catch a ride back to the city. I can come back to pick you up."

"I think I can catch a ride from someone." Aphrodite's smile curved knowingly. "Don't worry about me."

Persephone was walking back off set, wondering if the Shades would be parked somewhere nearby or if she really did need to catch a ride, when a voice called, "Mrs. Ubeli?"

She almost didn't turn, but a car slid up beside her and a man in a suit leaned through the driver side window, smiling. "Persephone?"

Her steps slowed. Was he a Shade? He had spiky blond hair and looked vaguely familiar, but her instincts told her to be cautious.

"Do I know you?" she asked the stranger and he grinned bigger. Something was off. The windows of the car were all tinted. None of Hades's cars were.

She noticed this at the same time the back doors opened and two thugs came at her. "If you come with us quietly, we won't hurt you."

Opening her mouth to scream, Persephone tripped and lost precious seconds she could've used to escape. One of the men jabbed her neck in a gesture almost too quick for her to see, and her scream came out a painful gurgle.

She choked and they took their opportunity to wrestle her into the back seat of the car. Kicking at them, she got in a few blows before one of the men slid next to her and caught her legs. No! She couldn't let them take her. She fought harder than ever.

But the other man came around the car, got in on the other side, and the two of them together subdued her easily. The man with blond spikes watched from the front seat.

By now Persephone had caught her breath, and she screamed. Please, someone hear her! The movie set had been bursting with people. But now all the car windows were closed. And they must have been soundproofed as well as tinted, because her three kidnappers didn't seem upset at her screaming.

They took their time tying her arms behind her back. One wrapped his hands around her throat, cutting off her air until spots swam before her eyes. Her ears were ringing, and she didn't know if she was still screaming or not. All she knew was that she couldn't breathe. Couldn't breathe.

Was this it? Was she going to die right here? *Oh Hades. It wasn't supposed to end this way. I never meant to...*

She kicked out again but weakly. It was no use. Spots danced before her eyes.

Dimly, she heard the driver cursing at the thugs, who growled back.

The world went black.

63

When Persephone came to, her head was lying in one of the men's lap. She started struggling immediately, but her hands and feet were bound. The man hauled her up to sit properly and she looked around. Her heart sank.

They were nowhere near the studio anymore, but driving down a large boulevard lined with abandoned and decrepit shops. She didn't recognize anything. She had no idea where they were. Wherever it was, though, the area seemed largely devoid of human life. She didn't see pedestrians around or anyone who might be able to help her.

The driver's face swam into focus as she blinked and looked around.

"We don't want to hurt you," said the spiky-haired blond man who was driving. "Do as we say and you'll be fine."

Persephone wanted to speak but her throat hurt. She caught a glimpse of herself in the rearview mirror. Her neck already showed bruises. Oh gods, what would these men do to her once they got where they were going? She had to get out of here.

She squirmed in her bonds, jerking her arms and trying to drive an elbow into one of the silent thugs flanking her. He caught it easily and looked down at her, face scary and blank. The pit of acid that was her stomach threatened to rebel.

"Behave, or I send men back to find that little spic hottie and make her pay," Spike Hair warned from upfront.

Persephone froze. She had no idea who these men were or if they had the power to make good on that threat. But the truth was, they'd bound her too well. Even if she could manage to disable one of them, she couldn't run anywhere, not with her ankles tied together like this.

Still, she made a point to glare at the driver in defiance until he turned back to steer the car. The men on either side of her were silent, and beyond light touches on her arms to steady her, at least they kept their hands to themselves.

From the position of the sun, Persephone realized they were heading south and a little east to a place below the city of New Olympus used mainly for shipping. They approached the large docks and Persephone recognized the border to an area of the city called the Styx. They were close to the territory her husband controlled. She felt a surge of hope.

The car went through gates into a fenced area. Beyond the vacant dock and warehouse, Persephone caught glimpses of the ocean. When they parked, she got another warning to stay silent, but now she realized the futility of struggling. They were in a wasteland of deserted commercial buildings by the docks. There would be no one to hear her scream.

Instead, she said to Spike Hair, "You know who I am, so I'm guessing you know who my husband is." Her voice was still raspy from that bastard strangling her earlier. It probably would be for a while.

One of the silent thugs took her arm as a warning, but Spike Hair nodded.

"So you know what he does to people who threaten me." Hades might not be here at the moment but he could still be her shield.

"We're not threatening you. Our boss wants to talk." Spike Hair motioned and they cut the tape binding her ankles and propelled her forward towards a building beyond the parking lot, into a hanger large enough to fit two small planes.

Stiffening her legs, Persephone resisted a little but her captors simply dragged her along. Her boots scraped across the ground. A wild thought gripped her—at least she'd worn the perfect outfit to be kidnapped, durable and comfy. She hoped their boss would approve. A laugh started to bubble out of her and caught in her dry, bruised throat. She wheezed and felt lightheaded.

They got her halfway across before she got her feet back under her, and worked up enough air in her lungs to ask, "Who's your boss?"

Spike Hair simply led the group to the stairs on the side of the building, up into a finished office, and she saw for herself who'd ordered her abduction. She gasped.

Poseidon wore a pinstripe suit, looking equal parts dapper and intimidating, if not more so, with the sun shining through the great windows over his giant form.

"Persephone Ubeli." He smiled, white teeth gleaming in his midnight skin. He came forward, greeting her like an old friend. She would have stopped in her tracks but the thugs prodded her forward. As the giant man came closer his gaze dropped to her collar bone and he sighed. "I said no force."

"She fought." Spike Hair held up her burner phone. "Her link to Ubeli."

"Which can be traced, you fool," Poseidon rumbled. Persephone trembled and felt the fear really start to sink in, even though his anger wasn't directed at her. This man was extremely dangerous. What would he do to her? His bald head jerked as he ordered, "Get rid of it."

She wasn't sure if she felt terror or satisfaction as she watched Spike Hair scurry off. She was alone with the two thugs and her terrifying 'host.'

"Apologies, Mrs. Ubeli. I promise, no more harm will come to you." Said the spider to the fly.

Licking her lips, she found her throat was too dry to answer him. She nodded instead.

"Can I offer you a drink?" Poseidon asked. He walked back to the windows where a few modern looking couches were arranged around a bar area. The ocean spread out behind him. "Something to soothe your throat, perhaps?"

"How about a ride home to my apartment?"

He glanced up at her from the bottle he was pouring, and her heart seized. A grin spread across his face and he laughed. "In due time, my lady."

So that meant he didn't mean to murder her where she stood? He and Hades had looked at each other with such hatred at that party... But if this was a game, her best bet was to start playing along. She couldn't run or fight anyway. If he liked her enough to laugh, maybe he wouldn't kill her. Either way, she shouldn't show fear. A predator would sense that weakness. Hades had taught her that much.

She held her head high as she walked forward and took one of the seats at the bar.

Poseidon poured different things into a glass and handed to her. She sipped politely, glad to taste something like a hot toddy.

"Are you turning this into a restaurant?" She looked around the large empty space with the one corner developed.

"Not a bad concept."

"The view is nice." She stared out at the ocean, wondering if she stood in the far corner and looked to the left, she'd see a way to escape down the built-up shore to the docks near the Styx.

"Ah, yes, my favorite. I was born on a ship, you know. I'm the son of illegal immigrants, who were smuggling themselves into the country. I received dual citizenship because of it. My first lucky break."

He offered his own drink and after a second, she clinked it. A kidnapper and kidnappee, hanging out, drinking like two old friends.

"It's a little late, but I want you to know I was intending to return your calls," she offered. "Your voicemail got deleted from my phone."

The white teeth were back with his grin. He reminded her of a shark. "I understand, lovely lady. I was happy to wait, but forces beyond my control moved up my timeline."

She stared at her drink, willing her hands not to shake. "So, you want a consult?"

"That won't be necessary at this juncture. For now, I simply wish the pleasure of your company. In a few hours, we'll be meeting with your husband, who is eager to trade for your release." His voice was smooth as silk.

Aha. So that's why she was here. She'd been used like this before. Ajax had used her as a hostage to force Hades to reveal the location of the shipping container. And look how that had turned out.

She'd tried to escape the dark but it kept pulling her back under. Maybe this was her penance.

Now she stared at Poseidon, taking in his calm, controlled demeanor. She wanted to ask what was going on, but didn't want to anger him. Did he know what was coming for him? Hades didn't look kindly on people who took what he considered his.

Deciding to keep with her plan to be the best hostage ever, she asked instead, "A few more hours?" She looked out at the sun, biting her lip and thinking of Cerberus whining, all alone in her apartment and wondering where she was.

"Our meeting is at dusk. Is there something you need?"

"My dog is in my apartment all alone...he'll need to be walked. He's a puppy."

"We'll send word that someone needs to take care of him." Poseidon assured her.

Persephone blinked at him, her eyebrows furrowing. "Thank you."

He chuckled. "Your concern is for your dog and not your own life?"

"I can do something about my dog. I can't stop you from doing anything to me." She squeezed her hands between her legs to stop her tremors.

"Practical as well as lovely," Poseidon toasted her and she looked up, surprised, into his dark brown eyes. "Hades is a very lucky man."

Continuing the most surreal conversation she'd had in her life, she blurted, "We're separated. I asked for a divorce."

Poseidon cocked his beautiful head. "Interesting. He made no mention of that in our last conversation."

"I told him I wanted a divorce. I've moved into my own apartment and started a business and everything." She didn't know why she was telling him this.

The door opened and they both watched Spike Hair walk back in. "Meet at six thirty. They agreed to every demand."

Water looked at Persephone smugly. "Despite everything, your husband still cares for you deeply. Two months trying to schedule a meet and no success. Two hours after picking you up and he gives me everything I want."

She sagged in her seat; she couldn't help it. She was Hades's weakness; everyone knew it. She needed to separate from him for his good as well as hers. But now that the criminal world associated them together, would it be too late?

Poseidon had come out from behind the bar to give orders to his men. Persephone turned when she heard her name. "Persephone's dog will need to be walked." He looked back at Persephone and she forced a small smile.

"Why do you want to meet with my husband?" she asked when the men had gone. Maybe this man could give her the answers that Hades never would.

Poseidon gave her a puzzled frown.

"Some parts of his business he keeps from me."

"Ah," he chuckled. "Perhaps this is the reason for your marital dispute?"

That hit a little too close to home, so she said nothing. Poseidon seemed tickled by this, and Persephone was glad, because it made him only too happy to share.

"He owes me money. Quite a lot of it actually. We had an agreement. Now we have a... disagreement. I'm confident it can be settled without too much bloodshed." Persephone cringed. *Too much?*

"It would help, actually, if you encouraged him to talk with me."

He said the last part eagerly, as if recruiting her as an ally would make her forget all the trouble he'd caused.

Still, Persephone pondered it. "Is my husband in danger?"

"Not from me. Not if I get what I want." A smile played around his lips. "For someone who wants to divorce your husband, you seem to care for him an awful lot."

She didn't answer.

64

Hades would kill Poseidon for this. The man had no excuse. He knew the Code. Women and children were left out of their business.

But there was no honor left in the world and Hades should have known it. He shouldn't have given Persephone a choice in that damn coffee shop. He should have thrown her over his shoulder and dragged her to the safe house with him. How many times would he make the same mistake? He'd never have the chance to win her over if she was dead.

His hands fisted and he wanted to break something, preferably Poseidon' face. But not yet. Not until he saw Persephone safe and sound. Hades strode behind Poseidon along the docks, Charon at his back.

"If only you'd been reasonable and taken my request for a meeting," Poseidon said, "it would never have come to this. Why don't we discussed terms and then I'll take you to her?"

"You're not getting jack shit until I see her," Hades growled, hands flexing.

Poseidon sighed. "This way." He led them into a large warehouse. "Here she is," he rumbled. "Safe and unharmed."

Safe?

One of Poseidon's thugs was holding a gun to her temple, and she was pale, her eyes wide with fear.

"I want to speak to her." Hades kept his voice tight and controlled. If that idiot holding the gun had even the tiniest slip of his finger... Hades's chest went cold with rage and a terror he didn't want to examine too closely.

"Be my guest," Poseidon said. "Let's sit, shall we?" He gestured towards a long table.

Hades didn't take his eyes off Persephone. The bastard with the gun to her head shoved her forward until she sat at one end of the table and Poseidon gestured for Hades to sit at the other end. Charon stood behind Hades, along with two more Shades.

Poseidon himself took a seat right beside Persephone. Another man bent down to chain her ankle to the table. Hades's fingers itched to riddle them all with bullets.

"Are you okay?" he asked Persephone, ignoring everyone else in the room.

She nodded shakily, attempting a smile and failing. "Poseidon just wants to talk. He's assured me that once you hear him out, he'll let me go."

Were those bruises around her neck? Hades clenched his teeth so hard he thought they might crack.

Don't think about it right now. Just get her out of here. Get her to safety. You weren't too late this time. You can still save her.

Hades fought down the rage bubbling inside him and set the large briefcase he'd brought with him on the table.

"Let's do this," he told Poseidon, not taking his eyes off Persephone.

Poseidon didn't beat around the bush. "This is a hostile meeting and you know why we're here. And yet, my hopes were for us to continue to do business with one another."

"Negotiation ends when you snatch one of ours. We leave family out of it."

"Ah yes, your Code. Well, I haven't harmed her, she's spent a quiet afternoon and is returning to you safe and sound." Poseidon smiled at Persephone as if she was sitting down at a meal, not a tense business negotiation with a gun to her head. "Like you, I merely want what's mine."

"The bruises on her neck say different," Hades couldn't help growling.

Poseidon frowned. "An unfortunate miscommunication with my men. It was never my intention for any harm to come to her as long as our business concludes on good terms."

Every word coming out of Poseidon's mouth only made Hades feel more murderous. He shoved the briefcase and it slid down the long shiny table. It stopped only inches from Poseidon's hand. Hades watched Persephone stare as the man opened it and checked the multiple stacks of large bills. The tension in the room heightened as Poseidon closed the briefcase, locked it and handed it off to one of his men.

"You've delivered, I've delivered," Poseidon waved a hand at Persephone. "Now, we talk. We will be nothing less than civil; you have my word."

Hades barely stopped himself from scoffing out loud. "That held weight up until the moment you took my wife. Now, your word means nothing to me."

"It meant something to your father." Poseidon folded his hands in front of him, his expression respectful.

"That cash is for Persephone's safe return. It has nothing to do with our business arrangement."

"And yet I don't think of it as a ransom, but as you settling up the debt you owe me." The temperature in the room plunged to subzero as Poseidon continued. "The original terms of our agreement was that we'd deliver the first shipment and receive payment. Instead, in return for our delivery, we received nothing but a formal governmental inquiry into our behavior in international waters."

"Terms changed when the police seized the shipment. You agreed to the change."

Persephone sat up straighter, obviously realizing Poseidon was referring to the night with Ajax on the docks. The last time Hades had failed her and put her life in danger.

"Yes, and then we reviewed things more carefully. We planned that meeting for months. You assured me there would be no trouble. I can only assume you or your silent partner didn't do your job." Poseidon paused and took a deep breath. Persephone's bowed head and her shoulders hunched as Poseidon grew angry beside her. Hades had to de-escalate this and fast. He didn't want Persephone any more traumatized than she already was.

"The events of that night were...regrettable," Hades said, keeping his voice calm and taking back control of the conversation.

"And your responsibility," Poseidon insisted.

"I am willing to accept the blame." Hades inclined his head, allowing Poseidon the point if only to drain the tension level in the room. Still, he couldn't help a caveat. "At least, until I know more about what really went down that night."

"That's all well and good," Poseidon said, his impatience rising to the surface again, "but we're receiving new reports that worry us. There's evidence that the shipment in question has already been distributed, without us getting a cut."

What? What was he talking about?

"There's been no distribution—not by my men."

"Someone is selling it, because people are buying a drug that sounds a lot like ours. If anything, this advance release proves how popular the drug will be."

Hades narrowed his eyes. "What do you want, Poseidon?"

"You have one week to prove the drugs are in your custody and you're back in control of distribution. If not, I will be forced to find other investors and distribution channels. I'm sure you agree it's in our best interest to find the best partner who can deliver."

"There's only one player who can deliver in the New Olympus market. You're looking at him." Hades stared Poseidon down, but the big man shrugged. His large fingers, bare but for his onyx ring, drummed the table.

"I'm being courted by a few others, and one group is especially eager. I'm notifying you out of courtesy, because if we choose to use them, the money they make off this deal may fund an incursion into your territory."

Charon spoke for the first time, but not to Poseidon. "He talking about who I think he's talking about?" he asked the room in general, his deep voice echoing.

"I am, in fact," Poseidon said. "If you can't provide me with what I want, I must seek other partners. And they very well may be your sworn enemies, the Titans."

Persephone's eyes widened just a fraction but otherwise she stayed still.

Hades kept his face bored. Few knew of his wife's connection to the Titans—that she was Demeter Titan's daughter—and he preferred it stay that way. "The Titans haven't been in this market for over a decade. I should know. I drove them out."

"And they're anxious to use their prior knowledge to rebuild." Poseidon spread his large hands as if to say, *What can I do?*

"You don't want to deal with them any more than we want to," Charon said.

"On the contrary, they don't hold a grudge against me." Poseidon was playing with his onyx ring again, twisting it.

"Give them time," Charon said, his voice heated.

Hades took over. "They won't be satisfied with letting you rule the water. They want it all." Back in the day, the Titans (secretly led by Demeter) had been ravenous for power and territory at any cost. Now that she was back in charge, she would suffer no challengers if she had her way. "And they don't operate by a Code. One day you'll want out, and you'll regret ever doing business with them."

"Given that you've been negotiating in bad faith, I'm not sure that I can trust a word you say." Poseidon looked at Hades. "Your father was honest. I'd hoped more of his son."

Hades glared the man down. "This meeting is over. You have your money. Give me my wife."

Poseidon nodded, rising. The men down the table did too. Persephone remained sitting, the gun still on her. "I'm sure you have enough courage to take on me and the Titans. But think of the price you might pay." He looked pointedly at Persephone.

He dared threaten Persephone to Hades's face? On top of all he'd already done? He was a dead man walking.

"Let her go," Hades ordered darkly.

Poseidon tossed a key on the table. "Free for the taking."

Hades was moving forward even as Poseidon left with his crew. Swiping the key, he knelt beside Persephone to unlock the shackle.

"You alright? We gotta go." He helped her up and hustled her to the far door. She trembled on his arm but he didn't dare stop. Poseidon definitely had eyes and guns on them still. Once they exited the warehouse, they were immediately surrounded by Shades, but Hades didn't breathe easy until they were in a black SUV headed out of the parking lot.

More than anything, Hades wanted to immediately send his men after Poseidon for daring to touch what was his, for making her tremble in fear. He wrapped his arm around Persephone and pulled her close to his side. She didn't resist at all, that was how fucking scared she was. Fury beat like an ugly creature with wings in his rib cage

Charon turned in the passenger seat and looked back at him. "You gonna order the hit?"

Hades glared at him. He knew better than to talk about business like that in front of Persephone. Charon nodded and turned back around front.

Hades put two hands on Persephone's shoulders and bent his head to hers. "He touch you?"

She curled her hands around his and looked into his eyes. Gods, it was everything to touch her. To be this close again.

"No. He was polite, actually."

She dropped her hands as he cupped her head, tilting it gently to study the marks those fuckers had made on her neck. His hand hovered over her pulse but he didn't dare brush the bruises marring her skin. The beast in his chest roared.

"They'll pay," he growled. "I'll make them pay for every bruise."

"I'm okay."

"They had a gun to your head."

Persephone bit her lip. "I think…I think he wanted this meeting to go well."

Hades's mouth tightened but he didn't say anything. He didn't trust himself at the moment and he didn't want to scare her any further. His family and Poseidon had long been allies but after today, they could be nothing but enemies.

Persephone frowned and grabbed his hand. "It's my fault."

What was she going on about now?

She clutched his hand tighter. "I slipped my guard at the movie set." Swallowing hard, she went on. "If I hadn't, they'd never have been able to take me."

Fuck but she was sweet. Too good for him, but he'd known that a long time now. She was looking down so he nudged her face up with a finger under her chin. When she still kept her eyes averted, he moved closer to her, pulling her legs over his lap. She resisted only a moment.

"Poseidon and me have been dancin' a long time." He shifted, lifting her into his lap. Maybe he was a bastard to use this to steal a moment of intimacy with her, but after getting Poseidon's call and hearing she'd been snatched, he needed her close. Apparently, she needed it too because she leaned into him.

He kept his voice soft as he murmured into her hair. "Taking you was his way of getting my attention. Now that he has it, we'll see what he does."

"So you're not mad at me?" she whispered, so soft like she was aware of everyone else in the car and wanted only him to hear.

"Mad? No. But every time you run," his arms squeezed her, "I get tempted to kidnap you myself and tie you to the bed."

She swallowed hard and her breath hitched. Maybe because underneath her, he was getting hard. He couldn't help it. Having her so close, her soft, delectable body finally in contact with his. Plus, after the showdown with Poseidon and the relief of finally having her back safe in his arms—he was only a man.

She obviously felt it but she didn't pull away. Sighing, she tucked herself under his chin, relaxing only when his arms slowly came back around to hold her. It was the most peaceful Hades had felt in months. This was right. This was as things should be. Together, they watched New Olympus's skyline loom closer.

When the car entered the city limits, she stirred. "Where are you taking me?"

"Somewhere safe—" Hades started, and her body suddenly went stiff as she yanked away from him. "No, I want to go home."

"We need to—"

"Don't take me to the Estate." She gripped the fabric of his shirt. "I don't care where else you take me, just don't make me go back there."

Was this a clue as to what had happened *that night*? Had Ajax actually dared to steal her off of Hades's own fucking family estate? But how? Hades had interviewed the guards on watch that night a dozen times over. He gazed at Persephone, waiting for her to give more away.

But she suddenly looked around as if realizing how still and silent the entire car had gone. She let go of Hades's shirt and looked out the window, shutting him out.

He wanted to press her. He wanted to know what had happened that night. But she'd been through another trauma and it would have to wait.

"Alright." He ordered the driver to head toward The Chariot Club instead.

Persephone looked back at him. "Okay. But once we get there, we're going to talk."

65

Once there, Hades guided Persephone to a private room in the back. Usually he came here for weekly poker nights with his associates and key lieutenants. A spread of food lay on the long table, reminiscent of the one they'd left.

Hades and Charon left her for a moment to speak with Shades in low voices. They came back in and sat down.

Persephone sat and waited. It felt like old times—Hades off doing business while she waited for him.

She took a deep breath and decided she wasn't going to wait anymore. When Hades turned from speaking to his men, she was standing in the door, arms folded.

His eyes warmed as he approached her, but her next words stopped him cold. "What's my mother up to? What's happening with the Titans?"

She watched, fascinated, as the mask slammed down over his features. She was so used to seeing him unguarded with her that watching him face her like she was one of his enemies was novel. Fascinating, even.

He moved into her, herding her back into the room with his body. She let him, even sitting in the seat he pulled out for her.

"Have you eaten?" He didn't wait for an answer before filling a plate from the family style dishes on the table. "You need to eat." He set the plate in front of her, full of chicken verdicchio. Her mouth watered; it did smell good.

Instead, she picked up her fork and pointed it at him. "You wanted me to talk to you. I'm here, listening. So talk. Tell me what I'm up against."

She couldn't be the girl who stuck her head in the sand anymore. She still wanted nothing to do with Hades's world. But it didn't look like his world was going to let go of her so easily. If she was going to live in the light, she had to be aware of the shadows and how to avoid them.

Taking his own plate, Hades sat next to her right, between her and the door. A slight smile quirked his lips. "And to think you were once a meek, country mouse."

He started eating, arching an eyebrow and nodding toward her own plate. She wouldn't get anything more out of him until he got his way, so she crammed food in her mouth. The second she did, flavor exploded on her tongue.

A moan of pleasure must have escaped her lips, because Hades bumped her elbow intentionally, and she turned into the full on blaze of his smile. Her mouth nearly dropped open at the sight of it. Instead, she gulped down her food and mumbled, "It's really good."

"Two months without Gio's cooking. You were due." He rested his hand on her knee, which sent electric little tingles straight to her core. Her body fell into old habits whenever she was around him. Her eyes fell closed. She should move her leg away. And she would. In another minute. Or five.

Gah, what was wrong with her?

She pulled her knee away from Hades's touch. "Tell me about my mother."

He let out a long-suffering sigh.

"I was gonna shield you from this—"

"Wake up, Hades, it's not working," she said, a little surprised at her own forthrightness. Athena's bluntness was rubbing off on her.

Hades went still, a sign he was surprised, too. Persephone put her hand over his, damning herself for the action because the electricity was back. Still, she didn't let go.

"You're not one hundred percent to blame. I've been trying to keep my head in the sand. But it's not working for me anymore and I need to stop. What's going on? I'm tired of being in the dark."

"Poseidon put you in the middle of this," Hades growled. "He's a dead man."

Persephone felt a chill; she knew all too well that he would make good on that promise. The image of Ajax's limp and disfigured body flashed through her head. And the sound of the wet saw as they prepared to cut him into pieces to send back to the Titans as a 'message.' She'd never forget the sound of the wet saw cutting through the night air.

The food didn't seem so appetizing anymore. She pushed her plate away, and taking a deep breath, she looked up and met Hades's gaze.

"I'm involved no matter what. Being married to you comes with a price. Not just late nights and hanging around men with guns, or the chance that I might get shot at while eating in a restaurant. I have to be a player too, and you're keeping information from me."

"It's not your fight."

"Hades, what I don't know *will* hurt me. I don't know what to look for, I don't know who the threat is. I don't know who your enemies are."

"You shouldn't have to worry about those things." The vein in his forehead was visible, a sure sign that he didn't like what she was saying.

Too bad. It was the truth. He thought he could control everything but as much as he might like to pretend otherwise, he wasn't a god. He couldn't see everything at once, be everywhere at once.

"You treat me like a child, but I'm not a child. I'm a grown woman. You married a *woman* and I need to know what we are facing."

"She's right," Charon put in. Persephone turned to him, blinking. She never expected support from his corner. Hades glared at him but the large man could take the heat. "She's not reckless because she's stupid. She's just ignorant."

"Thank you," Persephone told him and frowned. "I think."

Hades glared at them both. "Another reason I don't want you involved. You get picked up by the cops, you can deny everything."

She scoffed and tossed her hands in the air. "Hades, I know Santonio has a stable of women. I know the DePetri brother's run shipments of contraband up and down the coast. I don't know what Rosco's men sell on the streets, but my guess is they'd sell anything you want."

He looked like he wanted to interrupt so she continued before he could, "We have dinner with them; they talk, and so do their girls. I'm not an idiot. I can put the pieces together."

Hades pushed his chair forward, getting right in her face.

"You don't get my business. It doesn't *touch* you," he slammed a pointed finger on the table. "You stay clean."

Maybe before, she would've felt intimidated. But not now. Not after all they'd been through together, the good and the bad and the ugly.

"No," she shook her head vehemently. "You don't get to make this decision for me anymore. I want to know. If you don't tell me, then I never want to see you again."

But he shook his head, too. Stubborn as ever. "You stay clean. My father always kept my mother out of it. When things got deeper, she had his back, but she only knew the surface."

"And look how well that turned out for her!"

Hades shot back in his chair as if she'd slapped him. She might as well have.

She cringed and ran a tired hand down her face. She was a horrible person to throw his mother's death in his face like that. "Hades, I— I'm sorry. I should never have—" She shook her head. "I can't do this."

She stood up, her chair shoving back, and ran for the staff bathroom. She couldn't handle being in the same room as him anymore. It was too hard. This was all too fucking hard.

Burying one's head in the sand had a bad rap. It was a great plan, really. Coming up for air, now that was the stupidest idea she'd had in a long time.

She slammed the bathroom door shut behind her and let out a deep breath. She walked to the sink and turned the faucets on full blast. She leaned over and splashed her face. Again and again and again.

But she couldn't get clean. She could never get fucking clean. No matter how many times she scrubbed her body top to bottom. Sometimes she took showers so hot her skin blistered, but still it didn't come off. Eurydice's blood had seeped through Persephone's pores down to her bones. She'd never be clean of it.

She didn't hear the door open at first, not until it slammed into the wall.

Her eyes lifted to the grimy mirror and there was Hades, shoving the door shut with as much force as he'd opened it with. "Wha—?"

But she didn't have time to finish her half-formed question or anything else, because before she could even turn off the water faucets, Hades had crossed the space between him and had her in his arms.

He pushed her up against the wall and cradled her face roughly in his hands.

"I will never let what happened to my mother happen to you. Never." His hands shook, and in the raw pain in his face she could see it.

Holy gods. He'd been right.

She really *had* held the power all along.

Oh Hades.

How was he breaking her heart when she didn't have any left to break? She wanted to wrap her arms around him. He looked so lost.

"I wanted you to be clean," he whispered.

"Then you don't want me!" She tried to shove him away but he didn't let her.

And the next moment, his lips were crashing down on hers. She grabbed his shoulders, not sure if she was trying to tug him closer or shove him away. But by the next moment, she was surging up to tiptoe, moaning into his mouth, and giving as good as she got.

Her hips pushed frantically at his, her right leg hooking around his hips so she could press her pelvis closer. She wanted, needed to be close to him as if he was her second half. When he was inside her, she became whole.

This, finally, wasn't a dream and she'd never needed it more.

"Persephone," Hades's groan was deep and feral, ripped from the depths of his heart. He palmed her head, fingers tangled in her wild hair. "I need..."

His eyes were wide, pupils blown. His chest rose and fell, the bellows of his lungs pumping as he teetered on the edge of control. Persephone nodded frantically, helping him claw up her skirt. She needed, too.

With a jerk, Hades's large hand tore her stockings to shreds. Somehow she undid the button on his pants and unzipped them enough for Hades to shove them down. And she was up, feet leaving the ground, legs twining around Hades's lean hips as he drove into her, bracing them both against the wall.

She writhed, adjusting to his great girth, scrabbling at his broad shoulders to pull him closer. He propped her higher, letting gravity slide her further onto his thick length, and she cried out as his cock hit spots inside her she'd forgotten existed.

He filled her beyond limit, invading more than her body. She felt him in every corner of herself, in her very soul.

Her eyes watered with the intimacy. It felt so right. She hated to love this powerful, infuriating man, but she'd never stopped needing him.

"Persephone," Hades's brow wrinkled at the sight of her tears.

"More," she ordered. "I need more."

With a groan, he thrust hard enough to bang her head on the wall. A shelf above them shuddered. A vase fell and shattered on the floor. Persephone didn't care. Neither apparently did Hades. Shards of glass crunching under his shoes, Hades's only reaction was to carry her to the opposite wall. He gripped her bottom, angling her body to slam his cock deeper.

It was coming, oh, *oh!* It was coming. Every muscle in Persephone's body spasmed as her orgasm shot through her. Her hand flung out, smacking the hand towel dispenser. With a whirring sound, the dispenser started spitting paper wipes in a long line.

"Fuck, Persephone, fuck," Hades shouted over the dispenser's whine. She was moaning, her body drawn taut as a bow. Before she snapped, she buried her hands in his dark, silky hair, hanging on for dear life as her orgasm crashed around her.

More paper towels poured out of the dispenser in a white flood, filling the sink. They triggered the soap dispenser, which squirted into the sink, causing the water faucet to start pouring.

Hades slapped his hand on the wall beside Persephone's head, growling through his climax. "Fuck me. That was—"

"Yeah," Persephone panted. Her body trembled in the wake of pleasure. The world was spinning too fast.

Her husband rested his head beside hers, his eyes closed. Beyond him, water gushed into the sink, soaking the paper towels, threatening to overflow onto the floor. The dispenser was still whirring. Soap squirted again and again, coating the glass shards with scented bubbles.

Hades and Persephone raised their heads at the same time to take in the destruction of the small room.

"Fuck," Hades swore again, resigned. He carried her to the far corner, away from the broken glass.

"Typical," Persephone muttered, wriggling away as soon as her feet touched the floor. She wrenched down her skirt. The stockings were a lost cause. She tore the remains off. She sighed. Being with him like this again... It felt good, she couldn't deny it. Great even. And after everything that had happened with Poseidon...she'd been so afraid when those gangsters had kidnapped her. She'd needed the reassurance of Hades's touch.

But it didn't change anything. She looked around them and shook her head. "This is why we shouldn't be together. We're like...fire and dynamite. We destroy everything we touch."

"We're certainly explosive," Hades said mildly. He tore off a clean sheet of paper, offering it to her. "But Persephone, we belong together. I'd lock you in this room, if I could."

Couldn't he see? "That's not going to work for me, Hades. If I have your back, I need to know who I'm backing. And I need to know what monsters are out in the darkness, so I can help defend us. So I can help fight."

His deep eyes stared into hers, pulling her into unfathomable darkness.

"You think that when your enemies come for me they're going to spare me because you never told me about them? I'm the weak link, Hades. I don't want to be anymore."

"Fine." He sighed. "You want to know my enemies. I'll give you the list."

Her eyes widened; he was actually going to share?

"I don't need to know everything, Hades. Maybe start with the major players and work down from there," she suggested.

His mouth twitched, and for a moment he looked like he would laugh. "Gods, I forgot," he said.

"What?"

"How cute you are."

"Hades. The list."

"You know Poseidon. Started in shipping, now owns the largest privately held fleet in the world. Ships oil and goods all over the world. My father helped him get his start, financed some of his first shipments, back when New Olympus was a major port."

"So what's the shipment?" She already knew what it was, but she wanted to know if Hades would tell her the truth finally.

"Drugs. Something new. Supposed to be more benign than coke."

"Didn't they say that about heroin?" She pushed out of the bathroom, needing to be out of the small space.

The back room was as empty as they'd left it, their food untouched.

Hades watched her pace. "You see why I didn't want to tell you."

"I know the business you're in. Better I find out from you than someone else, or worse, just catch a stray bullet."

He came after her, caught her in his arms. "Never, ever joke about that." He gave her a little shake.

She put her hands on his arms. "You made your bed. I married you. We both lie in it."

"I live by a Code. And if I didn't control the drug market, someone else would. We sell to adults, not kids. The Shades are disciplined; if anyone else moves in, things would get worse. It'd be war."

"The Titans," she said, searching his face. "My mother and uncles. They want to move in."

Hades swore. He let her go, but she cupped his face with both hands. "Tell me."

"If we don't deliver Poseidon's shipment and his cut of our take, he'll bring his business to the Titans."

"Can you stop them?"

"Not if they ally with Poseidon. If that happens, things get ugly."

"What's ugly?" Persephone asked, even though she could guess.

"War," Hades confirmed.

Persephone blew out a long breath. The Titans aligning with someone like Poseidon would give them enough power to make a move on New Olympus.

"We've been preparing. I wanted to make peace with Poseidon, but the missing shipment is a sticking point. This drug is his baby, and he wants it back."

For a moment they sat in silence while Hades poured a glass of wine and tasted it. He offered it to Persephone but didn't release it. Instead, he tipped the glass until the red liquid washed her lips.

"What about the death threats?" Persephone asked.

"What about them?"

"You said you were getting them, going to go into hiding."

"I'm certain that either the Titans or Poseidon are behind them. I can't retreat now, not with things heating up." He reached out and tucked a strand of hair behind her ear. "At some point this shit is going to blow over, and we're going to talk about *us*."

She let out a sigh and leaned her head against his chest. She liked hearing his heartbeat and it meant she didn't have to look him in the face. "Maybe once the death threats let up."

He ran his fingers through her hair. "You're going to have nightmares after all this." He muttered, sounding unhappy.

"I already do," she said before she thought it through, and wanted to kick herself when his entire body tensed.

"When we work things out, I'll help you get over them."

His words let loose a flood of desire. She couldn't stop the shiver that started at the core of her and radiated out into the rest of her body. Hades's face got intense and she knew he saw it.

"Come on." She smoothed down her hair. "They'll be missing us."

"Later," he promised. "Soon."

At his words, she felt another shiver, but fortunately he didn't see this one. He was busy pulling open the door, no doubt to signal Charon it was safe to return. Soon after, Charon reappeared.

"We good?" Charon rumbled.

Hades raised his eyebrows at her.

"For now," Persephone didn't take her eyes off her husband.

"Good. Because we got a situation."

Hades straightened, waved a hand to Charon to continue talking in front of Persephone. She sat quietly, feeling oddly pleased.

"Got word from my contacts inside the force. The shipment was large so they put it in a warehouse for confiscated evidence. One box was opened in his sight, dusted for prints."

"No way only one box was opened."

Charon confirmed. "They opened the rest of them after checking them. Only Ajax's prints on them; our guys wore gloves. But now the boxes are empty. Contents removed. My guy checked."

"How'd he miss it before?"

"Because he's fucking stupid. Checked one box, didn't think to check the others."

Hades cocked his head, and Persephone could tell he was

supremely annoyed. "So someone got to the boxes when they were in evidence."

"Not unlike what we were planning."

"Who would do that?" Persephone asked. "Who had access?"

Hades leaned back in his chair thoughtfully. "I think it's time we revisited our friend the Mayor."

Persephone bit her lip. She'd been there the night the mayor's man had promised that the shipment would be returned to Hades within the week. Obviously that hadn't happened.

"You won't get anywhere near him." Charon said. "He hasn't returned our messages for two months—what makes you think you can do it now?"

Hades glanced at Persephone. "A little persistence will wear anyone down."

Persephone resisted the urge to roll her eyes. Hades was already counting himself the victor.

"Send Persephone," Charon said. "I bet we can get a meet with the mayor, if she's the front."

Persephone's body tightened.

"Absolutely not," Hades lost his cool and growled at his second in command.

"What choice do we have?" Charon shot back. "We've tried every channel. She could walk right in, no problem."

"I don't want her involved," Hades said.

"Like it or not, Poseidon made the right play," Charon said and the room turned arctic.

"What?" Hades breathed, facing his underboss with enough rancor that Persephone put her hand on his arm.

"Don't like that he took her, but it got you to sit down and chat. Maybe we've been going around the wrong way. Someone like her can walk right in—no one sees her as a threat."

"She's not—" Hades started.

"Is it safe?" Persephone interrupted.

The two men stared at her.

"You'd be covered. It's the mayor's office. No one will touch you,"

Charon said, but her husband spun his chair around and pulled hers closer.

"No, babe," Hades cupped her face. "You don't have to do this."

It was her fault the cops grabbed the shipment in the first place. Maybe if she could make it right, Hades would forgive her once he found out what she'd done.

"I want to. I want to help." She looked into his deep brown eyes, drawing strength from them. "What do I have to do?"

66

"Is this really necessary?" Persephone asked right before Hades grabbed her from behind and wrapped an arm around her throat.

"I'm not letting you walk into an unknown situation," he growled in her ear, "I don't care how public it is, until I'm confident you have some basic skills to take care of yourself. That's twice you've been kidnapped so you'll forgive me if I'm a tad overprotective of what's mine. Now. Again." His arm around her neck cinched tighter.

Just for his comment about her being *his*, she jabbed especially hard with her elbow into his gut, like he'd spent the last few hours teaching her. She went to stomp on his instep, too, but he maneuvered out of the way. She growled in frustration and he only tightened his arm more.

The bastard had the audacity to laugh. He was fucking *laughing* at her?

She tried to scream her fury but it was muffled by his giant stupid arm restricting her airflow. Not completely, but enough to be uncomfortable.

The next thing she knew, he'd swept her legs and had her on the mat, his big body crouched over hers.

"How many times do I have to tell you to turn your head to the side to free your airway? You get too excited about jabbing me but you'd be passed out before you had the chance to do any real damage or escape if you don't remember the basics."

She bit the inside of her bottom lip. *Don't scream in his face. Don't scream in his face. It'll only make him more smug.*

They'd been at this for hours and she swore they spent far more time down on the mat, him pinning her and droning on *about* defensive moves than actually *practicing* them. She'd told him that yesterday in the bathroom had been a one time slip up and she meant it. They were *not* back together.

"Turn your head to the right so your windpipe isn't obstructed, then attack only long enough to get free."

For once she'd like to get the jump on *him*.

"All right." She raised her arms above her head, giving a little stretch that made her breasts jiggle. A thrill of satisfaction went through her when Hades's gaze dropped to her form-fitting t-shirt.

"I'm sooo tired," she mock-yawned. "You're so big and strong. Fighting you is hard work."

Hades's brows knitted together. Oops, she overdid it. Rubbing a hand over her upper chest to distract him, she offered an innocent smile. "Grab me again?"

This time when his arms closed around her, she turned her head. Her hand went to his groin, but instead of striking, she cupped the hard ridge and gave it a good rub with her palm. Hades stilled, holding his breath as if wondering what she'd do next.

She lifted her legs, creating unexpected dead weight. When he lurched forward, off balance, she twisted out of his grip and scurried away. Hades landed on the floor.

"Ha!" She did a victory dance. Her would-be attacker lay face down on the ground, unmoving. Oh crap. "Hades? Hades? Did I hurt you?"

She worried her lip, tip-toeing closer. He'd hit the floor pretty hard. Had she hurt him somehow?

Her foot nudged his side and he snapped into action, grabbing her ankle, pulling her leg out from under her. She shrieked but he caught her and cushioned her landing.

Persephone found herself once again on her back with a large, aroused male rearing over her. With a stone expression, Hades grabbed her hand and brought it back to the front of his workout shorts, using her palm to stroke himself, harder than she would've done. His eyes were steel. "You think this is funny? A game?"

She shook her head, wide-eyed. Her hair spilled over the floor. "Hades, I was just—"

"You touch anyone else like that, I'll kill them."

She flinched at the vow. He smiled, the corners of his mouth turning sharp. "Other than that, well done." He raised her palm and kissed it.

She gave a tentative smile. "Thank you?" Her voice went breathless as he licked up her lifeline, a tongue stroke she felt in her groin.

"Hades," she wriggled. "Let me go."

He shook his head. "You made a mistake, angel." Slowly he lowered himself over her, keeping her pinned. He shook his dark hair from his face. "You should've run while you had the chance."

With a hard hand gripping her right breast, he lowered his head to nip and suck at the vulnerable junction of her throat. And everything in her rose up—all the longing and bone-aching need—a dizzying rush of arousal. Yesterday hadn't been enough. It would never be enough.

She was almost too far gone when Hades slid his hand up to lightly collar her throat.

"Persephone," he growled. "My own." His hand flexed, lightly squeezing the way she used to love, used to beg for, when she was old Persephone and willing to succumb, to let him subsume her until she was completely under—

"Mine," he said, and it was enough to jar her back to reality.

She jerked her knee up—he twisted to block it, but she rammed his inner thigh until he rolled off of her.

She rose, tugging her clothes back into place, willing herself not to face her husband. She could see him in the wall mirror, though. He sat, face carefully blank, watching her from the floor. Part of her longed to comfort him, but to what end? There was a chasm between them, filled with secrets and lies. She couldn't breach it, not even for a moment. Not even for him.

It was better this way. She would leave and shower and change, and stick to the plan.

"I told you earlier. Yesterday was a mistake. I'm not yours." She headed for the door. "Not anymore."

67

When Persephone left the locker room, Hades was already waiting for her, his tall form devastating in one of his tailored suits. His wet hair slicked back from his face was the only sign he'd spent the last hour exerting himself. Proud of the cool nod she gave him, Persephone strode past him, only to have her heart and limbs quiver when he fell into step beside her.

"What are you doing?" she snapped when he opened the door for her and followed her out as if he had a right to be there. As if she'd invited him along when he knew that wasn't the case. When he knew—despite the longing in her chest—that he wasn't wanted.

"Seeing you home." The corners of his mouth turned up as if she amused him.

"You said your driver would take me." She hated the petulant sound of her voice. Especially since *he* was the unreasonable one. "You said it was safe, that you swept my apartment and it was clear."

"We did," he shrugged. "But I'm going the same way. Why waste gas?" He opened the car door for her, looking so sensible and innocent she wanted to kick him.

She spent the entire trip with her arms crossed over her chest, refusing to look at his handsome profile. Her cold shower hadn't helped. She was so aroused, so aware of him, it physically hurt not to turn and throw herself into his arms.

"One more block," she whispered to herself, and when the car pulled up to the curb, she threw open the door and leapt onto the sidewalk. Only to find Hades opening his door and following her again.

"No," she almost shouted, enraged. "Hades, you can't be here. This is my apartment—"

"It's not, actually," he murmured, walking right up to the keypad and entering a code. Her mouth almost fell open when the gate unlocked and he opened it for her. "You don't own the place, you're only renting." With a sweep of his palm, he indicated she should precede him. "After you."

She was inside before she realized she'd obeyed his subtle command. Once he shut the door, she whirled to confront him in the inner courtyard. "Hades, what are you doing?"

"Seeing you home." In the dark garden, his body seemed to grow larger, his shadow swallowing her whole.

"Where did you get the keycode?" If he'd had one of his Shades watching over her shoulder while she or one of the other residents entered the building, she swore she'd—

"I got it when I bought the building." A dimple flashed in his cheek as he gave her a panty-drenching smile.

Persephone forgot about how hot he looked as her brain processed this. "You...what?"

"I own the whole building."

"You own the building." She put a hand to her temples; she could feel a headache coming on.

"I bought it." He moved closer and she watched him warily, wishing he didn't fill out his suits so well. His hair was a little long, brushing the edges of his collar. It made his professional garb look somehow...a little bad boy, a little dangerous, as if he knew the line of decorum and chose to step over it.

"You bought the building." Even in the dim light of early evening, she could see his eyes crinkling in his almost smile. She mentally shook herself for parroting everything he said. "So...the new upgrades the landlord's been doing lately..."

A new security system had been installed, including the call box up to the apartments. Along with a second entryway door and a doorman. The guy didn't wear all black, but yeah, thinking back now, it was so obvious that he was a Shade. How had she not seen it before?

"My requirements." Hades inclined his head, shadows falling over the planes of his face, making his features look sharper. "When I heard you were touring the place, I made inquiries. The owner has some debt he needed clearing. Gambling is such an unfortunate vice." Hades shrugged. "He was really very grateful."

Persephone made a noise and inadvertently took a step back towards the front door. She wondered why, whenever her husband said something that scared her, she had the burning desire to go to him and rip his clothes off.

"No wonder Athena thought I was getting a steal on rent. You fixed this whole thing, didn't you?" She held up a hand. "Never mind, I don't want to know."

She pulled out her keys, but just her luck, fumbled and dropped them.

"Here, let me help you," Hades said in his sexy, gravelly voice. His hands were graceful as he reached down and swept up her keys. Her heart stilled, remembering his long fingers moving with a different task.

She wouldn't jump him, she wouldn't. *No, no, no, no.* She crossed her arms over her chest.

He held open the door for her and, deciding it would be petulant to keep standing out here in the courtyard, she went through and smiled at Dennis, the doorman, before remembering that he was working for Hades. Thinking about it now, he rarely even opened the door for people. Well, other than Persephone. He sat at the desk, ignoring the computer on it and staring stoically at the outer door.

Seeing Hades, though, Dennis hopped to his feet and opened the second door that led up to the apartments. Persephone rolled her eyes and continued up the stairs.

Loud feet sounded on the stairs behind her. She spun around to face Hades when she got to her door. "I don't care if you own the building, you aren't coming in here, buddy."

He arched an eyebrow as if to say, *buddy?*

"I thought nothing of the sort," he said. "I'm merely heading home to my own apartment after a long, exhausting day."

He pulled out his keys, turned to the apartment across the hallway from hers and turned the lock. "Sleep tight, *neighbor*." He didn't turn around but she heard the grin in his voice.

Her hands squeezed into fists and she wanted to hit something really, really badly. Instead she let out a very unladylike frustrated grunt, unlocked her own door, and slammed it shut behind her.

She went straight for the wine.

"The nerve of him," she muttered, pacing back and forth two hours later. She'd tried everything to distract herself. Watching reruns of her favorite TV shows. Trying to get into a new TV show on her favorite streaming service. Picking up the book that had her captivated only the night before.

Nothing worked.

After a few minutes, inevitably her mind would wander to the apartment across the hallway. What was Hades doing? Was he thinking about her? Was he working? Was he watching porn and jerking off?

She took another swig of wine. It was only her second glass. She never allowed herself more when she was home alone, and usually not even that.

She glared at the clock on the wall. 9:30. That was a perfectly acceptable time to go to bed right? Responsible grown-ups went to bed at 9:30. She went to the bathroom and spent longer than usual on her nighttime routine, but when she climbed in bed, still only fifteen minutes had passed.

She sighed and flopped her head down onto her pillow. *Fates be kind, please, for once, let me* sleep.

Two hours later, she was laying on her stomach and banging her forehead repeatedly into her pillow.

Sleep deprivation was a form of torture. They had rules against this under the Genoa Convention.

So finally she gave up and went to the bathroom to seek out the little baggie with Hermes's pills. Tomorrow was important. A text had come through an hour ago from Hades letting her know they'd arranged a meeting with the mayor. He and Charon would be by early in the morning to prep her.

She couldn't be a zombie with only an hour of sleep, if that, and dark circles under her eyes. She frowned at the little baggie. The pills were almost gone. She bit her lip. Every time she took one, it was a little easier for her to justify.

Oh, screw it. She popped one in her mouth and swallowed it down with a cup of water. There. Now to lie in bed and drift off. And who knew? Maybe she'd have a nice dream like the one before, imagining Hades coming to her...

No, no, no. She did *not* want to dream about her husband. *Ex.* Wus-band.

Persephone rolled over and punched her pillow. She'd picked the softest sheets and mattress when she moved in, so why did her bed feel so hard? And why was it so damn hot? She clawed her clothes off and flopped one way and the other.

She wasn't falling asleep. Shit. She'd swear she almost felt...like, *more* energetic, a little frenetic almost. What if the pill didn't work tonight? Hadn't she heard you started getting immune to sleep medication if you took it too often?

She had to sleep tonight. *Had* to. After another few minutes tossing and turning, she went back into the bathroom and took out the second to last pill in the baggie. And before she could think better of it, she threw it in her mouth, swallowed it, and drank another half glass of water.

She went back to bed and waited.

Her room wasn't large, but the darkness made it seem endless, cavern-like. The shadows on the wall made weird shapes. The one in the door looked like Hades's profile—

"Can't sleep?"

Persephone let out a little scream, slamming back into the headboard. "Hades?"

His shadow stretched over her as he moved into the depths of her bedroom.

"Gods, you scared me."

"I can't sleep either." Hades looked down at his hands and Persephone sensed his frustration. He would hate anything he considered weakness or a lack of control. *Oh, Hades.*

"You shouldn't be in here," she forced herself to say. Even though what she really wanted was to invite him in for the night and wrap her arms and body around him. Sleep would come, cool and delicious. She'd rest peacefully knowing the monster was in her bed.

He paused at the end of her bed. "You lied to me."

Her heart plummeted to the floor. *He knew.* Her breath came in short gasps. *How did he guess? What would he do now that he'd figured out her betrayal?*

"What?" she managed to squeak.

"Earlier." His hands were at his tie, unknotting it. "Back at the gym."

"The gym?" she repeated, mind blank with relief. He hadn't guessed her part in the bust at the docks.

"You remember." His hand closed over her ankle, and before she knew it, she was on her back under him. He straddled her hips, loosely binding her wrists with his tie before securing them to the headboard. Her pulse pounded in her pussy, the throbbing beat so loud she was sure he could hear it.

This was it. He'd broken into her bedroom and now he was going to claim her.

He smiled down at her, gray eyes flashing. "You said you didn't belong to me." His voice deepened, roughened. "You lied."

He shifted off her and her moan caught in her throat. She wanted him back, his weight, his heat. He stood looking down at her as if he owned her. She felt his gaze like a touch but it wasn't enough.

He ran a finger down the middle of her collarbone, between her breasts. Of course she would be naked when he decided to invade her bedroom.

"I wasn't lying." Her breath caught as his finger traced down, down.

"No?" An arrogant brow arched. "What's this then?"

His finger trespassed between her soft folds. Persephone's body curled in on itself, dying for more. "You're wet for what, no reason?"

"No…"

"Then why, angel?" His finger twisted, probed, not quite filling her. She bit her tongue so she wouldn't ask for more. "Is it for me?" A second finger. Her toes curled into the bed.

"Hades, please—"

"Please, what?" His cheek curved in the darkness. A devil's smile. "'Please stop'?" His fingers stilled and her hips pressed upwards, seeking. "Or 'please more'?"

This was a bad idea. There were so many reasons she should stop this. Kick him out. Never let him touch her again.

His fingers stroked the wet grooves on either side of her clit. So many reasons to tell him 'no', but she couldn't think of a single one.

"More," she begged, breathless. "Don't stop."

"Sweetheart," that devastating curl of his lip. "I'm never gonna stop."

His fingers hit her sweet spot, setting off white hot electric flashes in her brain. He stretched over her, lips close, his scent washing over her. She sucked in lungfuls, growing dizzy drunk on him.

His fingers rubbed along her sensitive furrows, finding her orgasm, drawing it out as he whispered against her mouth.

"You're mine. You've always been mine. 'Til the day we die and beyond. 'Til stars fall and this world is forgotten. Forever."

"Hades," she cried as her orgasm blew up, a storm, a supernova. Sparks shot through her, her torso tensing, her limbs trembling, mouth opening to his as the climax consumed her. Transformed her atoms, turned her cells into shining suns. If she hadn't been tied to her bed she'd have floated.

In the corner of her eye, Hades reared up, wearing a shark's smile as he undid his shirt cuffs.

The biggest orgasm of her life and he wasn't done with her. He'd never be done.

She wrenched free of the tie and ran to the door. The knob wouldn't turn. Locked.

She pounded on the door, begging, "Let me out, let me out."

The darkness danced behind her, gathering into a potent form, a monster made of all her deepest desires. Her fist uncurled and she slapped the door, sobbing as it opened—

"Persephone?" The shadows dissolved and Persephone blinked in the light. Staggered backwards.

She was in the hall of her apartment building, standing in front of Hades, who'd opened his door. The door she'd been pounding on —*in her dream.*

Sleepwalking? Oh shit. Well, this was new.

Hades's eyes dropped to her body and flared with heat. "Persephone, you're *naked*." Her head jerked down to look at herself. Double shit. He was right, she was naked, well, underneath the sheet she had loosely drawn around herself.

"Get in here." Hades backed up to let her in.

She went forward on his command. When her legs wobbled, she balanced herself on the wall. Hades pushed the door closed and came to help her. She stopped him with a raised hand.

"What happened? Are you okay?" He stopped at her outstretched hand, respecting her request for space.

"I'm sorry. I wanted to sleep. I must have had a dream." She averted her eyes. She couldn't look at him. Her skin still crackled with sensitivity, dying to have her husband close the last few inches and put his hands on her.

A dream, it was only a dream. Except her pussy throbbed and she felt the wrung-out weakness of an incredible orgasm. *Don't think about that—*

"Sweetheart, you don't look well." His fingers brushed her forehead lightly. The single touch sent runners of heat through her. She gasped.

Hades's forehead furrowed. "What's going on?"

"I wanted to sleep," her words came slurred and heavy. "I can never sleep."

"Your pupils are dilated—"

"Hades." She couldn't think with him touching her. She grabbed his hand and he stilled. Her body convulsed. Not in climax, not quite. But close. She'd almost cum from his touch alone.

Hades's eyes widened, wild. He knew. He was always so attuned to her. "What the—"

"Hades," she moaned. "Touch me, *please*."

And she pressed his hand to her breast.

He stared a moment. His hair was tousled, wild, as if he'd been running a hand through it. She imagined him sitting on his couch, drinking scotch and debating whether to knock on her door. Never knowing he'd already invaded her dreams.

With a groan, a helpless sound, he bowed his head, shoved her sheet to the floor, and took her nipple into his mouth. Lightning sizzled through her. She arched upwards.

"Hades, *Hades*." Her hands dug into his silky raven dark hair, mussing it further. He was always so buttoned up, so in control. Except when he was with her. With her the beast broke free.

68

Hades's tongue circled his wife's nipple and she hissed, clawing him closer. With a growl, he raised his head, grabbed her wrists and trapped them above her head, against the door. Something wasn't right. This wasn't the same woman who'd been so cold to him only earlier today.

I'm not yours. Not anymore.

But here she was, her body stretched before him, legs thrashing, trying to hook his hips and pull him to her. He fixed her with a glare.

He wanted what she was so freely offering. By the gods, he wanted it. It was all he'd been able to think about from the second he'd pulled out of her yesterday in that damned bathroom. He wanted to impale her for about a month until she forgot everything else in the world but his name.

"Hades, please," she panted, struggling. Her flesh was so hot, rosy with lust. "I need—"

He thrust his fingers into her cunt. He would always give her what she needed. Her head flew back, slamming the wood. Hades watched her, jaw rigid, as one orgasm rocked through her, and another.

What the hell was going on? His woman was sensitive, it was true, but not usually *this* hair-trigger. He twisted his fingers in a way that would have been painful if she wasn't so wet, and her convulsions only increased. She went absolutely wild on his hand. He'd never seen anything like it. He frowned even as his cock stiffened past the point of painful.

"Easy," he crooned when she kept thrusting against his hand even though she'd come a handful of times. "You can have all you want. There's no rush." But he slid his fingers out. He needed to figure out what the hell was going on.

Persephone blinked, her features turning devastated. "You just said—"

"You want more?"

"Yes." She nodded furiously. "Yes, I need more." She licked her lips and his eyes followed. "I need you."

"Are you sure? After what you said today—"

"I was wrong."

Hades's whole body jerked. Did she really mean that? Or was she—

"I was wrong," she said louder, cutting into his thoughts. "I belong to you. In every way. And I need you." Her voice edged on a whine. "Now. I'll die if you don't take me." He couldn't remember the last time he'd heard anyone so desperate.

The breath left his chest in a harsh rush. He wrenched her around, making her face the wall. She sobbed, obviously thinking he meant to deny her.

Didn't she know? He could never do anything that would hurt her. No matter how much it might kill him to touch her now and have her deny him tomorrow.

But he didn't know what this was. Her inhibitions were obviously lowered. He didn't smell any alcohol on her breath, though, and he couldn't imagine her taking any kind of drug— He shook his head even at the thought. Was she on some sort of medication?

He wasn't the sort of man to take advantage of a woman in a vulnerable state.

"Hades," Persephone begged, almost sounding in pain. His fingers returned to her pussy, probing as he tried to think. But she was driving him fucking insane. Pushing him away only to show up like this?

"So wet." His voice was edged with cruelty. "So desperate. Are you always this wet?"

"Only when you're near."

"You lied to me earlier?" He worked his fingers more roughly. "What does that make you?"

"A liar," she cried out.

"Do good girls lie?"

"No." She twitched her hips to invite his touch. "I'm a bad girl."

Her words made Hades's cock pulse painfully. "You are a bad girl. You gonna cum again?"

Her escalating whimpers said yes. She arched her back, pressing her nipples to the hard wall. "Yes. Please, I need it."

"Not so fast." Hades spun her around and tossed her over his shoulder. She shrieked and grabbed onto him. The floorboards creaked as he carried her down the hall and dropped her on his bed. She landed on her back and when he didn't immediately follow her, her whines immediately started up again.

"Please, Hades. Please. Fuck me. Fuck me now."

She reached for him and when he backed out of her grasp, her hands went to her own pussy. She started rubbing herself frantically, her face pinched with frustration as she sought release. "It's not enough. I need your cock. I need your big, fat cock stuffed in my pussy. Right now. Please fuck me. Fuck me, Hades!"

"That's enough," he barked, putting a knee on the bed and grabbing her wrists, wrenching them above her head and slamming them into the bed. "Stop this right now."

"That's right," she breathed out, big, innocent blue eyes blinking up at him. "Punish me, Daddy. Punish your bad girl."

For fuck's sake.

"I'll tie you to this bed if that's what it takes," he growled, "but you *will* tell me what the fuck is going on."

"I need you. Fuck me. Fuck my cunt. Fuck my ass. I need it all. Fuck all my holes. Hades, *please*—" Her body writhed under his, her knee rubbing against his rock-hard cock. Like yesterday, but this time, he knew she had every intention of seeing her promise through.

He wanted to give in, to plunder her depths, to fuck her so hard she wouldn't be able to walk for a week, to mark her as *his*—

But then her eyes flashed with a different fire. "If you don't give it to me, I swear I will walk out this door, naked, and jump the first guy I see. But I will get a cock, any cock, in this cunt, within the hour."

Raw fury and terror scrambled over one another in his guts. It was not something he'd ever felt before.

Hades forced himself to let go of her and step back from the bed. She scrambled up as well, eyes flicking to the door like she might make good on her threat.

He casually moved in front of it as he slowly began unbuttoning his shirt. She tried to dart around him but his hand shot out, slamming the door shut.

"No, sweetheart." He gave her a cruel smile. "You came to me. We do this my way."

He grabbed her by the waist and felt her body melt into his touch. Which only pissed him the fuck off. Would she melt the same way if he was any other man? Would she squeal so good for a fucking stranger?

He forced her face-down on the bed and smacked her ass. She pushed her bottom up higher, inviting his touch.

"You're a bad girl? You need discipline."

"Yes, yes, please, Hades—"

"Enough. I think you've said quite enough. Now keep your hands on the bed." Hades yanked his belt out of his slacks and doubled it up. He slid the leather across his palm.

Persephone took a peek over her shoulder and he watched her eyes widen in excitement. *I'll die without it*, she'd said. For whatever reason, she needed this. So much so, she'd take any fucking cock and lie to him about wanting him, trying to manipulate him into—

Leather cracked against her ass. He'd teach her a lesson, that was for sure. He'd teach her a lesson and they'd be done with this. But as soon as the blow landed, her back arched, followed by a little mewl of pleasure.

She sobbed out a sigh and snarled when Hades paused too long. "Again! Give it to me again."

Hades paused. He'd been careful with his force, no matter how angry he was. But he hadn't taken it easy on her, either. He swung again. The belt bit her bottom once, twice, a third time.

Persephone tensed and melted into the bed with each strike momentarily before rising back up on her haunches and waving that lovely, now bright pink ass at him again.

When she next turned to look over her shoulder at him, tear tracks marked her cheeks and her brows were furrowed in need. "Please. Hades. Can't you see how much I need you?"

She looked helpless. Desperate. His beautiful wife. Literally on her knees.

Whatever was happening to her, she'd come to *him*. She'd been in need and come to her husband for help. As it should be.

A thud sounded as Hades threw away the belt, dropped to his knees behind her and buried his face in her pussy.

"Fuck, you're so wet." He sounded awestruck because he was. He gripped her wriggling hips, forcing her to remain still as he dived in and began making a meal of her.

He'd never in all their time together seen her so drenched. Her wetness was sloppy on his five o'clock shadow. He could barely slurp down one mouthful before more of her juice spurted forth.

Persephone raked the sheets, sobbing his name, "Hades, *Hades,*" her legs shaking on either side of his head as if an earthquake had struck, it's epicenter at her pussy.

"No, no, it's too much," she moaned, writhing and thrusting against his mouth in contradiction of her words. "I can't."

"You will," he growled. "You belong to me. You said so. You admitted it." He didn't care about the circumstances, he was fucking holding her to her admission. "So when I say cum, you cum. Now do it. *Cum.*"

She writhed, her climax hitting again and again, an unstoppable tide. It was fucking incredible to witness. Each crest seemed to bring her higher and higher. Her cries became higher and higher pitched until finally she was gasping out little high-pitched whimpers.

And Hades's cock had never been harder in his entire fucking life.

Hades flipped her over and she grabbed his shoulders. He withdrew her hands and pinned her to the bed.

"You don't touch me, not without permission." At this point he wanted, no, *needed* her, with an insane vehemence that might even match her own. But he *would* remain in control. No matter the fact that his thighs shook with the need to thrust inside her.

More tears slipped down her cheeks.

"Hades, please."

Shifting forward, he thumbed away her tears. He couldn't stop himself from tasting them. Her breasts arched outward as if that was the most erotic thing she'd ever seen.

"*Bellissima,*" he whispered, body tense with restraint. "If this is what you want..."

"It is. I need it. I need you. Now, Hades, you have to—"

"Shh, Persephone, *cara*, calm down. Let me be gentle—"

"I don't want you to be gentle," she shrieked. "I need it now, please, gods, please, Hades. I need you now."

His hand shot out and collared her neck. At the same time he shifted, angled his hips and slammed into her.

Persephone's eyes lit with ecstasy, her body seizing around him in orgasm.

"Is this what you want?" Hades snapped his hips, forcing his cock deeper. She was tight, so fucking tight, but so wet that he slid right in. Made so perfectly for him. He hitched her legs up over his shoulders and bent her in half, hammering savagely.

"Hades, yes. Fuck me harder." She closed her eyes. Her cunt milked him, sucking him deeper as he groaned above her. "*Harder,* Hades."

It was good she kept saying his name. The thought that she might have gone and shared this with some other man—

He pulled out and thrust in again, hard. But as soon as he was rooted deep in her, his heart calmed.

"Persephone. *Mi amore. Ho bisogno di te.*" *My love. I need you.* Could she not see what she did to him? How the two months apart had been hell on him?

"Hades," she whispered as shockwaves flowed through her. Gods, the way her pussy kept clamping on his cock—she was cumming non-stop, her legs shaking uncontrollably. Her hands scrabbled against the hard wall of his chest, fighting to bring him closer.

He let himself lay flush against her, coarse hair scratching her oversensitive nipples. "I'm here. I'm here. *Baciami. Abbraciami.*" *Kiss me. Hold me.*

His cock nudged deeper, sliding against her sensitive walls, and as his lips touched hers, the largest climax yet detonated. Her eyes rolled back in her head.

"Persephone? Persephone?"

After a moment of silence, she blinked again, mouth open and eyes wide like she'd seen a holy fucking vision or something.

"Persephone," he called again, cupping her cheek, smoothing her hair, almost frantic. "Persephone?"

"I'm here," she panted. Her gaze connected with his and she giggled. "I think I came so hard I passed out for a second."

She reached up and dragged his head down, nuzzling his forehead against hers. She sounded a little more like herself. He was still inside her, filling her, and she clenched around him with a low groan.

He didn't know whether to laugh, cum, or spank her ass again. This woman would be the death of him. But he didn't fucking care. He buried his hands in the back of her hair and kissed her hard. Their tongues tangled, Persephone clawing at him.

"Will you take my ass now? Please, Hades? I need to feel you everywhere."

Hades shook his head. Cumming so hard she passed out wasn't fucking enough? "You were unconscious." He sat up and pulled out of her.

She reached for him but he grabbed her wrists again to stop her. "Please, Hades. Please fuck my ass."

"And if I don't, you'll go get any random bastard off the street to assfuck you, is that right?" He'd never been so horny and so angry at the same time before.

She winced. "I'm sorry. I'm sorry. I took some sleeping medication and I think it's making me act weird— But please, Hades. I'm so *empty*."

Sleeping medication? Hades supposed he'd heard of people sleepwalking on sleep meds and maybe getting up in the middle of the night to eat a pint of ice cream. But this?

"I know it's a lot to ask." Persephone looked pained. "But please, will you fuck my ass? Fill me up?"

Tears poured down her face. She was more herself but her need wasn't any less. Her nipples were beaded so tight they looked like they could cut glass. She was the most beautiful thing he'd ever seen in his life. He knew the merest brush would set her off.

And she wanted him in her ass. His beautiful wife was begging for him to claim her *completely*.

He'd vowed he'd always see to her every need. He inhaled deeply. Her scent was thick in the air and his cock twitched, still wet with her juices.

In one swift movement, Hades tumbled her over his hard thighs.

"You will never," he punctuated his words with sharp smacks to her already pink rear, "ever, *ever*, touch another man ever again."

He shoved his fingers into her pussy, making her buck. Her spine seized with another jaw-breaking climax before he slid his hand out and spread her ample slick over her asshole. He probed her ass, invading the tight ring of muscle with one, two, three fingers.

"You want my cock in your ass?" he demanded.

"Yes." Her reply was muffled by the bed. Not good enough. He spanked her so hard she gasped.

"Tell me."

"Yes," she shouted. "I want your cock in my ass. Fuck my ass, Hades, please. Fuck my ass!"

For all his rough discipline, when he lined his cock up and started to invade her ass, he was exceedingly gentle.

His cock breached her tight hole in stages as she moaned into the comforter. This time Hades was afraid *his* eyes would roll back in his head.

So. Tight.

So fucking tight. They'd done this only once before, the night before she'd left and he'd lived off those memories for so many lonely nights—

She flexed, clenching on him and he lost his damn breath. He was trying to keep in control, he really was. But gods, she was testing him. Having his perfect, innocent little wife whimpering and thrusting her hips against the bed, searching for friction while he fucked her all-but-virgin ass—he almost came right there on the spot.

But no. Fuck no. He was gonna draw this out. She might have demanded it, but he was gonna make sure they squeezed every pleasurable drop out of this claiming.

Once he was fully seated, the hair on his chest brushed her back and he wrapped a strong arm around her middle.

"Is this what you wanted?" he asked, barely managing to keep his voice measured.

"This is what I wanted." She reached down and caressed his thigh, and looked back at him over her shoulder. "You're so strong. All that power, sometimes I can feel it, you know? How you're barely keeping it inside. Barely keeping it on a leash." She squeezed his thigh, a line appearing between her brows. "But you don't have to. Not with me."

"I'm yours, Hades." Her blue eyes were crystal clear as she admitted the truth. "I always will be. You know it and I know it. So claim what's yours and don't hold back."

Her words flipped a switch. She was his. She was his and she trusted him completely. He propped himself up with his fists on either side of her hips. With a roar, he did as she asked. He stopped holding back.

He thrust his hips forward, pounding her into the sheets, filling her. When her knees buckled, he wrapped an arm around her waist, fingers seeking her clit. She screamed and bucked back against him, mouth slack as her entire body—including her ass—clenched and spasmed with her orgasm.

Oh gods, so tight. His wife. His. Fucking *his*. Forever. Electricity rolled down his spine, but still he drove into her, his thrusts growing harder and wilder. His weight drove her hips into the bed, her raw pussy stuttering orgasm after orgasm until she was sobbing and writhing on the bed.

"*Mia moglie. Sono pazzo di te.*" *My wife. I'm crazy for you.* Gentle words as his body was anything but.

He'd never known passion like this in his life. Never knew it could exist. Never knew he could love anyone or anything so much. So fucking much.

He held her body cemented to his as his hips thrust more violently than ever, her sweat and his and her slick all mixed up together and soaking the bed.

"Cum," he shouted. "One last time. Cum with me."

His huge palm massaged her swollen pussy, fingers sawing in and out of her as he filled her up from behind. She screamed out as Hades's orgasm tore through him.

His cum filled her, dripping from her ass as he pulled out, joining the already wet sheets.

His gorgeous wife had never been more perfect than when she smiled up at him, a blissful grin on her face, finally satiated.

"Thank you," she rolled to her side, reaching blindly for him. He collapsed beside her.

Her fingers traced his face, his jaw, the blade of his nose, his eyebrows, up to his forehead. She smoothed the lines there. He sighed and let his cheek rest in her palm.

"I've missed this." She stole the words right out of his mouth.

But before he could ask her why she left or demand any answers, her eyes had fallen closed and she was gently snoring.

69

Persephone woke up to a splitting headache. Ugh. She clutched her head with both hands and moaned.

Gods, what was that racket? She fumbled around on the nightstand and frowned, really opening her eyes this time.

What the—? She wasn't in her apartment.

She knifed up into a sitting position. Ow! She grabbed her head again. Okay, okay, no sharp movements. Got it. But what the hell? She'd never gotten migraines before.

She looked around. Where the hell was she?

Then it all came rushing back. The dream.

Because that's all it had been, right? That's all it ever was. Dreams. She shifted and winced at the soreness in her...in her *bum*.

Shit! *Not* a dream.

That meant— Persephone swiveled, looking this way and that. She was in a bedroom, decorated in cool, masculine tones.

No, no, no.

She got to her feet, wincing again, and walked slightly bowlegged to the door. She pushed it open and peeked her head out.

"Hello?" she called.

No response but the noise that had woken her up sounded again.

Her cell phone ringing. She all but jumped out of her skin at the noise. "Crap!" She shrieked, hand to her chest as she made her way back towards the nightstand by the bed.

She frowned as she picked up her phone. According to her muddy recollection, she'd shown up at Hades's door in nothing more than a sheet. So how did her cell phone get here?

She touched the button to answer the call. "Hello?"

"You up, sleeping beauty?"

Hades's voice. He sounded like he was smiling. Persephone sank back down onto the bed. She missed the sound of Hades when he was happy.

"Yeah," she said tentatively.

"Good," he said. "You feeling okay?"

Persephone blinked, a thousand thoughts shooting through her head. *No, I have a headache from hell and for some reason I can't explain, I think I sorta came by your place last night accidently and screwed your brains out, had about a gazillion orgasms and begged you to fuck my backside, but ya know, apart from that...*

"Yeah," she said instead. "Feeling good. A little tired."

Hades chuckled and her toes curled hearing the noise. Why did he always have to sound so damn sexy?

"I bet."

Persephone felt her cheeks heat to about a thousand degrees. "Is there a reason you're calling?"

"As a matter-of-fact, there is," he said, continuing to sound amused. But then he sobered. "The mayor's schedule has been reshuffled due to a ribbon-cutting of some sort, but he can still see you. The meeting has been moved to 9:30 instead of 11:00."

Persephone's eyes shot to the clock on the nightstand. "It's already a quarter after eight!" she shrieked, jumping to her feet. She had no idea what she looked like, but considering last night's activities, she didn't even want to imagine.

"That's why I'm calling. I had to step out to deal with some unresolved business—" he definitely sounded less than pleased about the fact "—but I'll be by in half an hour to pick you up. We'll debrief in the car on the way."

"Half an hour?" she squeaked. "But I have to go shower. I have to do my hair. And makeup. And— Shit!"

"Calm down, baby. We got this. Now hop to it, see you in 30."

"Right." She reminded herself that she'd offered to help, convinced him to accept her help. She couldn't start bitching about it now.

"Oh, and put on some clothes before you leave the bedroom." With that he hung up the phone.

And Persephone commenced freaking out about how in the world she would be able to get ready in time. She was meeting with the mayor. The *mayor*. He was in Hades's pocket, or at least he used to be, but still, he was one of the most powerful men in the city.

Persephone threw on one of Hades's shirts and hurried out of his apartment. Rushing, she threw open the door to hers, and stopped short with a scream when she saw a man in all black sitting on her couch.

"Easy, Mrs. Ubeli, I'm here on your husband's orders." The man courteously averted his eyes towards the wall. He was identical to every other Shade—black slacks, black shirt and dark shades, sitting right in her living room. Meanwhile her hair was a mess and she was wearing nothing but one of Hades's oversized undershirts.

"I thought you guys were supposed to wait outside." A thought hit her and she asked with not a little bit of horror, "How long have you been in here?"

"Since about sunrise."

Was that when Hades had left the apartment? Gods, so obviously these guys knew she'd been sleeping over at his place. Biting her lip, she warred over whether to turn and shower, or go make coffee. She didn't have time, like *really* didn't have time.

But in the end, she couldn't imagine facing the day without caffeine. Maybe it would help with this damn headache. Ignoring the man, she crossed the room and started a pot, feeding Cerberus while it brewed.

"I'll take him out, if you want," the Shade offered. "I like dogs."

"Uh, thanks. If it's not too much trouble."

"My partner Fats will be in to wait in the living room while you get ready," he warned her. "You're to have a man with you at all times."

"Ok," she mumbled, rolling her eyes. At least they hadn't been ordered to wait in the bedroom.

The man waited until Cerberus was done eating, clipped his leash on and walked him outside. A tall, gangly man walked in.

"Fats?" she asked, eyebrows going up.

The man grinned. Grabbing a mug of coffee, she went to hide in the bedroom.

She showered and dressed in record time, putting on only a light dusting of makeup. When she was ready, the Shades were waiting to walk her to Hades's car.

Hades himself got out to hold the door for her. Persephone's breath caught at the sight of his handsome figure, broad shoulders and narrow waist with a suit tailored to show them off perfectly.

And every moment from last night came back in vivid, high-res detail. Shamelessly grinding against him right in the doorway. Begging him to fuck her. Cumming around his fingers. His cock. Begging for him in her ass—

"You need a robe," Hades said after they'd slid into the back seat.

"I know," she said, blushing. The Shade must have turned in a report.

"Come here," he demanded.

Shit. Because the other thing she remembered from last night?

Other than orgasm after orgasm after *orgasm*?

I'm yours, Hades. I always will be. You know it and I know it.

What. The. Hell. Was. Wrong. With. Her?

More like, what was wrong with those pills? She was never taking another one again, that was for damn sure. She should never have taken two, she got that, but damn—couldn't Hermes have warned her about possible side effects? And what the hell kind of side effects were those anyway??

And now here Hades was, gray eyes expectant. And she had to go face the mayor and try to get him to give up information about the shipment—

She scooted a little closer to Hades but not too close, pulling her dress down as she did so. Her outfit was professional, yet flirty, the dress a coral color with a scoop neck that skimmed the top of her cleavage. It showed off her figure perfectly and the color made her skin glow. Hades's eyes swept over her and they narrowed, but he didn't say anything.

"You sure you're ok this morning?"

Now her face was really red. "Coffee's helping the headache." She held up the travel mug she'd brought from home, crossing her legs, reversing the movement once she realized what she'd done.

Hades mistook her unease as nervousness. "You don't have to do this if you don't want to."

"You got a meeting with the mayor in less than twelve hours. I think it's too late for me to back out now. How did you manage that, by the way?"

"Called in favors. Hermes helped."

"Hermes?" Persephone wanted to ask how her friend had an in with the mayor, but of course, Hermes was a Merche. His last name carried all sorts of weight with the highest echelon, disowned son or not.

Hades started drilling her again on what to say. They spent the next fifteen minutes as they crept through morning traffic going over it.

"The mayor will toy with you. And he's good at reading people—it's probably his number one skill. But you, more than anyone of us, have nothing to hide."

Persephone nodded, thinking of the phone call she made to the detective before she ran from the Estate and set all this mess in motion. Right. Nothing to hide...

Her husband was still talking. "...and relax. Stick to the script and remember, you have an advantage."

"What advantage?" Persephone asked, worry starting to gnaw at her.

"Your legs look fucking great in that dress."

"Hades," she protested, and tugged at her hem.

His dark head darted close to hers. "As soon as this business is done, we're settling things between us once and for all."

If she looked at him anymore, she'd drown. She stared out the window for the rest of the ride, running over the script in her head.

"Mrs. Ubeli? This way please." A young man in a navy suit motioned Persephone to go into the office.

Inside Zeus Sturm stood, the leader of the most powerful city in the world, with his short blond curls, bouncing with boyish energy.

"Please call me Zeus." He took Persephone's hand and kissed it, guiding her into a seat as his gaze raked up and down her body.

"Thanks for meeting me on such short notice." She flashed him a smile.

"No trouble at all," he said smoothly, even though Persephone knew it must have been a lot of trouble. Between nine and noon was prime time for a politician, and they'd arranged the meet twelve hours prior. If he was annoyed, though, he didn't show it.

"Please, help yourself." Zeus gestured to the silver coffee and tea service on the desk. She waited, but instead of going back to sit in his chair, he leaned against the desk and looked down at her.

His position offered him a perfect view of her cleavage, she realized, but his smile was mild and nothing more than friendly.

"So," he started, "you're here to talk me into being the guest of honor at the fundraiser for the animal shelters?"

"A fashion show." Persephone leaned forward in her seat. She and Hecate had come up with the idea ages ago, and last night Hades and Charon decided it was a good enough cover for her to meet with Zeus. "Models and pooches. And Hermes and his team at Fortune are in charge of the designs."

Zeus grinned. "Fashion is going to the dogs," he quipped and she laughed.

"Exactly. Just show up to cut the ribbon for the new dog park, and a quick photo op. Your constituents will love it."

"Never hurts to support a good cause. Alright," he said, slapping the side of the desk. "I'll do it."

"Really? That's great...Thank you."

Zeus's face also held a smile, but it looked wrong somehow. "Is that it? Your husband pulled every string to get you in front of me and that's all you want?"

She flushed under his piercing gaze and he spread his hands apologetically. "I'm a busy man, Mrs. Ubeli. No sense beating around the bush."

She cleared her throat. "He did have a question for you. Some property was collected from the docks a while ago. He'd like his personal effects returned to him."

Now Zeus looked amused but he stayed quiet as she went on.

"He thinks the boxes have been tampered with and the contents removed." Before continuing, she glanced into the corner, where a mounted camera fixed her with its glossy eye. Under its impassive watch, she tried to remember everything Hades and Charon had drilled her on this morning.

"She's walking into a lion's den," Hades had said, almost calling the whole thing off right before she'd gotten out of the car.

"In the daylight, the lion's muzzled." Charon had responded, looking for all the world like he was at ease. Persephone knew better.

"Zeus does not do business in the daylight, never forget that. Most of his shit is buried deep, like an iceberg. But it's there," Hades said, and answered her question before she asked. "I've known him a long time."

Now, staring into the mayor's cutting blue eyes, she told herself to breathe. "Can you help us?"

Zeus paused, letting his gaze drift over her. "They were smart, sending you," he said finally. "I like a new sweet little thing in a sundress, every spring." He picked up a pen off his desk and pretended to study it. "How far did your husband tell you to go to soften me up?"

Persephone stiffened and, gripping the hem of her dress, drew it down.

He laughed at her. "Relax. I don't want you."

Lion's den, she reminded herself.

"Good, because you can't have me," she bit out.

Zeus tossed the pen he'd been toying with on his desk. "Tell Ubeli that I can't do anything to return his personal effects. They're part of a police investigation. If he submits a claim I'm sure it will be filled in… a few years."

She stood. The conversation was obviously over. He wasn't going to give them anything. "See you at the fundraiser."

He inclined his head, his blond curls falling attractively into his face. "I hear you and Ubeli were separated. Are you working something out?"

Persephone wanted to tell him it was none of his business. "We're talking."

He studied her with quick, cutting blue eyes. "If you want to divorce him, I can protect you."

"Thank you," she said politely. "I'll let you know." She didn't tell him that she'd been with her husband long enough to know that protection came with a price.

"Practicing your husband's poker face?" Zeus seemed amused and she'd had it.

"Thank you for your time. I also appreciate you giving us the use of your penthouse suite at the Crown Hotel. We do *so* enjoy it."

Anger flashed on his face; she turned on her heel and hurried out, frightened and elated to have scored at least one hit.

70

Hades sat, tense and on edge inside the back of the SUV outside the mayor's office waiting for Persephone. He glared up at the building.

"She's been in there too long," he growled.

Charon glanced back at him in the rearview mirror. "Only been 45 minutes. And you know Zeus. He probably had her wait outside an extra half hour because he could."

"I've had about enough of Mayor Zeus Sturm flexing his muscles. It's time to remind him of who is really in charge of this city."

Charon raised a brow. "Maybe don't declare war on the mayor's office until you heard what he's gotta say. And maybe when you don't got a target on your own forehead."

Hades grumbled under his breath and glared back out the window.

Finally. There she was. Persephone was pushing through the exit. Hades took a deep breath, the first it felt like he'd taken in 45 minutes.

He should never have let her go in there alone. Never again. He didn't care what sort of sense it made. It was his job to be her shield and he couldn't do that if he was outside waiting in the Fucking car.

She hurried down the steps, looking as beautiful as ever in her sharp, knee-length pencil skirt and tailored vest that was buttoned to accentuate her narrow waist and womanly curves. She'd been wearing a coat on the way in. Probably a good thing because if he'd seen that outfit, no way would he have even let her out of the car.

Charon jumped out and moved around swiftly to open the door for her.

She slid gracefully into the car, staying near the door as Charon closed it. As if she thought Hades would allow her to put distance between them. After last night? He didn't think so.

He quickly disabused her of the notion by grabbing her around her tiny waist and sliding her across the seat until she was flush by his side.

She let out a little squeak but that was her only protest.

"How'd it go?" asked Charon from the driver's seat.

Persephone frowned, still wiggling to put distance between herself and Hades. "Not well. He won't help us."

Hades was far from surprised. There was a reason Zeus had been ducking meetings with him. Something was wrong. Either Zeus had double-crossed him and sold the shipment to someone else—a fatal mistake, Zeus would soon find if Hades discovered it was true—or something else had happened that Zeus was trying to hide. Either way, Hades would get to the bottom of it. With or without the mayor's help.

"Tell me what he said. Don't leave out a single detail."

So Persephone did, replaying the conversation blow-by-blow. She looked nervous as she came to the end of her story, like she expected Hades to lose his shit. She ought to know him better by now. He valued control far too much to lose it over someone like Zeus Sturm.

"It's okay, babe." Hades patted her thigh. "We'll get the shipment back; we have other ways."

She didn't look convinced. "What if you don't by the end of the week? What will Poseidon do?"

"Worried about me?" Hades grinned.

She sniffed and looked away. "Making sure that I get alimony."

Hades laughed and, hooking her close, kissed the top of her head.

He cupped her cheek and slowly turned her face back toward his. "But things are getting serious now. I need to go back to the safe house. And you need to come with me."

Her head immediately started shaking no.

Not this again.

He lifted his other hand so that now he cupped both cheeks, holding her face still as he dropped his forehead to hers. "Stop denying what we have. Who you are. You are my wife and you belong by my side. Last night proved that. You said it yourself."

She pulled back from him, quick enough that he lost hold of her. "Last night didn't change anything. It was..." She shook her head and threw her hands up in the air. "Okay, well, I don't know exactly what last night was. A timeout from the real world. Two adults blowing off steam, I guess."

What. The. Fuck?

A timeout? "Blowing off steam?" He got right in her face. "You saying that you're mine forever and begging me to claim your pussy and your ass was blowing off fucking steam?"

Her cheeks went pink and she tried to look away but he cupped her face, forcing her to look at him. "Why did I know you were gonna try to pull this shit?"

"Hades, I wasn't myself. I'd taken some sleeping medication and—"

"What the hell are you taking sleeping medication for? And who prescribed it? Because they should lose their license. It was irresponsible and—"

"Stop it. Stop it!" She jerked away from him. "You don't get to control every little thing in my life anymore. I'm my own person. I can go to whatever doctor I want to. You don't own me. I can do what I want, when I want—"

Hades glared at her, his chest in a vice, her words from the night before ringing in his ears about how any cock would do. "You better not be blowing off steam with any other adults."

"Of course I'm not!" She looked appalled and his stomach unclenched, but only a little.

"Then come with me."

"No. How many times do I have to tell you that it's over?"

He got right in her face again. "As many times as it takes for you to get it through your head that it'll *never* be over between us. And deep down, you know it too. Otherwise, you wouldn't have ended up on my doorstep at two in the morning begging me to fuck you."

Her head jerked quickly back and forth in the negative. "I— I wasn't— That wasn't like me. I couldn't sleep and I was in bed and I got to thinking about you—"

"Please, do go on."

Her cheeks flushed and she stopped, her lips hardening into a thin line. "You know why I'll never go with you? Never be with you again? Because you're an ass!"

"You certainly seemed to like my ass last night," he leaned in and hissed in her ear, "the way you were grabbing it and demanding, 'harder, Hades, fuck me *harder*.' I have the fingernail scratches to prove it."

If he thought her cheeks were bright pink before, they were nothing to the cherry red they went now.

"I did not."

"I'll turn around and drop my drawers right here, right now. It's nothing Charon hasn't seen before." It was true, since Charon had once helped to dig fragments from a ricochet bullet out of Hades's ass. Hades would be proud to add Persephone's marks to his other scars.

"Don't you dare," Persephone bit out, her tiny hand batting at his bicep.

He grinned at her. "So it's settled. You're coming to the safe house with me."

"Charon?" Persephone knocked on the glass partition Charon had raised once they'd gotten on the road. "Charon!" Persephone yelled when he didn't respond at first.

Hades could imagine the wary sigh as Charon finally pushed a button and the partition began to retract. "Thanks Charon. Could you drop me off at my apartment?"

Okay, now she was really pissing him off.

"This isn't a game, Persephone." Hades gripped her thigh. "People have died."

Her head spun his direction. "You think I don't know that?" She said it so forcefully, almost like she was accusing him of something.

It felt like being doused with ice. Was she thinking of his mother? Of Chiara? Was she thinking of how women in his family had a habit of dying, because of their proximity to Ubeli men?

My father always kept my mother out of it.

And look how well that turned out for her!

Hades sat back hard in his seat. Was she right? Was the safest place for her far away from him?

"You heard her," Hades barked to Charon. "Take her to her apartment."

He ignored her surprise. Charon merely said, "You got it, boss," and turned the SUV to go uptown instead of toward the south side.

Persephone didn't say a thing for the ten-minute drive it took to get there and neither did Hades. He did feel her eyes on him occasionally. He wanted to growl at her to keep her eyes to herself because he was three seconds away from changing his mind, dragging her to the safe house with him, and chaining her to a bed again. Every mile they drove it sounded like a better and better idea.

Finally the SUV stopped in front of her apartment building. She paused before opening the door and Hades clenched his fists to stop himself from reaching for her.

"Hades—"

"Don't," he cut her off. The only way he was making it out of here at all was if he left right this second. "Stay safe. Don't go anywhere without the Shades."

He didn't wait for her acknowledgment. The second she'd stepped from the car, he ordered Charon, "Drive."

71

Hades had definitely been pissed at her when he dropped her at her apartment two days ago. And Persephone understood. She really did. After their night together, for her to turn so cold and bitchy...ugh, she didn't want to think about it anymore.

But thinking about it was all she'd been doing nonstop ever since she'd last seen him. She felt horrible. To raise his hopes like that was cruel.

She hadn't been completely in control of her faculties when she'd sleepwalked to his door, though! Okay, so she remembered almost everything that happened that night. In far too great of detail. She didn't even know how to describe the overwhelming, all-consuming need and desperation she'd felt.

And when Hades had finally given in... Persephone's eyes fell closed, a shiver running through her at the memory.

It was like her deepest and filthiest desires had bubbled up and she had to have them fulfilled, no matter what. No matter what she had to say, how she had to manipulate or... She wished she could say, no matter how she had to *lie*.

But that was the thing. Other than the one off comment about going out and looking for another man if Hades didn't satisfy her, she was afraid that everything else she'd said had been the truth.

It was like some damn truth serum had been poured down her throat. Things she'd never even admitted to herself had popped right out of her mouth. Thank the Fates but she'd been too concerned with servicing her libido to make any other confessions...

And when Hades had cornered her in the car after the meeting with the mayor, what was she supposed to do? Go hole up with him at a safe house? The two of them, alone?

No. The night before had been a temporary madness.

It was unfair to keep sending Hades such mixed messages, she knew that. Jumping him one moment and telling him to stay away the next—first in the back of the club and then again the next night? Gods, sometimes she didn't even know her own mind.

Because she couldn't want him. She wanted the light. She wanted nothing to do with the darkness Hades's life was drenched in.

So she couldn't let herself be swallowed back up by him, by his world. No matter how tempting. No matter that some pills had mixed up her head for a little while. No matter that she couldn't stop thinking about his strong hands on her body, the commanding bass of his voice, the taste of his lips on hers...

All of it kept her awake at night. And after the sleepwalking incident, she didn't dare take the last sleeping pill. She flushed it down the toilet. Wednesday rolled into Thursday rolled into Friday with her imagining more and more horrible things. What would happen on Monday when Poseidon's countdown clock wound down?

If she came clean and told them all everything—both Hades and Poseidon—would it help? Or was it too late for it to make a difference?

A stronger woman would have come clean, no matter the consequences. A stronger woman would have *tried*.

The couple of hours she actually managed to sleep at night were always filled with nightmares. She woke each morning feeling heavy and sluggish, like her body was full of concrete. Even walking

Cerberus didn't limber her up much; her torso ached and she had a headache that wouldn't quit.

With no end to the tension in sight, and no word from Hades, she took some painkillers and puttered around her house trying to focus on getting back to normal. Maybe if she settled into her normal routine and relaxed with her friends like she used to, she'd think of a solution.

Which was how she found herself wearing a little black dress, her hair teased around her face with smoky makeup, walking into a large row house on Park Avenue. Two Shades tailed her, looking unhappy.

Hermes met her at the door, in his signature rock star look—tousled hair, Fortune jeans, black band tee, and bare feet. He looked effortlessly sexy, and not for the first time Persephone wondered if she would've dated him if she hadn't met her husband first.

"Darling, you look fabulous," he said. "This little get together isn't as elegant as the party Perceptions put on, but the canapés are to die for and the booze is free."

"Sounds perfect," she mumbled. She was *so* tired. She'd slept maybe a total of three hours in the last three days. But Hermes had called and enticed her, saying Aphrodite would be attending.

"You okay?"

"I'm tired." She didn't quite know how to describe the achy, horny malaise that had settled in her bones, but she was chalking it up to worry and missing Hades.

"You sleeping?"

"Sometimes." Right now probably wasn't the time to ask him what the hell was in those pills. She was likely in the minority who had extreme side effects, anyway.

"Who are the suits?" Hermes looked over her shoulder.

"My bodyguards. Fats and Slim."

"Nice to meet you." Hermes grinned big at them.

"No fraternizing with the muscle," Persephone ordered, taking Hermes's arm and steering him into the house.

"Darling, I wasn't going to stop at fraternizing..." Hermes craned his neck to watch the two men follow them in before hurrying along as she swatted him. The back of his t-shirt was ripped a little so the tops of his angel wing's tattoo peeked out.

As Hermes rounded the corner, a demanding female voice boomed his name. "Hermes, there you are. The caterers ran out of ice, and I can't find Buddy. Without him they're too stupid to know what to do."

Persephone peeked around Hermes to see the tall woman who'd stopped him. She wore a long white and gold caftan that swirled around her arms and legs, allowing a peek of light brown skin. She stopped short once Persephone rounded the corner. "Hello, I didn't know we had new company."

She didn't smile, though, as her eyes swept over Persephone. Her dark hair was pulled back taut from her face and only made her look more severe.

Shrinking a little under the woman's frowning perusal, Persephone felt like a child playing dress up in her mother's clothes: weighed in the balance and found wanting.

"I'll find Buddy," Hermes promised, putting his arm around Persephone. "Olympia, meet my friend Persephone. Persephone, this is Olympia Leone, the lady of the house."

"Persephone? As in Persephone Ubeli?" Olympia fixed Persephone with a hawk-like stare and Persephone's greeting died in her throat. "I know all about your husband." The look on her face told Persephone that she didn't approve of Hades Ubeli at all.

"We're separated," Persephone blurted out, quailing under the woman's glare, and giving thanks that it was technically true. Athena always told her she couldn't lie "for beans."

Hermes, however, seemed impervious. "Come on, Persephone belle, let's round up the head caterer and I'll introduce you to the people here."

"Wait," Olympia said. "Who are they?" She pointed to the Shades. "Ubeli's men aren't welcome in my home. Not now, not ever."

"Relax, they're Persephone's bodyguards. I have my eye on them." Hermes grinned impishly. He pulled Persephone past Olympia, slipping in a quick cheek kiss that seemed to soften Athena's harsh countenance a hair.

"Right, let's check on the ice situation," Hermes said, leading the way through the long, open living room/dining room into the back kitchen. A few guests already milled around the table laden with food.

"Is Aphrodite here yet?" Persephone asked. It was so weird, going from living with Aphrodite and Athena, seeing them every day, to now having little idea what was going on with her good friends. She missed both of them, badly.

"Supposed to be arriving soon. With Max Mars. Are they a thing?"

"I saw them together at the studio where they are filming their movie. They are most definitely a thing." Persephone smiled as she gave this piece of juicy gossip, watching Hermes's eyes flash happily as he devoured it.

It felt good to be here, talking about frivolous things, forgetting her heavy reality for a moment. It made her feel young, like she could reverse the hands on the clock and go back, back to before...

"Let's hope they ditch the paparazzi before coming here," Hermes said. "The rest of us would rather not be so famous."

Persephone shook off her melancholic thoughts and threw herself fully into the moment. "Who else here is famous?"

"Olympia used to be the DA of the city. She's thinking of running for mayor now."

"Against Zeus Sturm?"

"Yep."

Persephone remembered that her meeting with the mayor the day before had been Hermes's doing. "Wait, how do you know Zeus so well?"

"I met him through Olympia."

Persephone's head went back a beat before she put two and two together. "Ok, right, she was the DA."

Hermes shrugged. "That, and she used to be married to him."

Persephone put a hand to her head, rubbing it. "I need a drink. It's been a long week and New Olympus is one big incestuous pool."

Hermes barked a laugh. "You got that right. Incestuous pit of sin." He slid up to the drinks table, getting her a white wine. He took a cocktail, raising it to salute someone across the room.

"Olympia is cool. She took me in when I was homeless, and made it clear that I'd always have a home here."

"Ok." Persephone felt a little better about the stern-faced matron. "She didn't seem to like me or Hades very much."

"Oh, she hates Hades. With a passion. District attorney, remember?" Hermes swigged his drink. "Of course, don't take it personally. Olympia hates everyone at first. By the way, how did the meet with our fair Mayor go?"

"Not great. Like I said, it's been a *loooong* week." She looked around at all the people laughing and having a good time. She felt envious.

It would be so lovely to get away from it all, even for one night. She wished she could be young and silly and get drunk off of neon colored drinks with umbrellas in them. But after her experience with the sleeping pills, she was not in the mood for anything even slightly mind-altering. "I don't suppose there's any coffee?"

"Coffee?" Hermes barked out a laugh. He tossed back the rest of his drink. "Girl, you have got to learn how to party."

Two hours later, Persephone wandered into the backyard, feeling so tired she was edging on delirious. The grass felt nice under her feet. If she lay down, would she finally be able to sleep? She twirled around, her arms out. She'd never realized before that you could reach a point of exhaustion where your limbs were so heavy they felt light again. A little like she was floating.

Aphrodite and Hermes stood on the patio, and Hermes started clapping. "Ladies and gentlemen, I give you: our friend plus a single glass of wine." Hermes flung out an arm towards Persephone.

Aphrodite giggled. "That's it? I guess she really isn't used to drinking. It's not even midnight and she's wasted."

What they didn't know: she hadn't even drunk that single glass of wine. She'd been sticking to bottled water all night. Her exhaustion was just finally catching up with her.

Fats and Slim stood on either side of the small garden space, looking even less happy than they had a few hours ago, but Persephone didn't care. She didn't care about anything. She was so damn tired. Tired didn't even begin to cover it. She was exhausted. Worn out. Pooped. Obliterated. Smashed. There weren't enough words in the thesaurus for how tired she felt.

Persephone teetered to the edge of the garden and leaned against a tree.

Aphrodite stepped off the edge of the stone patio and her five-inch spike heels sank right into the grass. She came towards Persephone anyway.

"Hey, are you okay, babe?" Aphrodite's brow furrowed with concern. "You've barely said two words tonight. You look tired."

Persephone started giggling as Aphrodite's thumbs ghosted over the bags that were undoubtedly underneath her eyes.

"I'm so exhausted," she confessed.

"Oh, honey," Aphrodite said, pulling her into a hug. "It's gonna be okay. Let's get you somewhere you can sit down. Maybe lay down."

"No, I don't want to leave," Persephone protested. "I never get to see you guys." And going back to her empty apartment was the last thing she wanted.

"How about a nap?" Hermes said, joining them. "There are rooms upstairs. Take a little power nap."

Persephone nodded. A power nap. Perfect.

"We can take care of her," the two Shades moved forward. Persephone stepped to follow them but stumbled and almost face planted.

"Whoa, I've got ya," Slim said, and the next thing Persephone knew, Slim had her over his shoulder and the whole world went topsy-turvy.

She went limp over his back. It actually felt nice not to have to hold herself upright anymore. She really, really needed that nap.

"Hades is going to kill me," Hermes muttered. Aphrodite patted his shoulder.

"I'll be back soon," Persephone mumbled, her eyelids already falling shut.

"We should take her home." Fats stepped forward, light from the tiki torches glinting off his shades.

"You're wearing sunglasses, at night." Persephone giggled, pointing. It all suddenly seemed so absurd.

"What did you give her?" Fats demanded, getting up in Hermes's face.

Persephone eyes watered and she felt dizzy as she looked between Fats and Hermes. Hermes was taller, but skinny compared to Fat's shorter, compact form. She didn't want them fighting over her. Thankfully Hermes backed down from Fat's challenging stance.

"Nothing but a glass of wine, I swear. And she only sipped at it. She didn't eat but it still shouldn't have affected her this badly."

"I'm just really tired, guys," Persephone tried to explain.

"Get her upstairs." Olympia appeared in the doorway to the kitchen, in her regal looking robe. "Now. You—" She pointed to Fats, "Out. You've overstayed your welcome."

"Go take care of Cerberus," Hermes muttered. "Persephone will be safe, we'll all be here to watch her."

Olympia kept giving orders. "Get her upstairs, put her to bed in the peacock room. There's a private bathroom in that one. You—" She pointed to Slim with a look on her face like she'd seen a cockroach. "Can stay. But don't cause trouble."

Olympia shook her head, obviously frustrated. "Andrea Doria just arrived and she brought a bunch of security with her, too. There are more bodyguards than guests." Olympia turned away, still muttering.

Slim nodded to Fats and carried Persephone down the hall with Hermes leading the way.

She dropped her head against Slim's chest, suddenly feeling more exhausted than she ever had before in her life. The good news was that she was pretty sure she'd be able to sleep the second she laid her head down on any kind of pillow.

In the upstairs hallway, she caught a glimpse of another tall black woman standing in a bedroom doorway, a giant blonde wig on her head and fabulous makeup highlighting her midnight skin. She stared in surprise down at Persephone in Slim's arms.

"So sorry, Andrea." Hermes sidled up to the woman as Persephone was carried on by. "Novice drinker."

"No problem, we've all been there," the tall woman laughed. Persephone craned her neck to stare at Andrea's heavily made up face under the outrageous blonde wig. She looked vaguely familiar, and Persephone almost had figured out why, but the thought escaped her when Slim put her in bed.

"I don't think coming out tonight was the best idea," Persephone murmured to him before the darkness of the room closed in on her and, exhausted, she finally slept.

72

In the Mayor's mansion, Zeus strode back from his study, tossing his cell phone to an aide. With his usual exuberance, he threw open the doors to the dining room and looked down the long table at the assembled guests.

Every night the same, like a boring joke, Zeus thought as he viewed their expectant faces. *A visiting dignitary, a decorated war hero, and a kiss-ass aide walk into a bar...* Out loud he said, "Apologies for my tardiness. I hope the first course was to your liking."

Polite murmurs came from up and down the table. Zeus made sure to share his smile all around. People could be so petty if they felt not enough attention had been directed their way.

"I'm told the chef received a gift from one of the ships docking in our ports," Zeus said as he sat down. "So tonight we dine on fresh sea bass. It was imported specifically for a particular shipping tycoon's meals, now graciously gifted to us."

The guests all expressed their appreciation.

"Please, enjoy." Zeus smiled and gestured, and took his first bite as everyone would wait on him. "Mmm," he said. "Much better than the way my ex-wife used to char it."

The guests around the table laughed, right on cue.

"What we call a sea bass is actually two species of toothfish, renamed to sound more palatable," said a man from midway down the table in a heavily accented voice. He had a neatly trimmed salt and pepper beard, and piercing blue eyes. He was a professor, if Zeus recalled correctly. Professor Wagner or Ziegler? Something like that.

"A fish by any other name...is still delicious." Zeus savored a forkful and motioned to the servers, calling for more wine around the table.

A round, bald headed man bustled up to the table. "My apologies for being so late."

"Commissioner," Zeus greeted the newcomer, and only the very astute would pick up the slight twitch of his lips, a micro-expression of annoyance. Zeus thought the bearded professor had noticed, though. Observant, that one.

"Sorry, boss," the heavy man breathed, tucking his napkin into his collar and grabbing a dinner roll. The man was the opposite of refinement and it was his position alone that afforded him a seat at the table. "This new drug has got us all scrambling."

Zeus wished he was sitting closer so he could kick the man under the table.

"New drug?" The dignitary from Metropolis, Claudius, perked up before Zeus could change the subject.

"Just hit the streets," the commissioner said, oblivious to Zeus's glare. But Bill wasn't the cleverest man and had always been slow at picking up on social cues.

"Limited quantity, but we think that will change. Couple of rich kids got picked up for indecent exposure, said they had taken something. Their parents went to swinger parties and came home with a couple pills. The kids know their stash; they try everything their parents do. We questioned them in the hospital and it all came out."

The commissioner finally paused in buttering his roll and realized that every eye around the table was trained on him in fascination.

"Are the kids ok?" a woman asked, Zeus forgot her name in his budding fury at his commissioner. Zeus had gotten re-elected, it was true, so he wasn't immediately worried about campaigning again. But a mayor was only as strong as the confidence he inspired. If his guests left with the impression that he couldn't control the drug traffic on his own streets—

"Oh yeah, effects wore off hours ago," Bill continued. "Just a little groggy, dehydrated. One of them still had a high, and he had an erection the size of—" Bill finally saw Zeus's face and bit off the rest of the sentence. Cheeks ruddy, he continued, "We rushed the labs to figure out what was going on."

"Interesting," Zeus said, his tone frosty.

The commissioner winced, having obviously caught onto Zeus's disapproval. Finally. But it was too late. The rest of the guests leaned in as one.

"What is the effect of the drug?" the professor asked in a scholarly tone.

"An extreme high, leading to almost uncontrollable arousal. Sets off...uh, climaxes that are...uh, off the charts, as it were."

"Again, nothing like my ex-wife," Zeus said, going for laughs and hoping to steer the conversation away from talk of drugs.

"Detrimental side effects?" the professor's fork was frozen halfway to his bearded mouth.

"Too soon to tell. But for some it seems to cause aggression. In all cases the high is followed by a crash. Sweating, shakes, a little dehydration, withdrawal headaches, that kind of thing." The commissioner, sweat beading on his forehead and obviously as desperate as Zeus was to end the conversation, shoved the entire roll into his mouth.

73

Persephone woke up in the dark, with a slight headache and screaming thirst. Her body was soaked with sweat. Ugh, gross. A glass of water waited on a side bed table; she downed it and staggered to the adjoining bathroom to drink some more.

Her shoes were gone, and gods, where was her purse?

She should never have come out when she was so tired. How long had she slept for? She looked around but she didn't see a clock. She searched for her purse so she could look at her phone, again, no luck.

She stumbled around the dark bedroom but still couldn't find her purse. She must have dropped it downstairs somewhere. Crap.

After looking around the bedroom one last time in vain, she slid into the dark hall. Pulling a shaky hand through her hair, she leaned on the wall to rest a moment. Where was Fats? Or Slim? The upstairs was one long hallway with rooms off of it.

Which direction led downstairs? Well, she wasn't getting anywhere just standing here, so she turned left and started walking. As she got closer to what she suspected was the front of the house, she heard a man talking. He sounded a little like Hermes.

It wasn't until she'd opened the door and was halfway inside that she realized she'd entered another bedroom.

And it was occupied.

In the low lamp light, she could clearly see the couple on the bed. She recognized Hermes immediately, he was the one on top, the angel wings tattooed on his back moving as his shoulder muscles worked. A woman's long legs wrapped around his body, as his rather beautiful backside pumped to the rhythm of the music.

Oh shit. She did not need to be seeing this. Persephone backed away in horror, fumbling for the door handle, but not fast enough.

A new partner entered from another side door, coming from the master bath, Persephone guessed. The newcomer was the blond, stunningly beautiful Andrea Doria. She put her hand up to straighten her wig, and Persephone saw the large onyx ring she wore. Andrea's robe fell open to reveal a very masculine chest and, lower down, male parts. Impressive, very aroused male parts.

"You all ready for me?" the drag queen drawled to the panting couple on the bed.

Hermes reared back and Persephone caught sight of the woman's face who was beneath him—it was Olympia. Her dark skin was slick with sweat, but her head was propped on the pillows and she looked as a regal as ever.

She saw Persephone, too, and glared daggers at her as she addressed Andrea, "He's ready. Climb on." Her toned arms pulled Hermes back down over her and Andrea leaned forward, climbing on the bed. Hermes hadn't seen Persephone and she'd rather it stayed that way.

Persephone backed into the hall before Olympia could alert anyone to her presence. Andrea noticed the movement by the door, though, and called to her, squinting through the darkness. "Come on in, honey, plenty of space on the bed."

Reversing hard, Persephone turned and hustled down the hall the other direction, hoping the tall drag queen didn't decide to chase her down and insist she join in.

Persephone passed a second door that had drifted open, but she didn't look. The noise of moans and cries made it sound like an entryway to hell, but she was sure the occupants were having a blast.

She hurried by. The hall turned and finally, stairs!

Persephone ended up in the kitchen, so it must have been a service stairwell. She looked around. Where was everybody? Her eyes moved to the digital clock on the stove. 1:30 a.m. Seriously, where was everyone?

More importantly, where were her bodyguards, shoes, cell phone and purse? Persephone was ready to get the hell out of here and curl up on her bed back in her apartment. Maybe she'd break her own rule and let Cerberus sleep up beside her on the mattress tonight. She could use a little comfort cuddling, even if it was only with her Great Dane.

Continuing her search, she walked out of the kitchen. The lights were low and all Persephone could hear was some sexy, throbbing music. Without thinking, she flipped on an overhead light, and gasped, her hand flying to her mouth.

Olympia's living and dining room was filled with naked people.

A few looked over at Persephone briefly when the lights turned on, but the rest were too caught up in the throes of lust to pay attention. For her part, Persephone couldn't move. Even her hand was frozen on the light switch.

The food had been cleared off the table, making way for the long, sexy body of a naked woman, who lay shuddering in pleasure as the mouths of three men traveled over her pale skin. One of the men briefly turned away, grabbed a spoonful of thick whipped cream, and dabbed it on her perky breasts before licking it off.

Beyond them, several couples were in a clinch, making out while leaning against the wall. Right before Persephone's eyes, one of the couples embraced as the man lifted the woman and started thrusting into her, pressing her against the wall. His partner moaned and wrapped her legs around his naked body, digging her nails into his muscular shoulders and urging him to go faster.

Above all of this, Aphrodite stood on the arm of a large armchair, naked but for her signature red lipstick, watching the goings on with a satisfied smile. Seated below her was Max Mars, his own legs spread with a woman kneeling between them.

As Persephone watched, the movie star reached up to Aphrodite, and Aphrodite stepped down so she was standing on the chair cushion with one leg cocked up on the armrest, straddling Mars's face. Gripping his blond hair, she thrust her pelvis forward, her head falling back as his mouth moved between her legs.

Persephone was blushing so hard, she was sure her face would explode. Hades had always teased her that she was naïve and sheltered. But even after two years living in the city watching Hermes flirt with every hot thing that moved and Athena delighting in saying the most graphic things to embarrass her...Persephone still wasn't prepared for this.

"Come on, babe," the man with the whipped cream beckoned to Persephone. When she still stood frozen, he grinned. "Oh, I get it. Here, there's a few left." He set down the whipped cream bowl onto the side board and reached for a little bag filled with white pills. "One of these will loosen you right up."

Persephone couldn't find air to speak. The man shook the bag impatiently. "Olympia won't mind. She scored them for all of us." He came towards her, a lanky Adonis, smiling as she stared at him, wide eyed. His own green eyes were long lashed and mesmerizing.

"Here, beautiful," he took a pill out of the baggie, and proffered it to her. "Down the rabbit hole."

A squeak may have escaped from her throat. She backed away even as she stared at the pill that looked identical in shape and color to the pills Hermes had given her.

"Persephone," she heard someone call, and she looked across the room, grateful for the interruption.

At first, her eyes flew to Aphrodite and Max Mars. Aphrodite had fallen to the couch, her body arched backwards over the arm of the chair as Mars's gorgeous muscular torso reared over her. The woman who'd been between his legs before now was kneeling behind him, still doing her best to lick him as he pounded Aphrodite aggressively.

Persephone reluctantly tore her eyes away from the threesome, looking past them to see the man who'd called her name. A man in an olive-green suit, dapper except for his hair, tufted unusually in blond spikes.

Oh shit. It was Spike Hair. Poseidon' thug, the one who'd been there when she was kidnapped.

Persephone didn't even stop to question what he was doing here. Her hand shot out and she hit the lights. As the entire room went dark, she jerked backwards, away from the man offering her the pill, back into the kitchen, escaping the man who'd called her name.

74

Around the Mayor's dinner table, conversation was stilted as all the guests waited for the poor commissioner to finish his mouthful.

"So this new drug, what's it called?" Claudius, the diplomat, piped up as soon as it looked like the man might be close to swallowing. Claudius took another bite of fish as he waited to hear the answer. He'd finished almost half his plate, not as put off his meal as the rest of the crowd by the conversation.

Glancing nervously at Zeus, the commissioner answered, "On the streets, it's now being called A, or Bro, or Brew. Short for Ambrosia."

"Sounds lovely," Claudius's wife said with a smile to her husband. "Causes extreme arousal? If the only cost is a little headache, might be something I'd want to try." She finished with a mischievous glance toward Zeus. "If it weren't illegal, of course."

"The libido is a powerful drive," said the professor. "Unexpressed emotions never die, but are merely buried alive to appear later in uglier ways. We suppress our desires to fit into society but when we suppress them too long, society may collapse."

"That's Freud, isn't it?" Zeus recognized the quote.

The professor nodded, looking pleased that someone had caught the reference, and raised his glass to Claudius's wife. "So you see, a woman such as yourself, keeping your libido under wraps could be dangerous to all."

She laughed delightedly, and the rest of the table looked impressed with the professor's musings. Zeus barely kept himself from rolling his eyes. The professor slipped down a few rungs in his estimation. He'd met academics like him before—old, self-important windbags who were relevant only to the campus bubble they lived in.

This was the last thought he had before he gasped involuntarily and hunched over a little. Fuck, his *stomach*. A cramping pain tore through his stomach and radiated outward to the rest of his body.

"Honey, what's wrong?" he heard Claudius's wife say. Looking up through watering eyes, Zeus saw Claudius collapse forward, face down into his meal, gagging.

Help. He needed *help*.

But when Zeus opened his mouth to shout for help, all he managed was another desperate, choking gurgle. The pain. Zeus had never felt anything so intense. Gods, he was going to die. He was going to die!

Zeus thrashed and plates and cutlery flew. His dinner partners jumped up as his hand went rigid, gripping the tablecloth as he slowly sank to the floor.

"Mr. Mayor?" The commissioner's voice was a distant shout.

Zeus's vision went blurry and he prayed to pass out because the pain, oh *fuck*. His eyes went wide as another spasm tore through his stomach.

The professor crouched beside him. "Get an ambulance!" he shouted in his thick accent.

"Is he choking?" someone cried out.

The professor stared down at Zeus and Zeus wanted to beg him for help, to do something, dammit. But all the man said was, "I do not think so." He looked down the table. "Two choking at the same time? It cannot be a coincidence."

A woman was screaming and Zeus peripherally registered that it was Claudius's wife, that her husband had collapsed, too.

"Madam!" The professor bellowed at her from the floor beside Zeus. "Does your husband have a food allergy?"

Zeus didn't hear her reply. All he knew was that the next moment, the professor was cradling his head and ordering someone, "Take his feet, now! We must carry him to the car."

"But, the ambulance—"

"It will be too late. We must go. *Now*."

"What about Signore Claudius?"

"He's already dead. Now hurry or we'll lose the mayor, too!"

75

*S*pike *Hair? Here?* Persephone could wonder why and how later, though. She wasn't about to let herself be a victim again. She rushed onto the patio. As she rounded the house, she tripped on a man's outstretched legs.

"Oh!" she screeched and slammed a hand over her mouth. Because it was Slim. Laid out and unconscious. Was he— Was he—?

She dropped down and put her fingers to his throat. But even before she felt his heart beat, she felt his chest moving up and down. He was breathing. But in the light from the back patio lamps, she could see a tiny trickle of blood marking the spot where he'd taken a blow to the head. Whimpering, she checked his pockets, but whoever had knocked him out and tied him up must've taken his weapon and his phone. Dammit!

It was only now as she looked closer that she realized that his hands and feet were tied together. But even if she could untie him, there was no way she could carry him. Her options were either: go back inside and interrupt her friends who were...otherwise engaged, or possibly get kidnapped by Spike Hair again.

Shit.

Or she could run and hope whoever had knocked her bodyguard out wouldn't come back and finish the job.

"I'm getting help," she whispered to Slim as if it would make a difference. "We'll come back for you."

Crap, how long had she been crouching here exposed? Time to get moving again. Barefoot, she escaped across the grass and ran straight into the foliage beside the back fence, oblivious to the briars scraping her.

A childhood in the country had taught her how to climb a tree. Which she did now, grabbing onto a low branch and swinging herself up until her legs got purchase. She climbed higher and higher, all the while waiting for one of Poseidon's soldiers to yank her down at any moment.

She was quick enough, though, to get up high and drop to the other side of the fence that divided Olympia's house from her neighbor. Scraped up and limping a little from the shock of landing on her bare feet, Persephone dashed around their house and slipped out to the street beyond.

After a few blocks running on the pavement, she slowed and reality set in. Shit. She had no money, scraped palms, no shoes, and no phone. Her bodyguard was hurt, maybe even dead if Spike Hair decided to come back and finish the job...all because of her frivolous desire to go to a party.

She kept trying to pretend that if she just closed her eyes and wished it all away, the reality of who she was would disappear. But it didn't work like that. She'd been foolish and childish, and now people might get hurt because of her.

Holding back tears, Persephone tried to think and take stock of her surroundings. Self-flagellation wouldn't do anyone any good right now. Hermes, Aphrodite, Olympia, Poseidon's man—she put them all out of her head so she could figure out what to do next. She was on Park Avenue, not the best place to be in New Olympus after midnight, but not the worst.

There was a place close by that she knew well—the Crown Hotel, where Hades had his penthouse.

Gathering her bearings, she slipped down back alleyways, moving as quickly as she could while still watching for broken glass that might cut her feet.

When the brilliant gold facade of the grand hotel appeared, she nearly sobbed. Even in the late hour, the door was busy with returning guests.

The senior doorman, Alphonse, recognized her. "Mrs, Ubeli, what—" His eyes widened at the sight of her bare feet and scraped arms. "Come," he said, wrapping her in his coat and ushering her quickly inside.

Wincing as the fabric brushed her raw arms, Persephone padded to the elevator, her head down, grateful for his help.

"I don't have my keycard on me," she said, feeling desperate.

"It's no trouble, Mrs. Ubeli. Your husband will want to see you right away."

"He's here?" Persephone asked. "I lost my cell phone. I was at a party and...it got wild."

"Ah," the doorman said in a kind tone. "No matter. You're home safe now." He used his own keycard to get her to the penthouse floor, and dropped her off, only leaving when she insisted she was fine. The penthouse lights blinked on as soon as she entered.

She hadn't been here since... She shook her head, taking it all in. The place was clean and perfect, but with maids that came through daily, that was no surprise. It looked the same, and nostalgia hit her hard.

Using the hotel phone, Persephone called the number she knew —Hades's cell. It went to voicemail; she left a message in a quavering voice. "Hey, it's me. Something went wrong at the party where I was tonight. I should never have gone. It was stupid, but I didn't think... Anyway, one of Poseidon's men was there. Slim is hurt...I didn't know how to help him, so I left him and ran and now I'm at the penthouse. I lost my cellphone," she ended awkwardly. "Call me."

After going to the bathroom and washing her dirty feet, she pulled off the little black dress and looked in the mirror. The sexy makeup she'd put on earlier seemed like a joke now. She wiped it off and threw her dress in the trash. She stared at herself in the mirror, cataloging her week so far.

Kidnapped, drugged, betrayed. She'd moved into a new apartment and gotten a bodyguard almost killed.

She glared at herself. "You wanted your own life, huh?"

She closed her eyes and breathed out a long breath through her teeth. It was time to stop running and grow up. For real this time.

She needed to talk to Hades and sort things out. He deserved to know everything. She didn't know what that meant for their relationship or what she even wanted it to mean... And she needed to confront Hermes.

Those pills he'd given her... What was happening to those people at the party looked an awful lot like what had happened to her the night she'd sleepwalked. Hermes had lied to her. Told her they were sleeping pills when they were actually... How could he have done that to her? And then on top of it all, invited her to a party like that? He had to have known what it would turn into, with them passing out the pills like candy. And he'd certainly been enthusiastically participating.

Persephone scrubbed at her eyes and headed for the closet. Her clothes lay just as she'd left them. Hades hadn't moved a thing. She opened one of his drawers and drew out one of his undershirts, lifting it to her face and inhaling. The familiar smell of his detergent made her feel calm and desperate at the same time.

She stepped further into the closet and ran her hands over his suit jackets. He was always so strong. She could use some strong right now.

Finally she pulled on a pair of her jeans, wincing slightly at the scrapes on her legs. She tugged a simple plain white tee over her head and went out to check the clock again.

Almost 2:00 a.m. No calls.

Waiting, she watched the clock until she was convinced she saw the second hand hesitate. Surely Hades would have gotten her message by now? Or wherever he was hiding out, did he not even have a cell phone? What about Charon? Where was he?

But Alphonse said Hades was here. Or had she just assumed? A big part of her had secretly hoped that this was his safe house—that he put out the word that he was going into hiding but he'd snuck back to the hotel to wait it out here.

She frowned, looking around. During their marriage Hades *did* like to work out before bed, usually opting for the private penthouse pool. Maybe he *was* here and had gone upstairs for a quick swim?

Okay, so maybe she was grasping at straws now, but she had to check. Anything was better than sitting here doing nothing.

Walking gingerly on bare, scraped feet, she left the penthouse and took the stairs to the top floor.

The top floor of the Crown Hotel had a spa and gym dedicated to the more elite guests, plus an open-air patio and a few small, shallow sunning pools outside, along with the Olympic sized indoor one. Persephone padded through the workout area, completely dark at this time of night, and through the women's dressing room. The lights turned on as she passed through.

She played out the conversation she would have with Hades in her head. He'd be angry, she knew. Two narrow misses was enough for her for one week. Her insistence that she be left alone to live her own life sounded stupid now.

Plus, would it *really* be so bad to be holed up alone with him? All week she'd been so lost and lonely without him.

The pool lay under a huge glass canopy, a dark pit that drew her eyes. One moment she was staring at its tar-like depths and then the lights blinked on and—

"Hades!" she screamed. "No!

A man floated face down in the blue water, fully clothed in a dark suit like the ones hanging in her husband's closet.

Persephone ran to the edge of the pool. "Hades!" His dark hair waved gently around his submerged head and his limbs were spread wide, completely limp.

Persephone didn't stop to think. She leapt into the water and swam towards her husband with everything she had.

It was only as she drew close that she saw the blood clouding the water around him.

"Hades!" she screamed as she grabbed him and flipped him over in the water. She let out another shriek, jerking backwards.

The man was dead. His head was bashed in.

But it wasn't her husband. It wasn't Hades.

"Persephone," Charon called and she spun around in the water. "Get out of there," he said. "Come on. Hurry."

Persephone swam towards the shallow end, tears clogging her vision. "Where's Hades? Is he safe?"

Charon met her at the edge of the pool, grabbing her elbow and all but dragging her out of the water. "I just got off the phone with Mr. Ubeli. He's safe. But that man is dead. And you can't be found here." Charon's voice was so deep she had trouble deciphering what he said.

Persephone shook her head as she stared into his black eyes, uncomprehending. Hades was safe. But a man was dead. Everything was happening too fast. "Who is he?"

"I don't know." Charon made an impatient sound as he bent and swept one arm under her knees, scooping her up. "We gotta get out of here."

The gory sight at the pool receded until Persephone saw it only in her mind's eye. She pressed her face into Charon's warm shoulder. She was getting him all wet, ruining his suit, but she couldn't care.

Back in the penthouse, Charon swung her down. She winced when her damaged feet hit the floor, but didn't sit when Charon motioned she should. She was drenched and dripping all over the carpet.

Charon already had a burner phone to his ear. "I got her," he said without greeting.

"Is that Hades? I want to talk to him." Persephone could feel her brain sizzling, the events of the night burned so deeply into her memory.

Charon answered her with a shake of his head.

Persephone went to stand in front of him, her body shadowed by his bulk. He hung up and glared down at her, imposing in black slacks and a black shirt stretched tight across his awesome muscular form.

"You don't move from my sight until Hades gets here."

"What about the body?" Her voice came out almost an octave higher than normal, but she felt near the edge of her rope. "What are we going to do?"

"Nothing."

"We can't just do nothing. We have to call the cops."

"And get fingered for murder? Not today." Charon ran his hand over his bald head, looking down at her. "What were you even doing up there?"

"Looking for Hades." She wrinkled her forehead, staring up at him. He was two hundred and fifty pounds of black muscle, and so scary most people wouldn't even look at him. Persephone wanted to smack him. "I didn't know it was going to be dangerous."

"Bet the body in the pool helped wake you up to that fact," he said sarcastically and she saw red.

"It's not funny!"

"Course it's not fucking funny." Charon loomed closer into her space. "You could've surprised the killer, taken a bullet. You're lucky to be alive."

"That man—who is he?"

"Don't know, probably some poor suit who got drunk downstairs tonight."

Persephone sucked in her breath.

"Our enemies don't care about the body count." He saw her pale face and paused, weighing his next statement. "It's a message to Hades from his enemies. They can't find him, so they get a guy with build and hair color that looks like Ubeli. We find the body; we get the message."

Biting her bottom lip so she wouldn't scream, Persephone barely dared to ask, "What message?"

"Death threat. Target: Ubeli. Now, go change outta those wet clothes before you catch your death and the boss kills me for not taking care of you right."

Persephone nodded, swaying on her feet.

"Gods, woman, sit." He took her shoulders and guided her down onto a leather settee. She should protest. The chlorinated water might mess up the leather—

But before Persephone could say anything, Charon left the room. He came back carrying another of Hades's undershirts and a pair of his boxers.

With the gentleness of a mother, Charon turned Persephone's back to him and peeled off her shirt, replacing it with Hades's. Next, he braced her while she stood and tugged off her jeans. He looked away while she kicked them off and tugged on the pair of black boxers.

He pulled her elbow so she sat back down. He sat next to her and, without a word, swung her feet into his lap to inspect them. After a second he grunted in annoyance and stood again, gathering her into his arms.

"What—?" She caught sight of his grim face and shut up.

He set her on the sink in the bathroom and fished around for first aid supplies. He found the first aid kit and lifted her foot to start treating her cuts.

Halfway through, his phone beeped and he checked the message. "Fats broke up the party."

"He did? Is Slim okay?"

Charon blinked at her. "You mean Jorge?"

"Fat's partner? I call him Slim," she said.

Shaking his head, Charon went back to cleaning her cuts. "You're lucky you're cute."

"What's that supposed to mean?" she bit her lip to keep from crying out as the antiseptic he applied started to sting.

"It means you're a fucking pain in the ass, but we'll put up with it." Charon finished with a soothing ointment and started bandaging. He went to work on the angry red marks she got from climbing that tree in a panic.

"Gods, woman." he muttered, turning her calves this way and that before treating the scratches. Persephone sat still, trying not to wince.

"I didn't know it was going to be an orgy," she said in a small voice.

"Right."

"I didn't," she insisted. "And obviously I didn't know Poseidon's man was going to be there, either. I wouldn't have gone if I'd known it would be dangerous!" She started to push up from the counter and Charon grabbed her waist to hold her in place, keeping her from standing up as he got in her face.

"Like you didn't go to the enemy's strip club for kicks?"

Not fair. That was completely different. "A girl was missing! I wanted to help!" she shouted back, not caring that his large, angry face was only a few inches away.

"You need to pull your head outta your ass. You put yourself in danger, and left to keep doing it. For all you know Ajax is still out there, waiting for his chance."

"Oh please, I know Ajax's dead," she said before she could stop herself. "I mean, I heard..." her voice trailed off at the blank, scary look on Charon's face.

"What do you know?" he asked quietly. No anger, no intimidation. Just scary quiet.

Persephone's heart was racing, finally realizing the danger. "I watched Hades kill him. I was hiding, I saw the whole thing. Hades beat him to death."

"That's why you ran." Charon looked almost satisfied. "Couldn't take it."

"He killed a man in cold blood." She gripped the edge of the countertop.

Charon's black eyes studied her face. "Fucker deserved it."

"I grew up in a world where people call the cops. Where they let them handle things."

"Yeah, for what? Scum like Ajax gets a fair trial, parole? Back on the streets."

"Yes, if that's the way the system works."

"Yeah, the system works sometimes. But when it doesn't, we fix it."

"You can't play god, Charon."

"We can't walk away. Not now."

"Oh, yes, because you're better than the Titans," Persephone said scornfully. "Because you follow some stupid Code—"

Charon's hand moved so quickly she only caught it out of the corner of her eye.

She flinched, but he didn't strike her. Instead, he stuck a thick finger in her face.

"Don't ever disrespect the Code," he said, and her stomach dropped at his tone. She could feel the angry tension in his body, but when he lifted her again in his arms and carried her, his arms were gentle.

He set her down on the bed. "Get some rest."

"Charon, where's Hades? When can I see him?"

"He's in hiding. Not even I know where he is. Total blackout until we flush Poseidon out."

"He didn't leave me a message?"

"He won't send anything to a phone that can be traced. But if you want a message, I'll give it to you—stay here, stay quiet." Charon looked her over, obviously noting the dark circles under her eyes. "And get some sleep."

"Great, orders. Definitely Hades." The penthouse was silent besides the two of them. "You don't have to babysit me, personally. I'm sure you have better things to do. Or did you draw the unlucky straw?"

"No," Charon said. "The lucky one. And your safety is top priority right now."

Persephone's head went back a beat. "Me?"

Charon chuckled, shocking her again. She'd expect the floor to open up at her feet before she'd ever witness Charon laughing.

The big man sensed her confusion. "Family always takes priority. Old Man Ubeli thought the same way. Protect the core." He walked closer slowly, until he towered over her. She still hadn't moved. "The world can tilt on its axis but when you're home, you're upright again."

Persephone waited, perfectly still, for the giant to finish what had to be the longest speech of his life.

"Hades and I made our choice long ago, when we lost all the family we'd ever had. Someone threatens you, we'll fight, bleed, and die before we see it carried out."

He gripped her chin gently. "You've got nothing to be afraid of, Persephone. Hades and I are tough because we have to be. We were made for this moment."

His finger slid under her jaw, tipping it up until she met his eyes. "Trust me."

76

Persephone lay in her and Hades's bed, cheek to the pillow, body curled in the blankets.

She didn't sleep, just lay staring at the ceiling, where the smooth paint turned into a pool with a body floating in it.

What would she have done if it had been Hades? Her chest clenched even at the thought. Reliving those moments in her head when she'd been so certain it was him, that she'd lost him, that it was all over...

Her breath hitched. She couldn't— How could she live in this world without him?

She raised her head when she heard voices outside. And barking. Cerberus!

She jumped out of bed, not caring that she was only wearing Hades's oversized undershirt and boxers.

She scurried into the living room and dropped to her knees when she saw Cerberus. She threw her arms around his neck and he barked happily, licking her face all over. Stupid tears sprouted as she hugged her dog, laughing and petting him on his tummy while he jumped and did little excited leaps at seeing her again.

The reunion was so sweet it took Persephone a second to realize that sitting opposite Charon in the living area was Fats.

He looked older, tired. The night had taken its toll.

Persephone's lower lip trembled as she looked at him. It was her fault his partner had been hurt, and now possibly— "You find Slim?"

"Slim's gone," Charon said succinctly. "Disappeared. Poseidon must have taken him."

Persephone willed herself not to spill more tears.

"We'll get him back," Fats told her. He didn't look like he blamed her at all. "You alright?"

"Just tired," she said. "I'm sorry about Slim. I should've gone to ground with Hades."

"Cops are swarming this place," Fats said. "They found the body in the pool."

"Took 'em long enough." Charon looked unimpressed.

"I'd say pretty quick, considering everyone's preoccupied with the situation with the mayor," Fats said.

"What situation with the mayor?" Persephone asked.

Fats glanced at Charon first and the underboss nodded permission. Persephone gritted her teeth but listened to the report.

"Mayor Sturm was taken to the hospital last night. They think it was poison. He had a late-night dinner party—one of his midnight specials. He's in critical condition, and another guest died."

"Persephone," Charon said and she fixed her eyes on the big man. "They think that Poseidon did it."

"Poseidon?"

"They're giving him credit for the body upstairs, too. At least, unofficially."

Persephone wanted to ask how Charon knew this, but she remembered his ties to the police and shut her mouth.

Fats agreed, "Two hits, one night. Trying to take out a major player and threaten the other. Gotta be Poseidon."

"You're sure it's not my—" Persephone swallowed. "You're sure it's not the Titans?"

Charon shook his head. "Doesn't make sense. They don't have any motive to hit the mayor. Doesn't do anything to forward their agenda."

"So why was Poseidon's man at the party last night?" Persephone asked, suspecting she already knew the answer.

"Looking for you," Charon confirmed, and, try as she might, she couldn't read his penetrating gaze.

She swallowed. "What do we do now?"

Fats got to his feet. "We let this guy out." He nodded to Cerberus. "I'll go with you. I need to stretch my legs for a bit."

Persephone looked to Charon for permission, and the bald head nodded. "Take the couple extra Shades downstairs to shadow you."

Fats nodded.

After a brief walk in the park across from the hotel, they waited for Cerberus to do his business while watching the lights from the cop cars wash over the golden facade.

"Will they come to question me?"

"Probably not. If they do, though, we'll brief you." Fats handed over her cellphone. "I found that winged fellow and got your purse."

Persephone took her phone, avoiding his eyes. "Thanks. You didn't have to do that."

"I had backup. Actually, it was my pleasure," he grinned.

"Charon said you broke up the party."

"Naw. Just flipped on the lights. Everyone had mostly finished."

Cheeks heating, Persephone hesitated. "I didn't know that was what the party was about." It was important to her that Fats understand. "And I didn't want to leave Slim behind."

"I know," the Shade said, so softly that she dared to look at his face. What she saw there was scarier than any rancor. Devotion. Loyalty.

She swallowed hard. "I'm going to follow orders from now on."

"Aww, don't say that." Fats winked at her. "It's more fun when you don't."

77

Persephone woke, her mouth dry and heart racing. Her hand was vibrating; her phone. She answered it before she realized it was an unknown number.

"Hello?" she held her breath, hoping it was Hades.

"Persephone?"

It took her a moment to recognize her friend's dulcet tone. "Aphrodite? Is that you?"

Aphrodite's voice sounded strained, weak. "I'm at the hospital."

"Oh my gods," Persephone swung out of bed. Cerberus's ears pricked up and he raised his head. "What happened?"

"Mars got in a fight." Aphrodite choked out. "I thought it was all fine. At the party, everyone took those pills and then it was, I don't know—it was just like, free love, ya know? Everyone kissing and hooking up with everybody else."

"A group of us went back to Mars's place and I thought it would be more of the same. Mars was fine with it at the party. I mean, we all were. But this one guy started kissing me and Mars went ballistic. He punched the guy and they got in this big fight, and a couple other guys joined in—"

She paused and Persephone could hear her crying. "And one of them started getting rough with me, slapping and hitting me. Mars didn't even notice, he was so busy beating the shit out of that other guy."

"Aphrodite, you're going to be ok," Persephone said, her heart breaking as she went to her closet to find shoes. "Tell me what hospital; I'm coming." Cradling the phone between shoulder and ear, she stuffed her bandaged feet into her sneakers.

"I don't want you to see me like this." Aphrodite's whisper was broken.

"Aphrodite, please. Let me come be with you." Persephone was already grabbing a large purse and shoving some essentials into it.

Aphrodite told her the name of the hospital. "Don't tell anyone yet, please."

"I won't."

A Shade sat in a chair by the door, not Fats or anyone else she knew. His head snapped up as Persephone came rushing out of her bedroom, her designer bag over her shoulder, heading to the kitchen to put out food and water for Cerberus.

"Good boy," she told the dog before racing to the door.

The Shade stood, his jaw set as if ready to stop her from leaving. She'd learned her lesson, though. She wasn't going anywhere without protection.

"I need to get to Main Hospital, right away," she said, and he blinked. Grabbing a jacket from the coat closet, she started out the door. "Come on."

A hand caught her arm before she was half gone. She looked back to see the Shade frowning at her. "Charon said you need to stay here."

"It's an emergency," she told him and watched orders war on his face.

"I drive," he said finally and she nodded.

Her phone rang again when they were almost at the hospital. This time a blocked number. Hades, or Charon, calling to scold her. In the second of hesitation, a car darted out suddenly and Persephone slid forward in her seat. The Shade cursed, reaching over to keep her still.

"Buckle up," he ordered.

Persephone clicked her seatbelt on, one hand on the dashboard. She silenced her phone with a swipe. As soon as they pulled into the emergency room parking lot a couple minutes later, she opened the door. "I'll be right inside, you can find me in there."

She ran for the building. The Shade wouldn't be far behind and Persephone couldn't stop replaying in her head how Aphrodite, strong, fearless Aphrodite, had sounded near broken on the phone earlier. Persephone had to see her. Now.

"She's in room 210," a nurse told Persephone. "We're not supposed to let people back here, but she asked for you specifically. You're her sister, right?"

"Right," Persephone lied straight-faced. "Her sister."

When the woman looked at her skeptically, Persephone straightened her shoulders and glared. "We have different fathers."

The nurse nodded and Persephone hurried down the hall to Aphrodite's room. She tried to brace herself mentally for what she might be walking into. What had happened to the man who hit Aphrodite? Who'd gotten her to the hospital? And what the hell was wrong with her supposed boyfriend that he would let a thing like that happen in front of him and not stop it?

The lights were out in the hospital room, but Persephone could still see the bruises blooming on her friend's face, looking dark and angry.

Aphrodite's lower lip trembled as Persephone approached. "Hey," Persephone said gently.

"It was my idea to move the party back to Mars's house. This is all my fault. I ruined everything."

"Shhh," Persephone shook her head. "No, honey, it's not your fault. You have to know it wasn't your fault."

Tears rolled down Aphrodite's face; Persephone held out a tissue. Aphrodite took it and mopped at her injured skin, wincing.

"It doesn't look that bad," Persephone said, studying the black half circle over the orbital bone.

Aphrodite laughed half-heartedly. "Thank you. You're a bad liar."

She sniffed. "The doctors want to keep me overnight, to make sure I don't have a head injury."

"From the blow?"

"The guy also pushed me down. I hit my head. I don't know, I came to and was seeing stars."

"I'm so sorry, Aphrodite. You don't have to talk about it if you don't want to."

"I have to tell someone or else I'll go crazy, but I don't want everyone to know." Aphrodite leaned back into the pillow, turning her head to hide the marred side of her face. Against the white pillow, her profile was perfection.

"After the party we went to his place... We were all having fun, drinking. Mars drank a lot. A few guys took some more of those pills we'd all had at the party. It seemed natural when our friend Nathan started kissing me. Like earlier. But Mars got pissed and started hitting Nathan. And one of Nathan's friends decided it was my fault." She shrugged, winced at the movement.

"And he just hit you?"

"I may have screamed that him and all his friends had tiny, limp little dicks. Then he just came at me."

"Mars didn't stop him?"

Aphrodite's eyes went distant. "I don't even think he could see me. He was consumed in this rage. There was no getting through to him. I thought he was going to kill the other guy he was busy pounding on. Someone called the cops. They showed up and pulled him off Nathan. It was only then he saw me and tried to get to me."

Aphrodite slumped into the pillows. "It took two officers to drag him away, he was fighting so hard to get to me. But I was glad they were taking him away. I hate violence. I could never be with someone like that. It's over between us."

Persephone bit her lip. Hades was violent. She'd witnessed him beating someone to death and there hadn't been any cops to pull him off Ajax at the last minute.

"I'm so sorry," Persephone whispered, almost too low for her friend to hear. Pulling up a chair, she smiled at Aphrodite until Aphrodite finally reciprocated with a wan smile of her own.

"Thanks for coming. I feel better already. The doctors are going to do a CAT scan and keep me for the night."

"That sounds really serious, Aphrodite."

"Oh, it's just my doctor being fussy." Aphrodite raised her head a little and confided, "He's a former client."

"Ah. So you're in good hands." Persephone smiled and pulled her purse into her lap. "In that case, it's good I brought you something to feel more normal."

She pulled out a small camisole and pajama shorts, a toothbrush still in its case, and a book. "And I barely use this makeup." Persephone waved a small case of eyeshadow and lip gloss.

When she looked up Aphrodite's eyes were shimmering with unshed tears. "Thank you. For everything. It's nice to have someone who cares."

"A lot of people care about you, Aphrodite. Athena, Hermes, pretty much everyone who meets you loves you."

"Not Mars." Her voice wavered. "He never said he loved me."

"Mars is a twisted, fucked up asshole." Persephone surprised herself with her own vehemence.

"Wow. I've never heard you use curse words. I didn't realize you knew any."

"Come on, I lived with Athena for a month and a half." Persephone grinned. "I'm a quick study. And seriously, Max Mars isn't worthy of you. If there was any justice, someone would kick his ass and teach him how to treat a lady."

Aphrodite nodded and sighed.

"Or tie him up and make him watch his own movies over and over," Persephone said with a wicked smile.

Aphrodite laughed, and this time, it sounded hearty. "Now that would be truly cruel."

78

Hades burst into the hospital hallway. He'd been running for the past forty-five minutes, ever since he got the message that Persephone had gone to the hospital for an 'emergency.' That was all his man could tell him. And that she'd been walking upright when she dashed into the hospital, but that was it.

The nurse at the desk wouldn't give his man any more information, declaring he wasn't family and saying she'd call security on him if he didn't back off.

She'd continued stonewalling until Hades himself arrived. He'd called the hospital Chief of Staff, a man who owed him more than one favor, so by the time Hades got there everyone was falling over themselves to guide him where he needed to go.

And now, at the end of the long hallway, sitting on the floor with her head in her hands, was his wife.

"Persephone."

Her head jerked up as Hades jogged down the hall towards her. He crouched down in front of her as she swiped at her eyes.

"You're okay?" he asked, heart in his throat even though he could see with his own eyes that she was all in one piece. "My man said you needed to come to the hospital."

She winced. "Not me. Aphrodite. A man beat her up. I should have explained."

What man had fucking dared lay a hand on his wife's friend? He would find out and make them pay. "She alright?"

"No." Persephone's eyes filled but she tilted her head back to keep in the tears. "She hit her head pretty bad when he knocked her to the ground. That's why they're keeping her overnight. The bruises will fade in a while. But her arm was wrenched out of its socket and she's got a concussion."

Persephone shrugged once, twice, and then her face crumpled. "I'm sorry," she sobbed lightly, putting her hand over her face. "It's hard seeing her like this."

Hades could relate, if it was anything like what he was feeling, seeing Persephone so torn up. His chest felt tight and all he wanted to do was make it better. She was trembling, and the thought of her sitting here all alone on this cold, antiseptic floor was enough to drive him nuts.

He pulled off his suit coat jacket and settled it over her shoulders. Her fingers grasped onto it like a lifeline as she pulled it around herself and leaned into his chest as she cried.

Hades waited. He exhaled, the tension he'd been carrying all week since he'd last seen her finally easing. It had been hell, sitting in that safe house, not being able to communicate with anyone, not knowing where she was or how she was or if she was safe.

He was done being Mr. Nice Guy. Persephone was going back with him. The only place she was safe was by his side. He was the only person he trusted with her safety. With her life.

When her tears finally subsided, Hades took his handkerchief and wiped her face. He watched her carefully.

"What did the doctors say?"

"They want her to talk to a cop. She's pressing charges. And breaking up with her boyfriend who was too involved in a brawl to realize what was happening and to stop it. Max Mars."

"Pretty boy. His movies suck," Hades said.

Persephone couldn't help herself, she laughed sadly. "Yeah, he sucks a lot."

Hades took her hand and brought it to his lips. He wanted to yank her into his arms or better yet, throw her over his shoulder and drag her to a basement somewhere he was sure she would be safe. Instead, he forced himself to let her hand go after pressing the briefest kiss.

He didn't know quite what to do with the two voices raging inside him, one screaming at him to go with his barbarian impulses and the other whispering to fight for his better nature. Things in his life used to be simple. So cut and dry.

But after knowing Persephone, he could never go back to simple. She was beautifully and wonderfully complex. She blazed with the light of the noonday sun and cast a prism of colors over his previously colorless life. He couldn't go back to black and white after living in glorious color.

But how did he let her be free and also make her do what he wanted her to do? What he *needed* her to do so that he knew she was safe?

Every day since she'd left him, he'd only grown more and more impatient treading that thin line. Yet still he knew, somewhere deep down, that the only way it would ever work was for her to *choose* him. She had to *choose* their life together.

Her puffy, tear-stained eyes met his, suddenly crinkling with concern. "Shouldn't you be in hiding?"

"I needed to make sure you were all right."

"Oh." She frowned. "Guess I'm still in the running for worst wife ever." Her lower lip trembled.

Hades blew out a breath in an almost laugh. "Come here." He stood and drew her up. He held out his arms. Offering comfort.

Persephone slid into his arms and his entire body relaxed at how right it felt. How natural. His arms closed around her and his eyes sank shut. He needed to memorize how she felt in his arms. She might pull away soon and he needed this to fuel him until she was in his arms again.

"Thank you," she said.

"Of course."

She stayed there for long minutes. "I can hear your heartbeat," she whispered into his shirt.

His arms tightened around her. He wanted to feel her heartbeat in the place he loved best, her pulse throbbing while he sucked her clit.

He wanted her back in his bed, underneath him, screaming his name, acknowledging she was his wife, that she was his, only *his*—not in the throes of one night's passion but in the morning and every morning for the rest of their lives.

She pulled back, and he forced himself to merely stroke the hair back from her face. For her, he could and would hold back. "What do you want me to do?"

Persephone bit her lip like she was actually considering his offer when a woman in a white coat cleared her throat.

Persephone swung around. "Yes? How is she?"

The doctor took them in with a dispassionate gaze. "She has a concussion, but no brain swelling we're worried about. Normally we'd discharge her but we want to monitor her through the night."

Hades nodded. "Thank you, doctor. Can you keep our numbers in case there's any change?"

"Of course, Mr. Ubeli."

Persephone looked startled, probably wondering how the doctor knew his name.

"She can bring this to the cops. Assault," the doctor said.

"We'll talk to her." Hades glanced at Persephone.

"She's sleeping now," the doctor put in. "I'd recommend letting her rest and visiting her in the morning."

Persephone nodded, blank like she was numb. Hades needed to get her out of here. He pulled the doctor aside for a moment and spoke to her for a few minutes about Aphrodite's continuing care, all the while watching Persephone. He came back to her as soon as he was done with the doctor.

"Persephone?"

She looked up blearily.

"You ok?" Stupid fucking question. Obviously she wasn't okay.

"I'm ok." She stared blankly at his shirt buttons. She looked so lost, it killed him.

He held out his hand. "Come on, goddess," he said. "Let's go home."

Without pause, she slid her small hand in his and followed him out.

79

After the hospital, Hades brought her home to her apartment. Cerberus greeted them; one of his Shades had brought him. Persephone relaxed as soon as they stepped foot into the apartment with its warm, welcoming design.

Hades stood in his trench coat, attending to messages on his phone as she got Cerberus's food, but really he watched her. Cerberus's bowl was already half full, so she only poured a little more in.

"When was the last time *you* ate?" he asked.

Closing her eyes, she shook her head.

She wasn't taking care of herself. There were dark circles underneath her eyes. She needed him. She needed to be taken in hand and—

Hades forced that line of thought quiet and breathed out through his nose. "I'll send a man with some food." He couldn't help following up with, "Go lie down."

He braced himself for her to snap back at him that he didn't own her and she could do as she liked in her own apartment, but instead she blinked wide, vulnerable blue eyes up at him.

"Can you...can you stay with me?" she asked.

His breath caught and he nodded, not trusting himself to speak because if he spoke, he might fuck it up.

He followed her as she moved toward the bedroom, taking off the coat he'd offered her earlier as she went.

She didn't turn any lights on, just went to the bed and lay down on her side, cheek to the pillow, staring at the wall.

There was a chair by her vanity and Hades sat down, still not daring to speak. Just being here was enough. Just the fact that she *wanted* him here... Was this the beginning of the way back? Or was this only for tonight because she'd been so affected by seeing her friend hurt?

Everything in him wanted to close the space between them and claim his wife in a way she'd never forget and could never again deny.

She was fragile like a flower right now, though. If he squeezed too tight, her bruised petals would never flourish again.

So he remained still. Gods help him, he remained still.

His beautiful wife turned her head towards him. The pain in her gaze cut straight through his gut.

He opened his mouth to say her name, to try to say something comforting, but she beat him to it.

"Will...could you hold me?"

She didn't have to ask twice. He was up off the chair and sliding onto the bed beside her in the blink of an eye.

And finally he did what he'd been longing to do all night. He wrapped his arms around her and slid his body into hers from behind, one leg tangling with hers.

It was a familiar position, one they usually settled into after sex, not before. Hades knew tonight wasn't about sex, though. It was about comfort and letting Persephone know she wasn't alone.

She never had to be alone again or to face anymore nightmares without him at her side. He'd fight all her battles, slay all her beasts. Things were bad now but they'd be good again. She'd see. He'd give her the most beautiful life anyone ever had.

He tucked her close to him and covered them with a blanket. He watched over her as she quickly fell into what he hoped was a dreamless sleep.

They stayed like that, her asleep in his arms and him memorizing the feel and smell and sight of her for over an hour. She only stirred when there was a knock at the door. A text pinged on his phone, letting him know that his Shade had left their food at the door.

Persephone lifted her head but Hades urged her to lay back on his chest.

"It's just the food," he said. "You hungry?"

"Not really." She wormed so that she was lying beside him, facing him.

"Why haven't you been able to sleep?" He lifted a gentle finger to caress the shadows underneath her eyes.

She didn't pull away. "I get these dreams. Nightmares really."

"Tell me."

"Mostly about Ajax."

Hades felt his entire body tighten but he forced himself to relax. He'd almost blown his lid when Charon told him that Persephone had seen him put Ajax down like the dog that he was. Somehow she'd been there and he couldn't imagine what it must have looked like to an innocent like her.

"That fucker doesn't deserve to take up any space in your head."

She hesitated. "I watched you kill him."

"Charon told me."

"It scared me." Hades thought of the violence of those last, brutal moments. Of course she'd been scared. Scared of *him*. Shit.

"He would've hurt more people. It was my responsibility to make it stop." He paused and took a breath. Justifying it wouldn't help anything. He wasn't sorry that he'd killed Ajax, but he was sorry that she'd seen it. She'd been an innocent when she married him. All he'd done since was corrupt her.

"I understand why you ran." He reached forward to sift his fingers through her light hair, but he couldn't quite meet her eyes. "You married a killer. It's a part of my life you were never meant to see. But if this is going to work, there can't be anymore lies between us. This is who I am. It's who I have to be."

"That's not what scared me."

He lifted his gaze to hers and she was the one reaching out this time, laying her hand on his chest. Her brows were scrunched together, upset. "I watched you smash his head in, and I was...I was *glad*. Ajax killed Eurydice like she was nothing. I wanted him to die. I *wanted* it to be brutal." Persephone's tortured gaze met his. "I hated him. I watched you kill a man in cold blood and I was glad."

She started to take her hand away, but Hades captured it and held it to his chest. Could she feel his heart beating?

Their gazes caught again. "I was glad," she repeated, gripping his shirt. "I wanted you to hurt him. All these months I've been telling myself that I had to get away from you because you were the darkness and I wanted to live in the light."

"But the darkness..." Fat tears trembled at the edges of her eyes. "The darkness was inside *me* all along."

Hades dragged her close to him and kissed her forehead before tucking her head under his chin. "You wanted justice."

They lay like that for a few moments. Her body shook and he held her tighter. His stomach tied in knots at seeing her suffering. She was in so much pain, he could feel it. And it was wrong, so wrong.

She was supposed to be kept separate from all of it. She was supposed to live up on a pedestal where only light shined. The darkness was never meant to touch her. But he had failed her, time and time again.

"I'm sorry I ran," she finally murmured.

He moved his head back so he could look at her. "Don't be sorry. You were frightened."

"I didn't leave because you killed him. I mean, I thought I did. It was what I told myself. I wanted to go back to a simpler time. A simpler life."

She frowned and shook her head. "But I think that was an illusion. Life's never been simple. The darkness has always been there. In the loneliness of my childhood. When my mom got mad and hit me. Even the whole reason we were hiding out on the farm—"

Her features scrunched with pain. "What my family did to your sister... You said to me once that the sins of the father would be visited upon the children."

"Gods, no, Persephone, I didn't mean—" Fuck. He had meant it at the time but that was before he'd gotten to know her, to love her. "That was a long time ago—"

"No, you were right. That's the legacy they left me." She sat up in bed and swung her legs off the side, pulling away from him. "I can't ignore it or pretend I'm not a part of it. The darkness is inside me."

"Persephone," Hades started, moving to sit beside her, but she cut him off, eyes distant.

"I wanted vengeance for what Ajax had done to my friends. I wanted it bloody and I wanted it brutal. With every blow you landed I wanted the next one to be twice as hard. I was disgusted with myself but I still couldn't look away."

She was killing him, didn't she know that? All Hades had wanted to do was protect her and yet here she was, the strongest, most resilient woman he'd ever met...and she was so close to breaking. Because of him. Because of his world.

Finally, finally, she looked at him, eyes wide and lost. "What does that make me? I was glad you got rid of him. He got what he deserved, but the more I thought about it, the more scared I got. Because, I mean, where is the line? How far is too far?"

"I draw the line," Hades said firmly, reaching down and grabbing her hand. If she felt lost, he'd be her anchor. He'd fix this, he swore he would.

"That's an awfully big responsibility, Hades."

"Yes. I take it seriously. And you're wrong. You aren't the darkness. Baby, I've looked into the face of the dark and depraved." He cupped both of her cheeks gently. "You are the light."

She started to shake her head but he held her still. "Okay, so you've seen some things. You were glad when a bad man died. You had a shit upbringing and fell into the clutches of a bastard with bad intentions."

Her eyebrows furrowed but he continued. "But *you changed* that man. A man most said was bound for hell, and good riddance. *You loved* me. And if you gotta have a little bit of darkness in you to love a man like me, then damn it, I'm glad you do. But goddess, otherwise, you shine so bright, you blind me most times."

Twin tears fell down her cheeks at the same time she leaned in and kissed him. Kissed him so sweet he thought he might die. The lightest press of her mouth, but she let her tongue stroke his lips lightly, asking, inviting.

His cock almost tore a hole through his suit pants, he went so hard so quick. But still he didn't press. He let her take the lead. He didn't dare scare her off, not now that it looked like she might finally be coming back to him. For real. Not for some frantic romp in a bathroom after getting kidnapped or a lusty madness in the middle of the night where any cock would do.

No, he'd take things slow, careful, making sure she was with him every step of the way. So he stayed perfectly still.

Persephone's eyes were closed and after a moment, she let her hands drop and moved back. Her brow furrowed and she looked at him uncertainly. Like she was afraid he didn't want her anymore.

Okay, fuck careful.

He stepped forward, his broad shoulders and body dominating the space between them as his arms closed around her.

And he kissed her back. He kissed her with everything he'd been withholding. He kissed her with his fury and with his longing and with his love because *fuck*, he loved her so fucking much.

He dragged her leg over his, positioning her on his lap and she kissed him back hungrily. Not with the sloppy insanity of that one strange night, but with the hunger of a woman who knew what she wanted. And what she wanted was *him*. Her arms wrapped around him and her fingers drove into his hair.

She shifted in his lap, gyrating her hips against his steel rod of a cock in a way that drove him absolutely fucking nuts.

Enough. He grabbed her tiny waist and flipped her so that she was beneath him on the bed. The next second, he hovered over her, grinding his body along the whole length of hers. Fuck. Yes. This was what he'd been dreaming about, ever since he'd let her out of his sight.

She was finally, finally, back where she belonged.

Apparently, she felt the same way, because her small hands were at his waist, tugging impatiently at his belt buckle and button.

"That's right, baby," he growled. "You want this?" He ground hard against her sweetness, imagining the liquid honey pooling inside her panties. He needed to taste her, but no, he needed inside her more.

He needed to reclaim what was his. This time wouldn't be sex. He was done with fucking his wife in a one-off here and there.

He'd given her space and they'd finally cleared the air between them. Now it was time for them to be man and wife again. It was time to make love to his wife.

He pulled her arms up, yanking her thin camisole off over her head. Damn, he'd forgotten how perfect her breasts were. He thought he'd memorized everything about her, but seeing her now, he knew his memory had done her no justice.

She trembled beneath him, her back arching underneath his gaze. Her nipples hardened to sharp little points.

He reached down and tweaked one. Her sharp gasp, followed by a breathy moan was almost his undoing. But no. This was important.

"What do you want, goddess?"

"I want you."

Fuck but that felt good to hear. He awarded her with a smile. "Tell me what you want *first*." He reared up over her, teasing his lips near to her mouth but not quite touching.

She arched her back, obviously needy with frustration. "Your mouth on me."

He dropped his lips to her skin, down her throat and ever so softly to her breasts, the barest whisper of a breath.

"Hades," she moaned. "Take over. Tell me what to do."

"Say my name," he whispered. "Say my name again." He felt

vulnerable the second it came out of his mouth but he couldn't help it. His name on her lips was everything. Her acknowledging who she belonged to while she was completely clear-headed.

"Hades. Hades. *Hades.*"

He dragged her nipple into his mouth, biting and suckling with all his might.

She screamed and bucked beneath him, her legs wrapping around his waist. Oh, his goddess liked that, did she?

He moved to the other nipple even as he reached his hand down between them. He slipped his fingers into her drenched panties. Always so eager for him, so ready.

His fingers were quickly slippery with her juices. His cock grew even harder, though he wouldn't have thought that was possible.

She writhed beneath him. "Please, I'll do anything."

"Anything? Then let go baby." He used his fingers, strumming her like an instrument until she broke perfectly under him. "Because all I ever wanted was you. Just as you are."

She was breathing hard when he shoved his pants down enough to glide into her.

Fuck but she was tight. So hot and so fucking tight. Made for him.

"Yes," she breathed in obvious satisfaction. "Hades, *yes.*"

He moved and all the world was perfect, there was never any wrong in it, as long as he was pounding into her. Imprinting himself on her.

"Who do you belong to?"

Persephone threw her head back. "You," she cried. "*You*, Hades."

"You better fucking believe it," he growled and grabbed the back of her neck, lifting her so that when his kiss landed, she felt it throughout her entire body as he continued his rhythmic attack on her senses. He grabbed her ass and shifted her position so he slid in deeper than ever.

She moaned into his mouth and clawed his scalp as her pleasure rose.

That's it. That's it, goddess. Give it all to me.

And she did. She didn't hold back a single damn thing. She

screamed his name as she came and thrust her hips against his, shamelessly seeking her own pleasure in a way that drove him absolutely crazy.

His own climax was lit by her going wild beneath him. He shoved in to the hilt, and as his seed shot out of him to coat her innermost depths, there was only one thing on his mind.

He crushed his wife close to him and whispered in her ear, over and over, "I love you."

She threw her arms around him and squeezed so hard he could barely breathe but he didn't care.

Because the next words that came out of her mouth were, "I love you too."

Four sweeter words had never been invented in the English language.

Hades pulled back, needing to look her in the eye. She was smiling but it was tentative, like she didn't trust this happiness.

"You done running, baby? Because if you come back to me, I don't know if I'll ever let you go." It had about killed him the first time and he wasn't sure if he'd be strong enough to ever do it again.

But her eyes were clear of doubt when she said, "I want to be with you. I want you back."

Hades couldn't remember feeling such stunning happiness ever before. He grinned. "I know."

She laughed and shook her head. "Cocky."

"Very cocky." He jerked his hips.

Her eyes widened at the reminder that he was still inside her.

She arched an eyebrow. "Ready for round two already?"

"Shoot me if my answer to that question is ever no." He dropped back down to kiss his wife. Once wasn't really enough to truly remind her of his claim. It might take all night.

80

Hermes lay in his canopy bed, messing on his phone. When he looked up, Olympia was standing in his bedroom doorway, wearing another one of her long silky robes and looking like an ancient priestess.

"You're up late," he said. When she came and sat on the side of his bed, he set his phone aside. "Worried about your ex?" She and Zeus had been married for years, no matter how acrimonious the divorce.

"I didn't realize how much I still miss the bastard," Olympia admitted.

"Aww, come here, Hermes will make it better." He opened his arms and she leaned into them. "I know something that will help you sleep," he whispered into the dark shell of her ear.

She pressed into him, fire in her tawny eyes.

Impishly, he plucked a bag of white pills out from under his pillow. "Sleepy time?" He shook them.

"Those aren't sleeping pills, *mon petit.*" She laughed at his confused look.

"I thought... I was wondering why you had sleeping pills at our little party." He studied the bag. "What are they?"

She dipped her head closer to his lips. "Ambrosia. Food of the gods."

Hermes blinked at her, still not sure what she meant, when she took the bag from him and tossed it on the bedside table. "But we don't need those tonight."

Putting a hand to his chest, she pushed him down to the pillows.

"Take off your pants, *mon petit*. Mistress is hungry."

81

For once Persephone woke up before Hades. She lay there a long while studying his face, her eyes tracing the strong jawline and the sexy hollows of his cheeks. He was masculinity personified. And how she loved him.

Being with him here, now, his big body so warm next to hers... She never wanted this moment to end.

But it would, wouldn't it? She bit her lip. Why hadn't she told him everything last night when they were finally opening up to one another?

It had been on the tip of her tongue numerous times. But after everything with Aphrodite... And then his arms were around her and it felt so good, so right, she wanted a little more, for it to last a little longer...

She wanted it still. She wanted to bury herself in her husband and hide away from the world for a little while more. Was that so wrong? To steal a little happiness while they could?

Hades frowned and stirred in his sleep.

She wanted to soothe him and promise she'd make it all better. But that was a promise she couldn't keep, so she did the next best thing.

Ever so gently, she tugged the bedsheet down. Her eyes immediately widened. Because while Hades might still be asleep, his cock certainly was not. The tent in his boxers was so tall, she was surprised the fabric was still containing him at all.

She was happy to remedy the situation.

She reached in through the slit in his boxers and tugged his shaft out. He stirred slightly but still didn't wake. She grinned as she bent over and took the tip of him in her mouth.

His hips shifted, effectively thrusting him several inches deeper. She smiled around him. What sort of dream was he having? It had better be about her.

She applied suction and bobbed up and down several times before bottoming out as far as she could take him down her throat.

Hades groaned. He shot up to a sitting position, his hand going to her head and tangling in her hair. "Fuck the Fates, you're real. You are actually here."

A wicked smile curled her mouth as she looked up his stomach to his face. "You bet your ass I am, baby."

"Alright." Sweat beaded a little on his forehead as his hips raised up involuntarily and he forced them back down to lie passively under her. He fell back to his pillow.

She pulled off of him and he closed his eyes as a muscle jerked in his cheek. She took him in her hand, working him slowly up and down. "You like that?"

He groaned. "I love it."

"I've missed this," she spoke to his dick, wet with her saliva. "I dreamt about it at night. I felt it in me."

She dropped her mouth back to the head of his cock and gave it a little suck, flicking her tongue along the slit the way he liked.

"Look at me," she ordered, and was thrilled when he obeyed.

Hades hands fisted in the sheets. She didn't take her eyes off his gray ones, knowing he was promising her retribution.

She opened her mouth and took him as far as she could go.

"Fuck," Hades squeezed out, his head thrown back. He was too thick for her to take all the way down, but she slid her mouth up and back, trying her best to go deeper.

"You're going to kill me," he groaned.

She came off with a pop, still holding him at the base. "Where do you want to come?"

"Inside you."

"Inside my mouth? Or inside my pussy?"

"Inside your pussy. I have plans for that mouth."

Turning so she faced his feet, she slid down on his cock, sighing with satisfaction. She canted her ass up and down, looking back at him with a sexy tilt of her mouth. "Like the view?"

"Oh yes." His hips were moving opposite hers and she could hear herself squelching around him.

"I'm so wet for you." She ground down.

"Yes, you are, baby." He gripped her hips, steadying her. "Ready for me?"

She tipped herself forward, steadying herself on her hands between his legs. "Ready, Daddy."

He drove his cock up into her and she lurched forward at the vehemence of his thrusts, shouting her pleasure to the ceiling when her climax hit.

It was over quickly; he came and pushed himself up hard, then fell back, breathing hard. He pulled her back to him, lifting her sweaty hair from her neck to kiss it. They lay together quietly, his hands stroking her pale breasts and belly.

She half thought he'd fallen back asleep when he finally asked, "Well, Mrs. Ubeli, where do we go from here?"

Persephone spiraled back into reality. "I have questions," she said. "Can you answer them for me, with total honesty?"

Even as she asked it, she felt her chest tighten. *Are you going to give him total honesty in return?*

Hades thought they'd cleared the air of what had happened the night she'd run. But he still had no clue what had set all the events into motion.

Her.

Her actions. Making the deal with Ajax, leaving the Estate, trying to rescue Eurydice with the help of the cops. How all of it had blown up in her face and resulted in his shipment being confiscated by the cops.

Hades sighed. "I can. For you, I can. I'll tell you when there's something that might not be good for you to know. But if you want, I'll tell you everything." He tugged her hair gently. "You gonna return the favor? Are you gonna talk to me?"

There it was. He was asking her straight out.

And instead of giving him a straight answer, she curved her hand around his face. "I missed you," she whispered. "I saw that man in the penthouse pool, dead, and I thought it was you."

There. That was the truth.

"Babe, you gotta be honest with me. You can't hold this all in." He stroked her hair and she closed her eyes, it felt so good. Being with him, in his arms, it all felt so good. Was it wrong of her to want to hold onto it for just a little longer? "You're going to keep getting bad dreams."

"I know," she whispered. Her brow furrowed. "Where's Slim?"

Hades matched her grim expression, but didn't answer right away. "We're looking."

"He's not dead?"

Hades pulled her back close and stroked her hair, a sweet, gentle act that belied their dark conversation.

"We have reason to believe Poseidon is holding him." The way they were positioned, she couldn't see Hades's face. But she could feel the tension in his body beneath hers.

"Why?"

"Power play. Maybe thinks he can turn Slim against me, or wants some collateral when we next go to talk."

"You're going to talk to him?"

A sharp shake of his dark head told her everything he felt about the subject.

"But...I thought you needed to ally with him. I thought it was the only way you could win a fight against the Titans." She lifted off of him so she could look him in the face, but he was staring off into the distance. "You can't let them win."

When he finally turned his attention back to her, his gray eyes looked straight through her, and she knew he was seeing something else.

"Hades," she said, and he snapped out of it.

"We can get through this, you and me," he said, changing the subject. "No matter what is ahead. I was taught that being married is for life, and you gotta control yourself, be faithful. But being married means you have each other's back, for all time."

"You may not feel like it," his eyes searched hers, "but I'll always, always have your best interest in mind. I'm not perfect, I'll make mistakes. So will you. We'll make them together and we'll talk them through."

"Okay, Hades," she said.

"You going to run from me?"

"Only if you chase me." She smiled, remembering the time he'd chased her at the art museum.

"Oh, I'll chase you," he growled, and smacked her ass lightly. "We'll play. We have two months of play to catch up on." He leaned in close and slid his nose along hers. "But right now, I need to hear it from you straight."

She froze. Did he know? Was this a test?

"I need to know that you meant what you said last night. No more running?"

She let out a breath of relief. "I'm done running. I think I was running from myself as much as you."

"Alright, babe." He kissed her lips. "How about we get some food?"

"Can we go to the hospital? I want to check up on Aphrodite."

Persephone would tell him everything. She would. She just wanted to soak in this happiness for a little while longer. A little while longer. Then she'd come clean.

"As long as you're doing it with me," he smiled at her, dimple appearing in a rare show, "we can do whatever you want, babe."

82

"Who's that?" Aphrodite craned her head after greeting Persephone, obviously having caught sight of Hades, or at least the shape of him through the hallway window. Persephone's shy smile must have told her the rest. "Hades. You two back together?"

Persephone nodded, and lifted a bag. "Fresh t-shirt, jeans, underwear, the works." She rummaged around and held up a bright yellow makeup bag.

"Thank you," Aphrodite sighed.

"When are you getting out?"

"Soon. Today. My producer friend is actually coming by to pick me up."

Persephone nodded. "So everything's still okay with the movie? Even though you'll have to go back to work with—"

"Max Mars," Aphrodite grimaced. "Don't remind me. He's been calling and texting nonstop."

Persephone glowered. "If he's not getting the message, Hades can—"

Aphrodite waved her hand. "No, it's fine. I can handle him."

"And your attacker? What did the police say is happening to him?"

"He's still in lockup." Shadows played across Aphrodite's bruised face. "Apparently Mars pulled some strings so he's not getting out on bail. It's something, anyway. They say he could serve up to five years for assault and battery."

Swallowing hard, Persephone took her friend's hand. The bastard deserved worse than five years. She couldn't think of anything more despicable than a man hitting a woman or child. "And the movie? What do you want to do?"

"I've wanted to be an actress all my life. I dragged my mom around to auditions, practiced for hours in front of a mirror. It's all I ever dreamed about." Aphrodite closed her eyes, her forehead creasing.

"There are other movies, other directors."

"Other asshole actors?" Aphrodite grimaced, shaking her head. "Not for me. You don't get it, Persephone. There's a time limit to my success. I need to break out now, while I'm young, and beautiful enough to let my looks make up for my lack of experience."

"If Mars doesn't back off or if he gives you a hard time in any way—"

"I've been taking care of myself a long time. I promise I'll be fine."

"But if you aren't, we can—"

"I said I'll be fine."

Persephone backed off at Aphrodite's sharp words, not wanting to upset her any more. But no way was she letting her deal with this alone. She was family now.

Aphrodite set her jaw and even bruised, her face was still lovely in a cold, untouchable way. When she spoke, Persephone had to listen hard to hear. "I'm going to do it. I'll do the movie and make my career. And then..."

"And then?" Persephone prompted. Even though she was looking straight at her friend, she saw a totally different woman.

"No one will ever touch me again."

A nurse stopped in, and the burning intensity in Aphrodite's eyes disappeared as she smiled and spoke charmingly to the woman.

When Persephone left the hospital room, she found Hades standing in the hall.

"All good, babe?"

Crossing the hall to him, she leaned close and took a deep breath.

"Babe?"

"Can your guys keep an eye on Max Mars? And...maybe send him a message to leave Aphrodite alone?"

Hades nodded. "He bothering her?"

"She broke up with him after what happened. But he's having a hard time taking no for an answer." She hurriedly added. "But he needs his face for the movie. So..."

"Got it." She thought she could see the ghost of a smile hovering around his mouth. "Anything else?"

"No." She came forward, put her arms around his suit-clad body, and pressed her cheek to his strong chest. He held her, while a few orderlies passed by and averted their eyes.

"Love you, babe."

She sighed, so content it hardly felt real. "I love you too."

"Well, if it isn't the two love birds. Marriage ain't killed your romance yet?"

Persephone jerked her head around to see a familiar figure in a dirty coat.

Pete. The cop who'd betrayed her.

He approached slowly, at a slight angle, as if he expected Hades to attack if he came at them straight on.

Which was exactly what he'd done when Persephone had last called him—he'd come in sideways and found Hades's weak spot—her. Pete had played her. And let a woman die so he could make his big bust. She wanted to claw his eyes out but she held back. Hades didn't know and he couldn't find out, not this way.

Pete slouched against the wall, tilting his shaved head towards them. "What'd you get her for an anniversary, Ubeli? The rest of

Ajax's dead body? I hear his head showed up in a gang zone in Metropolis. Right on the Titan's doorstep, so to speak."

Persephone couldn't help it; she gasped, and Hades's arms got tighter. "Let's go," he muttered.

"Aww, what's the matter? No respect for the man who busted ya?" Pete flashed his badge and smirked. "How 'bout you, Persephone? Haven't heard from you in a while."

"I'll thank you not to address my wife informally," Hades said to the man over her head. "Or at all."

"Let's go," Persephone said, ducking her head as her husband steered her away.

Pete loped along next to them, keeping his distance but staying close enough that Persephone could hear him plainly. "Last conversation I had with her, she was real friendly."

Hades stopped dead, but Persephone stepped between him and the detective. "You're despicable," she snapped.

"Your friends get in a bind again, you can always call me." Pete gave a mirthless smile and Persephone realized he was almost as tall as her husband.

Whirling, she tucked herself into Hades's side and marched with him down the hall. Hades's arms squeezed her a bit tighter, but other than that, he didn't acknowledge the man watching them retreat.

Persephone slid into the backseat of the car, feeling sick to her stomach. The nerve of the detective, after he didn't offer any backup. He didn't care about the women in need, about Eurydice *dying* on his watch, just his own career enhancement.

It took a while to realize there was stony silence coming from the other side of the back seat.

"Hades?"

Her husband stared out the window. "How does that dick know you?" he asked, voice deceptively quiet.

Persephone felt her heart drop out. "I—uh—met with him once. Well, twice. The first time, he cornered me with Aphrodite. He knew her. The second time…I asked him to help me find Eurydice. Orpheus's fiancée." Persephone could still see the picture of the lovely young woman and the angelic looking singer, both dead now. Two beautiful lives snuffed out.

Her husband breathed in hard through his nose. "That all?"

Persephone breathed out as her eyes fell closed. *Now or never.* She couldn't sit here and continue to lie to him. Honesty. He'd asked her for complete honesty only this morning and there was no more putting it off. "I may have called him before I went to find Aphrodite and Eurydice."

"I see," Hades said.

"I was trying to do the right thing. I never meant for any of it to—"

Hades raised a hand and she fell silent. He leaned forward and ordered the driver, "Crown Hotel. Now."

"Hades, please—"

"*Enough.*"

Persephone jumped at the barked word. They drove on in silence for five minutes. Ten minutes. Fifteen.

Hades stared out the window. Why wouldn't he say anything else? What was he thinking? She wanted to explain it all. The words were tumbling inside her, spilling over one another to get out. If she could just explain it right, she could make him understand.

Her stomach twisted in knots as they arrived at the Crown and Hades took her elbow in a vice-like grip as he led her up to the penthouse.

The whole time, she prayed silently. He had to forgive her. He *had* to.

Finally, they were in the apartment and the door slammed behind them.

Someone had removed the flowers that usually graced the foyer without bothering to replace them. Even though the place was clean, the shades were drawn over the tinted glass, making the place dim and stuffy, a shell instead of a home.

Hades went and poured a Scotch, neat, and now studied the amber liquid. "I think you better tell me what happened the night you ran. Starting with when I left, please."

Her eyes darted around the penthouse. She wanted to look anywhere but at him. Instead, she forced her gaze to meet his.

The truth had weighed heavy as a lead ball in her stomach for months, stealing her sleep, sullying her dreams. She had to tell him everything and hold nothing back, even if, when she was done, he hated her.

"You said you *went* to find Aphrodite and Eurydice?"

"Y-yes," she whispered, hating the tremble in her voice. "Ajax took them. Eurydice and Aphrodite. He called me and said if I didn't come with the ransom money right away, he'd kill them and—"

Shit, she wasn't explaining this right. "I wasn't going to go like he ordered. I knew it was a trap. But Athena had cracked Eurydice's phone and we had his address. You were gone and I thought I could get ahead of Ajax, surprise him at his safe house and have the police with me to bust him—" She broke off, hating how stupid and naïve she sounded. It had all seemed like such a brilliant plan at the time. Fail proof.

She took a deep breath. If she didn't get it all out now, she never would. "When I got there, I was supposed to go inside, to offer myself in exchange for Aphrodite and Eurydice, and as soon I said the safe word, the cops were supposed to come in and bust Ajax."

Hades studied the empty glass in his hand. He still hadn't looked at her, she realized, not since the car. "You gambled with your life."

"I knew Ajax would be too afraid of you to hurt me. And the cops were right there," she broke off, swallowing hard. She outlined what had happened when she reached Ajax's house.

"But the cops didn't come to the rescue?" Hades was at the bar, refilling his drink. Persephone still hadn't moved from the small landing in front of the door.

"They were listening in but when they heard Ajax call you, they obviously decided they wanted a bigger bust. I used the safe word over and over but it didn't matter." Persephone's voice cracked. "They let her die. They left Eurydice to die, right in front of me."

"So let me get this straight. You left the Estate of your own volition. You called a cop, thinking he'd keep you safe from a psycho who'd already taken two women."

Persephone licked her lips, staring at her husband's dark silhouette.

"Is that right?" Hades prompted.

"He had a SWAT team with him," she offered weakly. "I tried to take as many precautions as I could."

"Except at no point did you tell me, your husband!" He put his glass down hard, not violent enough to break it, but she jumped when it clunked against the cabinet. "At no point did you share."

"You were busy with the shipment—"

"You didn't trust me. My own *wife*."

"I'm sorry," she cried. "Gods, I'd change it if I could. It's my fault the cops came. It's my fault..." She couldn't finish, thinking of the way the blood poured from Eurydice's wound. How her eyes went vacant as her soul left her body.

"This is why you ran. You were afraid to tell me." She couldn't see Hades's expression in the shadows.

"Yes," she whispered. She'd lied to herself about it—his violence had given her an excuse—but ultimately, this was why she'd run.

"It's getting late," he said. "I got things to do. I'll get someone to take you back." Already his phone was out.

Persephone's heart thudded slowly, painfully. "Back where?"

"Your apartment."

"Hades, I'm sorry." The words burned in her throat. Everything she'd wanted to say, but couldn't bring herself to. "I never should have gone to Ajax. I should've trusted you."

She wanted to go to him, to convince him, to beg him to believe her. But he was now standing by the windows, drink in hand, and her feet were rooted to the spot. "I'll tell Poseidon it was my fault the cops were there. It was an accident."

"You stay away from Poseidon," Hades whirled and snarled so violently her feet came unstuck and, even though she was across the room, she took a step back. "It's over. You've done enough."

The door opened behind her, startling her, and a Shade walked in, glancing back and forth between the two Ubelis, before focusing on the one who gave him orders.

"Yeah, boss?"

"Please escort Ms. Persephone back to her apartment. Or anywhere she wants."

"Yes, sir." The Shade held the door open, waiting.

"Hades," Persephone whispered.

"Ma'am," the Shade called. He was obviously picking up on the tension in the room and thought it wise to give her a hint.

With one last look at her husband's straight back, Persephone took her exit.

In two days, time would run out. They didn't have Poseidon's shipment. At least Hades finally knew the truth. The fact was cold comfort. Especially when it hit her, in the car halfway to her place, that Hades had called her Ms. Persephone.

Not Mrs. Ubeli.

83

The rest of the day Persephone wandered around her apartment in a daze, analyzing Hades's every move.
It's over. You've done enough.
At dusk, she lost the battle with herself and dialed his private number. "Hades, we need to talk. I can explain." She stopped there because she didn't know if she *could* explain. Did it matter if she'd been trying to do the right thing when it all turned out so wrong? "Please call me," she finished lamely.

Pacing restlessly, she checked the fridge for anything appetizing. No luck. She started drawing open a bottle of wine. When her phone buzzed with a text message alert, she dropped the wine opener to grab it.

M. Ubeli not at this number. It's being monitored. Emergencies only.

She slapped her phone down with more force than necessary. Her husband was gone, disappeared behind the faceless Shades he used as an army. When she ran, she had to fight for her space, but he changes his number and, boom, she was cut off from him.

It wasn't fair.

"What can I do?" she ranted as Cerberus watched. "He holds all the cards in the relationship."

Her dog cocked his head and rubbed against her, trying to offer comfort. She scratched his ears. "It's okay, boy, I'm not mad at you. You sit and stay when you're told."

She laughed at this as she finished opening the wine.

A FEW HOURS later there came a rap at her door.

"Who is it?" Persephone paused in her slightly off-key rendition of the song playing on her phone's radio.

The heavy knock sounded again and Persephone groaned, not wanting to move from her spot. She'd just gotten comfortable.

Hades. What if it was Hades? Her drink sloshed as she set it on the floor.

In a wine-induced haze, she barely remembered to peek through the peephole.

The man outside was so tall she could only see his neck.

"No," Persephone said. Oops. She said that out loud. Shit. Maybe she could hide in the bedroom until Charon went away.

"Open the door," Charon commanded, in a voice that made it clear that he shouldn't have to ask twice. Had Hades dispatched his second-in-command to kill her for ruining his business? She giggled, the wine making that thought more fascinating than scary.

She opened the door and looked up, and then up some more. Charon was tall, like *really* tall. "Hey," she hiccuped. "What do you want?"

"Came to check on you."

"Did Hades send you?" She squinted up into the midnight black face.

"He doesn't know I'm here."

That gave her pause. Charon was intensely loyal, and as far as she knew nothing would entice him to go behind Hades's back.

Hades. Who hadn't sent him to check up on her. Who'd sent her away without even a backward glance.

"Well, I'm alive. Thanks for checking." She started to swing the door shut but Charon's foot stopped it.

"Charon, I want to be alone." He didn't budge at all and it only made her madder. "I can't believe you. Move, you big mountain."

But Charon just herded her back into the apartment until he could close the door.

Cerberus ambled over and sniffed the big man's hand.

"Fantastic guard dog you are." Persephone glared at the Great Dane, who gave a *woof* and went to lie down on the hearth.

Meanwhile, Charon was stalking through her apartment, first heading to her sound dock and cutting off the music.

"Hey!" she cried, but he ignored her, going to the balcony and looking out. He pulled the curtains firmly together, went back to the front door, and reached around her to dim the overhead light. The dimmer had been magically installed after she moved in, part of the 'upgrades' the super had instituted at the new building owner's—aka Hades's—command.

"What the hell—" she sputtered.

Charon leaned down and got in her face.

"People can see in here when you have the light on," he rumbled, looking down at her.

Persephone stared up at him with wide eyes. Losing all sense, she shoved him in the chest with both her hands. "I was having a nice, quiet," she grunted as she pushed, not caring that she didn't make a dent of difference, "night in. Alone!"

"Not so quiet. I could hear you singing down the hall."

With a final grunt, Persephone gave up pushing and stalked away. "Well, what am I supposed to do now that Hades has decided we're on a break? Sit in the corner and knit?" She flopped onto the couch and fished around on the floor for her wine glass, nearly tipping it and herself over when Charon sat down beside her. When he settled on his own cushion, she noticed he took up almost half the couch.

Lifting the bottle to inspect it, he gave her an amused glance. There was only about a glass and a half missing.

She raised her chin. "What? So I'm a lightweight."

Shaking his head, he leaned over and, before she knew it, he'd relieved her of her glass.

"Hey, I was drinking that." She struggled but was no match for him. He held her off with one large hand planted on her chest while he drained the rest of the red liquid in one gulp.

"I don't believe this," she fumed. "What are you even doing here?"

"Got your message."

She swallowed hard. "I thought that was Hades's line."

"It is, but he's gone to ground again."

"Did... Did something else happen?"

"More threats. Poseidon is on the move. A few of our men have been attacked, but he seems to prefer kidnapping over murder. No demands yet."

Persephone's temples were starting to pound with another one of the headaches she'd been getting lately and ugh, she felt like she was going to throw up. She rubbed her forehead and tried to focus on what Charon was telling her.

"Poseidon is holed up somewhere, but he's in the city. Gotta be. There's a warrant for his arrest in connection to the Mayor's poisoning." Charon grabbed the wine bottle and poured himself a glass. She'd never seen him drink before. "We think he's working with the Titans."

"The Titans want back in, don't they?" she whispered. "She won't stop, will she? My mother?"

He looked her in the eye and shook his head. "The Titans want back in and they're gonna get in, unless we can get Poseidon to join us. But with him scooping up Shades, it's not looking good."

"What can I do to help?"

"Nothing. Unless you can magically produce Poseidon."

She bit her lip.

Stay away from Poseidon. It's over. You've done enough.

It's over.

"Why are you telling me this?" Persephone tried not to sound sad and failed. Her mother was up to no good as always, trying to hurt her husband. She winced, the pain slicing deep. *Was* Hades even still her husband? Did he want to be? "He doesn't want me involved."

"You gonna give up that easy?"

She stared at Charon but he didn't look at her.

"What do you mean? I hurt him, I know that. I know he feels betrayed. But he won't even *talk* to me."

Charon chuckled without mirth. "Not fun being shut out, is it?"

"No," she said, chin dropping to her chest. She'd given Hades the same treatment for months after she'd left him.

"Two months gone and you grew a backbone. But you still haven't grown up."

Would she break her hand if she punched him? She'd probably break her hand. "Maybe when you all stop treating me like a child."

Charon just shook his head, taking a long drink. "You wanna know what he's thinking? You wanna know everything?"

Persephone frowned but nodded, tucking her legs underneath her on the couch, making her into the smallest ball possible. Cerberus sat close by, looking unhappy until she reached out and stroked his soft gray head.

"You sure?" Charon finally looked at her and the warning in his dark eyes was serious.

"Yes."

"You sure you wanna wake up? After this you may never sleep again."

Somehow she knew he wasn't talking about literal sleep. She nodded.

"Alright." He toyed with his empty glass, pausing for so long that she wondered if he forgot she was there. But she didn't dare break the silence. "You know Hades's sister?"

"Chiara."

"You know how she died?" He picked up the wine, refilling his drink and keeping his hand on the bottle's neck.

Persephone looked at her hands. "My mom killed her."

Charon downed his second drink. "That wasn't till after. First the Titan brothers raped her. All three of them. She was stabbed, multiple times—I guess when your mom came in and found what they'd done. Maybe she was mad at Karl for cheating on her. Maybe she hated old man Ubeli that much. Or maybe it was for the power. But Chiara bled out on the mattress where they had her chained up."

Persephone sat frozen, her hand still on Cerberus's head. She'd never thought through the particulars of that night so long ago. She hadn't wanted to, she saw now. She was going to be sick.

But Charon wasn't having any mercy on her. He was going to tell the story no matter how much it hurt either of them. And it hurt him, that was clear enough to see by the glaze in his eyes and the hitch in his voice.

"Chiara was safe at the Estate, but she got a wild hair and took off. That's when they snatched her. We knew she was missing, pulled every fucking string we could to find her. In the end, a snitch found her. Too late. She'd been dead for a day. Fuckers left her alone to die, stabbed, covered in their filth."

Charon's hand shook a bit on the bottle, a gold ring he wore on his right hand's ring finger clinking against the glass until he clenched it, hard enough for his knuckles to pale.

"Hades saw her and lost it. He was still a kid." Charon looked across the couch at her, his eyes filled with black memories. "But that was the day he grew up. Not the day they took his parents, not the year after. It was the day we found Chiara, that was when he left. Didn't even wait until she was laid to rest. Cried, last time I'd see him cry, and disappeared."

Persephone gripped her arms around her legs to keep from shaking. Her eyes were dry; she had no tears for this. Charon kept speaking, his deep voice echoing in the pit of this bottomless night.

"Took me a year to find him. He was fucking homeless for months before he found his way. Trained as a fighter, and came back to New Olympus. By that time, the Titans had been in power two years, and most of Old Man Ubeli's empire was gone. Hades built it back, and didn't stop until the last one of them was driven out."

Silence.

So this was why he'd left her. "I betrayed him and gave the Titans an in."

"Woman." Charon shook his head at her like she was dense. "He sent you away because he can't deal. Everything he's done has been to protect you. And you leave your safe home—just like Chiara—and run to the bad guys. Doesn't matter why you did it. He already lost his family once. He can't lose you too."

Persephone didn't know what to say to that. He was wrong, though. He didn't see the look on Hades's face. He didn't hear how cold Hades's voice was when he told her it was over. Hades was a man who valued loyalty above all else. And she'd betrayed him. Without trust, what was left?

"You remind me of her, you know?" Charon said, breaking the silence. "Chiara. She was sweet, but underneath was fire." His voice dropped, so she strained to hear. "We'd do anything to protect that."

The tenderness in his deep voice made her turn to look at him. Charon's muscular form was balanced, rigid, but he'd let the mask slip from his face enough for her to see the man beneath, the years of pain and torment.

Persephone leaned against the arm of the couch, suddenly seeing so much.

"You loved her," she whispered. Her stomach swam with nausea. "How can you even stand to look at me, Charon?"

"Get some rest, Persephone," he murmured. And that was it. He walked out the door.

But all Persephone could see was that young girl, violated over and over again by Persephone's uncles...by her *father*. And Mom had finished the job by...

Persephone barely made it to the toilet before emptying the contents of her stomach.

84

Zeus eyed the male nurse with thick, curly hair and enough muscles in his arms to suggest a fine body lay under his scrubs. He had to applaud his concierge medical care service—they'd hired a young man who was exactly his type. Watching the curly-headed lad move around the room, he contemplated pushing away the portable desk that was hiding his erection so that the nurse—Paul was his name—wouldn't be able to miss it. With these young bucks, that was sometimes all it took.

"Sir, it's almost midnight. You need to rest." The nurse bent to pick up some clothes that had fallen to the floor and Zeus got a glimpse of his bright red thong peeking out from his turquoise scrubs. *Bingo.*

"I've been resting all day," Zeus said, and it was true. The doctors had released him from the ICU and he'd done a photo shoot meant to assure the public their mayor was on the road to health, but that was about it for the day. He'd insisted on coming home to sleep in his own bed, under the care of his private doctor. "I have so much to do… it's hard for me to relax."

The nurse—Paul—straightened slowly and grinned at him.

Voices outside the room interrupted.

Zeus frowned and jerked his head. "Go find out what that's all about."

The nurse only had time to open the door before an aide popped in. "Sir, Hermes Merche is here to see you."

Zeus lifted an eyebrow. What was the young Merche doing here? "Send him in. And, take the night off, Jones. I'm in good hands here."

"Yessir." The aide disappeared and Hermes popped into his place, his thick hair wild over his more staid suit.

"Am I interrupting something?" Hermes wore his usual mischievous grin.

Zeus sighed. "No, no, come on in." He watched the young nurse leave along with his aide and didn't bother to hide his disappointment.

As usual, Hermes picked up on it. "Glad to see you're feeling better. Any luck on nailing the bastard who did this to you?"

"We have a warrant out for Poseidon. We traced things back enough to charge him, but for the life of me I can't think why he'd want me dead."

"I can." Hermes sashayed up to the bed, drawing off his suit jacket and tossing it on a chair. Underneath he wore a lavender shirt, its slim cut outlining his lean, attractive torso. He held up a bag of white pills and Zeus immediately snapped to attention.

"Are those what I think they are?" Zeus held out his hand and Hermes dutifully gave him the bag.

"Ambrosia. Brew, or Bro, they call it on the streets now."

"Have you tried them?"

"I have actually. I thought they were sleeping pills. Took one and..." Hermes smiled coyly. "Well, it turned into a pretty good night actually, but that's neither here nor there."

"I see." Zeus wasn't in the mood. The fact that Hermes had this contraband was a problem. "And how did you come by these?"

Eschewing the chair, Hermes seated himself right on Zeus's bed, facing him. "Your own police office. You have a breach."

Dammit. Zeus frowned. "Who?"

"Your charming ex-wife."

"Olympia?" Zeus tried to lift off his bed, but then groaned and laid back. "I guess I shouldn't be surprised. She used to treat the evidence room as her own personal locker."

He tossed the pills down the bed and Hermes picked them up again. "Why'd she risk it?" Zeus asked. "Stealing evidence isn't a great career move for a former D.A., especially if she has designs on running for my office."

Hermes shrugged, fingering the bag longingly. "I guess she still cares about you. She knew they were Poseidon's and returned them to him."

"Poseidon has the pills back? Is he distributing?" The news just got worse and worse.

"Last I heard he's in talks with the Titans to distribute."

Zeus closed his eyes, feeling a headache coming on. Most of the effects of the poison had worn off, but he felt as exhausted as if he'd run a marathon or two. And now all of this was coming to a head while he was waylaid. "Bypassing Ubeli will mean war."

Zeus stared off for a second, thinking about the Titans moving in on New Olympus again. What would that mean for him and his office?

Hermes's face was carefully blank. "You know my personal stake in the dark lord's success. Speaking of which, how'd the meeting with the Ubelis go?"

"Oh, fine." Zeus pushed his desk back a little. "He sent his pretty little wife alone. I couldn't produce the drugs, and she got me to agree to do some stupid fundraiser that was the pretext for the meeting. Which reminds me, I have to wriggle out of that." He leaned forward to make a note.

"Don't even think about it." Hermes leaned forward and caught Zeus's hand with the pen. "You're putting in an appearance at the fashion show. I'm also helping with it."

"She's got you wrapped around her little finger, too?" Zeus might be tired but it didn't mean he was off his game. He arched an eyebrow at Hermes. "Too bad Ubeli's got his claws into her. Of course," he mused, "she said they were separated, and I'm sure, in light of the recent death threat, Ubeli's gone 'to the mattresses.' We should invite her up here so she's not lonely. Put her on all fours, our own private dog show. Remember how we used to—"

"I remember," Hermes cut him off, looking cross, and Zeus grinned to himself. So Hermes had a soft spot for Mrs. Ubeli. Zeus filed this information away for later.

"What are you going to do about Poseidon?"

Zeus went along with the subject change without comment. "Ball's in his court. He has his shipment back. When did you say Olympia returned it?"

"Thursday morning, I believe."

"But—" Zeus thought rapidly. "Who ordered the hit on me and Ubeli's look alike Thursday night? If Poseidon already had his product back by then?"

Hermes shrugged. "Your guess is as good as mine."

"What do you know?" Zeus narrowed his eyes.

Hermes laughed. "Only what Olympia tells me. She wanted me to give these pills to you, and let you know Poseidon has the rest back. Minus a few she took as her cut."

Zeus studied Hermes, but found no clues on the winsome face. Coming here hadn't been a social call, or even to check on his health. Hermes wanted him to know that it wasn't Poseidon who'd ordered the hit. Interesting. What exactly was his stake in all this? "Be sure to thank Olympia. How is she, by the way?"

"She misses you, but most days she won't admit it. Just like you."

Zeus harrumphed and Hermes chuckled. "So cranky. There's still one part of you that's honest, though, isn't there?"

Hermes lifted the portable desk away, taking care not to let any of the papers spill. Zeus's erection was clearly outlined under the thin sheet and he didn't try to hide it.

"Ah, there it is. Although it looks cranky, too."

"It misses you." Zeus stared Hermes directly in the eye. Hermes hadn't come here for this, or at least not *only* for this, but with their history, things usually always ended up here. Hermes was a beautiful boy who'd grown into a beautiful man.

A smile played around Hermes's mouth and his nostrils flared. "I missed him too, which is why I thought I'd pay a little visit. Of course, it's more fun when there's a third, so I invited a friend to play. Paul?" Hermes raised his voice to call the nurse's name.

The curly-headed nurse came back in, this time wearing nothing but his red thong. As Zeus stared, Paul shut the door and Hermes stood back, looking mischievous.

"Mr. Mayor," Paul posed for a moment before crawling up from the bottom of the bed. "Let's see if we can get you started on tonight's physical therapy."

85

Monday morning came, and Persephone woke, hearing the ghost echo of the phone ringing. But when she checked it: nothing.

She padded out of the bedroom to be greeted by Cerberus. No Shade stood guard in her apartment, no bodyguard blocked her door.

She checked her phone again: no messages.

Aphrodite would be getting out of the hospital soon, and Athena returning from her trip. It was Monday, the deadline Poseidon had set for Hades to return his shipment to him. What was happening? Would Poseidon make another move against Hades when he couldn't deliver? Or would he simply go to the Titans immediately to strike a deal with them? Worry had her pacing, wearing a trail in her hardwood floors.

An hour later, there was a knock on the door. Persephone checked the peephole and opened it. A line of Shades poured through, carrying boxes upon boxes.

"What on earth—?"

"From the penthouse, Miss. Mr. Ubeli wanted you to have them."

Finding a box with a loose strip of tape, she peeked in and recognized her clothes. Stunned, she ducked around the Shades swarming around her and shut herself in the bathroom.

She called the number she had for Charon, and the emergency line she thought was Hades's, Charon's rang and rang until she hung up, and the emergency line gave her a dial tone.

Every hope she had drained away at that empty sound. She dialed it again, confirming she hadn't made a mistake. Nope. No one there. She slammed her phone on the sink.

So that was it. It was that easy.

Hades had cut her out of his life. Cut off her very access to him.

You didn't trust me. My own wife.

All this time, she'd been running, and she hadn't known what she was running from. It hadn't been from Hades, but from this. This was her worst fear made real. But once he knew, he could never forgive her. She'd broken the bond between them and could never go back.

It's over.

It hit her as she exited the bathroom and made her way across her apartment through a sea of brown boxes. She was finally alone.

"You got what you wanted," she whispered to herself

Locking the door after the Shades, she slid down to the floor, tears spilling over faster than Cerberus could lick.

"Persephone!"

Persephone's head flew up as Athena charged into her office. "Is everything alright?"

"Fine. Move." Athena leaned over Persephone and grabbed her mouse. She was back from her trip and as much of volcanic force as ever.

"What's going on?" Persephone leaned back and watched Athena surf the web at lightning speed, pulling up a popular news blog.

"Max Mars didn't show up on set today." Aphrodite sashayed in, looking lovely and well rested. Two weeks since she'd been released from the hospital, and her bruises had healed. Glowing and glamorous, she looked like the fledgling movie star she was.

"Here it is," Athena navigated to the side news bar, reading the headline, "Max Mars beaten in bar brawl. Unknown assailant, man in black."

"Oh my gods," Aphrodite pushed her way closer to the computer screen and commandeered the mouse to click around the article. "He got totally busted up."

"There goes the movie," Athena muttered.

"Not necessarily," Aphrodite kept reading. "Says here they were careful not to touch his face."

Persephone thought of her conversation with Hades in the hospital hall and allowed herself a private smile.

Two weeks, and she hadn't seen Charon or her husband, or even evidence of a bodyguard following her.

Her anger had subsided into a dull ache as she watched and waited for the silence to break. Reading about Hades's activities and knowing they were his felt like a secret message, an inside joke between lovers. It hurt and gave her hope at the same time.

"Thank the gods we've already shot his topless scenes. He'll be in pain, but he can work through it," Aphrodite said.

Athena snorted. "He looked like he was in pain through the entire God of War movie. Either that or he was constipated."

"No, that's his acting face," Aphrodite said. "Oh, look, Persephone, there's a picture of you here."

"Really?" Persephone leaned forward but suddenly Athena and Aphrodite were blocking her way.

"Never mind, I was wrong," Aphrodite said hurriedly, facing Persephone while Athena clicked furiously, navigating away.

"Yeah, it's not that flattering at all," Athena muttered.

"Stop it, guys, let me see." Persephone elbowed Athena out of the way.

Aphrodite and Athena exchanged worried looks.

"You can't hide it from me; I'll just pull it up on my phone." Persephone rolled her eyes at them.

Reluctantly, both stepped away and Persephone clicked back until she saw what made them cringe.

It was a candid picture of her and Hades, with a line down the middle. "Known crime boss and his wife split."

Another picture of her looking depressed and lonely, walking Cerberus on the tree-lined sidewalk outside her apartment. She kept scrolling down, unable to stop herself.

"Who cheated on who?" she read the histrionic red text, and clicked on the thumbnails to see a picture of her with Poseidon at Hermes's party. The two of them had been standing close enough to talk, and their pose in the lavish setting did look rather intimate, especially with his hand hovering near her arm protectively.

She clicked to the next picture and saw Hades walking with a tall, buxom blonde. His hand was at her elbow, helping her down the red line steps outside the Crown Hotel.

"What the fuck?" Persephone hissed.

"Damn," Athena said. "I never heard you swear before."

"You're rubbing off on her," Aphrodite said. "Persephone, honey, are you okay?"

"Seen exiting the Crown Hotel last night, Hades Ubeli and on again off again flame, Lucinda Charles." Persephone read the last words with a shriek.

"Oh no, he didn't." Athena ducked closer to read the article.

"Maybe it's best if we don't jump to conclusions." Aphrodite leaned over Persephone's opposite shoulder.

"I can't believe this," Persephone shouted. "I'm going to kill that bitch! And put Hades's nutsack through the shredder!"

"There you go, that's the spirit," Athena encouraged.

"Stop," Aphrodite reached around Persephone to poke Athena. "Maybe it's a misunderstanding. An old picture like the one of you and Poseidon."

But Persephone was already shaking her head, her whole body trembling as she yanked her phone out of her purse. "He's wearing the tie I gave him for Christmas. That picture is recent."

Persephone was so furious she could barely dial the number she knew would reach Charon. She leapt up and paced while her friends watched, and ended the call with a curse. "Oh no, he does not get to do this to me."

"What are you going to do?" Aphrodite said.

Hesitating, Persephone was saved from having to answer by her phone ringing. "Charon?"

"What?" She couldn't read Charon's deep voice.

"I need a meet with Hades."

"Not gonna happen. Shit's going down; he's buried deep."

"Then why am I looking at a picture of him and fucking *Lucinda* outside the Crown?"

A pause. "Fuck."

"Yeah, that's right," Persephone ranted. "I want to speak with him, and I mean now."

Another pause, this one longer, like Charon was speaking to someone close by.

"Uh oh," Persephone heard Aphrodite say, and turned to see that Athena had pulled another picture up on screen, this one of Persephone standing between Hermes and Poseidon, again from the party two months ago. *Ménage a trois?* the caption read.

"Aww, they cropped me out," Athena huffed.

"Charon?" Persephone called, her eyes on the two men flanking her in the picture, one white tux, one black.

"Yeah." The underboss's voice was muffled now.

"Did you find Hermes?" He'd all but disappeared after the orgy. Maybe a good thing considering Hades had wanted to tear him apart once they'd realized the so-called 'sleeping pills' he'd given Persephone had actually been Ambrosia.

"In the wind. We didn't get to pick him up and he hasn't returned to his place."

"What happened with Poseidon when the deadline passed?"

Charon didn't answer.

"And Hades?" she pressed.

"He's…busy."

The image of Hades and that bottle blonde bitch flashed through her mind's eye. "Fuck that. You tell him," her vision swam a little as she swayed with anger, "Tell him that, after this, he'll be lucky if I ever want him back." And she hung up.

Her two friends stood at her desk, staring at her.

Athena snorted. "Somebody grew a backbone."

"Men." Aphrodite shook her head. "They're all assholes."

"Oh shit," Persephone said, her anger draining from her. "Does this mean it's really over? What am I going to do?"

"Get drunk," Athena suggested. "Have an orgy."

"Been there, got the T-shirt," Persephone muttered, and plopped into her desk chair.

"You want to go get coffee and talk about it?" Aphrodite asked.

"No, no, I have stuff to do. The shelter fundraiser is less than two weeks away, and the mayor is scheduled to show up. I have to get cracking."

"You sure you don't want to go out and get wasted?" Athena sounded hopeful, but Aphrodite was already pulling her towards the door.

"Come on, Athena. Leave her alone. We have to finish recording my vocals for your computer game, anyway."

"It's not a game, it's a software program we're designing to be capable of recursive self-improvement so it can achieve singularity…"

"Oooh," Aphrodite cooed. "talk nerdy to me…"

As her office door closed on her friends' banter, Persephone pulled up the article on her and Hades. She stared at the picture of Hades and Lucinda until it hurt too much to look. Two weeks? Was that really all it took for him to replace her with someone else to warm his bed?

She started to click away from the site, but her mouse slipped and a picture of Poseidon from the party popped up instead. In the white tux his midnight skin was all the more striking, and the large onyx ring he wore caught her eye.

Wait a second. She froze and squinted at the screen. She zoomed in.

Holy shit.

She remembered that ring. She remembered it from the long hours of her abduction, but she'd seen it again, hadn't she? At Olympia's place on the second most unforgettable night of her life.

The one that began with an orgy.

86

After pausing a minute on Olympia's doorstep, Persephone finally rang the doorbell. With the sound still chiming throughout the large row house, she pounded on the door for good measure.

The heavy door opened and the mistress of the house herself opened the front door. Olympia wore a tight red leather top and black skirt. Barefoot, she still had enough height to look down her nose at Persephone.

"Mrs. Ubeli. Do you need something? I'm getting ready and need to be on my way to court."

"I need to speak with your guest. Andrea Doria." Persephone kept her backbone ramrod straight. At this point, she had everything and nothing to lose.

"What business do you have with her?" Olympia's tone was borderline rude.

"Personal business. I mean her no harm. I just want to talk." Then Persephone tilted her head. "Although I do wonder what would happen to a lawyer if they found a fugitive hiding in her home…"

Olympia's nostril's flared at the threat but she opened the door.

Persephone stalked past her into the house, straight down the hall and into the large living/dining room that had been the scene of an orgy the last time she'd been here.

"Darling, do you have anything besides dairy milk?" A voice called from the kitchen. A pleasant tenor voice that could be modified either up or down.

The voice of Poseidon.

The person who appeared in the doorway had a bald head, but full makeup. Andrea Doria, halfway to her full persona.

The drag queen stopped when she saw Persephone approaching.

"Hello, Ms. Doria. Or do you prefer Poseidon?"

Olympia had followed Persephone into the room. "I told you not to shit where you eat," Olympia said to the tall crossdresser, then glared again at Persephone. "I need to get to court. Flax milk's in the fridge." She stalked away.

"I'm not here to hurt you," Persephone said to Poseidon/Andrea Doria. "You paid me the same courtesy."

Poseidon/Andrea asked, "How could you have known who I was?"

"Your ring. The one with the large onyx stone. You wore it the night of the party. There was a lot going on, but I never forget a statement accessory."

Poseidon/Andrea raised one perfectly penciled eyebrow. "Are you mocking me?"

"Not at all. I don't mock people, especially if I'm planning to ask them for makeup tips." Persephone smiled.

A small smile appeared on the fabulously contoured face. "So why are you here?"

"You said it yourself when you kidnapped me. I'm easy to talk to. I'm here to lay some things out in the open and see if we can come to an agreement."

The smile disappeared. "Your husband sent you."

"No, he didn't. We are very much separated, and I am very much alone." She held up a printout of the picture of Hades and Lucinda and handed it over. "This was taken yesterday. I haven't seen my husband in a couple of weeks."

The queen studied the picture and flashed Persephone a look of pity. "Very well. Let's talk. Coffee?"

"Please." Persephone followed the cross-dresser into Olympia's kitchen, and leaned on the beautiful quartz countertop of the large island as her former kidnapper went to the cabinet and took down two mugs.

"For the time being, I'd appreciate it if we kept to my disguise. I never thought my recreational activities would serve a serious purpose, but then I found myself hunted by my allies and wanted for double homicide." Poseidon/Andrea poured the coffee and winked at Persephone. "So call me Andrea."

"Pleased to meet you, Andrea."

"You're rather brave to come here, after the last time." Andrea placed a steaming mug on the island close enough for Persephone to reach it.

Persephone studied Andrea. "I don't think you ever meant to hurt me. Although, FYI, kidnapping me didn't give you any points with Hades. He killed the last guy who did that."

"I'll keep it in mind."

"So, you're wanted by the police." Persephone took her mug and fixed it with flax milk and honey.

"You going to turn me in?"

Persephone shook her head, tested her impromptu flax-milk latte, and then added more honey. "Turn you in, Ms. Doria? For what? They want Poseidon."

"So this is a game." Andrea paced along the long island, keeping it between them.

"The more I thought about it...I don't think you did it. Poisoning the mayor, threatening Hades—any of it. I think someone's setting you up." Persephone sipped her creation again and smiled. "Perfect."

Andrea fixed her with an intense stare. "Who do you think did it?"

"Someone who stands to gain from Hades and the mayor fighting with you."

"That could be any number of players."

"Who stands to gain the most from Hades and Zeus cutting ties with you?"

"Who would you guess?" Andrea didn't touch her drink, but folded her long arms across her chest.

"My mother."

Andrea did a double take. "Fuck the Fates, how did I not see it? Apart from the blonde hair..." She shook her head. "I assumed she died along with Karl. They always send Ivan as their contact when they try to negotiate with me."

"She didn't die. She took me into hiding. When I came out, Hades found me."

Andrea's sculpted eyebrows all but hit her hairline as she took a drink from her mug. "And you ended up married to him? I bet that's some story."

"For another day," Persephone said. "What's important now is that my mother is back. She's the brains behind the Titans, she hates Hades, and she wants to regain control of the New Olympus rackets."

"Well, young lady, you've figured it all out. You a gangster now?"

"Nope, just married to one." Persephone shrugged. "And the daughter of another. But I'm neutral ground. No one expects anything from me. That is my weakness, and my strength." She watched Andrea ponder this. "Why didn't you tell us you found the rest of the shipment?"

"I found it Thursday night, at Olympia's party. She'd recovered it for me. By morning, I was a wanted fugitive."

Andrea sighed. "And now Ubeli is pressing me on all sides, not to mention the mayor's legal arm. Our only hope of holding New Olympus from the Titans is to align our interests. Yet I am stuck here. I can't return to my ships."

Her eyes glittered and Persephone was reminded of how dangerous this person was. Andrea/Poseidon owned the seas and had for decades. "It's been too long already. If things don't break, I will give my men orders to extract me with whatever level of violence is necessary. Lives will be lost on both sides, and your husband and

Zeus will hold me responsible. Then I will be forced to deal with the Titans."

"Which is exactly what my mother wants."

Andrea nodded. "At the same time, I'm prevented from extending an olive branch to Ubeli, because then the Titans will know I've chosen sides."

Persephone thought about this. "Is that why you're snatching Shades and going through the motions of war? To look like you're fighting with Hades, when you're really not hurting anyone, just keeping his men prisoner somewhere?"

Andrea's face was scarily blank. "How do you know I didn't kill them?"

"I don't. Except that Slim's body hasn't been found anywhere. And if I were you and wanted to threaten Hades, I'd leave a body. So..." Persephone met Andrea's stare head-on with one of her own. "Where is he?"

Andrea laughed. "You're certainly giving new meaning to the phrase, 'Out of the mouth of babes.'" She leaned forward on the island opposite Persephone. "I suspect you only *look* like a babe, though."

"My aura of innocence helps. And it'll work to your favor. I can be a bridge between you and Hades, and I'm here to tell you that's what I'm willing to do."

"Your husband has broken ties with you."

"I still have his ear. And I have it on good authority that he prefers an alliance with you to all-out war. He will listen to reason." At least, she hoped he would. At this point, Persephone thought more of dealing with Charon than Hades, the lying two-faced SOB.

"Very well." Andrea drummed her fingers against the quartz countertop. "If you were me, how would you go about breaching the gap between you and Ubeli, as well as the mayor, when we can hardly be in the same room together without killing each other or our enemies finding out?"

Persephone put down her mug and smiled. "I thought you'd never ask."

87

Persephone and Andrea had just finished their conversation when Hermes walked in.

Son of a— So this was where he'd been hiding out all this time? His hair was adorably tousled, adding to his sleepy dishevelment Bare-chested and barefoot, he stopped when he saw Persephone standing in the kitchen with Andrea.

"Persephone, what are you doing here?"

She didn't think, she just threw her empty coffee mug straight at him. Fortunately for him, her aim was horrible.

Hermes jerked out of the way as the mug hit the rug near his foot and bounced. Open mouthed, he gaped at her.

Smiling, Andrea left for the dining room. "I see you two have some things to talk through."

Persephone stood glaring at Hermes.

"Did you just throw a mug at me? Who are you and what have you done with Persephone?" Hermes moved forward but she threw a hand up.

"Sleeping pills, Hermes?"

He stopped dead in his tracks and turned white. "Oh, gods, I forgot I gave you some. I didn't know they weren't sleeping pills, I swear."

"Well I trusted you and I took them. Once even when I was still at Athena's." She could feel the blush coming over her face, but didn't lose her grip on her pique. "And had...dreams. Crazy, crazy dreams. I thought I was going out of my mind. Another night I even sleep-walked!" Right to her estranged husband's apartment.

"So...nothing happened? With Aphrodite, or even Athena?" he perked up, and Persephone could see the lesbian fantasy start up in his mind's eye. To stall it, she looked around for another mug to throw.

He came at her, and she tried to dodge him, then wrestled with him as he grappled with her. Even with his lean build, he still had enough strength to catch her questing hands, and force them down.

"Are you really very mad at me?" He gave her hurt, puppy dog eyes.

She tried to stomp on his foot and missed when he jumped away. "Yes!"

"Persephone, I didn't know. I swear. Olympia had them, and I raided them, thinking they were her sleeping pills. They looked the same. I'm sorry."

"You're lucky nothing happened when I took them."

"Nothing? Not even with Hades?" He looked hopeful.

She wriggled away and he let her, but watched her in case she lunged again for a mug. He didn't deserve an answer. Especially one that was too painful to give right now. "Haven't you seen the news? He left me for his old flame. That Lucinda bitch."

"No way," Hermes gasped.

She pushed the photo of Hades and the woman towards him.

"This has got to be photoshopped. There's no way...damn. He's wearing the tie you gave him for Christmas." Hermes rubbed his hand through his unruly hair, making it stand up even further.

"Hades is looking for you," she told him quietly. "After what happened that night at Olympia's party, Hades put it together...

Remember when I told you I'd sleepwalked? Well I walked right to Hades's door and...wasn't behaving like myself."

Persephone felt her cheeks blaze hot. "Anyway, Hades made the connection after I told him I'd gotten the pills from you. He connected you to the shipment."

"I know. I heard he was looking for me. That's why I'm hiding out here with Andrea. Olympia's being a good sport about all of it."

"What Hades *doesn't* know is that Poseidon already has his missing shipment back. I'm going to tell Charon today. So you'll be off the hook."

"The Mayor knows, too," Hermes said. "Poseidon allowed me to tell him."

"Good. So you'll help me with the next phase of the plan."

"Operation Win Back Hades?" Hermes said, and lunged to grab Persephone's wrists again when she started to go for her ceramic weapon of choice. This time he whirled her around so her arms were crossed in front of her. For a moment she struggled but he just crushed her tighter with his wiry biceps on either side of her arms.

She sagged forward.

"I want to help you." His voice was muffled in her hair. "That, and I bet Athena a grand that you two would be back together within a month of the party."

Persephone couldn't help it, she laughed. He let her go, crossing to the other side of the island, keeping it between them. His hair was wild, sticking up in every direction, but his brown eyes were wary.

"Will you forgive me?"

"Not a chance," she said. "You invite me to a party, I get drunk and wake up to an orgy!"

He winced.

"Before that you accidentally drug me! And help my husband corner me at a party I helped you throw." The more she spoke the more she was geared up to charge around the island and tackle him. "And you tip my husband off to my new address and he ends up buying the entire building..."

"Now, that, I'll take credit for. Also, you're welcome."

"Just shut up," she said. "I don't know whether to hug you or put a hit out on you."

"Definitely all for hugs here."

"At this point, you're too valuable to kill."

"Good to know." He leaned on the island across from her, back to his shit-eating-grin. "Seriously, I'm sorry. Tell me what I can do to make it up to you."

"Well, other than never giving me medical help ever again, there's one thing."

"Name it."

She sobered. "I need to pull off this fundraiser."

"Done. My design team is working on it as we speak."

"That's not all I need help with." She bit her lip, wondering how far to bring Hermes in.

"There are two sides to this fundraiser," Andrea Doria said from the door. She stalked towards the coffee pot for a warm-up. "One is for the dogs. The other," she motioned with the coffee pot, "is for the city." She looked pointedly at Persephone, who sighed and explained to her friend.

"Are you on board with the plan?" Hermes asked Andrea when Persephone was finished.

Andrea nodded. "It's risky. And we only have two weeks to pull everything together, and to make sure it doesn't fall apart. No easy feat."

"Yes," Persephone said, "but it's going to work." *It has to.*

"For all our sakes," Andrea said. "I hope you're right."

88

Persephone paced her apartment while waiting for Charon to answer his phone, then said, "Poseidon found the missing shipment two weeks ago. Zeus Sturm can confirm. Also, Poseidon is keeping the Shades alive. He can't communicate with you because he's stringing the Titans along until you can meet. You need to act like you're at war with Poseidon to fool the Titans, but don't escalate things further." She took a deep breath to finish. "Don't ask me how I know all this."

A pause, then, "Why didn't Zeus report this to us sooner?"

"Why do you think?" Persephone retorted. Poseidon and Hermes had discussed the Mayor at length with her. Apparently, Zeus was a consummate politician, waiting to see which way the wind blew before doing anything or choosing sides.

Charon's sigh told her that he understood.

"Give me two weeks," she said. "I'll have more for you then."

"Woman, what are you planning?"

"Two weeks," she repeated and hung up.

The phone rang again and she let it go to voicemail, bustling around her apartment. When her door buzzer went off she shook her head and muttered to Cerberus, "See? Can't just sit and do as they're told, but they expect me to..."

She checked the peephole and froze when she recognized the spiky blond head.

"I know you're in there," Poseidon's bodyguard breathed.

"Did Andrea send you?" she called through the door.

"Poor Persephone. Husband left her all alone." Spike Hair tilted his head and she saw his bloodshot eyes. Checking the locks, she leaned against the door, heart pounding. She jumped when he rapped on the door. "Open up, little girl. I'll keep you company."

"Please, please go away," she whispered to herself. Her cell phone lay on the countertop, but she couldn't bring herself to move and get it.

Sensing her tension, Cerberus came to her side. She curled into him, but he stood at attention, vibrating with alertness. When Spike Hair spoke again, the dog barked, three times. A warning.

Shaking, Persephone kept hold of her dog. Had Poseidon sent his thug to threaten her? Could he be trusted to follow through on the plan, or was he playing her? If so, why send Spike Hair to threaten her like this?

As she waited for him to leave, she ran through all her memories of Poseidon. In every instance he'd acted like a gentleman, a man of his word. But he'd said it himself—with the Titans closing in, he'd be forced to turn against Hades. Did that include her? Damn it, she should never have volunteered the information about who her mother was. What if he'd contacted Demeter and made a deal that included turning Persephone over to her?

"You can't hide forever," the thug outside the door said finally, and when Cerberus relaxed, Persephone knew the threat was gone. She squeezed her eyes shut. Maybe Poseidon wasn't backing out of their deal and his man was acting independently? Or was she just deluding herself like the naïve idiot she'd always been? Still, it was ages before she would feel safe enough to open the door.

"Two weeks." She hugged Cerberus, and hoped she would last that long without her husband's protection.

89

"You ready, belle?" Hermes called, and Persephone straightened from the front of the rented stage where she was pinning up bunting.

"Looks good," Hermes said. "And it's almost three. Just enough time to go home, take a nap, and get ready for tonight."

Easing backwards, Persephone took in the product of a month's planning. The large tent took up half the new dog park. Three hundred chairs faced the long T shaped stage—a real cat walk. Or should she say, *dog* walk.

Behind the stage, Persephone knew, the models were getting ready, both human and canine. Hecate was back there somewhere, along with Cerberus and about fifty volunteers.

"Okay," Persephone said. "Just a sec."

Two weeks had flown by. After the incident in her apartment, Athena had inexplicably volunteered to pick her up and take her to and from the office. That meant Persephone worked eighteen-hour days, but Hecate was only too willing to check in on Cerberus, sometimes even taking him to visit the shelter and all his old doggie friends.

Hermes had also been exceptionally sweet, flitting in and out of her life, showing up at her apartment with Chinese takeout, leaning against the fireplace and cracking jokes about the Shades, watching her closely to make sure she ate.

She didn't tell anyone about Spike Hair, or his threats. The truce between Poseidon and the rest of the city leaders was too important for her or a wild card bodyguard to muddle it. She kept her head down, worked outrageous hours to draw every detail of the fundraiser together, and didn't go anywhere without at least one friend by her side.

Now the work and the wait would pay off. At least she hoped so. Everything hung on the success of tonight.

"What are you still doing here?" Hecate came out from behind the stage curtain, holding an adorable, tiny mutt. "You need to go change. You can't be the belle of the ball smelling like dog."

"Everything is going to smell like dog tonight. That's the whole point," Hermes joked. "Besides, she's not the belle of the ball. That would be Queenie."

The little dog barked when she heard her name, part Chihuahua, part terrier: all attitude.

Hecate laughed, and Persephone tried to smile, but it crumpled quickly under the weight of everything she had on her mind.

"Go on home, Persephone," Hermes spoke up. "We have it under control, at least until things get underway at seven."

"All right." She gave the bunting a final frown and straightened. "Are you my ride?"

"I've got my stuff here to change into. I was going to check out the old theater."

Persephone nodded absently. The theater was a brick building at the end of the park. Too small for the fashion show, it played an important role in the second half of the night's events—the events that would make or break the alliance between three powerful players and decide the fate of New Olympus.

"Persephone," Hecate called, and Persephone realized her friend had called her name twice. "There's someone here to pick you up." Hermes motioned her out of the tent.

"Fine." Persephone headed out of the tent, ignoring the worried looks her friends exchanged over her head. She knew she wasn't acting like herself, and everyone who knew her had picked up on it, but she couldn't help it.

A month and she hadn't seen or heard from the man whose last name she still bore. Divorce papers hadn't arrived, but then, he'd been busy fighting a mock war with Poseidon.

At least there were no more pictures of Hades in the paper with his arm around other women.

Other than reports of escalating violence between New Olympus and Metropolis gangs—street confrontations, drive by shootings, and vandalized buildings owned by Hades's holding companies—she'd had no sight or sound from her husband, not even from Charon.

Which is why, when she saw the large black man hulking behind the wheel of a car, she stopped short. Charon got out of the car and opened the door. Habit propelled her forward into the back seat, until she sat secure behind bulletproof glass. Her heart ached, being this close to her past life.

"How have you been?" Charon's dark sunglasses wrapped around his head and she couldn't see his face.

"Fine."

Charon turned the car into traffic, pulling out of it a minute later to cut down a back alley. "You eating?"

"Yes. Did you get my last message?" She'd left a voicemail last night. "Are we on?"

"All systems go." He stayed silent for the few miles the car crawled through thick traffic. "He's doing well."

She let out a breath. Now tears came, pooling in the corners of her eyes and stinging. Crap. She couldn't afford puffy eyes today. But Charon sitting there made the loss too fresh, too raw. She took several deep breaths, though, and managed to get herself under control.

After parking, Charon followed her into her apartment. Cerberus was already at the pavilion, a lead in the doggie fashion show.

Her thoughts on Hades, Persephone left Charon in the living room while she showered. Her dress, an ethereal blue, lay on the bed.

She dried her hair quickly, then pulled it back in an antique silver clip, curling the ends. She put on just enough make up to give her a dewy glow. She looked like a teen ready for prom, except for the distant look in her eyes.

The dress came on like a second skin, the neckline plunging to the point where she couldn't wear a bra. Try as she might, leaning over and shifting, the final few inches of the dress's zipper escaped her. The last time she'd worn it, she'd been on Hades's arm. He'd helped her with it. She felt a twinge of pain at the memory.

Trotting out of the bedroom, heels in hand, she waited until Charon turned away from the balcony doors.

"Will you zip me? I can't reach it." She went to him and turned, head bowed. A pause, then the dress bodice tightened as he obliged. For such a big man, his hands were nimble, zipping her up and hooking the little hook without so much as touching her.

Once she felt the hook catch, she stepped away and bowed to slip on her shoes, heels like skyscrapers. She'd be among powerful men tonight, and she needed the height, the authority.

The dress's baby blue color gave her an innocent air, complemented by the pink of her cheeks. An approachable sweetness, until someone got close and realized the fit was so tight they could pick out the goosebumps on her legs if they wanted to, and just one twitch to the side and her nipples would be exposed. All the more sexy, because it was unexpected.

Charon must have felt the effect, because as she straightened, she felt large hands brushing her back, lifting her curls and fixing them so they flowed down her back. It felt nice.

"You were right," Charon said out of the blue. "I loved Chiara. We were engaged."

Charon's voice was so deep, and he was usually so quiet, she almost thought she'd imagined it.

She kept her head bowed, hoping he'd take the hint and keep talking and fussing with her hair.

"We kept it a secret. People didn't need to know. We knew. From the first time we saw each other, we knew we would be together."

His hands on her shoulders turned her gently to face him. Even in her skyscraper heels, he dwarfed her. "She was in danger, just because she was born. Her father had so many enemies. And she was just this little, shy thing, until you got to know her. Then she was feisty."

He looked like he was about to laugh, and he tugged one of Persephone's curls. Then his face darkened. "I was young. Cocky. I thought I was strong enough to keep her safe."

He paused so long, Persephone wrapped her hands around his wrists, as if her touch would bring him back to her.

"You hate it when we keep you in the dark, or on a pedestal. But I'm telling you, if I could bring Chiara back, I'd take her far, far away and lock her in a tower if that's what it took to keep her safe."

Oh Charon. Persephone wanted to reach out and comfort him, but she didn't want to break the spell. He was opening up to her and she saw the truth, that inside the large, brutal man before her, there was a gentle giant. Or at least, there once had been. Was there anything left of the boy who had once loved a girl, before he'd lost her so brutally?

Her eyes searched his black ones. She found nothing but darkness.

And suddenly, she was crying. She felt like she'd cried an ocean of tears lately. But how could she not? First Hades, then Charon. How was it possible for two men to lose so much?

Charon shushed her, pulling her to him and holding her in a giant hug. His heat wrapped around her as she pressed her face to his suit as if that would stop her tears. She'd need to redo her makeup but she didn't care.

A big hand cupped her head. "I had a childhood growing up with her. Watching over her. And when we were older, we had a year together. A good year. Then her parents died, and she got shut up at the Estate. One good year, and one bad. Then she died."

He put his head close to Persephone's, making sure she heard him. "She was sneaking out of the Estate, trying to meet me."

"Oh, gods." The image played in Persephone's head, immediate and full of color: sweet Chiara, young Chiara, running over the green lawn to meet her love. Then— Then—

Persephone's stomach spun and she squeezed her eyes shut. No. She couldn't lose it now. Charon deserved for her to hear him out.

"Hades and I found her a week later." Charon reached out and took her hand. "We'd told her it wasn't safe. She knew that and went anyway, no guard on her, no protection, she just got a mad idea and ran off to find me."

Persephone wiped her eyes, pressing her fingers to her skin as if they could hold back tears. "So when I snuck out—"

"It was Chiara all over again. And her death is something he's never dealt with. It was too much. It could've been Chiara all over again, and it was too much."

She dropped heavily on the couch. "Then why aren't *you* mad at me? You of all people have every reason. My parents—"

"Aren't you," he said firmly, sitting beside her. "And I've dealt with her death, Persephone. I buried her. I loved her, and she died, but she's not gone. Not while I have my memory. She was the love of my life and I'll never lose her."

He sighed. "But Hades fights it. He thinks if he works hard enough, long enough, wraps up every inch of this city so tight that nothing happens without his say so, that he'll somehow save Chiara, and bring her and his parents back. He's spent all these years running."

Persephone sat up beside him, searching his face. "What does that mean?"

Charon tilted his head towards her. "Means he needs a woman by his side who understands, and who can be there for him. In his world, men destroy, women heal. He needs you."

"He sent me away."

He squeezed her hand. "He needs you."

"Will I ever see him again?" she whispered.

Charon let his features soften into a smile. A happy ache went through her at the tender sight. The gentle giant was still there. That boy who'd once loved a girl remained inside the man today. "That can be arranged."

Persephone's lower lip trembled, but she nodded. "Okay."

His wrapped a big arm around her, and she relaxed into the hug, letting his steady heartbeat calm her.

He said Hades needed her. Wrapped in Charon's warmth, she felt like anything was possible.

A thought struck her.

"What about you, Charon? Are you going to fall in love again?"

He turned and lightly—very lightly—kissed the top of her head.

Her cheek pressed to his huge chest, she blinked. She let him hold her for a beat, then, she shifted away, avoiding his eyes.

"I should fix my makeup." When she let her eyes drift up to his face, she could barely look at his tender expression. He looked ten years younger, closer to her age.

With a nod, he let her up and she stood up.

Back in the car, they shared a taut silence. Charon's large hand rested on his leg; she reached forward and touched the gold band he wore on his right ring finger.

He looked down at her, eyes still gentle.

"Thank you," she said, touching the ring she now knew he wore for Chiara. Her throat closed before she could elaborate—*thank you for sharing, for watching over me.*

His eyes crinkled into a smile and she knew he heard her unspoken words.

Then his gaze slid down to her cleavage and back up. "I've got your back tonight," he said, and he didn't sound happy. "Don't let anyone get too close."

She read his displeasure and couldn't help smiling. "Hades bought me this dress," she reminded him, and his nostrils flared.

"You were mine, I wouldn't let you out of the house in that thing."

"Good thing I'm my own woman then," she said. "Because you boys couldn't pull this off without me."

90

The first half of the night went well. The dogs paraded next to the models, and everyone was on their best behavior.

"Are they all house-trained?" Persephone looked up at Andrea Doria, who'd joined her backstage.

"The dogs are. Can't say for sure about the models." Andrea smiled. Her blonde wig was glorious, teased around her perfectly made up face.

"You look amazing," Persephone told her honestly.

"Thanks, darling. You're sweet."

"I'm serious. And I was serious about getting a makeup lesson, I want to know all your secrets." Persephone admired the contours of Andrea's cheekbones, then turned back around to watch the mayor give his speech.

"It's my honor to dedicate this park to our four-legged friends. My father taught me that you measure a man's humanity by how he treats his fellow creatures."

"Talks a good game, doesn't he?" Andrea muttered.

"Mmhmm," Persephone agreed.

"And so we are here to honor the most loving and loyal of creatures. My friends, I never thought I'd say this with any pride, but here

I am to tell you: this city is going...to the dogs!" Zeus said to the crowd's happy applause.

"See you after half time," Andrea said, and when Persephone turned around, she was gone.

Striding carefully in her high heels, Persephone met the mayor backstage.

"That went well," Zeus said briskly.

"Yes, thank you, Mr. Mayor." Persephone stepped forward before his aides could intervene. "Could we trouble you for a quick photo op in the back building, where the light is good? The photographer has a setup back there."

The mayor blinked at her, and Persephone realized he didn't completely recognize her. "Just back here," she repeated. "There's someone I want to introduce you to."

"Sure, sure," Zeus said, waving at his aides. "Just a few minutes."

"Certainly." Persephone smiled and led the entourage across the park lawn to the old theater. Inside, she led them to the stage. The space was big and open, which was the main point. There were few hidden corners other than backstage—but Poseidon's men had secured it beforehand, and otherwise, everything was out in the open.

"Interesting spot," Zeus commented. He and his aides slowed when they saw Andrea Doria's tall form flanked by two guards. Andrea also held Cerberus's leash; Persephone hurried to take it and then positioned herself between the two parties.

"Mr. Mayor, meet Andrea Doria."

Zeus barely hesitated, extending his hand for the tall drag queen to shake. "A pleasure, ma'am."

"All mine, Mayor Sturm." Andrea didn't bother to alter her voice's smooth tenor. "I'm so glad you have recovered so well after the poisoning."

"Yes, bit of a scare, but all's well that ends well." The mayor gave his fake chuckle and looked around. "Where are the cameras?"

"I believe you know Ms. Doria under a different name," Persephone said, stepping between the two.

The mayor's eyes narrowed and Persephone knew then he recognized her. He opened his mouth, but Poseidon stole the show by removing his platinum blonde wig and stating his name clearly.

The mayor's people reacted immediately, drawing their weapons and forming a hedge around Zeus. Persephone found herself at the center of a deadly circle as Poseidon's men also responded.

"Stop, just stop," she cried out. Stretching out her hands in a 'stop' sign, Persephone looked from one powerful man to the other. "This is neutral territory. We are just going to talk."

"Well, well," Zeus said, staring at the tall black man. "This is an interesting way to get my attention. Although you had it as soon as you tried to poison me."

"I'm innocent of that," Poseidon said. The wig lay at his feet, and even wearing a dress and backed by only two men, he looked more than a match for the mayor's posse. "You're the one who allowed my shipment to be taken, and then reneged on our deal."

"Enough," Persephone said and, at her feet, Cerberus barked—a deep, dangerous sound that stilled the men who heard it. "Poseidon never tried to kill you, or my husband. And the matter of the shipment has been settled, are we agreed?" She glared at all of them. "The real issue is that you're being played."

"The only issue I have—" Zeus began but Persephone quickly cut him off.

"Don't you get it? The Titans are setting you against each other. They'd like nothing better than to watch you take each other out. Then they can take the city with no one in their way."

Persephone's outburst seemed to silence the mayor, if only because he wasn't used to being interrupted.

"Mr. Mayor, look at him," Persephone snapped. "Does he look like he's hiding anything from you?"

Zeus Sturm took in Poseidon from head to toe. Then, to everybody's shock, he laughed, and it was a genuine, pleasant sound.

"Lower your weapons," Zeus ordered his men, and Poseidon's men mirrored them.

"This is unbelievable," the mayor shook his head, but he had a smile on his face. "You planned this ambush?"

Poseidon also grinned. "Mrs. Ubeli did. I come in peace."

"An alliance, eh? You, me, and Ubeli, all united against the Titans?"

"So says the lady," Poseidon nodded.

The mayor studied Persephone. "Do you speak for your husband?"

"She does," a voice echoed from near the ceiling, and Hades Ubeli sauntered down the stairs at the side of the stage, flanked by several Shades.

At the sight of him, all the air rushed out of Persephone's lungs. Down at the base of the stairs, the curtain rippled and Charon stepped out of his hiding place, nodding to her. She nodded back and retreated from center stage to watch the mayor, the shipping mogul and the mob boss converse.

"An alliance, then." Zeus actually sounded pleased. "Me in office, Poseidon controlling the sea and Ubeli," he waved his hand as if that would encompass Ubeli's activities on both sides of the law.

"Agreed," Poseidon said, and looked to Hades, who fixed him with a dark stare.

"Return my men."

"Done," Poseidon said. "Although I'd like to hire them as muscle. The Titans took their shots at offing the two of you. Once they know I have no intention of aligning myself with them, they will come for me."

"Very well," Hades said. "I'll give the orders. We'll keep staging skirmishes to get the Titans thinking we're at war. Then, when the timing's right, we strike."

Persephone turned in a slow circle, looking at all three of the men, almost disbelieving at how well this was all turning out.

"So, if we're all agreed—" Zeus began, when movement caught Persephone's eye.

"Get down," she shrieked, and the men around the mayor reacted instantly, pulling him to the floor and raising their weapons.

They were too slow for Spike Hair, who darted out of the wings and fired before any of the mayor's men could react.

But he didn't aim for the mayor.

"Hades," Persephone cried and Charon threw himself forward, but he was too late. The gun went off, and Hades dropped.

Someone jerked Persephone back. "Come, Mrs. Ubeli, I've got to get you out of here."

It was a Shade, Angelo she thought his name was. But she had to get to Hades, to see if he was okay—

But no matter how she struggled, Angelo pulled her backwards from the scene, stronger than he looked. Charon had rolled off Hades but she couldn't see— She couldn't see if—

Spike Hair continued to fire. Bullets ricocheted around the stage. It had all happened in seconds and Persephone couldn't, she couldn't—

Angelo was pulling her from the room and out down a hallway. "I have orders to get you to the back exit if anything happens," he said, dragging her away from Hades and Charon.

She wanted to wrench away from him and run back, but gods, she could still hear the gunfire. What good would she really do Hades if she went back in there, though? She'd only be a distraction from him getting himself to safety.

He'd ordered his Shades to get her out should something happen. For once in her life, she could obey and not screw things up worse.

So no matter how much she wanted to punch Angelo in the face and run back to help the others, she went along with him as he hurried her down the hallway and out the exit into the warm evening air.

And right into an alley where her mother, Demeter Titan, stood with half a dozen armed guards waiting.

"Baby, it's so good to finally see you again."

91

In the blink of an eye, Persephone saw it also clearly. How her mother had manipulated them all. She'd only had to flip two men after all—one inside Poseidon' camp, and one inside Hades's. Spike Hair and Angelo, who, now that Persephone thought about it, Hades had mentioned had been troublesome in the past.

And now here she was. Caught like a fly in a spider's web.

"Call off the attack," Persephone said. "You have me."

Demeter laughed. She looked nothing like the woman Persephone had grown up with, who wore overalls and rarely conditioned her hair.

Now Demeter's dark brown hair was styled in big curls, she wore dramatic makeup, and she had on a power skirt-suit. "Not that you aren't special, darling, but this is about so much more than you. This is about history. And righting wrongs. Ubeli stole this city from me and I mean to have it back."

"Righting wrongs?" Persephone scoffed. "Sixteen years ago, you murdered an innocent girl. After my father and uncles *raped* her."

Demeter's face went cold. "I thought I knew what I was getting into when I married a Titan brother. But I was young. Karl was handsome and said he loved me. I never had a real home or real family so marrying into his seemed like a dream come true. But he was weak."

Demeter took a step towards her. "So I did what needed doing while he drank and whored his way across town. Then he finally managed to do something right—he caught the Ubeli girl, but of course he couldn't keep his dick in his pants."

Demeter shook her head in disgust. "So again I had to come in and clean up his mess."

"You stabbed her over and over!" Persephone shouted. "You're as much a monster as he was."

Demeter crossed the last of the space between them and grabbed Persephone's wrist in a painful, bruising grip. "You will not disrespect me in front of my men. You've embarrassed me long enough, running around and consorting with the enemy. It ends here. Today."

"What are you going to do?" Persephone glared hatefully, only inches from her mother's face. "Kill me in cold blood? That's what you're good at, right?"

"I do what has to be done," Demeter said through gritted teeth. "Something a girl like you would never understand. But you will. I'll take you home and you will get an introduction to the way the real world works. You are my daughter and one way or another, you will behave as such."

"Never—" Persephone started to shout, right as the back door to the theater swung open and a deep voice called, "Persephone!"

"No!" Persephone shouted but it was too late. The shooting had already begun.

"Charon!" Persephone cried.

He had his weapon out and managed to take down three of Demeter's guards before falling to his knees, blood gushing from several wounds on his chest.

"No, Charon!"

Persephone fought to get away from her mother but Demeter caught her from behind in a chokehold and started dragging her towards the SUV parked several feet away.

Persephone wheezed and tried to scream, but she couldn't get any breath, her mother's hold on her was too tight.

How many times do I have to tell you to turn your head to the side to free your airway?

The self-defense lessons with Hades.

Persephone swung her head to the right, immediately freeing her airway, just like Hades said. She sucked in a deep breath, then she elbowed her mother hard in the side, once, twice, three times, until Demeter's hold loosened. For good measure, Persephone stomped on her instep, then, when Demeter was wheezing, Persephone grabbed one of Demeter's arms and planted her feet, using her firm stance as a fulcrum to launch Demeter to the ground.

Demeter screamed as her face slammed into the pavement and she rolled over once. She landed right by Charon. He'd been immobile, Persephone feared dead, but he suddenly reared up and slammed a knife straight through Demeter's heart. And then he collapsed.

"Charon!" Persephone cried, right as the back door of the theater opened and a handful of more Shades poured out. They made quick work of the rest of Demeter's guards, but all Persephone could see was Charon.

"Charon, please," she sobbed, crouched at his side, pressing her hands to the wounds on his chest. They had to stop the bleeding. There was so much *blood*. It was like Eurydice all over again. "You're going to be all right."

He lifted his hand to caress her face. "Loved—"

"You loved her, I know. You told me. You're going to be okay. You're going to love again, you'll see." She choked on her tears as the big man's eyes closed. "No. No! Help me! Someone! Help me!"

Hades was beside her, prying her hands away as several Shades moved in to put pressure on Charon's wounds.

"Hades?" She grabbed him with bloody hands. "You're alive?"

At the same time, an ambulance pulled into the back alley and sped their direction. Its lights weren't flashing and the sirens didn't sound, but as soon as it came to a stop, several EMTs poured from the back and Hades barked orders at them.

Charon was immediately put on a gurney and wheeled inside where the EMTs started working on him.

Persephone looked on in stark shock.

Hades finally took her hand as the ambulance sped away, this time with lights flashing.

"I had an ambulance nearby in case things went wrong. And I was wearing a vest," Hades said gently as she finally turned to him, parting his shirt and touching the Kevlar. "I should have insisted Charon wear one, too."

Persephone heard the pain in his voice but she was too raw to be able to comfort him.

"Come with me, now, Persephone—"

He tried to put his arm around her but she wrenched away. "Will they be able to save him? Charon saved me, he killed my mother. He has to be okay—"

"It's over. Honey, it's over now."

She glared up at him, fury and grief warring within her. "No, it's not. But it will be."

92

Persephone sat on the edge of the limo seat, tense as they passed a long line of drab, squat buildings marked with graffiti. If New Olympus was the glittering belle of the ball, Metropolis was its ugly step-sister.

"Almost there," Fats said from the driver's seat.

"Any sign they're on to us?" Persephone straightened her wig.

"Not if we've come this far." Poseidon shooed Persephone's hands away and fixed her dark brown curls. Andrea had given Persephone a makeup lesson after all. Heavy makeup designed to make her look older.

Like her mother.

"How do I look?" Persephone smiled at Poseidon carefully so the thick makeup wouldn't crack.

"Like a mob mistress."

"Good. Because that's what I am."

"Checkpoint ahead. Get your game faces on," Fats instructed as he slowed the car. Two men with machine guns blocked the road as a third approached the driver's side.

"Confidence," Poseidon murmured to Persephone as Fats rolled his window down.

"Mrs. Titan and guest," Fats announced.

"Mrs. Titan?" the guard asked.

Persephone leaned forward so the Titan's men saw her. "Of course it's me," she snapped in her mother's voice.

"What's with the tail?" The man motioned to the three cars following them.

"They're mine." Persephone waved a hand.

"I don't recognize them."

"They're new. My personal guard died in New Olympus. Once we forged our alliance, Poseidon was kind enough to loan me a few of his." Persephone's heart pounded as she waited for the guard to call her on her lie.

"I got orders not to let anyone I don't recognize through. The Titan brothers won't like it."

"They really won't like it when they find out Poseidon withdrew his offer of alliance because you wouldn't let him through to the meet."

On cue, Poseidon rolled his window down.

"You're wasting my time," Poseidon informed the man in his deep, grave voice. The checkpoint guard paled.

Persephone sat back, sliding a large pair of sunglasses on and looking straight ahead as if the checkpoint didn't exist.

"Hurry up and drive," she barked at Fats. "Alex and Ivan are waiting."

Persephone remained in 'Demeter Titan' mode as the guard waved them on. As soon as Fats drove past the machine guns, Poseidon chuckled. "That was perfect."

Persephone squeezed his big hand. The next stage of the plan wouldn't be so easy.

"We're here," Fats reported as the car stopped in front of an old church. "The Titans holed up here three days ago. Both are inside, expecting Demeter and Poseidon. They're meeting with their capos in an hour."

"Plenty of time to take out the trash." Poseidon straightened his collar and exited the car, offering a hand to help 'Demeter' out.

As they strode ahead, arm and arm, three more black cars pulled up to the church. Men poured out—some Shades, some Poseidon's men. They'd infiltrate the church, quietly taking out any of the Titan's men and assuming their places.

Persephone and Poseidon waited in the foyer until Slim strode in. "All clear. Your uncles are in the basement, oblivious. Alone."

This is it. Persephone kept the big sunglasses on and let Poseidon guide her with a hand on her back down the stairs.

"Ready?" he rumbled when she paused to stare at the doors leading to the basement hall. In a second she'd meet both her uncles for the first and last time.

"Ready," she said finally, and pushed the doors open.

The basement was hot and stuffy, smelling of onions and sausage. Two blond men sat at a plastic table, playing cards in their shirt sleeves. They stopped when she marched in, a phalanx of guards fanning out around her, and Poseidon at her side.

"Demeter? About fuckin' time." One of the blond men turned. Ivan. She recognized him from an old photo. "Poseidon," he said, getting to his feet. "Glad to see you here. It's good that you've come to see reason. Your product will be safe in our hands."

Persephone stopped just inside the door, keeping to the shadows, and let her and Poseidon's guards surround the room. "Yes, he and I have come to an agreement," she said.

"The alliance is a done deal, then?" the second Titan asked, also standing. Her uncle Alexander. He glared at Fats and Slim and the rest, obviously suspecting something, but not going for his gun.

He wouldn't dare in front of Poseidon.

"The alliance is done." Persephone said. "But you two and I have unfinished business." She slowly pulled her sunglasses off and put them in her pocket.

Alex scowled. "What's that supposed to—" He stopped short when Poseidon pulled a gun from his pocket and, before he could even blink, shot him. He slumped forward.

"What the fuck?" Ivan shouted and went for his gun, but every man in the room pulled a gun on him before he could.

"Stand down," Persephone said coolly.

There was a riot of action as the Shades swarmed the table, securing Ivan and Alex, who was moaning in pain.

"You're not Demeter," Ivan snarled.

"Hello, uncle," she greeted him, tugging off the wig. "Nice of you to join me for this family reunion."

Her uncle's eyes bulged. "Where's Demeter?"

"My mother is busy at the moment." Busy being dead. "She sent me."

"You bitch—" Ivan started, only to choke when Slim looped a belt around his neck and tightened it.

Meanwhile two Shades had bound and gagged Alex. "What should we do with this one?"

"Is he dead?" Poseidon asked, coming to join Persephone.

"Nope," Fats reported. "You got him in the stomach."

"I'm getting rusty." Poseidon grinned. "But then again, belly shots are so perfectly painful."

"Make sure he gets to my husband in one piece," Persephone instructed and turned to Slim and the Shades who held Ivan. "Him too."

Ivan gurgled something and Persephone motioned for his throat to be freed.

"What's the meaning of this?" Ivan rasped. On his knees, surrounded by her thugs with guns, he didn't look so big.

"In a minute, I'll explain everything," she informed him sweetly. "But not to you. Your reign is over. You're going away for a while. At least, until Charon can hold a knife again. I'm sure he'll recover faster, knowing he has you waiting for him to take his revenge out on."

Before Ivan could shout anything else, Slim stuffed a gag into his mouth and dragged him off with his brother.

The doors closed, leaving her and Poseidon alone. Persephone let her shoulders slump.

"Well done," Poseidon said. "That went quicker than I expected." He bent to study her face. "You didn't want to talk to your uncles?"

She shook her head. "Honestly, I had nothing to say to them."

The doors opened and one of Poseidon's men reported, "The Titan capos are starting to gather in the sanctuary. Do you want us to relieve them of their weapons?"

Poseidon nodded and the man disappeared. He watched Persephone wander around the room, lost in thought, touching the table where her uncles had sat.

"You talk to Hades yet?"

Persephone blinked as if coming awake. "Not yet. Time was of the essence. We had to get here before they got too suspicious when Demeter didn't get into contact."

Poseidon tilted his head. "He wants to talk to you."

"He will. I have to do this first."

Poseidon's man returned. "We're ready for you."

"The capos are unarmed?" Poseidon asked.

"Not all of them were happy but we used that Aurum pulse thing Mrs. Ubeli picked up for us on the way, and their guns jammed. Excuse me, I meant Mrs. Titan."

"Ms. Titan," Persephone corrected. "Tell them the Titans are now allied with Poseidon and loyalty will be greatly rewarded. We'll be with them shortly."

The man scuttled off and Persephone smiled. Turned out she liked giving orders.

"Ms. Titan?" Poseidon asked. "You taking back your maiden name?"

"I've never been a Titan, actually." Persephone took his offered arm. "But it's my birthright, so I better get used to it. So will everyone else."

With a smile of his own, Poseidon nodded. Persephone let him escort her to the sanctuary before pulling away.

"I have to do this alone."

He nodded again. She reached up and touched his cheek. "Thank you," she said simply, before dropping her hand and striding into the sanctuary. Poseidon covered his cheek with his hand.

The capos sat in the front pews like oversized, disgruntled altar boys in ill-fitting suits. Above them, in the balcony and choir loft,

Shades and Poseidon's men stood guard, outfitted with special guns that Athena had designed to withstand her patented weapon-jamming device. Turned out Athena had been up to more on her West Coast adventures than just pestering suppliers. She'd come home bearing new toys.

With a nod to Fats and Slim, Persephone climbed the stage to address her new capos.

"Welcome," she called and waited while they all took her in.

"Who da fuck are you?" one man called.

"We've never met. I'm Persephone Titan. You will treat me with respect."

"Or?"

"You die," Slim shot back.

Persephone smiled. "I understand you have questions," she said. "In a minute I will answer them, but for now know this. There's a new Titan in town. As of now, I'm running the show."

The capos murmured to each other. "Who died and put you in charge?" another asked.

"My mother and uncles, actually. If they're not dead, they will be soon." Beeping sounds filled the room and the capos patted their pockets, pulling out their vibrating cellphones en masse.

Thank you, Athena.

"You've just been texted pictures of my deceased mother. Note the resemblance." Persephone tilted her head to the side, giving them a profile.

"Fucking spittin' image," an older capo murmured. "Demeter and the old man, what's his face, Karl."

"You'll find I have a lot in common with both my parents," Persephone said. "With one difference. While they enjoyed war, I prefer the alternative. Peace."

"Peace," a capo echoed.

"Indeed. After all, it's so much better for business." Persephone spread her hands. "Imagine this. A city at peace. Men and women visiting your brothels. Hordes of partygoers sampling Ambrosia, returning again and again to buy from your distributors. We have a new alliance with our good friend, Poseidon."

She turned to smile at Poseidon as he ambled in. She paused a moment to let him greet the capos and shake a few hands. He took a seat at the end of one pew, his great height dwarfing the rest.

"With Poseidon at our side and unlimited access to overseas imports, profits will roll in. Imagine the streets alive with people who've come for the party. New Olympus is where they do business. Metropolis is where they come to have fun."

"I like it," the older capo said. "Especially the part about the profits, and alliance with ole Poseidon here. I knew your father," he said to Poseidon.

"What about the cops?" another capo called.

Persephone dropped her next bombshell. "Tomorrow the mayor of New Olympus introduces a proposal to make Ambrosia legal. A controlled substance. It'll be the new Viagra, but recreational, and for both men and women. We can expect the mayor of Metropolis to follow suit."

Yep, the mayor was on her side too, and she saw the impact the news had on the crowd. It hadn't taken much convincing to get Zeus and Poseidon to throw in behind her, once she explained that her assuming control of the Titan gang was the quickest way to bring lasting peace to the streets. "With a few bribes, we'll buy all the rights to distribute. Legally."

"This true?" a capo demanded of Poseidon.

"Every word," he confirmed, and the murmurs got louder.

"Damn. Never thought I'd go straight in my old age," the gray-haired capo muttered. "But if there's profit in it, who cares?"

"This is bull." One capo shot to his feet. "You're a lying whore." His shout echoed to the rafters. So did the sound of a hundred guns trained on him.

Persephone raised a hand. "Stand down," she drawled. "I like a rigorous debate among my leaders. As long as they remember their place."

Fats and Slim grabbed the man and brought him cursing before her, forcing him to his knees. "But there's no room for men who don't see my vision."

A glint of metal and she had a knife at the man's throat. "Do you pledge your loyalty to the Titans?"

"You ain't no Titan," the man spat, and then died with a gurgle as she slit his jugular.

Her stomach rebelled at the sight. But this one act of violence now could stop endless violence later. She had to prove she was strong and ruthless or these men would never respect her rule. She understood now some of the choices and sacrifices Hades had to make every day to hold his city in check. She would now do the same.

Poseidon strolled to her side and offered a white handkerchief. Persephone wiped the blood from her face and hands, but didn't bother with her white dress. She'd expected to be christened tonight. Once she'd handed back the handkerchief, she fixed the capos with a cold stare she'd learned from her husband. "Anyone else?"

Dead silence answered her until the older capo chuckled. "She's a Titan all right. Fuckin' visionary, like her parents. Spittin' image."

"Any other questions?"

"What about Ubeli? With all due respect," the capo added. "We just gonna roll over and let him win?"

Persephone smiled. "Not at all. From now consider war at an end between us. You handle business as usual. I'll handle my husband."

Another chuckle from the oldest capo. He elbowed his neighbor while the others exchanged knowing glances.

"I know a few of you won't be happy with the new arrangements," Persephone continued. "I expect you to come discuss things with me. Respectfully. Otherwise, you'll feel the full force of the Shades and Poseidon's men, not to mention the trouble you'll get into with the law. Oh yes, the cops have orders to back me. The mayor of New Olympus introduced me to the Metropolis chief of police, and we're fast friends." She laughed lightly.

Another chorus of beeps had the capos checking their phones again.

Slim held out a screen to show Persephone the grisly image.

"Looks like my husband got my little peace offering. A sign of goodwill. Alexander Titan had some use after all. He was your main leader, correct?"

A few of the capos had turned green.

"I don't have to warn you what will happen if you ever cross me," Persephone said. "I expect we'll all get along beautifully, especially when profits start rolling in. I'll be by to visit each of your businesses this week. Expect me. I'll expect you to be on your best behavior. Behave and you won't get on my bad side."

A bark broke the silence. Cerberus broke from his handler in the back, and bounded to Persephone's side. She knelt to stroke his head a moment before rising. Slim came to her side with a red coat. With his help, she shrugged it on over her dress.

"Now, Poseidon and I are going to dinner. You're all invited to pay your respects." She'd know who was loyal if they came to kiss her ring. "If not, I'll see you later this week."

Signaling Cerberus, she strode down the aisle, her guards at her back and her dog at her side. Poseidon paused a moment before following.

"The king is dead," he rumbled. "Long live the queen."

93

A week later, Slim pulled the limo up to the docks.

"You gonna be all right?" Poseidon asked. They'd spent the week in Metropolis, cementing Persephone's rule over the Titan's businesses.

Persephone raised her chin. "Don't worry about me." The capos weren't all happy she'd moved in, but they'd put down the ones most likely to betray her, and placated the rest with a bigger cut of profits.

"That's the spirit." He chucked her under the chin. "You let me know if anyone causes you trouble."

"I will. Thank you, for everything."

"Don't thank me yet," he announced as he got out and went around to open her door. "In a minute you're gonna want to yell at me."

"What? Why?"

"This is my limo. Your ride's over there." He stepped away and she looked down the pier to a black car idling at the curb. A familiar form waited, hands in pockets, dark head bent.

Hades.

Persephone drew in a sharp breath.

Hades and Persephone

"He's been calling me like crazy," Poseidon grumbled. "Demanding proof that you were okay. Me and Slim and Fats all had to report hourly."

Persephone put a hand to her neck, gaze fixed on the dark form of her husband. "I don't...we didn't leave things in a good place. I know he came through at the theater, but I don't know..."

"He's here, isn't he?" Poseidon put out a hand and Persephone automatically took it. When she was out of the car, he gave her a little push. "Go get him, kid."

She started across the blacktop. Hades looked so sober, leaning against his car. She'd talked to him on the phone over the past week, but only about Charon's progress after his multiple surgeries. Whenever he tried to turn the conversation to deeper topics, she made excuses and hung up.

There was so much between them. So many lies. So many scars. Could he forgive her? If he really had been with Lucinda, could she forgive him? Had he moved on? Did he even want her?

She wobbled on her heels and stopped.

"Persephone." He called her name and her head snapped up. His arms opened.

Kicking off her high heels, she ran.

HADES HUGGED her as soon as she'd jumped into his arms, but she'd turned her head aside when he lowered his mouth for a kiss.

She might have completed her coup in Metropolis, but there was unfinished business between them.

"Thanks for the ride," Persephone said from her side of the limo. She made no move to bridge the awkward space between them.

Easy. Gently. Give her time, Hades could practically hear Charon coaching him. He missed his friend more than he could say. Charon had been put in a medically induced coma, but the doctor said all indications were positive that he would have a full recovery. But they wouldn't know for sure until he woke up. It had been days, though, and he still hadn't opened his eyes.

You better not die, brother. I don't need you haunting me. Hades could almost hear Charon's chuckle filling the car.

They'd spent hours talking in the weeks Hades was separated from Persephone and Hades tried to muster all of that advice now.

All right, brother. We'll try it your way.

"You were magnificent." Hades drank in his wife's slim form, barely believing she was real. She looked different. Older. Not hard or jaded, just wiser somehow. "Poseidon and the Shades told me everything. I made them get footage."

She shrugged, then looked at him anxiously. "How's Charon?"

"No change. Yet."

She bit her lip and he had to clench his hand into a fist to keep from brushing his thumb against it until she relaxed. Then she asked, "You really think so? You really think I can do this? Lead the Titans?"

"Don't believe me. Check it out." He grabbed the paper on the seat and showed her. "*Queen of the Underworld*. You're gonna have to get used to getting dogged by the press."

"I'm already used to it. I married you, remember."

"Mmm." He'd always hated being called King of the Underworld but he'd embrace the term as long as she was by his side as his Queen.

His Queen looked exhausted, though, as she glanced his way. And she was sitting much too far away, almost hugging the opposite door.

"Come here." He held out his arm.

She sighed. "Hades, just because this is all over…" She shook her head and looked out the window, her expression far away. "It doesn't mean—" She broke off, hands going to her face.

She'd been as powerful as any general back there demanding her due as head of the Titan Empire but here with him, she was as vulnerable as always.

And he was done allowing her to put distance between them. He went to her and gathered her in his arms. "I almost lost you and I'll be damned if I spend another minute apart from you."

She struggled, though, and when she pushed away from him, her eyes flashed fire. "It was easy enough for you to walk away from me three weeks ago. And I saw the picture of you with that woman. Your lover."

She had to mean Lucinda. Hades had raged when he first saw the picture but now he grinned. "Jealous, kitten?" He could stand anything but her indifference.

If he thought her eyes were fiery before, it was nothing to the fury that sparked at his words.

"Get off of me, you oversized oaf." She shoved ineffectually at him but he only tightened his arms around her.

"I didn't touch her. I ran into her outside the Crown and she stumbled into me. Probably on purpose. Come to think of it, it was probably her who'd called the paparazzi. She always was an attention whore. I steadied her and then continued on my way. That was the full extent of our interaction."

Nice work, Charon said. *Now tell her the truth.*

Get out of my head, Hades almost muttered aloud before taking his advice. Tilting his head at his beautiful wife, he said, "There's no replacing you, love. There never could be."

Her countenance immediately changed. Instead of pushing him away, she gripped the lapels of his suit coat. "I was so scared. When you went down, I was so scared." Her eyes filled with tears. "And then Charon."

"We're heading to New Olympus General now. I knew you'd want to see him, first thing."

"Good." Persephone sank against him, her head to his chest. "Is it really over?"

He squeezed her close to him and breathed in the sweet aroma of her hair. "Yes, goddess. It's over. But the rest of our life is just beginning."

He felt her nod against his chest. But the next second she was pulling away. "Charon tried to explain. I'm sorry. I'm sorry that I left the Estate like that and headed straight into danger. I had no idea about Chiara."

Tears spilled down her cheeks and he cupped them, shaking his head. "You couldn't have known. I just— I just couldn't—" He looked down and huffed out a frustrated breath.

But then he forced himself to meet her gaze again. "I swore to protect you. No matter what. Even if it meant the safest place for you was away from me. It killed me, being away from you. Worse than the first time. So much worse, because I was afraid it was forever."

He didn't want to think about what the past three weeks had been like. He'd thrown himself into his work but not even that could distract him from missing her. Or from wondering, every hour of every day, every minute, if she was okay, what she was doing, if she hated him. If she was moving on. His sleep had been tormented by nightmares of her happy—in the arms of another man, wearing another man's ring.

Ten times a day, he'd had to wrestle himself back from saying fuck it, and getting in his car and breaking every traffic law known to man to go back to her. All his discipline, all his control, none of it counted when it came to her.

Maybe she saw something of his torment on his face because she lifted a hand to his cheek and whispered, "Never again. From here on out, it's you and me together. Always. No more secrets. No more lies. No matter if you think it's for my good or not. We're partners in everything now. Swear it?"

He met her eyes solemnly. "I vow to you, Persephone Ubeli, never to lie to you again."

"Not even if you think it's for my own good? I need you to say it, Hades."

He smiled at her tenacity. "I will never leave you nor forsake you. I will never lie to you again or keep secrets, even if I think it's for your own good. Now your turn."

She clasped his hands and there was no smile on her face. She was taking this dead seriously.

"I, Persephone Ubeli, vow to never leave nor forsake you, and I will never lie to you or keep secrets from you again, even if I think it's for your own good."

"Now all that's left is to seal it with a kiss," Hades said, moving his head slowly towards hers.

She rose to him and when their lips met, Hades thought he might just die after all at the angel soft touch of her lips.

In his worst moments, he thought he'd never get to experience this again. Even remembering how that felt made him crazy. He couldn't do gentle, not right now. Not after all they'd been through and their separation.

He crushed her to him and she threw her arms around his neck, apparently just as desperate for him in return. Their mouths met in a hungry tangle. Lips, tongues, teeth. He couldn't get enough of her. He needed all of her. Now.

But just as he shifted her to straddle him, the SUV came to a stop and the driver's voice sounded over the speaker. "We're here."

Persephone broke from Hades's mouth, eyes wide. "Charon."

She barely bothered to rearrange her clothing before shoving open the door. Hades had to run after her; she was halfway to the hospital entrance by the time he got out his own door.

THEY SPENT TWO DAYS' vigil at Charon's bedside before he finally opened his eyes.

It was sunset when his large brow finally scrunched and he blinked his eyes open.

"Charon!" Persephone cried, jumping up and grabbing his huge hand in her tiny one. "You're awake. Hades, he's awake!"

Hades stood behind Persephone, smiling down at his oldest friend, at his brother. "Thank the Fates," he breathed out. Charon had been such a steady constant in his life. He couldn't imagine going on without him. He was family.

Charon looked around, obviously confused.

"Here." Persephone let go of his hand only long enough to grab a cup of water with a straw in it from the bedside table to hold it up to Charon's mouth.

He took several swallows before leaning back on his pillows. "What— Happened?"

Persephone took his hand again. "You saved the day. You saved my *life*." She squeezed his hand.

"And for that, you have my eternal gratitude, brother," Hades said.

Charon met his eyes over Persephone's head and they shared a silent look. Charon nodded and Hades knew he understood. Hades owed him everything. It was a debt Hades could never repay but he'd spend the rest of his life trying anyway.

"My mother would've gotten away with all of it if you hadn't showed up when you did," Persephone continued. "And then you got shot. So many times," her voice broke. "I thought you were dead. The doctor says we're lucky that you're alive. If one of the bullets had even been half an inch closer to the left." She broke off, shaking her head, tears falling down her cheeks.

"I'm okay," Charon croaked, and Persephone immediately held the water back up to his lips.

Then Persephone swung around to look at Hades. "He's awake. We need to get the doctor. They said to call him when he woke up."

Hades nodded and pressed the button for the nurse to come in.

The nurse and then the doctor arrived several minutes later. Hades and Persephone were hustled out of the room while the doctor attended to Charon.

As soon as they left the room, Persephone's shoulders slumped. She was exhausted. No matter how Hades had tried to coax her to go home to get some rest, she'd refused to leave. She'd gotten a few hours sleep on a little cot they'd set up in the room, but not much.

Now that Charon was awake, though, he was insisting. She'd go home and get a full night's rest.

Her hand slid into his, fingers intertwining.

"I love you, Hades." She paused in the middle of the hospital hallway and looked up at him. "Thank you for giving me this life. Thank you for everything. You know how much I love you? Can you even fathom it?"

Hades smiled down at her, the woman he loved more than life itself.

He was about to leaned down to kiss her when her eyes suddenly rolled back in her head and she collapsed. He barely had time to catch her before she hit the ground.

94

All was dark and there were no stars.

"Hello?" Persephone called into the darkness.

No one responded.

Persephone stretched her arms out and felt all around her. Nothing. There was nothing.

"Hades? Hades?" Her voice was high-pitched, nearing on frantic. Where was she? Why couldn't she see anything? She spun around but there was only more nothingness, until, arms outstretched, her hand finally ran into a brick wall.

The air smelled sour and dank and that was when Persephone knew.

Mama had locked her in the cellar again.

It had all been a dream. Hades. New Olympus. None of it had ever been real.

Hades had never been real. He'd never loved her. He never would. Because he didn't exist. None of it had. Athena. Aphrodite. Charon. Hermes. She'd made them all up in her head.

How many days had she been down here? How long since she'd had food or water? How long since she'd slept?

She'd experienced it before, the delirium that came with being confined in the solitary space for long stretches.

She sank to her knees.

She was alone.

Unloved.

Her mother had finally driven her mad.

"Noooooo!" she cried, banging her fists on the earthen ground. "Please!" She didn't know what she was begging for. Maybe for the earth to open and swallow her up whole.

But then she froze. Because she heard something.

She sat up and craned her ears.

"Persephone. Persephone!"

The sound was coming from so far away, Persephone could barely hear it. But it was there. Either that, or it was an auditory hallucination.

But she was so desperate, she didn't care.

"Hello?" She stumbled towards the sound. "Hello?"

"Persephone," came the voice, louder this time. "Persephone, baby, come back to me."

Hades. It was Hades's voice.

Persephone started running towards it. She should have run into the back wall of the cellar but she didn't. The darkness just went on and on and as she ran, it began to lighten. First to a dark gray and then...and then...

Persephone blinked her eyes open and winced at the painfully bright lights.

"Persephone!" Hades's blurry face loomed over hers. He was smiling and crying at the same time. She'd never seen Hades cry in the entire time she'd known him.

Wait. Was this real? Or was it just another hallucination?

But when Hades dropped his lips to hers, she decided she didn't give a damn. She was staying.

95

Persephone had taken about ten years off Hades's life when she collapsed in the hospital hallway.

But then she was blinking up at him, awake, only ten minutes later. And if she had to pass out, she couldn't have picked a better place to do it.

Nurses and doctors had immediately rushed to their aid and gotten her on a gurney and into a room.

She was dehydrated, something Hades would never forgive himself for—he should have been making sure she'd drank more fluids while they watched over Charon, especially after the traumatic events of the days beforehand.

The doctors had taken some blood and they were waiting on the results. Hades had never been a praying man but he prayed now, to every god he knew and even those he didn't, that the bloodwork would come back fine and nothing was wrong with her.

They'd been waiting for what felt like hours even though he'd threatened the doctor to prioritize Persephone's bloodwork with his most menacing face. In reality, it was only a little over 45 minutes before the doctor came pushing through the door.

Hades leapt to his feet. The doctor was carrying a folder and he was smiling. Smiling had to mean good news, right? If it didn't, Hades would do more than smash this guy's face in.

"What is it?" Hades demanded. "Tell us."

"Hades." Persephone squeezed his hand gently. "Give the man a chance to take a breath."

Hades looked down at his wife in the hospital bed. She was too pale for his liking. And ever since she woke up, she kept asking him if he was real and clutching his hand like he would disappear if she let go even for a second.

"Other than the slight dehydration issue, you are in wonderful health," the doctor said to Persephone, avoiding Hades's gaze and walking to the other side of her bed.

"And I have good news." Persephone frowned up at him but then he continued, "You're pregnant!"

"What?" both Persephone and Hades said at the same time.

Persephone gasped and stared at the doctor in shock. Then she looked up at Hades with a tremulous smile on her face. She clasped his hand even tighter as she blinked rapidly. "I guess, I mean— I forgot to re-up my birth control shot because—"

Because they'd been separated.

Persephone shook her head and let out a little laugh. "And then I didn't even think about it but I should have gotten my period three weeks ago. Everything has just been so nuts preparing for the fundraiser and everything else." She broke off with another laugh.

But Hades wasn't laughing. He looked at the doctor. "So how far along is she?"

"When was the date of your last period?" the doctor asked Persephone.

She was still shaking her head in wonder, and then her eyes went to the ceiling as she calculated. "Um, about six weeks ago? Maybe seven? The second week of last month, I think."

Hades did the math in his head. He wasn't that well-versed in women's reproductive health but he'd had a woman once try to falsely claim he'd fathered her child and had learned a little about it. If her last period was seven weeks ago, that meant the baby had been conceived five weeks ago...right around the time they'd first gotten back together and first had sex.

But if she was off, even by a little bit... They'd been separated for months. She'd left him and he never asked if there was any one else during that time.

Frankly, he hadn't wanted to know. Okay, that was a lie. He had wanted to know, with a vengeance, but he also knew himself too well. If any other man had touched Persephone, whether she welcomed it or not, that man would not remain breathing for long after Hades discovered his name.

But now there was a child...

His jaw locked and he could hear his heartbeat racing in his ears. There was a child. No matter what, the child was half Persephone's. And anything that was half of her, he would love until his dying breath.

He reached down and retook her hand. "I will love this child as my own, no matter what."

Persephone blinked up at him in confusion. "What do you mean? It *is* your child." Then understanding seemed to dawn on her. And she threw his hand away. "I didn't sleep with anyone else while we were separated. Did *you*?" Her eyes spit fire and color flushed back into her previously pale cheeks. "So help me, if you so much as—"

Hades roared with laughter and then sat down on the bed, pulling her into his arms. "No. Never. Never anyone but you."

He kissed her hard. At first she was unresponsive but then her lips softened and she gave in to him. His sweet Persephone. His powerful, ball-busting Queen.

He pulled back from her and pressed his forehead to hers. "We're going to have a baby," he whispered.

Her big blue eyes blinked up at him, wide with astonishment. Her hand slid between them to her stomach. "A baby," she said in awe. "Your baby."

"You've made me the happiest man alive. I love you. Forever." The words were an understatement. They always would be.

But he would spend the rest of his life proving them to his wife. His beloved. His Queen.

EPILOGUE

Three years later...

PERSEPHONE KNEW the moment her husband entered the ballroom. Her spine prickled. Behind her, close to the door, the murmuring crowd quieted.

"Incoming, twelve o'clock," Hermes waggled his brows at her. Persephone pivoted in her gold dress and instantly picked Hades out. He was suave and knee-weakeningly handsome in his tux.

"No costume?" Hermes pouted, putting a fake-monocle to his eye. Persephone swatted his arm.

"He wouldn't wear it. But does he even need one?"

Hades had caught sight of her. His stubbled jaw creased into a smile. Mmm, five-o'clock shadow, her favorite. He had been working a lot lately, and hadn't had time to shave before the ball. He'd make it up to her later with the burn of his beard against her thighs...

Pressing two fingers to his lips, Hades blew her a kiss.

"Damn. He makes an entrance." Hermes dropped his monocle.

"I know," Persephone murmured.

"I was talking about Poseidon."

"Oh." The big shipping tycoon had just wandered in with a group of giggling women in skimpy sea foam green costumes.

"Water nymphs. Very, very clever," Hermes admired their costumes. "Shall we go greet your husband?"

"I think not," Persephone said. "Let him placate his supplicants." As usual, Hades was surrounded by people wanting to shake his hand and whisper in his ear.

"You make him sound like he's an emperor," Hermes lifted a critical brow. "What does that make you?"

"A goddess." Persephone smiled into her drink. "Leave Hades alone. He'll come to me."

"Of course he will. You two are glued to the hip. Or...other parts." He cast a pointed glance at her rounded belly.

"Hermes!" She put a hand to her baby bump.

"Aaaand you're blushing. I still got it."

"You're worse than Athena." Persephone pretended to look prim.

"Thank you. What number is this?" Hermes hovered his hand over her belly. "Two of ten? Eleven?"

"Two of two, thank you very much. We wanted a boy and a girl."

"You already have little Vito, so that makes this one..."

"A girl." Persephone's flushed skin seemed to glow. "We found out last week."

"Mrs. Ubeli!"

Both Persephone and Hermes turned to greet a gray-haired man in a white coat.

"Dr. Laurel," the man reminded them, raising bushy eyebrows that'd make Einstein jealous. "We met at the last gala. I can't tell you how grateful we are for all your charity. We're on the brink of a breakthrough."

"Dr. Laurel," Persephone murmured, letting him pump her hand. "Of course I remember."

A willowy young woman in a white toga and a headband of green leaves hovered at the Dr.'s elbow until he dragged her forward. "Allow me to introduce my daughter, Daphne."

"Hello." Daphne gave a shy little wave, laughing when Hermes executed a bow.

"Please to meet you, dear," Persephone said. The girl was a beauty with olive skin and almond shaped green eyes. She looked barely out of high school. "Are you in college?"

Daphne flushed as her dad guffawed. "College? My girl graduated already. On track for a Ph.D. Genius. Takes after her mother."

"And you as well, Dr. Laurel, I'm sure." Persephone smiled gently at the young woman. "Would you mind spinning around and showing us your costume? Let me guess what you are."

With a graceful nod, Daphne spun on her heel.

"Her specialty is biochemistry," Dr. Laurel was telling Hermes. "Her research is already making waves. Youngest recipient of the Avicennius grant."

"Very impressive," Hermes said.

"She didn't want to come," her father announced. "But she's spent too much time cooped up behind a microscope. You're still young." He waggled a finger at his daughter.

"You look beautiful," Persephone told Daphne. "I'm still trying to guess what you are. White robes and a wreath on your head?"

"I'm an ancient Olympic athlete," Daphne explained. "A winner. These are my laurels."

"Clever," Hermes said and Daphne blushed further.

"You can't be an Olympic athlete," a deep voice interrupted. A tall, dark-haired man stepped between Daphne and everyone else. "Olympic athletes performed naked."

"Oh my," Hermes raised his fake monocle to his eye and peered at the newcomer. "Hello there."

"Logan, stop being such a stuffed shirt," Dr. Laurel chided with a grin. "Mrs. Ubeli, may I introduce Dr. Logan Wulfe, unparalleled medical researcher and apparently an expert on ancient sports customs."

"Not an expert," Dr. Wulfe said. His face was stern but there was a mischievous tilt to his lips. His fingers traced the edge of Daphne's laurel leaves. "You could be Daphne, chased by Apollo, who turned into a laurel tree."

"That's a sad story," Daphne said, a bit breathlessly. She gazed up at Logan Wulfe as if he was a god come to life.

And no wonder. With his height, dark hair, and raw-boned features, he wasn't handsome but overwhelmingly masculine. Perfect to play the part of a brooding gothic hero. Daphne wasn't the only one under his spell. Hermes didn't rip his gaze away until Persephone elbowed him in the ribs. Everyone looked at him when he sputtered.

"She could be a military conqueror," Hermes covered smoothly. "The Romans stole the practice of crowning winners with laurels, and gave wreaths to their successful generals."

"That fits," Logan nodded to Daphne, who looked like she might faint with happiness. She had hearts in her eyes.

"Do you want to dance?" she asked and a shadow fell over the tall man's face.

"I don't dance. Not even for you."

"I'll dance with you."

The shadows on Logan's face deepened as a model-handsome blond broke into the circle.

"Here's my other star student. Adam Archer, of Archer Industries," Dr. Laurel babbled as the blond and Logan glared at each other. "His partnership has been essential to the success of our company."

"Happy to be of service." Adam flashed a toothpaste smile to everyone but Logan. "Daphne, shall we?"

The young woman put her hand in his outstretched one, letting him lead her away. But as the song began, her eyes drifted back to Logan.

"Excuse me," Logan muttered, pushing a hand through his thick hair before walking off.

"Forgive my protege's rudeness," Dr. Laurel said to break the awkward silence. "Logan and Adam used to be like brothers, but recently had a...a falling out."

"Business or personal?" Hermes asked, studying how Logan glared at Daphne and Adam on the dance floor.

Dr. Laurel blinked. "Business, of course."

"A bitter rivalry. How delicious," Hermes murmured and Persephone nudged him again. "Excuse me, I must go...see if I can offer comfort." He and the doctor wandered off in Logan's direction.

A strong hand on Persephone's back made her turn.

"Hades," she exclaimed. There were a few silver hairs at her husband's temple but he was even more handsome than ever.

"My love," he dropped a kiss on her shoulder. "Are you feeling all right?"

"Better, now you're here." Persephone cupped his cheek. They exchanged what Athena called an "ooey-gooey" look.

"I got away as soon as I could. Poseidon has a new delivery for us. Charon's overseeing it now."

"He's not coming to the party?"

"He says he's too busy." After Charon recovered, he insisted on helping Persephone secure her hold on Metropolis. He hunted out dissenters and put down any coups. With his responsibilities in two cities, he did nothing but work.

Persephone frowned. "He needs a girl."

"That's what I told him. That cute little physical therapist he mentioned a few times. I could get the Shades to pick her up, deliver her to him..."

"You are not going to kidnap Charon a bride."

"Why not? Worked out well for me." His hands slid over her hips, tugging her flush to him.

"Hades, not here, people will see..."

"Like I care." But he pulled her into a private alcove before claiming her mouth.

"Hades," Persephone gasped when he let her come up for air. "You're mussing my hair."

"I'll muss more than that." With a shark's grin he reached for her again. "I can't get enough of you, woman." But once he had her in his arms, he simply held her.

Persephone rubbed her chafed cheeks. Stubble burn. Perfect.

"Just wait until your daughter gets here. She's gonna have you wrapped around her little finger."

Hades's hands framed her belly.

"Have you thought about a name?" he whispered huskily in her ear.

"Of course. Chiara."

"You sure?"

Persephone turned to face her husband fully. "Are you okay with that?"

"I am if you are." He toyed with a strand of her hair.

"Hades," she covered his hand. "What is it?"

"I wanna name our daughter something good. Something happy and light. Untainted."

"Your sister was all those things." Persephone pressed her forehead against her husband's. "My love, the past will always be with us. A part of us. The pain will never go away. But we are strong. We can remember the good and bring it with us. Let's name our daughter after your beautiful sister, and remember Chiara the way she'd want."

Holding her husband close, Persephone rubbed her face against his. And if her cheek came away wet, there was no way to tell who cried the tears.

"You're so beautiful," Hades whispered. His thumb rubbed circles on her soft skin. "How is it you're also so wise?"

"Are you implying beautiful women don't have brains?" Persephone raised a brow. Hades shook his head. "I'm kidding. I know you're in awe of me."

"Of you. And the fact you're with a guy like me. Why is that anyway?"

"Hmmm," Persephone twined her arms around his neck. "I thought I had a few reasons but I don't know. You better kiss me before I forget."

"I'll do more than kiss you," Hades bent her back in his arms, claiming her mouth as she laughed, moving his lips down her throat until she gasped.

"We're missing the party," she murmured as he tugged her zipper down.

"Fuck the party."

"Hades." She laughed and gave in. With any luck, no one would come investigate her disappearance. If they did, the happy sounds emanating from the alcove would give her away. "Hades," she panted.

After a moment he raised his head. "Yes, my love?"

"I love you."

"And I love you," he said.

"Say it again."

"I love you. *Per sempre.* Forever." He whispered it over and over, imprinting his kisses on her cheeks, her eyelids, her fingers and fluttering pulse. He had forever to make her feel his love for her.

Forever started now.

***

Read several extra scenes from Hades' perspective: sign up at https://geni.us/Hadesextras

A NOTE FROM THE AUTHORS

A note from Lee:

Whew! What a ride! Stasia and I are so glad you made it to the end of Hades & Persephone's story. Without our readers and fans, none of this would be possible. Big fat thanks to our author friends who cheer us on and provide moral support through the writing doldrums.

When I first started writing Hades & Persephone's story in college, I had no idea what their books would become. Thank you for reading!

A note from Stasia:

I agree, writing this trilogy has been one insane, exciting ride!!! Thanks for coming along with us! We lived with these characters, cried with these characters, celebrated with them, almost killed some of them before days later, deciding, nooooooooo! We can't kill them!

So yay, most of them have survived and yes, we will be writing another trilogy, in the world telling Daphne's story (mixing mythology with a little bit of our favorite fairytale, Beauty & the Beast), and omg, already the ideas are stirring and soon we'll begin outlining and starting all over again!!!

***

Want more dark and epic romance from Lee & Stasia? Check out the Beauty trilogy. Start with Beauty's Beast.

The Beauty trilogy

Beauty's Beast
Beauty & the Thorns
Beauty & the Rose

Want more mafia romance? Check out the Mafia Brides series by Lee Savino… start with Revenge is Sweet

Mafia Brides
Revenge is Sweet
Vengeance is Mine

FREE BOOK

Lee's dark lumberjack romance, Beauty & the Lumberjacks, is free right now for newsletter subscribers
     Grab it here: https://BookHip.com/WZLTMQX

Beauty & the Lumberjacks

After this logging season, I'm never having sex again. Because: *reasons*.

But first, I have a gig earning room and board and ten thousand dollars by 'entertaining' eight lumberjacks. **Eight strong and strapping Paul Bunyan types, big enough to break me in two.**

There's Lincoln, the leader, the stern, silent type...

Jagger, the Kurt Cobain look-alike, with a soul full of music and rockstar moves...

Elon & Oren, ginger twins who share everything...

Saint, the quiet genius with a monster in his pants...

Roy and Tommy, who just want to watch...

And Mason, who hates me and won't say why, but on his night tries to break me with pleasure...

They own me: body, mind and orgasms.

But when they discover my secret—the reason I'm hiding from the world—everything changes.

ABOUT STASIA BLACK

STASIA BLACK is a USA Today Bestselling Author of dark contemporary romance and paranormal romance novels.

Stasia grew up in Texas, recently spent a freezing five-year stint in Minnesota, and now is happily planted in sunny California, which she will never, ever leave. She loves writing, reading, listening to podcasts, and going to concerts any time she can manage.

Stasia's drawn to romantic stories that don't take the easy way out. She wants to see beneath people's veneer and poke into their dark places, their twisted motives, and their deepest desires. Basically, she wants to create characters that make readers alternately laugh, cry ugly tears, want to toss their kindles across the room, and then declare they have a new FBB (forever book boyfriend).

~

Join Stasia's Facebook Group for Readers for access to deleted scenes, to chat with me and other fans and also get access to exclusive giveaways:

Stasia's Facebook Reader Group

~

Want to read an EXCLUSIVE, FREE novella, Indecent: a Taboo Proposal, that is available ONLY to my newsletter subscribers, along with news about upcoming releases, sales, exclusive giveaways, and more?

Get **Indecent: a Taboo Proposal**

When Mia's boyfriend takes her out to her favorite restaurant on their six-year anniversary, she's expecting one kind of proposal. What she didn't expect was her boyfriend's longtime rival, Vaughn McBride, to show up and make a completely different sort of offer: all her boyfriend's debts will be wiped clear. The price?

One night with her.

∽

Connect with me on social media!

Website: stasiablack.com

- tiktok.com/@stasiablackauthor
- facebook.com/StasiaBlackAuthor
- x.com/stasiawritesmut
- instagram.com/stasiablackauthor
- amazon.com/Stasia-Black/e/B01MY5PIUH
- bookbub.com/authors/stasia-black
- goodreads.com/stasiablack

ALSO BY STASIA BLACK

Reverse Harem Romances
Marriage Raffle Series
Theirs To Protect

Theirs To Pleasure

Theirs To Wed

Theirs To Defy

Theirs To Ransom

Marriage Raffle Boxset Part I (Boxset)

Marriage Raffle Boxset Part II (Boxset)

Who's Your Daddy
Who's Your Daddy

Who's Your Baby Daddy

Who's Your Alpha Daddy

Freebie
Their Honeymoon

Dark Contemporary Romances
Vasiliev Bratva Series
Without Remorse

Stud Ranch Series
The Virgin and the Beast

Hunter

The Virgin Next Door

Reece

Jeremiah

Breaking Belles Series

Elegant Sins

Beautiful Lies

Opulent Obsession

Inherited Malice

Delicate Revenge

Lavish Corruption (Coming soon...)

Dark Mafia Series

Innocence

Awakening

Queen of the Underworld

Persephone & Hades (Boxset)

Beauty and the Rose Series

Beauty's Beast

Beauty and the Thorns

Beauty and the Rose

Billionaire's Captive (Boxset)

Love So Dark Duology

Cut So Deep

Break So Soft

Love So Dark (Boxset)

Taboo Series

Daddy's Sweet Girl

Hurt So Good

Taboo: a Dark Romance Boxset Collection (Boxset)

FREEBIE

Indecent: A Taboo Proposal

MONSTERS' CONSORT SERIES

Monster's Bride

Thing

Between Brothers

DRACI ALIEN SERIES

My Alien's Obsession

My Alien's Baby

My Alien's Beast

ABOUT LEE SAVINO

Lee Savino has plans to take over the world, but most days can't find her keys or her phone, so she just stays home and writes smexy (smart + sexy) romance. She loves chocolate, lives in yoga pants, and looks great in hats.

For tons of crazy fun, join her Goddess Group on Facebook or visit www.leesavino.com to sign up for her mailing list and get a free book.

Website: www.leesavino.com

Facebook: Goddess Group: https://www.facebook.com/groups/LeeSavino/

ALSO BY LEE SAVINO

Want more dark romance? Check out the my Mafia Brides series.

Dark Mafia Romance

Mafia Brides
Revenge is Sweet
Vengeance is Mine

A Dark Mafia Romance trilogy with Stasia Black
Innocence
Awakening
Queen of the Underworld

Beauty and the Rose trilogy with Stasia Black
Beauty's Beast
Beauty & the Thorns
Beauty & the Rose

Contemporary Romance

Royal Bad Boy
Royally Fake Fiancé
Beauty & The Lumberjacks
Her Marine Daddy

Her Dueling Daddies

Paranormal romance

Berserker Saga
Sold to the Berserkers
Mated to the Berserkers
Bred by the Berserkers (FREE novella only available at www.leesavino.com)
Taken by the Berserkers
Given to the Berserkers
Claimed by the Berserkers
Rescued by the Berserker
Captured by the Berserkers
Kidnapped by the Berserkers
Bonded to the Berserkers
Berserker Babies
Night of the Berserkers
Owned by the Berserkers
Tamed by the Berserkers
Mastered by the Berserkers
Surrendered to the Berserkers

Berserker Warriors
Aegir
Siebold with Ines Johnson

Bad Boy Alphas with Renee Rose
Alpha's Temptation
Alpha's Danger
Alpha's Prize
Alpha's Challenge
Alpha's Obsession

Alpha's Desire
Alpha's War
Alpha's Mission
Alpha's Bane
Alpha's Secret
Alpha's Prey
Alpha's Sun

Shifter Ops with Renee Rose
Alpha's Moon
Alpha's Vow
Alpha's Revenge
Alpha's Fire
Alpha's Rescue
Alpha's Command

Midnight Doms with Renee Rose
Alpha's Blood
His Captive Mortal
All Souls Night

Sci fi romance

Planet of Kings with Tabitha Black
Brutal Mate
Brutal Claim
Brutal Capture
Brutal Beast
Brutal Demon

Tsenturion Warriors with Golden Angel
Alien Captive
Alien Tribute

Alien Abduction

Dragons in Exile with Lili Zander
Draekon Mate
Draekon Fire
Draekon Heart
Draekon Abduction
Draekon Destiny
Daughter of Draekons
Draekon Fever
Draekon Rogue
Draekon Holiday

Draekon Rebel Force with Lili Zander
Draekon Warrior
Draekon Conqueror
Draekon Pirate
Draekon Warlord
Draekon Guardian

Cowboy Romance

Wild Whip Ranch with Tristan River
Cowboy's Babygirl
Taming His Wild Girl

Made in the USA
Las Vegas, NV
27 July 2024

93002357R10439